# One

# One Duty

## What Happened At Falls Gate Keep

### J.M.Cressy

Copyright © 2022 JMCressy, Eurthantian Press

Cover Art, Maps and Illustrations by JMCressy

ISBN 978-1-958327-01-2

EURTHANTIAN
PRESS
© 2013

In Memory of Elizabeth Griggs

Who was there at the beginning

With special thanks to Amy Farrell for her help and support through the years.

# Contents

# MAPS

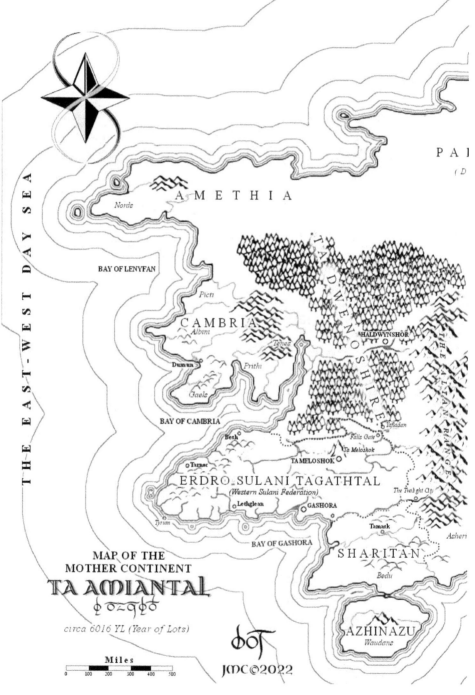

THE EAST-WEST DAY SEA

AMETHIA

Norde

BAY OF LENYFAN

Picti

CAMBRIA
Albini

Tenes

Dunvun

Prithi

Gaels

BAY OF CAMBRIA

Besh

Tarnac

TAMELOSHOK

ERDRO SULANI TAGATHTAL
(Western Sulani Federation)

Lethglean

GASHORA

Tyrun

BAY OF GASHORA

PAI
( D

TA DWENOSHIRE

HALDWYNSHOR

THE TAITAN RANGE

Yafladan

Falls Gate

Ta Meloshok

The Twilight City

Tamæk

Asheri

SHARITAN

Bedu

AZHINAZU
Waudano

MAP OF THE
MOTHER CONTINENT

TA AMIANTAL

circa 6016 YL (Year of Lots)

Miles

0    100    200    300    400    500

JMC©2022

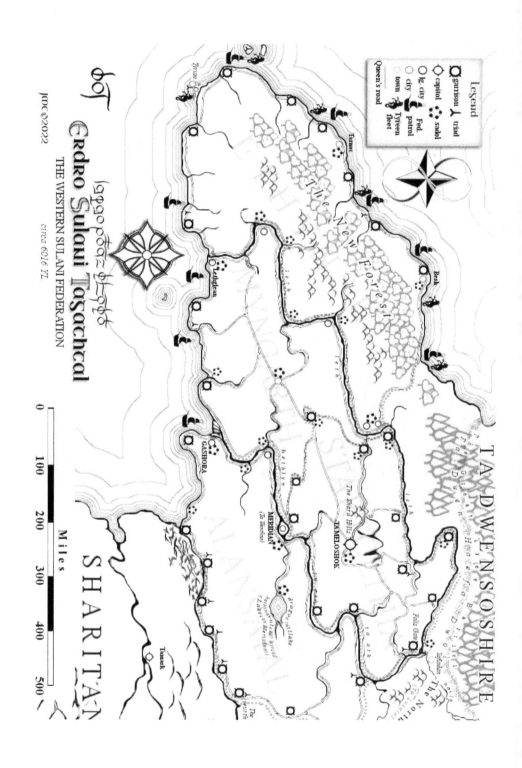

ᏦᎡ

ᏋᏛᏗᎠᏖᏋᏖᏋ ᏋᏖᏋᏘᏋᏖ

# Erdro Sulani Taṣachcal
## THE WESTERN SULANI FEDERATION

JDC ©2022

circa 6016 YL

### Legend

- 🏛 garrison ⚔ triad
- ◈ capitol
- ◇ lg. city · Fed.
- ○ city · patrol
- ○ town · Tyreen fleet

Queen's road

| 0 | 100 | 200 | 300 | 400 | 500 |

Miles

Tyvran

Tanwe

The New Forest

Beih

Leshglean

leth

leth

GASSHORA

bethlyn

MERIDIAN
(As Merithel)

The Shara Hills

TAMELOSHOK

leth

draco solitaire

aath

Falls Gate

The North

Tamask

SHARITAN

TAYDWENSOSHIRE

ALAN

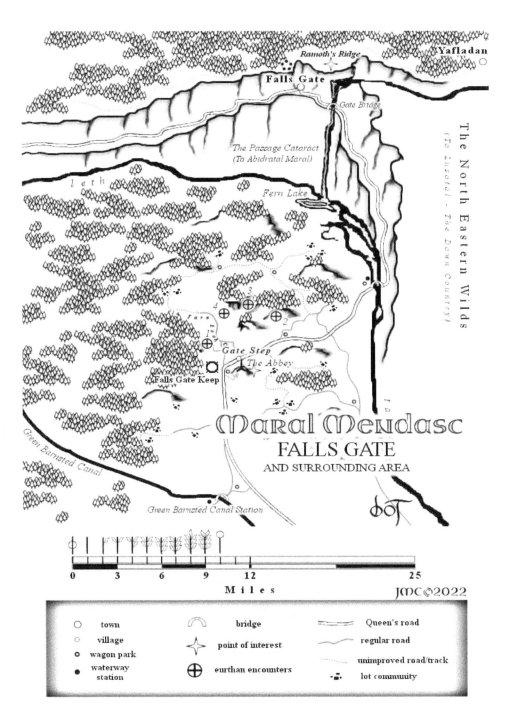

Ramoth's Ridge

**Yafladan**

**Falls Gate**

Gate Bridge

The Passage Cataract
(Ta Abidratal Maral)

The North Eastern Wilds

(Ta Lusetal - The Dawn Country)

l e t h

Fern Lake

3

4

2

1

Gate Step

The Abbey

Falls Gate Keep

**Maral Mendasc**

FALLS GATE

AND SURROUNDING AREA

Green Barnsted Canal

Green Barnsted Canal Station

Miles

0    3    6    9    12        25

JMC©2022

| town | bridge | Queen's road |
| village | point of interest | regular road |
| wagon park | | unimproved road/track |
| waterway station | eurthan encounters | lot community |

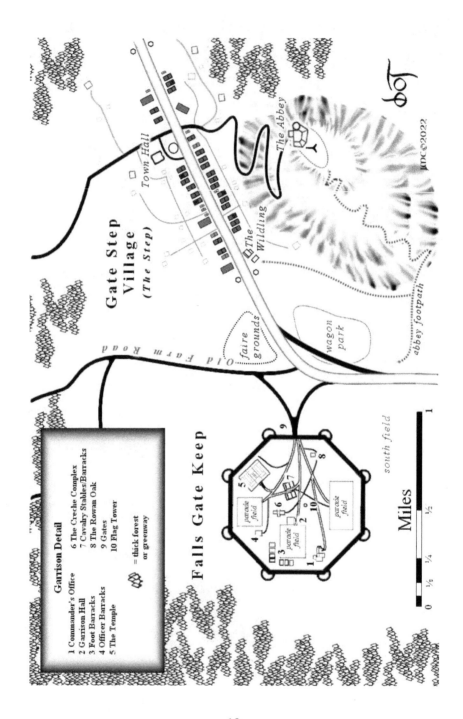

Gate Step Village
*(The Step)*

Town Hall

The Abbey

The Wildling

Old Farm Road

faire grounds

wagon park

abbey footpath

μα©2022

**Falls Gate Keep**

**Garrison Detail**

1 Commander's Office   6 The Creche Complex
2 Garrison Hall   7 Cavalry Stables/Barracks
3 Foot Barracks   8 The Rowan Oak
4 Officer Barracks   9 Gates
5 The Temple   10 Flag Tower

= thick forest or greenway

parade field

south field

**Miles**

0   1/8   1/4   1/2   1

# Eurath

In Ta Pangeal, the Net of Time, Eurath hangs among the stars like a sapphire gem in the black Void. The Orb of Eurath and her companion Lun had existed for eons beyond counting before the rise of her caretakers, the Elfyn of Er. They were a sister race to the humyn, clever in the use of magic or essence as humyn were clever in the use of their hands. Under the watchfulness and works Er, for millennia there was no want, famine or war, no storm was too harsh, nor weather too fraught for the peoples or creatures of the Orb to thrive. And thus it was for many eons, the elfyn mothers nurturing all within the Orb.

Then, from the deeps of the Void, the Dying Star came, a wayward behemoth of iron as large as a city, flying faster than the winds of a hurricane, striking the Orb, setting the air on fire, boiling seas and shattering the hardest earth.

In a moment of memory Er was destroyed, the works the elfyn had built for so long wiped away. On that horrible day their powers were changed and diminished, one people were divided into five great Diaspora, cleaving to those parts of Eurath they had the best affinity for, then driven to find shelter in the Long Winter after, helpless to assist the beasts and humyn who were left to their fate.

Yet somehow the Orb survived, and the humyn and the beasts. One day spring returned, then summer and then all the days of life after. The world would never be the same again and neither would the elfyn, forever scarred and changed. But they remained in essence one people with one duty dedicated to protect and care for the Orb as had their foremothers in Er, though the memory of the failure in the face of the Dying Star would haunt them ever after.

After a long time peace and tranquility had returned to the many lands. Forests and beasts thrived, crops and medicine were found, and the oceans were full of life again. The many skills of hands and essence were rediscovered, and though not as perfect as those times long past, the Orb thrived well enough for the mother who wanted nothing more than for her children to thrive.

Yet for all this abundance, the scars of minds full of fears and fascinations of horror lingered. The old understanding was gone, links between minds and nations weakened, thus it was easier for weeds of greed and aggression to find a place to take hold in any untended garden of souls. Those who sought to advance themselves at the expense of others – the greedy, the grasping, those always wanting more, though they had plenty and were willing to barter to lives and security of others – such souls never completely vanished, and some put on a cunning face to hide their true intentions.

Thus whether in the lands of the Athlantal or Eurthantal (distinguished as being above or below the surface of Eurath respectively), watchfulness was a duty of every mother nation. But how that manifested and who was perceived as ally or enemy varied greatly with tribe, culture and history. Only one thing stayed constant among the elfyn mother cultures: that as people with a duty to protect the Orb, war, though it did happen, was taboo between elfyn. For if the mother cultures fell to fighting amongst each other, they would fail as surely as if another dying star struck Eurath and that was not to be thought on.

Duty to the Orb defined elfyn culture. A mother's duty was to be challenged only at a soul's peril.

# PART I

# AN ~ DUTY

## Chapter 1

# Coming to Falls Gate Keep

The company had ridden hard from Tolith Keep to Falls Gate on the white paved Queen's road since noon the day before, and Lancer Elderyn Farthal was pleased to see the misty ridge ahead of them, a sign their journey was at an end.   The formidable cliff face was called Ramoth's Ridge, named after the legendary sleeping dragon said to be encased in Eurath until the End of the Days of Life.   Over the ridge spilled a great waterfall, the Passage Cataract, slowly coming into Eld's sight, the late afternoon sun striking a glimmer of rainbow when the spray blew just right in the wind. It was fed by the river Halva in the east far above, birthed of many glacial streams, dropping in countless mountain falls in dense fern filled, forested ravines before cutting its way through the foothills of the Altan range. Once birthed, the waters of the Halva had a short but dramatic journey as rapids over a high riverbed, scattered with great boulders dropped by the ice rivers of the Long Winter. Finally after barely thirty leagues, the river's life ended falling over the ridge a thousand feet into Fern Lake below.   It was at the exact point the water leaped into the air as it poured over the long worn down cliff jutting from the foothills of the Altan mountains, that the North Eastern Wilds ended and the Sulani Federation began.

The Sulani Federation was the largest known ethno state of Sula, the elfyn tribe blessed with the inherent ability to magically manipulate fire and light, or as they called it, sulessence.   Their territories and influence spanned most of the continent west of the Altan range and, to fulfill their duty of watchfulness, the Sula had the most visible standing military forces or hosts, both foot and mounted.  Fortifying garrisons built by the Sun-queens over six millennia past guarded the borders and supply routes dedicated to the army.  Falls Gate Keep was one of these many garrisons, where Eld's company would be quartered for the next three months. The host companies were rotated once per quarter by a system the average soldier and cavalier was sure only the Voice and Parliament could fathom.  This company's journey was one of these spring rotations and their speed was an exercise in itself.  The garrisons had been built with the idea that mounted reinforcements were a day's ride away, thus they were spaced about a hundred miles apart, a distance a cavalier could cover going at an easy speed with light provisions. In the practice, they left Tolith Keep at noon and covered half the distance before camping and continuing on in the morning.  The speed and freshness of the horses was assisted by their riders; as long as she stayed in her saddle, Eld could alleviate Fiorseth's tiredness through their linked auras. This effect was greater in sunlight; the last two days had been clear so they made good time. Spring was still new, winter only recently loosening its grip and the scent of snow was still in the crisp air. The month of Merdow was just beginning, the small pale flowers of many trees blooming, though their leaves were yet to come. They would be at their new home until the end of Quol, at Sol Suldan, the summer solstice.

"That's it there," Lancer Danshor said, nodding out over the land falling away to their right the higher the road climbed. Danshor was the war-sister closest to Eld, though they had many differences. "Still several hours to go."

The constant jingling of their tackle and the clopping of hooves on stone was starting to wear on Eld's ears. It was always the same during a rotation: the first couple hours were full of the excitement of being on the road. Then the tiredness of traveling in full gear set in. At least their coats and capes hadn't been soaked by rain, but they had slept without bathing and that always put Eld in a bad mood. Like many, she'd taken time in the early morning to scorch as much of her lingering sweat and dirt she could standing naked in the dawn sun. Remounting her pale mare Fiorseth was a chore, knowing she would be holding her lance in its foot rest for most of the day as they rode again without further rest. At least her sword was in the saddle sheath, keeping it from pulling on her belt and baldric for hours. Even Fiorseth was tiring of the adventure; a horse left to itself would never canter so relentlessly unless pursued by a wild beast. At least Fiorseth wasn't wearing barding. And so Eld looked eagerly out over the land for their destination, wishing she was already there drinking barley-mead and whatever else they'd be offered during their welcome.

Spreading south and west, the wilds were slowly tamed into communities of farming lots, divided by bright white stones. Amidst a series of ravines, hills and fields that had the mixed character of wildness and cultivation, Eld could see a distant road winding through a level gap of scrub woodland between a couple of rocky hills; beyond those hills were the white walls of a keep. It appeared as small as a child's sand castle, but Eld's keen eyes saw it was a typical octagonal fort, a cannon set in the middle of four alternating walls; in the center was a community complex, surrounded by barracks and other buildings. The sky banner rippled from the staff pole on the messenger's tower, a yellow gold sun with four dart shaped rays, circled with a white halo on a pale blue field. This was the ensign of the Federation, the flintsun symbol evoking the ancient blessings of the Court of Heaven where the early settlers of the Bright Plains imagined pagan Mother-Gods watching over the affairs of the Orb. Such spiritual literalism still lingered here in the outer lots, where it was said the mothers, or more precisely their men, lived by many superstitions abandoned elsewhere and relied overmuch on dreams to communicate news.

"Do they even have a communing circle here?" Eld asked of no one in particular.

"The closest sadol stones are in Falls Gate," Patrycan said. She rode just ahead of Eld.

"I thought there was a Triad of stones," Torin said, beside Pat and directly ahead of Danshor.

"There's a Triad at the Abbey," Althone put in. Althone was a couple horses behind. "It's on a hill near the keep. A cousin of mine spent a summer in the village Step doing accounts for a quarry."

Eld looked out over the countryside, trying to spy a hill near the fortress. There were several likely outcrops, all thick with trees on their slopes, the dark grey and green of pines and fir hovering between the haze of the mostly empty branches of oaks, maples and beeches. Any green was from freshly growing herbs and grasses, and emerald patches of moss on damp shadowed ground. But only one hill near the keep had a tower and buildings at the top.

"That must be it," Eld said. "The perfect place for stargazers and mystical recluses."

"Actually they run a school for the village," Althone said. " A road goes right up the hill to their front gates. The only mysterious thing are the ruins."

"The ruins?" Torin asked, voice wavering with slight worry; she was a credulous soul.

"Yes," Danshor said using a stage voice. "Haunted by ghosts of souls ripped from bodies by mad sorcerers who wanted to live forever ..."

"The ruins are a humyn temple," Althone said. "So I think we'll all sleep soundly, sister."

"Humyn have souls," Torin said.

"But they don't have the essence force to linger," Eld reminded her. "The magi can't be too mad if they're running the village school."

"And what in the Orb would a wizard want with a body that would barely last a century?" Patrycan said.

"I'm not the one who started talk about ghosts!" Torin objected.

"You should learn to ignore Danshor's bait," Eld said.

"Because you are expert in this," Danshor drawled.

19

Eld looked away as if she was concerned about the road. This quickly stopped being pretense when the land sloping down the right side steepened, until it was a cliff with aught but large stone markers at intervals to keep a wanderer from falling. The forest side was little better, rising until bare rocky soil made a wall on their left, the roots of trees hanging over them. As if that wasn't enough a coach horn sounded behind them, and they had to yield to a single file path between the road and the markers. There was ample room for a sound rider, but Fiorseth didn't like to go closer to the 'dropping danger' as her mind thought, and Eld didn't blame her. It took firm minds to both guide their mounts and reassure them the elflings did in fact know what they were doing. An elfyn cavalier controlled her horse through a mind link, not reins. The same was not true of the coaches that passed them.

Many travelers and tourists visited to take in the majesty of the Passage Cataract and the view from Falls Gate before resuming adventure in the wild lands and rural farm lots near the mountains. The first of the coaches had the character of a light touring vehicle, bone white and rounded, elaborately decorated with scrolls and whorls, that seemed to bounce like a bauble on its suspension. It had a team of four horses and the driver held the reins firmly, though she would also be linked. The upper walls and door had as large windows as possible without compromising the integrity of the cab. It was full of laughing boys and men in bright robes decorated with many ribbons. One of them leaned out of a window, long white blond hair streaming on the wind as he shouted merrily, "Al met, defenders of the Orb!" before being pulled back into his seat.

"That one's Torin's," Danshor said.

"Because he's bright and bold?" Torin asked, looking after the rolling coach hopefully.

"Because he also doesn't have a spark of sense," Althone muttered to laughter.

Torin glared back, only to have her hair fly right into her face. Like all of the women, her hair was pulled up in a tail bound in a flout at the top of her head. Torin's horse, Holden, wavered and Eld was glad Patrycan reached back to hold his reins until Torin had shaken her hair out of her face.

"Spawn of the Bane, all of you!" Torin said.

Then the other coach passed them, a more formal affair of black lacquered wood with dark bronze fittings, marking it as a vehicle for tradeswomen or local officials. No mother or man within greeted the company, but the driver and their sergeant exchanged salutes. After the vehicles passed the company returned to trotting in double file.

20

The road started to wind gently, cleaving to the folds of the cliff face that was now sheer on the north side. They could hear the roar of the cascading water now, and the rays of the sun that had moved further west behind them struck the eternal spray of water making many rainbows shifting in the mists.

"The ridge of the dragon," Danshor sighed looking up. She wasn't a romantic, but one had to be a completely dead soul to not appreciate the view.

"Which dragon is that?" Torin asked.

"Black Ramoth, of course," Althone said.

"Ai, the companion of Selis of the Fold."

"Or a shape of herself," Patrycan said.

"The same dragon that's supposed to wake when the Orb dies?" Danshor asked.

"Ramoth is in many tales," Eld offered. "At the beginning when Sul made the Orb. Or Ramoth is the Orb. Or a companion of the ancient wizard Selis. Or Selis in disguise to protect Sul's daughter. Or--"

"See what I put up with?" Danshor opined. "Poets are as bad as magi if you want a direct answer."

"Whereas braggarts always have an answer on every subject whether it's known to them or not," Eld shot back.

The women whistled with appreciation. Hanmet Danshor could be amusing but was often too much for herself. The general thought was it was good for her to be humbled now and then.

But Danshor was crafty and adept at distraction. "Look! Trees!" she said.

They made the last turn before the township of Falls Gate proper. Here a shallow narrow valley cut into the cliff, sitting between a wall of rock and scree and Ramoth's Ridge that loomed ahead. A road of darker local stone branched and curved into the township, built up and against both cliffs, the buildings on the side facing them being larger and grander, arching windows reflecting the afternoon sun. The architecture was typical of the region, wood frames on stone foundations, with graceful, peaked, gate arches. Stone and white ash-lime, a type of cement plaster, filled gaps between beams, over which decorative panels of wood were placed, fine tracery formed with magically twisted wood. For the "trees" Danshor spotted weren't the many tall spreading oaks around the town center, still bare of leaf, but a couple of Dwen women speaking with a white robed man outside an important looking building.

Like all elfyn the Dwen had accented ears and brows. But unlike the man, a typical Sula with gold hair and warm pale skin, the women were tan, their hair shades of red and brown blending together. They wore leggings of sage green leaf-felt, a fabric flexible to those with wood-essence, and close fitting vests of reddish brown bark cloth, decorated and reinforced with thin strips of wood. These two were barefoot with twinings around their ankles to just below the knee. Twinings were unique to Dwen, finger length tentacles of wood or vine that helped them walk through branches. Vinings were a similar accessory for the forearms, but could be purely decorative, often freshly plucked ivy with living leaves or flowers grafted for the day. One woman wore vinings as basic and functional as her ankle twinings; the other appeared to have bright green leaves sprouting off her elbows. But the most culturally distinctive item of wear was the yastol, a wooden crown-like headdress that looked like leaves growing behind the hairline just above their foreheads. A yastol was said to extend a Dwen's aura, especially when she walked through trees.

"I didn't realize there were Dwen here," Eld said.

"Ai," Althone said. "Falls Gate is right on the border with Ta Dwenoshire, our Forest allies. Ramoth's Ridge is a tactical position. There's a sister township above on the banks of the Halva. In Dwenhilish it's called Yafladan."

"And civilized souls call it Haflad," Danshor said snorting derisively.

Danshor's dismissive attitude wasn't rare. Yafladan, like most Dwen towns, would be built with a mix of living trees, and magically twisted wood, leaving an impression of interwoven nested dwellings apparently growing around, out of and among the branches of great oaks. It was hard for a Sula soul to tell if such a place was a village or town, or exactly how one navigated the paths between dwellings little more than branches the width of a foot, or how the Treerunners made their way through the forest without touching the ground. And the average Dwen mother, tired of condescension, wasn't interested in helping her. All Sula needed to know was that Dwen too watched the 'Gate to the Dawn County', the old name for Falls Gate, and not one leaf or acorn, nor fish nor fowl, nor mushroom nor game in the Forest would be poached without consequence. The Forest and the Federation were allies now, but there was a time it was not so.

Yet in spite of lingering bad feeling, many Dwen traded with Sula or even sought employment in their gardens or farms to earn the only currency Sula merchants accepted: coins in the denomination of 'queens'. Dwen bought the solstone lamps that released sun-soaked light at night, and shiny metal jewelry, though they had no care for the difference between gold, silver or even brass. Metalwork beyond twisting wire was a nonexistent industry in the Forest. And so the local Dwen joined the tourists as regular visitors of Falls Gate and the environs.  The Dwen might be day laborers. The man speaking with them waved  to the company; the Dwen stared and did not, their yastol leaves lowering slightly. Eld had a feeling the women didn't trust armed Sula on principle.

Soon a small crowd of children and the curious had gathered as the company passed, having slowed to a walk as more wagons, carts and coaches navigated the roads around them.  There were whistles and cheers and some soul belatedly started the Federation March on a flute.   But the company was passing out of sight before the instrument was warmed enough to make a true tune.

Now the grade leveled and gave indications of dipping in elevation.  The air was humid, the spray from the cataract like a constant misty rain, and Sergeant Tarl forbade them from going faster than a walk until they crossed the bridge and the road was dry.  A  horse with an elfyn rider did not magically make the wet stones of the Queen's Road any less slick.  The hiss of the water falling and distant roar of it crashing into the lake below echoed off the cliff side like the bellows of Soltarlu Firewind, smith of the Mother-Gods.  Talk died away as the roar increased.  The warm light of Sul was gradually shifting from bright yellow to orange as She considered Her coming evening sleep.

Suddenly the darting small shape of a fly zigzagged in front of Eld.  She waved it away with her lance free hand, and it zoomed to hover around Danshor's stallion's head.

"It's too early for horse-flies," Eld said in confusion.

"It's mine," Danshor said, hefting her lance from its foot rest and gripping it under her arm.  She let the length of smooth solstone enameled steel slide down through her hand until she risked hitting the ground behind Tuiric.  Eld knew she was trying to aim with the tip but worried the discharge would hit Torin in front of her.

Then there was a bright flash in the air just over Tuiric's head, making the stallion shy and leaving spots in Eld's eyes.  The fly had been vanquished to aught.

"Lancer Danshor!" Sergeant Tarl bellowed, trotting her horse over.  "Did you discharge your lance?"

Eld felt guilty about waving the fly away.

"Ai," Danshor said lazily.

"Why?"

"Horsefly, sergeant, harassing my lovely stallion."

"It's not even Sol Suldan, cavalier!  There are no horseflies!"

"With respect, it looked like one," Eld put in. "I felt fading dreams of blood hunger. It think its dying."

"It's dead now!" Danshor said smirking.

"It would come from the greenhouse barns by the lake below," Althone said. "Harbors them out of season."

"Well, be that the case, it is not part of our duty to wage war on horseflies," Tarl said.

"Pardon, sergeant," Danshor said. "But Tuiric would strongly disagree."

"Well, lancer, until Tuiric can prove he's Thyn and earns a command rank, you'll continue to take direction from command protocols, not dumb horses!"

"Ai and the Orb," Danshor muttered,

"What was that?" Tarl yelled.

"Ai, sergeant!"

Eld waited until Tarl returned to her place near the front of the column.

"At least she's not a lieutenant, or Sul help us, a cornet."

Danshor snorted. "We won't be graced with either of those minted nits out here. The garrisons are too small to bother for the cavalry host. We'll just have a captain until we rotate closer to the capitol. Assuming my dear Tuiric doesn't catch a blood disease." Danshor glared at Sergeant Tarl's back.

"You have to be subtle," Eld said. "Watch."

Now, even with the moist air, they were in warm sunlight, and more stray flies came, refugees who had survived the winter unnaturally. Eld gripped her lance, but kept it in place, using it to draw heat from sunlight into her aura while keeping one fly in sight. When she felt she had enough, she focused it on the fly and with a small flash and pop it was gone.

"Good one!" Torin said, looking back.

"Bah," Danshor said in a bored tone.

"I understand it might be hard as it requires patience, sister."

"Did you become a man suddenly? Patience is for virgins."

Eld laughed as she killed another fly in a flash. "That bait is stale. I'm wise to all your gambits."

"Is there a poem to go with that wisdom?" Danshor ventured. "Surely by now you've memorized every word said or reported from an ancient poet."

"Is there something wrong with literacy and poetry?"

"No, unless you're a dreaming scholar with a cold empty bed."

"You understand that it's the body of elfyn poetry that distinguishes us from the savage and uncivilized, correct? It's a record of our history, aspirations and dreams-"

"Inspired by lustful poets with cold empty beds. Why else are there so many men falling to, or being saved from, rapine?"

"It's a metaphor! A symbol for the struggle between the hungers of passion and commitment to duty in civilized life! The men represent the vulnerability of mothers through their sons, and heroes are the best of the virtuous woman who is willing to sacrifice all to ..."

"Save the man so she can coit him herself."

"That's not at all the point!"

"Ah, but you are ignoring me so adeptly."

Eld opened her mouth, then closed it as she seethed, realizing she'd been baited and trapped. Finally she snarled, "You are Athmod's first daughter!"

"And you have a cold empty bed ..."

"You know well that is not true ..."

"Cold as the white peaks we march towards!"

"Be silent!"

Danshor laughed like a hyena, like always her joy was the greatest when she'd made chaos in another soul's mind. There was nothing for it but to let her have her moment and plot revenge. Soon Eld was smiling to herself as they passed the ever crashing white water, over the Gate Bridge, descending in a gentle grade passing farm house estates, smithies and weaving shops, through hills and fields until they came to the quiet village of Gate Step or "The Step" as it was known locally. It sat near the hill where the magi lurked in their Abbey. It was only a short way now, a mile through the village to Falls Gate Keep, its white walls seen through the bare branches of the village trees. It seemed every local man (or boy old enough to be mistaken for one) was present in the welcoming throng of villagers. Among the celebratory whistles and horns, the men spun in their long robes, white and yellow, embroidered with red, blue and purple threads in patterns of leaves and vines and spiraling geometries. Unlike the man speaking to the Dwen women in Falls Gate, they had gilded gold lips and their hair shimmered with glimmer. Such men of the lots, unmarried sons bored of local passion trysts, sought the attention of soldiers as a matter of course.

While most military women acquired a man where she was stationed, Danshor was known to have a harem of them, shifting with her mood and interest, modified by their availability; not all mothers approved of their sons cavorting with soldiers. But though Danshor was lousy with admirers, Eld had a knack for catching the eye of the best of them, the well read man, who spoke intelligently and asked thoughtful questions. Such a man would quickly tire of waiting for Danshor's forever wandering eye to return. It was only a matter of time before he fell first into conversation with Eld, and then into her bed. It was a fine system and in many ways saved Eld a lot of hassle pursuing the boys herself. The best part was Danshor didn't even notice most of the time. This private jest warmed Eld's soul when Danshor irritated her in the extreme.

So Eld was smug she didn't need to reverie to know how this tale of rival wooing would end, only that she'd have the better man, whoever he was. What Eld could not foresee was that moment of revenge would come in the strangest guise and that it would change the course of her military career forever.

*Chapter 2*

# The Seduction of Lun

A few weeks later the spring was warming, the earliest bulbs, the white snowdrops, were about spent, soon to be replaced by a mix of silver blue crocuses and primroses both white and pink. But the nights were still cold and, unfortunately, that meant Danshor had been right: Eld's bed was cold and empty. But so was every other soul's bed, because men weren't allowed.

It was a command regulation made to mollify concerns estates had of their men being dragged off and debauched by the sorts of hard riding mothers they all imagined themselves to be. The truth was even the most talented and enthusiastic harlot would have trouble holding himself in to satisfy all two score women of the company, willing or not. Garrisons varied widely about which regulations were enforced and how strict. Falls Gate Keep seemed to allow anything that did not disrupt discipline during duty hours and wasn't felonious, always provided a soul didn't get caught. A couple of times they brought men in, but the hassle of getting them out meant no one was interested in making it a regular habit. And for some reason the only boys that seemed interested so far were high spirited to the point of mania or the sorts who laughed at every utterance. None of these appealed to Eld and so she read at such times or went for a walk. She might have haunted the public house or inn with Danshor as she usually did. But, unbeknownst to the company, or even Danshor, she'd found a man and there were plenty of other places to tryst.

When Eld found a beautiful man with a compatible temperament, that was as good as could be expected. But when she found a man who loved poetry as much as she did it was the best. And the man Eld had met wasn't just beautiful, he was stunning. His recall of the ancients' poetry was so perfect they didn't even need to practice lines, but threw them out as if they were speaking naturally until it became a game and then something more.

The man stood alone in the glade, draped in white, a figure of brightness. His long pale hair swayed loose as if in a light breeze, but the air was mostly still, the strands dancing with a life of their own. Willowy, yet statuesque and well formed, he was the image of a Goddi of legend, the male deities of nature who consorted with the Mother-Gods. One was inclined to credit much of this effect to the noon sun that shined unhindered, or the individual essence of the man in question, and there was much to credit there. But this man preferred not to rely overmuch on magical effort , for it was a distraction from passion. And so he used an abundance of glimmer, the finely ground leavings of the solstone trade, the basis of Sula magical technology. The dust was used in cosmetics by elfyn men of Sula ancestry, the powder dusted lightly over the skin or hair. In this case it had to be both, for Seth looked the literal image of a son of the Mother-God Sul.

Eld smiled to herself from where she lurked in the shadow of a yew tree. It was an ironic image for it had been agreed Seth would be the goddi Lun, the only male deity in the Court of Heaven who remained unmarried, yet never abandoned his fraught romance with Sul. Lun was, as the poets described, the patron of dreams, magic and passion. And such passion was not limited to Mother-Gods, or so the ancients liked to imagine. Eld waited until Seth stretched his arms out, like a dancer brushing the air below him away with his fingertips. Then she stepped away from the tree, still shadowed, but visible. Seth froze, but did not turn to look at Eld as he spoke:

"What bold mortal thing are you,
To disturb this my nightly dance,
On this part of the face of Eurath,
Open to the step of my rays as they rest
before they journey on?
Know you not, the danger you face,
To be struck dumb or blind,
At sight?"
Eld took a step forward, hand over her breast and bowed low, saying:
"Forgive me, and my simple shepherd soul,
For the beasts sleep, and the night is dull,
Then you came! Appearing like a dream,
And I cannot resist, for what woman could?
And if I do be struck without sight,
I shall see thee forevermore;
Such a vision to haunt an elf's mind--
There are fates far more unkind!"
Then Seth turned to face Eld, gold eyes flashing almost white in the glare of the sun, the glitter sparkling on the surface of his pale warm hued skin.

"Do not presume, mortal, your flattery, will save you," Seth intoned using his deeper tone, so his voice carried like an actor projecting to the far reaches of a theater.

Eld kept her tone in a middle range, perhaps slightly higher than her regular speaking voice, suitable for a peasant shepherd in awe of meeting the divine.

"Never, great Laird of the Night,

For I know I am at the mercy of your might!
I was doomed from the start,
When I laid eyes on your white heart."

Then Eld, now within arm's reach, fell to one knee and bowed her head, her own hair bound on the top in a bun of a common laborer. She waited, her faced brushing the white linen of Seth's robe, until she felt Seth's hand hover over her head.

"Look at me, mortal!" he commanded.

Eld's head snapped up, as if compelled by divine power. Seth was astonishingly striking, a vision of Lun the demanding lover, marred only slightly by being back lit with the sun, not the moon. Eld wondered if she could wait until the end of this stanza.

"And into my eyes," Seth continued, his voice falling way, luring her deeper into his aura.

"And thus do I curse you, for behold!
I am merciful!
You will keep your sight,
That you may know nothing
And no man from this moment forth you do see,
Will ever compare to my image
that will forever taunt thee!"

Eld's eyes widened, as if in shock and wonder, but then she asked:

"But if that be true, I am cursed so forevermore,
"Then what loss is it to dare more?"

She stood suddenly, and would have been a couple inches taller, had Seth not picked a slight rise in the glade to stand on, keeping the illusion of his divine stature.

"For mortal I may be,
and you divine,
but still a man and must feel
the same thing I feel now."

"You dare? You feel as you do because it amuses me to move women so."

Seth voice was a hiss of outrage that sounded far too real.

Eld seized his hands in her own, her soldier's hands more than strong enough to mimic the firm grip of the shepherd from the poem.

"Now you may not escape," Eld said, voice wavering in excitement.

"Nor turn into your many forms and leave the earth,
"Until perhaps I may have a kiss."

"Unhand me, grubby peasant of the Orb,

Your unworthy leaden feet drag at my spirit,
Your dim soul and simple essence,
Nothing compared to the romances of
Mother-Gods ...”
“And yet you are here on the earth,
In opposition of your beloved,
Showing your fullness to mortal women,
And so a mortal may wonder,
If all these words of threat and spite,
Are not to eclipse the light,
of a passion denied.”

Seth paused, lips parted, and Eld knew he was also ready to abandon the poem.  Playwrights abridged the old works for reasons of time and convenience.  Eld and Seth  abridged poems when the purpose of arousal had been served.

“Then kiss me quickly mortal, but be warned: the wrath of Sul may follow you if I am not released after.”

“Simple shepherd though I be,
I speak honestly and will release thee
once the token is paid.
But I wonder ...will you flee so quickly after?”

“I would flee now, if I could!”

Seth pulled his hands back, but Eld pulled him towards her, slightly unbalancing him so when she kissed him it felt a bit like she caught him with her lips.  For a moment they stood, Eld enjoying the familiar heat of his mouth against hers.  Then they abandoned their charade and got to the business of trysting.

The white mantel, fastened lightly with gold clips in an imitation of ancient wear, was the first to go, revealing Seth’s nakedness and fullness. With the grace of a dancer he let himself fall back on the mantel, while Eld pulled the bun free, her hair falling as she shed her loose bracs, trousers of heavy cloth every farmer wore for labor and many other mothers as causal wear. She also shed her vest. Neither of them wore their shoes: simple shepherds of that time often went barefoot and, of course, gods needed no footwear. For a moment they caressed each others bodies amid a flurry of kisses, at which some point, Seth had managed to pull Eld’s shirt off.  He considered it particularly unromantic for her to remain so covered when they were joined and in general she agreed. But today her drive was high, the company had ridden hard in the morning and she had not trysted with Seth for a week. So she was more eager than usual to settle around him.  Without her shirt, the sun hit her back as they rode together and this was generally a favorable thing. As a Sula Eld felt the light intensify all her senses. Like Seth, she made no conscious effort to move essence to enhance their love-making. But neither of them had to. They were both coiting in full sunlight, in a cloud of Seth's glimmer dust such that not only was every feeling en-hanced, Eld occasionally worried the air might explode in fire around them one day. It would be awkward returning to the garrison without a stitch of clothing.

And then Eld didn't care. She might not be literally around the Goddi of Passion, Seth's grip driving her to take him with more vigor, but the orgasm that came was certainly worthy of a seduction of Lun.

They laid on the mantel in silence a while, feeling the warmth of the sun and the waves of essence between them, echoes of their shared pleasure gently fading away like ripples in a great lake.

Presently, Eld kissed Seth once affectionately, then put her hands behind her head. He in turn stroked her lean muscled torso, caressing a breast briefly before being distracted by her noteworthy biceps.

"Perhaps it's time to switch poems," he said.

"You have one in mind?"

"I was considering Ramlachi and Amer."

Eld thought a moment. "I'm not sure I want to be the Mother-God of War. It sounds like more work than passion."

"Hmm. Perhaps you're not up to the challenge."

Eld laughed. "That trick might work on your sister. Did that ever work on your sister?" Eld was genuinely curious. The commander like most offi-cers was reserved about her personal life outside intimates.

Seth laughed. "When we were young. I made profit from it while it lasted. Then she got wise to the ways of men."

"Whatever we consider, it shouldn't take much longer. Remember the time we take to get here away from prying eyes."

The reason they trysted so far in the wilds way from the garrison was Sethshorn Alhern was no vagrant freeman or common harlot. He was the the brother of the Falls Gate Keep's commander and Eld was a simple lancer. Unless she had prospects, implying a rank equal or above the women in the man's mother's house, and her intentions were serious- - and, for these purposes, soldiers without command ranks were not considered se-rious no matter their feelings - - Eld had no business courting, and certainly not coiting, a man in her commander's house. These things were only toler-ated provided discretion was observed, hence their choice of this forest glade far from both the garrison and road, and the incongruous setting conflicting with the night scene of the poem. There was nothing for it. At night they would both be missed: Seth had duties managing his sister's house and Eld's absence would be noted in both the pub and the barracks.

A slight pain scraped the insides of Eld's belly, the constant companion of an active soldier making itself known.

"I'm hungry," she said getting up and walking to the basket in the shade of the tree. Seth brought their luncheon, prepared by himself from his sister's stores (a thought that Eld tried not to feel guilty about) and Eld brought the mead and light snacks, sweets and sometimes pastries, things it would not seem suspicious for a soldier to take on a causal ride in the country by herself. Still naked, Eld crouched down to open the basket. It was a bit like Hal Suldan, the midwinter festival where gifting children was custom. What would she discover wrapped in waxed paper when she pulled open the blue and white linen that covered the basket?

"Traveler sandwiches and apricots!" she exclaimed. "That will do." She carried the basket back to where Seth lay.

"I hope so," Seth said now lounging on his side. "Honestly, the apricots would have gone to waste. But I do hope the travelers are large enough for your ...appetite."

Eld smiled at the entendre and offered the basket to Seth.

"So noble and chivalrous," he said taking one of the wax-paper wrapped buns thick with meats and garden trimmings.

"Well, if I don't, there is a real danger I might consume them both without noticing."

"But that's where you're mistaken," Seth said around a mouthful. Sex was the one thing that made men as hungry as mothers. "I packed two for you."

Eld looked closer and sure enough, there was another sandwich underneath the apricots. "You are a blessed man," she said.

"I know."

"I should marry you."

"You can't afford it."

"I wonder can your sister afford my appetite?"

"What she doesn't know, the cook's accounts don't need to manage."

They relaxed in silence a while, finishing their sandwiches. Halfway through her second one, Eld asked, "Should I pour some mead?"

"I want to get dressed first. I feel exposed."

Eld bit back any obvious comment as Seth, though rising gracefully to retrieve his proper clothes, did have parts of him hanging exhausted and certainly exposed. The mantel was a frivolous costume thing Seth might wear on his moon meets, but it wasn't a real garment. Like many adult men he wore no underpants, only a narrow kilt skirt that hung on his hips and fell just above his knees. Slit at the sides for mobility, it had been stiffened with starch so that the front minimized any unintended display of excitement. Over this was the main male garment, the linen kirtle-shirt, in this case a pale, yellow, sleeveless shift, with a squared neckline. It fell to the ankles and was cut with a slight fullness for ease of walking. Seth did not wear the pillar style gowns everyday like some men. Over this was an open robe, a rich reddish brown, woven with gold leaves. It had long sleeves of the old fashioned sort that hung from the wrists, as well as more practical pockets. And thus masculine modesty was restored. Only his hair looked untidy, but presently he retrieved a comb from a pocket and set to rectifying that.

"Are you going to dress? Or stare at me all day?"

"If I'm permitted to do the latter ..."

Seth threw the comb at Eld. She caught it and tossed it back, but made sure it would be an easy catch. Seth sighed and returned to grooming. He set to dividing his hair into trilocks, a common style for both women and men, the hair to either side of the face tied or clipped in a lock near or behind the ears, the rest falling free in the back. Individuals who could not easily part their hair pulled the top part back as well to hang in a lesser high tail. Often this was done for fashion as Seth did now. Eld let her own hair hang freely, like the poet she was often accused of being.

"I don't mean to fuss, but I do feel we should be watchful," Seth said.

Eld shrugged. Her second sandwich now finished, she corralled her shirt, bracs and vest, casual cloths of a soldier off duty, and set to dressing herself. At many times she would tease a man for over caution, but she also felt something was odd. A quality of the sunlight perhaps, or a shift in the wind. Whatever it was it moved her to retrieve her belt and boots, bringing Seth's walking slippers with her. With her mind, she reached out to Fiorseth, who was loosely hitched to a tree near the road. Fiorseth acted as a lookout. While she was no Thyn horse, that is, she did not have the intelligence of elfyn or humyn, her link to Eld's mind through Eld's training as a cavalier in the Federation Host meant if the horse was upset or disturbed, Eld would know it.

But Fiorseth's mind was calm, even bored, as she browsed on grass nearby and thought of running across vast fields as she loved to do. If there was danger, the horse knew aught of it.

The greatest danger Eld could think of was being found out. She didn't usually hide her trysts from her stable mates, certainly not Danshor, but she just didn't trust them to keep their mouths, minds, and dreams for that matter, to themselves. Eld was no adept with her mind. They said elfyn were racially telepathic, but in the modern world very few mothers became so proficient they could eschew speech like professional magi. But times like this she wondered if she should have kept her studies up as an animal healer. She had an affinity with animals' minds, and most souls who had that talent could learn to read thought. For now her best course was to continue to act with discretion.

"Am I finally presentable?" Eld said, standing over Seth who had re-clined again, to snack on the apricots.

"Pour me a goblet and I'll tell you."

He had already retrieved the simple pewter traveling goblets and set them in firm places on the ground.

Eld uncorked the bottle and poured the mead, filling the goblets until the sun was reflected in the twin golden pools. They toasted each other and drank, Eld settling beside Seth, enjoying his natural scent, accented with a touch of clary sage.

"Well?" Eld asked.

"Never."

Eld laughed. "Now tell me, noble laird, the secrets of your house."

It was Seth's turn to laugh. "I fear our trysts are the result of two bored individuals diverting themselves and not a sprawling tale of dark intrigue."

"And thank the Heavens for that. I might be a romantic, but I abhor melodrama."

"Still, it might interest a cavalier in my sister's service that our nephew is coming to visit. It's a small thing, or so I tell myself."

"You do not like your nephew?"

Seth shook his head. "He's a pleasant enough boy. His keeper however will always try to run any house he's in as if it was his wife's."

Eld smiled. "This was why I visit kitchens only long enough to feed my-self."

"You haven't visited mine at all."

"And, if I don't want to be stationed on the edge of the wilds in the Alansatal, I'm going to keep it that way!"

Seth chuckled. "The apricots are finished."

"'And thus is the hour'", Eld quoted.

"It's been a bit more than an hour. We should discus our next tryst, then return….."

But as Eld was about to reply, a shimmer in the air made her sit up and look about. In an instant she became a soldier, surveying the land and their place in a moment:

They were in a small glade, a patch of meadow full of crocus and emerging wild flowers, the new grass surrounded by a mix of pine and oak forest. The oak to their right, that shaded the basket and Eld's travel cloak, lay to the south of them. That too was the direction of the road Eld had ridden. Behind them, to the west, was the hunters track Seth had taken by foot. Before, them to the east and north, looming over the tree tops, were the sharp white peaks of the Altans, the mountain range that bounded the far eastern edge of the Sulani Federation. Technically Eld was already stationed at the edge of the wilds. But no one thought of Falls Gate as wilderness. It might be the farthest north-eastern corner of the Federation, but, out of the churning froth and mist of Fern Lake birthed the two great rivers of the nation: the Leth that flowed west marking the border between the Federation and Dwenoshire for hundreds of miles before turning south to wend through the center of the nation; and the Ath, flowing south and east, before it bent west making a snakelike winding not quite parallel to the Leth. This area was the Gate to the Crownland in the province of the same name, and as Eld had seen during their rotation, it had a steady trade of travelers to see its sights and history. And while Dwenoshire might appear to be an unsophisticated land of tree-house villages, it was well populated and patrolled by Dwen. They were on the borders of the nation, but they were in no backwater. Thus real danger was unlikely. Perhaps a great bear or similar animal, drawn by the scent of food, stalked them?

As Eld stood, her mind flew back to Fiorseth. The mare wasn't frightened, but she was no longer relaxed, tense and still, as she too scented out possible danger.

"What is it?" Seth said, standing to join her. He was practiced in the company of soldiers to know to keep his voice down and wait for direction.

"Something is wrong." Eld shivered. "Fiorseth senses it."

"Wolves?"

"Not at this time. Perhaps a bear ..."

Seth gasped, and grabbed one of Eld's arms. A figure stepped from the shadow of the eastern tree line, maybe twenty yards away from them. It was joined a moment later by two others, spaced apart like beaters in an infantry line. Eld shivered again. They were women, but like no women Eld had ever seen:

Like herself, they were tall and well formed, frames expected from mothers who lived away from the easy conveniences of township life. But they moved exactly like infantry, stepping together with purpose, each individual's move reinforcing the others. They wore dark red jackets with broad bands of gold around their shoulders, certainly not dressed for stealth, though their bracs and boots were black. Like soldiers, they had swords and daggers hanging from their baldrics, but didn't seem to use either, instead holding a contraption much like one would hold a crossbow: instead of a bow, it was mounted with a triangular cluster of three, two-foot long rods, bound together, pointing at them. These were made of a shiny black metal, with green and blue shimmer, and ends of the rods that faced them glowed in three red points. The air seemed to crackle, like before a great storm, though the sky remained clear of any storm clouds; Eld knew both she and Seth were in a great danger.   But the most shocking thing about the women, even more so than their bluntly cropped hair, were the glowing eyes in their dark faces. These were Eurthani, earth elfyn from the rumored Eurthantian Empire.

While Eld had never seen them, she'd heard stories, mostly dismissed as drunken dream tales. There were many tales in the outer lots, hawk women who carried boys away, dream lovers,  men telling of dark skinned lovers, or worse. Hunters claimed to follow women with eyes like fire to a mountain door, then the door disappeared before their eyes. But these women did not disappear or run. They advanced,  hesitating slightly before stepping into the sunlight. A more scholarly soul might be awash in curiosity and questions, eager to spill ink into a notebook to share with other obsessive scholars. But Eld had only two goals: keep Seth safe and get out alive. She didn't know what the contraptions did, but the women put a lot of confidence in them. But the worst was Eld didn't have her sword. It hung next to her other gear in the stables, because who needed a sword when going for a picnic? All she had was a hunting knife and her lance, unhelpfully resting against a tree near the road. She needed no strategist to tell her the best course was retreat. She couldn't hold off three armed elves with only a knife for long.

"We seem to be caught out ..." Seth breathed. "I wonder what they want?"

Eld wished he hadn't said it. The women stopped their advance, and one, with eyes like smoldering orange coals said, "Give zah man do uz and yew live."

It was heavily accented Sulanilish, as if trying to speak around a mouthful of gravel, suggesting their native elfyn dialect was full of hard vibrating consonants. Their voices were much deeper than Sula or even Dwen, though that could be aggression. Women used their deeper voice in fighting or anger.

"What do you want!" Eld shouted to buy time. She didn't dare pull her knife yet. She hoped they had not marked her for a soldier and she could surprise them.

"Move when I move," she added to Seth.

Seth said nothing, but released her arm. The strange contraption held by the lead woman  hummed while she leered. Oh, Eld knew her intentions. And just as certainly she knew these women were not to be bargained with. Feeling the sun on her skin, she reached for Seth's hand and prepared to run in a race for both of their lives.  Her hand barely brushed the tips of Seth's fingers, her body in mid turn, when the air erupted around her with a peal of thunder and her side was hit by a fork of blue lightening.

They screamed together, Eld from pain, Seth from shock. Eld tried to force herself to move but something was desperately wrong and she couldn't breath properly. Reflexively she grabbed her side with a hand, sure enough, there was a hole, a bubbling wound where her ribs and lung had been breached.  Waxed paper, she thought foolishly. There was some in Seth's basket. In emergencies, oil soaked muslin gauze. But there was no time for any of these measures.  Eld sank to her knees knowing she would die and Seth, poor Seth,  would be used and it was her fault....

In agony, Eld's sight dimmed a moment, on the edge of fainting from shock, as Seth tried to keep her from falling.  The women rushed them. Their steps where heavy and Seth shouted, his own voice deep, no ingénue begging for mercy, but the brother of a respected commander who expected to be obeyed.  Oh Seth, women like this do not care, Eld thought. Then Seth ordered: "Close your eyes!"

Eld did, for it was easy. The next second the redness behind her eyelids glowed bright  as if she had turned to face the sun. The women cried out, swearing harshly in their tongue, and Seth shoved something against her brutalized ribs, forcing her hand over it. Waxed paper. Maybe there was hope.

"I can't carry you," Seth protested.

But the small victory acted like a tonic and Eld found the strength to lope with Seth's support into the shade of the tree, then beyond it, abandoning the remains of their meal.  Reemerging into the sunlight, now Eld saw they were covered thickly with glimmer dust, as if they had been targeted by a naughty child's prank.

"We've been gilded," Eld breathed.

"It blinded them. Briefly." Seth looked back.

Eld heard sounds of stumbling pursuit. "Fiorseth," she said out loud, as if addressing the horse.  She reached out with her mind in greeting, urgency, and a rare instruction she might regret later. Fiorseth's lead was loosely looped to a post, something any Thyn could undo easily. In fact Thyn often "freed" riding horses this way, pulling the leads with their teeth, never mind the horses would return on their own. Cavaliers were strongly discouraged from teaching their horses this trick, but now wasn't the time to worry about Fiorseth learning she could run in a field anytime she wanted. While Eld leaned on Seth, loping as fast as they could in her state, she showed Fiorseth how to untie herself, with the urgency that they must do this to escape danger.

"Fiorseth should be meeting us soon," Eld said.

"We're almost at the road aren't we?"

"It's near but not near enough. This way," Eld directed them to an elm. "My lance should be there."

She never needed her lance for protection in the country, but liked to practice with it. She breathed a sigh to see it was propped where she left it, its twelve foot metal haft unmolested, one tip as sharp as a needle and enameled with solstone dust, glittering in the sunlight. Eld grabbed it for support. She rested with her back against the tree, holding her side, letting Seth stand free. His hair was untidy again and his robes covered with burrs and bedstraw. The snapping of twigs from women without woodcraft grew louder.

"When Fiorseth comes, ride her back," Eld said, trying to catch her breath. That would not be possible without a healer.

"What about you? I'm not abandoning you!" Seth exclaimed.

"No choice. Fiorseth is a light cavalry horse. She won't be able to run fast with two of us. You're lighter. And ..." Eld gasped for breath. "And it's my duty."

"Hak," Seth swore. "They'll kill you!"

"So the faster you go and return with help, the faster you can keep me on this side of the Door."

Seth's eyes grew wide. Dying, even with the certain expectation of being retrieved, was a risk. Anything could happen, the soul could drift through the Door, or wander in confusion long enough the body had reached rigor and was beyond viability. It was obvious but bore repeating to the new recruit: death was to be avoided, even if the best healers were in a tent nearby.

The crashing grew louder. Eld gripped her lance and braced herself against the tree facing the Eurthani in as much sunlight as she could. The air around her grew brighter. The lance shivered as if it too was excited.

Behind her she heard Fiorseth break from cover and Eld gently directed the horse to circle the tree to her. A light gray muzzle nuzzled Eld's head.

"Well done, girl," Eld murmured. "Now you will carry this man back to the stables as fast as you are able."

Fiorseth's mind was full of hesitation, uncertainty and worry.

"Leave me. I am always with you." To Seth, Eld said harshly, "Get up and get out of here!"

Seth didn't argue. No sooner than he was seated, Fiorseth broke into a fast canter, disappearing in the direction of the road.

A moment later the Eurthani appeared, covered like herself in the remains of glimmer dust.

Eld didn't wait this time, no warning shouts, no wary words of a mother wanting to avoid a fight. They had shown they intended to kill her for the basest of reasons. They would die, if she was able.

Then the lance was part of her, and Eld didn't feel her weakness or injury as she channeled the sun's rays along the metal haft and focused them in the tip, which she lowered at the woman who charged her, the same one who had struck her with the fell weapon. A ray of light, as strong as a ray from Sul herself, hit the Eurthan and she screamed.

A solstone cannon could burn a body to ash in sunlight in a second. Lances could only do a fraction of that damage. But a fraction was enough. The glare faded and Eld saw the woman had dropped the contraption, cradling one of her arms. Her sleeve was burnt to ash up to the elbow, the hand blackened and shriveled, white bone revealed in places. It would take at least a year to heal such an injury with elfyn medicine.

The woman fell back, halting the advance of her companions. Perhaps they assumed they were the only ones with essence technology and Sula were a simple people of wood spears and bronze knives.

Eld didn't strike again because they lurked in shadow and she wanted to avoid a fire if she could. Already the place the contraption dropped smoldered, it's metal heated to scorching by the strike.

Eld waited, watching in the sunlight.

She could now mark the shimmer of air around where the Eurthani hid. Why didn't they advance? Perhaps it wasn't worth it now their quarry was gone and Eld had proven to be no simple elf.

Then why didn't they retreat?

And Eld understood. They were loath to leave without the dropped contraption. It was even likely part of their military protocol. Rarely were Eurthani artifacts found, not even an eating utensil. And the injury was serious;

the woman would be in no mood for rapine. Eld smiled and warmed her lance for another strike.

A woman darted out, a different one, a little thinner, with amber eyes, almost Sula like, except they glowed from within. She had a paler hue, a charcoal gray, but more notably her hands were raised, in a universal gesture of truce. Eld laughed humorlessly to herself. Yes, I will let you retrieve your Bane weapon, and kill me with it...

~We need to take it back!~ a voice in Eld's mind said in perfectly clear Sulanilish.

But mind speech was not in any language. If minds were compatible, they were mutually intelligible.

Eld could reply even though she was inexpert at sending.

~And let you kill me with it?~ She aimed the point of the lance at the woman. ~ Flee, debased hood!~

~ It's too hot to hold and is starting a fire,~ the woman protested.

There was something about the urgent intent that felt honest. Eld wasn't trained to read truth, but if she was inclined to consider it...

The woman decided to risk a dash, diving to the weapon as Eld struck the place where she'd stood. The strike instead hit a pine tree turning it into a roaring pillar of flames.

Eld blinked. She might have passed out. Now the lance lay before her on the ground, pointing to the tree licking with flames, the women long gone and the sun beginning Her descent to the west. Her rays hit Eld more fully, warmer, but the quality of light had diminished. Eld doubted she could use her essence to make a brake. It was ridiculous. She'd need to be at her peak and now, with the threat gone, her power ebbed. She sank to sit at the base of the tree, pulling the lance to her in one hand, the waxed paper pressed against her side under her other arm. She should try to move to the road, away from the flames, but they were far enough away. Smoke was starting to fill the air. At least she'd be easy to find.

And though the fire grew brighter, Eld's sight dimmed as finally, after all her injuries and labors, she sank into unconsciousness.

*Chapter 3*

# Dreams Present and Past

Eld woke in a dream, walking over a familiar field under a sun too bright to be real. She was on a well worn track in the grass, so trafficked the grass had abandoned the center and stones had been revealed with the passage of time. They seemed to have symbols and them; Eld stooped to pick one up, expecting very little to be readable. Even in true dreams she has trouble reading writing of any sort. Sure enough, the closer she looked , the symbols on the stones danced, shifting through all the scripts she knew: Queen's Capitol from monuments and common documents, River, the first alphabet of mothers after the clay pressed Rays of the Field, distinct themselves from the much later Orb and Ray alphabet poets used. Eld made it a hobby to read the myths in their original text. The script finally settled in Queen's. One word on a stone became clear, then she saw it repeated over every stone: NAN. In Sulanilish, even in ancient Erhilish, it was the imperative for "stop". Looking up, Eld saw a door in the distance, a frame of light at the end of the path. A slight breeze blew over her shoulders, pressing her in that direction. And there was music. She remembered something about the music beyond the door…

Behind her children's voices called: "Ama! Ama! We haven't seen you for a week! Why are you leaving us?"

Traith and Shedann. Her children. Memory came back, hitting her mind like an anvil. The door, no, it was the Door. Eld backed up, feeling a chill, looking wildly around for anything to hold on to. The wind was growing stronger and she knew she might have to grip something real to keep it from taking her, to give the healers time.

Eld turned around and the wound in her side caused her to gasp. Most dreams were without pain, but if the body was mortally injured a soul could feel it. Still, this was a good sign. It meant her body was hale enough to recover. And that was well, because lying in dreams was almost impossible. Now her children hugged her knees, she was glad she would not be saying a final good bye.

"And what do you have there?" she said to Shedann. He was the youngest, a toddler sprite, still clinging to old toys for comfort.

"This is Vineflower, remember?" he said, holding out his tree doll, a popular toy imported from Dwenoshire. It was very basic, a thick length of hemp or linen rope , separated in parts to give the impression of legs, arms and branch-like hair. Traditional Dwen toys looked like stuffed trees, those made for export were given eyes and other details. This one was remarkable because it was alive, like a small tree figure doll. It reached its arms out to Eld and the ends erupted in a mass of tentacle like vines. "Vineflower always likes you!"

Eld couldn't say the same. She preferred Vineflower in non dream form, an inert mass of fiber not animated by a child's dreaming mind. But maybe this was good. Vineflower might keep her soul anchored.

"Well, I haven't seen Vineflower for a while," Eld said heartily, picking up the doll. Sure enough, as soon as she held it, its dark eyes crinkled in what would be a smile if it had a mouth, and the vine fingers wrapped around her hands and wrists. It always made her shudder and this time was no different. "Hello, Vineflower, I don't want to take you away from Shed so here you go."

Eld tried to give the toy back, but it wouldn't let go.

"Are you in trouble. Ama?" Traith asked, always the cool one. She wasn't much older than Shed, but had already accepted it was her duty to look after him while her mother was away.

"Ama's just having an interesting day," Eld said.

"Only, Vineflower does that when Shed thinks someone is in danger."

Traith was already much more advanced in her understanding of essence and dreams than her brother. Vineflower was only a magical animated toy in dreams, because Vineflower was a projection of Shed's soul and essence. As elfyn children matured, such projections faded, dream forms more closely matching actual forms, unless an object was truly alive with essence itself. For instance Eld's dagger, though sheathed shined with a light because of the solstone enamel covering its blade. Traith had no magically improbable toys though a black cat sat on her shoulder. It looked much like Tad, her actual cat, but dreams could be tricky. It could be Tad, or it could just mean Tad was in her thoughts. This was much closer to how Eld dreamed as a child: she had a host of animal companions.

Meanwhile Shed, through Vineflower, was trying to make Eld safe the only way he knew how. And it was making her skin crawl. The one animal she had little affection for was the snake.

"That's very nice to think of Ama like that," Eld said in a hearty fluting voice she never used with anyone except children. "You know what would be helpful, Shed?"

He smiled eagerly, brushing long blond hair out of his face. "Yes?"

"It would help very much for you to take Vineflower back and get Silalin." Sil was the chief keeper of children in Eld's family's estate.

With relief the snakelike vines unwrapped and Shed took his toy back. Almost instantly, Sil appeared. And thankfully, Sil had a faint aura, marking him as a real dreamer and not just a Thought.

"Emha Farthal!" he exclaimed, glancing down once at his perfect white linen house robe. It was a common fear of men to appear naked to a woman in any type of dream. "What in the Heavens? The Door is open behind you!"

Like all well informed dreamers, Sil seized Eld's wrists. It wouldn't keep her alive if her body was lost, but it would buy time for her soul to be returned. Unfortunately being reminded the Door stood ajar behind her made Eld more aware of it. The wind rose and the fell music touched her ears, music so beautiful and haunting, it was known even to humyn souls.

Eld started to panic. Time flowed very differently in dreams but it had seemed a while. Where were the healers? Had something happened to Seth? To Fiorseth? She didn't know which thought troubled her more: the loss of her lover or her horse. She'd never confess this dilemma to Seth.

Then the wind stopped and the singing was silenced. Sil looked up with relief over Eld's shoulder and let her arms go.

"You're a garrison healer?" he asked.

Eld looked around to see a woman in a white robe and a round fitted green hat. "Leave her to me," she said. "She's not for the Door no matter how much she tried."

Eld exhaled with relief though it was entirely unnecessary. Most acted in dreams as they did waking.

"Ama, don't leave us!" Shed said.

"She has to go anchor herself," Sil explained as they all started to disappear into mist.

Eld was annoyed she was unable to call out any words of comfort before they faded away.

"I should take you back," the healer said, taking Eld's arm briskly, as if her soul was a stray hound.

"Why can't I just wake?" Eld said, annoyed at being shepherded.

"You were too close to death. Your body isn't ready to wake on its own. And that invites wandering. Since you wandered near the Door, it's best we secure you."

Eld looked around. The landscape was a misty and indistinct twilight. They walked through the grass on a newer path, one laid with well dressed white stones. Eld had seen it before, a healers path back to waking soundly. The Door was was nowhere to be seen.

"We'll be back soon," the healer said.

Already Eld felt herself falling down into wakefulness, everything grew dark and it seemed to take forever. She was floating, alone, a man's face drifting in her sight a moment. Seth?

"Come back," he said.

A whinny. Fiorseth. Eld knew her voice in dreams.

Then three bright figures appeared, one at her head, one at her feet, the other hovering over her wounded side. This was how healers appeared in dreams, so bright with essence they where shadows of light. A light also shone from her side, as if her essence was leaking. Then a cool breeze blew through her soul, and slowly the light faded. The wound was sealed, and she was able to breath deep invigorating breaths, her own essence activated to engage healing. She wanted to thank the figures, but couldn't speak. Soon they disappeared and she faded into simple dreams, mostly forgettable, excepts for the last one, a dream of the memory of her arrival at the garrison, several weeks ago:

Eld was with the company again, on the wide and even Queen's Road, the breeze brisk, the sun shining, the sky clear of all but the finest of clouds, Payeen's feathered wings high in the heavens. Along their left, marching with them was the deep darkness of the great trees, the border of Ta Dwenoshire, the Forest nation. Here the trees tended to be oak, broad and thick, even the youngest trees well over a century. But traveling east, closer to the uneven hills that would became the Altan mountains, the character of the forest changed, the oaks with wide welcoming branches, soon to be laden with the new green leaves, now mixed with looming dark conifers, glowering from the gaps between oak, maple and ash, as if questioning the intentions of the new arrivals. The elevation grew and with it the air was both cooler and dryer. This suited the company as there was nothing like riding free under a bright sun and a clement clear sky making this routine rotation of troops during peacetime much more pleasant than it would have been during rainy weather. During a soldier's twenty years of service, she could be expected to have been stationed in every federation garrison at least once. The first ten years a soul was rotated by season. After that a mother was stationed according to skill and need, with a small consideration for preference. Eld had served for eight years at this point and, being an elite cavalry woman with good pay, she had no particular desire to settle to a post. Unless there was a chance to stay close to her children, in the province Myngarth, all posts were the same to her.

They bivouacked overnight in a wagon park, the fields maintained at intervals along the Queen's roads. They were open to all travelers, itinerant laborers, vagrant tradeswomen and Wildlings, but Federation troops had first right to the facilities. With them had been a family of tinkers with some of the strongest mead Eld had ever drunk. The next day they rode the last stretch, up the east mountain road, through Falls Gate, passed the Passage Cataract, and through the hamlet of Gate Step that cheered their passing. It was said one could see the lay of the Crownland from the Gate Bridge. This was clearly an exaggeration. On a clear day, an elf might be able to sight the bright spires of Ta Meloshok, the capital city that lay south and west. But often mist descended over the lowlands by evening, meaning only the tops of the tallest trees and the hamlet towers would be seen. They arrived in Falls Gate Keep as Sul stepped onto the western horizon. As they rode in, the leaving company saluted as they passed each other in single file, horses prancing, lances angled out to the left, so that company made a line of fire above them, to merge with the leaving company that did the same, a bright snake of light twisting and burning in the air above them, to the delight of local children had come for the sight. Some fool had made Torin one of the banner bearers, holding a dragon streamer that sang shrilly when the wind blew through it. It needed to be held just so for the effect while, at the same time, their mother host banner, night black and sky blue, riven with a fork of lightening, rippled out underneath it. But, to the surprise of many, Torin did this ably.

Then they were inside the walls and they cooled their lances, turned their horses over to the garrison grooms and rushed into the cavalry barracks to pluck whichever cots appealed to them. Eld had looked forward to resting in a proper bed; though the army had made tents standard over a millennia ago, old souls like Sergeant Tarl felt their character was better served by bunking under the open stars, with a saddle blanket for a pillow. It was late spring and they're been lucky to avoid rain.

So they lay briefly in their new cots, then bathed before settling into the stable barracks, built aptly against the side of the stables proper. This was where cavaliers were usually quartered. Later they found themselves in the garrison public house, socializing informally with soldiers and other garrison residents. And the next day they were feted in a more formal welcome, though this always appeared to be an event invented to give the officer's men something to do.

Not that Eld or any healthy soldier or cavalier would complain. A party was a party, and no hard riding or hard marching woman ever turned down food, whether literally or in the more suggestive sense of the word. Romancing a free man was always better than a harlot and usually cheaper; even if one failed, it was worth a tale to be shared later.

The Garrison Hall -- a serviceable, marble, rectangular building with a vaulted roof -- was surrounded by round pillars more for decoration than support, and was filled with light: solstone beads strung on silk lined the tall, arched windows; grand lamps stood in the corners, light filtered by globes of frosted glass perched on helix twined brass stands; bauble lamps, no larger than a child's ball, perched on small stands down the centers of the tables in military precision. All this, as well as the open flaming braziers that flanked the entrance, it was easy to forget it was night long after Sul fell asleep. To the right side were tables laden with food that drew the newly arrived women like bees to honey. To the left was another temptation, local men, men of the commander's house and others attached to resident officers. They stood in their best robes and glimmered hair, watching the arriving soldiers keenly while doing their best to imply they had no care. Musicians played on a stage usually used for entertainment or announcements, but the strains of flute and string were far less interesting than the man Eld had sighted.

He sat to one side of the important women dressed in coats of fawn ocher and sage green, the color of most Federation officer uniforms. He was not part of a pack of men; instead a small group of women, a mix of soldiers, foot and cavalier, stood around the high chair he perched on, so that he sat more or less at eye level. His top locks were pulled back and fastened with a gold filigree clasp. In addition, his guardlocks, the hair at the sides many civilian women left hanging free, but men preferred not to leave to chance, were tightly braided with gold foil, their ends attached to the clasp so they hung in wide loops. The rest of his hair, blond white and straight as finely retted linen, hung down his back. His hair shimmered slightly, but not excessively, like some men who had glimmered themselves so much, one might think their skin had been gilded. Men never understood, or perhaps were too keen in competition with each other, that the shimmer women preferred wasn't cosmetic but in the eyes of a man who returned her interest. But this one seemed to return every woman's interest. His gold eyes flashed, crinkling as he laughed at some clever or foolish thing, thin smooth hands gesturing with perfect though unpainted nails, his white linen kirtle-shirt much stiffer and restricted than anything Eld would see Seth wear day to day. For this was the first time she'd seen Seth, basking in a circle of admirers, yet speaking to them all as bold and plainly as if they were his sisters about any and all subjects: art, history, the soldier's life and poetry. The open gold brocade robe he wore over the tunic had a stiff wide collar and body to the fabric that acted like armor, so he found it easy to dissuade the closeness of an over eager admirer with just a slight turn of his shoulders.

Thus he trained them in short order to petition for his favors directly and not attempt to take them by proximity or stealth. Eld had assumed he was the commander's consort.

"Like the look of the brother," Danshor said. Danshor, fit as a hero, always bold, never sad to lose a man, for she assumed an eager one would appear soon enough. It was all the more aggravating because she appeared to be right. One might say it was down to men's fascination with a woman in uniform, but what other sorts of men was a soldier expect to meet regularly apart from harlots?

"Wait," Eld said, confused. "Brother?"

"Oh yes, he's the commander's brother. Sethshorn Alhern. Commander Major Alhern is not married so he manages her house. And there are stories ..."

"Full of hak," Eld interrupted, wondering why she felt moved to defend the honor of a man she didn't know. "Brother or not, if he was anything less than discreet, he wouldn't be allowed to manage an officer's house."

Danshor shrugged, her eyes never leaving the man. "I didn't say they were scandalous stories. Obviously he's discreet."

"You are bold, captain!" Sethshorn said. "But I must not let my limited time be so worried away by frivolity. I will walk a turn in the garden ...such as it is in this solder's lot--" Here the women laughed. Gardening beyond food was not a priority of garrison grounds. "I will walk a turn, even in the moonlight if Lun be generous, with the woman who can recite a perfect stanza from the Old Poets. Nay, not the fluff of light musicals popular on the modern stage, the true poetry of the ancients."

It always amazed Eld how ignorant women were who imagined themselves masters of verse. They assumed men like Seth wouldn't know better. Or in the attempt they might win with charm. But this was no pampered ingénue. Sethshorn was educated, polished and worldly. And privileged men like himself, once their duties were tended, had little to do but indulge their hobbies . Eld would never assume a shoddy effort would succeed. She and Danshor listened a bit at the halfhearted ventures, some serious, some for the japes. A field captain made the best start, but faltered, to the sympathetic jeers of her fellows.

Suddenly Danshor slapped Eld's shoulder roughly. "Don't save a drink for me. I expect this will be a long night!" She winked, walking forward with all the confidence of a woman who never doubted herself.

Eld didn't know why she was annoyed as she watched Danshor kneel before Sethshorn, in a passing imitation of chivalry, then launched ambitiously into the Lament of Jaro, after she defeated the Spined Eel, but lay mortally wounded.

"There you be and bright, the beautiful Lun,
changeling of the many stars
in the same visage you appeared to me
an aeon ago.
I longed to see you once again,
brightly fair and fullsome ..."

Eld could not bear it. She knew all the poets, read the originals in the River script of the Bright Plains. She had even mastered the poets' script of Orbs and Rays. She did not usually vie with Danshor over a man, but this, butchering of the master mother poets, this could not stand.

And, after being mocked for having a "cold empty bed" there was the matter of revenge yet to be paid.

Eld swept forward, driven by her passion to put the old verse right. In one motion she was on one knee, hand over her breast as many actors affected, and gazed up into Seth's mildly surprised face. Surprised, but amused. His eyes had flecks of gold....

Eld recited, intoning in a vibrant voice that soon had the hall quiet:
"There you are, bright and beautiful Lun,
changeless as the stars
with the same visage you appeared to me
an aeon ago.
I hoped to see you once again,
bright fair and fullness
but bright and fair must do."

Eld paused, uncertain if she should continue Jaro's lines or if Seth would take up those of Lun. Seth stood, and Eld felt her aura shiver. It forced her to crane her neck more and for himself Seth looked down with a face now full of pity and woe, also taking cues from the theater.

"Oh what have you done,
boldest of mothers that
ever walked Eurath?"

His voice was high and thin, as if traveling through the ether from his heavenly orb.

Eld replied:
"The Spined Eel is dead.
its poison made medicine that the queen's heir may live.
The mothers are safe and the lands will return to fruitfulness in time.
Sul will shine, my duty discharged and I will return to Her."

Seth turned his head, as if to deny a great pain.
"But only one was to die this long day!"
Eld took a sanguine tone:
"Are you not happy at last?
In victory is my defeat.
The poison consumes me
I do not have long."
"Fool!" Seth exclaimed. "I never wanted this!
All I wanted I denied
and fought against,
Such a foolish waste of time!
But I thought, once I released you from my curse,
and with many daughters birthed,
our time together would be at least as long
as the time we fought."
Eld changed her tune, more understanding, also projecting regret:
"But it is not your nature to be consistent,
ever changing White Laird of the Night,
Nor is it mine, a Daughter of the Sun,
to settle in the quiet life.
Perhaps we were doomed
before the stars first sang.
Leave aside our old quarrels
perhaps you may grace my house
and many daughters daughters with your light
not just to entice or promise
gallivanting in the night
But in remembrance of our time past
and all their times to come.
And when they walk beneath the stars
in the dew before the dawn
know those were my tears of sorrow
that I must leave themselves and all that is dear.
Though I lived long in the ways of the mothers of the earth
there is never enough life for all that we would wish.
I hear the Song of those who have gone before.
I hear the Door."
"Nay," said Seth, in a voice full of eternal regret, "You are the first child
of Sul,
Jaro of the Dawn,

the Living Daughter of the Sun,
You are not meant for such a fate.
A place has been made,
you have but to step between the stars ...and take my hand."

Eld had known it would come to this, had prepared as soon as she knelt, Seth's thin graceful hand lowering , fingers parted in expectation. There would be no other rivals. Out of the corner of her eye Eld saw Danshor staring at her, seething. It was a good thing they were inside at night. An angry elf strong in essence, could scorch one by sight in sunlight. Then Eld took Seth's hand and Danshor fled her thoughts.

His touch was electrifying.

She had to have him. Surely he wanted the same? She could not be alone feeling this deep passion that needed to be sated as soon as mortally possible. But whatever she felt or he shared, she simply stood and let him lead her away in his wake under the applause of the hall. Behind them one of souls chanted the coda, taking an ironic tone:

"And the mothers of the Orb will weep
to see their great champion leave the earth,
Jaro of the Dawn,
The Great Leaper,
The Bull Stealer,
 Once Queen of the Bright Lands,
Mother of many heroes, and Dragon friend ..."

"Oh shut up!" Danshor bellowed.

"Hardly seems a fair contest after only a handful of challengers," another woman opined.

"Men are as changeable as Lun himself ..."

Eld knew nothing more of the conversation after. Seth led her to the back doors that opened out onto a portico with a round fountain, still in the dim night. It was here, just outside the light from the hall Seth kissed Eld once, almost chastely on the lips. Her lips burned, hungry for him. The man she had in Toleth Keep was a pleasant boy, but they had little in common. In Seth Eld felt she'd captured a prince of the old Lors, despised for their stolen wealth, but lusted after for their glamorous scarcity. Seth paused after the kiss, the cool air between them misting portentously. Then their eyes met and Eld kissed him almost savagely, the deepest part of her on fire. She pressed his lithe form against her, feeling his responding fullness even beneath the layers of modest garments worn to hide this very thing.

 Seth tried to take them to a gazebo, but alas, another tryst had beat them there.

They laughed together quietly, Eld not entirely in good humor, and made a scheme to meet far away from prying eyes. Then they managed – though Fates knew how! – to restrain themselves and discuss their mutual passion for poetry for the rest of the evening.

The memory faded and Eld realized she had been dreaming. Now she was waking to a room of muted early morning light. She lay in a bed, firm but comfortable, covered with the plain white linen sheets used in healing temples throughout the Federation. In the distance an owl hooted, a long warbling cry, a farewell to the fading night. Even though the windows were shuttered, the crisp predawn air filled the room, heavy with the scent of dew. There was no lamp shining: any elf could see well enough, and most of the cheap solstone lamps would have been exhausted over the night. Eld looked around: it was a single room, with a high vaulted ceiling, the kind a temple used to concentrate essence on a seriously wounded patient. Usually there was an array of mirrors and solglass hanging in the center, in front of the high windows at the peak, but Eld's vision was still foggy. The predawn was lighting the peak of the vault, being built so they rose above the roof of the Temple patient ward. Near her a figure sat on the lone chair next to a small table by her bed.

A voice said, "So you are a romantic."

Eld tried to make her eyes obey, looking at the figure as best she could in the dim light. A narrow face with familiar proportions peered closely at her a moment, then pulled away.

"Seth?" Eld asked.

"Our uncles always said we looked alike as sprites." The voice was middling, but vibrated, as if it was used to projecting and found the predawn quiet confining.

Eld blinked, and finally perceived a woman in the casual loose shirt and bracs a soldier off duty might wear; bracs were inspired by a trouser like garment worn by Cambrian tribes and now worn by most women, even officers, off duty. The awareness of the woman's identity was half formed in Eld's mind, and the part of her that understood felt the first stirrings of panic.

The woman did look vaguely like Seth, if he had trained and lived as a soldier for over thirty years with the form to match. It wasn't that men couldn't be as vigorous as mothers, just few of them bothered.

But she was nothing like Seth in aura. Seth filled Eld full of ardor. This woman filled Eld with terror. Finally Eld remembered her name: Commander Major Selind Alhern of Falls Gate Keep.

"Commander," Eld said in a whisper that could be passed off as weakness, and not abject terror at what happened to the careers of women in her position.

"Disappointing, I'm certain. If it gives you comfort, my brother has made a vigil of visiting you at dusk and dawn. He should be here in an hour or so."

"At dusk and dawn ..." Eld tried to think. "How long..?"

"You've been malingering for three days, cavalier."

"Oh."

"After quite an adventure. The entire cavalry host of two companies was dispatched for your rescue; a good portion of the forest you were found in had not only burned, but burned a swath through a Greenway, which will require formal reports. It's a good thing we're not in the Forest or Sul knows what the Trees would demand."

"Tree" could be a mildly derogatory, when used by conservative Sula mothers who considered Dwen both savage and obsessed with protecting any foliage however meager. But Alhern could simply be irritated about the paperwork the forest fire created.

"In all it was an exciting event, the lot mothers in The Step are still discussing it, and you'll be a hero. Of course your greatest feat was sending my brother back first." Alhern paused. "Now tell me: what exactly were you doing with my brother out in the middle of the forest?"

"Say nothing and tell no lies" was the first prohibition children learned when wanting to keep secrets from their elders. But Eld could not refuse to answer, it was her duty to obey, and the commander almost certainly had training to sense truth and the practice of decades. So Eld had to answer craftily. Fortunately she had prepared for this since her first tryst with Seth.

"Poetry," she breathed, as if speaking was a chore. In truth she felt mostly healed, though she wouldn't be running races any time soon. But maybe if the commander assumed she was still weak, she wouldn't question Eld as vigorously.

"Poetry," Alhern said flatly.

"We share an interest," Eld added.

"Your shared interest in poetry inspires you to take my brother into the forest far from the safety of the garrison, instead of, say, the library in the Abbey above the village."

"We never thought there were dangers beyond the odd wandering bear."

"Really." It was a question, but the commander made it a statement, her way of forcing a contrary assertion.

"I knew I could protect him from any rabid animal if need be."

"Indeed."

"That's why he felt comfortable meeting me on foot."

"My brother regularly walked over a mile, where you thought he was at risk for wild animal attacks, to meet you in the middle of the forest, for poetry."

Eld decided to be quiet and hope it was taken for exhaustion. Hearing the commander repeat her tale, it sounded like a handkerchief thin excuse invented by a sprite.

The commander was quiet a moment.

"I looked over your service records, Farthal. You were a good student in your First Circle, Second Ring, and you were going to be an animal healer. You completed the basic magi tests. But then you left and joined the army. Your affinity for beasts was noted, and you were all but ordered to test for cavalry, passing first in your student host."

"Don't tell Danshor. She always brags she was second in her student host. She would be so disappointed."

The commander laughed. "You have a strange friendship. The Braggart and the Poet. So why did you abandon your earlier profession?"

Eld didn't like to discuss it, but it was better than making excuses for trysting with Seth. "When you meet their minds, animal minds, even those not Thyn, you are reminded of how similar we are. And their emotions do not filter, their fears are raw, their affection direct and without artifice. But they are like that all their life, and the burden of tending innocents, especially those that are destined for meat ...I could not do it."

"Yet you hunt."

"We have not made a dishonest relationship with those beasts, claiming to be their caretakers, planning one day to betray them."

"In modern slaughter, the soul of the beast is sent through the Door before its body dies. It knows no pain."

"But I would know I had befriended it. I would know I was complicit in the killing of one I befriended."

"Even Jaro lost her innocence thusly."

"That is not a poem I like."

"No, you prefer the ones with beautiful Goddi trysting with mortals."

The light slowly filled the ceiling vault while Eld considered her reply. The commander seemed to be giving her time. Beyond the walls of her room she could hear the small movements of morning activity, healers and assistants making rounds, more for practice than tending. Eld was certain she was the only serious patient at this time. A horn sounded from a parade field; Eld couldn't remember if it was her time to drill or not.

"I should be out there," Eld finally ventured.

"Regaling your fellows with poetry?"

Eld started to feel despair. Being stationed in the Alansatal probably wasn't so bad. She was a strong enough dreamer her children wouldn't miss her. She only hoped to see them properly before she was transferred. She would miss Seth. It had been a good romance while it lasted. She wondered what Danshor would say when she left the company....

Suddenly Seth's voice echoed in the room.

"Are you pestering her?" he demanded. "You know she needs rest."

Eld's eyes flew open. She must have dozed off. The room was much brighter and she could see the grounds clearly through the window, the shutters now open. The parade field was empty. They would be galloping over the fields for exercise. Eld turned her head to see Seth looming over the still seated commander, wearing a modest workaday crottle brown robe over a white kirtle-shirt. The top of his hair was pulled back, the rest falling loose. He wore no cosmetics today. The commander was unmoved by his remonstrations.

"Before your hero drifted off, she was clarifying her preference for certain poems."

Seth sighed impatiently, brushing past his sister's chair to the small table by Eld. He poured water out of a metal pitcher into a pewter cup and offered it to her. Grateful she took it, not realizing how thirsty she was. It was cool and refreshing. Eld drained the water in on long gulp while Seth said:

"It's well known she is a practiced poet, from the very day of her arrival. Unless you were asleep, dear sister."

Seth took the cup, inquiring with his eyes if Eld wanted more. She shook her head ever so slightly, then closed her eyes. She might get out of this yet. All she had to do was malinger.

"Just because something is not said, does not mean it goes unnoted," Alhren said. "For instance, after your impromptu performance, you took this cavalier for a walk ..."

"In the gardens like I promised any worthy woman who could recite from the masters well," Seth cut in, something no soldier serving under Alhern would dare to do, in public or private.

"And it was noted," the commander continued, a warning deepness creeping into her voice, " that for all the sparseness of these garrison gardens, your absence during this walk was quite long."

"I brought her back in the end , didn't I?" Seth said. "Does Federation protocol state how long I may discuss poetry informally with one of your soldiers?"

"You seem to forget how many freedoms you enjoy, brother."

"I work for my keep," Seth said, his own voice taking a deeper tone.

"True, and I am grateful. But you are not entitled to any soldier's society. As you know that privilege is dependent on discretion."

"I have always been discreet," Seth breathed, in subdued outrage. "I would never neglect my duty to uphold household dignity ..."

"And yet lot helpers gossip in The Step predicted for the fortnight is of how the commander's brother fled on a cavalier's horse, while the cavalier in question battled brigands that threatened his dignity. I understand it's shaping up to be quite a tale, at the end of which, you might find yourself assumed to be ravished by a demonic host many times over. The poor thing."

"That would be a ridiculous slander!" Seth was shaking and Eld couldn't tell whether it was outrage at the story elaborated at his expense, or the harsh fact that he had come close to that exact fate. Before Eld realized what she was doing, she reached out to touch his nearest hand. Just as reflexively, Seth seized it. Slowly his shaking stopped. In a more controlled voice, he added, "I'm sorry if escaping danger and seeking help was a cause for notoriety or embarrassment. In the future, surely I will find a way to escape ravishment calmly so as not to cause a fuss."

"My point, dear brother, is they would not be talking, and nor would you have needed to escape anything, were you not trysting so far from safety."

Seth opened his mouth, the reflexive denial, then, knowing it would be worse to say the lie, shut it  But the commander had marked their clasped hands, her eyes meeting Eld's, making Eld shiver in shock. Gently she let Seth's hand go.

"I'll be honest," Alhern said. "I prefer to not know of these adventures. Even so, I've known about most of them. And yes, you have been discreet. The only time I have interfered, was when the woman was not."

Suddenly Seth crossed his arms in offense. "You had  Ardvess transferred in retaliation? I knew it."

"She did it to herself, brother. Her strong hints over hard mead about her lover only sealed a fate already spun from unpaid debts, tardiness and lax discipline. I never understood what you saw in that one."

Something clicked in Eld's mind, her subconscious abacus finishing an occulted calculation.

"You were sifting my dreams!" Eld exclaimed, sitting up in outrage. Belatedly she realized her plan to malinger was shattered.

Seth turned back to his sister. "Is this true? Even a commander is bound to respect a mother's mind."

Alhren shook her head and stood. "Not I, but the night healer in the course of her duties. But enough of it bled to confirm what I already knew. Be easy, cavalier. You will not be banished from Falls Gate and transferred for 'irregular discipline' to languish watching for savages threatening our southern borders. Do you know why?"

Eld felt off footed. She was vaguely aware of her long hair hanging unkempt, unflouted, or otherwise groomed, as if that mattered. Even though Alhern was near the door, her presence felt overwhelming. "I wouldn't care to chance a guess," Eld finally said, hopefully with the right mix of dignity and humility. "Because I have true respect for Effa Alhern?"

"No, not that, or the sentimental twaddle of having deep affection you probably wanted to say. Though it is true, and a fondness for you is blooming because of that, it is not important in matters of duty. There are many cowards with 'true affections'. No, because you sent Seth back to safety first."

Usually Eld would say something like "any woman would", but since this was literally saving her career, she kept quiet.

"And you knew you could die. There might even be a medal in it."

Eld looked up, horrified. "But that would mean ..."

"And finally the understanding of the subtleties beyond facile chivalry manifest." Alhern's eyes had hardened. Whatever friendliness she professed clearly had its limit. "It's easy to make grand gestures, sweep seats clean, hold doors ajar, offer a hand to assist, all in the hopes of romance. It is a much harder thing to think in advance of the moment to ensure the spirit of chivalry is equal to the appearance. And making a spectacle that calls into question a man's dignity is contrary to the spirit of chivalry, no matter how many grand and glorious deeds transpired.

"Think on it cavalier. In the meanwhile, you will promise, once you have left the Temple, to abstain from my brother's company until told otherwise. He will inform you of how you will fraternize from that point forth, after it has been discussed in house."

"In house" could literally mean a decision made among the mothers, and sometimes men, of the household. But in this case it obviously meant sister and brother would be having long talks, possibly arguments, late into the night.

"Hence, rest well hero. You will be released soon. One more thing: deny it to yourselves, but your auras are becoming entwined. Be certain of your intentions before your next scheduled transfer, Farthal."

Then Commander Alhern left.

Eld let herself sink back into the bed. She felt drained from the exchange and found herself gazing on the sunlight shimmering on strands of Seth's hair. The room was now bright, and the array far above her was too bright to look at directly as it channeled and filtered the sunlight directly onto her. Seth settled in the chair his sister vacated, sitting uneasily, slightly to the side.

"That was not expected," he said.

"It went better than we had a right to."

"Oh, bother her coddling!" Seth was annoyed.

"She cares about you."

"Yes, and many other things. Let me pray for patience!"

"Do you expect a row?"

"It's certain. She'll torture me into the night, leaving no part of me unscorched until she has her will."

The hyperbole dated from feudal times, before the Sunqueens, when tyrannical Lors did such things to indentured mothers who displeased them.

"And what do you think that will be?"

"I honestly don't know. It's never come to this before. I never ..." Seth looked unnerved with himself. "It's never been this complicated."

"Did you ever talk about me?" Eld asked. "Not trysting, obviously. I mean in general."

" 'Oh see that brave mother on her horse, I bet she's a fine rider' ?" Seth said.

Eld laughed.

"No. I make a habit of avoiding such statements about women I tryst with. I'm sorry it came to this."

"I'm not."

"Oh I'm not sorry for all we've done. Just that it's over."

"Is it?" Eld asked. "Your sister seemed like she's considering something."

"I can't imagine what. In gossip that I forbid you to repeat ..." Seth paused to look at Eld, marking her nod before continuing, "The West Marshal's son was trysting with a captain from the borders. From the Alansatal. They were caught in a much less dignified position."

Eld smirked. "Is he a stallion? Were ropes involved?"

"It's not funny. Since the captain was attached to guarding Meridian nobility and couldn't be stationed on the far side of the Day-Sea on a whim, they were absolutely banished from each other's company. And a man of the Marshal's house is always with her son to enforce this."

"Tresses," Eld swore softly.

"Exactly. I will move to our mother's house before I am chaperoned like a boy with a keeper again. And that is saying quite a bit if you knew how much fati and I rowed."

Eld looked at him, waiting until she caught his agitated gaze. "I'd miss you if you left."

"You hopeless romantic. I know my quality but there are plenty of men who would gladly fall in a cavalier's bed."

"But few who know poetry the way you do."

"Is it true then? What my sister thinks she sees? Are our auras becoming entwined? Because I know I would miss you dreadfully and … "

Eld was surprised at her annoyance when he didn't finish his thought. She too wanted to express feelings she wasn't certain about. But what had made Seth pause was the sound of rambunctious women breaking the quiet, an invasion of high spirited souls in booted feet ruffling the native calm of the Temple.

Seth stood abruptly, eying the door warily. "If I'm not mistaken I think you have visitors. Possibly the entire host."

"Neh, probably just Danshor and a couple of raffins. Danshor often leaves the impression of being a host in one soul."

They exchanged a look. It was the look soon parted lovers gave on stage, a look Eld rarely felt moved to once past adolescence. Suddenly Seth swooped down and kissed her, quick and furtive.

"Whatever happens, look for me in dreams."

Eld opened her mouth to speak, but, eager to avoid meeting her fellows and the gossip it would birth, Seth was gone.

## Chapter 4

# Return to Company Life

Eld would have liked to have been with her thoughts but that was impossible. In moments Danshor strode in, leading with a hand determined to seize Eld's forearm in such a sisterly grip she might never free it.

"There she is, the layabout!" Danshor said, as expected clasping Eld arm in a soldier's greeting. To Eld's surprise, she let go without making it a wrestling match. The healers must have been very stern. "We cantered up and down most of the valley while you were playing truant!"

Eld smiled weakly. It was almost as if she was meeting Danshor for the first time.

Danshor looked much like herself, a little taller than Eld, a little broader in the shoulders, in fact a little more of everything. That was part of her character. Her blond hair was brassy, and her gold eyes, rich. She was still in uniform, so her hair was pulled up on the top of her head through a flout, a metal and leather cone that Federation cavalry wore. The chest of her leather coat was covered with a gorget and heart plate impressed with the titular signet of the Wasps, the elite cavalry of the Federation army. Brown leather and beige linen canvas were the main tone of their uniform breeches and coats, save the solstone gem epaulets mounted on their shoulders to regulate sulessence around a soldier's aura. They had a dress uniform trimmed in gold facings, but this was rarely worn. The roughness of cavalry attire was its own elegance. Riding on a fast steed, running like the wind, was the greatest high an elfyn mother of the Bright Plains could enjoy. Very occasionally, cavalry would wear sky blue capes, trimmed in gold. But these were always prone to scorching in anything but the calmest of maneuvers. They were best reserved for fetes in the cool of evening, while seeking the company of willing men in the afterglow of a bright day.

Danshor fell into the chair Alhern and Seth had used in turn, stretching her legs out in front of her, hands behind her head. "We'd have brought you daisies but there were only white ones."

Traditionally, yellow daisies were for women, white ones, for men.

The next two souls who invaded Eld's retreat were Patrycan and Torin. Patrycan had yellow-white eyes and was a dead shot with any weapon. She also managed the barracks' petty cash and ran shifting trade out of her barracks chest: anything you needed and a few things you perhaps ought not have, Patrycan could scrounge it. Torin was a fey soul, slightly superstitious and given to drink and merriment. She was in awe of Danshor, certainly the only reason Danshor put up with her. Eld didn't dislike Torin exactly, but a little of Torin's company could last a while. It was understandable why souls like Althone were impatient with Torin's flightiness.

For instance now Torin was looking up into the bright roof and spinning like a child. "You can feel the sunlight right through you!" she said.

"Indeed," Eld said politely, trying to hide her annoyance, but Patrycan grinned knowingly.

"Looking bright?" Pat said, as they clasped wrists firmly.

"Never brighter," Eld said grinning. She liked Patrycan. "For having been shot through."

"Just imagine! You fought the Bane!" Torin said. She'd stopped spinning and was looking at Eld's torso as if expecting to still see a hole in her side.

"Don't be a dwep," Danshor said. "We don't know what it was and whoever attacked wasn't Bane because Bane don't exist outside of poetic metaphors for the 'Evils of the Orb'. Am I correct, poet?"

Eld sighed. "More or less."

"Well, then what were they? They say their eyes glowed like demons!" Torin said.

"Eurthani." Eld had mulled it over. It was the only explanation.

"I thought they were a myth," Patrycan said. "Tales to frighten children of the lots to come in before dark."

Eld frowned. She did not approve of "cosy lies" to manage children. "Well, they seemed real enough. My lung is strongly opinionated on the subject."

They laughed, Torin perhaps louder and longer than necessary.

"But consider, sister, is there a more likely explanation? " Patrycan continued. "You were found unconscious. Could you have dreamed the Eurthani? Or perhaps a group of hoods were playing a prank that went wrong."

Eld frowned. "We were attacked. And if Se--, the commander's brother, saw them too it couldn't be my wounded mind."

"An accident? Could not your wound have been produced by lance fire?"

Eld remembered how her lance scorched the woman's arm to the bone. It was true: no Bane weapon was needed to scorch a hole through her lungs. "I would need to speak to a healer. If there was a difference, they would know."

"And they'll still know for days to come," Danshor said. "You'll be released at noon and so will have plenty of time to rest before we revel tonight."

This was exactly what Eld feared. "Revel? What kind of revel?"

"The usual kind, of course. Rounds of mead."

"And merry men!" Torin put in.

"A full account of the adventure," Pat added.

"And merry men!" Torin repeated.

"I venture Torin is lacking men in her bed," Eld said, making the other two laugh. "But honestly, do I look fit to revel?"

Eld's objections were interrupted by a white robed healer who entered with a tray of covered food. Eld smelled stewed venison and almost swooned with weakness. She hadn't realized how hungry she was.

"Look! An early luncheon for visitors!" Danshor said.

"Not if you value your striking hand," the young woman said, setting the tray down. "How long have you been here?"

"Mere moments," Danshor said, looking innocent.

"Liar. You can be heard throughout the ward." She stood up, waved Torin back (Torin had taken to basking in the ceiling rays), and looked first up into the ceiling, then at Eld. Eld knew from her training it sometimes helped to follow the rays by sight to see how they interacted with the aura. "Well, there's no reason to stay longer than this day if you feel hale. But you will be on light duty: simple exercises, only casual riding, energy forms, and simple food. No excess of barley-mead or--" this she directed at them all, – " ...men."

"There are ways to have men without exertion," Danshor said.

"See that that's the case. You can leave as early as noon, but you must eat first. And take your return to life easy."

With those stern word's, the healer left.

"She's a jolly soul," Danshor said. "I bet you can't bear to leave this paradise."

"I didn't wake properly until this morning," Eld said. "I had dreams ..."

"We had a bet on how long it'd be till you came back," Torin said a bit too cheerful for Eld's taste.

"Who won?"

"Danshor, of course," Torin muttered with less enthusiasm.

"How did you cheat with that one?" Eld asked. She said to Patrycan, "Did she tell you how she got that tree flask she favors?"

"Fairly won, beating a dreaming poet at Gains," Danshor said.

"Stolen from the heart of a mother," Eld said, allowing herself to glower. "It was a gift."

"Ai and the Orb, so you say," Danshor. "Are you going to badger me about it until the day we walk through the Door?"

"While I still have breath," Eld said. She closed her eyes, surprised the banter was wearing so quickly.

Then a horn sounded, a couple long notes, a sign to return to duty.

Danshor surged to her feet. "We must abandon you, sister."

"Tah!" Patrycan and Torin echoed waving as they left.

"Tah," Eld replied. She sighed with relief when they left. She loved her war-sisters, but wasn't up to their high spirited company yet.

Eld devoured the stew. It was venison thickened with acorn roux, with chestnuts, mushrooms and parsnip, a local dish. Elsewhere it was served in late autumn but up north, near the Forest, it was eaten year round, based as it was on Dwen cuisine. Sweet, savory and filling. After Eld ate she was tempted to linger in bed. But she knew if she didn't leave today, she most certainly would the next. And if she didn't get back to the stables before the company finished maneuvers, she'd have absolutely no hope of a peaceful rest before her return was celebrated.

So Eld dragged herself out of the comfort of the Temple bed, bare feet on the cool stone floor, her mutterings under her breath not inspiring confidence in the young healer who'd come in for general tidying. She was extremely thin, almost waifish, and had an angular but not unattractive face. Then Eld scented the air and felt a fool.

"Are you certain you should be about?" the healer said in a medium toned, stern voice. He --for his amphermones clearly advertised his sex to the elfyn senses regardless of clothing or musculature--eyed her dubiously.

"I didn't know we had men working in the garrison Temple," Eld said by way of avoiding his question. She was still wearing the long white patient's shift that was so much like a man's robe she felt ridiculous. "Where's my garb?"

The man strode to a cupboard as he spoke. "As I understand it, you arrived unshod and your shirt was almost scorched off you. Here are your bracs, and a leaving shirt. Please return it at your convenience." He handed the garments to Eld. "And I've been working in this temple for nearly a fortnight, long before your misadventure."

Eld eyed him closely. They were about the same height, but he was wearing shoes and she wasn't. His hair under his green cap was pulled back in a simple tail, bound with a thong at the nape of his neck and his face had the plainness of a girl. "You don't wear glimmer."

"Why in all of Sul's holy names would I wear glimmer working in a temple?" He looked for a second as if to engage in a spirited debate. Then he seemed to remember he had duties and set about denuding the bedding as if it had insulted him personally.

62

"Well," Eld said carefully, "You wouldn't be mistaken for a girl."

"What? Did the Bane rogues scorch your soul and nose as well as your lungs? Might it occur to you being marked as a man is not my greatest priority while working in a temple?"

"I see I've offended. I would be sorry if I knew exactly what I said. But I'll apologize anyway. Now I'd like to dress."

"Oh carry on!" the man said, his voice slightly higher as he wound the sheets up into a ball to carry. "I've seen it all before."

"Well, I'm not in the habit of exhibiting myself. So if you wouldn't mind ..."

The man sighed huffily. "I was going to take the shift with me, but very well. Just leave it on the mattress."

Then he left.

Eld pushed the door shut and changed. She didn't have shoes or boots and wondered if the rescue party retrieved their belongings or whether they'd burnt up in the fire she started. After digging around in the cupboard she found a pair of Dwen style rope sandals, that could be wound over the foot and heel in a woven pattern, but needed to be tied if one didn't have wood-essence. Eld tied them on, thinking grimly she'd look like a Wildling vagrant walking around the garrison. All she needed was a yastol on her head. Sandals secured, she made her way out the door, navigating around white and green robed figures in the halls until she emerged outside.

Eld blinked in the sunlight, a light breeze ruffling her free hanging hair. The brightness only bothered her for a second. Then, as if highlighted in a dream, she saw everything suddenly clearer In her fragile state it was both energizing and dizzying.

The garrison was a planned thing and thus more regular than the truly ancient edifices of the Shard hills, The New Forest or the south border. The New Forts, as they were called, were part of that building enthusiasm credited to the Sunqueen Selastimor the Great, but were probably the collected work of later monarchs based on Selastimor's concepts and philosophy. The New Forts definitely postdated the Queen's Roads but predated the canal system. All were surrounded in an octagon of eight walls, their length and angle often variable based on terrain. But the Falls Gate Keep was built on a flat rise of hilly ground and so was almost perfectly symmetrical in plan.

The eight towers were the most important part of the keep; that would be where the longest line of sight and strike was. On the walls between the towers was perched a cannon, a two yard long, foot thick tube of solid solstone, mounted traditionally in bronze and stone, but now more often in cast iron. It sat in a round rest on the top of the outer wall, set to strike the ground up to a hundred yards away. It could be angled with effort, but not ease. And Eld would bet a week's worth of mead, these had never been moved since their construction, much less fired in a real battle. Cannons in use near fraught borders, or on patrolling ships, were built to be adjustable. It said something for the complete absence of action that these sculptures of war had sat for centuries in place, their only action being regularly polished and fired during quarterly exercises. Women spent many an idle time arguing the benefits and detriments of cannon.

In the center of the garrison was the Crèche but it was more precise to say the Crèche complex was built over the well. All Federation garrisons were to have their own independent water supply, assisted by rain catching. Combining with the practical needs of mothers placed to share duties, bathing and assorted tasks, the Crèche looked much like a spa or lodge in a reinforced stone building. Its plan was roughly cross shaped, aligned with the walls and gates, a large building with a wing on each quarter: in the east was the crèche proper, where children were kept and watched; the south, the Kettle, where food was made and served to troops; the west, was a sport and recreation area; and in the north were the baths. Their main functions still in use, over time they had changed subtlety. For instance, the common soldier usually kept her children in the family estate or fostered away. And so the crèche was now used by visiting officers or as a default meeting area for informal meetings. It was the one place men were regularly seen as they were often employed by a mother's estate to travel with and watch children. The Kettle might be primarily the place to eat, but outside eating times it was also used for study and informal gatherings. The same was the true of the sport hall, dedicated to acrobatic equipment, bars to pull up, and hanging rings and chains. It had a small amount of bound stone and cast iron for mothers who liked to test their strength. But though Eld liked to recite Jaro's words in poetry, she felt no need to literally look her image. She felt her regular training, with her daily addition of a score pull-ups, was enough exercise. Only the baths were nearly unchanged since the garrison's construction a millennia ago. This was Eld's goal, a good bath.

As refreshed as Eld felt in the sun, she knew she'd feel better after an immersion in water. Neither the moist toweling of healers, nor the impromptu wash from driving a mount through a ford was a substitute. Eld set to walking towards the Crèche, glad that it would be relatively clear this part of the day. It was then her enhanced sight landed on something on the ground near her foot. A stone. She picked it up. There was a faint symbol inscribed on it, a four pointed star at the intersection of two curves that suggested a helix.

Eld shivered in recognition. It was the Astalyn, the Helix Star, the ancient symbol of the lost city of Er.

This was a felkinoc, or luck stone, and technically wasn't a stone. Felkinoc were made by the first mother settlers of the Bright Plains as objects of devotion or gratitude to Eurath, for Her clay, and Sul, for Her heat that made Sulani early pottery culture possible. Felkinoc came in all sizes and were often found by farmers or wanderers in disturbed earth near the remains of millennia old lots. Eld wondered where this one came from. Since there was no construction currently she assumed it came in with soil for the gardens. Or someone had dropped it. It was small, a little over an inch at its widest, and was in excellent condition considering its age. The Astalyn was still sharp. Briefly Eld wondered if it was a more modern curio, often sold to tourists. But in the sunlight she felt the felkinoc's age: the clay fired to stone hardness had been made by a mother's hands before the time of the Sunqueens, perhaps even before the Lot Lors. Which meant that it could be no less than six to ten millennia old, probably older. Felkinoc were considered lucky, even in these post-literalist times. While Eld would have freely given it back to the owner if she was asked, by the nature of any offering to Felkeni, the Goddi of Luck and Chance, the finding was Eld's blessing and she was under no obligation to seek to return it like with an ordinary possession. Eld silently thanked Felkeni's memory and slipped the felkinoc in her pocket, then continued on her way.

No sooner had she walked a few more yards than someone called out:

"What Wildling vagrant invades our keep?"

"Tis not a vagrant think I, but the saddest thing in the Orb: a cavalier on foot!"

"A fig for a wasp!" added a third voice, and Eld knew what to expect.

Reflexes tuned to light, sound and past experience all worked tandem, compensating for her weakened vigor so that, a second later, Eld had caught the fig a soldier had thrown, without breaking stride. She took a bite. It was ripe but not too much so. This time of year they would be imported and so were not at their best.

"My thanks," Eld said around a mouthful. "Though, as a hero, I was expecting to be showered with, say, flowers."

"She's eating your fig," one soldier of the group said.

"That's a quarter flint you owe me."

"Then you shouldn't have thrown it away." Eld swallowed the last bite. "Have anything else? A roast ham? A bacon traveler? And I could do with some mead to wash it down." Eld held up the nub of the fig in the sunlight on the tip of a finger and was pleased it took only a moment to pull the force of the sun into her aura and scorch it to ash. Which then immediately flew into her face, electing laughter from her new companions.

"Looks like she's recovered! Will you grace us with the tale?"

Two of the women, dressed in sage and dun, were regular infantry who carried swords and spears as part of their duties. The spear was much like a cavalier lance, with a slicing tip. In many ways their military dress wasn't much different from cavalry: they both wore the padded leather military jacket, but they had armored plates on the shoulders as well as the chest. But women in the foot host infantry had longer and thicker wrist guards, and similarly the front of their boots were protected by shin guards. Metal loops on the shoulders and sides of their coats anchored their packs when marching. A foot soldier of the army host could travel twelve leagues in a day over road or plains, sixteen under clear skies. Their boots were made for it, not actually ugly, but laced and reinforced in a way that made them heavier and less elegant than the smooth, snug cavalry boots. They of course had no flouts; that was a cavalry custom and considered ever so slightly masculate. Instead they had helm bands, not the full helmet worn during practice maneuvers and in a real battle, but a cap of metal surrounded by a band that had a basic nose guard. Like a full helmet it buckled under the chin. Under this their hair hung in the trilocke style unchanged since the time of Sun-queens: most of the hair hanging or pulled back, except for the guardlocks on either side of the face, bound not in pretty ribbons like men, but in stiff leather and metal sheathes. Both women were known to Eld: Tracan had thrown the fig, she had a merry heart and enjoyed theater. The other, Ollyn, Eld didn't know as well. They were both on guard duty, patrolling the garrison and grounds. With them were three others, also infantry, but in the light duty uniforms of sage tunics and hunter's caps. They carried no weapons except for hunting knives but one held an unstrung bow.

"Alas, friend," Eld said in response to the query, "My tale is only for the commander's ears."

"Oh, go on," one of the unknown women said.

Eld shook her head and walked on, but the women dogged her heels.

"Is it true they looked like Bane?"

"Given no one has seen a Bane because they don't exist, I wouldn't know."

"Now she thinks she's clever."

"But they did have eyes like burning embers, right?" one pressed.

"Yes."

For a second Eld remembered the glowing eyes, red, yellow and orange, and she paused, shuddering. The eyes, the malice, the brutality....their intent to rape Seth. She had a sudden urge to see Seth, to know he was well, but of course he was. He was safely in his sister's house. Eld became aware the women, surrounding her, where watching keenly, hoping her pause of consideration would lead her to speak. And what soul could blame them? Very little exciting of a military nature happened these days or had for centuries.

They were at the far northeast border of the Federation and war, real war, had not happened on Federation lands since the Battle of the Bluefields almost five millennia ago. The Federation Hosts protected the four provinces: Star-tolthia or Crownland, the ancient seat of the monarchy and the same province Falls Gate occupied; Ethynsul, the mineral rich forested hills next to the western shore; Myngarth, south and center agricultural lands, and Alansatal, in the southeast, a warm and fertile land, the main source of oranges, figs and other produce that loved the sun.

To the far west, near Cambria by the sea, now and then there was strife. Northwest of the Federation there were a small collection of barbarian, that is humyn, tribal lands. Tenes, Prithi and Gaels lived in a reluctant truce, greatly midwifed by the Federation government, helped in part by the semi divine reverence Cambrians still gave elfyn, or the Sídh Mór as the Gaels called them. The worst threats in the north of the continent came from the Nords, northern humyn tribes who due to a mix of social instability, fragile agriculture and bad luck, always seemed to be tempted into piracy, at least until the Federation Patrols and the Tyreen Navy scorched their long boats out of the water.

Threats came from the south as well, near the Gulf of Sharitan, from the humyn empire of the same name. Unlike the elf-tall, pale skinned and gray eyed Cambrians, the Shari were sun darkened, slight and clever. While they never worshiped elfyn as gods, they did fear them. Now and then across the centuries there would rise an ambitious ruler whose greed was greater than their fear and there would be war, if one called a decisive rout after a brief engagement "war". That's the worst that had ever happened. There were occasional skirmishes at the southern border, merchant caravans raided, farm lots vandalized, livestock stolen, even households looted. And while this was all exciting work for those soldiers stationed there, the less spoken truth was the worst events were caused not by barbaric humyn, but vagrant workers with grievances, or even bandits, those women who for whatever reason heard Athmod's song of darkness and violence in their souls and found it sweet. If not executed for their crimes they were banished for life, and found fellowship and common cause to harry the nation that rejected them.

But humyn attacks, much less war, were rare. When humyns were caught in feral actions, they were dealt with according to laws of legal compassion: thieves and vandals were captured, interrogated, and deposited outside the nearest border. Those who tried to murder or act with similar malice, were executed without ceremony and their ashes scattered. This was the middle ground of those who warred over the duty of elfyn to their sister race: some believed humyn should be nurtured and taught better ways; others that only by culling the minds harboring malice would the humyn herd improve. In any case, war with humyn had been unknown for centuries.

Yet, because it had happened, readiness was a duty. Elfyn did not so quickly forget tragedy, no matter how long ago. And a soldier's training wasn't completely wasted. Once or twice a year, they assisted in rescue after stormy weather or floods. Now and then the Hounds Master and her sheriffs requested help managing Wildlings or other migrating itinerants that the landed found troublesome. And then there was the odd herd, be it horse, cow or sheep to help round up. But while all these things were honorable ways to keep a military woman busy, they could hardly be considered glorious. Eld felt she was being stingy. She was already going to share an abbreviated version of her adventure with the company; what harm would it be to invite souls from the infantry companies?

"Look, sisters, I still feel weak. I need a bath." A small gust of wind blew several of her tresses into her mouth as she tried to speak. "And a dammed thong if anyone has one," she added impatiently brushing her hair aside. "But I have every faith this evening Danshor will want to revel my return. Come to the stable barracks and you will hear more then. Fair enough?"

"Ai, good, I guess," Tracan said.

The woman with the bow handed Eld a length of black stained suede.

"Elam," Eld said in thanks, tying back her hair. "Practicing?"

"Neh. A farmer has trouble with rabbits near her lot. We are welcome to hunt as much as we want."

"Better practice than a target," another woman added. "And some for the Kettle if there's spare."

"Good luck," Eld said. "I look forward to rabbit stew. "

They bade each other goodbye and went their separate ways, the hunters to the gates, Tracan and Ollyn to continue their patrol, and Eld to the Crèche building.

There was a main entrance between the west and north wings, nearly opposite the gates. But each wing also had its own door some preferred. Not Eld. Today she walked through the north door, a tall and imposing peaked arch of dark stone.   In an alcove to either side stood a bronze statue, as tall as a woman, but standing on pedestals to look down on all visitors.

One was a man in scale armor so fine it fitted him like a second skin.  An ancient mantel draped around him improbably, and his graceful pose and form pandered to a romantic masculinity that belied his alleged identity as a War-king.  One of his curved swords he held loosely at his side almost forgotten, the other still sheathed on his back; the back of his other hand rested against his brow, eyes lowered, as if mourning a great sorrow.  A great raven sat at his feet, another on a shoulder, the children of his wife transformed by the vindictive magic of Lun.  Opposite  him stood his wife Amer, Ameram of old, once the Mother-God of midwives and surgeons, now the Mother-God of War. She was also the matron of the blood colored star modern scholars knew to be an Orb not unlike Eurath.  As usual, she was cast as a bold woman, built with a physique the greatest athletes would envy.  Mother Sul was often imagined taller and even broader than Amer, but never as muscular. And that was saying quite a bit.  Only Jaro was depicted as physically Amer's equal, but understood never to be as skilled a fighter, for Amer was the personification of war, of the hot blood that only a mother could know when she must kill or be killed, murder or allow murder, birth or die of the effort.  Jaro was bravery, boldness and hope, but Amer fought on even when hope was lost, even when the reason to fight was forgotten.  In some tales she was said to have gone insane and that was why weaker races had been infected with the greed for violence without sense.  Still she was the soldier's matron of all things.   Here she was depicted in ancient armor, breastplate and armored skirt, with greaves and sandals.  She had a helmet of the kind that had a narrow "T" shaped opening in front of its graceful sides.  Yet even in that dimness the artist had managed to convey Amer's deadly baleful gaze, her thin lips pursed eternally in relentless certainty, whether it was wooing or slaughter.  Her stance was wide, one hand above her holding her signature Janus Scythe, Ta Helsyn, an inverted double ax, concave crescent blades as keen as moonlight. It was the only thing that could kill the Bane and Amer was the only Mother-God who could wield it, until a later poet imagined her loaning this power to Jaro.  In Amer's other hand was the Dragon Shield, a buckler made from one great dragon scale stolen from the Sky Mother while she slept.

The statues were magnificent work, but did not make for calm reflection.  The man was Ramlachi, or Eclipse, a brother of the primordial twins, Light and Dark, the only man Amer wifed, though she had taken many men in her time.  They had met in circumstances that invoked the wrath of Lun, and for their offense, their children were cursed for centuries to be ravens.  It was a tragic story, one that should have warned men away from marrying soldiers, but instead fueled romantic fascination to this day. Coins were left at their feet, impromptu prayers, petitions or expressions of gratitude: women, usually a wish for family leave or a good post; men, the usual certainties in matters of wooing and love. Eld thought they would be better off praying privately to Sul herself than depend on this tragic couple to send their hopes to heaven.

Passing under the arch, Eld walked through double doors that stood open during the day from the spring to autumn equinox. The short hall led to a circular atrium in the center of the crèche complex where the roof opened directly above a round pool. This was not the actual well, but a folly above it. The wide stone rim was embedded with seats and planters with attractive but practical garden greens, flowers and herbs. It was a calm place. Currently a soldier was sitting reading letters, smiling occasionally in amusement. Another woman reclined in a bench against a wall in civilian garb, holding a simple flute and looking pensive at the sky. Presently, she raised the instrument to her mouth and started simple scales. Eld was reasonably competent with a flute, though she was more expert with a signal whistle. The sunlight reflected off the slightly rippling water to reflect on the stone walls above. Eld exchanged a nod with the soldier who glanced up from her letters before entering the door to the baths on her left.

The baths were only for women's use and so very little in the way of privacy had been built into the design. The forecourt was built in the old style, a bare entrance area ending before a row of decorative pillars that lined the edge of the shallow square pool that was just deep enough to do laps. In fact most women could stand up head above water in all but the center point. It would take a mix of accident, determination and a failure to alert any soul in dreaming to die by drowning in the bathing pool. It had not ever happened as far as Eld knew.

Nonetheless, a woman was on duty to keep the baths during the day, as well as manage their maintenance. The woman, a soldier assigned during drudge duty, handed Eld a towel and offered to hold her things. Eld waved her away. Like most she preferred to chose a place outside of the sight of the door and strip, keeping her garb nearby. It wasn't fear of thieves, which were rare, but pranksters. Few served in a garrison for more than a month before being the target of a prank or retaliation for the same. It was a war that never ended and so every sister was watchful.

Eld made her way through the pillars feeling the filtered light touch her skin, its force dimmed by its journey through the round skylight above, reflecting off the water's surface in glimmering ripples. She shed her clothes, folding them carefully and setting them in a neat pile next to her sandals, the folded towel over them. The air was cool on her skin, but not chilly. The water, while not hot, was warmed just enough to be clement and warm the air with its moisture. She stepped off the marble edge, one foot landing on the seat ledge two feet below the surface that surrounded the pool. The water was cool and refreshing and she quickly took the next step, not quite as deep, to first sit, then submerge herself up to the neck. Eld closed her eyes, bouncing in the water, then took the final step, a full foot, and her feet were touching to bottom of the pool. She pushed off, legs bent, gliding onto the surface of the water and did a lap across and back.

She paused at the center, treading water under the sky light, feeling the rays of sunlight, reminded of her Temple recovery room. Here the bottom of the pool was deepest and she couldn't easily touch it with her feet. The garden pool of her mother's estate suddenly came to mind. Shedann didn't like water much; he stayed in the shallows. Traith always wanted to out swim ama, but she too old to pretend ama "lost" anymore. Eld smiled, thinking of her daughter at a younger age, so gleeful she'd "won". Traith needed girls her own age to challenge. Eld would suggest this to her mother and grandam in her next letter.

Letters, Eld mused as she glided back to the edge with easy strokes. Writing letters, another thing soldiers spent more time at than they ever would as civilian mothers. Their life roving around the Federation made them inevitable. Not everyone dreamed well in the alloted time between sleep and waking for duty. And while it was a duty to a woman's house to keep them informed, it was a necessity to sooth the spirits of their children who, second to their mother's presence, wanted nothing more than to brag about their bold mothers to any who would listen. Eld settled on the submerged seat, letting herself float slightly, nipples breaking the surface of the water. She didn't know when she'd have time to write. Danshor wasn't going to let her sleep tonight and she wanted to ride with the company on the morrow...

"Are you asleep?" Torin asked.

Eld's eyes flew open. Her heart raced as if she'd fled the Eurthani again. With relief Eld noted her side was whole. Of course it was whole. That was days ago. She was fine, in the baths, with Torin of all people.

"I must have been," Eld muttered, her eyes roving the pool. There were a handful more women now, except for a couple, all solitary, the early arrivals after the end of a day of duty. In an hour the pool would be seething like a Meer orgy. "What are you doing here?"

Torin was crouching fully clothed, still in her field browns. "I'm on a secret mission."

"To keep me from the stables while Danshor plans a debauchery?" Eld said, pushing herself out of the water to sit at the pool's edge.

"How did you know?"

Eld didn't answer. She reached for her towel, but her hand landed on bare marble.

Eld snapped her head around, looking for the towel, and her clothes for that matter, her eyes landing on a couple of women on the far side of the pool who at that moment laughed. The echo sounded like a confession, until, glancing back, she saw her towel laying roughly where she put it, only slightly rumpled by the hands of the prankster who could only have been Torin. Eld must be in miserable shape indeed to be fooled by Torin, however briefly. She snatched at the towel while Torin grinned, giggling like a boy.

"Watch your back sister," Eld said. "You will never be safe."

"I'm terrified," Torin said, still grinning.

"You should be. I assume you have my clothes as well ..."

Torin's face fell. It was one of the sporting conventions of such pranks that if the victim asked the prankster directly, they confessed and rectified the situation instantly. Torin dragged over Eld's clothes, still more or less in a neat pile, having been pushed up near a wall.

"And sandals."

"They're underneath."

Eld checked and this was true. She dried herself quickly.

"You know, Torin," she said as she dressed, "That wasn't necessary to keep me. I was planning to go The Rowan Oak afterwards for some piece of mind."

"No, that was just fun. It's rare to get a jump on you."

"Congratulations on your victory over a recovering sister who just escaped the Temple. You should get a medal for chivalry."

Eld knew she was being unreasonably cross and Torin wasn't helping it by looking like a wary hound. Torin always cared too much about what her fellows thought.

"Stop sulking. You got me. Tell the Orb for all I care. I'll be in the Rowan Oak when Danshor is ready."

"Very well. See you, Ai?"

"Ai and the Orb! Go on!"

72

## Chapter 5

# The Rowan Oak

Torin ambled away, greeting other soldiers she knew, while Eld, after first checking nothing else was missing, left the baths.

Outside Eld shook her damp hair and combed it with her fingers into something presentable before letting the sunlight into it to gently warm it dry. It was a small feat of essence all Sula children learned before they could walk. Normally Eld would have stopped in the stables to use a comb, but given Danshor's plans… She shrugged to herself. She also wanted to see Fiorseth; stretching her mind out to the building as she passed it, she was troubled she didn't sense the horse's mind. But she sensed no other horse either. They were gone, being walked and watered to cool down after exercises. Eld sighed, tied her hair back with the thong and walked on without pausing, her destination the garrison public house, the Rowan Oak.

The Rowan Oak was a privately owned alehouse placed conveniently, some said too conveniently, near the gates. It was a log wood building in the old style of the ancient settling mothers, long before the Federation, the roof, doors and larger windows framed with arches of intertwining branches that met in pointed peak, typical of gate style architecture. It was quite similar in fact to the buildings they saw passing the town, Falls Gate. No one was certain exactly how old the modest two story building was. Several centuries, though not as old as the garrison. Through the maintenance of skilled Dwen crafters most of the original wood of the main frame was well preserved, the corner joins fused with wood-essence and decorated in forest spirals, giving the impression of pillars. It had a roof of fused bark shingles, fashioned cleverly so that the rain flowed into water catch pools that fed the only garden of note, that being the one of the Rowan Oak's kettle. In times past whitewashed daub or ash-lime had patched much of the outer facing as the wood decayed from wind and rain, and the previous owners had found it troublesome, time consuming or expensive to arrange repairs with Dwen. But the current owner was well able for this work and would tolerate no clay or duab, much less cement plaster, in place of woodwork. Now every outer wall was covered with a decorative mass of intertwined branch-work, grown from the support beams on either side. All once bare wood was covered with a scale of finishing bark as Dwen preferred. The only allowance for civilized custom were the windows with shutters. Their frames were kept intact, for Sula did not favor the style of netted screens or open windows at night. Even the foundation had been repaired, the building not just sitting on the stone, but now thick roots gripped the stone before sinking directly into the soil. The ground around the alehouse had its own patch of green, grasses feed from the water that seeped from the garden. It was one of the greenest places inside the garrison, where most grass was brown by summer from overuse of both elf and horse. This led to some peculiar amusements, as Eld observed approaching the building.

A wide welcoming porch with shallow stone steps covered most of the building's front. A couple of simple round tables of woven wood stood with several mismatching, but well crafted chairs. Women sat at the tables with chalice style tin cups, one resting her boots on an empty chair. But they were looking at a patch of grass several yards in from of the porch, where five soldiers, still in sage and brown and full baldrics, clustered talking urgently, and none too quietly.

"Mark ...he returns," one said, eyes bright and eager with some mischief.

Eld looked where the woman gestured and sure enough a man had walked through the gate. He was tall, though not notably so, with medium nut brown skin and swept back roan hair, auburn red at the crown, slowly fading to dark brown where the ends touched his shoulders. Unlike most respectable Sula men, his legs were visible, though covered with leaf-felt leggings of variegated greens. This was somewhat mitigated by the knee length tunic of brown barkcloth, though the garment's side openings rose to his waist for ease of movement, thus any coverage was negated. He wore the same type of sandals Eld did, but they appeared to twine around his ankles as if they were part of him. His arms were bare except for the vinings he wore like the Dwen in Falls Gate, an ornamentation specific to those with wood essence. The living vines wrapped around his arm and wrist, but without leaves or flowers. They didn't last more than a couple days in any case; then, like spent flowers in a vase, they were cast aside. But what confirmed the man was Dwen was his yastol.

Each yastol was unique to the Dwen in question, a crown of thin wooden leaves seeming to sprout from the hair just above their forehead. The wood would be the same as the leaves represented, though some yastols were made from wood with still attached leaves, renewed by the essence of the wearer. But these rarely lasted more than a season. In addition to the leaves, individuals would often attach decorative danglings at the sides, like ear clips, flowers for men, berries or seeds for women. For instance the man's yastol was in the shape of rowan leaves, making a fine filigree effect, with a small cluster of white flowers hanging on either side. Eld knew from close examination the "flowers" were not real, but made of painted or stained wood shavings, like many crafted imitations. But the man was not solely a creature of the Forest. Like many who made a living engaging the public, he had a taste for cosmetics and baubles. Brass bangles, bright and gaudy, hung on his wrists. He also loved glimmer and paint, though he had no skill in application. Instead of the light dusting Seth favored, his lips were gilded, and he often shadowed his eyes the same way, something Sula men only did for Moon Meets. The closer he came, the clearer his figure was, attractive, lithe, but wildly exotic, a thin dancer's body with a wiry, dangerous strength. And he had delightful green eyes. Many women found Tafli compelling, but he deigned to share his bed with few. Had Eld not met Seth almost as soon as she dismounted at Falls Gate Keep, she might have wooed him.

As it was, they were reasonably friendly, and as a friend Eld wondered what this group of overly merry soldiers had planned. Tafli confused some women who took his directness as promiscuous immodesty and an invitation for solicitation. Eld had to admit she enjoyed watching the humiliation of such troll-mothers. She stepped onto the porch and rested against a support, watching what would transpire.

The soldiers nudged their friend, who looked dubious and uncertain the closer Tafli came. He waved at women he knew, a couple of drivers and one woman on patrol. Then he quickened his pace, striding to the porch. At which point a soldier started stamping on on the grass.

Eld frowned. At first it was just a couple times, like a horse might stamp a hoof. Then there was a pause as the whole group stared at Tafli waiting for a response. The stamp was repeated, followed by a couple strangled laughs by two mothers who couldn't contain themselves.

Tafli stepped on the first stair, looking at them quizzically. The soldier smirked and stamped several more times, then her fellows joined her, stamping all together.

Tafli sighed as if all patience had left him and ascended the porch, saying, "No, this thing you think, that I am being angered at the abuse of every blade of grass, is not true. Or why would I be serving cavalry host in my house?"

The soldiers roared with laughter. So annoyed was Tafli he didn't notice Eld as he walked through the open door. Eld followed him, shaking her head at the antics worthy of a sprite of forty.

Inside the pub was a perfect mix of Dwen and Sula artistry: the commons room was on the south side, the high ceilings with exposed beams and trimmed log joints, inside all bare and oil finished with spiral and coiling branchings where they met each other, the wall or ceiling. The windows themselves, four tall and narrow multi-panes set along the south wall, had a top valance. This was open now so air circulated as the light fell clear and bright over modest round tables throughout the center of the floor. They were also of Dwen construction, the top round being a blank of fused fibers, that could be wood, but were often grasses or other planting material no respectable Sula woodworker would consider viable. But that was the advantage of moving wood-essence; a Dwen could make the sturdiest objects from materials any other elf would consider shop waste. The tables did not move, being rooted to the floor like the trees their crafters loved. Similarly a bench extended around certain parts of the outer walls, under a couple of round windows, as if growing out in a shelf a couple feet high from the floor for a seat width before curling down to merge into a series of "legs" that rooted in the floor. A handful of plain ordinary chairs of the gate style stood around the tables.   A cold hearth sat in the corner of the room, rarely used except during winter Eld was told. Tafli did not like burnings in his house, not even candles. The long lanterns that hung on chains from the rafters were solstone lit. Dwen had eagerly adopted cheap passive solstone lamps in the ancient days of trade before even the Sunqueens ruled. The lamps would not shine until dusk but there was plenty of light for now, slightly subdued as Sul prepared for Her nightly sleep, restful but not too dim.

Ordinarily Eld took a place in the commons, favoring a small table near the hearth with a bench seat. It was rarely occupied, though after the fall equinox that would change.   But today Eld took a seat on one of the tall stools at the bar, itself a mass of fused hazel wands that seemed to grow from the floor  near the entrance to wind like a flat-topped wall in shallow curves before ending and merging with the entrance of the common room, making a place for women to retrieve orders if needed. Eld took a seat at a shallow point in the curve, putting her closer to Tafli as he checked taps on the barrels against the back wall.

"Haven't run out I hope," Eld said by way of greeting.

Tafli glanced quickly at her, green eyes still simmering with annoyance. But his expression changed at recognition.

"There is our hero being returned from death, I see. After saving men and burning trees." Tafli looked at Eld seriously. "A man who is worth the lives of those trees, I hope."

"I think even a Dwen warrior would accept the burning of trees to save a man," Eld said, hoping she was diplomatic.

"We men of the forest are not being so helpless as men you are used to," Tafli said, now sorting tin cups, his bangles ringing slightly against the metal. "I would be having any woman with perverse intentions bound in vines at a thought."

"I'm sure you would."

"Still, you are right. Your duty was first to be protecting the commander's brother. The trees will return. How are you now?"

"Healed, but I am warned against exertion. And I am forbidden to go to my quarters because Danshor-"

Here Tafli made a noise, somewhere between a groan and a sigh.

" – Is apparently planning to celebrate my return. It'll probably send me through the Door."

Tafli laughed. "She is good comrade to you."

"You don't like her."

"No. She is loud with her own praises and laughs at her own bad joking. But she is loyal to her sister. This I respect."

Eld nodded. "What did you get from town?"

Tafli's expression turned sour. "Nothing. They have no gruit. Already it is being late two days. And they are thinking is accidentally sent to Falls Gate. The wagon will not be returning until the day after tomorrow."

"Is that bad?"

"What are you thinking I make ale from? Water and moonlight? Without gruit I have barley water with no flavor. I have malted already. Now I might have to dessicate it all to save it from spoiling."

"I'm no brewer, but isn't that how it's stored?"

"By lazy mothers and men who do not know how to keep the taste of the green!"

Luckily at this juncture a couple of new souls requested service. After pouring a couple cups of barley-mead and taking their coin, Tafli returned, eyes bright with passion. Heavens help the mother who offended a Dwen epicure.

"Listen, you know why most forest food is untouched by fire?"

"Yes, you forbid 'burnings'." Eld stared pointedly at a large sign made apparently by Tafli, a thin plank impressed with capitol letters: "NO BURN-INGS". "I've always wondered how anyone stays warm in the Forest during winter ..."

"The reason is because it kills the flavor of life in grown things. To save, we ferment and sun-dry. But to dessicate is the most extreme drying, for only food stored against famine. Not for taste. If I do this, I will not be pleased."

"You could always use it for mead."

Tafli acted as if Eld hasn't said anything. There was a rumor the barley-mead Tafli sold wasn't true barley-mead, brewed directly from barley-malt sugar and honey, but a blunt mix of mead and ale. It was something a house helper might do in desperate straights or youths might mix as an experiment. But for an alehouse to do it, usually to cut costs, would be risking fines and loss of licensing. Eld suspected there was some truth to this rumor on two counts: there was no "barley-mead" as such offered. Tafli called it "ale mead" and everyone assumed it was a quirk of his less than fluent Sulanilish. Secondly, he never acknowledged, much less answered questions on the subject, avoiding the chance of uttering a lie. Not that Eld would rat him out. She was just curious.

"It is being busier," Tafli said by way of changing the subject. "I cannot speak with you all the night. If you fill the lamps, I will give you a good drink."

"You'd think being a hero would gift me a drink."

"Yes, but many trees died, even if this is unavoidable. "

Eld glance at the lights high on the chains. "I was warned against exerting myself."

Tafli leaned on the bar with his elbows, and let his over glided eyelashes lower, greens eyes smoldering in an imitation of passion. "You can be my hero."

Eld was thrown a moment. He smelled like spruce and wood cinnamon, lips hinting at skills Eld had never been privy to. If she hadn't have met Seth first, what would have been?

"Very well, fine," Eld agreed. "But if something happens, expect the physicians to scorch you."

"Nothing is happening. You are strong, agile, riding mother, not drunken bear."

"Well, not yet."

Eld slipped off the stool to retrieve the ladder from the back. It wasn't her first time helping for a free drink. The ladder, basic and serviceable, was long enough to easily ascend the eaves and was stored in a shed outside. Eld parted a newly arrived group of soldiers, evaded their attempts to engage her over her adventure, and set to getting the ladder, as well as collecting the handful of solstone gems sitting on the top of the shed, where they had been soaking light all day. They were cut in the common dodek, or twelve sided gem, to sit flat and cast as much light from the faces as possible for the least cost. They were slightly less than a couple inches wide and all twelve of the dodeks fit a tin with a handy handle. Eld took the ladder down, hoisted it mid length on her shoulder and picked up the tin with the other hand.

"Clear the door!" she called ahead, forcing a group to part. Women already seated rose to stand aside, expecting her arrival. Already the light was less bright. Eld set the tin, the gems inside already glowing slightly, on an empty table while she maneuvered the ladder against a rafter, briefly wishing she was Dwen so she could tack it in place with wood-essence. Then she took a gem and ascended while a woman called out:

"Why don't the lamps lower like in a civilized place?"

"Sula never get enough exercise over flat land!" Tafli said. "It is good for Sun mothers to climb."

Now fifteen or so feet above the floor, Eld had only to reach for the lamp chain, pull it to her, and drop a stone into the foot long, six sided, glass chamber. She set the lamp back, minimizing its sway then looked at the next one.

It occurred to her at this point she could climb three more steps up the ladder and step on the beam and finish one entire row before having to descend. The beam was sturdy, a full six inches wide, and, thankfully, flat. It would be no effort.

"No!" a voice called up from below. Eld looked down to see Patrycan sitting on the edge of a table below her, setting down her cup.

"I thought you'd be in the stable helping Danshor."

"Why do you think I'm here? They sent me to get you. And she won't be impressed if I have to drag you to the Temple instead because you thought you could dance like a Tree."

Before Eld could answer, Tafli interrupted. "Who do you say is a 'tree'?"

"No offense , Effa," Patrycan said easily. "Just that our sister here shouldn't think she's Dwen."

"Then you should say that," Tafli said, glaring before returning to wiping the bar down.

Patrycan made a face like a child might behind a father or keeper they thought was being overwrought.

"Be careful," Eld said. "I value a friendship that yields free mead."

"Be careful yourself. Do not think I'm going to let you dance on a beam. Just do the lot, come down, and do the rest."

Eld felt contrary. She didn't like anyone thinking her less able, or worse that she was shirking. But she also knew Patrycan was right. Annoyingly Pat added, "And you should be asking for someone to steady you. Fortunately, I'm here."

Patrycan put on hand on a rung, holding it secure against the rafter while she took a sip from her cup.

"Well aren't I lucky," Eld grumbled trying not to sound ungrateful. She'd have to accept the help; it would go quicker that way.

She came down, sliding freely with two hands, moved the ladder and ascended again. She'd just dropped another gem in the lamp when she heard a woman say, "I wouldn't do that," from the vicinity of the door. Caution made her grab the beam as she looked over, seeing a small group of new arrivals in sage uniforms with black facings, the army rangers.

Federation Army Rangers tended to be taciturn, grim women with an odd humor, their time in the wilds making them less adept at civilized life. Mounted or on foot, they cut a dark romantic figure, at least for men who pined after the dark charismatic mother who they found fascinating in spite of her aloof contempt of all ordinary things. They weren't all self-centered hoods, rangers, but they were odd. There weren't many of them in any garrison and they tended to mingle with their own. In the wild they were deadly fighters, night hunters and dreamers. In a keep, they could forget civilized conventions, perhaps because they were so used to being laws unto themselves. If they were terrible at mixing with sisters, they could be disastrous with men.

The group was four. All were seasoned except one scout who had the aspect of one newly come into their profession. She smiled arrogantly, presuming many things while Tafli reached over the bar, exposing his legs further, his tunic shifting to make more of his form visible. The woman probably thought it was a jest, or even he'd welcome the attention, for didn't all men want women to mark them? As Eld watched, too far away to do anything, the woman's hand hovered over the back of Tafli's upper thigh. Then she took the liberty of patting her hand on his rump. Or that had been her intent. But between Tafli's reaction and her alarm at his speed, her hand slipped suddenly up his inner thigh almost to Tafli's nethers. She started to laugh nervously but the next moment she shouted with alarm.

Tafli had grabbed her wrist and stood, his twinings wrapping around the woman's hand, binding them together in a parody of a Dwen marriage ritual. Worse, what had been decorative twisting of wood on the planks of the floor wrapped around the woman's feet. She was able to move one foot free, but the twinings around her wrist kept her from escaping. Women nearby leapt back to keep distance from the seething vines.

"Tresses! Are you mad!" the ranger exclaimed.

"I do not let women take liberties," Tafli hissed, as he pulled the woman close.

"Heavens, you crazed man, it was an accident!"

"What is accident? That you are grabbing? Or than you grab so badly?"

"It was a jest!"

"Oh. Then I jest too." Suddenly Tafli freed the woman from his wrist twinings. She fell back awkwardly against a wall, her ankle still held by the floor.

"Tree witch harlot!" she snarled, reaching for a small ax at her belt.

"You will not use an ax in my house!" Tafli bellowed in a voice deeper than Eld had ever heard him use.

"Then free her," another woman said, her voice also deep and firm. She appeared to be the lead ranger. "I will deal with her."

"You should not have let her take liberties in the first place!" Tafli said, eyes flashing and lips pursed. "You think this is funny perhaps? Are you her commander?"

"Her captain, yes."

"Fine." The ranger's foot was released and the floor returned to normal. "But she is gone for a fortnight and you pay double."

The ranger glared at Tafli, reluctant to obey. But the captain jerked her head towards the door, and the scout left without further protest.

Tafli looked around at the matrons, green eyes flashing.

"No mother tries to stop this? This is entertainment yes? Then you make gratuity." Here he slammed down a tall tin jug. "Or leave for the night."

Slowly, one by one, women made their way to the bar. A couple walked out, but most put at least a couple coins in. To Eld, Tafli looked up, accusingly, then seemed to remember her precarious state. "Hurry up," he called crossly. "It is not the eve of Yafelram Astersh and it will be dark soon."

"The eve of what?" Patrycan asked.

"The Long Night of the Stars," Eld explained. "What Dwen have at the winter solstice instead of Hal Suldan."

They finished the lights with no further adventure, transforming the inside of the Rowan Oak from calm, sheltered quiet into a glittering beacon of merriment for the coming night. Eld was regretful they were leaving. She'd prefer a drink with a book of poetry in a quiet corner near merry society. But there was nothing for it. Patrycan was chivying her out, carrying the ladder on her shoulder. Eld was going to leave quietly. It was quite busy and Tafli had lost a serving boy a couple weeks back. But even annoyed as he was, Tafli intercepted Eld with two bottles of mead and a hamper of the pastries left from the morning, usually given for penny-shards at supper.

"It is not being the best mead, it is too fresh, but you will be merry, yes?"

"Thank you."

Tafli did not smile, but pecked Eld's cheek.  "Good night, hero."

## Chapter 6

# Revelry

"He's an odd one," Patrycan said as they walked back to the stables. "Flashes his legs, then takes umbrage at a woman's eye."

"Groping is hardly 'a woman's eye'," Eld said, a little annoyed with Pat; she was usually a reasonable soul.

Patrycan shrugged.

The air had cooled as the night darkened, black ink washed over the violet-blue of late evening, stars scattered across the firmament. Behind them the increased sounds of merriment from the Rowan Oak faded among the casual mutterings of clusters of women gathered together outside informally. Some lit fires in designated places for the joy of it or to prepare a light snack, perhaps something hunted or caught during the day. Others used solstone lanterns, enjoying the echo of the sun, even entertaining each other with simple light and fire tricks. Still others, like Dwen, drifted away from the light, speaking quietly as they watched the stars appear, walking to the darkest fields as the night wore on. Even elfyn needed darkness to see the stars best. Eld would like to have taken Fiorseth for an evening walk, enjoying the peaceful calm and the brisk air. She could feel Fiorseth's mind nearby now, sleepy, then suddenly alert, feeling her desire and want to go. Fiorseth was always game for an outing. But, once through the stable gate, Patrycan firmly steered Eld away from the horse stalls.

The garrison stables were several buildings, housing all the horses used by the outpost. But only a couple were set aside for cavaliers, with barracks en suite. These buildings faced each other, stable gates opening onto their own inner covered court where horses could be walked during inclement weather. While the ground was bare and the foundations stone, the buildings themselves where made of Dwen formed wood. It was a superstition that horses were best housed in buildings made of forested materials as opposed to stone, this being considered more natural. Never mind horses in nature neither dwelt in caves or forests, but on open plains. But it was true there was a lightness to such buildings that felt less oppressive to a soul who preferred the open sky. Being a functional building, little ornamentation was wasted though it was well made and had a pleasing shape, the vaulted roof evoking aesthetic simplicity. One of the distinctions of elfyn architecture was beauty and grace married to function; this was considered a requirement by elfyn builders and architects, especially for public works.

Inside the double barn style gates, the inner court was hard packed dirt. Lanterns hung along the stalls to the far right; to the left, a large door with a gate style peak was shut, a lantern hanging above it. Muffled laughter could be heard from within; this was their stable barracks. Above, the vaulted ceiling faded into darkness, the earthy scent of horse and straw ever in the air. The actual purpose of the inner courts was to muster before charging, each rider attended by army grooms in case they needed to muster at a moment. They hadn't had such a drill at Falls Gate Keep yet, though their captain threatened them intermittently. To Eld's eye even in the dimness the ground seemed less even. But she couldn't look closer because an officious woman suddenly blocked her path.

She held the simple spear of a footer and was dressed in basic gear: band, boots, jacket, one sword, one spear and a whistle. She was young, maybe in her eleventh decade, probably enlisted soon after her majority.

"Stand and reveal yourself!" she demanded.

"What is Sul's blazing tresses ..." Eld began.

"Should have warned you," Pat said. "The entire outpost is in Watchfulness. Hence the guard."

Eld tried not to roll her eyes. It was their duty to comply and it made sense. The only times she'd practiced watchfulness was drilling and quarterly exercises. She wanted to laugh at the girl who was unlikely to repel an invasion of one, much less a battalion of Bane warriors.

With great reluctance, Eld stood to, as if in review, raised one hand at her side, facing outward, the basic greeting of ghosts, gods and superiors. "Lancer Elderyn Farthal, 2$^{nd}$ Company Cavalry," she recited. Every garrison cavalry host had two companies: the newly arrived and the resident 1st Company. In a month and a half the 1$^{st}$ Company would be rotated out, Eld's company would replace them and the new arrivals would be the 2$^{nd}$ Company. She kept her hand raised as this callow elf stared into her eyes, presumably to discern truth. Whether she had that skill or not, which Eld doubted, a couple seconds later, the girl stood to, raised her spear and allowed her to pass.

Then she did the exact thing to Patrycan.

Eld smirked at Pat's astonished face, before she yielded to the ritual: "Lancer Heled Patrycan ..."

The soldier let her pass, then returned to face outside, looking satisfied with herself.

They walked to the door, glancing back, laughing together once they were far enough not to be offensive.

"We'll rest easy with that one guarding us!" Pat snickered.

"She's just doing her duty," Eld said, but couldn't stop sniggering. Had she been that serious when she was green? Surely not.

Then Patrycan knocked and the door was thrown open so forcefully Eld had to dodge out of the way.

"There she is!" Danshor said. Eld had barely a moment to note her running tunic, flouted hair and a garland of daffodils before being yanked into the barracks.

It was like being thrown in the midst of a parade, a really wild one, like the Recognition Day celebration of the elfborn on the island city of Tyrum. There women donned rustic tricorn hats, festooned with blue daisies, many with costume armor, with sea shells over their breasts, mimicking the well known but fantastical inaccurate statue of the Mother-God Maer, Queen of the Sea. In this ridiculous get up, elfborn would take to their currach, or what ever vessels they had, and "raid" the surrounding coasts of the Ethynsul, a festival game where communities set out "booty" to be taken and men allowed themselves to be "captured". This was done to commemorate the real historical fact that, before being recognized as a Federation city and incorporated, with the funding and support that went with it, Tyrum's residents raided coasts for supplies and ship building. Eld wasn't sure it was exactly the right way to express gratitude for their piracy being forgiven. But the revels were popular and had the resident Exiles', that is, the descendants of the abdicated monarchy, blessing, so it became a tourist attraction. Eld had never been to the Recognition Revels, but she imagined they might be much like the throng that had overtaken her barracks.

The barracks were crammed with not just Eld's company sisters, but other soldiers and outliers she didn't know. She had to fight to get near her own cot and almost gave up until Torin, being helpful once in her life, shooed the revelers away.

"Get up! That's the hero's bed !" she said, yanking on a particularly slow elf who gulped on her goblet of mead as she was turfed out.

"Sorry!" she said, then immediately fell onto another bed. "She's not planning to sleep is she?"

This was considered extremely amusing by all nearby, their laughter going through Eld's head. She looked around, at the glittering lamps, the bottles of mead, Tafli's additions being swept up by the greedy crowd. Eld found a goblet shoved into her hand; a taste told her it was cheap barley-mead. She sighed. Barley-mead made an elf cheerful, but had no hope of putting one to sleep. She also found herself inundated with nuts, small cakes and sugar lozenges imbued with herbal flavoring, allegedly for health. She took these politely because they tasted good, though she didn't put stock in such things like cures of lot helpers. Temple potions were the only thing she trusted as medicine. She also found herself draped with their mother host banner. Most women wore their bracs, light tunics or vests, a couple like Danshor embracing the revelry as an excuse to let themselves dance freely. Someone started plucking a lyre and another played a whistle and a dance started down the center row between the beds. The men – for a hand-ful of men had been scrounged from somewhere – found it awkward; there was little room to properly spin without their long robes catching on the ends of the beds. Thus the dancing was kept to the sideways hopping sort, more for fun, than skill. The men were fine enough, from Gate Step or the lots around, all blond Sula except for one who had red hair. Whether that was natural, from Dwen or other ancestry, or a glamour or henna, was im-possible to tell.

Eld leaned to shout at Patrycan, "How did the men get past the Guardian of Amer's Keep?"

Pat, in the middle of a swig, pointed to a window and the floor. It was shut now, but a ladder was lying under the beds on the opposite side of the room.

"Want one?" Torin said, appearing at Eld's side, a man in a pale blue robe in tow. He was thin, not actually pretty, but with enough glimmer it didn't matter. Torin had dragged him over, but once there he retrieved his arm.

"Unhand me, you scrawny rabbit!" he said. "I'm not sure about this hero," he added, appraising Eld. "She looks half dead!"

"You have a good eye, effa," Eld said, amid the laughter. "I feel half dead and I'm certain I'm going through the Door before the night is out!"

"Not before you tell us the tale!" a woman said. It was Tracan. "We even brought the Rabbit Stew!"

"Then what are you waiting for! Give me some!"

"The tale first!"

The room took this up, until they made such a din Eld wondered no one came to discipline them. Was the guard paid off? Danshor suddenly loomed, her tunic disturbingly short, and clapped her hands like thunder. The throng was subdued a moment.

"Get her a bowl of stew! She won't be telling any tale if she faints from hunger. Then we will have the tale." This she added with a steely eye, as if making a threat. Then she laughed, joined by Torin and most of the men. Tafli was right: that was an obnoxious habit.

By the time Eld finished her first bowl, the throng was settled on beds and around the floor, more or less like well mannered children in front of a

charcoal fire at the end of a day, waiting for ama to tell a tale. Eld took this
mood as she told them, telling no falsehood, but obscuring details that
would reveal her liaison with Seth. Patrycan's eyes glittered in particular at
some phrase; she was insightful and intelligent. Eld hoped she didn't have
to draw Pat into her confidence to prevent speculative gossip. But no one
challenged Eld on truthfulness and she thought the tale went well, the lyre
player doing a particularly good job plucking tones to match the mood.
Eld even added her venture near the Door, which seemed to impress her audience more than the actual attack. When she was done, the man Torin
dragged over sat next to her, looking deeply impressed.

"Did you see an Amerling?" he asked.

Before her brush with the Door, Eld would have scoffed. But she herself
had been curious at the time. Amerlings, the Reapers of Souls, were a myth.
Some saw them, but Eld was certain that was a phantasm like her dreaming
son's toy Vineflower.

"I don't think I came close enough to the Door," she said diplomatically,
accepting another helping of stew.

"I'm Althas," the man said.

Eld nodded, her mouth still full of stew. In short order Althas had taken
possession of all tasks regarding Eld's person. She had only to glance at
her cup, and he was ready to fill it with a bottle of wine. Eld decided to enjoy this service. She suspected Danshor or someone had made arrangements
as were done with free men. She doubted they were professionals because
she knew harlots. Even the ones who liked to appear not to be prostituting,
became expert with cosmetics and glamors to fit the time and place. Althas
and his fellows, while not as garish as Tafli, still made the same mistakes
unsophisticated men made when imitating what they thought was cosmopolitan. In short, they looked more gilded, than glimmered. And their
garb would not be found on any fashionable boy in Ta Meloshok. In Althas'
case, under the open blue robe was a white linen kirtle-shirt with red tulips
embroidered on the hems. It was bound by wide gold bandages under the
chest and he wore green shoes. While all well made individually, it made
an unsophisticated ensemble. Added to that was the bright brass jewelry,
necklaces and rings, all cheap and flashy. The most sophisticated thing
about Althas was his hair: the sides fell in guard locks, but a close braid
wove from the peak of his forehead, down where otherwise a part would be,
to hang in the back, bound by a brass clip halfway down it's length, the rest
hanging free. It was a very Meridian style; he probably saw it in a maga-
zine. He really wasn't that hard on the eyes. When Althas snuggled up
against her holding his own cup, Eld didn't object, draping her arm around

him. His scent was meadowsweet and green fern. If she couldn't be with Seth for who knew how long ...

A thought intruded. "Now I have discharged my duty," Eld said, "will some elf tell me the whole of what happened after?"

There was a brief contest of wills; Danshor wanted to be the voice, of course. But Patrycan overruled her without much difficulty, for Danshor really preferred her present activity of dancing with two men in her increasingly less modest runner's tunic. It was an ancient garment, held at the shoulders with two clips and a rope or girdle at the waist. Though professional runners – footers, messengers, couriers and the like – wore the tunic over modern bracs, breeches or some such, many women running for athletic games or simple exercise wore nothing underneath it. It was obvious to every soul in the barracks that Danshor had taken the latter habit in high spirits, Torin mimicking her, even down to having found a man to put up with her, or at least her purse. Nobody minded this exhibition, it was all in good fun, the kind of thing high spirited girls at university got up to. But Eld did not want Danshor standing over or near her, exposing herself however inadvertently. So Pat spoke, while Danshor added commentary, never pausing her salacious dancing.

"Effa Alhern came riding Fiorseth. The mustering bell rang. We should have been on the road in seconds. The captain wasn't happy ... "

"As if we'd expect to be mustered this far north!" Danshor exclaimed.

"The cavalry on duty was divided between the Rowan Oak and the Kettle. I think three were ready in time ...Tanamin, Algath and Reon." She nodded to the three women to one side of the room, two on a cot, one perched on a window sill. They all toasted and drank to them.

"It was just luck you know," Reon began.

"Shut up!" Danshor bellowed to laughter. "Gods save us from the humble, " 'I was dutiful and prepared and have so many medals I can barely stand, but it was nothing!' "

"Anyway," Patrycan continued as Danshor exchanged rude gestures with Reon and her fellows, "They galloped ahead, and our company followed after almost a quarter an hour. The 1$^{st}$ Company stayed in reserve. A messenger was sent to the Falls Gate Hound's Office and the surrounding communities were put on watch. I think the farmers are still drilling with firelances.

"Those of us with the company galloped at speed. In a couple minutes we saw smoke and knew that had to be you."

"If we go to war with the Forest, we're just turning you over to the Dwen," Althone said.

"You would too," Eld replied. Althone was a strict soul.

"We went in with hot lances," Pat continued. "Algath and Tanamin dragged you out to the road for the healers to tend while some of us pursued the enemy tracks. The rest made a firebreak. The ambulance cart took you back as soon as they arrived. We were scouring the area until dusk. Then we returned."

Eld was disappointed. "You found nothing?"

"The fire didn't help. There were footsteps and a track. A magi reported strong essence auras from several souls. Oh, there was a lot of glimmer on a patch of meadow grass. Something Effa Alhern dropped?"

"Yes, we had to leave everything behind."

"We?" Althas said.

Eld laughed nervously to cover her horrible gaffe.

"I meant 'he', of course."

"There was the charred remains of a basket," Tanamin said.

"What were you doing out there anyway?" Reon asked.

Eld felt her insides freeze as the women made the usual jests.

"You're not hiding something from us are you?"

"Seth is too far above your station ..."

"Yes!" Eld agreed forcefully. "And that is EFFA Alhern! He was picnicking obviously." Eld had to go very carefully. Even without notary training, many a mother could sense deviations from the truth just by the sound of a voice. "Say nothing, and tell no lies." But Eld had no choice; she had to speak to keep them from the whole truth.

"I don't think we should be gossiping about the commander's brother."

"She's so chivalrous," Danshor put in.

"But correct," Patrycan added, a knowing glint in her eye. "Besides, who needs to moon over a pampered Lun with such lovely men nearby?"

This was well received by all, and with that distraction the throng returned to the usual interests of military women off duty: good food, good drink and willing men.

At one point there was a rap on the window and the ladder was dragged out to allow a couple more men in, while a couple took the opportunity to leave, their paramours taking the door to meet with them outside. Another dance tune began, and some of the beds were shifted so that they could do the 'skip and tag', moon reels and even a Cambrian hornpipe.

By midnight, Eld had moved to a bed the farthest from the activity, Althas still ensconced at her side. She found herself kissing him and then fell back on the bed, suddenly very tired.

"I'm sorry," Eld said. "My desire has outstripped my vigor. And the Temple warned me not to exert myself."

"Danshor told us that."

"Did she now?" Eld stared at the rafters that appeared to have grown in place. The lanterns had been dimmed but she decided it was safest to look up. "What is Danshor doing now?"

Althas inhaled. "Well, they are obscured. But if you prefer not to watch a sister with a man ..."

Eld groaned and closed her eyes. "I enlisted to serve my nation for twenty years and I end up in a bawdy house."

"Don't mind her." A hand tentatively drifted from Eld's knee to her inner thigh. "I can do everything."

Eld lay back as Althas unbuttoned her bracs, thinking how she wanted to be on him, how she had no energy for it, and how she really wished he was Seth. But that last was a dangerous thought. Perhaps a frivolous dalliance was the cure. She put two fingers on his gold lips, stopping him before he went further.

"Shutter that lamp first."

No one was watching, but the deepening darkness of the extinguished light was a relief. Soon Eld felt Althas lips doing things below he'd obviously practiced quite a bit. It was pleasing but Eld was so weary it was hard to know if she had finished awake or in a dream. Languid tides of pleasure washed over her as Eld finally drifted to sleep.

## Chapter 7

# Spying the Enemy

Eld prided herself on being an early riser. If not actually awake before dawn, she was near enough rising wasn't a trial: at the first sound of the horns at first light she usually rose without effort. But she was exhausted from healing and the revelry of the night before, so Eld didn't stir until after the first horn had blown and it was bright enough all the lamps had been shuttered and hung outside to be renewed for the night. Some rude elf was rattling her cot with a foot. Eld blinked at the blurry image of a woman standing over her, apparently naked. She certainly didn't have her gear on, though her hair seemed to be flouted. Eld blinked and her vision cleared. The woman wasn't naked, but dressed in laced leather shorts and vest, her hair tied on the top of her head. It was the usual garb for taking exercise.

"Up with the light, Jaro of the Dawn," the woman said impatiently. "And get out of my bed."

Eld looked wildly around. She was at the far end of the long barracks room in one of the five beds at that end. The head boards of all the narrow cot like beds sat against a wall. Only the area around the door, in the middle of the wall facing the windows was free of cots, instead having a large table on each side, a place for drink and light refreshments. Currently the tables were overflowing with spent cups, crumb filled platters, empty bottles and other detritus of the night before. Eld's cot was slightly opposite the door, to the right, six cots down from where she was and underneath a window.

"Sorry," Eld muttered. She looked down at herself. A blanket lay aslant, not so much covering her as covering her still open bracs. There was no sign of the men. "Help?" she said, holding out her hand.

The woman, Tartreacha was her name, seized her hand and yanked Eld up.

"Elam," Eld said. The room spun a bit as she walked to her own bed. The entire room was currently in the chaos of running to and from the baths, dressing and tidying beds, wrapping the mattresses with sheets and folding their blankets neatly at the end of the bed. They were all the same, the beds, hard wood frames made in Federation shops with supply contracts. Four legged, cross frame, with a pad "a hand width deep and full of fine thistle down" as the phrase went, though these days it was likely to be scrap wool or rag. Their sheets were white linen, property of the garrison, laundered weekly like towels, but the blankets were the same woven light wool they traveled with.    The standard wool twill traveling blanket for foot and cav-alry was densely woven light wool, and dyed with lichens in a process that produced a dark brown color on one side, and a sage green or ocher on the other.    Rangers wore cloaks of the same material for its camouflage ability in twilight.    The material wasn't exactly cozy, but it held heat even wet, and shed water unless submerged for hours.    Even in the cooler northern Crown-land, the heat of the day lasted most of the night.    During winter, garrisons provided a comforter of heavy wool felt.    Those were now be stored in cedar cupboards, wrapped in waxed paper.    Thank the Court of Heaven for waxed paper, Eld thought, holding her side.    It didn't hurt, but her side still felt wan and fragile.

At her own bed, she saw the impression where someone had slept, her blanket rumpled.    She shrugged and set to making it.

"Sorry," Reon called a couple beds down.    "But you have a better mat-tress than mine.    And since you weren't using it ..."

Eld shook her head.    "I didn't make the one I slept in so we're blessed."

"Some of us more than others," Reon said, staring at Eld's bracs, or more specifically her crotch.    Eld had just been in the middle of shedding them to change into her training garb.    Looking down, Eld saw the heavy dark twill trouser cloth was smeared with glimmer around the closing fly.    In fact, Eld was somewhat appalled the down of her privates was similarly decorated. This never happened with Seth.

Danshor was suddenly there, cot already made, laced up to run or what-ever they would be doing.    The vest and shorts left a small band of midriff. Most women, even those who had birthed, were smooth toned.    But Danshor retained a couple ripples of stretch marks.    They were barely visible but she was proud of them.    Eld wondered if it was that thought that resisted her body healing completely.    Danshor snatched Eld's bracs, holding them up for all to see.

"Beware, young mothers," she said, taking the mocking tone of a moral scold, "the depravities of being kissed by loose men from farm lots who in-dulge over much in glimmer!"

"Save us from the Bane, are you gilded down there?" Crandal said.    She was usually a quiet poetic soul.

The laughter was deafening and an impromptu game of keep away began as Eld fruitlessly grasped at her garment as it was tossed from hand to hand like a football.    Eld was quick and fit, but the problem was so was her entire company, and they weren't recovering from having their side torn open by deadly strike.

"Oh dear," Fenath said, mimicking the fussy tone of a dowager uncle, "You must save these as an heirloom for your descendants. Shall we bronze them? Or are they gilded enough, sweetest?"

Her act was particularly ridiculous as she had a scarf left by one of the men wrapped around her shoulders like a shawl against the night chill.

Crandal pulled Fenath to her side and deepened her voice like an old matriarch. "Indeed, my dear. The tradition of The Gilded Trousers shall always be upheld in this house! For twenty-five generations it has been passed down from mother to daughter. It is on our coat-of-arms...."

Finally Eld was able to snatch the garment back.

"Very amusing! I hope everyone has been entertained!"

If anything the laughter grew louder as Eld opened her chest under the cot, and threw the bracs in while dragging her gear out. "Some souls might wonder when the wedding is, they way you two carry on."

Torin in particular laughed louder at this, and Danshor smirked nastily. But neither Fenath nor Crandal were fussed. They were both from theatrical families and thought nothing of playing roles.

"Well might you ask," Fenath said, looking at Crandal affronted. "She hasn't asked me yet!"

"You better see to that, Cran," Patrycan said. "Men become deadly over marriage matters."

"I'm waiting for the right moment," Crandal said. "Danshor is thinking the same thing no doubt."

Eld had just gotten her gear on and was about to tighten it. "Hold on!" she shouted. "Why would Danshor be the mother here?"

"Well, isn't it obvious?" Fenath said as she unwrapped the scarf and threw it in the chest under her bed. "Between the two of you, you're prettier."

This suited Danshor, who grinned like a devil, though the company had greatly muted their mirth. They could feel the potential for a real fight.

"She's right, " Danshor said. "You are prettier than me."

"I am not prettier!" Eld shouted. She knew she was being baited, but felt unable to stop herself.

Danshor rolled her eyes. "Helpers, they get so excitable, don't they?"

"I'll help you through the Door ..." Eld growled.

The mustering horn sounded and the company abandoned their horseplay and jogged out the door, a couple like Eld still tightening their laces. The vest ended just above the ribs, with lacing at the sides and front. The shorts laced at the sides and were reasonable secure. Eld, still fuming, was still tightening her fronts when they arrived at parade feild. She'd only loosely tied her hair in a tail at the nape of her neck, unlike most who tied it higher, as if they were all wearing invisible flouts. They ran out between the stable houses, through the center garrison road, then to the south parade field. It was flagged with work stone, an amalgam of rock scraps bonded with cement formed to mimic the hex flags of the Queen's roads. One of the drudge duties was scorching the fields clear fortnightly. A couple utility barrels were placed near the street side. They were full of clusters of lacquered wooden poles, twice as thick as broomsticks, and the length of a woman high. These were called "lances" and in fact were made of the same way lance poles had been before the enameled steel battle lance was standard. Each woman grabbed a lance before they trotted around the field, the length of the four sides perhaps a total of a quarter mile, before running into rows they were well practiced making, so that when they finished the company was arranged in rows of ten, six deep, each woman in the center of a ten foot sided square. Those at the front, the first to stop, immediately knelt on their left knee in the center of their square, lance held upright with both hands, left hand high, the right across so that the right forearm was parallel with the ground. Head high, at attention they waited until the rows filled behind them and the whistle was sounded by a driver, a woman charged with training garrison troops. She had not arrived yet and until the whistle sounded they would stay at attention, unspeaking. This was part of discipline, a thing reviewed quarterly under truth. A soul never knew what exactly they'd be asked, and so even impulsive wastrels like Danshor, or fey sparkwits like Torin, found it within themselves to resist shirking during duty hours. Only if they were told to be at ease would they chat while waiting.

The women of the company exercised like most of the military twice a fortnight. They would often start with the Dance, the martial art form of magi energy exercises, but today these would be done afterward. That meant they would do the usual calisthenics: squat presses, press ups and hand stand presses. Eld wasn't sure if she was able to do a handstand yet, much less a stand press. The short trot out had been fair, but she felt more winded than she expected. At least the sun was clearing the buildings to bathe them in a watery dawn light. Eld closed her eyes, feeling much better as her skin drank in the rays. She stayed a while like that until a sharp voice still a ways off shouted:

"I see several sisters asleep!"

Eld's eyes flew open. An athletic woman in black training garb was striding forward, fondling the long whistle around her neck. Like many of the women her hair was tied on the top of her head, but in an laborer's bun.

Master Sergeant Tershol wasn't notably tall or broad, like, say Danshor, but she was extremely muscular and had little to no fat. Eld heard she was an amateur wizard, which would explain it. Essence users burned more energy than the regular mother. Tershol had a darker complexion than most Sula, almost a bronze. She wasn't tanned, for no Sula ever burned or tanned. Sunlight was a tonic to Sula and at worst an excess might make a woman giddy or drunk. In rare cases, spontaneous fluorescence discharge might happen, but a mother would have to be in a desert for hours with no shelter for such a thing to happen. Even then her own fire would not hurt her, though the same could not be said about her clothes or those in close proximity. So Tershol's skin was likely due to a Dwen stream in her family; many oak Dwen, like Tafli, were tannin complected. In all Tershol looked like a bronze statue of an ancient hero come to life.

Tershol blew her whistle and shouted, "Company, stand to!"

As one they stood, lance still at their side, right arm now straight.

"Much improved!" Tershol said as she walked in front of them, scanning the women. "Nothing to rectify nightly merriment than taking good exercise. Isn't that right, Lancer Patrycan?" she said.

Tershol had paused near Patrycan who stood in the front row to the far right. This was why Eld always dawdled a bit before running out. The first out the door usually landed at the front.

"Well said, Master!"

"Indeed," Tershol drawled looking away from Pat, seeking her next victim. Alert to the threat, the company was now on its best behavior, discipline as fine as a tuned harpsichord. Finding nothing more to criticize, Tershol said, "Stand easy!"

It was the closest thing to a casual countenance during maneuvers. Right now, for exercise, it simply meant they did not have to be at attention or move as a unit. Many woman took the opportunity to use their lance for a couple quick stretches and twists before the proper exercises started.

Tershol was about to withdraw, her weight had shifted, then paused, an elk halted in the act of springing away. Tershol looked right at Eld, who had her lance overhead in both hands in the middle of a stretch.

"What are you doing here, Farthal?" she demanded.

"Taking exercise with my company?" Eld ventured.

Tershol started at her, as if she expected her to be half dead.

"The Temple released you? Or did you stubbornly drag yourself out like most of these idiots would?"

"Not me!" Algath called from the back rows. There was a smattering of laughter from others who were also not so shy to confess their duty did not extend to giving up a short holiday in the Temple.

"Silence! Farthal?"

"Master, I was given permission to leave yesterday. But they did say they preferred I stayed another night."

"I see. And what did they say about activities?"

Eld lowered her lance and prepared to be dismissed. "To take it easy and not overexert myself."

Hearing this sent half the company into a fit of sniggers. Their bodies might be present, but their minds were in a brothel.

"And so you will not," Tershol said.

"Too late!" Danshor crowed, causing another fit of laughter.

"That must have been quite a revel last night," Tershol ventured. "I won't banish you if you feel you are able, Farthal. But I'll not have you collapse either. Move from your square to the side of the field and go at your own pace if you feel over wrought."

"Master!" Eld said in acknowledgement then trotted to the side of the field to stand in one of the border squares. As she went, Reon called out, "Company, salute our Gilded Hero!"

Eld wasn't surprised to see Danshor joined a handful of wags with their hands over their hearts in a mock honor salute. They found 'Gilded Hero' amusing because that was what winning arena fighters and gladiators were called, the 'gilding' being draped and wound with a long length of gold satin before being presented for the awards. Danshor in particular would find this double meaning comical; she made a tidy sum wagering on fighters, both professional and otherwise.

Eld struck her lance down on the ground, and flipped off the wags, fingers parted in pairs, back of the hand facing out, to make a "V", a common lewd gesture. The fingers could be either up or down. Then Eld called brightly to Tershol: "Master, I want a transfer to 1$^{st}$ Company!"

"Enough!" Tershol shouted. "Stand ready! Arms up! Press up! Squat down! Stand up, arms down! Press up, squat down...."

The squat press was the basic conditioning exercise of the military. It was said, using progressive weighted lances or training weights, a soldier could be trained on nothing more and become champion material. It was simple but required flexibility and balance. It was performed thusly:

While standing with feet shoulder width apart, the "lance" was first held below the waist with both hands, slightly shoulder width apart. Then it was jerked up to shoulder height with a precision that was perfunctory with a wooden pole, but became essential with a proper lance or weighted bar. It was pressed up overhead, then, with arms still straight, one squatted down as far as one could, with the lance balanced overhead. Then one stood up, let the lance fall to shoulder level, pressed it up overhead again before squatting down, and so on, repeating the process for however many times.

Basic required fitness of a soldier, using a 40 pound 'lance', was a minimum of twenty squat-presses, in addition to twenty pull-ups, forty press-ups and the ability to run a mile in five minutes. The ancients required hand stand dips, but while part of training, they were not part of regulations. Even the most athletic and virile elf was unlikely to practically walk on her hands fully armed and equipped, and definitely not a cavalier on a horse.

It was each woman's responsibility to make time to take regular general exercise off duty during peacetime. In watchfulness frequency was increased to twice a week to ensure conditioning.

Eld had felt able enough when they started, but when they were done with the squat-presses she felt winded. While twenty was the standard to keep a mother from being thrown out as unfit, a company of elite cavalry women rarely did less than fifty and today was no exception. Eld was certain the only reason she lasted was because the sun, glorious Mother Sul, was bathing them with Her light. Eld stood at attention with her eyes closed, facing the sun. Sergeant Tershol was interrogating Althlyn. Eld remembered Althlyn had a harder than usual birth a couple years ago. She should have been healed and hale, but she kept over doing it. If she wasn't careful, she'd get jailed in the Temple.

"What about you, Gilded Hero?" Tershol said.

Eld's eyes flew open realizing she was being addressed. She was too tired to even be annoyed at the mocking name.

"Hale, Master!" she said, sharp and spry as a new recruit.

"You don't look hale," Tershol said. "You look like you're going to faint. Stop marking time with the company and dance at your pace until we run."

"Yes, Master!"

Eld no longer objected nor felt her pride was wounded. She was light headed, as if her blood was enfeebled. Her side didn't hurt but clearly the rest of her being wasn't yet recovered. So while the company went on to do a 80 press-ups and 20 handstand dips (while not a tested exercise, it was still popular with trainers), Eld went through the paces of the Dance slowly, feeling her breath and essence, as she pivoted and spun from foot to foot. It was strange to watch the company like an instructor, powerful women's bodies springing up from the ground and falling again as they did presses. As Eld always suspected but could never confirm when she was participating, at around fifty repetitions only a handful of women kept strict form, Danshor being one. At the end most sprang to their feet, as if eager for more. This was a lie; it was relief and the satisfaction one had enough energy left to spring anywhere. Eld was definitely relieved she'd been excused from the regular exercises.

Then the company Danced, not the slow gentle motions Eld was practicing, but the deadly martial form that trained each elf to be lethal in her own person, whether armed or not. But mothers of the nation were jealous of the lives of their daughters, and ancient conflicts, even with weaker opponents with crude weapons had taught the foremothers of the Federation that the risk of loss was nearly eliminated by a soldier having a full kit. The Dance was good exercise, but practically only used by troops in the direst of straits. It did however have another function of substituting for the ancient duels of honor, as it was easier to prevent two women from accidentally killing each other in their passions.

Eld moved slightly away from the whirling figures striking the air with feet and fists. The dance done at a martial pace, by Sula, in sunlight, was dangerous to be near. The aura of each woman became so energized it could be seen with the naked eye even by humyn, a sphere surrounding each elf. Now with every strike in the air, a burst of bright light and heat blossomed, a discharge of active essence. With some of the more powerful individuals, including Reon, Patrycan, Danshor and Torin of all souls, their movements left fiery tracings, like afterimages of a fire dancer's spinning lanterns. There was a reason this discipline was practiced on stone or tiled floors in Sula countries. Here, it helped keep any weeds down that tending had missed. As the Dance ended, Eld prepared to leap aside. Most of the company made a game of seeing who could fluorescence the most afterwards, a discharge they tried to direct upwards. But since few were magi trained, high spirits could result in scorched garb or hair. No one was ever seriously injured. As Eld covered her eyes at the sudden brightness , the wind rushing in the heated air as women shouted, dodged and laughed, she saw more clearly the main reason for lack of injury was because, as elfyn, they were fast enough to evade it.

The company fell out, preparing to run, and Eld found herself blinking. She hadn't closed her eyes fast enough and bright spots interrupted her vision.

"Still hale, Farthal?" Eld heard Tershol ask while she blinked.

"Ai, just dazzled."

"Good. You'll run with Althlyn at the tail, three quarter speed."

"Yes, Master."

The company sprinted in double files past the Rowan Oak, then out the gate onto the road. They would run towards the village, then take a left fork before the inn, turning on The Old Farm Road as it wended between two hills, the boundary of two farm lots, then rose through a Greenway, part of which was a copping wood of old oak. It was a little easterly of the place Eld and Seth had trysted. The mountains weren't actually nearer, but the land dipped in such a way the view to the east was clear for miles.

When speaking of the Altans, one wasn't speaking of a series of tame ridges like the western forested coast of the Ethynsul and Dwenoshire, and certainly not the bald mounds in Cambrian lands that might as well be glorified hills. As scholars told it, the Altans grew where two or more lands strove against one another, driven by forces of Eurath so powerful they pushed and buckled over timeless eons into the tallest white peaks of the continent. If there were ever greater mountains, they were long gone before the coming of othyn, elfyn or humyn. The dense cluster of ridges included hundreds of peaks, most unknown except for the most prominent like Amerdwol or Amer's Rise, Skyrie and Othynde, the Dragon Seat. Amerdwol was to the south; Eld doubted even in sunlight she could pick out that peak. Skyrie was said to be the tallest, but deep in the thick of the range, the spine of which divided the continent, giving the range other names like Ramoth's Ridge. The mountains were thought to be the inspiration for the mythic Spined Eel, the fatal nemesis of the hero Jaro. The Nord humyn had a comparable myth, a serpent so large it circled the Orb. Even looking on the peaks in the distance, bright in the late morning sun, stark white, hovering over green foothills fading to blue in the distance, one could imagine the unlimited possibilities of exotic adventure. The lands in the shadow of the mountains inspired tales of gnomes blessing worthy mothers with treasure, dragon moots apparently for the sole purpose of giving wisdom to the intrepid seeker and underground cities of diamonds and jewels. That last one was probably based on a truth, Eld mused darkly, thinking of her Bane-like adversaries.

Eurthani. The more she thought on it, the more certain she was. They had been elfyn and used weapons not known to magi or any crafter of the Shard Hills, where laired the largest consortium of blast furnace shops that supplied the Federation military.

So what did the Eurthani want? Apart from despoiling Sula men? That was a puzzle Eld turned over as she jogged with Althlyn, the company easily a quarter mile ahead of them. They chatted on and off about the weather or other inconsequential things, but Eld was always looking to their right, to the mountains, the purpose of the Eurthani weighing on her mind.

The women with glowing eyes had been soldiers. Soldiers were part of a force, and a force was sent with a purpose, by a power, with a goal. Whatever it was, it didn't require them to hide their presence. Were they lost? No, their goal would be to return, not detour in an alien country and molest men. There had to be a greater force of them nearby. Surely other strategists better than Eld were considering these matters at the same time. However, Eld would feel more secure knowing the answers now.

"They're coming back," Althlyn said as they trotted up on a high ridge. It leveled out for the rest of the way, the course turning around in a great grassy field used to practice cavalry maneuvers. The total run was about five miles. But Eld and Althlyn would cut their jogging two miles short because they'd be running back with the company when they passed them.

"Thank Paradise," Eld said. She wasn't actually exhausted, but she could feel her body would run out of energy sooner than she expected. Maybe she should have stayed in Temple another day.

They yielded to the side of the grassy lane to avoid being overrun by their returning fellows and paused to catch their breath. As they turned Eld saw a flash in the corner of her vision, something she didn't expect. She looked more carefully. A bird with white flashing landing in a distant tree perhaps? She scanned the trees, then mountains.

From this vantage on a low rise, looking east early in the morning, everything was still shadowed and mists rose from valleys as Sul released the night dew into the air. Ramoth's Ridge jutted darkly into the sky in the distance to the left of Eld's field of vision, a haze of mist from the Passage Cataract merging with low gray clouds above the horizon. From this rise it was obvious how the ridge sloped away to the south abruptly, revealing what the first settlers called the Dawn Country, a lay of meadow and hills that seemed to rise together to be immediately overshadowed by steep foothills of the Altans, either bare of trees or harboring clusters of tall stubborn conifers. In the early days of the Federation humyn tribes of various sorts migrated through high steppes and mountain meadows in the north Altans. The ancestors of the Nords, Tenes and Picti took paths through Dwenoshire, perhaps explaining how the runes of the Tenes-Cambri and Nords came to be, as they were almost certainly copied from Dwen scripts pressed into wood. The Gaels and Prithi migrated along the border between Sula lands and the Forest. All these tribes were allowed to pass provided they caused no mischief to mother, man, child or beast. And ever after they carried tales of the fairies or elves who had marked their souls.

The only tribes that were trouble were the steppe riders who drove their people to raid the Bright Plains of the early Federation. Even that wasn't a proper war. Mothers and men across the Crownland rose up at the first news of children kidnapped, and the raiding humyns were burned alive in droves. Some escaped to the east but most died. Slaves or thralls of the raiders were allowed to leave and their descendants lived still in north mountain valleys, peacefully tending their herds. Legends of the angry Bright Ones who had been offended were still told and for this reason humyns of the steppes never crossed the Ath. They rarely came to the high meadows except for festivals and rites of passage, always with many rituals to avoid offending the spirits that dwelt near.

Althone had been a great resource, satisfying many a curiosity with her knowledge of the region. It was why Eld scanned the distant meadows and foothills, and then closer to them where the Ath lay hidden as it wended from Fern Lake, flowing south and east, before it bent west, passing around the ancient island principality of Meridian. Meridian was the only ancestral estate whose nobles still had a legal right to rule in the modern nation. After Meridian, the Ath became the river Hethlyn and eventually turned south to empty into the Bay of Gashora. It was possible the flash she saw came from a reflection on the water. But the Ath was still a narrow mountain river and its course cut a shallow canyon through rock before it grew and turned, somewhere to the south of where they were. It could not be the source of the flashing.

Had it come from the sky? Now and then one did see Thyngalu, the fly-ing dragons, above the peaks. But not today. Eld was about to abandon the search and accept the flash had been her tired eyes and essence when she saw it again. It was a distinctly mirror-like flash, and then another, not from the mountains or meadowland, but a hill ridge much closer, perhaps only a league away, nearer to them, west of the Ath. Eld stopped and stared, letting her natural essence use the sunlight to enhance her vision. The longer she looked, the clearer it became: in a place the pines grew, figures moved up where the trees thinned, glittering, beetle-black with a greenish blue cast. If Eld could guess, these figures were armored in bright, dark metal, moving slow but not clumsily. Eld's heart hammered. They disappeared up the path, going behind an outcrop and not returning. Eld became aware she wasn't alone.

"See something, Farthal?" Tershol said in a calm, even tone, as if not to startle a shy cat. Soldiers knew not to spook a mother sighting in the sun.

"Yes," Eld said. "I think they're soldiers. I'll have to report this."

Eld felt Althlyn and Tershol join her sighting, the air around them shivering.

"Those women are wearing armor," Althyn said. "Champion armor. But how are they moving so fast?"

"Fast" was relative. Champion armor, the form fitting, interlocking plates of past ages, was obsolete in war; speed and strike were what made victory, not armored behemoths battling their equals on a field. And since the fall of the corrupt Lot Lors millennia past, there were no champions of hostile powers that required an answering force. A handful of gear remained in modern military costume: the gorget, wrist guards and of course the helmet. Other than that, champion armor was only used in champion tournaments and on stage. Actors made false armor out of painted paper paste.

At its height, when power hungry women poured their wealth into fitting out their champions to the point of virtual indestructibility, the pieces were still designed to allow as much movement as possible. For an elf agility and speed were considered essential. But even at the height of skill, the best armorers could not make a full suit a woman could easily run in for long distances. Eld had worn one of these suits once in a study on ancient war. She could lope if the ground was even and even run if she was in sunlight. It was not easy to see and ears in particular were muffled, not just by the metal, but by batting to protect from short term hearing loss. While heavy, the suits supported themselves in many ways and one didn't really notice the weight until one needed to move suddenly or reach beyond the center of gravity. Then again, mounted champions weren't expected to need to run.

But these black armored figures trotted as easily as foot soldiers in standard kit. If Eld didn't know better she'd think they were insect creatures and the armor was their natural hide. The line of figures disappeared after several minutes. The panorama of the Altan foothills was again free of Bane like mysteries, at least for now.

"Mark the place, cavalier," Tershol said. "Report to the commander instantly on our return."

Eld took a moment to commit the vision to memory, and then ran back to join the rest of the company.

## Chapter 8

# Conference

When they reentered Falls Gate Keep the company mustered before being counted, then dismissed to their regular duties for the day. But Eld ran on, away from the parade field, and to the grand house that was reserved for the garrison commander.

It was an old building with classical inspired architecture: circular and semi circular archways of the Sula style. There were only two stories, with a raised watch platform near the roof. The first floor was larger than the second, much added on centuries after the original building, now looking like the sprawling matriarchal estates in the suburbs of the southern seaside city Gashora. But the proper entrance was still obvious, a solar arch, that is, a whole circle arch and facade covered by a pillared porch, at the top of wide, white, ash-lime cement steps. One knew the conceit of the builders, married to both brightness and thrift, by their use of lime. In contrast, local stone buildings were made from dark or greenish hued rock. Still ash lime did last, and when it wore, it was easier to repair and replace, though many insisted modern ash-lime was never as good as that made under the rule of Queens. And if all this did not give a soul a certainty they were at a place of importance, the sign above the lintel, marking it as "Falls Gate Keep; Commander's Residence" would leave no doubt.

Two guards stood at ease at the base of the steps. They were only required to snap to attention if an officer or member of the commander's household passed them. It was considered a plush post, a chance to relax, do mental work, or chat, assuming the women were agreeable. The worst thing for such a post was a scatter brained helper always returning for something forgotten, or children who would deliberately try the guard's patience until their keepers or mothers ordered them to stop. Since Commander Alhern had neither helper nor children, the duty was reported to be the most pleasant of any place Eld had been stationed.

As Eld approached, the women pulled the lances they were leaning on straighter, but then relaxed. Eld had no helix on her running habit marking her as an officer. They nodded to Eld as she walked between them.

Halfway up the steps, Eld paused, turning back. "Aren't we in Watchfulness?"

The women looked at her, then at each other.

"True," one said. "But I'm not sure how that changes our duty ..."

"Aren't you supposed to challenge me? At least that's what the spark did outside the stables last night."

"That's night, knownt?" the other woman explained. "During daylight, no difference."

"Very well," Eld said and continued on her way.

It sounded less reassuring as she thought on it, walking through the open doors and into the shadowed vestibule. She and Seth had been attacked in full daylight. Just beyond the entrance, Eld had an impression of spacious stoic decor, brilliant, white, holly-wood furniture, tables covered with glass and spare of frivolities except feminine accents like a porcelain river vase or a bronze horse sculpture. The drapes, pulled back from the long window for the day, were dark wine picked out in gold tracery. There was no carpet, the checkered floor inlays of alternating white and gray tile declaring this was a floor of purpose, not a place of idleness. The simple hard chairs and divan with minimal cushions seemed to echo this.

"Cavalier?" a voice queried. It was the butler, dressed in traditional dark green complete with a somber cast.

There were few places women wore cosmetics outside of parties, pranks and theater. Domestic service was one such place. The casts or moods dated from the Sunqueens, who, like actors, wanted their expressions to be seen by the eyes farthest in a theater. The ancient monarchs lined their eyes and brows with dark kohl, gall ink or charcoal to advertise their mood. Then the original point was to be neutral and inscrutable, the Queen having no favorites. Now butlers and others in service seemed to make their cast one of permanent seriousness, as if perpetually mourning the death of a dear pet.

"I am Emha Sonamor. How can I serve you?" the woman asked. Many mocked butlers as condescending, but this woman's voice and mood was truly neutral.

"I've seen something the commander should be informed of immediately," Eld said. She prepared to launch into an explanation, but the butler simply nodded and beckoned Eld to follow.

She was led through the main sitting room and down a corridor. They paused outside a pair of closed double doors.

"Wait here," the butler said and went inside. Briefly Eld saw officers around a long table before the door was shut. If she was very quiet she might be able to hear what they were saying....

"Eld?" a man's voice called out behind her.

She turned to see Seth. He was wearing pale green over a cream kirtle, an empty basket in hand.

Eld didn't know what to say, but it was nice to look on him. "Are you traveling somewhere?"

Seth set the basket on a table before walking to her.

"I have to tend to the accounts in the village. Just frivolities."

"Isn't that servants work?"

"I need to get out."

"Get out or get away from your sister?"

"Both," he said darkly, his voice taking a deeper tone. "I will not be caged." Seth looked at her, smiling slightly. "Not overdoing it are you?"

"No, our master trainer saw to that." Eld became aware she wasn't standing at ready and corrected herself, turning her eyes to the door. "Sorry. I am on duty."

Seth walked around so that he was in Eld's sight without her needing to change position. He was warm and smelled sweet....

"You smell like honey," Eld said quietly.

"You smell like ...a strong woman of vigor."

"Sweat you mean," Eld said smiling.

Seth leaned in, his lips close to hers but not touching.

"I could pull a bath," he breathed.

Eld felt her eye brows involuntarily raise. "Here?" she breathed.

"I didn't say a tryst. Just a bath." Seth's eyes drifted to the closed door. "They'll be there for hours. I've seen the schedule."

Then the air between them shifted and Eld could feel Seth's aura touching hers. Feeling their essence spiraling together almost made Eld reckless....

But then the image of Commander Alhern interrogating her in the Temple loomed from memory and Eld did her best to pull her aura in. It would not do to stretch her luck and certainly not under the roof of the woman who held Eld's career in the palm of her hand.

Instead Eld asked, "What agreement did you come to?"

Seth pulled back, clearly piqued. "If you must know I left before we come to an accord."

Eld looked around, wide eyed in spite of herself.

"We were rowing and I left." Seth paused. "I'm not proud of it. She's ..."

The door opened, interrupting Seth. Eld was grateful beyond measure she had controlled the urge to kiss him. She was looking down the long table at the end of which was the commander. Even from this distance Eld knew from her stare she marked how close Seth was to her.

"You may enter," Sonamor was saying.

Doing her best to act as if Seth was a random knave she had no regard for, Eld marched inside and saluted. "Commander!"

Alhern stared at Eld for moments, more moments than a superior usually did before acknowledging a salute. The door shut behind her and still Alhern stared. Finally she said, "At ease cavalier. For those of you who are unfamiliar, this is the worthy horsewoman who rescued my brother."

Amid the murmurs of praise and approval, Eld said, "It was my duty and I was pleased to discharge it."

"Indeed," the commander said, her smile not reaching her cold unfriendly gaze. Eld could only imagine the row. "Now tell us of this sighting."

Eld forced herself to calm her mind to convey the particulars, every detail no matter how slight. When she was finished, the women regarded her. Eld was relieved that the news had diverted the commander's mind in so far as she no longer glared at Eld with foreboding.

But it was another woman who spoke next, a field captain in a dark ranger garb. Eld recognized her from the Rowan Oak.

"How are you certain they are the same entities?" she queried. "The women you encountered were not armored."

"I can't explain it, captain," Eld replied. "But they have the same feel about them."

"A taste for our men?" quipped Captain Hawthorn. Half the women chuckled with amusement, women more daring that Eld. The commander did not join in.

"That is my brother your are speaking of," Alhern said icily.

Hawthorn coughed, muttering an apology, while the other women busied themselves with their documents or drinks. "Farthal, is there more to add?" Alhern asked.

"I don't think so, emha."

"No more signs of these fell weapons?" Hawthorn put in, looking as serious as possible. "Captain Draeyn is understandably anxious to avoid Bane weapons in the wilds."

The ranger twisted her mouth in an ironic smile. "Thing is, for as many stories told of the elusive Druai or Eurthani, there is very little physical evidence. But I have listened to treerunners and others of the Dwen nation ..."

Here a couple women snorted. The narrow minded thought the idea that Dwenoshire was a proper "nation" was stretching the tale. Draeyn ignored them.

"Treerunners I've spoken to tell of encounters and trade with Eurthani individuals of a less Bane-like character. They live further north, in the highest peaks of the Altans. They are said to be as swarthy as these villains our lancer met, but given to long, wild hair, barbarian kilted plaids and strong drink. They hunt by starlight and have weapons of a strange make, black metal, like this."

Captain Draeyn pulled a sheathed knife from inside her coat and set it in the center of the table, sliding it close enough to Alhern that she could pick it up. The sheath was typical, well made, but from a scaled animal, or perhaps a facade of scales, for it was too sturdy to be only fish or lizard scaled as it appeared. The handle was black, in the cunning shape of a roosting bat, delicate folded wings and details picked out in the same way of frosting glass, perhaps an acid applied with skill. Alhern seized the knife in one hand, the sheath in the other. Eld was very still, wanting to see this wonder, fearing if her presence was remembered she'd be banished. She held her breath while Alhern unsheathed the knife.

The light from the skylight fell into the liquid black blade and seemed to ripple along the edge. There were two qualities, a deep fine sparkle, like that found in the blackest aventurine glass, betraying a crystalline quality. But there was also a surface shimmer with hint of green and blue. Eld shivered. Unbidden she exclaimed, "It's the same metal as the armor! And the Bane-weapon!"

Alhern met Eld's eye's briefly. Then she stared back at the blade. "It is quite cold," she said. "Like marble or stone." Holding the edge up to the light, she added, "And sharp."

"But rather small," Major Galledan said. The troops called her "The Red Major" because of her reddish underlockes. "Is it a fruit knife? Do Eurthani even eat fruit?"

Alhern passed the the knife around to be examined. "How did you come by this?" she asked Draeyn.

"A housetrade. There is a Dwen custom for visiting guests: on the eve before departure, after dinning, exchanges are offered. It's from a time when trade was infrequent and unsophisticated."

"You mean last century?" a young lieutenant put in to rude snickers at the expense of the Dwen. Eld didn't know her, but decided to mark her if she visited the Rowan Oak. Leave her to Tafli. Alhern said nothing, but Draeyn glared at the young woman.

"It's just a jest," the lieutenant said. "Tresses, live among Trees too long you'll turn into one."

"That will do, lieutenant. " Alhern said with finality.

"They didn't want to part with it," Draeyn continued. "It took a bag of lamp gems and more queens than I care to admit."

"The Dwen are not unsophisticated savages, sisters," Alhern said. "Their ways and talents are different from ours, but they know value. And rangers are perhaps not the subtlest barters."

Draeyn shrugged. Someone gasped. Eld looked with the rest at the young lieutenant and stifled a laugh. She'd cut herself examining the blade.

"Damn thing bites," the woman said defensively, sucking a finger and resentfully pushing it to the next woman. "Bane weapon."

"Bane weapon or not, Lieutenant Roel, it is simply sharp!" an unknown officer said as she examined it. "Perhaps you should not be using live steel? Kit you out in the finest training wood, should we?"

Buffeted by laughter, Roel made a face. "How extraordinarily droll," she sneered.

The blade passed near Eld and she yearned to touch it. But something jogged her memory.

"Permission to speak," she said.

"Yes?" Alhern said.

"I don't think I've said this. You have Seth's testimony...."

Alhern stared at Eld as if she wanted to set her on fire by sight.

"Effa Alhern," Eld amended. "He wouldn't know what had happened after he left ..."

Eld told them of the strike exchange and the soldier who retrieved the Bane-weapon. "She was very insistent they not leave anything behind. Yet they're selling paring knives to Dwen."

The women murmured in agreement.

"Perhaps this is cheap and common to Eurthans?"

"Maybe they are only jealous of military equipment. The Federation has prohibitions against trading steel with savages."

"Humyn you mean."

"Yes. Trees don't care about metal ..."

"Perhaps that's why they parted with it?"

"Maybe ..."

A woman near Eld was turning over the knife, careful after Roel's mishap. For a second Eld saw her gold eye reflected in the blade, a slice of the blackest pool of midnight. Eld so wanted to touch it. Then Alhern said, "If that is all cavalier, we should not keep you."

Disappointed, Eld saluted smartly, turned on heel and left, perhaps shutting the door behind her sharper than necessary.

Selfish hoods, Eld thought in bad humor. She shivered. She'd long since cooled down from the run and it was cool in the shade of the house. She needed a bath and honestly wasn't sure where to report to. They weren't doing more maneuvers today. Perhaps they'd let her take Fiorseth out for a turn. It was good for a cavalier to reconnect with her mount after a mishap. But first she had to get out of the commander's house and without Sonamor's help, if felt like a maze. How many sitting rooms and galleries did a woman need? They seemed to perpetually lead into one another.

Then she saw a basket sitting on a table outside a room with a heavy door standing ajar. It was the same basket Seth had earlier, now with a small sheaf of paper notes. The door opened onto a private library, a small room by floor space, but the walls rose to over twenty feet high, covered with shelves of books, so high it had library ladders along the walls. A solstone domed skylight drew the light in so efficiently it was like standing in a sunny field. Seth was half sitting at the edge of one of the tables, a small book in hand, while flickers of light flashed along his hair. He glanced up once then back to his book. He was marking notes in charcoal.

"Back from your important meeting with important mothers?"

"Your sister must be very upset with you. I think she wanted to burn me alive on the spot."

"Don't be ridiculous. How can she award you medals for bravery if you've been cremated?"

"If there was a way, I don't doubt she'd find it."

Seth looked up, with an air of impatience. "So why are you still here?"

"You seem irritated with me as well."

"You seem to care more about what my sister thinks than my presence."

"You want me to be reckless enough to be stationed on the border of Sharitan? Didn't you warn me you yourself could be chaperoned?"

Seth glared in frustration then exploded. "Very well! I know I'm not being rational! But it offends me! I'm not a boy! I should be able to consort with whom I wish!" He sighed, then added more calmly, "And I should not take it out on you, my most brave and worthy cavalier. Will you forgive me?"

The light seemed to brighten, the finest part of the air allowing more brightness than should be possible. Seth's gold eyes flickered warmly. His lips parted.

"Well, that depends," Eld said.

The door to the study opened inward so it was an easy thing for Eld to push it shut. It was made so well she didn't even need stealth; it swung silently, shutting with a quiet snap. "There should be a price of some sort."

As she stepped towards Seth, he set the book and charcoal pen on the table. "Perhaps a kiss, like the Lakeson gave Amer before he took her to the Janus Scythe?"

Eld leaned into Seth, her hands on either side of the table, 'trapping' him. "There is no Lun to restrain Amer from taking you as she yearned to do with the Lakeson."

"So you will be Amer after all," Seth breathed. "And I will wear water and dew. But unlike the Lakeson, I will happily let you take me ..."

And then Eld was kissing him and she felt the air would explode. It would madness to coit here, surely they had some semblance of self control. But part of Eld knew the time was apt and Seth was right; the over serious officers would be in council for who knew how long and with the door shut they would be unobserved. The only real danger was perhaps setting a book or two on fire.

Eld had pulled Seth's robe and kirtle-shirt up, the shield a simple thing to force aside. But when Eld felt Seth's fingers at lacing on her shorts, her wiser self took command of her mind and she seized his hands, stopping him. Gasping, she closed her eyes, and forced herself to pull back. In a low voice she said:

"We have reviews, Seth. They are not always read for truth, but they could be. One never knows what might be asked and I could not hide this if I was asked. I'm sorry. I can't do that to my children, be sent so far away from them. But come to me in dreams and I will take you any way you want."

Then, not daring to look at him, Eld threw herself at the door, yanked it open and fled the study. Soon she stumbled over a servant who help her escape the commander's house and the temptation within.

## Chapter 9

# The Hero's Doom

The mists parted as Eld walked in the light of a sun that was brighter yet cooler than it ever was in waking. She followed Fiorseth, no longer her mount, but a pale, wise horse guiding her foals to safety. Eld understood she was one of the foals and Danshor, walking next to her was the other. They were secure, confident their dame knew all the best places with the finest tasting grass…

Then the scene shifted, Fiorseth disappeared, and Eld and Danshor were back at the welcoming fete, watching a glamorous Seth wrangle admirers. Seth moved closer, and the scene shifted again; Eld was no longer at the fete, but in some woman's private study, where a woman and man argued with fading heat, both exhausted from the battle. Eld was standing in the doorway and became aware she was awake in a true dream.

"Why don't you join us?" Commander Alhern said, looking at her with a foreboding intensity.

"You are awake too?" Eld asked.

"Don't you see our auras? It seems the argument between myself and my dear brother, having failed to be resolved in waking, has drifted into Dreams. But not before I saw him wandering towards the thought of your barracks."

Seth sighed, standing. "Perhaps I should inquire why exactly you, dear sister, were wandering towards the Rowan Oak. Surely if you are going to Travel, you don't need to dream of cheap barley-mead."

"Some of us do dream of merry times with sisters and men we can't indulge in waking. But that is not the subject. Sit down, Farthal, and join us. Perhaps we can resolve this before we all wake."

Eld walked into the room carefully. She didn't actually have to obey. Dreams and thought were part of a mother's rights in her person and soul. But Eld didn't fancy the fate of her service if she refused. She met Seth's eyes. Seth looked alarmed. He looked her up and down sharply, then looked away. Eld became aware her feelings of being exposed had manifested: she was nude.

Eld tried not to panic to keep her body from waking, jolted with adrenaline. Eld focused, moving her feelings of vulnerability into thoughts of defense and was satisfied to be garbed in ancient armor, like the statue of Amer at the doors of the Crèche. She was over dressed and looked theatrical in comparison: Alhern wore a vest and loose trousers and Seth had a thin kirtle-shirt. But she wasn't an embarrassment. Eld hoped Alhern hadn't noticed, but the remains of a smile played at the commander's lips as she met Eld's eyes again and gestured to a chair.

Eld sat. Immediately she felt the chair subtly squeeze her, channeling the commander's thought she should not leave until she was allowed.

"I have been yelled at in my own house for longer than I care about being an unromantic troll, thwarting passions," Alhern said. "Let both of you know that, were it not for the circumstances of all our stations, I would not care one jot what you did with each other.

"But, Seth, as my brother and the manager of a commander's house, it is your duty to maintain the plausible appearance of masculine modesty and an aura of dignity. Farthal, as a soldier of humble station and indifferent ambition, it is your duty to respect the ranks of your betters and their household. If your intentions are no more than a summer fling, then I can forbid you from fraternizing with my brother."

"No regulations stipulate that, and you know it!" Seth objected.

"But they do stipulate an officer may forbid soldiers of a lower station from openly wooing men of their household. Practically that includes liaisons and trysts. Elderyn Farthal cannot woo you. Oh yes, should the thought birth in your mind, you are forbidden cavalier, because I cannot allow my brother to waste his time with a woman of no prospects, at least not while he is living in my house. It is my duty to look after his interests."

Alhern paused, letting the various meanings be understood.

"Now, that said, there does seem to be a genuine affection beyond the heat of trysting and 'poetry' between you. While you are at this time forbidden from wooing my brother, if your station or prospects change, that might change as well. But I see no ambition, Farthal. You are a solid mother, but have no drive to go up the ranks, much less seek a commission. It is good enough for women, but men married to such a mother rarely live in the comfort they prefer.

"If you can respect these terms, and never boast or brag about your liaison, we may come to an agreement."

Multi colored pale mists swirled around Seth, leaving brief images, impressions of his seething thoughts. "I feel disposed of like the estate chattel," Seth opined.

"Don't be ridiculous," Alhern said.

"I am not a child," Seth added.

"No, you are not," Alhern said. "Else I would have sent you back to the Alhern estate already. Farthal, your thoughts?'

Eld reminded herself lying was unwise in dreams, if not impossible. So she chose her words carefully.

"Considering your position, I think you are being fair." Seth snorted, but Eld looked at him seriously. "Truly she is. She could forbid us each others' company if she wanted. I admit to being surprised at my affection for your brother, and though I was willing to set him aside, I would prefer not to."

"I would prefer not to be spoken of as if I wasn't here," Seth said.

"I think you have spoken enough over the days," Alhern said as if Seth was a soldier.

Seth glared but was silent.

"It is also true I cannot say my intentions are more than a summer dream," Eld continued. "I have never sought a helper, but I would not reject the right man were I to meet him. But it is true, I am not worthy of Seth's hand today were it to come to that. What are you saying, commander?" Eld spoke more boldly, and she noticed her clothes change from armor to her regular uniform, unbuttoned as if having just finished duty for the day. "I will abide by any reasonable terms. Else abstain from effa's company except in dreams. Yes, commander," Eld said as Alhern seemed to want to inter- ject. "Dreams are the right and province of every mother and man's soul. Anything we decide here is but an agreement between mothers. It has no le- gal weight. However I will agree to formalize arrangements when we wake."

Alhern sat back, looking Eld once over. "I should be pleased you can be bold with me. Any mother pursuing my brother had better have an iron gut ..."

"She values both obedience and bravery in her soldiers," Seth put in. "Just not at the same time."

"They are not mutually exclusive," Alhern said. "Men never understand this. Very well, Farthal, then this is our agreement: provided you remain discreet, and you do not reveal in any way, even in dreams, your liaison with my brother, at my pleasure, to be revoked at any time, you are allowed to tryst only in my house."

Eld was so shocked that her soul shivered. The room started to smear out of focus, like a child's watercolor painting fallen into a pool. The comman- der and Seth's voices became distant and Eld felt herself falling.

"Now look what you've done," Seth said. You've shocked her awake ..."

Eld opened her eyes in the barracks. It was still dark. A couple of women wheezed in their sleep, the closest elfyn came to snoring. Eld sat up in her cot, wondering at the dream.

Surely the commander wasn't suggesting she sneak in to tryst with Seth in her own house? But true dreams never lied. Perhaps she was wrong and it was just a dream. How would she know? She supposed if it was true she'd find out soon enough.

Eld looked out the window. The sky was clear and the stars were bright. She rose, quietly dressing in her basic riding gear.

"Where are you going?" Danshor muttered sleepily from the cot next to her.

"Taking Fiorseth for a ride.."

"Today's your big day, Gilded Hero."

"Return to your dreams of endless harlots. I'll be back in plenty of time."

It was to be a bright day, cloudless except for the lingering mists that lurked around the horizon, biding their time for the evening chill. Now noon, the entire outpost had turned out for the ceremony. So too had the surrounding communities, who seemed to to have taken the events of the past week as an excuse for a holiday. A field nearby had been opened for a gathering, with farmers and townsfolk trading and an abundance of music and dance. Eld expected the Rowan Oak would be doing quite some trade. At times like this, with farmers gathered to sell, Tafli would be up early to select the best produce, a task he trusted to no one but himself. Often men, and even women, would follow in his wake, marking the farmers he bought from. Snide though many could be about the sophistication of Dwen, they were unequaled at judging the worth of vegetables and produce.

A more refined celebration would be held at the commander's house, showcasing the work of the men of the house, their crafts as well as good food. The household had grown in the last couple days after the arrival of the commander's nephew, his keeper and tutor. He was a pleasant enough looking boy, now standing in the ranks of the commander's household near the heroes' dais, a platform that had been raised outside the doors of the Garrison Hall. Eld forgot the nephew's name, but he was wearing layers of white, embroidered thickly with patterns of bright yellow, with a pale silk mantle draped around his shoulders. In all he reminded one of a daffodil. His face was free of glimmer except for the faintest dusting of the lips, undoubtedly the influence of the tall, stern man who stood next to him in chaste white linen accented with the barest of decoration at the hems.

The nephew's keeper was a man of a certain age, usually between his second and third century. Though youthful in appearance, he was dour, if not by temperament, then by profession. For it was his duty to be a model of masculine modesty and virtue, guiding and watching his charge that he remain free of wayward influences. If the keeper had a lover, she was unknown to the household that paid him and might only visit through dreams. If he valued his position, he never mentioned his paramour, unless he was being wooed in seriousness for marriage. It wasn't unheard of for a keeper of boys to be married, but it wasn't common. Most married men had enough to manage in their wife's household. His livelihood depended on him being a cool forbidding presence, protective of his duties, yet politic enough to navigate the household where other men out ranked him. Eld could see where this could be awkward for Seth: Seth would be the senior man in the commander's household, and expect to be deferred to. But the keeper answered directly to the commander's sister, and in the mother's absence might consider the commander his direct superior and any of Seth's considerations simply a courtesy. Seth's lifestyle would work against him, for any of the keeper's concerns could be framed as being for the good of the nephew's future. Eld understood why many mother's hated household strife.

Both the nephew and his keeper wore trilocks, the boy with a circlet of glass that shimmered brassily. Eld's son had one that in sunlight sent flickers of light running around the rim in fascinating patterns children found amusing. If it was a similar band, it was unactivated. It was considered rude to distract formal proceedings with private artifacts. Other than that the boy was pretty in the vague way all young men were, but to Eld's eye far too unfinished to take an interest in. He might be past his first fire, but not by much. If it was uncertain by appearance whether a boy was over his majority, it was best a soul sought companionship elsewhere.

Eld had no need to look far for what she sought. In the row forward of the boy and his grim keeper stood Seth. He looked like a laird of the old lots, wearing mail today, a jewelry fabric of fine links of gold. It draped decoratively over a sleeveless pillar robe of bright, white linen, the open links like metallic lace, falling to hang in a fringe of opal beads off his shoulders and to just above his knees. Loosely linked chains at the sides kept the mail in place. On Seth's head was a hastol, a crown like headdress of metal and solstone glass men wore for formal occasions. It was somewhat inspired by the Dwen yastol and was meant to shine at the climax of ceremony. Seth's bright blond hair was in loose trilocks, the guardlocks bound with gold clips, the back hanging straight down to his waist. As always his glimmer was discreet, enough to accent his beauty, but never cheapen it. His hands with perfect unpainted nails were bare of jewelry or decoration. He could have been a consort of the Sunqueens, manifested from the memory of history, except he wore no aspect kohl. Though he was not the focus of this event, he bore himself like nobility, correctly assuming any woman would have her eye on him.

As Alhern prepared to speak, Seth ascended the dais from steps at the side to stand by his sister, slightly in her shadow. Alhern was in formal military garb as they all were, in her case in fawn and sage, white facings and a short sage cape with white lining, with white breeches and black boots. On each lapel was embroidered a gold helix, the mark of an officer; the dress coat would also have a helix in the center of the back. Alhern's trilocked hair was parted, her guardlocks in regulation helix clips, and on her head was a command circlet, a feminine form of the hastol, a crown with four acute points, a circlet of solstone enameled brass sitting on the points. Unlike Seth's hastol, the command circlet was part of the garb of a commander of a military station when performing ceremonial duties. It would not flicker or glimmer notably. But it was said on the head of a popular commander with a happy host it might shine brightly. As Alhern was a firm but fair disciplinarian, it glowed modestly.

Among the ranks of foot and cavalry companies, the rangers stood apart, their dress uniforms identical to their duty uniforms, except for silver leaves on their black facings. Both companies of the cavalry host wore their rarely seen pale blue, gold lined capes. Except for women on duty, no one wore helmets or bands. In ancient days the Queen's Beasts, the Thyn horses who chose to serve the monarch, stood in ranks behind the host, usually on a rise or platform for better viewing. Scholars who studied these things said the Thyn mounts only did this out of courtesy, being bored by excessive proceedings. Thyn horses drifted away from the Sula army host since the abdication of the monarchy, the last herds serving in the battle of the Blue Fields. Now and then a Thyn horse might befriend a Sula soul as an individual. But the alliance between cultures had faded, the interests of horses and elfyn becoming too greatly divided. The only horses who still served were the simple beasts Eld and the rest of the cavalry host sat on, though Eld could tell a scholar even dumb horses were bored with elfyn ceremonial proceedings. Every mounts' mind was full of questions: why, if they were doing nothing, could they not wander in fields nibbling grass?

Eld patted Fiorseth's neck. ~It shouldn't be too long, girl,~ she thought.

"Nothing better to see on a fine bright day than a fine bright host!" Alhern said in a vibrating voice that carried across the grounds. Civilians from the fringes whistled and clapped, but every service woman stood in her ranks, with her company, at attention. A time would come for cheering later.

"I ascended this command at Falls Gate Keep a decade ago," Alhern continued, "and I can honestly say I am proud of this garrison and the women who serve therein. Those of you familiar with wishes and wants of soldiers know that many of us came to this path dreaming of glory in days gone by, deeds done in the name of Sunqueens, serving the mothers of the Bright Plains ...and not just in the cause of rounding up thunder scared sheep."

Alhern paused for the expected laughter, a rolling chuckle through the ranks, the civilians  loud and free with their mirth.

"In time wisdom settles in our souls and we appreciate the peace and safety our foremothers  worked so hard to build in the Queen's Commonwealth and continued under the government of mothers.  Yet still we maintain watchfulness and that preparation is part of security, for times may come when our peace must be defended.  It is with this foresight a modern soldier trains, to discharge her duty when the unexpected arises.

"A fortnight ago such an event arose.  A man was attacked in our peaceful forests, by persons unknown.  In the ways of Felkeni, a cavalier was nearby and came to this man's aid, at great risk and almost to her mortal peril.  For her actions saving this man and securing his safety, we are empowered to present this cavalier with the Rose Shield. In respect of mortal injuries sustained during her actions that brought her to the step of the Door, she is also presented with the Red Phoenix.  Step forward Lancer Elderyn Farthal and accept your doom!"

Eld dismounted, gave her lance to Danshor to hold, then stepped smartly from her ranks and turned to march to the dais as she'd practiced the day before, her cape swirling around her.  While she marched, the infantry host started pounding their spears against the ground.  The cavalry host did the same with their lances, dropping the foot to the ground.  Some commanders forbade vulgar applause and tasked the band with beating out such acknowledgement, but Eld heard Alhern believed every opportunity for mothers to participate reinforced garrison unity and cohesion. Excessive discipline could be as problematic as lax discipline.  Meanwhile there were mutterings in the ranks:  a Red Phoenix was rare in peacetime, at least on land.  Rose Shields weren't uncommon: they could be awarded saving civilians from banditry or fire and storm.  What exactly had happened? they all wondered.

Eld felt she'd never reach the dais.  Then she was suddenly  ascending the stairs while the commander and a couple of women from her staff watched her.  Slowly Seth emerged from the shadows, looking even more so like a king consort from the Old Realm.  He was so beautiful, mail glittering like a thousand gems in the sunlight, his hastol glowing with a hint of a rainbow halo as only the finest made hastols shined. Eld suddenly noticed her cape hung straight down, and was not thrown back over her shoulder rakishly as she planned. If she did it now she'd look ridiculous, vain or both. She'd just have to settle for the medals.

Eld stood directly in front of the commander. The pounding of hafts had stopped. She'd never noted until now the commander was ever so slightly, perhaps a half an inch, shorter than herself. Alhern was holding a thin plain box of aged cedar. She looked into Eld's eyes, her own piercing, then opened it.

The Rose Shield was an enameled black medallion with a stylized five petaled white rose in the center. The Red Phoenix was a less pretty thing, an eagle's head in the halo of a setting sun surrounded by flames. But it was cast in bare iron, treated with red oxide giving it a patina effect. Untreated it would fall to rust; Eld expected her mother would insist it was sealed with lacquer. Though the same size as the Rose Shield, it was heavier, carrying the weight of the risk of death. Alhern asked formally:

"Do you accept these deeds truthfully as your own?"

"I do."

"Do you accept these honors and the responsibilities that go with carrying them?"

"I do."

"Effa Alhern has requested to do the honors."

The commander still held the box open, but stepped to the side so that Seth, beautiful Seth, could stand before Eld.

"I still think she's earned a Battle Lion," Seth murmured as he lifted the Rose Shield. Eld dipped her head so he could reach over her flout as he placed it around her neck.

"Dear brother, a Battle Lion is reserved for declared wars and actions," Alhern breathed.

"Well, then a Ruby Torch," Seth said, reaching for the Red Phoenix. "She did raise the alarm."

"Just put the damn things around her neck. And if anyone earned a Ruby Torch, is was her horse, being as Farthal was unconscious at that point."

"My sister is so stingy," Seth breathed, as the weight of the last medallion settled on Eld's breast.

"Let's ask our hero; do you think me stingy?"

"Not at all, Commander," Eld said keeping her voice light. "I think you're the most generous and understanding commander in the garrison."

The corner of Alhern's mouth turned up in a smirk, acknowledging the joke.

"Damn right I am," she said quietly. "Now face the Host and let them deafen you with applause."

The applause was deafening but not as overwhelming as the salutes that followed, for it was the duty of those presented with honors to stand with the command staff and review the garrison host as the companies marched by: first the heralds, holding dragon streamers and banners; then the band, with deep drums and flute cries, only musical in the skill of the players with instruments whose primary purpose was signaling. A marching orchestra was a modern thing. Such tunes might sound martial, but they were too cheerful. For this ceremony the only tunes heard were dread drums and fluted notes so high they pierced the soul. Duty, longing and loss was the theme of soldier tunes. It would be left to tongues well wetted by barley-mead to sing of cheer or victory. Somewhere in the distant past singing joyously of victory after battle was seen in bad taste and the mood had barely changed millennia later.

The cavalry companies came next, horses prancing and turning in a way some found fun, others tedious. Fiorseth led them all, guided by an army groom, as if she was the hero of the day and in a way she had been. Fiorseth was supposed to walk with dignity. But, knowing her paces, she pranced to laughter, pulling on her lead until the poor girl holding it allowed the horse to move as she wished. Eld smiled. That was her girl.

The foot hosts marched after, their pace quick and crisp, mounted officers leading them. Eld spied Roel, noted her hair shimmered in the sun. She wasn't the only woman to dust her hair with glimmer, to give a hint of being touched by the Grace of Heaven, but Roel was one of the brightest.

And when the review was over, and the troops had returned to their formations, about an hour later, they were finally dismissed.

Eld looked down to find Fiorseth, but the groom was already leading her away with the other horses; her company, like the rest of the host, milling briefly on the field before going separate ways: some to the Crèche, some to the Rowan Oak, many to the fair just outside the gates; a few to the barracks to change clothes. Eld wasn't sure where to go. She looked at Seth, but he was already descending the dais to join the men returning to the commander's house.

"You will join us for refreshment, Farthal?" Alhern asked.

Eld started like a girl caught watching a boy bathing.

"Yes, certainly, thank you, Commander."

Eld swallowed under Alhern's piercing gaze.

"Good," the commander said. "My brother is showing his paintings in our many halls."

"Oh?" Eld said. Dimly she remembered Seth discussing certain plants he collected for pigments. But nothing in particular that she could add intelligently.

"Yes. My brother is a man of many talents. He has a good eye ...usually. We will see you there, Lancer." The commander gave Eld a curt nod, then trotted down the steps to join her staff following in the wake of the men.

"A man of many talents?" Danshor said, materializing by Eld's side. She had thrown her cape back already, knowing it was just a matter of time before a man drawn to dashing uniforms came into her sights.

Eld shook herself, shrugging outwardly. Inwardly she chose her words with caution:

"He's the brother of a respected commander, from the Alherns. They have ancient estates from the time of Lors. Of course he's well educated."

"Your house has an ancient estate."

Eld shook her head. "It's barely three millennia. Gallens was a gifted stream from the Galeenwol, through the matriarch's eldest son. The daughter he begat inherited the new charter. His wife was born of a vagrant mother, Farthal; they chose his mother's name, Gallens, for the prestige. After several centuries, one my ancestors, a third daughter wanted her own branch and she reclaimed 'Farthal'. Legally we're Gallens-Farthal, but no soul says that."

"I've been serving with a jumped up Wildling all this time?"

"Hardly. We have no Dwen streams and no ties to the New Forest."

"You know what I mean."

"They say vagrant mothers carry the gift of vitality. You noble farmers would be inbred millennia ago if not for us."

Danshor grinned. "Is that what you're trying to do? Swim upstream like a salmon back to a noble source?"

It was the worst time to blush. The sun, while not over hot, was shining brightly, with not a cloud in the sky. So when Eld's face flushed she saw a brief shimmer of rainbow lights. The medals suddenly felt heavy, the weight of their responsibility like a living thing. Eld became hyper aware, in all of the thronging souls, sighting the commander from the porch steps of her house as she looked back, as if to warn Eld about a boastful tongue. It was a coincidence surely. Then she was aware she still stood on the dais and jumped down. Danshor sauntered down the steps after her.

"The commander's brother," Danshor drawled. "A rich meal ..."

Eld prayed to the Court of Heaven that something, anything, would shut Danshor up. Ideally a thunderbolt.

Instead Eld heard a shrill chorus of "Ama!"

She spun on her heels, heart in her throat. Traith and Shedann were bearing down on her as fast as they could run, eyes bright, smiles blazing like the sun. A second later they leaped into her embrace, still small enough to be held in each arm. The three of them clutched each other, Eld pulling them close, not just because they were present with her in life, in her aura and in her soul, but there was a very real danger she would weep for joy.

## Chapter 10

# Keepers and Children

After kissing both children Eld managed to say, "How?"

"We came on the canal boat!" Traith said. She frowned. "I had to leave Tad behind."

"Well, you know cats don't travel."

"Vineflower is here," Shedann offered, showing his doll that was pleasantly inert. "We sang on the boat!" he added.

Walking up to join them was Silalin, in his usual long silver gray robes woven with vining patterns. His kirtle-shirt was bright white linen, his hair in simple trilocks. His only frivolity was a thin silver circlet, hammered to glitter in the sunlight. Keepers of children, when on duty, were expected to dress modestly and not seek to call attention to themselves.

"How do the leaves fall?" Sil asked, smiling.

"Oh, so brightly now!" Eld exclaimed. She put her children down to look at them better. Traith was wearing a white shirt with a vest of green fabric woven with leaf patterns. Like most active girls she wore bracs. Shedann liked to wear bracs too, so he could follow his sister up trees and share in her adventures. Not all families allowed young boys to do so. Eld had been badgered by the men of the house about the dangers of boys wearing bracs. She didn't like to argue with them. They worked hard to keep the children and the productivity of the estate. But Eld knew most boys abandoned bracs around their first fire, the age they became interested in catching a girl's eye. And the ridiculous concern he'd become a 'brother' for wearing girl's clothes was exactly that. Even brothers of passion tried to outdo each other in fashion. For now it was more important to protect Shedann from briars and nettles. As a compromise he wore a long kirtle-shirt over them. Both children wore leather slippers; soon Traith would be old enough to have proper shoes and boots. They were both clean, if a bit windswept.

"How did you get here so quickly?" Eld asked Sil.

"A juxtaposition of many fortunes," Sil said airily. "Your mother was sent a missive after we dreamed, but a missive from the Temple must have been sent at the same time because the house received it posthaste with word you had survived. The next day we received another, detailing your deeds and proposed honors. You can thank these two for badgering the estate if they could go to the awards. It was a long night of calculations between Salthyn, Reonalt and Eldshorn."

Eldshorn was Eld's mother. She'd served twenty years as a foot soldier and another fifty as a postmaster. Her sisters Salthyn and Reonalt served in the fleet and merchant canal respectively. They would all know the general timetables of such things.

"It would have been too close to rush about," Sil continued, "except it was announced the locks would open to release the last of the spring runoff."

"And all the canals would run high and fast," Eld finished. Now Traith and Shedann were chasing each other around Danshor. Eld smiled. The first time they met Danshor they were in awe of her. Now they treated her like furniture.

"Exactly," Sil was saying. "It took about half the time it usually would. We rode to Falls Gate Station from there, arriving last night. Thank Paradise they were so tired they fell asleep instantly."

Shedann squealed as he found himself spinning in Danshor's hands. Vineflower got loose, and Eld reached for the toy, but Sil adroitly snatched it out of the air.

"I am well practiced," Sil said languidly.

"Be still my little Wildlings!" Eld said affectionately, but in her deep mother's voice. She went to snatch Traith up but the girl darted away.

"I'm not a sprite anymore!" she objected.

"Very well then, my aged heir, calm your spirits if you want to meet the company in my dotage."

Instantly Traith stood still as if at attention. Shedann joined her, Danshor taking the cue from Eld to put him down. Danshor, typically an inconsiderate hood, was strangely good with children. The children's sudden self mastery came with an agenda: they enjoyed the attention the company gave them when they visited a garrison, particularly the endless treats and gifts from women who missed their own children. They knew they would be sent away if they remained unruly, probably indoors with Sil, doing dull activities like tutoring or drills.

Eld felt a vague obligation to put in a showing at the commander's house. But the children wanted to visit the barracks, and to ride Fiorseth and go to the fair, and all at once if they could wish it. And they were hungry. For that matter so was Eld. After conferring with Sil, Eld decided they should go to the barracks, freshen up and store her medals. Then they could go to the fair with Fiorseth, feed themselves, and Sil could watch them while she and Danshor put in a showing at the commanders house.

It went much as planned except that they were held up at the stables as Traith and Shedann charmed the company. It wasn't so bad: Eld was given ample time to recover from the sun and straighten her uniform, and the children had a light meal of raisin buns, fruits, nuts and sundry snacks that abounded in their barracks. After, they gamboled in the yard and insisted on helping a groom feed the horses.

"I think they cleaned us out," Eld said drying her face with a towel as she met Sil outside the door. No keeper ever was caught inside a woman's private chambers, much less an entire barrack, if he cared about his references.

"They have livened up," Sil said, watching as Traith, bored of feeding horses, was taking another turn being spun around by her hands by Reon. At the end Reon pulled her in and up, then let her go to somersault and land on her feet. When Traith was younger and lighter, she would land adroitly on Eld's shoulders, but those days had passed. Sil clapped while the women cheered.

"I'd only offer there has been a dearth of meat and savories," Sil added.

"We'll feed them up at the fair."

To their disappointment Fiorseth was one of the horses still being walked by the grooms, so they set out on foot. Traith, no longer concerned about being seen as a sprite, sat on Eld's shoulders. Shedann rode on Danshor, Vineflower safely tucked in Eld's cot under the coverings. Sil strode beside them, looking more relaxed than he usually did.

"It's like a holiday for me as well while you and your sisters are present," he explained. "I expect to be more engaged once we arrive in the midst of the throng."

"Can I have a firelance?" Traith asked, watching a group of girls somewhat recklessly play with a scorcher, a low powered farm tool much like a lance.

"Get down," Eld said boosting Traith up so she could scissor her legs around and back, dropping behind Eld. Eld was looking for a woman in charge, but Danshor was already striding over, Shedann still on her shoulders.

"That's a bold lance," Danshor said. "Can I see it?"

The girls eagerly handed it to her, proud of their activity. "I can get it hot enough to scorch a fly!"

Danshor nodded, holding the rod. "But you know, if it's hot enough to kill flies, you could start a fire unknowing."

The girl looked wary. "Who are you?"

"I'm not as important as that mother there," Danshor said, pointing to Eld. "That's the hero of the day, Ai."

The girl's eye's lit up and soon Eld was surrounded by her and her friends.

"Is it true you fought the Bane?"

"And struck down a forest with strike?"

"And rescued a prince?"

"Where is your lance?"

"Can you show us strike?"

Eld was rescued by a group of women who had been notified of the girls' reckless behavior.

"No lances for you," one woman said, now holding the rod. "There are plenty of flash sticks, that's more your speed."

"But we want to see strike!" they chorused.

Traith helpfully added, "Maybe we can invite them to the barracks, ama."

Eld adored her children. But herding a mob of lot children into the garrison all so they could watch her strike a bale or log was not what she'd had planned.

Luckily some inspired soul had already come up with the idea of having a game of strike for some prizes, a common thing at these type of fairs. The lance was old and worn, decommissioned surplus, its flashing enamel in need of retouching. But the sky was clear and the sun was bright. And so when Eld was directed to strike the perched log, it was an easy thing. It exploded in flames, the flash blinding many for a second. The crowed cheered with applause.

Traith and Shedann became instant celebrities among the children who vied with each other to reenact Eld's deeds. Meanwhile Eld was given a ball of straw a foot across bound in red ribbons, a common prize for such feats at fairs. The prize in the center was either a locally made snack or sweet, else inexpensive bright ribbons or scarves or even baubles. Eld handed the ball to Sil. It was common enough to give such prizes to men and he seemed happy with it.

Free of the children, Danshor reverted to type, eying certain games because she could never resist showing off. There were rings one had to toss over rods. Normally they hovered in sunlight, to gently light on each other. But the rods used here were bright, flashy metal and made it difficult to set the rings straight. Then there were the usual darts and archery games, that Eld considered downright unsporting for soldiers to partake in until she saw the old bows offered for use. It wasn't a grift so much as part of the expected experience at these kinds of fairs. The games were not serious and had their origins, like gambling, in offerings to Felkeni, the Goddi of Fortune. As such, losses were a sacrifice, winnings were blessings. Neither should be ruinous for that would offend Him and more importantly his wife Myngar, the Mother-God of industry and prosperity.

But if Eld was irreligious, Danshor was downright apostate, and ruthlessly won at archery, darts and knives until she gathered enough straw prizes she was gifting them to any man who caught her eye. Eld saw her gambit, for soon she had the usual men orbiting her, impressed with the sight of a uniform and dressed to outdo each over in the eyes of women. Aggressive men made a game of "accidentally" trodding on the feet of rivals or causing other small accidents, until only a handful who considered themselves the most important of the local beauty were within Danshor's reach.

Eld left Danshor to it, helping Sil chivvy the children so they could buy a meal of mutton pies and honey tonic. Traith had developed a desire for a firelance. Eld managed, with Sil's help, to get her to accept a flashing lance instead. It was five feet long, made of reasonably sturdy white brass, had a blunted tip and, in sunlight, could produce a bright blinding flash, if the girl could concentrate. Traith could barely make it flicker, so it would have the double duty of training her essence as well as being a toy. Shedann wanted a yastol, because he'd sighted Tafli and found him interesting and exotic. Both children loved Dwen culture, but this was the first time they'd seen a Dwenifee closely

"And see, he's wearing bracs without anything!" Shedann cried.

Sil made a disapproving noise. "Dwen have different ways," he said. "And I am sure the House would not approve of one of their boys running about so exposed."

"I think the House might be more concerned with the quantity of glimmer," Eld said diplomatically. "I might be concerned something might catch fire."

Shedann giggled. Eld decided between the two scandalous prospects of Dwen leggings and a boy gilded with glimmer, a yastol was perfectly acceptable. But there were none to be had, only the Wildling yastols of twisted branches and sticks, decorated with moss and lichens, and wound with glass beads and copper. Shedann was happy enough with this substitute once they found a small enough one. Both the children begged for wishing orbs, a small glass ball with mica glitter in colored water. Eld resisted until Traith explained they would use them to make sure ama visited the estate more often. It was a mix of true desire and conniving, but the thought warmed Eld's heart so much she relented. They bought the orbs from a Wildling crafter wearing a shimmering gold vest; Shedann's had rose-gold water, Traith's blue.

When they had time to talk, Eld caught up with Sil on the activities of the house. Eldshorn was continuing with the construction of the "great barrier", a low wall she'd commissioned to keep the local sheep and cattle off a part of the property. Unfortunately a Greenway passed through that area, and for a decade they had argued with the provincial office over where exactly the Greenway ended and the estate property began. One of Eld's cousins, Tolen, Salthyn's third daughter, was growing and planned to return home to birth. The problem was, instead of managing affairs, Tolen's helper Eroli was coming with her and Salthyn's helper Tiyed hated him. Tiyed was from a generation who believed in duty and his temperament abhorred frivolity. Eroli was an actor and singer and had continued on the stage when it did not interfere with his duties as a helper.

"It is Tiyed's strong opinion a man with interests outside his marriage ..."

"Cannot focus on his duty," Eld finished. "I'm familiar with all of Tiyed's opinions. It's part of the reason I don't live there!"

Sil laughed. "And the reason I am pleased to be married to no one."

"Truly?" Eld asked.

"Oh, you do not understand the fate of a man, new to marriage, thrown into the brutal politics of a matriarchal estate!"

"I suppose I don't," Eld mused.

"I am protected from machinations by my contract with the dame of the estate, currently your grandam. My duties are to tutor and manage children. I cannot be bullied into more labor, nor pressured by affection to bend my pride at my expense. I must be careful even of my kindnesses to young men in these straights, and can only give advice and shelter provided it is free of gossip. I have advised legal council once."

Eld nodded. She was certain she knew why and it explained why one uncle was cool with Sil ever after.

"I am well," Sil continued, "My finances are secure, my investments healthy and I enjoy my duties. Barring becoming suddenly besotted, I have no desire to complicate my life."

Now Eld was curious. "Then I have an impertinent curiosity," Eld said.

Sil laughed. "How do I live without the company of women?"

"Yes."

Sil looked off into the clear blue sky. "I don't. But I am discreet."

"Obviously."

"Outings offer opportunities."

"I see. I suppose moon circles can as well."

Sil rolled his eyes. "Save me from Moon Meets!"

"I thought all men enjoyed them!" Eld was taken aback.

"Young men love them. Dancing in Lun's brightest light! Singing like the ancient pagans!"

"And looking like them as well," Eld said, grinning. "Savage humyn wear more than silk loincloths. Not that I've ever seen such a sight."

"Don't lie to me. We know every mother is a sneaker if she thinks she can get away with it. The one's we catch we string up as a lesson to the rest."

"Oh, I know," Eld nodded. "We found a cousin like that during an early morning hunt. At least she had her clothes on."

"She was young, correct? It's only women old enough to know better who are stripped and gilded before being hung by their ankles."

Eld looked at Sil, so proper and poised. "I'm beginning to worry about your suitability."

Sil laughed. "I could tell you tales. Most women and girls get away from us, losing at most a shirt. And they laugh all the while they are dusted with glimmer. It's a great sport, to you women. For us? Well, when you're younger it's all so exciting. So mysterious! But once you've been to a hundred or so, they lose their mystery. And the same men who like to rule houses manage to rule Moon Meets too."

Eld though a moment. Moon Meets were customary free times given to male servants. "So you don't ever, say, let people assume you're going to a meet, then go somewhere else for the night?"

Sil froze, meeting Eld's eye, a moment of understanding passing between them. Then he stood abruptly. "I should take the children to the Rowan Oak so you may present yourself in the commander's house, Emha Farthal. "

Eld stood, matching Sil's clouded distant expression. "An excellent idea, effa. You'll tell Danshor to follow after if you see her?"

"Of course."

Eld had no intention of revealing Sil's secret such as it was. If it didn't interfere with his duties it didn't matter. Still Eld couldn't keep her mind from wondering who Sil met. Was it the smith, known for juggling men? One of her many daughters? Or perhaps another servant, like a coach driver, or someone who came through regularly? Was there an arrangement with tribes of women and men with no attachments to meet at such times? Eld was certain this was a theme of a couple of the new novels popular with men, but she'd never read one. The arrangements soldiers made with men were a matter of convenience: free men and harlots who haunted the places military women gathered.

And now it was time for Eld to go to another haunt, the commander's house. It was late afternoon and the sky had grown hazy, as if Payeen had thrown shoddily made puffs of vapor across the heavens that did not occult all Her mother's light, yet hindered the best of it. It would not rain, Eld thought as she peered at the sky, but there would be little starlight that night.

As she reached the steps, the guards were for all purposes not on duty as soldiers and local sightseers milled around, above and even on the steps. Eld would have tried to get such a post, but cavalier watches were more patrolling the surrounding area. Hers was coming soon. She trotted up the stairs, making a path where she could between people, nodding in acknowledgment at the greetings. She'd never been this popular before with people she didn't know. It was strange, she thought in the shadow of the porch. Would someone write a ballad? She didn't know if she should be expectant or terrified. A few of the younger women of her estate still in the studies fancied themselves poets. She tried not to think about listening to earnest but feeble glorification of her deeds. This must also be the "doom of a hero".

Inside was much changed from the day Eld had come to report the Eurthans. The furnishings were the same, but strings of lights that would shine come dusk hung around the upper walls. There were also giant easels in every parlor with a work of paint on parchment or stretched canvas. But they weren't in the grand style of the old masters who painted in ground colored stone and glasses, mixed with spirits and balsam. These were pigments extracted from plants, coached out by arts known to chemists and kitchen helpers, that the savage and ignorant called magic: bright yellows, vivid reds and mauve, a touch of pale lichen purple, shadowed in black gall, with copper rusted green giving them all life. And at the bottom center of every piece, was a scrolling letter done with such artistry, at first even the keen eye took it to be part of the work, Seth's signature. A man of many talents indeed.

Like the humble materials, so too were the subjects; bowls of floating flowers, emerging spring crocuses, full blossomed roses, often backlit by sunlight or just a single ray of light. The deepest shadows of such paintings had the fainest cast of deep dark blue, perhaps a wash of indigo. Eld wasn't an expert in such things, her own surviving paintings from childhood being simple things on paper kept by Eldshorn only out of a mother's sentiment. But these were art, perhaps not as grand as Tochrohan or Jendalis, but they had spirit and the light of the house put them in their best aspect. Like all good elfyn art, looking on an image one could discern the phantom of the essence behind it and these made one feel as if standing in the garden or glade where the subjects had been seen. As she wandered the house, room to room, looking at the works, Eld marveled at Seth's soul and that he chose to be embraced by her. She took vicarious pride in hearing the murmurs of praise at Seth's talents. She found herself smiling, then became self conscious, as if any might mark her thoughts. She made her face neutral before walking into the next room, pleased to suddenly hear Seth's voice.

No longer wearing his hastol, he was speaking to a group clustered around a painting that seemed to strike one's eyes with its brightness. The center and top burst with shaded yellow and white, accented with reds, starkly contrasted with a background of dark blue and black. Then Eld saw the subject departed sharply from most of Seth's works: it was a glowing spear, lit by the sun and surrounded by blue lightning, as if it was rising above a sea of stormy clouds. Unlike the other paintings, this had a placard nearby with a title: The Spear. It seemed to be his latest work. Eld looked at it and knew it was a tribute to her and her deeds: she could feel the strike, the urgency, the boldness, even the sunlight from the image. For a second Seth's eye's met hers. He smiled slightly as he continued to speak.

"I did use quite a bit of my stores of pale ocher and yellow lakes," he said to appreciative chuckles.

"But what of that pale blue on the strike?" a woman asked. "My sister is an apothecary in Ta Mel and she has said blue is not something plants yield easily."

"This is true," Seth affirmed. "A few plants harbor blue, but they guard it jealously, especially in the north. I grow a small plot of woad from Cambria for this purpose. But the color is dark and must be heated and mixed with clay to give it a sky blue. Else I might lake some flowers of blue columbine. But these, though pretty, do not last."

"I wish I had a man who made paintings inspired by my deeds," Danshor whispered quietly, startling Eld. Eld stared at Danshor, who was smirking. A small cluster of men trailed behind her.

"If you're going to be a hood ..." Eld hissed.

"Wouldn't dream of such a thing." Danshor turned her attention to the painting. "My, that is bright."

Eld saw Seth break away from his admirers to walk over, so she abandoned the retort she was forming.

"Effa Alhern," Eld said, inclining her head in a bow. She elbowed Danshor, who belatedly nodded her head as well.

"Oh, be at ease, cavaliers. You have earned a rest from formalities. You will be attending dinner?"

"I don't think I have a choice, effa," Eld said.

"Being a hero must be a trial," Danshor drawled.

"That it is," Seth said seriously. "For a hero accepts her sacrifice might mean death in duty."

"With respect, effa, she did not die," Danshor said. "And so lives to enjoy her ...rewards."

Eld wanted to strike Danshor down right then and there. Seth still smiled politely, but his eyes had cooled. Eld shook her head ever so slightly, trying to communicate her disapproval.

"Is this cavalier a close war-sister, Lancer Farthal?" Seth asked Eld.

"You know those fraught families in novels where sisters vie to the death over fortune or men?" Eld said. "She's that kind of sister."

Danshor of course found this very amusing and laughed loudly causing heads to turn. Seth stared at Danshor as if she was humyn. Finally Seth said, "Dinner will be late. Your war-sister shouldn't feel compelled to attend if she has other obligations."

Eld forced herself not to laugh at this slight. But before she could wallow in her smugness, Danshor's men caught up. They of course had nothing but praise for Seth's clothes, paintings and general appearance. These were the victors of the battle for Danshor's attention. They would be equally ruthless in ingratiating themselves with the highest status male in the garrison. And Seth, being a creature of class, would indulge them to a reasonable degree

Then a man cried out, "Ai and al met, my Gilded Hero! One of your sisters told me that! A sparking jape, is it not?"

Eld's cheeks burned. The man was Althas from the barrack's throng. And while he had reduced his glimmer to something much less garish and now wore a pale green robe with embroidered vines, making a more presentable ensemble, he was still the bold son of a simple lot farmer, with a bold laugh and no sense for the shifting mood. Whether it was his familiar words, or how he grasped Eld's arm as if he was about to drag her off to matrimony, or the allusion to Eld's new nick name and how it came about, Seth's eyes flashed in anger, first looking at Althas as if he was a harlot, then at Eld as if she was a convicted traitor. Then Seth eyes slid above away from both them, as if he was stepping up to Paradise and had no use for such low creatures.

Seth smiled gregariously to the other men. "For those who wish, let us take a turn of my modest garden where I grow the most difficult of herbs ..."

Just like that, Eld felt frozen out, as if she didn't exist. It was a blow to the soul. How had she become so entangled with Seth?

Most of the men followed in Seth's wake while Althas and a couple others lingered with Eld and Danshor.

To Danshor, Eld hissed, "Why did you do that?"

"Careful, hero. I didn't do anything but bring the company of the best lot men for women who have none."

The last words were said with an edge. Danshor knew. Or suspected. But then surely she knew she shouldn't make a jest of the matter? Oh, she didn't care, not when it came to men. Maybe she even thought she was doing Eld a favor, distracting her from a career-ending temptation.

Meanwhile Althas, oblivious, was chattering. "He's so fashionable, our commander's son. Just like in the magazines. Or theater boys. Do you suppose he acts?"

"Not likely," Eld said. "It's not considered respectable for a man of his station. Singing perhaps."

"You seem unsorted," Althas said.

"Nothing to do with you," Eld said, bending the truth to breaking. She looked around for a distraction. "My children might be around here."

"Oh, you have mites? How many?" Many men either adored children or thought it politic to pretend they did if they wanted to marry well. Eld's wasn't sure which one Althas was.

"A girl and a boy. They're just leaving spritehood."

"A perfect age!"

"An exhausting age. I don't know how vagrant mothers do it."

"Don't they have their own crèche camps? Like Wildlings?"

"I think so. Every time we bivouac near Wildlings we're more interested in their mead. I know dinner is this eve, but isn't there a spread somewhere around here?"

Having been at other events when the commander's house was open to the public, Althas knew where to go. A path turned off from the main entrance and wide steps descended to a lower hall that led to the kitchens. Other doors opened at the side, probably to cellars, pantries or even servants' quarters. Against one wall were tables covered with white linen holding a spread of the sort of food one took on picnics or left out for salon guests: breads, cakes, pastries and cold meats, as well as nuts and cheeses, and sliced sausage spiced with juniper, a local favorite. Many local foods were Dwen inspired: many cakes and biscuits were made with chestnut, acorn or nut flours. There were also sliced fruits and fresh vegetables arranged in a way Eld thought was familiar. Then she realized they must have been ordered from the Rowan Oak. Tafli would be the most prosperous Dwen in the area at this rate, though what exactly Dwen exchanged queens for in the Forest Eld was still unclear about. Surely he had enough lamps and brass bangles. There was wine too, but these bottles came from highly recommended vinters. Seth's tolerance of the Rowan Oak's quirks did not extend to serving inferior wine and spirits. Eld and Althas set about piling their plates high with food. Eld took especial interest in the pastries and jellied fish and anything else she didn't have regular access to. In this same spirit she poured herself a measure of white brandy from the west coast of the Ethynsul. It was distilled from the cider of a particular apple. Althas found a bench for them to sit on while they ate. Eld did her best to pretend she didn't notice the "scavenging" done by soldiers and cavaliers, Patrycan among the more mercenary of them. The company would not lack for snacks in the barracks.

"These are so good!" Althas said, eating an acorn pancake cake flavored with honey.

"Don't you eat those daily?"

Althas shook his head. "Mine never come out right. Either scorched on one side, or too thin and flat. They're okay if I use an oven, but my uncle says cooking with coal is cheating."

The acorn cake was a staple in these parts, leavened with soda and egg. Eld had a couple of them with slices of white farm cheese.

While she ate, she heard a loud young woman exclaim, "I do hope we'll not be eating nuts and pine cones this evening at dinner! I want proper food: a good roast, leavened bread and the best mead."

Eld stared at the woman, a tall, thin army officer with a narrow drawn face, as if spite had dried her out from within even in youth. Eld recognized her as the same officer who had jested about Dwen in the commander's meeting. Roel, was her name. Lieutenant Roel.

"I suppose it's good enough for Trees," Roel carried on, a man hanging on her every word. Eld couldn't tell if he was a like narrow minded soul or simply harloting himself and willing to put up with any woman's drivel to get paid. "What can you expect living in branches and swinging around like, what do you call those animals? The ones from Sharitan ..."

"Monkeys," the man said indifferently.

"Yes, like monkeys. Worse than humyn. At least humyn have adopted bits of civilization like plumbing. Dwen don't even have toilets, just holes in the ground ..."

"That's not true," Eld found herself saying. "The garrison toilets pour into a composting sink, which is nothing more than a "hole" as you might say. And there are some individual sheds indistinguishable from Dwen facilities."

"I mean proper toilets, where you settle down, not just hover over a hole. I know every soldier is friends with our resident Dwen free agent and I imagine he's quite a ride. Dwen men are obviously all harlots. But savage is as savage does. What in the Orb is the matter, cavalier?"

Eld hadn't noticed rising to her feet. It was fortunate the light was dim or she might be fluorescing. If one had asked Eld when her blood was cold if men needed defending, she'd have said something vague about the duties of a house to sons and brothers. She wasn't the type of romantic fool who defended any man whether he was family or no. But Tafli, well, she saw him as one of them, as good as being part of the company. A brother in spirit if not by duty. And he was no harlot whatever women like Roel preferred to think.

However, Roel was Eld's superior. She was younger, but she was an officer and Eld's privileges as hero of the day had its limits. She had to be clever; she'd already promised herself to leave this one to Tafli.

"I just remembered my family is visiting," Eld said to cover her suddenly rising. She handed her plate to Althas. "Sorry, I have to go."

"Well, yes, you shouldn't keep them waiting," Roel continued, now taking a slightly maternal tone. Eld seethed inside. It was just possible Roel had a child, but if so, it would be a babe kept in a family estate like Eld's were, no older than a sprite. "Nothing more than our Staties likes to do than make much of their heroes."

"Indeed, emha," Eld said, squeezing some semblance of friendliness into her voice. "On your previous subject, emha, the Rowan Oak is a good mother's inn. Some say ...well I'm sure you already know."

"Know? Know what?" Roel asked.

"Well, the favors of some Dwen can be wooed , if you get my meaning."

"Oh?" Roel asked, oblivious to the slight annoyance of her companion. Even Danshor wasn't this much of a hood. "Wooed with queens?"

"I never have," Eld clarified. "But I hear some don't charge at all."

"Except for drink," Roel nodded, warming to the idea. "They all look like harlots certainly. Something for a night when I'm free. Thank you, cavalier!"

Eld walked away as fast as she could breathing hard. The bait was laid better than she could have hoped for. It was hard not to laugh at the moment as she imagined Roel tied up in Tafli's vines.

"Wait!" Althas called, dogging Eld's heels, still holding both their plates. "Don't you want this?"

"You can have it. Or give it to a friend. I have to rejoin my children."

"Will I see you later?"

Eld tried to answer. Then the hall wavered and she heard men's screams and woman shouting.

It was a Reverie, a memory of the future. The lights seemed to go out and the tables were knocked over. Then the vision was gone and she was still standing on the steps to the hall above, Althas in front of her holding the plates. The tables were still upright. It took Eld another moment to understand then she said to Althas urgently:

"Put the food down or take it with you, whichever. But run home to safety and barricade yourselves. An attack is coming. If you stay here, you will be trapped."

Then Eld ran up the stairs and out of the house to seek an officer on duty.

## Chapter 11

# Invasion of the Bane

It was still light. The clouds had thickened as Eld had suspected, Sul obscured slightly with a couple hours before She set. Eld shivered and set off to find the officer in charge of the house guards. She had reveried and Reverie was never wrong. But it was inscrutable and vague. Failing to find the officer she wanted, she sighted the ranger, Draeyn.

"Captain!" Eld said.

"Yes, Lancer, what can I do for our hero?"

"There's going to be an attack soon! I had a reverie!"

Draeyn was instantly serious. Rangers never joked about reverie; they relied on it too much in the wilds. "How soon?"

"I don't know. After dark, but not later than tonight. The tables from the kitchens will still be there."

In short order Draeyn had the ears of other officers.

"Reverie is fickle," Captain Hawthorn said. "I don't doubt you, Farthal, but until we know the nature of the event we can't do more than put the garrison in watchfullness. Which we are already. Just be thankful the Crèche is empty ..."

Eld stopped listening started running to the Rowan Oak before she knew what she was doing. She didn't even know what she should do, only that she had to get Traith and Shedann to safety.

Before she was halfway there the mustering bell clanged. Instantly the crowds that obstructed her path yielded to the sides, civilians running either to the gates to get out before they closed, or retreating further in for safety. It was divided by sex: mothers wanted to defend their property, while most men felt they'd be safer inside the garrison. Foot soldiers ran to form ranks, in the stables the army grooms would be outfitting the horses. Anyone not on duty was running to reserve stations. It looked like utter chaos but every mother and man ran with a purpose. Eld was running to the Rowan Oak, dimly aware of voices shouting at her. They didn't matter, not until she saw her children. Why, oh why, had they come? Why had grandam let them come?

The thud of horses' hooves nearby was muffled by the roar of panic in her ears. Just before she reached the Rowan Oak's porch, out of the open doorway Sil emerged with the children. They didn't look scared. They were too young to understand it wasn't just another entertaining event. With them was Tafli and, unexpectedly, Althas.

"Why are you here?" Tafli yelled. "You are riding! We take them to shelter! Go!" He pointed to Eld's left where she finally heard the galloping column of horses through the fog of panic and clamoring of the bell. A split second later a mounted Danshor was bearing down on her, Fiorseth running next to her while Danshor held the mare's reins. Eld stopped thinking and her training took over, changing her course to run by her horse then mount her in a leap. Danshor let go and they drove their mounts back to the column in time to exit through the gate in formation, catching the lances cast at them by pages as they passed.

"What were you thinking!" Danshor was shouting. It was strange to be berated by Danshor of all people.

"My children, of course!" Eld shot back. She was angry at being judged, angry at being scared, and angry with herself for losing her head. Some hero.

"You are not the only mother in the Host!"

"Shut up!" Eld shouted back, more enraged that Danshor was right.

They rode hard out of the gate, down the white Queen's road, then turned sharply left, first onto the Old Farm Road then into a Greenway. Of course it would not be simple. No hostile force was going to conveniently attack them on well paved roads, and certainly not Bane-like Eurthani. For a moment Eld panicked looking at the ground. Would they rise up like gnomes?

The ground muffled the sound of hooves, as the horses churned the earth like rooting pigs. This was a time a cavalier gave her horse more rein than usual, trusting the equine's training and sense to pick a way across the uneven turf. They were near a tree line, maple and conifer, then the ground dipped into a rocky ravine full of gorse and small bushes. It looked as if it could be river bed but wasn't long enough; it might have held water recently from the run-off but was drying. Eld seemed to remember there was an old quarry or ruin nearby. She shivered as they slowed to a walk. She gripped her lance. The company seemed to have the same feeling as they came to the open ravine. They heard a crunching sound, as if a host of souls were stamping in rhythm on flakes of slate. A couple rays of sunlight filtered through the clouds and tall pines above, and lit something familiar on their far left. At first Eld thought it was the small body of a babe wrapped in green canvas, a gruesome thing fitting a gruesome hour. But it was just a pack of the sort a foot soldier would drop fleeing in terror. They were in the shadows of a hilly rise where the trees stood. A signal was given to ready lances. Eld let her aura flow into hers, though the light was dim, she could feel it hungry to channel the sun when they cleared.

Then they charged as one, circling around into the full light of the late day sun to face a host like none of them had seen or prepared for:

At a distance they seemed to be ants. Now much closer, they were armored behemoths. Each woman – for surely there was a woman inside, not some hideous eldritch Bane from legends? – towered seven to eight feet in black armor that covered any possible flesh. The armor in general functioned like champion armor but was more complete than any craft known to Sula could make. Armor plated legs that Eld had worn were secured by a leather girdle. But these seemed to be sealed completely, as smooth as if they were a clan of beetle like creatures. Their shoulders sat higher than elfyn, making the figures looked hunched. But this was a functional design, for attached to their shoulders were bane weapons like the one that had struck Eld in the side. Their helmets peaked in a shallow point, but the visors were eerie, semi-translucent white, as if made of frosted glass. This last convinced Eld they were mortal, for bane creatures would have exposed eyes. In count there were at least two score.

Eld forced herself to remain in formation but she didn't know how long they would be able to. Strike had worked against the unarmored but she had no idea how effective it would be against these. The only thing besides her training that kept panic at bay was the knowledge if strike was to have a chance, they needed to do it collectively. Of course, her fellow soldiers had no idea what the Bane weapon strike was like and were full of the boldness of righteousness and revenge. They were not used to thinking in terms of vulnerability. But they were more vulnerable than they knew. A cavalier's greatest asset, after her lance, was her horse. They were not at a time of war, so none of the horses had barding. Eld prayed they could surprise and rout the Bane force before any beast was hurt.

And then there were only the orders and actions of two forces using their training to the best of their ability, to serve the powers that sent them. Even in the weakening sun, lances exploded with strike either hitting their targets who staggered or collapsed, or else the ground near them, the stones splitting or even exploding with the concentrated heat normally only found in forges and potter's furnaces. A small pine tree erupted in flames as it fell, landing on a couple soldiers of the Bane-force. A second later it exploded from the heat, showering both forces with splinters and flaming pitch. Smoke and dust rose up to obscure the ground. Horses whinnied, excited and not at all pleased with being involved in this endeavor, while women shouted boldly and looking to be heroes themselves.

But as Eld fired a second strike it disturbed her that the armored women did not run. A few had fallen over but managed to crouch defensively. In fact quite a few had strange metal bracings extending from their lower legs and ankles as if to keep them from falling over. As Eld looked the bracings disappeared on one, melting into the metal like liquid, and she stood straighter, the Bane weapon on her shoulder rotating suddenly to find a target.

Eld yelled incoherently, but it was enough to warn the company. There was a peal of thunder and blue forked lightning from a handful of the bane troops erupted. By luck they found no mother, but a horse screamed as it was struck. Glad only that it was not Fiorseth, Eld drove her forward while shouting at Danshor:

"It's the weapon on their shoulders! If we can get it off ..."

Danshor, glaring with determination, surged forward with Eld. Eld hit one of the soldiers with strike, getting her off balance, while Danshor drove her lance in the gap between the helmet and shoulder where the weapon sat. Then she drove Tuiric in a tight circle, using all of their combined weight and leverage. Danshor shouted as blue strike hit her arm, but it was a flashing wound and only scorched her jacket. Meanwhile the bane soldier, making alarmed strangled cries Eld could just barely hear, fell over just as the Bane-weapon released from its housing to fall hard to the stony ground. The soldier fell on her back and something strange happened. The visor cleared and snapped up, sliding smoothly on fine hinges.

The face was a dark charcoal gray, like wet slate, and the eyes could have been Sula, a warm gold, had they not shined with a light from within. Eld was doubly shocked she recognized the woman as one of Seth's attackers, the one who had retrieved the bane weapon.

"You!" Eld shouted, driving at the stunned elf with the tip of her lance. She forgot about strike. Eld would just run her through.

But the woman moved with an alacrity that belied the armor that encased her. She first rolled on her stomach and rocked back into a crouch. Danshor gamely tried to use the full weight of Tuiric to crush her, but as soon as her stallion's hooves struck the curved back of the armor, the woman seemed to freeze, falling back as if stuck. Eld understood: the armor had many magical properties, one of which was to protect their wearer by freezing solidly in one piece. The next moment the woman had rolled free, and was on her feet again. Eld drove Fiorseth at her, to keep her from retrieving her bane-weapon. But she hadn't gone for it, instead drawing a sword, a short, blunt, unlovely thing. As Eld ran her down the woman swung the sword wide and low. Fiorseth screamed and reared. Eld couldn't worry about her mare, hoping she could drive her lance into this troll before retreating to check Fiorseth. But instead the Eurthani soldier caught the end of the lance haft under an arm and next thing Eld knew she was ripped from her saddle, and flying through the air before her back slammed into what felt like the entire Altan mountain range. Then everything went black…

They had been racing their horses neck and neck. It was a drab windy day and the company was bored. It didn't help that Feilithon Keep was run by the most hide bound commander Eld had ever served under before or since. Rules were followed to the last drop of ink and no blind eye was turned to to anything: exchanging watches, barracks spreads, shifting or scrounging, and certainly not men. Duty days were grim and free days eagerly anticipated and not a soul returned a second sooner than she had to. Into this dull barracks Eld and Danshor had been thrown together and grated on each other almost instantly.

While it was understood the dislike, then rivalry, was mutual, Eld had the worst of it for Danshor had that knack of knowing the exact moment to break off a fight so as to look, if not exactly innocent, then less culpable. Danshor didn't go out of her way to attack Eld or even to obviously bait her. But she quickly knew what annoyed Eld because it was the same thing that annoyed most soldiers except Eld had trouble letting it go. And so with one thing leading to another, and with an escalation in challenges and bets, Eld found herself racing Fiorseth to outdo Danshor's stallion Tuiric.

Tuiric, a dark and glossy rich brown, was a powerful horse. But Fiorseth was a strong, tall mare, long legged, but not as heavy. Eld suspected Danshor knew she was going to be beaten in a flat run and that's why she took the road over the Ghost Bridge. It was a local joke, because the bridge that had been there was long gone, washed away by a storm and no longer needed because of the new canals. Thus the province saw no reason to replace it. But riders still liked to jump it on a dare and that's what Danshor intended to do, perhaps hoping to spook Eld into yielding.

"My son rides faster than you!" Danshor taunted in one of the few mentions of her child. All Eld really knew was Danshor had him when she was very young. Danshor was more like an older sister than a mother, her son being raised by her large, old and very wealthy family of estate farmers. Not so old as to be Lors before the Sunqueens, but Eld wondered. The fall of the Lors' feudal grasp was so total and sudden, it would not be unthinkable some had blended in with the new commonwealth to keep their assets. Danshor's sense of entitlement certainly seemed to come from a previous, less enlightened time.

And so Eld drove Fiorseth faster. Fiorseth for her part had long since lost interest or enjoyment and continued on only because Eld drove her and promised in thought to give the mare her favorite foods. Eld would have the fattest horse in the company, but if she beat Danshor at her game it wouldn't matter.

Eld had Danshor's way blocked and was in the lead. But Danshor was coming by her side, using the stallion's bulk to try to push Eld off before she got to the Ghost Bridge. Fiorseth put on a burst of speed, Eld looking at the ground, mostly short grasses right up to the edge. But Eld had misjudged the lay of the grass. Unmaintained, the overhang was further by a foot. So when Fiorseth's hooves hit the ground to launch her leap, instead of sailing over the ravine, they both fell horribly down.

It was the worst feeling a rider could have, falling and knowing there was nothing to do but pray the horse found her footing. Even then it might have been alright if the river had been high enough. They would have fallen into water and it would have been an embarrassment, with nothing more than hurt pride. But the river wasn't more than a couple feet high in summer and the fall, while only six or so feet, was awkward. The lightest horse was the weight of over six average mothers. There was a horrible snap and Fiorseth screamed as Eld tumbled off her, barely landing on her own feet. And then Eld screamed herself, a sound she had never made before and hoped to never make again: Fiorseth's right front leg was broken.

It wasn't just the horror of seeing it, but she could feel Fiorseth's terror and pain too. Eld would have been sick except she had nothing in her stomach: she had taken the maxim of many athletes that competing was best early in the day before breaking fast. In despair of what to do she screamed again. In old days it was a mother's duty to send an injured horse through the Door if there was no way to bring a healer. If Eld left her to get help, a predator might find Fiorseth, and that would be a truly terrible way to die. She only had a knife on her and wasn't sure she was able to do it. Delaying the grim choice, her healer's training took over and she laid her hands on Fiorseth's neck, calming her own mind so she could calm her horse, and feel the part of her mind that screamed in pain. Eld quieted it, but didn't silence it. The mare need to feel just enough pain to not want to move. Then Eld moved further into her mind, calming nerves to make her numb. Fiorseth relaxed, and appeared to be on the edge of consciousness. Eld could knit the bones of the leg, but it was no good: it needed time to heal properly or wouldn't be strong enough to use, much less climb out of the river bed. There were no crutches for horses, only a cart and winch. And Eld didn't dare leave her to get one from the garrison Temple. Eld started to weep in despair.

"Was that you screaming like a boy?" Danshor called above her. Eld had completely forgotten about Danshor and the race. Now she remembered, guilt weighted on her like a mill stone. This was her fault...

"Did you fall and muddy your kirtle-shirt and robe?" Danshor continued to jeer.

Eld wasn't even angry. She just wanted to shout back without her voice cracking. She had to do it for Fiorseth's sake.

"Let's just say I win this one ..."

"Shut up!" Eld finally screamed. "Fiorseth needs a cart and winch ..." Then her voice broke into sobs.

Everything was in a fog before the cart arrived. Eld felt she must think on Fiorseth's health every moment without fail for her to survive. Danshor had slid down the embankment moments later, murmuring something to Eld, words one said to someone in sickness or grief, not at all her usual voice. Eld stared into Fiorseth's eyes, willing her to live, to not leave. She hoped the only injury was the leg. Horses could break backs and necks. It was rare, but of course it was only the leg. That was bad enough. A cart and winch, Eld had repeated like an invocation. Then Danshor said something reminding Eld to stabilize the leg. Splints. Wraps. Danshor disappeared then reappeared with wood and leather straps. Much layer Eld realized the leather was from the reins and tackle of both horses. They set and stabilized Fiorseth's leg, Eld fusing the bones to keep them in place even if they couldn't be used yet. But Fiorseth would not be able to stand on it until proper healers had knitted it and even then she'd be in a sling for at least a fortnight.

Danshor sat with Eld to wait, talking about anything and nothing, horses, men, anything to keep Eld's mind busy. She knew Danshor had told her a messenger from the inn she shifted the wood from had been sent to a temple. The Temple knew how to retrieve an injured horse. But Eld could never remember the exact words. Only her soul was bereft and she was lost and Fiorseth could not die. And through it all she was grateful Danshor was there.

Slow hours crawled by until the wagon arrived as a fine mist of rain started to fall on them. The winch and sling raised Fiorseth from the riverbed and Eld let the healers put her under a healing sleep. Eld walked exhausted behind the wagon, Danshor besides her, Tuiric following as placid as a hound. Eld expected in the coming days for Danshor to make some dig about her panicking like a boy and bawling like a baby, but Danshor never said anything about the accident after. While they walked back to the garrison Danshor had said, "A mother who cares not for her horse is worthless."

In the days that followed Danshor slowly returned to type, the arrogant, lecherous braggart. But now she counted Eld as her closest war-sister and Eld accepted the awkward fact they were friends...

The mist of rain was much heaver now. Large drops landed on Eld's face. Then a splash of water hit her forehead and she sat up sputtering. From the light, it had not been long since she'd been knocked unconscious; her back was against the tree she had been thrown against. Danshor stood over her, dusty and scorched, screwing her canteen shut.

"See? She's fine."

With Danshor's offered hand, Eld stood up, looking around. Nearby Commander Alhern was on a horse surveying the area and the wounded. "Cavalier, you sleep too much," she said to Eld before moving on.

Eld glanced at the empty ravine, the women dousing smoldering fires and the line of cavaliers on watch at the end of the dry bed.

"Fiorseth?" Eld said.

"She's down here," Danshor said leading them down a slope out of the trees Eld had been thrown up into. "She was cut but not badly. It was your saddle and tackle the Bane was after, to unseat you."

"And it worked. Score one to Team Bane," Eld snarled.

Fiorseth was full of impatient thoughts to return to the outpost. She did not like fire at all and wondered why there was suddenly so much of it.

"I'm sorry," Eld said, patting her neck. The healing had been done well enough. The hide was still tender, but it would be sound in a couple of days. If they all lived that long. "What happened while I dreamed?" Eld asked.

"I danced with our friend a while," Danshor said as they mounted and waited for orders. "She can use a sword and even on the ground didn't seem to be at much of a disadvantage. But then she took an opening to break off, retrieve the Bane-striker and return to her formation."

"I remember their ranks didn't seem to be much affected by our strike. They crouched but barely moved."

"They rallied square," Danshor said certainly. "The entire Bane host made one gargantuan square with Bane weapons pointed outward, outer ranks on one knee. They weren't crouching from fear; they're infantry who knows how to fight cavalry."

"That would mean they have horses underground."

Danshor shrugged. "Maybe. Or they learned from watching us."

"If they have horses do they have cavalry?"

"You are asking the wrong soul," Danshor said.

A signal whistle blew. They were to fall out and assist the wounded, collect stray gear and anything else required, then wait for the next muster.

Miraculously most horses had evaded the worst of the Bane-strike. The exception was one stallion with a horrible hole scorched in his flank. He could walk, but he limped hard as the healers led him away, his rider trailing behind him looking shaken. Eld knew exactly how she felt.

Other mounts had simple cuts or burns like Fiorseth and were patched up enough to serve for the moment. Some women were not so lucky. The worst had somehow fallen into wrestling with an armored Eurthani and had both her wrists broken from her trouble. She, along with the worst of those hit by strike, left with the healers to return to the garrison. At least there were no deaths. The rest would stay in case the Eurthani returned.

Gloom deepened as Eld and Danshor picked over the rocky ground. They were tasked with retrieving anything the Eurthans left, no matter how small, while their horses rested and grazed. Even in battle the Eurthans were spare, but a handful of things were found:

Small clasps and links that might be broken off armor; a couple broken pieces of plate; and an awl-like tool, all of the same black metal. Above them a flock of ravens flew overhead to land in the trees nearby. Eld wondered what they saw.

~more and less than thee, elfling~ a thought came.

"They're thyn!" Eld called out.

The ranger captain Draeyn pulled up on a roan mare, returned from tracking the Eurthan troops. She scanned the trees, darker by the minute, then made a bird call, indistinguishable from a raven's croak. In reply one figure launched from the trees to land on a rock before them. Black eyes looked at them and Eld felt amusement from the mind.

~that was a terrible sound. like a crow with throat sickness,~ the raven thought.

"We do what we can with what fate gives us," Draeyn said. "Know you aught of what we seek?"

~elflings from below in hides of black metal. yes. neither of you has left anything for us to eat.~

"This is why I hate ravens," Danshor said. "Ghoulish bloodthirsty scroungers."

~if walkers did not spill blood there would be nothing to scrounge.~

"Could you wait until the ranger has questioned the raven before insulting it?" Eld hissed.

Danshor shrugged but said nothing more. Luckily the bird did not take offense.

~we know aught of those you fought except they come out of mountain doors inside caves made for the purpose. "

"Where are these caves?" Draeyn asked.

~here. there. they are everywhere on paths leading to the mountains.~

"How long have they been there?"

The raven croaked. ~long long before my dame's, dame's dame was an egg. the doors have always been there."

"What?" the three elfyn said together.

"Always?" Draeyn echoed.

"~yes. always. in all ways. in all times. that we know. have your thoughts strayed from sense?~

"Then why don't we have this knowledge?" Draeyn asked.

~have you asked for it?~ the raven replied.

"If the position of the Raven Nation is a child's gambit of 'you never asked', I might roast you like a chicken," Danshor said.

"Danshor!" Eld exclaimed.

~you would have to catch me first, wingless one.~

The raven fluttered away with ease.

Draeyn looked at Danshor with eyes like death.

"What?," Danshor said. "She wasn't going to tell us anything we don't know and was going to taunt us while doing it."

"Are you certain you are talking about the raven, cavalier?" Draeyn asked. "And not yourself?"

Draeyn rode away leaving Danshor standing open mouthed. Eld turned away in disgust.

"Bird probably didn't know anything anyway," Danshor muttered.

Eld pretended she didn't hear.

They were brushing down the horses and making repairs to tackle when Danshor came back from refilling their canteens.

"So the gossip is the rangers lost the trail inside a shallow cave. They went in but there was just a bare chamber. Though clearly constructed. A room without a door."

"That we could see."

"Or feel. It's as if they walked through a stone wall. And it's solid stone, not bricks or blocks."

Eld thought of how the Bane armor froze protectively. "There's much strange magic we don't know. That's why we've never found these doors, though they've 'always' been here."

"According to one raven," Danshor snorted.

"I wonder if there's another one nearby. That one won't be used."

"Unless they return with a greater force."

"Aren't you the optimist this eve."

"Consider it: they were exercising a small force."

"Just an exercise?"

"Of course. Who could they possibly attack with two score women?"

"A small target? A rescue mission? Maybe they underestimate our forces ..."

"So, it's a small force," Danshor continued. "They get routed. What do you do?"

"Well, it depends," Eld said.

"On?"

"On why my forces are here. If I was just drilling, I'd go someplace else. Why aggravate the savages?"

"And if you weren't just drilling?"

An owl gave a warbling hoot while Eld thought. "If I wasn't drilling – If I was trying to gain ground ..."

"Yes?"

"I'd come back better armed, with more numbers. With cavalry and magi."

"And that's why we're going back to the outpost double time or rout speed," Danshor said certainly. "When they return we will be outnumbered."

Eld shook her head. "You're just making guesses."

"You want to bet?"

"No."

"Five queens we'll be galloping back to the garrison before midnight."

"Fine."

The owl hooted again, sounding more insistent. Even the birds didn't want them there. Maybe the ravens told it about Danshor. Were there Thyn owls?

"At least we know the men and children are safe in the cellars," Danshor added.

Something slid in Eld's brain, planting a seed of panic. A cascade of logical thoughts made the seed sprout.

"If as the raven said, the doors have always been here, then they know this area and everything in it."

"Probably," Danshor agreed.

"That means they know about Falls Gate Keep and what its purpose is."

"Likely."

"If I was a force trying to gain ground, I would have plans to depower any local military force."

"The walls are thick enough to hold these black champions off. Hey, maybe someone will get to fire a cannon at a live target for the first time in history!"

"Forget the walls!" Eld said, starting to panic. "They don't need to go over walls; they will tunnel from below!"

"That's a good point ..."

"And that means the cellars aren't safe at all!"

Danshor grabbed Eld's shoulder as she tried to mount Fiorseth.

"Hold! Even if you're correct, the fortress is full of soldiers who know their business."

"But they don't know they need to watch the stores and cellars!"

Even in the dark Eld saw worry grow in Danshor's eyes.

"Very well, but go to the commander. Don't just gallop off like a green recruit."

Eld stalked away trying not to think of her children in whichever cellar, waiting to be snatched by eldritch forces from below. Alhern was conferring with Draeyn, the cavalry host captain, Aynath, and a couple of black robed magi investigating the path the Eurthans had disappeared.

"The lights in town have been shuttered," one of the wizards was saying. "We can watch most of this area from the abbey. But it's an occulted night. Soon there won't even be starlight."

Eld glanced overhead at the black sky where only a couple stars peered between clouds.

"What is it, Farthal?" Captain Aynath asked.

Eld explained the concerns of a force tunneling up through the keep grounds.

"A grim thought," Alhern said. "And well considered."

"And embarrassingly obvious," Draeyn put in. "Still, my understanding is tunnel roads and shafts are closer to the bulk of the mountains, where stone is solid and deep."

"But tunneling through earth is possible, if not preferable," Alhern said. "It doesn't have to be permanent. It could only be for a task, like a mine. They are perfectly capable of that. If only we knew why--"

"One of our scouts observing minds says they hear a host!" a magi inter-rupted.

"Listen!" Draeyn said.

They all became silent, listening as only elfyn could. Because their con-versation, while low, was not meant to be secret, every woman within ear paused to listen as well. It was like the hiss of a thousand cats, one could even feel a vibrations through the ground. Many many more feet than be-fore were marching over the slate and stones of the ravine. Imperceptibly it grew louder until it matched the same sound Eld had heard just before the company engaged the Eurthans an hour or so ago. She shivered and took comfort in thinking that surely, if they were here, the children and men hid-ing were safe in the fortress. Her eyes strained to find some image in the dark night. Finally she saw them, a vast shadow moving revealed only by a flicker of dimming starlight.

"Aynath, hold this position for as long as you can," Alhern said as she mounted her horse. "Don't fight them to the Door. I don't want losses, just delay them. Then return to the garrison."

"Emha," Aynath acknowledged. Alhern rode away. "Cavaliers, prepare for action."

"Emha," Eld and Danshor acknowledged. It looked like Danshor was go-ing to have her five queens. But before Eld had stepped far, one magi was speaking urgently.

"Emhas, we have grossly miscalculated our defensive measures."

"How?" Aynath demanded.

"From the brief sight into their minds, they are not hindered by the lack of light."

"What?"

"And they can see us clearly though no fire is burning, without moon or even starlight. But they can see your weapons and gear even better. In their eyes metal and stone glows."

"So we're standing here like gormless Cambrians looking out to sea for a Federation patrol, while elfyn eyes see them down to the weave of their plaids?"

"Essentially."

"The Eurthans can see by the light of essence shining from the center of Eurath, I was told," Draeyn added. "And Eurath never sleeps."

"And you didn't think this might be worth mentioning before now?" Ay-nath snapped.

"We didn't understand what it meant!"

"Well, apparently it means they can see in pitch dark better than even Dwen! What exactly do they see, wizard?"

"Our bodies are like dark shadows, as are the trees and anything living. But metal and stone shines brightly ..."

"We can't hold this position if they can see our weapons and we are virtually blind!" Aynath said. "All the lances have one charge left if we're lucky. Can you do anything to stop them?"

"Give us a moment. You have a few minutes. Let us try something."

A sudden hiss filled Eld's mind, urgent thoughts being passed back and forth quickly. Suddenly she was aware both magi had risen into the air, shadowy ghosts rising to hover above them. With their black robes, only because Eld knew exactly where could she still see them, as they exploited the invisible treadle of Orb forces with essence to defy the pull of the ground. They stopped fifty feet above the Host.

The marching continued. Eld held her lance and gripped Fiorseth's sides with her knees, boots firm in her stirrups, ready to strike or flee. Suddenly the air shifted and the sounds of marching wavered. Eld was heartened to hear clattering, as if individuals had somehow stumbled. What had the magi done? Could the Eurthans see the magi? They wore only robes.

Then the night darkness was shattered by a fork of blue lightening and a deafening peal of thunder, as if they were at the source of a storm. They were in a sense: the fork erupted from the marching black armored host, reaching above their heads, to strike a magi. A woman made a short sharp cry, then fell like a stone, only the quick action of Captain Draeyn, charging with her horse to catch the wizard broke her fall, preventing worse injury. Eld caught a glimpse of Draeyn holding a woman, eyes staring with horror, black robes smoking, before the light vanished and they were in the dark again.

In moments the other magi returned to the ground, one speaking with alarm to Captain Aynath.

"They spied us quickly by the solstone around our hats. There aren't enough of us to use flame strike at night. We'll scout the ridge above the host and try to turning the ground into slurry, make it impassible. But it could be a trap for the horses..."

"She's for the Temple," Draeyn interrupted, the wounded magi draped over her horse in front of her unceremoniously. Draeyn rode off.

"Do what you can to delay them!" Aynath said. Then the captain blew her signal whistle in code: prepare to muster for a guarded to retreat, galloping at route speed on command.

"Told you," Danshor said smugly as she mounted Tuiric and snatched up her lance. Eld patted Fiorseth, checking she felt settled, reassuring her they were leaving. Eld felt shaken the magi had been so quickly dispatched. But Fiorseth's spirits raised instantly.

"She's glad to be leaving this place," Eld said.

"So am I," Danshor said. "That spawn bent my lance head and cracked the enamel."

Eld considered her lance. She'd been thrown free and the metal was undamaged. It might have a strike left in it.

They moved their horses into their usual formation and waited. The marching of the Eurthans had resumed. Now the sound of that host could be heard without effort, the hiss of metal crunching on stone and slate palpably vibrating through the ground. A scout was sent off on a light horse in the direction of town, perhaps to warn them darkness was no protection. The magi had vanished, melting into the darkness to seek a clever gambit not yet thought of. Eld was glad they were returning to the keep, even if it cost her five queens. There was clearly more they needed to know if they were to be victorious over the Eurthans.

Suddenly a fork of blue lightning rose vertically in the air perhaps fifty feet above the Bane-host. Like a demonic finger a fork branched off, angling crookedly to the stand of trees on the embankment. There was a cry as it hit a soul, another magi. A flock of ravens exploded from the trees to fly to safety. Another couple bouts of blue strike discharged, this time in the direction of the trees. But one discharged in the air, many fingers of light failing to find a target. The other grounded in a tree that promptly exploded, then fell over the ravine, hopefully on the heads of the Eurthan troops. Tafli would not be pleased.

Finally the whistle sounded for them to move and they left the way they came, cantering until they were out of sight of the ravine. Then they galloped as fast as they could back to the garrison.

Once through the gates, the company rode to the stables to rest the horses and prepare for the next muster. The second cavalry company was at the ready, horses in order, saddled and bridled, riders ready to mount at the mustering horn. But Eld broke away from the column, racing Fiorseth to the commander's house. She had been thinking while they rode back of the places her children might be sheltering and there were two she wanted to check before doing anything else: the Crèche cellars and the commander's house.

"Where are you going?" Danshor shouted, but Eld didn't slow to explain. At the steps Eld jumped down, throwing her lance aside. The guards were absent, which was not as it should be, and the house still glowed with the lights from earlier but seemed to be abandoned. Distant crashes could be heard, and then a scream but whether from children or men Eld couldn't tell.

Small stones flew into Eld's legs as Danshor's stallion skidded to a halt behind her.

"Take Fiorseth to the stables!" Eld yelled as she ran up the steps taking three at a time.

Inside, a small table had fallen in such a way as to suggest a great force pushing past it with no regard for the commander's station or possessions. One of its legs was ripped of, the white splinters reaching futilely for where they had once been moored, the end of the leg crushed by a great weight. It spoke to the fear of the fleeing crowds. The ground shook. Instantly Eld took the stair down to the kitchens, skidding into the hall where she had left Althas.

And there she caught up with her reverie.

Danshor also caught up with her.

"You didn't take Fiorseth to the stables?"

"I'm not your groom! The horses will make their way back."

The building shook again. Eld and Danshor looked around, above them, then at each other. Eld ran towards where she presumed the kitchen and pantries were. She spun in the center of the grand kitchen, a blur of white porcelain tiles, smoked white oak, with gleaming copper pots over head. A few had fallen and she kicked one accidentally while looking for a cellar door. The clanging echoed like bells breaking.

"Over here!" Danshor shouted from outside the hall, then a man screamed and Danshor yelled.

Eld rushed out in time to see Danshor pull back from a iron bound door that had been so damaged, its hinges ripped off, it was propped against its frame as a facade. Beyond a crowd gathered, mostly men but a couple of soldiers. Traith and Shedann were among them.

"Ama!" they chorused, pulling free of Sil's grasp. But Tafli caught them both by the scruff with his vinings.

"You are staying safe so your mother can be fighting!" he said.

In a moment Eld's mind cleared.

"He's right," Eld said but walked to them, crouching down so they wouldn't leave as she hugged them, relieved to see them alive and whole.

"Sorry, cavalier," a man's familiar voice was saying to Danshor. "I thought you were the Bane." It was Seth. His robes were smudged with dust and ash, his hair free and wild and he looked no less beautiful for it.

"I live," Danshor grumbled. " I'm sure I didn't need my flouted hair ..."

152

Eld let the children slip out of her arms and saw the scorch stick Seth was holding. It was a kind of firelance used in cooking. It couldn't kill but it could burn an eye out, or in this case, scorch a lock of hair.

"What do you mean, the Bane?" Eld asked.

"How do you think the door was broken down?" Seth said.

"She didn't come from within?" Eld looked as far as the pantry went, men and soldiers incongruously huddling among barrels, jars and crates of staples. But the walls behind them were intact.

"No," a soldier said. "It -she-kicked the door down. We ..." here the woman looked ashamed. "Our swords did nothing, just scraped against the black skin like it was marble. Only the fire stick had any effect--"

"Stuck it right in it's neck, he did," Althas added. "Gave her a start!"

"Then she is fleeing," Tafli affirmed.

Seth looked meaningfully into Eld's eyes and murmured, "Almost as good as glimmer."

"The commander tells me you are a talented man," Eld said smiling.

Eld was pleased events seemed to have driven Seth's earlier annoyance with her away, but she remained doubtful of their safety. Eld didn't disparage Seth's courage, but it was unlikely the Eurthan warrior fled due to this impromptu defense with cookware. The warrior was probably looking for something. The rest of her company? Were there more of them in the house?

"Stay with the men!" Eld ordered her children, before she and Danshor ran out to look for the warrior, hoping she had no fellows. It didn't take long to find the breach in the cellar wall, not in a room, but in an alcove near a toilet, at the end of the hall. They peered over the masonry blocks scattered on the floor into the darkness, a strangely smooth tunnel slightly arched, that would give semipermanent support even through solid earth. Here it was a mix of earth and stone, not actual bedrock, but it's quality had changed so the rocks in the roof and wall of the tunnel had fused into a dense aggregate where they touched. To either side were still abundant remains of loose earth and stone that had not been removed, as if the work of miners pressed for time to make a path through, not bothering to clear it. The width was about four women abreast and at least eight feet high.

"What Bane magic made this?" Danshor breathed. Just then the entire house shook again.

Eld didn't know which was a more frightening thought, meeting one bane warrior loose or a column of invaders from this dark hole. It was impossible to see anything very far within but Eld listened.

"I don't hear footsteps or breath," she said.

"Block it up?" Danshor asked.

"Do we want to? Shouldn't we make it easier for her to go back?"

Protocol for a hostile invader was capture. But Eld knew she and Danshor were unlikely to be able to hold an Eurthan in armor.

"If there as a way to peel them ..." Danshor mused.

Then the house shook again. They had to do something, even if it was just track its movements. They ran upstairs and through the halls. At some point Danshor said, "I'll get the lances" and ran outside. Eld didn't argue though she thought it was futile. Lances were for open warfare under a day sky. But if there was any essence left, maybe they could scorch the woman out. Eld ran past the library where she and Seth had almost trysted, then into one of the still brightly lit parlors where empty easels still sat. The black behemoth was waiting for her.

Even several yards away Eld felt she was too close. The warrior was not gargantuan in full light, but still larger than Eld would ever want to battle. She could extrapolate the woman inside was about her size. But the greaved boots had platform soles that made her seem a whole foot taller. She had to be carrying at least half the weight of a horse. The hulking shoulders added to the imposing effect, the Bane-weapon instantly pivoting to aim itself at Eld, the three red points at the end glowing. Instinctively Eld dived behind a divan as a peal of thunder clapped and blue strike cut the air, hitting her behind the knee, but with little force.

The strike was more alarming in that it did not seem to need a perfect line of sight. It was as if it followed the will of its operator to her target. As if to prove this point, the air was split again by the sound of shrill thunder and the divan was blown apart with a fork that would have hit Eld fully, but was absorbed by the ruined wood. Eld had a moment to see the occluded helmet peer down at her, the triangular head of the bane weapon turning to sight her again with its three red points. Then Eld rolled away, onto her feet, and drew her rarely used sword. Maybe she could concuss the Eurthan if nothing else. Leaping from a table, Eld swung as hard as she could at the woman's neck, only to be batted aside by an armored arm, blocking her as if they were sparring barehanded. The force was so strong, the metal so hard, Eld fell to the floor on her stomach with an inelegant thud. At least she was able to hold onto her sword...

Then a reckless soul threw a hunk of masonry that hit the warrior just as the Bane-weapon turned on Eld again. It distracted her, but the stone bounced hard and would have hit Eld's head if she hadn't rolled away in time.

"You want to play?" Danshor taunted. "Let's warm you up!" She was holding a lance pointed at the warrior head. Suddenly the end of its tip flashed brightly. Eld blinked. There was no strike for it was spent.

"Huh," Danshor said, dropping it with disgust. "That must have been mine."

Suddenly she launched it at the Bane warrior, and the Eurthan ducked reflexively, something Danshor was counting on to keep her from focusing on Eld or striking.

"Now this one is my war-sister's and it still has a heart ..." Danshor said, holding it with confidence.

Eld scrambled to her feet and raised an arm to shield her eyes as the lance she'd dropped in the ravine skirmish struck the warrior with a beautiful ray of heat and light. Danshor didn't let it disperse in a flash but kept the strike flowing, concentrating it until it was spent. A strangled scream emerged from the warrior. While the armor did not break or split, or even change color, the air rippled above the place the strike hit, the left shoulder where the weapon sat. So, even armored they could be hurt. Then with a flash the strike was spent. Danshor threw the lance aside and drew her own sword while the Eurthan stumbled.

"It's going to be work," Danshor said.

"Any thing of worth is," Eld replied.

Then they set on the Eurthan who also drew her blunt sword and a long narrow knife. The knife reminded Eld of the stilettos used during the Lot wars to dispatch a champion through an eye. The thought made Eld shiver. Eyes were easy to heal with elfyn medicine but Eld had no intention of learning first hand.

They worked the warrior between them, like a couple of Cambrian hounds baiting a bear. The woman was slower in the armor, but not as slow as Eld would have liked, and she made up for it having an impenetrable skin. As they fought, another disadvantage of the Eurthan was revealed: she was slow on her feet and took the care any warrior did in champion armor not to drift from her center.

"If we can knock her over," Eld shouted as she ducked under the grim knife and deflected the black sword, "we might be able to bind her!"

"With what?" Danshor shouted back, kicking into the back of an armored knee and instantly regretting it. "Bane spawned whoring sodomite!" Danshor yelled. Riding boots weren't enough protection to kick the Eurthan armor. "I think I broke a toe!"

That was the least of Danshor's problems. While she hopped away the Eurthan rushed her and shoved her against the wall with an armored arm to her throat. Danshor was winded and it appeared the Eurthan was going to use all of her weight and her armor to crush Danshor against the stone wall.

Eld dropped her sword, leaping on a sideboard where one of the many bronze horse sculptures sat. Grabbing it with both hands, she ran half up the wall above Danshor's head and brought the bronze horse on the top of the warrior's head with all the force she could.

Sparks flew and a mighty clang echoed throughout the room. Eld landed on her feet and retrieved her sword to see the warrior stagger. Danshor recovered, glaring murderously, then rushed the warrior, using her sword to try to leverage the Bane weapon from the shoulder like they'd done in the ravine. Eld shoved the remains of a table between armored legs and twisted, making the warrior fall. Between these two forces the Bane-weapon popped free of its mooring.

Danshor dropped her sword as she caught the weapon gleefully. "How does this work?" she asked.

"I don't know," Eld replied trying to think of a way to bind the warrior. "The one who attacked me used it like a crossbow...."

The curtains. Of course. They were made of fine, gold, velvet linen drape, but the cords that hung and kept them drawn were silk, as strong as any rope. Eld swung her sword to free several lengths then set to ripping the ropes free for use.

She turned to find Danshor holding the Bane-weapon more or less like the Eurthan Eld remembered. The warrior had risen to her knees. Eld was about to leap on her to knock her down, but would be in the line of strike if she did.

"Lets see how you like a hole struck in your side!" Danshor said nastily. The air around her flickered, much like it did when using a lance but all that happened was a faint shimmer of blue light, like a pale flame from burnt out peat.

The Eurthan laughed. "Liddle zavage! Yew hazh nod dee ezzenze!"

Then there was a commotion outside the door. "It's in here!" some blessed soul shouted.

Help had arrived. A cluster of lances aimed at the warrior. If only half of them had strike, she'd be cooked. Eld prepared to wrap the cords around the woman's ankles, the Eurthan wouldn't have leverage to move if she was bound.

But the warrior was quicker than Eld thought possible. Suddenly the Eurthan was on her feet and wrested the weapon out of Danshor's hands. She made a wide backward swipe of her sword as lance strike discharged, lighting up the room and setting scraps of curtain on fire. Eld jumped back, avoiding the blade, but there was no intention to battle. Instead the woman, abandoning the stiletto while she dodged most of the lance strike, ran to a tall door-sized window and crashed through it. Eld and Danshor dodged the falling glass to rush after her; the woman ran to the north garrison wall.

The night air was cool and the grounds well lit as it was when drilling for an attack. Figures on the wall whistled orders back and forth: they were to try to catch the Eurthan if possible.

"She can't get through!" Eld said as they sprinted.

"Unless they have a tunnel waiting!" Danshor said.

The heavy armored boots left great gouges in the ground. Eld was certain they had been gaining on her. But the closer they came to the wall, near where the ground became more stone and gravel, the faster the warrior ran, as if she drew power directly from contact with stone. The wall might not be such a barrier to her. But then why had they bothered tunneling?

Eld's thoughts were answered as the woman reached the wall, then improbably, started to climb it.

"What in Sul's tresses?"

"Stop!" Danshor said, yanking Eld back with a hand on her shoulder. Archers had prepared to strike and a second later a mass of arrows flew at the figure for all the good it did. Maybe it gave the woman a headache. But the arrows fell away, many broken as the woman climbed the wall. It shouldn't be possible. The stones were faced smoothly. From what Eld could see it was the armor that did the climbing, by some magic where the gloves and knees gripped the stone making it momentarily pliable. The weapon was back on the womans shoulder and turned to discharge forks of blue strike behind her, discouraging pursuit. Whether she couldn't focus without a line of sight or for some other reason, no one was hit. But that gave Eld and idea.

"The strike towers."

She set off, Danshor on her heels. They didn't run to where the woman climbed, where she'd be at the top in seconds, but to where the nearest sol-cannon was housed. They couldn't be adjusted at a moment, but at some point the warrior would have to pass through its range. And maybe, for the first time in history, the cannons would be used in battle.

They ran up a couple stairs switching back in the walls, then to the final one that spiraled to the top. In the turret a sergeant with the gold facing of a cannon striker glanced at them laconically, a telescope in her hand.

"Up here for the show?"

The cylinder of amber solstone rested in a semicircular gap in the parapet wall a short way from the tower. A brass cap the size of a small shield covered the butt, with grim steel veins spidering out down half its length. This made striking more precise and easier for the less experienced. A gap in the top of the brass cap allowed an elf to put place her hand where her palm would contact the stone. Since it was night, there would only be one charge. But the sergeant wasn't standing near it, much less touching it.

"Where is she?" Eld demanded. "You haven't struck yet, have you?"

"No."

"She can't have climbed down already," Danshor said looking along the wall. They could not see their quarry.

The sergeant laughed. "Oh, you're a couple of summer sprites! She didn't bother climbing down. She jumped. Or fell rather. Thought it might kill her, but there she is."

Eld could just make out a figure moving between the low bushes near the end of the illumination beyond the walls. The black armor was well in cannon range.

"What are you waiting for?" Eld shouted. "Strike her!"

"That cannot be, sadly," the sergeant said, folding her telescope and putting it in a pocket.

"Why?" Danshor yelled.

"Because she is in retreat."

"What?" Eld yelled.

"Even if war was declared, cannon is never used on retreating troops without explicit orders."

"The Battle of the Blues Fields ..." Eld started.

" ...The humyn were given ample warning and chose their doom. Check your own code cavalier: you might imagine you're free to run every which way under the sun on your pretty horse, striking like Payeen juggling lightning bolts, but you are forbidden to strike a force in retreat unless explicitly ordered."

## Chapter 12

# Entwined

"Then an hour later the order to strike on sight was given," Danshor was saying in disgust.

There were few times Eld and Danshor were in complete agreement on the absurdity of regulations, and this was one.

They were sitting in the Rowan Oak at one of the larger tables under the tall windows. It was three days after the engagement and, after a couple days of hazy rain, the sky was bright and clear, the late afternoon sun lighting up the interior of the commons so that few shadows lingered. The weather was a balm, making mothers bold and men secure, and seemed to underscore the general feeling the Eurthani had been driven back to their dark subterranean realm by the bright and the bold of the nation.

The reality was the Eurthani had raised a defensive barrier across the ravine at the site of the recent skirmish. Scouts with good eyes and long telescopes reported a low wall, no more than four to five feet high, but thick enough that horses couldn't clear it easily. Behind it the Eurthani had built a complex of metal or glass domes, surrounded by tents typical of a military encampment. That it all appeared overnight was alarming. But there were no further military incursions and the line was far enough away from the the keep and village to give the residents of the Step a misplaced sense of security. But Falls Gate Keep remained in watchfulness.

Inside the Rowan Oak, spirits were lively; Eld and Danshor had been recently joined by Patrycan and Torin, Sil, and Eld's children; Traith was engaged in a vigorous telling of her mother's heroic deeds to a group of girls about her age.

"And then she charged at the Bane, standing on Fiorseth while she struck ...Pesh! Pesh! And the Bane army fled!"

"I don't remember that detail," Danshor drawled while they laughed.

"And we wonder why tales grow so," Eld said. "I should talk to her later."

Sil's eyes twinkled, as if to say "Yes, most certainly". But it was not given to men in Sil's position to publicly criticize mothers in the matter of her own children.

Instead Sil said, "We are packed for our return, assuming it's safe."

Eld's spirits dipped a little. Though she had returned to regular drills and they were still in watchfulness, every spare moment had been spent with the spritelings, riding, swimming and picnicking in the fallow fields nearby.

They spent one day in the village making gall eggs at the Wildling Inn, a spring custom common in the region: eggs were boiled in the water left from leaching acorns from the winter, then decorated with beeswax and brushed with a mixture of iron and vinegar, making the shell black with white where the beeswax sat. Traith had done a great work of art, two cats with knotted tails, but it was long gone, the egg eaten in her impulsive hunger. Shedann's egg was covered with moons and stars, now also gone.

Once Seth had contrived to join them during a picnic, ostensibly by chance on his walks. But Eld knew he could have walked any place else if he desired.

Shedann had run off suddenly after a butterfly, and Danshor and Sil had gone after him. Somehow Eld's tiny boy gave them the slip, darting in circles to evade their grasp, squealing in delight at this new game. Traith had been daydreaming, looking at clouds and almost asleep after exhausting herself earlier trying to climb one of the tallest trees; she'd refused to come down until Eld threatened to retrieve her. When Seth arrived, Traith was wide awake taking amusement at her brother's antics.

"You're not going to help?" Seth had said, standing slightly apart, as if he thought sitting with them would look improper.

"If he goes too far I will," Eld replied. "Oh, come on, he's a tiny boy!" she added laughing.

"But he's fast!" Traith said with sibling pride.

"So much for the hero of the vale," Eld shook her head.

"You're all heroes now," Seth said.

"When do we get our Battle Lions?"

"She's almost regretting those honors," Seth mused. "If she'd just waited a little longer, she'd have given yours in the coming batch."

"Thrift and economy in awards," Eld said. In a softer voice, trusting Traith was distracted, she added, "You forgive me?"

Seth looked at the sky. "I know you're a mother and a soldier. I have no claim on you. It was just a shock at the moment."

"It surprised me too. I wasn't expecting Althas to be there, truly. Don't blame him, it was Danshor."

"When men are forced together in danger, it is hard to hold grudges. At last! Your child has been retrieved. I should go. Look for my missive."

Sure enough, Danshor was carrying a squealing Shedann like a sack of flour on her shoulder, a less amused and harried Sil following close behind. Eld turned to say goodbye, but Seth was already a good ways away, walking quickly to the shade of an old apple wood.

"He's pretty," Traith said.

This surprised Eld. Traith was usually of the opinion that boys, with the exception of her brother, were 'useless'. She was far too young to have serious romantic interests, but Eld supposed even before the first fire, a young mother could see the dream of a man she would want when the time came. Or perhaps it was because Seth was more beautiful than most men. Or, being Eld's daughter, Traith picked up on the essence link Eld shared with Seth.

"Yes," Eld said simply. "He is."

Suddenly Traith smiled impishly. "You like him."

"He is a pleasant and generous keeper of my commander's house," Eld said in her firm mother's voice. "We all like him."

Eld hoped that put the matter to rest.

The memory had taken Eld out of the moment while Danshor abused the command and regulations and all the tiny grouses soldiers nurtured like babes in their wombs. It worried Eld ever so slightly. Children were never the best confidants, in waking or dreams. As much as she'd miss them, it was best the sprites return to the estate, both for safety and discretion.

"Yes," Eld said in response to Sil, "It's a good time to go. We're still in watchfulness and the magi haven't left their post in the commander's house. The force massing nearby is reported as sedentary."

"Sedentary?" Sil queried.

"They are holding a position. But reports through dreaming reveal there are still designs on us. It's like some twisted game. So it's best you leave while it's safe to."

"Reinforcements are coming from Dethglan and Farsnah," Pat said. "Avoid traveling at night."

"Unless you're on a canal boat," Danshor added. "The ground near canals should be safe from tunneling. Tell the drivers not to stop."

"Let's meet for one last meal in the Kettle?" Eld suggested.

Torin groaned. "Why not the Wildling? Isn't that where they're lodging?" Torin favored the Wildling's savories.

"Because for them the treat is eating like a soldier," Eld explained.

Suddenly Tafli called out from the bar, "Ai! This is not a forest of trees to be climbing!"

All mothers who heard words like this were bidden to look around sharply in the event their children were involved. Eld knew before she looked her own daughter was the cause of the mischief. Sure enough, a group of girls clustered together near a bench, one of them with a metal pot on her head, holding another against the wall, while Traith, about to bring a small wood block down on her head, was perched on the bench back.

Eld stood up so fast her chair toppled, but Danshor caught it deftly before it fell.

"Verily little soldiers!" Eld barked as if she was directing a company. "Reenact our great deeds outside! sprightly!"

Traith looked sheepish. "Sorry, ama." Then the excitement of play took over again and she commanded the throng, "Come on!" They ran out as one horde, adroitly avoiding the other matrons, most of whom were amused. Suddenly Shedann slipped off his chair.

"You don't have to go, metti," Eld said.

"I want to! Traith said I could be rescued!" He darted away, holding his perpetual companion, Vineflower.

With a sigh, Sil stood. "My duty is now without." He left in a rustle of silver-grey vestments.

"He's kinda nice," Torin said once Sil was out the door. "For a man of his age."

Pat laughed. "And has too much class to give the likes of you a look much less a kiss. Of any kind."

Eld was glad Pat said something. It kept her from having to be the dragon. "I don't know," Eld ventured. "Sil is adept at managing children."

"Ha!" Torin said a bit too shrilly. "You're all so amusing! As if you're not thinking it yourselves -- what vision is this?"

Torin was distracted by the arrival of a young man who looked as if he'd walked through an explosion of glimmer. His eyes were outlined in dark kohl, as well as his brows, exaggerating their accent to a theatrical degree. This was one of the current styles of boys in Ta Mel. It was striking, but gave him a startled look. His lips were gilded, and glimmer was dusted over his cheeks and hair, the last pulled back in an imitation of the Dwen style. But instead of a yastol, a Wildling made twisted half-moon band of wood pulled his hair back so it hung mane-like around his face. The fullness of his locks suggested they'd been braided in sleep, and they glowed red from henna. Eld was certain what he was wearing few mothers and no mother's helper would have let him outside of the house with: tight, dark brown leggings with a short red tunic, belted with a woven cord. The tunic was slit up the side, cut amateurishly. If Eld could guess, the young man was trying to imitate Tafli's style, right down to the wrist bangles.

The man grinned, pleased at the effect he had on seasoned soldiers, if Torin could be included in that count.

"Afternoon, heroes of the Vale!" he said. "I've been sent to see if you desire anything."

Danshor snorted.

"More mead? Bread? Roast? Only we're wondering if the table will be free soon."

"Where did you come from?" Danshor asked.

"Oh Taffellyni is ever so busy these days!" the man said enthusiastically. "So when I asked if I could help, he agreed!"

Eld had the feeling the man did this more for excitement than money. She also felt he was familiar, but she couldn't place him.

"Are you on the menu?" Torin asked, looking the man up and down.

He giggled but Eld and Pat looked at her sharply.

"Are you trying to get use evicted?" Eld hissed.

"You are risking the Rowan Oak's lease by suggesting solicitation," Pat said grimly.

"Sorry!" Torin said. "I thought that's where we got the other boys--"

"We'll have another round of house mead, thank you," Danshor said loudly.

"Verily and anon!" the man said and bounced back to the bar.

"Now look at that – end," Danshor said, watching the barely covered curves of the man's rear.

Torin hooted with laughter then gulped self consciously.

"Too raw for me," Pat said taking a swig from her goblet. "What is he? Five hours past a century?"

A century was understood in most elfyn nations as the age of adulthood.

"All men have their uses," Danshor said wisely. "The mature have experience, the young, have enthusiasm. Depends what one is in the mood for."

"Well, I prefer someone who might be able to hold a conversation," Pat said.

"I'll find you a nice virginal, accountant's son," Danshor needled.

"I can scrounge my own men, thank you," Pat retorted.

Eld heard Tafli say, "Why yes! I am to be teaching this to Farni? He is wanting to dance." Tafli was talking to one of many women who tried their luck with Tafli under the guise of casual conversation. "Do you know it?"

"Know what?" some elf said.

"Some loud souls are saying all men have purpose," Tafli said. Eld cringed inside but Tafli didn't even look at their table much less Danshor. "But such souls should be careful who she is twining with."

"A gorgeous drake like you can twine with me anytime!" a footer fresh from duty proclaimed.

Tafli smiled, "You are sure? Sometimes there's more twining than expected."

While still wiping out a tin cup Tafli started singing :

*In a wood, by a field, near the fence, on the plain*
*Saun saw a bright Dwen play*
*Not a man, not a boy, he was quick, he was bold*
*And he danced across to say ...*
~

*Twine with me, twine with me!*
*By the tree, in the lee;*
*Dine with me, wine with me!*
*Have no care! for I am free!*
~

It was a Wilding or Dwen folk tune, cheerful and lively, the chorus easily joined even by souls unfamiliar with it, and easy to dance to as Farni did, spinning on his toes as he served the matrons.

*They danced in the glen, they dance in a fen,*
*They danced the day away*
*They danced under trees, they danced with the bees*
*And as they danced the man sang away:*
~

*Twine with me, twine with me!*
*By the tree, in the lee;*
*Dine with me, Wine with me!*
*Have no care! for I am free!*
~

*At the end of the dance, in a copse by chance,*
*They found a bower of fray,*
*They fell to the task, in a soft ferny mass,*
*Blooming kisses for the rest of the day:*
~

*Twine they be, twine they be,*
*By the tree in the lee*
*Twine they be, twine they be,*
*They had no care twining free!*
~

By this time Farni was doing all the serving, skipping on his feet while a couple soldiers cavorted with Tafli on the floor before the hearth. Spinning with linked arms, Tafli skipped between then in well known steps of farm lot dances. Most matrons either sang with the chorus or whistled the tune as

Tafli sang. Tafli had a higher voice than many Dwen, but he could be imitating Sula fashion.

Two new and slightly deeper voices joined; a couple of Dwen women had stepped inside, one was much like Tafli, the other had both darker skin and black hair; both had oak yastols. They suddenly looked grim and foreboding but the lyrics explained why:

~

*Gone was the sun and the dusk had come*
*When came the mother as they lay,*
*Before Saun could run, in vines she was spun*
*And the mother dragged her boy away!*

~

*Twine thee be, twine thee be,*
*bound in tree for a night and day*
*Twine thee be, twine thee be,*
*If you dance with Dwen boys that stray!*

~

There was much whistling and cheering as the song ended.

"I'm never going take liberties with a man of the wood if I sight his mother, mark that!" the footwoman said.

"You are being wiser than many," Tafli said before greeting the Dwen and handing them a full mesh bag. They left, that being their only business.

A couple soldiers Eld didn't know engaged Pat briefly over the matter of a horse, a ring and a couple pounds of sausage. There was some tricky situation but Eld was too distracted by something happening at one of the small center tables.

Tafli was standing nearby, holding an empty tray after delivering drinks. He looked as he usually did, today with vinings attached with fern, making his forearms look like leafy armor. The woman he was waiting on was an army officer in uniform with a man of the sort that had attended the stable throng: local, unsophisticated, but adventurous and happy to harlot as a hobby. He was dressed better than most, wearing a sleeveless green kirtle-shirt of light fabric that flowed to the floor. He had minimum glimmer except for his lips which were gilded and bright. His hands were toying with the helix decorated lapels of the officer while she spoke with Tafli. There were so many voices, Eld couldn't hear at first, but she knew Tafli's moods and he looked stiff and haughty when he suspected disrespect. Eld concentrated and finally found the thread of their words:

"What is this thing?" Tafli queried.

"I had heard you might be available," the officer said. Her voice sounded familiar.

"Available? How is this? I am available now. That is why this house is open?"

"Not as a public house. You know. Privately. Not right now of course ..."

Eld marveled that the man on the officer's arm didn't get up and leave. She must be paying him a lot. But now Eld was starting to get the gist of the intent and then, with a thrill of mixed excitement and terror, she realized who the officer was: Lieutenant Roel.

"You are asking to pay for my private time?" Tafli said.

"I understand you have other visitors ..."

"Others?" Tafli's voice rose very slightly in register.

"I was recommended by a mutual friend ..."

Tafli's head snapped around like an owl's. In a second his eyes met Eld's, then looked back at the officer.

"I am having no friends who say I am selling my private time!" Tafli said loudly.

"Well, she didn't say that exactly ..."

"I certainly am hoping no mother said that exactly or not!" Tafli shouted. "I am not harloting now or ever, and any mother who is thinking this is not welcome!"

It was Roel's turn to be outraged. "Well, if you're going to prance around exposing your legs you can't get upset if some elf thinks you're for sale!"

Tafli turned back to the officer and smiled terribly at her, like a vengeful Goddi eager to eat her soul.

"But I can be upset about anything here because this is being my house!"

Then the officer's companion screamed.

"Snakes!" he shouted, leaping to his feet. Eld found herself on her feet, along with half the matrons, their collective chivalry triggered to rescue any laird in need. But there were no serpents as such, only vinings that had grown out of the chair the officer sat in and seethed like snakes to bind her limbs. She shouted, too late to free herself.

"Now you will be sitting a moment to thinking on your wrongness," Tafli said as he sauntered to the bar.

"I hate snakes!" the companion man shrieked. He grabbed his bag and fled.

"Get back here, you stupid slet!" Roel yelled. "I've paid for you!"

"Maybe you do not pay enough," Tafli mused lightly polishing the bar at leisure.

The entire house was so silent one could hear heartbeats. Unlike the humiliation of the ranger, this was an officer. Roel was in uniform and the soldiers were duty bound to respect her station. Eld thought she'd pass out between the tension of keeping herself from laughter; it was certain as soon as the officer left the commons would explode like fireworks at a carnival. But, for now, the women hoped Tafli would release Roel before their control dissolved, even if most mothers joyed in Roel's humiliation. Tafli was great value.

Lieutenant Roel was oblivious to their collective dilemma and started spitting like a snared cat.

"Unbind me at once, bar knave!" Roel snarled.

"I am not a knave," Tafli said. "I am owning this lease. I know it is hard for mothers to understand a man can own things."

"Your lease can be voided!" Roel shouted. "Insubordination! Assault on an federation officer! You lost me my harlot ..."

"Maybe do not be calling men harlots if you want to keep them?"

Several women couldn't help snorting at this. Every mother knew the basic rules of harlots: pay them what they ask and treat them like princes.

"I could have you evicted!"

"You are to have me court-martialed next, yes? But you are wrong. It is I who evict you." The vinings retreated into the chair. Eld shivered. They did move like snakes. "You insult me in my house. Get out. Do not let me see you here again."

Roel lurched to her feet, relieved to be free. But the next moment, eyes smoldering, she turned on Tafli, who backed up with alarm.

"Dwen Harlot!" Roel snarled as she bore down on him. "How dare you--"

Eld found herself rushing Roel with a handful of women who leapt to Tafli's defense. Eld stood in front of Tafli while a couple other women firmly seized Roel's arms and guided her to the door. Just before she was dragged out, her head snapped back. She looked straight at Eld.

"You!" Roel said. "You did this!"

Eld stood her ground, shrugging at the confused looks as Roel was dragged out.

"Are you alright?" Eld asked.

Tafli looked shaken. "I didn't think she would threaten me in seriousness."

"I thought the entire bar was going to erupt in branches and strangle her."

"Yes, that would have happened. If she touched me. I would not be able to help it. But I might have killed her. I do not think I have been that afraid before. Not here."

"Knave!" Eld called to the new man. "Get your boss something strong." Eld guided Tafli to their table to sit down. "You shouldn't waste a thought on that hood. If you had killed her, the Temple would have her back among the living for a court-martial in the hour."

The boy put down a tin mug of something strong.

"Thank you," Tafli muttered and drank, while the boy rushed around the commons cleaning tables and catching orders. "He's keen," Tafli said. "I forget how much work this is without helping."

Then his eyes fell on Eld. "Is what she said true?"

Guilt weighed on Eld's shoulders. She hadn't expected Roel to be so reckless or Tafli to be frightened.

"I ..." Eld found the words hard. "Roel was comparing Dwen to savages. Claiming you had no toilets and generally being a disrespectful bigot. I'm a bit surprised she bothered to come here if she thinks so low of Dwen."

"Perhaps she comes because you tell her?"

Tafli was recovering fast, narrow green eyes watching with every word.

"I didn't say it like that. She was already calling Dwen men harlots. After that bold scout, I thought I'd send her to you to discipline."

Eld stopped speaking. Tafli stared at her for a few moments. Eld felt like a small child caught in some mischief.

Finally, Tafli called sharply to the new knave, "Farni! I am being gifted another tall drink by this one. Bring it quick so she can pay." To Eld he added, "Then I forgive you. Next time tell me of these plots. Then it can be funny for both of us, see?"

"Yes," Eld breathed, thankful to be not cast out of Tafli's society. "I am sorry."

Tafli patted her hand. "Yes, you are."

"Since we're settling accounts and you're not about to be strangled by vines," Danshor ventured, "Perhaps I can get my five queens."

Eld had pulled out a small purse from inside her jacket. Expenses entertaining the children had depleted much of her free funds, but debt didn't get less for the waiting. She only had four queen coins, but made up the last in flints, and threw down seven shards, the greater portion of a flint, for Tafli's drink.

"Not to be a vulture," Pat said, "But you still have seven flints on the stable accounts." The stable or barracks accounts were managed by a responsible soldier and used for petty expenses for all those in residence.

Eld looked at her nearly bare purse. Normally she didn't care, but if she had the children visiting she liked a few shard coins for the odd treat. "Can I catch up you up later? Only the children still might want."

Patrycan waved a hand. "Any day anon."

"Elam," Eld breathed. She'd have to draw funds from the estate if she didn't want to wait for her quarterly pay. Where did it all go? At least she didn't gamble as a habit.

"Soon I am ready to work again," Tafli said. "I am needing a hero to retrieve my stones for the night." He looked at Eld inquiringly.

"Let some other bold elf help," Eld said. "Torin could use the exercise."

Torin tore her eye off the new knave and said, "What?"

"You can help Tafli with the lamp stones."

Torin's smirked in an imitation of Danshor at her most lecherous. "What's my reward?"

"I give you free drink," Tafli said lazily.

Torin pouted. "That's all?"

Tafli laughed suddenly, then wagged his finger at Torin, his bangles jingling. "You do not want this thing you are imagining. Yes, I know you jest. But it is few Sula who join with Dwen who like it."

False disappointment on Torin's face was replaced by curiosity. "Why? Dwen men are so – fulsome."

"Dwen like to coit in a form of mutual sodomy," Danshor said smugly, taking joy in making Torin uncomfortable.

"What?" Torin said, no longer leering at Tafli.

Tafli stood, looking down at Danshor as if she was a dirty worm. "It is not being like that at all."

"So it's not true you entwine your bower vines and prod each other?"

"When together we are rooted and sharing essence together. It is nothing like this 'sodomy' of Sula women obsessed with domination on men."

"Sounds like mutual sodomy to me. With wood-essence. And roots, I suppose. Maybe you could demonstrate one day ..."

"Danshor," Eld breathed, "For once in your life, shut up."

"It is no bother. Your sister should not being worried. No Dwen man, or woman for that matter, would be wanting to touch her stagnant essence."

Tafli stalked off while Danshor shrugged still smirking.

" 'Stagnant essence' ," Pat said. "That has to be a sharp cut in the original Dwenifee."

"So should I still help with his stones?" Torin asked causing Danshor to bark with laughter.

"Not unless you want to be 'mutually rooted'!"

"And I thought the children were outside," Eld opined. "In seriousness, yes, you should," she added to Torin. "It might save us from being banned from the Rowan Oak. Just don't try to flirt anymore, verily?"

Torin nodded seriously and left. There were few fates worse than being barred from the only public house in a garrison.

As the conversation drifted away from Dwen to issues of leave and duties, Eld finished her drink and rose to get more with some coins Pat offered.

"Are you sure your sisters should have more?" Tafli said, giving the knave a tray with traveler sandwiches and three goblets to deliver.

"You know how she is," Eld said. "Probably read 'the Sodomy of the Trees' one too many times."

"The how of the trees?" Tafli looked as offended as if he'd seen a burning tree.

Eld shrugged. "It's a notorious work of pornography read in brothel lounges."

Tafli's kohled and glimmered eyes looked even more baleful if possible. "I see. My nation is fetish for amusement."

"Let's just agree she's an idiotic hood. She always makes assumptions about men who don't have women."

Tafli arched a brow. "Who is saying I do not have a woman? I prefer not to go too long without being entwined and ..."

"Stop!" Eld said, holding up a hand. "I don't need to know!"

Tafli grinned at her discomfort. "Sula say they are so sophisticated, but are bothered by little things like wood-essence...."

"It would help if all the wood-essence I've seen didn't look like moving snakes. So, you only coit Dwen women I assume?"

"And some who are not Dwen but open."

"Anyone I know?"

"Here are your drinks," Tafli said, ending the subject by shoving a tray into her hands and turning to a new matron.

## Chapter 13

# The Wildling

Intriguing though it was that Tafli might have a Sula lover, it wasn't Eld's concern and the children needed to be taken to the Kettle soon if they were going to eat in the garrison. Afterwards, Eld might go with them to the Wildling and take the time to put them to bed. That would be nice. She even had a Dwen story picked out, "The Last Leaf of Summer". Traith and Shedann both liked Dwen stories in preference to all others.

As if answering her thoughts, Sil and the children reentered.

"Everyone's gone home for dinner," Traith volunteered.

"My little heroes," Eld said as Shedann climbed into her lap, still clutching Vineflower. Traith climbed onto a chair, standing on it briefly, smiling at her boldness, then sitting down under Eld's suddenly stern eye. "Much better," Eld said. "Before you tell us of your heroic deeds, we should make our way to the Kettle while the food is at its best."

"I've just started!" Torin's voice called from overhead where she was perched on a beam.

"Join us when you're done," Eld said. "You haven't forgotten where the Kettle is, have you?"

Eld immediately regretted her sarcasm as Traith sniggered along with Danshor. It was one thing to poke fellows among themselves, but it should be out of the ear of children or the impressionable. Torin muttered to herself in bad humor, mocking Eld's sarcasm.

"Then it would be wise to put these to rest," Sil suggested. "They don't appear to be, but they are weary."

"So am I," Eld said, draining her cup then standing, hoisting Shedann on her hip. "You want to ride?"

"Yes!" It was usually Traith that rode on her shoulders.

"Let's wait until we get outside." They walked as a group to the door while navigating new arrivals. "Good eve!" Eld called to Tafli who nodded acknowledgement while taking a moment to glower at Danshor. The knave grinned and waved.

"You're going to fix that," Eld said to Danshor as they stepped onto the porch.

"The knave? Well, I can think of a couple of things ..."

"No, Tafli, you depraved hood!"

Danshor laughed. "Sorry, I'm not interested in being 'mutually rooted'."

Sil looked sharply at her, Eld, then the children.

"I mean clear your offense, you ogre. So we can still get drinks at a reasonable price."

"Maybe I'll visit The Wildling instead."

"You're too lazy to walk that far and the men aren't as bold."

"They're not allowed to be because they're under family eyes."

"A difference without a distinction."

"Fine. I'll tip him some of your queens soon. You worry too much."

Suddenly someone shouted, "Lancer Farthal!" and Eld's blood turned to ice.

They were in the middle of a patch of green that divided the main road and a parade field and were about to join the straggling line of women walking to the Kettle in the Crèche. Shedann was now on Eld's shoulders, Traith on Danshor's, Pat and Sil in low conversation sharing violet sugar lozenges they both favored. There was still plenty of light though Sul struggled through a haze of clouds that had layered themselves above the western horizon. The general mood of the garrison was genial and Eld wasn't the only one who had visiting children. But the voice that called out was so full of rage that heads turned, children cleaved closer to their mothers or her tribe, and women looked with the alertness of judging whether a fight was imminent and what role they should play.

But a second later most relaxed, for they understood the matter in the broadest soldier's terms: one of them had run afoul an officer who was full of her importance. The only reason eyes lingered after was the subject was Eld herself. How did the hero who saved the commander's brother come under such censure?

Lieutenant Roel, eyes glinting, bore down on Eld's group with an open sneer. Eld eased Shedann off her shoulders passing him to Sil's hands.

"Go on without me," Eld murmured.

"I called for you, cavalier!" Roel barked. "And you! Yes, the bold one trying to escape with the keeper."

Danshor looked askance, for once Eld thinking her justified in her expression of innocence.

"Now!" Roel yelled. Danshor removed Traith, who found Sil's hand, holding onto her keeper for comfort. She was not used to soldiers being anything less than motherly and indulgent. Eld could feel the girl's anxiety and it sparked anger.

"Emha, whatever your cause for anger with us, you will do my family the courtesy of not upsetting the mites," Eld said in a tone navigating her respect for Roel's rank and her obligations as a mother.

"In that case cavalier, bid them move out of hearing range smartly!" Roel snarled.

Eld glanced at Sil and Patrycan, now joined by a confused Torin. Eld nodded at them curtly. "I'll join you as soon as I am able."

As Sil grabbed the children's hands to hurry away, escorted by Pat and Torin, Roel loomed closer to Eld and Danshor. Suddenly she shouted at them:

"Stand straight when I speak to you!"

Eld and Danshor snapped to attention, but Eld said:

"You don't lead us. You're not our captain."

"What is this?" Roel demanded waving a hand over the fronts of her fawn and sage uniform, where the twining gold helix officer braids graced her lapels. "Decoration for the stage?"

Eld and Danshor said nothing.

"I asked you a question!" Roel bellowed.

"It sounded rhetorical ..." Danshor began.

"Officer twinings!" Eld answered as smartly as a new recruit.

"Yet with an officer in sight you did not salute my presence."

This was stretching discipline to absurdity. An officer should be acknowledged on sight while on duty with a salute, off duty with a nod, and only required when reasonably within immediate line of sight. Roel was playing with them.

"With respect," Danshor unwisely began, "You were not within our sight."

"Not within sight?" Roel mocked. "I was right over there ..." She pointed about thirty yards away where, true, technically she would have been visible. But practically, with the many souls passing hither and yon, they would hardly noticed her unless they'd been looking for her. "Do you have dim humyn eyes?"

"No, emha!"

"Are you aelg, a result of your mother's dalliance with dim humyn, having inherited their dim essence?

"No, emha!" they chorused again.

"Then by Her Holy Tresses salute!"

Eld could refuse. She could make a formal objection to harassment. But she knew that could be worse. The same urge that drove soldiers into harmless pranks, could drive an officer with wounded pride to revenge.

They saluted smartly, open hands reaching for the sky above as if to snatch a star from the zenith.

Roel stared at them a long while, frozen in a position they could not yield until she returned it. Roel leaned close to Eld's ear, her sweat the scent of anger and violent arousal.

"I hope you enjoyed your prank, Farthal," she hissed. "Hero or not, if you ever toy with me again you'll find yourself rooted and it won't be by your Dwen harlot!"

Stepping away, Roel returned the salute, allowing them to lower their hands. "Now, cavaliers, boldly march yourselves to the commander's office. You have an account to make of your behavior. Meanwhile, I have to replace my harlot. That man, Althas, he'll be available, won't he?" Roel leered taking joy in Eld's sudden worry.

"He's not a harlot."

"He acts like a harlot and gets paid like a harlot, correct?"

"I've never paid him," Eld said.

Suddenly Roel was at her ear again. "Are you trying to be clever, Farthal?"

"No, emha. I'm simply saying you should not expect him to be for sale."

"Well, I guess we'll see, Farthal."

"He's probably not even around," Danshor volunteered.

"Why would you say that, cavalier?"

"We're in watchfulness and a lot of mothers like children and men of their house inside before dusk."

This was true, but Eld wished Danshor had not chosen this time to express a motherly interest in a man's welfare. As long as Althas was not around that would be good enough.

"Well, aren't you both the souls of chivalry. Perhaps later you can introduce me properly and we'll find out whether he's a harlot or not. Why are you still standing here? The commander is waiting!"

Eld and Danshor saluted, then pivoted onto the road to the commander's house walking at a clip, highly aware of the eyes who had witnessed their humiliation.

"If she touched Althas unwillingly ..."

"You need to stop worrying about the honor of every man," Danshor said. "She's not going to rape him. Maybe offer him enough money for a night to humiliate you though."

"I don't care if it's his will."

"I thought you were close."

"He's a laugh, but I have no more than brotherly feelings for him."

"You trysting with your brothers? Now who is depraved?"

"Be silent, we're here. Though I have no idea what you've done wrong."

"I confess being mystified as well. I did snort at her entanglement ..."

"She'd have to have reported every mother there.... Yes, we're here to see the commander," Eld said to Sonamor who had appeared.

The house was mostly cleaned up, though repairs remained to be finished, stone masons and architects passing in and out as they were guided through the corridors. They came to Alhern's office, a room in the east overlooking the parade grounds and gates. The door was open revealing the usual sparse furnishings of white holly wood and bronze sculptures; in a place of prominence was a particularly gorgeous work of art, a rearing horse with a flowing mane and tail. There were three clocks on the fireplace mantle, one set to regular time, the other two to mark the Day-Sea/Cambrian coast and the East Altans and Sharitan respectively.

Sonamor knocked once on the door.

"The cavaliers you sent for."

"Enter," Alhern said.

Eld and Danshor walked in at an easy march, shuffled their feet to face the desk in smooth dancelike motions and saluted, saying, "Commander". Then they stood at attention, all in perfect synchrony like dance partners. In fact there was a soldier's musical hall line dance that began exactly like the formal protocol before abruptly and amusingly breaking into a hornpipe. It was common in whimsical military theatrical productions. But Alhern didn't look like the whimsical type to jest about breaking into song. In fact she hadn't looked up from her desk or even said, "At ease" as was common if a soldier had to wait for a moment. Instead she left them at attention in silence while she finished reading a document, then signed it with gold tipped metal quill pen. Only then did she look up, leaning back in her chair. Still Alhern did not give them leave to be at ease.

"Cavaliers remind me of girls who never grew up, still playing with horses."

Had they been at ease Eld might have smiled. But after the encounter with Roel that would be presumptuous. She still couldn't fathom why Danshor was there.

Alhern moved a leaf of paper in front of her, glancing at it once before addressing Danshor:

"Lancer Hanmet Danshor, are you a ranger or qualified Thyn consultant?"

Eld cringed inside as Danshor gave an ill considered chuckle. Alhern stared at her icily until Danshor coughed apologetically then answered, "No, emha."

"Were you asked for your opinion while Captain Draeyn was interrogating T'hen 'Ok of the Third Branch?"

"No, emha." This time Danshor's voice was perfectly disciplined.

"Are you trying to sabotage our efforts to gather intelligence in the course of our duty to the Federation, cavalier? Perhaps working as a spy for the Eurthani?"

"No, emha." Now Danshor sounded positively grim.

"I'm glad to hear that, Lancer Danshor. The next time Draeyn or any ranger is querying Thyn you will keep your words and thoughts to yourself, and let others with talent in such matters take the lead. Understood?"

"Yes, emha."

"I don't care how heroic you are on the field. Interfere with rangers or magi in the course of their duties and I'll have you in drudges on road repair and woodworks for a month."

"Yes, emha."

"Dismissed."

Eld and Danshor exchanged a glance.

"What, cavalier?" Alhern demanded. "Need a mother to hold your hand?"

"Emha," Eld said, "My children and their keeper are waiting in the Kettle. If I need to stay longer, I need Danshor to look after them until I'm finished."

Alhern's eyes flickered between them, her face neutral.

"Very well. Now she knows. Dismissed."

Danshor saluted, turned about face, and left.

Alhern's eyes lingered after her as the sound of Danshor's boot steps faded away. Eld mentally marshaled her defenses, trying to put her loathing of Roel into reasonable terms on short notice. So she was surprised when Alhern said:

"At ease, Farthal. And close the door."

Relieved yet cautious, Eld complied, then returned to stand easy. Alhern was was pouring a drink but had only set out one goblet. She leaned back and sipped it before speaking.

"Tell me what happened between you and Roel in the Rowan Oak."

Eld stitched the tale as loosely as she could, focusing mostly on Roel's presumptions.

" ...And I consider Tafli a friend, though I should be clear we have no liaison."

"Uh hum," Alhern murmured eying Eld.

"Not that he doesn't glow. He's just more like a brother. And he was clearly offended at Roel's offer, yet she didn't take the hint and kept pushing. Well, you know Tafli ..."

"Do I?" Alhern asked.

"I mean, any regular knows Tafli. He's a bold Dwen man and not to be tested in his own house. So of course he tangled Roel to teach her a lesson. I admit I laughed. We all did."

"And then?"

Eld decided to omit Roel's words for now.

"Then some women, other officers I think, threw Roel out. We left shortly after to go to the Kettle. Roel – Lieutenant Roel – waylaid us and told us to report here. After shouting a lot."

Alhern's lips turned in a wry smile. "I can imagine."

"Commander, she baited us unreasonably."

"Did she."

"Yes. She startled the children."

"Ah," Alhern nodded. "No mother likes to lose face in front of her birthed."

"I care not about that! They were frightened!"

"Have a care, Farthal. Calm yourself."

Eld glared outside a window while Alhern continued.

"Would you say Roel was popular with the troops?"

"It's surely not my place to say ..."

"Farthal," Alhern said with an edge, "Don't waste our time."

Eld shrugged. "I don't know her. She is not an officer that inspires respect. "

"You don't like her."

"No."

"Why?"

Eld paused, choosing her words. "I did not like how she spoke of 'Trees' and mocked our Dwen allies."

Alhern set down her goblet and leaned back looking up at Eld. " 'Tree' isn't always a slur, lancer, but I trust your judgment in this context. Roel tells me you suggested Tafli harloted on the side."

Eld said nothing.

"Is this true?"

"I admit I said words that could be taken that way. I never said Tafli was a harlot."

Alhern leaned forward, elbows on the desk, looking into Eld's eyes.

"You set Roel up."

It was a statement.

"Roel was not obligated to proposition Tafli. She had a man on her arm already...."

But Alhern waved a hand, as if swatting a midge.

"Sit down Farthal and say no more words on the subject, lest you trip and utter a lie, forcing me to discipline you."

Eld sat down carefully, but did not relax.

"You are lucky," Alhern continued. "Roel seems satisfied with the opportunity to scream at you on the grounds and has waved away her right further satisfaction. Of course we both know that has more to do with avoiding a recount of her humiliation by not just a man, but a Dwen man, in front of a military court. I promised her you would be rebuked in the strongest terms you deserve."

Eld held her breath.

"Consider yourself rebuked. Yes, Farthal, that is all. But don't swagger about it. I also abhor bigots. Unfortunately they are not uncommon in Federation service. You will be satisfied to know I impressed on Roel that the Rowan Oak is a valued contract with the garrison, and its owner, whether they are a bright desirable man or an Aeon matriarch, is not to be harassed with unwelcome advances. Even if they were lured by a soldier's prank."

"Will she apologize to Tafli?"

"That is not your concern, cavalier. You've done enough for the day."

"Yes, emha."

"I will advise Roel about her conduct in front of children. But since you did bait her first, you should otherwise consider yourselves even."

Eld stood and left Alhern's office as smartly as she arrived. Once in the hall, she saw it was later than she thought, as if Sul, eager for sleep, had sped up in Her courses. Eld found the door with little trouble this time; soon she'd know the building like the stables. Eld paused in the entrance, hearing activity down the stair that led to the kitchens. Black robed magi speaking in serious tones emerged while more ran down the steps.

" ...And dreamers report a camp of sorts at the end of a warren of tunnels."

"And the commander hasn't sent a ranger? Isn't this what they live for?"

"Remember the formidable magi minds reported? They need to be prepared to send a foot company ..."

The women broke off their conversation on sighting Eld, nodding in acknowledgement as they passed her.

"Here to help?" Seth said, startling Eld with his voice. She was watching the magi leave thinking on the words she heard. Seth was in a workaday robe again, though he was lightly glimmered.

"There's an encampment in the tunnel?" Eld said.

"As I understand, it's deep in, past the garrison walls and a quarter mile downward. They want to block it up, but we don't know if that will make a difference. Selind is in correspondence with engineers. The best course might be Dwen craft. It won't stop them, but we'll know when they're coming. I think the tunnel is trapped to that effect. So, to what do we owe this visit?"

"Oh, you know. The commander likes to yell at her heroes."

"Truly?"

"I exaggerate a bit. I have to leave. I'm to be meeting the sprites in the Kettle."

"The choice portions will be gone now."

"I know," Eld growled. "Damn Roel."

"Lieutenant Roel?"

"I don't think it's wise to speak about her." Eld looked outside, through the open door, then at Seth's bright slender form. "I have to go."

Seth stepped near Eld, placing a hand on her arm. Eld felt a stiff folded paper under it as another magi passed them. Adroitly she moved a hand to catch it when Seth removed his. "Read it."

Eld glanced in her hand and saw it was a small sealed letter, apparently meant to be sent. She broke the waxed decorative letter that sounded 'S' and unfolded it, the words making her smile:


My Bold Cavalier;

If you have forgiven my envies ... for even the Lake son is jealous of his lovers' admirers! ...and you find yourself nearby in the aspect of Amer after the lights are dimmed, but before the midnight hour, then take a turn on the paths on the east back of the house. You will find a door unlocked, its handle wound by a string of pearls.

~ The Lakeson


"We're decided then on the scene, but which stanza ..." Eld asked, looking up. But Seth had slipped away in the bustle of patrolling soldiers, magi and servants, the latter becoming almost martial in their duties.

"Could a soul wrangle these wizards out of the way of my knaves?" a sharp man's voice shouted from the direction of the kitchens. "Surely there's a circle of stones or a star tower that needs tending ..."

Eld folded the letter, slipping it in her jacket as she hurried herself out the door to evade dinner preparations. She walked as briskly as she could towards the Kettle, elated at the thought of meeting Seth later. But she worried about the time, for she would not miss this one last chance to tend to her children before they left. At least she wasn't seriously in trouble over Roel, though she would be careful not to gloat about it. No reason to bait the weasel.

The light was fading early, Sul occulted by a cloud bank before She ended the day. It was hard to know when exactly She set as the bluish air of the twilight gloom settled around them. The illuminated interior of the Kettle still looked active as Eld was about to pass a group of cavaliers leaving, many women having removed their flouts, their hair hovering free on their shoulders. The truth was, Eld yearned to be free of hers. Yet, while they were allowed to drop their hair after the duty of the day, watchfulness made her wary to be completely out of uniform outside of sleep.

"Well met, Gilded Hero!" Alcas, a trumpeter, said. With a slight start Eld recognized her own company.

"The cast of jealousy is a rot to the soul," Eld quoted. "Besides aren't we all heroes now?"

"No mother is getting a Lion until watchfulness is over," Patrycan said.

"I'll meet you all anon. Sil and the mites are waiting," Eld said.

"Oh, they've gone on," Pat said, stopping Eld in her tracks.

"What?"

"Don't worry," Reon said. "They were well fed. For some reason the Kettle has a surfeit of rabbit. Then we were schooled by your heir about all your deeds and were bidden to mark how you must be the bravest and boldest mother in the Orb. She's quite a little advocate."

Eld laughed with the rest. "If I hadn't given the medals to Sil for keeping, I expect she'd be wearing them. Where are they now?" Eld asked Pat.

"When Danshor finally showed up and told us you were still being scorched, the mites were fading. Your boy had fallen asleep in Sil's lap. Danshor took them all to The Wildling."

The women were as eager to get to the Rowan Oak as Eld was to meet her children so they parted merrily. But Eld stood, unsure of what to do.

She could go on to the Kettle and wolf down the over-warm remains of rabbit, bread, the daily potage, cheese and weak barley-mead, then run to The Wildling, hoping the children were still awake. But if they were, she might not have time to meet Seth. Or maybe she should just eat her meal at a easy pace and turn in early to dream. But then she'd miss her tryst with Seth for certain. Eld sighed to herself grimly. Seth was dear, and she burned to be with him, but he wasn't going anywhere. He would understand. Eld strode to the mess, planning to leave a note of regret if she could not meet the hour.

The Kettle was built, like the stables, with the most minimum nod to elfyn architectural sensibilities, free of excessive decoration. The tall, narrow windows made it brilliant on a summer day. Now they were dark mirrors, reflecting the light of the same type of lamps used in the Rowan Oak, except these were arranged to be lowered. No soldier was to be caught cavorting in the open rafters, though some did it on a dare. Few women remained at the long tables of aged oak planks, rumored to have been around since the garrison's first days. The benches, on the other hand, though well made, could be no more than a century or two old. The furnishings were all made out of the less desired portions of lumber and designed with an eye to seat as many souls efficiently as possible in a large space. Yet, in other lands with less craftsmanship, even with the common designs of apprentice scrolls and compass stars, the benches would be considered master works. Each bench was half the length of a table and seated four women on average, and while they had no cushioning, the top sculpted for comfort. Now the benches sat aslant, women leaving in haste to public houses to meet fellows and men. The Kettle staff was starting their last labor of cleaning and straightening as Eld walked up to the serving tables.

"The hour is late," the woman in a white military chef's tunic said. Her hair, on the top of her head in an artisan bun, was hidden in a white regulation scarf wrap. Only the pin on a lapel marked her as a kettle sergeant.

"Yes, I know my poets," Eld said.

"So I hear. I'll get you what we have left. Beware; the potage is grim."

"I'll take what you have."

It could have been worse. The pewter bowl of potage was simply very thick, the pulses, grains, vegetables and herbs having merged into the consistency of pea soup. But it was flavored with bacon scraps and tasty. The rabbit on the other hand , while well seasoned, had gone dry, like skinned chicken sun-broiled by an inexpert helper. As always the bread, a quarter round, was excellent, slightly yellow from a mix of egg and the best yeasts to make it light and moist. It wasn't sweet like bread for the road, where honey was added to help it keep. But there was butter a plenty. Alas, except for crumbs, all the cheese for the day was gone.

All this was given to Eld on a trencher with a plate, bowl, tin fork and spoon. Every mother carried her own eating knife. She also had a generous tall cup of barely-mead.

"Try not to linger," the cook warned. "There's an hour of work to be done yet and a man is waiting."

Eld nodded her thanks and found a place to sit just as the last woman left. She ate quickly while she considered her next action.

She'd never found out the exact lodging room apart from the inn's name. That might take a few moments, as they would be in the midst of the evening revelers. Or maybe most of the village was staying home at night in respect of watchfulness. Still, Eld had to expect Traith and Shedann would be asleep by the time she arrived if they were as tired as reported. She sighed to herself, having finished the potage, and set to working unenthusiastically on the over-warm rabbit legs while she reviewed the story she'd memorized. Maybe she could pick up a tastier snack at The Wildling. Then she remembered her purse was as good as empty and cursed to herself. Wasn't there a soul that owed her something? But she couldn't think of one, not even Torin who made a habit of petty borrowing. Sadly for Eld, even fey Torin paid her debts promptly. Eld knew she'd have to wait for the estate funds or their next quarter pay. She washed down the dry rabbit with the last of the barley-mead and grabbed the last potion of bread to eat on the way. Grim thoughts about her finances followed in her wake as she left the Kettle.

Eld couldn't even depend on her hero's award, because she knew she was going to exchange most of it for a boon, the most important thing a cavalier could ask for. And their Lion's awards and pay would be lucky to arrive before the next quarter. Well, that was then her further doom, she would live a poor soldier until next pay day.

It was dark as she walked to the gate. Crossing the center of the grounds, she glanced at the commander's house, a beacon of light shining across the sparse grass and stone. The dining room was visible, Eld easily picking out Seth, now draped in a basic white robe, talking animatedly to his sister's guests. Eld turned away and made for the gate, passing the now boisterous Rowan Oak where music played, pipes, mandolins and drums merging like tonal herbs in a acoustic stew. Tafli would have placed the musicians by the unused hearth. Eld waved greetings to odd souls she knew, but did not pause as she walked on, past the watch at the gate.

"Remember it's watchfulness," one woman called.

"Yes, I'll be back before midnight," Eld said. "Just like in a Cambrian child's tale."

Such tales always had warnings of dire magic or being stolen by fairies. But the Cambrian word for "fairy", sióg, was the same they used for elfyn. Eld could never fathom why the humyn Gaels would think elfyn would want to steal a humyn child. Probably an excuse invented by a wayward child late for supper to avoid punishment. Eld wasn't bigoted against humyn exactly, but all the evidence showed they were overly given to superstitious ways and, being an empiricist, she found that unsettling. No wonder the Cambrian Sea lanes were fraught with conflict before the Protectorate.

The town wasn't far, the road full of foot traffic at this time, the odd horse cantering by. Street lamps lined the way, more for the visibility of troops than for civilian convenience, but these gave the townsfolk the experience of a lit night, which was not always desired in rural communities. A truce was made between those who wanted a cosmopolitan feel and those who loved to watch the starry night: all street lamps were shuttered at midnight. Thus, if the streets were dark, Eld knew she was in for discipline and possibly unable to return to the stables before dawn.

Gate Step was a typical village, with gate plinths to mark the roads entering the town proper. There was no wall or guard as in lot towns near the southern border, though now in watchfulness a civil guard in livery, a blue arch over a rising sun, stood with a sheriff's Hound, a woman in hunter's green, trimmed in dark red. The guard was from Falls Gate, the village being too small to support its own guard office. She might have a handful of fellows working with her in the village. The Hound was part of the provincial office of the Hound's master, so called because of the mind-linked dog packs they used for search and rescue, and for hunting down suspected criminals. In the outer lots, near the wilds, the Hound's Master was the law that had the most respect. They were armed as expected, service swords, hunting knives; the Hound had a bow, the guard a crossbow. Propped against a wall nearby were also light spears, not actually spears, but spear shafts topped with a large marble of solstone. Like a fire lance, they were used to strike, though with much less power. Their point was to dazzle and distract, not to kill, though one could be burned. And, just like a fire lance, they would have no more than a charge after night had fallen. Thus the reason they sat aside as if discarded.

The truth was, against the current foe, there was little either woman could do, even if her whole force was with her. They could protect themselves to effect an escape and that was surely what they were there for: to call the alarm and lead citizens to safety.

Eld exchanged respectful nods with the women as she walked into town. Before her injury, it had been a couple weeks since she visited the Step.

Now she seemed to be going every other night. The white stones of the Queen's road made the center street, which, truth told, was the only one graced with commerce. The pavements, once perfunctory cobbled stones, were now raised a couple feet above the streets like most cities, laid with brick or stone, but these were uncharacteristically empty for the early eve. What townswomen Eld caught sight of who did not work at the inn, were locking and securing their buildings, to either retreat within or seek safety with others in estate houses better fortified against storm or attacks. Above, on the hilly escarpment that overlooked the town, twinkled lights from the Abbey and the ruins of an old temple the magi had taken over. The bulk of the people walking about the village now were soldiers and cavaliers like herself. She saw Captain Draeyn on the porch of her destination, The Wildling.

One would think an establishment with such a name would look a bit like it's namesake, exotic and adventurous, perhaps with a woven stick conical roof, evoking the temporary pole shelters that nomadic culture used. But such was not the case. On the contrary, The Wildling was "wild" in name only, otherwise being a conventional travelers' inn built of local stone on a base of ash-lime, with slate roofing. Only the outer facade of the porch suggested the exotic life of the Forest Travelers displaced by fire centuries ago. Dwen crafted gate arches welcomed the visitor, branching decorations formed in attractive knotted and twisting patterns it would take any without wood-essence a great labor to match. It was said Dwen craft was the inspiration of the knot art of the Cambrian Gaels who had always lived close to the forest. One could stare at the patterns for hours and still find new facets in a familiar piece. In this way the porch might be slightly authentic. Wildlings Eld had met didn't fuss about the twinings and decoration of their travel huts. These were saved for their wagons and carts, their most valued permanent possessions.

The farce didn't stop there. Lanterns of hollow logs pierced with spiral patterns of light hung intermittently, as did willow wicker orbs with lights shining inside. These were frauds, the only commonality with Wildling culture being their construction in wood. Like the Dwen they were closely related to, Wildlings used basic solstone lamps with glass or empty sides. The entire point was illumination, not exotic ambiance.

But such cultural inaccuracies didn't deter matrons from enjoyment and Eld had trouble getting through the door, sidestepping affronted mothers who assumed she was pushing forward out of turn.

"My children are lodging with the family keeper," she said, finally able to get the man's eye who was directing staff. He was about Sil's age and draped in gold and sapphire blue. There seemed to be a private party in one of the rooms. "I need to know which room."

"Estate?" he asked.

"Farthal. Maybe Gallens-Farthal. Sil is the keeper with them."

"And you are?"

"Lancer Elderyn Farthal, Cavalry Host, 2nd company."

"And you are entitled to access?"

Here the man looked at Eld, gold eyes flickering ominous red hints from the charcoal fire burning in the common room fireplace. Eld shivered a moment. The man was trained in hearing basic truth, having more precision than the senses of the average mother or man. It was a common skill acquired by those in trade with the public.

"Yes!" Eld said.

The man's eyes lowered, glancing at the book without otherwise moving.

"Second floor, two rooms. The children are in 24, the Keeper, 23. Unfortunately we did not have one room large enough for both available."

"Elam!" Eld said. She removed herself from the annoyed matrons to break through the scrum to the stairs. They weren't carpeted; one of the conceits of the inn in appealing to the woody rustic life was certain typical decor was lacking, uncharitably assumed by some as meanness. By the same token there was no wallpaper or hangings, though there were panels of woven wood in the most basic, some might say trite, patterns. Eld slowed her pace, not wanting to make more noise than necessary. Once she was on the second floor, the hanging lamps were fitted with red tinted glass to be more restful to the eyes of those retiring. The center of the halls, while not carpeted, were covered in fabric backed matting of the kind used to cover the ground in outdoor fairs and produce stalls. Oh, this certainly was quite the rustic experience, Eld thought sarcastically.

The walls, both in the halls and throughout the inn, had images of the true thing, paintings in life and portraits of actual Wildlings: a barrel-shaped round wagon, fantastically molded and carved, for the diaspora of Wildling culture spread so far that some had taken men who where not Dwen and not all children had the strong wood-essence of their foremothers. This was why the Wildling yastol was often a headdress of inert sticks, not the quasi living extension Tafli wore. A grand matriarch sat in one portrait, wearing what looked to be a true yastol of hazel leaves, bright blond hair fading to red at the ends, in the common roan effect of many Oak Dwen. Her skin was lighter and warmer than Tafli's; perhaps she had a Sula ancestor. Thick kohl-like black lines had been applied to her green eyes, similar to aspect, but much heavier, making her look like a creature of the wood. This would not be lampblack or kohl, for Wildlings, though they were known to use fire, avoided burnings for ceremonies and sacred practices. This would be gall or acorn ink, freshly made, that would stain the skin for days. There were other marks on the woman's face, thin spiral lines that could be tattooing, another reason the respectable considered the Wildling too much for civilized company. A layered garment of sage green leaf felt rose to cover the woman's neck, over it a bark vest impressed with twining designs, the collar and shoulders covering in moss and lichens. Around her neck was a long scarf or stole, woven with lichen dyed yarns of gold and purple, shot with threads of madder red. The woman looked ageless, being a painting one felt, however old she had been, her essence had authority. She certainly looked no younger than Eld's mother, but she could be an Aeon for all Eld knew.

It was then Eld remembered Wildlings did not call themselves so. It would be an absurd name. But Eld couldn't remembered exactly what the did call themselves. "The Yinno?" "Tree Travelers" or " Tree Wanders"? She wasn't certain. A further thought disturbed her: was "Wildling" offensive? She'd never known a Wildling to object. Perhaps they felt too dependent on charity to protest.

There were also images of travel huts, and a series that showed women working together with a bundle of long poles, first binding one end to set them up like a cone, its base maybe twenty feet in diameter, and finally molded by wood-essence to balloon into a domed hut, the top ends either folded over, else folded down circularly to make a smoke hole if needed. Finally panels of oiled canvas, hide or heavy bark cloth were wrapped around the frame, to be secured by another set of lighter poles and found wood. The structures were quite sturdy except in the worst of storms. Wildlings might camp in one round for a couple months to a whole season before moving on, if not driven off.

It occurred to Eld, as cheap and kitsch as the establishment was, it was perfect for her children who loved all things Dwen. They would in particular be fascinated with light impressions, a newer archival craft that transferred observed images directly to mineral treated metal plates. They captured what the eye saw in perfect though monochromatic detail, as if a godlike hand had taken a rubbing not of stone carvings, but the images of life. Eld, like many, preferred paintings to impressions that felt empty and lifeless. But children adored them and scholars found their cold, precise eye invaluable. So there were impressions of Wildlings and Dwen among the paintings, looking somehow more savage in the starkness of muted grays.

Eld found the rooms and put her ear to 24 to see if they slept. She didn't knock in case they were dreaming, and she didn't feel she should disturb Sil in his time of rest. Eld heard nothing, so she gently turned turned the handle.

A shockingly peculiar custom on the outer lots of the federation – or shocking to those used to city life with an abundance of strangers – was the infrequency of locking doors. It wasn't that theft or other crime was rampant in elfyn cities. It had more to do with privacy; the thoughts and essence of strangers were many in a city and thus the greater desire to be secure that the peace of one's place would not be intruded on. Otherwise souls were apt to trespass by pure accident, especially while dreaming. Restricting access to spaces kept the paths on the minds that resided there free. However, in small lot communities, few souls were unknown to each other and fewer still completely ignorant of the boundaries and space, and what was expected of them. Houses weren't even locked, though now in watchfulness they would be. But as the likelihood of the bane warriors wandering into the inn to get lodging was non-existent, locking internal doors wasn't seen as essential.

Eld cracked the door, opening it soundlessly until a ray of dim orange light told her what she expected. Traith and Shedann lay in the center of one bed, lightly covered with linen sheets and a patterned blanket with the image of a great tree. The bed itself was made to evoke a Dwen bower, branches curving up from the headboard and foot, as if it was a giant cradle in the top branches of a great tree. Eld knew they were delighted to "sleep like Dwen", as they imagined it. The building's air flow was sound and, being on the second floor, the room benefited from heat drafting up through cleverly designed vents such that, in this late spring, blankets were almost unnecessary. But children often liked them for comfort after the ages they stopped sleeping in their mother's bed. Traith's arm was around Shedann's neck, while the younger boy laid his head on his sister's chest, much like he'd done with Eld when he was a baby. Eld watched them a moment; calmness filled her, the visceral pleasure of knowing her mites were safe. She noticed she was smiling and didn't bother stopping, for who would see or care? There would be no tale tonight. It was better that they sleep undisturbed.

Then Traith opened her eyes and murmured, "Ama?"

Eld stepped in and shut the door quietly, and strode over to sit on a wood twisted stool. Now the room was only lit from the street lights; Eld left the lamp on the table shuttered.

"There's my little hero," Eld whispered.

"You didn't come to the Kettle,"

"Soldier things that couldn't wait. Sorry, mite."

"I'm not a mite."

"Of course you're not."

"Aged heir."

Eld grinned. "That you are. You should return to sleep. You have a long journey tomorrow."

"I hope we can dance on the canal boat again ..." Traith's voice drifted away as her eyes closed.

Eld kissed her forehead and Shedann's hair before standing to leave. She wanted now more than ever to be certain they would safely return to the estate, that all would be well, that the Eurthans, curse them, would be driven away, never to return.

The air shimmered and Eld saw Traith, but she looked different. Though still young, she was older, perhaps with the development of a ten year old humyn.

"I'm not a mite," she said in a slightly deeper voice and with much more irritation.

"Then do not act so and no one with make that disagreeable mistake," a familiar man's voice said.

Eld's heart thumped. Was it possible?

Traith frowned then smiled in a way she did when angling for a favor. "You're so pretty," she said. "Shedann thinks so too."

"Now you're trying to charm me...."

The reverie faded leaving Eld shaken to the core with excitement. Traith had been in her own estate rooms and the voice was not Sil's.

Reverie never lied, but it was rarely the complete tale. The man could just be visiting. But few visiting men had the privilege of seeing a mother's children to sleep unobserved. And because the implications touched on Eld's recently growing desires, a superstition took hold of her otherwise rational soul. She would speak of it to no one. It would be a quiet light to privately guide her when events seemed dark and unknowable. Unbidden her hand reached into her pocket and found a stone. The Felkinoc. Another thing she did not share with other souls. She held the ancient talisman and, whether it was its provenance, age or it really did have some essence of luck, Eld felt warmed with hope. She focused on what the Reverie told her was certain: Traith and Shedann would live, and so would the man, and that was a comfort. But Eld also noted with a chill her own fate was not clear. Felkeni was never to be taken for granted.

Now the children were well into their dreams. The story would wait. Eld took a step to the door then, hearing voices outside Sil's door, froze.

"Hush, bold one," Sil whispered in barely more than a breath. Eld held her own breath to better hear. Sil turned the lock on his room; men often locked their rooms, especially if they were visiting a new place. There were sounds of shuffling, then the faintest snap as the door shut. Then Eld wished her ears would go deaf as the muffled but unmistakable sounds of Sil being romanced into seduction commenced. Sil and the woman said little more, but the moment they fell on the bed Eld heard as the furniture shifted slightly.

Now Eld held her breath so not to be heard as she stalked out of her children's room and closed the door as quietly as a ghost. By this time she heard Sil gasp; at a guess, his paramour had mounted him. Eld hurried away down the hall, slowing only at the stairs. And to think she'd been curious about Sil's private life. She could almost hear Felkeni laughing at her from the Court of Heaven.

Eld didn't begrudge Sil. The only question she had was where he'd been; she preferred him to be nearby, especially as the children's rooms were unlocked. But there was no way to know without revealing him and, reasonably, he'd probably been in the inn all the time. The children were never in danger. Eld walked down the stairs, now clear of the early evening scrum as most matrons had found their places, whether in the commons room, or one of the dining halls where Eld saw in passing a cluster of officers. To her disgust she spotted Roel, laughing over boldly, much like if someone had actually commissioned Torin and she was surrounded by souls beholden to pretend to find her amusing. Eld glanced around and saw few men except those who were clearly consorts, keepers or sons in the commons dining. At least the lot men were safely out of Roel's reach, at least for the night.

Eld waved a hurried thanks to the man still fortifying the entrance and left.

## Chapter 14

# The Lake Son

The sharp air of late spring was a tonic and wiped away most of Eld's disgust at sighting Roel, as well as significantly diminishing her new knowledge about Sil. It wasn't her business as long as the mites weren't neglected. Eld put it out of her mind and took Seth's letter out to reread by the street lamps. It was well before midnight, but perhaps not late enough for Seth to be available. Eld decided to walk at a leisurely pace, recalling the lines she knew relevant to Amer and the Lakeson. She would avoid the Rowan Oak, for if she was sighted and suspicions arose, the time could be calculated at Seth's expense.

The clouds parted and Eld saw a few stars from the Mother Bear, but they were soon obscured by new cloudy trappings. The wind shifted and a scent of lilac hovered on the air, fading as she approached the garrison gates. She was challenged like before, those on guard already bored with the task. Once inside, Eld went to the stables. With her purse so light, she'd avail herself of whatever was on the tables. Her timing was perfect. No one was there; after snacking on small cakes and nut biscuits, she drank a good goblet of spring mead flavored with woodruff. Before setting off again, she took a few sugar lozenges of various flavors to suck on.

By the time Eld left the stables and made her way, avoiding the brightest of lights, the commander's house was in repose, lights dimmed throughout the lower floor, the dinning hall darkened. Eld judged it would be a good time to approach, with ample space to drift away were she intercepted by a soul. But no one marked her, and once she's turned a corner to the backside of the building, she was impressed how the night made an impenetrable area of persistent darkness, the very lights fronting the building to increase illumination casting deep shadows. Eld walked into the dark gloom, passing two rooms, one window dark, the other covered with thick curtains that leaked light at their edges. Then there was a bush of some white flower with a lilac-like scent by darkened windows and she almost passed on. She spotted a string of white beads, not actually pearls, but a pearlescent glass imitation. Eld paused, heart skipping as she looked into the dark glass. A blue light appeared as if glowing from the depths of a distant lake and Eld let herself be taken by the scene, where Amer had arrived to retrieve Ta Helsyn, the Labrys Inverted, the weapon forged by Soltarlu Firewind, in a Cauldron of Eurath, from Amer's ax handle and two perfect crescents of moonlight gifted by Lun. Ta Helsyn was the only thing that could kill the Bane.

But first the Lakeson must take Amer on his mother's boat and the Lakeson was a dangerously bold boy...

As Eld watched, her reflection was slowly replaced by Seth's face back-lit by the blue light to give his skin a pale, watery cast. His hair fell in waves, darkened by green henna or ink. A loose shift of light blue fabric clung to his form, and strings of pearls seemed to swath him. His feet were bare, of course, and dark green straps of leather suggesting weeds circled his wrists and arms. The faintest of glimmer dusted his skin, and his lips were now adorned with blue shimmer, something used by actors or the young to shock their elders. On Seth's head more pearls hung from a circlet more apt for a prince of Maer. But one did what one could on short notice. Certainly Eld in her cavalier's uniform was far from the image of Amer. The poetry would have to carry the rest.

Seth pushed the unlocked glass door open. Eld slipped quickly inside and shut it.

"What brings you to this my mother's watery home,
The deepest lake in the center of all lands,
That few have seen since Eurath's earliest days?"

As Seth spoke he drew the curtains over the windows with sweeping theatrical gestures, as if showing the lake in question.

"Are you truly so ignorant, fresh faced boy," Eld began,
"So unknowingly, unseeing,
that the light beyond does not inform your mind?"
"Oh that! I see my distant aunt has dropped a thing.
She does this often,
it is nothing."
"Nothing but the salvation of the Mothers of the Orb,
of all those that turn to us to uphold our duty of care.
But you know this, oh wayward boy,
and play with our time for your amusements.
Have a care, for I am Amer,
And the only games I play are death and wrath."
"Very well, I confess when I sighted you true,
A Mother-god from the Court of Heaven
 among the mortal bound,
I was moved in a way never before,
your dark visage, masterful aspect
has taken me before my own will was formed.
So forgive me my impertinence, for I know your goal:
You need dame's boat to ferry you there.

192

But payment is custom and payment I will have,
For I am the Lakeson and my mother's will is law."
"Then take my coin and quickly boy,
For the weapon cools, and the Bane stills roams free
and blood calls out for vengeance."
Eld offered a flint coin, the only use she could see for it being a prop.
"Fie!" cried Seth knocking the coin out of Eld's hand where it fell to the floor which was carpeted.
Eld was surprised. There were several versions of this tale. Many did not end in the ravishment of the Lakeson. But all where he refused coin did...
"What mean thing do you offer?" Seth continued in theatrical umbrage.
"What am I to do with a common coin?
You can pay more, much more!
For are you not a Mother-God?
Is this not a task to save the mothers of the Orb?
I demand no less than a kiss!
For I know you have kissed many men and I will not be denied!"
Eld stepped forward, glowering as best she could. This turn in the tale did not  move her, but Seth's scent did.
"You were begat from a fool,
Slovenly slet of a soul,
For by denying me my rightful own
I am freed from the contract and
may take revenge in passion that drives me as ever it does."
Eld seized Seth by the waist, drawing him to her forcefully; she felt every part of his arousal.
"You will have your kiss, foolish boy,
And so much more.
I will feed on you until you are dry of vigor and tears
and men of the world will forever be warned
against standing between a mother and her righteous work!"
Eld kissed Seth long and deep, his body melting in her arms with no further resistance.
In his own voice Seth whispered, "Unlike the Lakeson, I welcome my ravishment."
Most of an hour later they still laid in Seth's bed.
"I wish you'd warned me you would chose that version," Eld said.
"The rape of fictitious persons hurts no one," Seth replied.
"The idea is odious."

Seth sighed. "Very well. We shall not do it this way again. It would be nice if you could come prepared."

It was Eld's turn to sigh. "Yes, disrobing and shedding my gear was a tedious delay. But if your sister insists I can't take you far from garrison, we will have to accept it. I'd look a tit walking around the garrison in ancient armor and sandals."

Seth laughed.

Eld was only in her shirt while Seth was naked except for some pearls and "weeds", his lake garb having been "striped forcibly from his form", another actors trick. The fabric had been tied with knots that pulled apart with ease and was lying somewhere on the floor.

Eld tried not to think about the Reverie. But she had to say something.

"Do you think it's possible for us to do more than coit like rabbits when we visit?"

"There's nothing to say we must coit at all. We could have a conversation about important issues of the day. How do you think the Voice will reply to the Bright Band's accusation today's mothers are weak and their sons morally wanting?"

Eld laughed. "Hopefully Ledowyn will say something about common morality not being the duty of the Mother's council."

"But they're trying to make it their duty. And don't forget Ledowyn has listened to concerns of 'sissies' grooming girls from crèches."

Seth's voice sounded pensive.

"It's all ridiculous," Eld said, sitting up. "Women can't be 'seduced' to change their passions. And this obsession about Aelg men painting their feet. Who does it harm how much cosmetics they use? I've never heard of a mother's children wanting for food because the men of the house were inexpert at glimmering. If that was so, and you'd seen the men of Gate Step, the entire village would be dead of starvation!"

Seth laughed. "Some might say it's a wayward influence on boys seeking to marry well."

"So we must be irritated to distraction because some mothers can't marry off their idle sons? That's what boys' schools are for!"

"But what if the schools don't want the idle boy obsessed with fashion and cosmetics?"

"You're arguing Athmod's case."

"Yes."

"Why?"

"So we can do more than 'rut like rabbits in heat'."

It was Eld's turn to laugh. "Fine. Here are my thoughts: cosmetics aren't the bane of boys so much as the judgment of the men of the house who think it so. And these men will also be the ones pressuring a boy they don't like out of the pool to be married. That won't stop a mother certain of her feelings, even if the couple must move to live in a town. But to the ambitious mother depending on her estate to support her advance, any man who does not please the uncles will find himself a casualty."

Seth looked at Eld oddly. "You have a peculiar insight and sympathy for the plight of men."

"I suppose. I talk to Sil who knows more on the subject than I ever will, and I want to protect Shedann from the extremes of this silliness. Does it ever occur to them, if they said nothing at all, whatever evils of the 'excesses of glimmer', the boys would just grow out of?"

"No, dearest. They are blinded by a misguided compulsion to control. The uncles fear for their reputation at the hint of impropriety. The demagogues of the Bright Band... I don't know if they are truly afraid of men joining in public society or use it to gather followers. Many women would prefer never to see men in the public sphere acting like mothers."

"They clearly don't know their men if they'd mistake them for mothers," Eld said pulling Seth close again.

"Excuse me, emha," Seth said with mock prissiness. "We are here for civil conversation, not to rut like rabbits."

Eld smothered his mouth with a kiss and they had another enjoyable hour together.

By the time Eld was making her way back to the stables most of the garrison was asleep except for those on watch. The clouds had cleared a bit and Eld paused to look up at the Mother Bear. Nearby was the Seat of Sel, seen as a warped "W" shape. Selis of the Fold, foster mother of Sul's daughter Jaro, and the greatest wizard in legend watched over them all. Alone of the mythic persons there was some evidence Sel had lived in the Orb. She was usually imagined in a black dragon cloak with a staff and orb, and had perhaps been a pioneer in the elfyn mastery of essence. But though Selis was a matron of magi and they her inheritors, her time was eons before the Sunqueens, before even the Cataclysm of the Dying Star. Most stories about her were lost to history. Only echoes in dreams and the places she touched remained. The standing stones, dolmens and circles were credited to be her works, and inspired the modern sadol of odd numbered stones, usually eleven or thirteen, that magi used for communication across distances. Much technology of the ancients was lost, but Selis remained sitting in the stars watching over her distant descendants. Eld found it a fetching idea that gave her soul comfort.

"Mind yourself, Farthal," Commander Alhern snapped, shocking Eld from her stargazing.

Eld stumbled, taking a moment to get her bearings. Alhern must have been walking around informally; she wore casual clothes, dark tunic and bracs, and a half circle cape wrapped loosely over her shoulders. Her hair was loose though Eld didn't hold this against her, her own hair was loose, flout and band in her hand, not wanting to wear it anymore. Apparently Eld had, like Torin, lost herself in the moment and almost run into the commander.

"Pardon, emha," Eld said, yielding before the commander's path. "I didn't expect to see you walking at night," she added.

"What is there to wonder at? You, yourself are wandering about."

"I ..." Eld stopped herself. Alhern was walking past her without pause and Eld knew saying nothing about her visit with Seth was the correct course.

"Good night, cavalier," Alhern said without looking back.

Eld stood a moment watching Alhern's back as the commander made her way to the steps of her house. On instinct, Eld turned her head in the direction Alhern had come, where the shadowed outline of the Rowan Oak sat. The lights in the commons were shuttered; Eld knew Tafli wrapped them in strips of dark fabric mat for the night. They wouldn't be spent until early morning. But there was another light in the upper rooms, one of which Eld knew one belonged to Tafli . Eld wasn't sure if the cook lived there  or in town.

As Eld watched, the lamp winked out, shuttered for the night.

Alhern. Tafli. It was the only answer that made sense. By Seth's clock, Eld had left well after midnight. And while the guards certainly weren't going to refuse the commander reentry even during watchfulness, no commander wanted to be an example of lax discipline. Eld could hear Tafli's words:

"But it is few Sula who join with Dwen who like it."

Eld tried not to think of the details. It was another secret for the Door.

## Chapter 15

# Allies

Two weeks later they were no closer to knowing the intentions of the Eurthani encampment, but there had been no hostile actions either. The tunnel under the commander's house had been partially blocked and set with traps by the magi. Eld didn't know exactly what, but if the Eurthans tried to emerge again they would be noted. One complication was that most of the male staff refused to sleep on premises even with a full guard present. After much wrangling, they were housed in The Wildling and a couple of private houses at the commander's expense. The exceptions were Seth, his nephew and the nephew's keeper, who all in their own way enjoyed the privacy, but found each other's company a trial.

Without the cook, a close friend of Seth's with clear duties the keeper respected, there was no buffer between them and Seth felt he was defending himself in his own house. Eld heard much on this subject after trysting.

"Yes, I know it's my sister's house. But who is he?"

"The protector of your nephew's virtue from your wanton lifestyle?" Eld ventured.

"He certainly sees himself that way. Now he consults Sonamor, questioning my every decision."

Sonamor was also Seth's friend, but was averse to involving herself in men's matters. Neither Seth nor Effa Melgan Tanmor were staff, so she did not have express authority over them.

"So go to your sister."

This suggestion was not welcome. Alhern had the custom of deferring management of the men to Seth. If he needed his sister to intervene, Alhern would question what Seth was failing to do to manage the keeper.

"Because Seli sees everything in terms of military discipline. I will soon go mad."

And to make matters more fraught the nephew Solafi had decided he could invite his friends from town, and they spent much of the day lounging in areas usually unoccupied, gossiping and playing music, and doing very little productive. When Seth bid Solafi to take the music out of doors because women in the offices were working, Melgan was affronted and demanded Seth come to him if ever there was discipline for the nephew. This led to an explosive row where Alhern had been forced to make it clear that her brother was her authority in her house and Effa Tanmor was to abide by that or pack his things and return to the family estate.

Affronted, Melgan was icy now; neither man said anything to each other if they didn't have to. Seth suspected Solafi enjoyed this immensely and leveraged more freedom for himself and his friends; they now had taken to haunting the Crèche, where they were welcomed by soldiers who found masculine company a pleasant diversion. It also had the effect of getting Melgan out of the house most of the day. At first Melgan tried to keep the Solafi in house, but the boy just went to his aunt directly to complain.

"The results were not pleasant," Seth said, barely hiding his glee at Melgan's expense. "Seli shouted, 'For Heaven's and Sul's sake, man, if you're worried about his moral liaisons, go watch him at the Crèche yourself!'"

Seth took obvious delight in repeating the words, words Eld knew never to repeat.

So, provided his duties and studies were finished, Solafi was free to spend the afternoon holding court in the Crèche while Effa Melgan looked balefully on. It also meant for much of the afternoon they were out of Seth's and the staff's way, and Seth was pleased that the house had returned to a form of normalcy.

Hearing these updates every other night after their trysting was a bit like reading a serial in a gazette. Eld found it all amusing mostly because it wasn't happening in a house she had to live in.

"This could be a play," Eld said at one point.

"I have friends in the theater," Seth replied. "But that would get me banished from my sister's service for life. The military does not forgive such things."

"The military picks and chooses what it likes to remember. Remember that hero's feast I was cheated out of?"

"Blame those dastardly Eurthans! No respect for the time!"

"Precisely! How else can I advance my career at the commander's table if they're always interrupting?"

That had been a couple nights ago.

Presently Eld waited with Danshor, Draeyn and Tafli in the morning mist at the edge of the forest, a mix of maple, pine and fir next to the field Eld and her children had picnicked in. Eld and Danshor were mounted, while Draeyn stood by her horse; Tafli did not ride of course. A couple rangers hung back, including the one Tafli rebuked, Scout Orinac. Orinac seemed much changed in her attitude and appeared to want to make peace with Tafli; now and then she tried to catch his eye with an awkward smile. But Tafli ignored her. Eld and Danshor were invited because of their experience with Eurthans. Magi reported another attack was imminent and finally a plan had been agreed on to confront the threat. In general, the commander planned to force the Eurthans to fight in the day. Other particulars would exploit assets Eurthans didn't expect, like the Federation's Dwen allies.

While the closest watchful Dwen community, Yafladan, was over twelve leagues away above Ramoth's Ridge, any undedicated forestland was considered an easement of the Forest Nation if it was contiguous. There were many arguments on what counted as contiguous. Sula land owners insisted on trees together with no root break. Most Dwen considered interwoven branches contiguous, so a treerunner, a type of Dwen messenger scout, did not need to touch the ground in the course of her duties. Still other Dwen and Wildlings claimed the Forest had only left when the last dreams of the trees once standing were gone and no daughter trees lived. In practice, though a Queen's road clearly demarcated the border along the north, peninsulas of forest that reached several leagues or more into the north of the Crownland were recognized as embassies of Ta Dwenoshire as a courtesy. Now the command office had summoned Dwen for assistance, they were to met them at a forest easement for an escort.

At the tree line a path could be seen, narrow and unfinished, used by locals and hunters. Eld and the other Sula watched it pensively, lost in their own expectations. Danshor was uncharacteristically quiet. The threat of laboring on roadworks had sobered her reckless tongue, and Captain Draeyn's presence was a constant reminder of her rebuke, though Draeyn herself was nothing less than civil. At least there were no ravens present to tempt Danshor.

Draeyn idly patted her mount while she looked over the treetops. Sparrows flitted through the low brush of gorse, snowberry and just flowering currant. A lone hawthorn, new leaves still tiny buds among long thorns, stood out slightly from the rest of the trees while its daughter saplings made clusters of thorny shrubbery. A thrush burst into song, its notes urgent and insistent, to Eld's ear a song yearning for companionship and a strong feeling that, at least for this morning, it had the sole possession of the branch it perched on. Then the essence of the air shifted and the thrush fluttered away with thoughts of alarm.

Fiorseth snorted and flicked her ears. She had also scented something, but since Eld wasn't worried neither was she. If anything the mare was bored. She didn't even start when the crown of a particularly tall maple shivered, its yellow flowers and new red-green leaves nodding in the morning sunlight. Danshor's stallion Tuiric didn't think much of this and cantered backwards until Danshor convinced him to halt.

Draeyn looked eager and expectant, Tafli stepping forward to join her. Neither seemed surprised at the quaking top of the maple, as if a giant child was shaking it. Then one of the longer forks from the bole, perhaps a couple hands thick, started to bend out and down, like a banana being gently peeled, until the leaves at the end came within four feet of the ground. Walking along the length as if it was nothing more than a narrow log over a bridge  descended the Dwen.

The first two women were much like Tafli, Oak Dwen with red and brown roan hair, tannin hued skin, arms and legs covered with leaf felt; their bark vests seemed sturdy enough to act like armor. They had thick vinings around their lean forearms, like snakes that had been petrified in wood. They were barefoot but around their ankles were twinings with multiple branchlets; Eld could see how they would stabilize a foot walking through tree tops. The Dwen also had wooden collars that acted like gorgets; they were clearly well versed in the expectations of encountering a hostile force. Both their yastols were oak, but free of acorns or other decoration.

The next Dwen was a man who rivaled Seth in beauty and grace. His skin was pale like aged holly wood, almost white. Whereas the Oak Dwen had thick, wavy hair, his dark ash locks hung straight, or would have if the strands didn't hover on the slightest breeze, much like his garments. While he also had a vest, it was of a silver gray wood, seeming to encase him in a sculpted girdle.  Underneath and over his leaf felt hung a pale green and white robe that was slit so he could move with ease.  It was made of tree silk, a fabric of Dwen manufactured from wood waste.  It was almost as valuable as real silk, though it was not as strong and did not retain heat.  He also had thick vinings, of some light colored wood; for a moment Eld thought he wore shoes but then saw they were simply thin strip-like twinings over bark slippers. His yastol was much like Tafli's, but true ash not rowan.  His face was the image of the Ash Dwen, a more cultured and sophisticated tribe of Dwen by Sula standards. Unlike Tafli he wore no glimmer, though his eyes had been darkened kohl-like with gall ink.

The last Dwen was beyond Eld's knowledge. She was a woman, but built such that she made most women appear like waifish girls. Her leanness equaled her muscularity, so that veins were clearly visible intertwining her limbs like vines and yet her step was as light as any of the other Dwen. She was slightly taller and of a tribe with deep reddish skin of a hue like aged cedar.  Her long dark hair was much like the Ash Dwen man, except thick and her cheekbones high with aquiline features stronger than the average elf. She wore a yastol of layered fans of cedar or cypress, but as she stepped down with the rest, the false leaves settled down on her head over each other making a wooden helmet. Her entire torso was covered in scale-like fans of wood encasing her completely though it flexed with her movements.  By necessity it left her ample arms free. Eld would not want to be on the opposing side of any force this women supported, whether on the battle field or a friendly game of ruger. Leaf-felt covered her legs – or Eld assumed it was leaf-felt, though it had an odd color: reddish tan instead of sage green. She had twinings on her arms and legs like the rest, and fans of cedar appeared to cover the tops of her feet. All the Dwen had green eyes, though this last one's was darker, with a hint of hazel, and lined with gall like the Ash Dwen man.

"How do the leaves fall?" Tafli was asking, but with an exactness of meaning Eld had never appreciated before. The common greeting was obviously of Dwen origin.

"Lightly and brightly," one of the Oak Dwen replied. "I am Yeladrin. This is my cousin, Olyeth." The other Oak Dwen nodded. "Aredheli is from the Ash City, that is, Haldwynshor, and has skill in healing. And from the Red Dwen nation to the east of the Altans this is Peyteor, though she answers mostly to Little Acorn."

Peyteor smiled at this, amused at the intentional contradiction in the nickname. "We are being glad to assist," Peyteor said, her Sulanilish much like Tafli's. "The Devourer's legions must be humbled."

Tafli nodded. "The time is over for their taking of liberties, with trees, lives and men. We will take you to the meeting now. This is ranger Captain Draeyn," Tafli said by introduction.

Yeladrin and Draeyn clasped hands smiling.

"We have met before," Draeyn said. "Your tree thrives?"

"Well enough," Yeladrin said.

"And this is the bold cavalier Lancer Elderyn who fought off three of the dark legion by herself."

"Al met," Eld said, thankful Tafli omitted how many trees were destroyed.

"This other cavalier is her war-sister. Now we take you to the commander's hall."

Eld stifled a laugh at Tafli's snub as Draeyn mounted her horse. They escorted the Dwen over the field and around to the inside of the garrison, and the branches of the maple returned upright as if they'd never been bent by wood magic. Eld and Danshor led them side by side, the Dwen behind, Draeyn and the rangers at the rear.

The mist was gone when they returned inside the walls. The foot and cavalry companies to be deployed all stood in ranks, at ease and equipped, ready to be released. Though quiet, the grounds inside the keep were full of the low murmur of women talking informally among themselves. At the fore of their minds was the expected reinforcements from Dethglan and Farsnah, two keeps also on the eastern border, but just south of the Ath. Without them, the reserve companies might be forced into the field when their entire purpose was to ensure garrison's safety. But Dethglan and Farsnah had not arrived and no one yet knew why. The existence of the Eurthan tunnel did nothing to quell these anxieties. What prevented the Eurthans from just tunneling up among them as they stood?

A light wind ruffled banners and flouted hair, the dragon streamers whistling intermittent sighing notes. Above a hawk cried. Eld and Danshor trotted their horses down the main road to the garrison hall before dismounting to lead the Dwen inside, Captain Draeyn and the rest of the rangers bringing up the rear.

Inside, the hall was packed and dim. Shades had been drawn over the windows and half shuttered sol-lamps, hanging and standing, were being used to focus attention on the stage where Alhern and her advisors clustered in front of a map projected by magi in the air over the wall behind them. The illusionary images, much like projections from the best bard performances, had a light of their own, making them more distinct in the calculated dimness. Eld and Danshor walked directly to the stage with the Dwen. Many women fell silent with curiosity, this being maybe the first time they had seen Dwen closely, not counting Tafli.

"How do the leaves fall?" Yeladrin greeted Alhern as they clasped hands.

"Hopefully a damn sight brighter and lighter now our Dwen allies have joined us," she said. "Tresses, maybe this sister could tie the Eurthans up all by herself!"

Little Acorn smiled as both Dwen and Sula laughed in appreciation of the Red Dwen's vigor. Eld heard the slightest huff from Danshor beside her.

"Bet she couldn't mount a horse," Danshor muttered.

Danshor was always irrationally in competition with women who could match her in strength or skill.

"You are being kind, Bright One," Little Acorn said. "But it would take more than myself and the strongest sunlight. Mothers and men must be working together for this victory."

"A welcome attitude," a male officer near Alhern said. Eld was surprised because she had never seen a male officer, or even soldier, at Falls Gate. Male soldiers were usually stationed around Ta Mel where they could be politically visible as proof of parity, or else in training camps. Eld's teacher on military history and protocol had been a man. Military men wore a uniform almost identical to women, except their coat hung to just below the knees, but was slit up the sides and back for ease of movement. The exception were male cavaliers, an even rarer breed, who wore exactly the same uniform style, cut to fit a male body. This man had a long sage green coat, with fawn facings, his hair in metal helix guard locks, and he wore no glimmer. His military bracs and boots, though obscured looked the same as the women's. He had the lowest commissioned rank, whether on land or at sea:

"Thank you, ensign, that will do," Alhern said with a familiar annoyance one reserved for close friends and family. Amidst the low chuckles, Eld suddenly recognized the man as Seth.

"What are you gaping at, Farthal?" Alhern barked.

Eld closed her mouth. "Nothing, emha!"

"Good. Because every mother's – and man's – attention needs to be on the task at hand. Before we start, let me address the common concern of every woman in the garrison that I share: the lack of reinforcements. Farsnah and Dethglan's forces mustered on time, but were thwarted by the flooding Afleen that feeds the Ath, forty miles south of Falls Gate. As if that wasn't bad enough, the bridge supports collapsed soon after. Sabotage is suspected but we don't have time to go into that. Just reassure your women command has not forgotten them. Tolith and Meltok might still come."

As Alhern spoke, the images changed for illustration.

"Now magi inform us an assault has been planned for this evening. As many of you know, we seem to be the target of a stress and training exercise. Eurthans have never made organized incursions this far into Federation territory. However, our Dwen allies tell of a different tale. The goal of the Eurthans, as we understand it, is to take the garrison and use the surviving local population in works of forced labor. If I understand this correctly."

"They take men as slaves," Tafli interjected loudly, green eyes flashing.

"The Forest loses men and boys every year," Yeladrin added. "Those used only for sport are lucky to be released. The rest are never seen again."

The hall was utterly silent in horror. What could be said about slavery and rape? Not committed by savages, but fellow elfyn, however alien? Every man was some mother's son, and a crime against a mother was a crime against decency, a crime against her nation. The idea was revolting enough that the taboo against war would be bent if not broken.

"And with this sober knowledge our duty is clear," Alhern said, her deep voice even and steady. "We must not let moral horror freeze us into inaction. We will surprise them by attacking in the middle of the day where we will have the essence advantage. We also have more information for our troops that should give them a better chance against Eurthans at close quarters:

"Women should  avoid hand to hand engagements, as the armor makes an individual Eurthan almost indestructible.  I give you over to Emha Remlan Pelan, master of the Falls Gate Smithy Guild."

Pelan was an older woman, nearing her third century.  She had the same eyes as Eld's grandmother. She didn't wear the greatcoat of industry, having taken to work vests and bracs, like most of the village women who felt they needed to be prepared for action on a moments notice.  Pelan probably rarely worked at a forge these days, unless for personal pleasure; she spoke with an air of excitement over the Eurthan metal and artifacts that sounded a little too cheerful for the moment.

"Thank you commander," Pelan said. "The Eurthani metal appears to be cast or formed in a manner that does not require heat.  This image," – here the semi transparent bat handled dagger hovered in air above and behind her – "does this artifact little justice.  It is made of an alloy mostly of the dark metal known as grim-steel.  But even the hottest blast furnaces of Shard Hills can only sublimate vapors to bond to lesser metals, such as along the edge of service swords, giving them a strength and keenness that exceeds the folding wave process. These blades, being wholly grim, I estimate could shatter a standard sword on forceful contact."

"It didn't shatter ours," Danshor blurted.

"But it chipped and bent them," Eld said with an edge to her voice.  Eld was certain Alhern would ask for their input at the right time.

"Even so, that was due to your skill and luck," Pelan said agreeably.  "Pound for pound, this grim alloy is stronger than any steel.  It is slightly resistant to conducting heat, but not significantly so.  There are multiple reports of Eurthans injured by heating their armor with strike.  It has the minor disadvantage of being partly crystalline and therefore brittle under great stress.  However the amount of stress exceeds the force of a typical battle between women.

"This stiletto was retrieved from the battle of the ravine.  Attempts to break or bend the dagger resulted in a dented anvil and tools, with the minutest of flakes separating from the blade.  Only when placed between a boulder of great size with a magi driven counter force of another boulder did the knife finally snap in two."

The women digested this a moment before someone said, "So we should drop boulders on the Bane troops?"

"It is a joke around the Step that our greatest resource is rocks," Pelan rejoined.  "Unfortunately, we do not have them corralled in a handy avalanche.  Using strike to burn them out is a better gambit, but with its own challenges as you will learn.  We should all take in the serious implications about their use of grimsteel. They must have a source so great they use it as the basis of their military technology like we use iron. Only the visors, that have changeable visibility, appear to be constructed out of different material, possibly quartz. That could be a weakness. And, as you know, grim is an excellent conductor of essence. This explained how they have entire suits of champion armor that yet move as if they are second skins to the women wearing them. There are observed to freeze solid to protect a wearer, probably in the event of rockfalls. The ankles and shins also send out anchors to keep a woman from falling over. While their swords and armor are formidable, nothing compares to the Blue Strike cannon that is held or mounted on the shoulder. I give you over to Ta Murdan."

A magi not directing the illustrative illusions stepped forward, long black robes swishing around her. Magi habit, a robe cut on a full circle, had changed little since the days of Sunqueen Selastimor who founded the order. Originally a quasi religious society tasked to commune with the Mother-Gods, they were now an empirical institution of magical knowledge, dedicated to serve the Sunqueens' successor, the Federation of Mothers. Their robes weren't plain black: in the right light, on the robes of a university graduated adept fine silvery threads glimmered, tracing the patterns of the flow of energy nodes through a soul's body as modern scholarship understood it. Thus the back of the robe had a series of circles outlined down the spine with paths weaving helix-like between them. The magi's hat was a short stiff cylinder, her hair contained under it, with a black scarf or veil pinned to cover it. The faces of the round hat had four nodes mounted with solstone cabochons, symbolic of the four directions as well as a practical essence regulators.

Ta Murdan was speaking and Eld tried to follow her thoughts. Even from where Eld stood, she could feel the edges of Murdan's aura. Was she an Aeon? She had to be quite powerful to touch Eld's aura from several yards away without trying.

"Blue Strike," Murdan was explaining in a clear carrying voice, "Is what we are calling the discharge from the Eurthani weapons. It acts like lightning in that it seeks a source, then discharges along a direct essence line to that source. Technically these weapons never miss." This caused a mutter of alarm. "Fortunately," Ta Medan continued, "Unerring does not equal unerring with full power. It can be blocked if a soul finds cover before discharge, and distance, distraction and dispersal will lessen the force, making a mortal wound simply damaging. The wounds themselves are a type of burn with a similar healing time. Beyond being essence induced, they have no long term effects on a soul."

"So if we march in close ranks that will minimize the Blue Strike's effect?" an officer asked.

"If only it was that easy," Ta Murdan replied. "Blue Strike seeks out targets guided by the will of the soldier. In the case of no clear target – and this is the most alarming effect discovered at the last encounter – Blue Strike will, without error, ground into the strongest essence source within range."

The room was completely silent for a moment absorbing this dread fact. Essence, the very thing that made elfyn the dominant power in the Orb, could be a liability. Eld remembered the forks of blue lightening striking the magi out of the air, then reaching to the wood where more magi lurked, and her soul shivered. Pikers, foots and cavaliers all gloried in their ability to dance in battle, but doing so without the security of magi assistance was a frightening thought.

"Yes, it is sobering. The strongest souls will be wounded or killed without effort, and those who survive are marked as targets. Even without magi present, the strike will seek the strongest mothers or the largest living force. Or both."

Eld exchanged a horrified look with Danshor. The horses. The horses would be dead before they could finished a charge...

"Are you saying we can't use strike at all?" a field captain demanded.

"Our weapons are useless and so is our magic?" another opined.

"What about armor and barding," Captain Aynath asked.

"Armor and barding is a barrier," Murdan said. "It will disperse some of the Blue Strike. Luckily it is not actually lightning but only acts like it."

"That will be a great comfort when I'm on the other side of the Door," Major Galledan said to grim barks of laughter.

"What are we going to do?" another soul asked.

"Run them under Ramoth's Ridge and hope for an avalanche, I suppose ..."

The angry muttering started to sound like a hives of wasps.

"Let her finish," Alhern ordered and the buzz died down. "We will come to strategy soon enough."

"We have a plan," Ta Murdan continued. She held up a palm sized cube of what looked like plaster or ash-lime. "This is a loci sink. It is cast ash-lime impregnated with solstone and grim. Magi and scholars use them to pick up essence signatures from places for research. They are extremely porous to ambient essence, as well as radiating their own when activated. We think they may act to ground Blue Strike, like drawing lightning. The sinks will be fitted to the rear part of all mounts in an ingenious way to deflect blue strike. Foot companies will be carrying at least one per elf to drop as the army sees fit to best act as a distraction. We warn you, however, these might not deflect a powerful strike from a determined individual. So we advise strategists to use tactics that avoid women acting alone."

Seth caught Eld's eye by abruptly brushing his hair, as if waving away a gnat. He looked around accusingly, as if someone had touched him, but the women were completely engrossed in the images on the wall and the problem the magi presented. Then Eld shivered as if a cold wind had passed through the hall. From the startled expressions around her, she wasn't the only woman to feel this. Ta Murdan stood stock still, eyes scanning the hall. Eld heard a whisper that wasn't a whisper by minds in communion.

"We have an intruder," Ta Murdan said.

The illuminated images winked out.

The magi were already moving, the rest of the women yielding to them, the Dwen clustering together to make a ring. This was exactly what the magi were doing, making a great circle of their bodies, with Ta Murdan moving to the center. Old eyes glowed in the dimness, and her hands started to move in the air, as if pulling invisible tangled ropes of a small vessel in a storm tossed sea. The air shivered, full of the soundless vibrations of forces and cross forces being manipulated. Finally Ta Murdan stood still, reaching out one final time to grasp the air with each hand high above her, then pull slowly down and towards her until her fists crossed her chest.

While Ta Murdan did this some of the officers milled, uncertain of what to do until she spoke.

"There is no need for any mother to move," the master adept said. "Except to yield so we can perfect the circle. "

Eld counted nine magi total. Seven made the edge of the circle and though there was no need for women to move, they yielded from the center as the seven women converged on something, the master adept in the center, her fists still holding the invisible air close. The seven shifted, their own hands moving, but with open graceful guiding motions. Then they stopped shifting their feet and a light flickered once around the circle of the seven. Only then did Ta Murdan open her hands, releasing essence she'd drawn and trapped, as the seven magi around her held their palms out as if they were collectively holding something in the center mid air. Ta Murdan crossed her arms, looking satisfied and curious, yet still alert.

"Ta Murdan, what is it?" Alhern asked in a careful calm voice used to avoid disturbing an essence thread, though the magi, being a professional, was hardly likely to lose her focus.

"A dreamer," Ta Murdan said. "We have expected something like this. Being experts with the construction of essence artifacts, they would have their own magi."

Eld's mind was rent with a screech of alarm, a mind angry and hostile, but elfyn. A hum vibrated around the circle, not women vocalizing temple chants like the ancients, but a palpable and audible effect of activated essence focused by wizards who knew their business.

"I have trapped it," Ta Murdan said. "She's quite agitated."

The hum subsided. Slowly an apparition appeared in front of Ta Murdan, much like the ghostly illustrations that hovered recently over the back wall. Someone dimmed the lights further for better visibility. It was a woman, dressed not unlike the soldiers who attacked Seth. But her coat was black instead of red, with white circles around where the sleeves attached to the shoulder. On each lapel was a stylized eight pointed star similar to a compass star or the star in the center of an Astalyn, the Helix Star of Er. If Eld was to guess, this soldier was rated as a magi. And even in sleep she saw herself as such, not a romantic image of a wizard, however that might appear in an Eurthan mind. This woman's self image was completely in tune with her task. Her bright hair was oddly cropped like most of her Eurthan compatriots. Most elfyn abhorred cutting their hair. But Eld could see this being an advantage in their champion armor.

"Release me, unholy savage!" the woman demanded, her voice thin and distant. Eld was shocked her Sulanilish was perfect.

"She is dreaming," Ta Murdan explained. "We have made a type of Sadol of our bodies and souls. You are not hearing her with our ears, but our minds, her projection is amplified for our convenience."

"She's dreaming?" Roel blurted. "That means ..."

"Silence, lieutenant," Alhern ordered. "Continue your interrogation, Magi."

"I'm sure even among your own people mental intrusion is rude," Ta Murdan said.

"All I do is in service of God and Avatar!"

"How diligent of you. Which God is this?"

"There is only one True God! God the Mother!"

"Ask about this Avatar," Alhern murmured.

"The Avatar, is this your ruler or queen?"

"The pagan High Queens are long dead. Our Avatar is Her incarnation in the Earth and we are Her chosen people!"

"That's convenient," Danshor muttered.

The trapped magi soldier's soul looked more frantic, her orange eyes blazing with panic. She wasn't bound in any apparent way, but she kept spinning around franticly as if she were looking for an exit. Finally she stopped and her eyes calmed.

"You will soon regret this, Agent of the Adversary. God and Avatar!"

The woman saluted in defiance, as if facing death.

Suddenly the whispering of magi minds gusted through all their thoughts. Two magi raised their palms outward on either side of the figure to hold her, while Ta Murdan pulled back the heel of her hand in a martial stance, then she struck the apparition in the heart. The place she hit flashed gold for a moment, and the Eurthan woman's face registered shock. Then the apparition flickered and disappeared, and the hum of the circle vanished.

The light returned to what is was, making Eld wonder if it was a side effect of the magi operation.

"I have struck her hard enough that the shock should knock her out into simple dreams," Ta Murdan said. "But expect her to wake within an hour to tell her tale. She was sending to her fellow magi to break free; now it will be some time before they know of our plans. The rest of the intelligence can wait."

"Thank you, Ta Murdan," Alhern said.

"But commander," Roel said, "If she was dreaming and they planned to attack at dusk ..."

"Yes, Roel, it means their camp is asleep and we have confirmed an element of surprise. Which we might have lost with you yapping in front of an enemy's spirit."

Eld smirked while Roel blushed deeply.

"We are out of time," Alhern said. "The Dwen will be assisting us in taking down the wall. Wood-essence is one of the few effects Eurthan craft is not resistant to. Those mounted will be issued with chains and other means of entanglement. If they don't run, get these trolls on the ground and strike them until they crack open like nuts in a fire. Our foremothers were Queens and they didn't build a nation to be slaves or sport for arrogant alien literalists. Rout this Bane-spawn back to the roots of the Altans whence they came!"

## Chapter 16

# Engagement

Everyone was dispersed with speed to their tasks, the Dwen clustering around Alhern's staff and the magi drifting out except for a couple who lingered with some officers around a table on the stage. Seth caught Eld's arm as she was exiting with Danshor to join their company.

"The women would follow an ensign as bright as you anywhere," Eld said.

"It's an emergency civilian commission," Seth explained. "I'm to assist Captain Vergant organizing reserves. And my sister wants to be certain her household has an unquestioned chain of command while she's absent."

"The sword gives me comfort," Eld said. "You know how to use it?"

"Yes," Seth said. "Men can use swords. I admit it has been a while, however I'm not expected to need to fight." Suddenly Seth pulled Eld's head down and rose on his toes to kiss her forehead like an ancient prince blessing a queen's champion. "Be bold, but not too bold."

With Seth's bright golden eyes on her, Eld's misgivings vanished and she felt her heart was as big as a dragon's. She could do anything...

"You can get kisses from all the men you want on your return, Lancer!" Captain Aynath shouted at her. "Join the muster!"

The bells were clanging as Eld ran after Danshor to mount the horses and found their steeds almost unrecognizable. While they had been in conference, the garrison grooms had been busy fitting all the horses in unicorn barding, a custom that inspired confusing tales among humyn. Contrary to fey imaginations, unicorns didn't actually exist outside of dreams, but one could hardly blame them for the misconception. The top of each horse's face was covered with the best plate steel, and over the hardest part of their forehead rose a spiral horn of steel a foot and a half long. Layers of plates descended to cover the neck and a breastplate covered their chest. It wasn't ideal for light cavalry but couldn't be helped. From what they had been told, without barding the horses didn't stand a chance against Blue Strike. They were already shoed, the better to kick at armor without injury, but the saddle was the strangest:

Just behind where Eld would sit, a loci sink was mounted in a leather case, stapled rudely to the leather of her saddle. Ingenious, indeed, Eld thought sarcastically. But that wasn't all. A thin wand of metal, tin or brass, rose up from it, maybe a foot. It was like a lightning rod. Next to Eld, Danshor fumbled her mounting, almost poking herself indecently, and Eld would have done the same had she not spotted it first. She worried it would get in the way, but once seated it was of minimum interference. Checking her saddle sword was secure, Eld noticed a loop of chain hanging where ranchers held lassos. In fact some horses did have lassos; if they managed to not catch fire, they might be useful.

"I wish I had barding," Danshor opined as they cantered to join the company.

"The barding is a burden for the horses as it is," Eld said, patting Fiorseth's neck. Fiorseth hated barding and wanted nothing more than to shed it all and wade in a cool stream. "I know," Eld murmured. "But duty comes first and it will keep you safe."

Fiorseth flicked her ears back. Eld was never certain how much Fiorseth understood of duty, or "the musts", as her mind understood it. All the mare saw were elves running into danger when they could run away from danger. Eld had tried to make image analogies to the threats of wolves or bears, but Fiorseth remained unconvinced. In her mind simply staying near the stables would suffice. All the danger that ever happened was when they went "out there".

As they rode to join their fellows, Eld saw Sergeant Tershol, armored and helmed like all the infantry host, passing out loci sinks to soldiers now at attention.

" ...When we arrive be prepared to tidy up after the cavalry foray!" a field sergeant was shouting. "Drop these away from yourself and any sister as you advance on a mark ..."

A mark was an instruction by whistle, the code understood by all Federation troops. The shrill signal for the cavalry to move out sounded as Eld and Danshor joined their company and they cantered out at a good clip through the gate. The sky was clear, the sun bright, the stones on the shoulders of Eld's jacket glowing excitedly, perhaps more activated by whatever essence flowed through the loci sink. Or maybe it was their collective excitement, to finally be deployed in the field to test their mettle against the alien force, this time at their strongest. The company kept a steady pace; it wouldn't do for the horses to be winded when they arrived, especially with the added weight of the barding. But the inherent advantage to having an elfyn rider in mental affinity with her horse came to fruition: while they rode in full sunlight, the horse benefited from her aura of essence. The practical effect was the horse stepped lighter and the barding felt much less than its actual weight. The mount would also benefit from the heightened senses of their elf's mind, and, provided affinity was unbroken, horse and rider would act as one, able to perform feats beyond the skill of the most talented animal trainer.

And so the company led the Host, riding down the lane to town, turning onto the Old Farm Road near The Wildling. They would have been a glorious sight, bright riders, lances blazing in the sun, on silvery, unicorn mounts, had anyone been there to see them. When Eld caught a glimpse of the village in the distance, it was deserted except for scattered guards and Hounds. At dawn the alarm bell had tolled and the Amynvar, such as she was – having a mayor in such a small village seemed unnecessary – had held a council and the mothers decided most men and all children should be sheltered in the Abbey with the magi, while women clustered in the larger and more defensible houses, including inns like The Wildling. Sil had sent Eld a brief missive from the canal station that he and the children had arrived without incident and expected to be at the estate in a day. They should be home now. Knowing that was a relief to Eld.

Turning off the Old Farm Road, after a quarter of an hour, the company ran through a passage of meadow much dryer than before, to the favor of the horse's hooves. Ahead was the mouth of the ravine, to their right the rise with the trees, presumably still held by the Eurthans. When the Dwen arrived that wouldn't last. To their left and northwest, there was a ragged tree line of scrub, young oak and apples from an ancient orchard long gone wild; Eld could just pick out the shapes where longbow snipers lurked in brush, the air around them shimmering like heat waves created by the archer's blind, a shield that gave an illusion of obscurity. There was no point in throwing masses of arrows against the grim-steel armored host. But if a soldier was burnt enough to crack, or a gap was spied, a sharpshooter with a horn and elm bow and sol-tipped arrows would be deadly. A skilled Sula archer could shoot a target in full sun at a distance of five hundred yards. But a sniper in the battle would not be shooting in conditions so favorable and must always be ready to change her position if threatened. At one time cavalry carried bows, but fire lances made them obsolete. The point of Sula cavalry was to ride down the enemy with godly fire, not take potshots with arrows from horseback.

As the company cantered into formation, the prelude to charge, Eld caught a glimpse of the wall. At four to five feet, it would come up, at the highest, to a woman's chest. At first she didn't see it as much of a barrier. Any horse could clear it, though not as easily with barding. But then she spied its proportions: it was thick, perhaps three feet, tricky to clear without a good head of speed. But the day was bright and the morning grew brighter. And beyond the wall no guard was to be seen.

Instead there were strange structures, domes made of thin frames of wood or metal, covered with light shimmering, gray cloth. The structures were perhaps a hundred yards beyond the wall, the largest further than that, half again as high, rising like a goose egg among a clutch of duck eggs. As the company arranged themselves into a line, Danshor on Eld's left, Eld was surprised to see no sign of guard or a watch.

A flash caught her eye from the trees on the rise. They had been spotted. Eld felt it, the imminence of the future threat. Soon, whatever would happen, would happen. Glancing to their rear Eld saw the tips of the foot host lances, just arriving, marching into position far behind them. The foot soldiers, unlike the cavaliers, were armored, coats reinforced with chest and shoulder plates, but carried no packs, so they would be even lighter on their feet.

The whistle to prepare sounded. Eld moved her lance into her left hand, pulling her cavalry sword out with her right. Until there was space to entangle, it was still the best way to start. Fiorseth would not need to be guided by anything but Eld's mind. Already the mare yielded to Eld, experience having taught her being open to Eld's aura reduced her fear and anxiety. Suddenly Eld could smell the grass much more strongly than she usually did.

A series of whistles sounded: they were to charge, with level strike, clear the wall if able, and route or strike as many Eurthans as they could. Harry their camp, then return for more instruction.

The final whistle to charge, high and piercing, sounded.

The company started slow, tackle jingling as they cantered to mark time with their fellows much as the foot host did while marching. Eld was porous to the sun as if she was being filled with light. They gathered speed and Fiorseth now seemed pleased, the barding oddly lighter, her senses enhanced by her link with Eld's mind almost as if she was a Thyn horse. Then they were galloping, closing the distance between themselves and the wall about a hundred yards away. It was like flying, the air bright around them, sunlight ready to bend to the Sula will.

And bend it did. Halfway across the field, now just rocky ravine with little grass, the lances, surrounded with an ambient glow, started to brighten at their tips. But instead of striking, the light of each lance sought the light of the one to either side to make a line of fire above them, a flaming salute to the heavens running over their heads. Once it was strong and secure, as one they slowly lowered their lances bringing the line of fire in front of them so that it would hover above the wall before they cleared it.

They were fast now, not the fastest a horse could go, but certainly as fast as an unarmored horse thanks to the auras of the riders. The light from the fire line was so bright, the glare was hard for even Sula eyes to see details of any sudden activity. If changing their course was needed, the field commander would signal....

As if reading her thought, a signal whistle warning of archers blew.

Archers? Eld though frantically, keeping Fiorseth's pace. The Eurthans had archers? She couldn't see anything, but if they had archer's shields like there own how would she?

Suddenly Eld spied dark, heavy projectiles flying through the air at them from over the wall. They were not long, elegant arrow shafts. With horror Eld saw they were crossbow bolts, made of the same black metal as the Eurthan armor. There were not many, but had heavy, triangular tips for large targets and were enough to make the line waver. Elfyn senses attuned, she saw five bolts in rapid succession crossing Fiorseth's path.

One would go high. She could flick that away with her sword.

Two would pass to either side, grazing one or both of them.

But two could not be avoided. One might glance off of Fiorseth's chest plate, but the other was a dead hit. Eld knew what she had to do. If she was lucky she could keep the fire line while she did it.

~Roll,~ Eld thought to Fiorseth, though linked as they were a command wasn't necessary. Fiorseth perceived the danger at the same time, and yielded to the strategy in Eld's mind.

As they both tipped together to the right side, falling slightly behind the line, Eld batted the high bolt away with her sword at the same time as she leaped from the saddle, aiming to roll clockwise while Fiorseth did the same, careful to keep distance to avoid each other and any other horse in the line. Fiorseth's training would keep her head tucked, so the horn on her barding would not stick in the ground. As Eld rolled, she continued to hold her lance, keeping the fireline though it was ragged and dragged behind. She prepared to leap back on Fiorseth once the mare had righted herself. They might still make the wall.

But Eld had lost track of the path of the bolts. While rolling had moved them both out of the path of the twin mortal shots, and cleared them completely from the one that might have grazed Eld's left shoulder, she had thrown herself much closer to the bolt that would have otherwise grazed Fiorseth's neck. Instead it struck the armor on the upper chest of Eld's jacket and gorget before bouncing away. Though a glancing blow, it was forceful and hurt, and the shock was enough that her lance's link to the fireline was broken.

Cursing, Eld ran to Fiorseth who was getting back on her hooves, though feeling heavier for the lack of Eld's aura. Eld scanned the air for more bolts while she secured their link and ran to leap back on Fiorseth, amid some of the worst noises she'd ever heard in her life: horses screaming. Luckily the horizontal fireline, which was just dispersing, had done some good: the crossbow archers, women in padded, black skin suits, were in retreat, some hobbling with sniper arrows, many leaving their bows behind, either because they had become too hot to hold or their strings had melted, the women themselves injured or blinded.

Back in the saddle, Eld switched her sword and lance hands. She preferred single strikes with her right. And not a moment too soon. One archer remained, her silvery hair marking her as she took aim. Eld struck her device with a glorious bolt of fiery light. If Eld had struck the woman there was a chance a bolt might have been released anyway and they were too close for another roll . The woman cried out, standing up to drop her ruined weapon just as Fiorseth wheeled near the wall, Eld cutting down with her sword. But the woman, green eyes blazing in a tan face, was elfyn quick, dodging the blade, then running, presumably to find her shell.

Now Eld's course was less clear. Those who had cleared the wall with the charge continued running through the camp, striking the round structures that then immediately burst into flames. They were metal framed, but the light cloth easily caught fire and cries of panic and alarm filled the Eurthan camp. Here and there Blue Strike erupted, soldiers striking with unmounted weapons. But, while some cavaliers seemed to be showered with a cascade of lightning forks, the horses were not hit nor did they fall. The loci sinks protected them, at least for now.

Eld's senses, along with Fiorseth's animal perceptions, told her to instantly wheel around. Archers hidden, crouched against the other side of the wall, aimed their crossbows at both elf and horse. Eld struck one in the arm, a flashing strike, but enough to set her clothes on fire, she dropped the bow and ran screaming while Eld warmed the lance for a sustained strike she drew along the back of the wall, flushing the remaining archers. A couple appeared suddenly, from behind  shield blinds. The shields fell, clanging like broken bells while the archers fled in earnest, for they had seen the infantry host making its way across the field, lance tips shinning bright and hot, ready to scorch on command.

Eld urged Fiorseth on, riding through the camp to where their war-sisters needed help. The mare kicked an Eurthan desperately trying to seal herself in her armor, forcing her to flee without a helmet and arm pieces, and, most importantly, her bane-weapon. As a precaution Eld struck the weapon; it didn't destroy it but would make it too hot to use for a while. Eld exchanged sword blows with a woman who had managed to get armored, visor still up, but she only had a sword. Being mounted with the momentum of a horse's weight, Eld enjoyed the advantage, but the woman did not retreat easily. Red eyes blazed in a bronze dark face and while they fought, other women in shells converged to help their sister. Eld wanted to avoid lethal strike; they were to drive them out. The taboo against waring between elfyn might be shattered, but if war they must, death should be avoided for only the living could make peace.

But there was no choice. Eld spied bane-weapons on armored shoulders and in hands, ends glowing, warming to strike, and Eld did not yet trust the magi device to protect her. She would not gamble with Fiorseth's life. Eld struck the woman she fought full in the face with sunstrike.

Or so Eld thought. When the brightness dispersed, the face was completely obscured, the visor having been lowered, protecting the warrior from mortal injury. But there was a muffled scream of agony. Not dead or blinded, the woman would still be burned. Meanwhile three Bane-shelled soldiers threatened to trap her. Eld struck again, this time to make an opening and Fiorseth broke through, knocking one woman down as they escaped while blue lightening showered them. Eld jumped as if shocked by static from a wool blanket during a storm. Another shock made Fiorseth skip a step, her mind full of alarm at this new feeling. Eld calmed her, they were safe, the loci sink having bled the strike somewhat. As Eld joined the scattered cavalry run, burning tents and striking at unarmored women, harrying them hopefully into flight, she became aware the wand of metal on her sink had broken off, probably when Fiorseth rolled. So it worked, it kept them from being seriously injured or killed, but a strike might still be dangerous.

And that was a greater risk of remaining in the encampment. Eld glimpsed Danshor riding through with the first charge, out of sight behind the great tent, presumably where the Eurthan field command lurked. Those cavaliers were now returning sun-wise, from the right and east of the field, burning and striking as they went.

A whistle sounded to rejoin the main Host.

"The command tent has armored walls!" Danshor shouted as she passed Eld.

"And the Bane spawn have found their shells...." Patrycan added, then screamed as she was surrounded by a shower of blue Bane-strike so dense it blinded their eyes a moment. Her horse reared, screaming in alarm and pain, while Pat was barely able to stay seated. Eld didn't hear so much as feel the loci sink behind Pat's saddle, a moment before as bright as a blue sun, shatter, instantly turning into fine gray sand. It probably saved her life. Residual blue forks of strike discharged through her mount's barding. Torin had the presence of mind to grab the horse's lead, forcing it to follow by habit and training. Eld cast about looking to strike the warriors who had done this, all thoughts of simply driving the Eurthans away evaporating. They would strike them through the Door into the Void.

But while it was true black armored figures were rallying, none had been nearby in a cluster to explain the density of that strike. Eld's eyes scanned the area as speedily as she could. East of the ravine was clear, the ground flat and rocky. Ahead the Eurthan camp seethed with activity, cavaliers still swerving between the tents, causing as much havoc as they could. The Eurthans had taken the ridge, the south and west side facing them in an almost sheer wall of rock and soil bordering the ravine, above which was woodland and tall pines, a prime place to watch. So far they seemed to be lucky the Eurthans had no snipers or even simple bow archers. But Eld's eye caught a flash of something black with a greenish hue. Fiorseth backed away, only keeping from turning because of Eld's mind; the mare had understood they were retreating and found this to be the best of all elfyn ideas. But Eld needed to sight this thing certainly while she could, in the sun. Finally she saw and was terrified.

"Scatter!" she shouted, letting Fiorseth turn and run as fast as the mare could, letting her pick her own way. "There is a bane weapon in the trees, greater than the rest! Run and scatter!"

No one questioned her as they abandoned their task of routing the encampment and made for the far west of the wall, where they would run around the oncoming host. In the clearing between the encampment and the wall there was nothing except abandoned and broken crossbows, bloodied sniper arrows, and discarded bolts; just beyond was the rumble of women marching under bright lances. In minutes they would be over the wall. Eld was surprised the Dwen had yet to dismantle it.

The Host needed to know the danger that awaited. At least there was not another great strike. Perhaps the weapon took time to use again. Or they were out of range. Most had enough speed to leap over the wall, those who didn't leaped on the wall, cantering along it before jumping down. Once over, Eld galloped to the field command as fast as she could.

The cavalry had to ride hard and fast in a broad arc around the northwest flank of the marching companies, who were now a mere score of yards away from the wall. If the wall didn't come down, Eld expected half the women would run and leap it while the other half covered them by scorching the air in front of them. Once over, their position would be held in the same way while the rest of the Host followed. Soon the entire Eurthan encampment would be alight with strike and flames, and bold women with eager swords, who could not believe a chance to make a glorious name for themselves in battle had come in their lifetimes.

But the Eurthans were rallying. Unshelled women were gone now, either retreating with wounds or, having found their armor, joining the glittering mass forming beyond the smoke and haze of the wreckage the first cavalry run had wrought. Eld kept her ears open for new orders as she neared the rise where the commander and her entourage watched.

Alhern sat on her horse near an old apple tree, wild and neglected, twisted by the elements but still alive, white flowers gamely gracing its branches, dreaming of summer fruit, free of the cares of the non-rooted things that ran to and fro around it. Around the commander were a handful of signalers, expertly trained with whistles to pass orders far into the field. In front of all of them were field archers, complete with shields that shimmered indistinct in the sunlight, making it hard for the eye to settle on them. Eld wondered if the effect was the same for Eurthans. And if the archers failed, a company of twenty pikers stood ready to defend the rise and, if necessary, the commander's retreat. Their lances, heavier than a regular foots', were extra long, meant in the most desperate case to be driven into the ground to remain as pikes while they battled with stars, though few women used stars, rods mounted with a spiked head, enameled to burn, so a victim impaled by its spikes would find herself roasted by a small flaming sun. It was a brutal weapon considered too dangerous to practice with except on straw padded mannequins.

Eld reached Alhern, her company riding on to regroup in the fields beyond. Tafli stood nearby, as if he'd just emerged from the branches of the apple. He was barefoot now, but his arms and ankles had twinings that looked like thick tree roots and vines. While Eld slowed Fiorseth to a trot, Tafli spoke.

"We cannot yet take it down," he said, his voice tense with frustration. "We are rooting deep, but it is not stone work made with hands and mortar. It is some way grown from the rock below."

"It's solid?" Alhern sounded terse. Eld knew it would be best for both the foot and the mounted companies to have the barrier removed.

"No, thank the rain, it is porous a bit. We can break it. But we need more time."

"How much?"

"Some minutes, we are hoping?"

Alhern swore under her breath then called out to the signalers, "Halt the foot host, form ranks in place." To Tafli she added, "I want that wall down!"

Tafli nodded before running away to the tree line near the escarpment, a bit too close to the danger for Eld's liking.

"Commander!" Eld said.

"Yes, Farthal?" Alhern didn't look at Eld, her gold eyes flashing in the sun as she stared out over the battlefield as the air was filled with signal whistles. She didn't wear her helmet, presumably to not limit her field of view, but it rested on the horn of her saddle while she watched the foot host stop a couple yards away from the wall. Then with a series of graceful gliding maneuvers, the companies split into ranks of women two deep, who further staggered themselves so that the row in the back was ready to strike while the row in the front either advanced or fought. They would advance switching positions as needed. Meanwhile, infantry on the far ends of the host to either side positioned themselves to change into column formations, ready to make a winding rank to advance or defend. Most officers on horses who were not with Alhern's command staff patrolled these ends. Field officers stood near their ranks, more clearly seen now the soldiers had spread out. Shouts and whistles sounded; Eld couldn't parse the details but there seemed to be a minor conflict about deployment of the loci sinks.

"The sinks," Eld said. "They can be destroyed if strike is strong enough. There's a massive bane weapon above, in the tree line. It almost killed Patrycan."

Alhern glanced at Eld, then the looming pines in the east above them. "Where?" she demanded, pulling a telescope out.

"Close to the ravine ...they struck at the eastern end of the wall. If you saw the shower of blue strike--"

"Yes. That was not several bane warriors?"

"No, just one source, and the ranks will be marching within range."

"Tresses, it's the size of a small cart with the shape of a field cannon!"

"With respect, some of us have been wondering...."

"Why we don't have field cannons like garrisons in the south?" Alhern lowered the telescope and blew several short sharp notes on her own whistle: rally and withdraw on the east. "Lack of savage upstarts nearby looking for elfyn loot I expect. You can take it up with Command if you like. If that's all, Farthal ..."

Eld saluted and rode to join the company where the horses were being quickly watered, and checked for wounds by field grooms. She wanted to check Fiorseth herself, but no sooner than she'd dismounted, their captain was shouting her name.

"Emha?" Eld queried.

"You were an animal healer, correct?" Aynath asked.

"I didn't finish my training."

The captain made a motion as if to wave away a midge. "You were first in your training host and the horses like you. Work with the healers patching the steeds and moving them off the field until the next foray."

Eld nodded, allowing Fiorseth to be led away and driving her lance into the ground for keeping. As an after thought, she darted forward to retrieve her sword from the saddle holster and snap in on her baldric. Suddenly Danshor was standing next to her.

"What did she mean, first?" Danshor demanded, the urgent business of battles being pushed aside in her competitive mind. But before Eld could answer a horrible scream sounded, piercing both ears and souls, the sound of abject bereavement. Eld knew before she saw a cavalier from the first company, a woman she didn't know, crumple to her knees, collapsing on the body of her still barded horse. Nearby a healer was standing up; helpless to do more, she moved to the next mount in need several yards away. Eld knew the woman and her closest sisters would try to remove the body, and return the soul later. But those not Thyn almost always passed straight through the Door. Even if they were in time for the body to be viable, the soul would be gone...

"That one is beyond help," Captain Aynath said firmly, but not without sympathy. "Others can yet survive."

Eld shook herself and ran into the field immediately, heading for another horse resting on its side. A figure was already there, not a healer, but a civilian man recruited from the lots. One of the advantages of rural villages was that many souls picked up basic healing skills tending to their animals. The man, thin and wearing a plain, undyed linen kirtle-shirt already stained with grass and mud, looked up franticly. His eyes were full of panic and he knew he was out of his depth. Eld sped towards him, one eye always watching the front lines for new danger, hoping they could work fast.

## Chapter 17

## Sunstrike meets Bluestrike

Being in the battlefield on foot was a different experience. Eld felt vulnerable, like a mouse in a vast field knowing hawks soared above out of sight. She had her natural speed, but she didn't have the height and bulk of a horse for protection. And her boots, well made for riding and walking on even ground, were not optimal for running over uneven turf recently churned up by a host of horses followed by the infantry and their much sturdier marching boots. In moments she fell by the side of the man and horse.

"Eld?" Althas said, mildly surprised, but not as surprised as Eld.

"What are you ..." Eld cut herself off. She knew what he was doing. "What's wrong?" she amended. "I trained as a healer before enlisting."

Althas nodded, his face, free of glimmer or cosmetics, looking wan and pale. "I thought all she needed was a tonic and ligament binding. But then she fell back down ..."

Eld put a hand on the horse's neck and another on the top of her heaving belly, the saddle pressing into her uncomfortably. Preferably one always tended an unknown animal from the back side for safety. The horse's breathing was shallow and she was shivering with the beginnings of shock.

"Where's the rider?" Eld asked.

"She was wounded. A bolt in her thigh. She was taken away."

Eld swore. A cavalry horse's rider was the best source of calm and comfort at times like these. She hoped the captain was right and the horse liked her enough to let Eld into its mind so she could find out where the injury was. It was possible the horse was lying on it ...

"I need to calm her mind and ...oh." Eld could feel the pain. She had to quiet the agony to find the source. "Check for a wound around the chest. Be careful."

Althas dashed in front the beast fearlessly. Hooves had broken the bones of many a farmer and her helper in similar straights. Through the horse – Hollar was what she was called--Eld felt Althas' quick hands looking for the wound. Then she felt it, a tear in the flesh under the chest piece, a lucky shot that landed in the fraction of a second when galloping legs lifted the chest plate up. The entire bolt had gone in, but hadn't cut more than the meat of the chest until further action had moved it close to an artery. A nick was causing bleeding inside. The worst thing was the bolt itself was keeping the horse from bleeding out completely.

This was no work for a common animal tender, or green healer.

"Get a healer instantly," Eld barked. "She will die and we can't move her."

Eld shed her baldric, jacket, and gorget as quickly as she could, and pushed up her sleeves. She knew they had to remove the bolt. While it was removed, the artery would have to be healed as it retreated, closing up behind in a perfect seal. The essence flow needed was so fine it was usually reserved for surgeons. Eld certainly hoped she wouldn't have to do it. A risk was the filling tissue clogging the artery completely and not being able to clear it fast enough before heart failure. And it was essential Hollar didn't lose more blood. With a healers tonic they could just get her on her feet; no wagon could be brought onto the field while maneuvers were active, if only for the safety of the drivers. Althas had been yelling for what Eld was sure was minutes. That was something she'd forgotten about healing: time flowed strangely when a mind was in the world of the unseen motes that made living bodies.

And then another mind joined her with a male presence.

Eld wasn't proud of her instant doubts. She wanted the surety of a mother's presence. But his mind was as sharp as any she'd worked with in stable infirmaries past. Before she could say anything or give instruction, he sent and spoke, "You have training?"

"Yes. The bolt needs to be removed with –"

" –A hand in essence around it," the man finished. "Calm the pain –"

"I can do that ," Althas interjected.

"Well. Be present, cavalier and tell me when you feel my hand around the bolt."

It was healer jargon. "Well" or "good", was an acknowledgement of a communication from an operation participant. "A hand" was the force of an elf's active essence, usually ready to do something. "Presence" was one's essence flowing in a body, ready to work or support work. Eld didn't have much experience working with other healers, but feeling the man and Althas with her made her oddly calm in spite of the seriousness of the wound. And she knew the less they were inclined to panic the more likely they were to succeed. Her biggest worry was any of them being shot or worse. But even this was calmed now to an intellectual concern, like an observer of a chess game.

Althas had no formal training so Hollar's pain, while greatly diminished, wasn't completely gone. Still, it was a help, as much as stilling the mare's body. Meanwhile Eld heard a rushing in her ears, the sound of the man's mind while at the same time she felt his essence flow side by side with hers, pouring himself into the horse's meat and bones. Eld was suddenly aroused, a not infrequent effect of a healer's body involved in the essence flow. It was a common joke healers fell to coiting after a hard operation, though in practice the lower number of men in theaters made this rarer than expected. The only women who fell together were sisters of that sort in nature; the arousal never changed a mother's preferences, though it might reveal something she had not known of herself before.

Once Hollar's pain was diminished, Eld slowly moved her hand into the wound, pulling flesh apart on the essence level where needed, trying to do as little damage as possible. The minute streams of blood, carrying motes of air the body depended on for life, pumped in alarm at her gross intrusion, as if they were aware of the catastrophic danger their world was in. The tips of Eld's fingers found the bolt, canting up and down with Hollar's shallow breaths. She gripped it gently, loose enough to let it move. Then the healers essence flowed around it and her hand, and Eld was seized with the urge to violently coit the man.

It was so unlike herself, she almost lost her grip in alarm. There were essence forms and meditations both magi and healers did regularly to control flow and focus. Eld, like many lay people, did these now and then for personal health, but she hadn't understood the consequences of failing regular practice could be this dire. She focused on keeping her grip and shielding her mind: the only thing more mortifying would be if the man knew.

And not a moment too soon. This time he only spoke in mind:

~Now pull, slowly.~

It was like a hard birth: Eld was the surgeon pulling the child, while the flesh of the vein the man closed behind was the effort of the mother to push the child out, only here to close up completely behind it. It seemed to take minutes, the sounds around Eld diminishing to distant hums, women's voices deepening in aggression, shouts stretched out for seconds. At least her arousal had been dampened. But she saw nothing in the outer world; instead her mind swam with the strange awareness of Hollar's body and her grip on the cold metal that had almost killed the mare.

Finally the bolt was free of the artery and Eld's hearing rushed back. She no longer had to be hyper-aware, only feeling her way out to safely remove the bolt from Hollar's body cavity. She sat back hard on her heels, still connected enough to be aware of the repaired great vein. With her left hand she kept her connection, moving flesh back into place and starting the repair of minor veins but the man said, "Leave it. We need to get her off the field."

Already two more healers were running over. Althas released the mare's mind so she could move, though keeping the pain suppressed. Instantly Hollar started clambering to her feet; she had no intention of staying in this strange place of painful stings. Part of Hollar's mind wondered where her rider was.

Eld grabbed her gear and rolled out of the horse's way and onto her feet. Her right hand was bloody to the elbow, the bolt still in hand; she wiped it off best she could before putting it in a jacket pocket. Then she donned her jacket again, and, while scanning the field, she replaced her gorget.

Magi hovered in the air near the commander on one side of the smoke-filled battlefield scattered with haze and flashing lances, while at the other side narrow flickers of blue strike tried to seek them only to fork into bright threads in the sky before dispersing. The magi were too far away to be hurt. But neither could they be as helpful. Magi could call a firestorm cyclone in sunlight, use the same counterforce from Eurath they used to fly to throw a body off her feet, rip weapons from hands, crush bones, even boil blood. But not if they were keep out of range because the Eurthan eldritch weapon was able to seek out and kill them by simply seeking essence. The Federation force of wizards was rendered ineffective while they labored to simply make a space where they could work.

Suddenly Eld saw another danger and shouted "Duck!"

Time slowed again but in a different way. Eld saw the errant bolts, shot from the cover at the far east portion of the wall, the same place covered by the great bane weapon lurking in the trees above. There were only two murderous darts of black metal cutting through the air, but their target was the same: Hollar. So the Eurthans did understand the value of a horse.

The male healer pulled on Hollar's bridle, correctly guessing the best direction to get her out of danger. Meanwhile one of the newly arrived healers was either greatly skilled or recklessly brave: she grabbed one of the bolts out of the air between the palms of both hands, while almost being struck by the second one that missed her by a hair's breath.

Eld was already in motion, diving not for the bolt but for Althas who, in ducking, inadvertently put himself directly in harm's way. Eld tackled him to the ground, the bolt skinning the back of her jacket before striking the earth, spent.

While they lay there, one of the healers shouted, "Get this horse off the field!"

Then Althas shouted, "Let go!"

Eld pulled back, alarmed, wondering if there was a new danger she should be aware of. But Althas just lay there, looking at her wide-eyed, breathing shallowly.

"Are you injured?" Eld asked.

"No!" Althas said, voice still sharp. Then he closed his eyes and exhaled. "Sorry. I was alarmed."

"Of course. You almost caught a Bane bolt."

Eld knew it was harder for men to laugh off these narrow scrapes. Althas grimaced wanly and started to rise. Eld sprang to her feet to help him, but he glared at her as if she was a Bane. Now she knew something was wrong.

"Althas, I don't know what's wrong, but we need to move." Eld looked around as she spoke, wary of more bolts on the air.

"I'm sorry. No, it's not you." Althas stood. "We'll go there next."

There were no horses left to remove, at least not those that still lived. But westward of them two foot soldiers crouched around a third, almost certainly the sign of an injury.

They trotted quickly, half crouching, ready to evade more missiles, Eld moving backwards to keep her eye on the air. Her sudden arousal was gone but it reminded her of an adjacent worry.

Trying to keep her voice calm, Eld asked, "Has Roel been harassing you?"

"Roel?" Althas queried. "I don't know that cavalier."

"She's not. She's an officer of the foot host. Young. Arrogant. More so than most young officers."

Eld glanced at Althas. Their eyes met briefly.

"She doesn't like you," Althas said. It was a statement.

"Did she ..." Eld couldn't bring herself to say the word "hurt", much less anything more serious. It wasn't to be thought on or Eld must kill Roel.

Althas stared stoically straight ahead, his natural sharp features even starker for lack of merriment.

"She paid me for my company like any woman."

Eld was having trouble watching the field, the snipers, the bright lines from the host striking near the wall. For all of the Dwen's craft the wall remained; it seemed Alhern had decided it would serve them as much as it had served the Eurthani.

"If she took liberties, she can be censured. You can make a complaint ..."

Althas barked a sharp laugh without mirth. "I have no intention of sharing what she did with another woman. And neither will you!"

This last was said with a finality that would not be brooked.

"Besides," Althas said in a subdued voice, "I could have refused. She didn't kidnap me. She offered so much I thought it would be worth it." He shook himself as if chilled. "They weren't things I like. But it was knowing why she used me that made me feel like a harlot for the first time. I was a tool of revenge. I think I shall keep to my own bed for awhile."

They had arrived at the trio of soldiers. One had a wound to her inner thigh that seemed to be easily stopped, but would start bleeding anytime they tried to move her. She had to spread her legs as if preparing for an awkward birth for Althas to see where her sisters had cut the bracs from her inner thigh. Eld wondered that he had no trouble tending to women this intimately, but supposed when it was all blood, flesh and bone to be managed like butcher meat, it was different. Eld felt Althas slipping away from her and it made her sad. She hadn't known he had cleaved a part to her soul until now. It wasn't anger or blame, but he was protecting himself; he had danced too close to the Gilded Hero and the brightness had burned him. What had Roel done? Eld thought in quiet rage.

The next moment a couple large masses bore down on her, one dark roan, the other white and gray with dappled hindquarters. Tuiric and Fiorseth.

Danshor was mounted on Tuiric, holding two lances, but a woman Eld didn't know was riding Fiorseth, at least until they stopped. From her look, a lean foot-soldier with light field shoes, a green and gray coat, and a horn and elm compound bow, she was an archer.

"Can I use your mount, sister?" the woman asked. Before Eld could answer the woman had pushed herself out of the seat and stirrups and jumped to stand on the saddle, all the while stringing an arrow to her bow and drawing. This was done in a couple of seconds and while Eld was impressed, she worried that the archer had made herself a target.

"Can't be helped," the woman said as if reading Eld's thought while she aimed. "The dense cover makes them impossible to see from the shield blinds, and besides, the Bane-weapon doesn't have the range."

"And they prefer to seek our magi," Danshor put in.

"But some of their crossbows do have range!" Eld said. "We just dodged some bolts while tending a horse!"

"Did you?" The archer sounded unperturbed. "Graced with Sul's touch I will not be long."

In full sunlight, at noon, it was said the best Sula archer on a hill could hit a target a thousand yards away. This was usually dismissed as an exaggeration; champions in the Games rarely went past six hundred. But military sniper's arrows weren't allowed in the Games. Not only were they coated with a solstone impregnated lacquer with solstone tips, but the metal holding the tip was gassed with grim. The arrow would fly higher in the sunlight like all Sula made arrows, but the grim gave it a memory of the archer's will and it would fly truer and straighter as a result. The memory was brief, but so was the flight of an arrow.

Eld glanced towards the distant tree covered hill where the Bane-weapon lurked. False thunder rolled over the field as a massive spray of bluestrike, pale in the sunlight, discharged, but it seemed to seek something further ahead of the Host, perhaps a foray or errant cavalier. Eld felt more than saw the air bend and her mind was for a moment taken with the archer's as she made a bright path of will to where the Bane-weapon sat with an eager woman, teeth bared in murderous glee, eyes bright and expectant. She was shell-less, wearing the padded, leather reinforced singlet Eld had seen the crossbow archers in. There was an impression of a couple more Eurthans, also in singlets, and armored women nearby, or perhaps the shells of the women visible. The woman reached out with something in her hand, too far away to hear, but shook her head, yielding a coin to the other observer who grinned, pocketing it. Like petty gods they gambled with Sula lives... "Unholy savages" they had called them...

A horse had died.

Hollar almost died.

Eld felt the essence in her aura become inflamed.

Then she heard the sniper arrow leave the bow.

Three seconds later it struck the Bane archer in front of her shoulder, right above her lung.

Eld joined the cheer from the command mound, where aids watched with telescopes and reported to observers. The essence empowered vision had vanished so she didn't get the satisfaction of seeing the jeering women humbled. But Eld had to join the muster and the archer was still on her horse.

"Patience, Gilded Hero," the woman said, taking another aim. "Like my fati says, a well made loaf is ready when it is ready."

Another arrow flew. Since Eld saw aught, she counted the seconds, waiting for the cheer. If anything it was louder.

"Surely they've fled!" Danshor said.

"No," the archer said shortly, drawing a third arrow. "They are soldiers like us. They have a duty. Though the last two have fallen to the ground seeking cover. Alas –"

The arrow flew.

" – I sighted them."

Now the cheer was echoed by both cavalry and infantry. Eld's spirit lightened.

"Now they have fled." The archer jumped directly to the ground.

"Are any dead?" Eld asked.

"No, though wounded badly. Camden, Company Par," she added by introduction.

"Danshor," Eld said jerking her head to the left. "Farthal."

"Everyone knows who you are!" Camden said smirking. "And the bold sister here?" she asked, nodding to the horse.

"Fiorseth."

"Sounds like a Gael name. My Gael is rusty. It means "true"or "truth". Thank you, horse-sister. Duty drives – see you anon!"

Camden ran off and Eld mounted Fiorseth.

"Was that well with you?" she murmured, pleased to feel Fiorseth's mind calm though the mare was hoping they would be returning to the stables soon.

"She's fine," Danshor said, giving Eld one of the lances as they trotted to rejoin the forming muster. "If all she did was let archers stand on her, she'd be as happy as a boar in rut."

"How colorful. She wants to return to the stables."

Danshor smiled. "Tuiric wants to run as fast as he can. He likes that."

"I wonder how he'll like getting stung by bolt."

"My horse never gets hit," Danshor said with alarming certainty.

"If Felkeni is listening, I plan to disown my association with you," Eld said.

Danshor laughed. "Remember, the Gods don't exist, correct, little poet?"

"Well, if any did exist, it would be the Laird of Chance and Fate."

"Who would think our Gilded Hero would be frightened of a fancy of poets."

"The only one of the Court of Heaven who did not fear Felkeni was Athmod. And we all know what happened to her."

Danshor laughed again. "Your moral saws are wasted on my ears sister. I will not be lost in the Void. Mark, what is she doing?"

Eld turned to where Danshor pointed. A woman was running, notable because she was not a foot soldier but a cavalier.

A cavalier on foot in a battle was never a good thing, even though a Sula cavalier on foot could run faster in the sun than a foot soldier because her gear was lighter. The woman had a lance in each hand, secured under each arm, so she made an odd spectacle, calling to mind a charging bull with the strangest of horns. Eld heard shouts from many souls attempting to stop her, the loudest being voices of alarmed officers. But the foot companies yielded to the mad woman and the implicit danger of close strike. She leaped the wall easily, then dropped over. Even from this distance the air around her was bright, an aura that could light things afire. No sooner than Eld had thought it, an Eurthan tent went up in flames.

"Who was that maniac?" Danshor breathed.

"The woman who lost her horse," Eld said. It was the only explanation for being so angry she didn't care about her own life or the loss it would be to her family.

Captain Aynath whistled repeated orders for her to come back, but the woman was beyond sense or reason. A couple moments later strike erupted behind the enemies lines, bright, gold and glorious. Eld hoped many Eurthans got a good roasting from it. Meanwhile the cavalry companies mustered, cantering together, ready to move into action.

Behind the wall, well outside of strike range, the Eurthans had regrouped into roughly two masses of women in armored shells. The bulk of their forces were west and center, slightly to the right of where Eld's company was massing to support the infantry. A smaller but not negligible force was further eastward, nearer the hill and the now silent Bane weapon. This force, knowing they had cover from above, had maneuvered to engage the foot host. Did they know their demonic familiar had been silenced? They were moving, the ground shaking with the weight of their steps, while Sula ranks reformed in front of them, spreading out so that women could strike at full force and minimize burning their fellows. Smoke from the ruined Eurthan encampment and its smoldering tents thickened the misty haze, but not thick enough to hinder their strike power. Eld looked at the sun, wondering how much time had passed since the engagement. It wasn't even two hours.

Whistles from the captain's aides laid out their task: support the foots, strike Eurthans when they could, and aim for entanglement.

"My sink is damaged!" Eld called out to Danshor as she loosened the chain on Fiorseth's harness.

"So it works?" Danshor called back.

"Yes, but we still feel it! I wish we'd had time to practice!"

"It'll be like rounding up stray calves!" Danshor said confidently. "Easy summer work!"

"Not all of us are wealthy farmers!"

"Your estate has farms! What were you doing in your youth? Memorizing poetry?"

Damn Danshor. Eld urged Fiorseth forward to avoid confirming the truth. But it did give Eld some confidence they could drag the shelled women off their feet. They were to seek pairs out if they weren't near their usual partner. Eld looked around to see if Patrycan had been allowed to rejoin the Host but couldn't see her. Hoping for the best, Eld continued to canter with Danshor, patrolling the edges of the strike lines.

Now it was certain the Eurthans felt bold and protected. The ground shivered as the bluish-green black metallic hulks loomed behind the wall, perhaps twenty yards away. What did the Eurthans plan to do if they drove the front lines back? Soldiers with lances now stood on the wall, gifted with the clearest shot any mother could wish for. A line of beaters were right behind them; several paces back another pair of lines waited for an opening. Eld was riding just behind the final row, maybe forty yards from the wall, when the Eurthan forces struck.

Searing blue light pierced Eld's eyes as the front-most line of armored figures sprayed the front ranks of the Sula forces with forks of deadly essence. Women jumped, crouched or even blinked, but not one was hit. Instead the lightning-like fingers forked into the nearby ground where the loci sinks had been scattered. One could feel the change in mood from anxious fear to joyful boldness. The Eurthans' power over the Sula mind had been broken.

The air erupted in sunstrike. Lances flared, sending bursts of powerful concentrated strike into the faces of the advancing line of Eurthani. No one could hear their cries, but Eld saw a couple stumble, one collapsing to her knees. The Eurthans struck again, but the Host was again unhurt, though some had to dodge.

And the women had learned. No longer were soldiers hitting women in the chest, expecting to kill or shock them off their feet. They had accepted strike alone wouldn't kill. For many this was a relief, for it meant they could use full force without further guilt from breaking the Taboo. Now they struck at faceplates, to blind, at the feet to roast, even at the weapons themselves in the hope the stress would damage them in some way. And it worked, the black armored ranks halted, though they didn't retreat. Without the cover of the great bane weapon, the battle might be a draw.

But Eld spotted something that made her worry. The little gray irregular cubes of ash-lime that sat on the ground among pebbles and thin grasses were not unscathed. Where some had been there was only crumbing plaster and sand. Perhaps a tenth of the sinks had been destroyed. So the Host too had lost some protection. Whistles from the field command seemed to confirm this. Women were told to reform with an eye for support and protection.

And not a moment too soon. Though the Sula forces had not stopped striking, the Eurthans sent a targeted volley. Eld watched as a sink exploded in a flash of blue lightning so strong it left some parts melted. To Eld's horror, one by one the sinks across the field and wall were targeted, greedily drinking the blue strike to their death. And then the Eurthans shifted in a move hard to catch, but they rotated out soldiers at the front for fresh women and now struck without mercy, hitting at least two soldiers. The Eurthan front resumed its march. They held shields now and there was a great hiss, as if an army of a thousand snakes had been released from Athmod's prison: the Eurthans had drawn their swords.

A whistle sounded and the front two strike ranks fell back. There was a real danger of a rout. The soldiers had seen the powdered and melted sinks, their enthusiasm melting with them. The second couple of ranks started to advance, but whistles told them sharply to stay were they were.

What was command thinking? Eld wondered, trotting behind Danshor. If the Eurthans made the wall...

She saw it in her mind: if the Eurthans made the wall, either the wall was about to crumble by Dwen magic or the Eurthans would rise on top of it. Eld smiled at the possibility she saw in her mind's eye.

"Ready yourself to round up some calves!" she shouted to Danshor.

The next whistle vindicated her hunch: cavaliers in pairs to entangle.

The cavalry host milled in that way observers thought was aimless. But like a court dance of interweaving steps where partners were exchanged but never lost, there was a pattern and plan, and out of chaos was birthed a deadly purpose. As the Eurthans reached the wall, they started to climb. Eld remembered some clusters of stones the crossbow archers were taking feeble cover from. It wasn't archer cover; they were steps for the shelled women. The company was already galloping, the wind whistling over Eld's ears as she fingered the chain in her left hand, wondering what to do with the lance in right. But as a shelled figure stepped onto the wall, years of training and practice manifested in the moment:

Eld drove the lance between the woman's feet, using Fiorseth's weight for torque. The black armored figure spun spectacularly before falling forward off the wall where she was run over by Tuiric's gleeful hooves. Danshor crowed.

"Well done!" she shouted.

"Ahead!" Eld called, as another armored figure mounted on the wall, turning her Bane-weapon on them. Eld threw out her chain and Danshor caught it, then took the slack up when Tuiric leaped onto, then over the wall.

It was pure brilliance, a maneuver hard to imagine without being caught in the moment of action. Eld and Danshor made the chain taunt between them. With Eld on one side of the wall and Danshor on the other, all they had to do was ride down and knock off any Eurthans standing on the wall. The Eurthan warrior must have seen her danger, but there was little to do except strike at them. They were both hit: Danshor's sink held; Eld felt the shock but was protected enough that it didn't matter. The chain hit the Eurthan around her knees and she fell with a horrible clang, first onto the top of the wall, then to the ground on Danshor's side with a thump.

Eld laughed with Danshor, whooping at the absurdity. Of course they weren't going to defeat the entire Eurthan Host with tricks like this. But they could make them look damn ridiculous while they worked to that victory. The horses gathered speed and two more warriors found themselves knocked off the wall, though the last had tried to dance over the chain but instead simply fell harder when it took her out at the ankle of one leg. But she had her revenge: the chain had been damaged, catching on some nook in the Eurthan armor. It broke on their fifth entanglement attempt, the long end whipping around in a deadly arc that almost hit Eld in the face. Instead she swung it counterclockwise around her head, and whipped it around the next woman's ankles. Eld held on, arm across her, using the saddle horn to keep her grip. There had been a satisfying shink of the chain forcibly looping, but a brief jerk of resistance. Abruptly the resistance was gone and Eld let the chain go, knowing its work was done, the warrior lying in an ignominious heap on the Sula side of the wall.

Now Eld wondered where Danshor was. Bright strike erupted and burned for several seconds. Danshor was trying to make an opening. Eld hesitated to jump over or even on the wall. But then Danshor leaped back over, followed by fingers of blue strike that grounded harmlessly into the sink behind her. They clapped their hands together, whooping to celebrate their boldness, Eld shouting, "Now where in Athmod's craw is my lance?"

The foot host had not been idle. While the Eurthans had been harried, entangled and humiliated, the footers struck with a vengeance, perhaps more so knowing the protection of the sinks was not to be depended on for much longer. And a new danger came from the larger westward force: a couple smaller groups broke from it, if Eld was to guess, to retrieve the three warriors fallen on the Sula side. The women could shed their shells and try to flee. But if the character of most of the troops was anything like the women Eld had spotted in the archer's vision, they didn't expect honorable treatment much as they didn't give it.

Fiorseth wheeled around, charging back the way they came. The first shelled warrior they'd toppled was struggling to her feet, surprisingly unhurt considering the full weight of Danshor's stallion with barding, and Danshor herself, had trampled her into the dry rocky soil. Eld marveled again at the construction of the Bane-armor. Now the warrior was faced with a new threat: four foot soldiers hungry to strike harried her. Eld thought she might have been trying to retreat. Given the general goal was to drive the Eurthans away,under regular circumstances Eld would urge the foots to let the Eurthan leave. But this was complicated by the fact that her lance was lying in the Eurthan's retreating path. It would be the perfect jest for Felkeni to play if the warrior stepped on it and snapped it as she fled. Matters were not improved by the fact this individual was quick on her feet even with a shell, and the foots were having trouble sustaining strike while wisely staying out of the reach of the black metal sword as it cut the air in clumsy but forceful swipes while the bane weapon rotated to strike. Eld saw no sinks on the ground, only powder. She stopped thinking and fell into Fiorseth's mind:

To be a horse was a joy in its own way. True, certain things were beyond a horse's mind: the necessity of this noise and danger for one. But the horses trusted their adoptive elfyn mothers who fed and sheltered them. And though Eld felt a part of Fiorseth's mind dwelled on the fallen horse, Fiorseth also knew through Eld they were both safest if they were bold and quick. So as one she drove her front hooves into the hard ground, twisted around as her hind quarters reared, Eld standing in her stirrups to give the horse less hindrance. A moment later Fiorseth gave a mighty kick with her back hooves, hitting the side of the armored woman so she rang like a bell throughout the valley. The ground shuddered as the Eurthan collapsed to her hand and knees, still gripping her sword.

But that bought time enough. Fiorseth cantered forward to the place the lance lay by the wall, but another foot soldier was already there, having sussed Eld's goal and grabbed it. So instead Eld turned Fiorseth to run past and she caught the lance as the soldier threw it.

"Elam!" Eld called out. Behind her the air erupted in bright strike. Eld expected the Eurthan would flee soon enough but decided not to leave it to that fickle heavenly harlot Chance. From a good distance she wheeled Fiorseth around and struck at the Eurthan's feet, driving her closer to the wall and her encampment. It would be painful to stand still, risking her feet roasting, and sure enough, reluctantly, the woman shuffled to the wall until she collapsed against it just as Eld needed to pause.

An individual Sula couldn't hold a sustained strike for more than minute in optimal conditions and no battle was optimal. The clear sky helped, as did the spring season when the power of Sul's rays was ascendant. But the reason beaters in a line took turns was so each striker could gather her essence for as powerful a stream as possible. Two rows taking turns was more reliable than one row when advancing. Only in holding or capturing a stationary target might the whole force strike at once, but it was considered bad tactics. There should always be reserves to respond in a moment.

Nearby foot soldiers acted as that reserve. The moment before Eld's stream faded, they were striking the Eurthan in turn, in short bursts. For some reason the Bane-weapon wasn't striking back. Eld wondered if the warrior was too injured or exhausted to command it.

But then it didn't matter. Suddenly a crossbow archer appeared, her blunt weapon propped on the top of the wall. Eld struck without thinking, hitting the woman in the chest. The Eurthan fell but it was too late. A shout of pain from a foot soldier revealed she'd been hit. The following stream of profanities damned the archer, the mother who birthed her and her harlot father to the deepest parts of the Void, but also told everyone within earshot the wound, while painful, wasn't mortal. The wounded soldier's war-sister laid down a sustained strike of flaming vengeance at the archer, but it was a wasted effort. The archer had disappeared, either fallen dead or wounded and dragged away. The armored Eurthan managed to drag herself over the wall, returning to her encampment.

Eld waited to see if the soldiers needed help, but the foot-soldier, though struck in the meaty part of her thigh, could limp. She was helped off the field, limping with her fellows, both angling lances in their retreat so they could strike if they needed to. The ranks closed up, waiting for more unwise Eurthans trying to pass.

Meanwhile the other two Eurthans who had fallen were making a nuisance of themselves on the eastern side, near the gap the Host was still hoping to break through. While their entangling ruse certainly upset and delayed the bulk of the force from coming over the wall, country rodeo tricks weren't going to keep an entire army at bay. And worse, three of the Bane-warriors had banded together and were making a good clearing around themselves as soldiers fell back before the strike that they were using to improved effect.

Much like line beaters, they took turns, presumably to conserve essence. Forks of blue fire erupted around them, destroying the remaining sinks. Then the strike became more focused, not fingers of seeking forks, but thick single forks, with minimal discharge, seeking targets among the Host while false thunder rolled over them. A crooked fork, perhaps thirty feet long , sought out an officer on her horse near the end of a line. Her horse reared as she was struck, the bluestrike wrapping around the horn of the unicorn barding before hitting the rider in a flash. Her sink protected her; instead of being roasted or maimed, she was blown out of her saddle, flying head over heels and somehow landing on her feet, though she fell to her knees. Her horse, having enough of this foolishness, bolted to the rear lines. The officer screamed curses at it as she got to her feet.

Then a whistle sounded: a command for feeding strike.

The women were angry and eager, and the sun was still bright. Two or three foot-soldiers started the stream. Soon they were joined by half a company. Feeding strike could be done on horseback or on foot, by anyone with a lance who saw a sister needed more strength to her fire. The stream was focused on one Eurthan, near her shoulder where the weapon sat. She would be blinded by the light, unless the helmet could protect against that too. In moments she'd be burning by the nimbus created, the singularity of sulessence as hot as a potter's furnace. As the rest of the company's strike joined it, the glare around the soldier becoming almost too bright to look at. Suddenly that individual fell back, not even striking, instead running in wild retreat.

But she struck behind her as she ran. That was when something strange happened: instead of seeking any one of the Sula soldiers, the strike forks curved back to discharge into the center of the remaining nimbus of the feeding strike. In seeking out the strongest source of essence, the blue strike sought the nimbus, to no effect on the troops. The Bane-warriors, perhaps perplexed and thinking they needed to use more magic, struck with a frenzy of blue strike, but every exploding fork recurved into the nimbus. And slowly the nimbus changed color, turning bright green. Eld had never seen such a thing as green strike.

The signal whistle warned the nimbus was losing its fire and to ground it at the Eurthans' feet. While most of the infantry continued feeding the singularity, a handful guided it with their lances to the ground, where it landed with a silent explosion of green light. The Eurthans nearby, uncertain of this new magic, dodged it as best they could. The light faded until only the bright green of grassy turfs remained.

Eld blinked. She looked back over the field. The grass stopped yards away, the main ravine where they were was rocky riverbed, almost completely dry after the early spring runoff. All along the wall the ground was the same, except for the place the nimbus had disappeared. Only here, perhaps six feet along the bottom length of the wall, was the grass bright and green, like after a rain, a little taller in the center than at the outside. Eld looked around for the Dwen. Perhaps this was the beginning of their work to take down the wall…

"You!" a voice shouted, insistent and demanding. Eld was not surprised to see the officer who had been thrown striding towards her on foot. But

Eld was slightly surprised it was Roel. Her black riding boots were dusty, but she otherwise wore similar gear over her dull green officer coat, including a plate and gorget much like Eld's. Her helmet was more substantial than Eld's metal flout and band, a pointed cap with graceful contours to protect the neck and cheeks, but not so closed as a foot-soldier's helmet that barely allowed a "T" shape in its face. Roel's long guardlocks swayed like twin metronomes as she stalked towards Fiorseth, Eld slowing the horse to a walk. Like all officers, Roel wore a sword as part of her gear, along with a service dagger and other sundry tools.

"Don't just stand there," Roel barked. "Turn around and let me up. I need to catch my idiot horse!"

Fiorseth shied back, picking up on Eld's reluctance to carry any dead weight, especially Roel.

"I'm not sure there's room with the sink," Eld said to stall while looking out over the field for a more pressing excuse. It would give her such joy to gallop off leaving Roel in a fit. But, alas, the Eurthans had stopped trying to break through for the moment, though the cavalry company was starting to mill. Eld listened for whistles, but there was nothing.

Meanwhile Roel had yanked off the remains of the damaged sink and was pulling herself up. Eld felt like the recipient of the unwanted attentions of a randy hound. Thankfully Roel was a good enough rider not to cling to Eld's back. Eld fought the urge to drive Fiorseth forward to make Roel fall. The quicker it was over with, the quicker they would be rid of her.

"Well, let's go!" Roel barked.

At least she was relatively light. Much like Eld, she was as fit as she needed to be, perhaps a little lighter, relying more on her elfyn vigor than regular exercise.

But Fiorseth was not pleased. No matter how strong a horse was, the fact was the medium weight mare was carrying two adult elfyn bodies that equaled at least twice weight of a foal and no horse was ever expected by fate to labor so. And that did not count the weight of the unicorn barding. Hoping to relieve more of the burden, Eld let her aura fill with the sun, then looked to get rid of Roel as quickly as possible. They trotted across the field making for the rear lines. Eld thought she saw a horse wandering in the scrub woods they passed, but it was shy. On their right was a healer's tent, sides open, a line of soldiers guarding the perimeter. Eld could just pick out Althas carrying a jug of water into the shade.

"Now there's a reason to malinger," Roel said. "That rut is a hungry harlot." Roel chuckled obscenely.

'Rut' was a much ruder word for a promiscuous man than 'slet'. Eld felt herself freeze, her whole body shivering with restraint.

"Some men are just drawn to motherly vigor--and purses, of course!" Roel laughed at her own wit. If Danshor's habit was annoying, Roel was positively revolting. "If your purse is heavy enough, you can get a harlot to agree to anything…"

Did Roel know who she was talking to? The dramatic conventions of revenge and murder contrived in the chaos of battle might occur more frequently on stage and in novels than in history, but they were based in fact. Roel could not possibly be stupid enough to provoke Eld in the midst of a battlefield. Eld endeavored to not reply, hoping Roel would tire of talking before they found her horse. But Roel was a curse, to herself and others.

"Many harlots will refuse to play with other brothers. But 'knowing a handle', they'll let you do that for only a little extra. My dagger hilt was deep in and well fertilized." She laughed again. "But it was the bindings that made it worth it. They wiggle so earnestly when they know they can't get away because they took your coin. He was hard all the same when I settled on him ..."

~Rear,~ Eld thought and Fiorseth enthusiastically obeyed, kicking the air in front of her with a great neigh. Keeping her seat was the most natural thing to Eld. But Roel wasn't expecting it and she tumbled off the back of Fiorseth's rump, landing face first on the ground.

Eld almost had Fiorseth gallop off. She thought briefly of lying, and claiming Fiorseth was spooked. Then she thought of trampling Roel into the ground and unfortunately Roel sprang to her feet and met Eld's murderous eyes while she shouted, "Can't you control your horse, you idiot cavalier?"

Fiorseth was champing, stamping her hooves dangerously. Eld started to understand her mind: Fiorseth didn't like Roel because she had seen Roel being harsh with horses.

And still Eld stared at Roel, gripping her lance, feeling the truth that, if she cared for no consequence, she could scorch Roel's eyes out.

Then Roel recognized her.

Instead of alarm or shock, she laughed. "Well, now you know he is a harlot! And is a fine ride, Gilded Hero. I didn't realize you were so sentimental. But you know men; they go with anyone who pays them." Then Roel's eyes hardened. "Now let me back up and find my horse, and I'll forget that little stunt."

"Sorry," Eld said, making no effort to hide her insincerity. "Fiorseth doesn't like you."

"It's just a damn horse and you're the rider."

Roel moved to mount. Fiorseth moved her hindquarters away, shuffling back without instruction from Eld, lowering her horn to wave it warningly; Eld didn't attempt to stop her.

"You used him to get to me," Eld said.

"Athmod's Legions, cavalier, he's a harlot! He takes money to be used. That's a harlot's business. And very pleasant business. Well, for me. He wasn't as enthused. But maybe his Gilded Hero will have learned a lesson from this ..."

"What's going on here?" Sergeant Tarl demanded, pulling her horse up beside Eld. Only then did Eld see the feeble grasses around Fiorseth's hooves had whithered with heat from her anger charged aura.

"This cavalier is refusing to help me find my horse after deliberately throwing me off!"

"Tresses, it this true?"

"Fiorseth doesn't like her," Eld said tonelessly.

The sergeant stared at Eld a moment, then said to Roel:

"Farthal is needed for the muster. You're going to have to find your horse on your own, emha."

Roel glared, then decided to say nothing more as she ran away.

"I heard truth in her voice," Tarl said. "I have to tell the captain!"

"Then tell her." Eld still seethed with rage.

"Farthal, after the battle, you will face discipline. Or a duel. Now stop burning the grass and muster!"

The air was suddenly less bright as Eld felt her anger fade to something controllable. Fiorseth fairly leapt forward, the mare also eager to burn off energy as they ran to join the muster.

The air was brighter again. But it wasn't the air, or the sun, or the day heating up to be equal to a day in midsummer, though it was still spring. It was Eld's lingering rage that, with her solstone epaulets and battle lance still in hand, made everything brighter and more energized than it ever appeared to calm eyes. And, Heavens above, could she see in the sunlight, as far as a hawk. The muster was nothing, just women on horses doing a country dance on a field. She saw a lone raven high in the trees on the ridge, watching the battle, flitting from tree to tree, wary of the peals of thunder and blue strike that erupted from the Eurthan forces lurking there. She spied a couple of Dwen slipping through the wood, presumably laying the roots of their woodcraft that were overdue to dismantle the wall. She spied also the details of the skirmish behind the Eurthan lines and saw the cavalier on foot finally surrounded, out powered and beyond any help from the Host. The woman clearly didn't care, moving like a demon, her sword flashing and clanging on the black armor of the five figures that surrounded her, fire running up and down its edge. They didn't even use strike; Eld expected they were toying with her, black swords batting her from woman to woman, yet she parried and danced well, still on her feet. But no soul needed Felkeni's eyes to see the end: they would crush her and she would join her horse beyond the Door.

No, Eld thought. Every soul counted.

Fiorseth was already moving while Eld hefted the lance. It would be a throw worthy of Jaro of the Dawn. For, while it was true a modern Sula battle lance was primarily a carrier for deadly sunstrike, it was still, in its nature, a lance. And a lance was just a fancy word for a spear.

First Fiorseth ran forward at a gallop, then twisted around, spinning Eld like a discus thrower. The mare stopped suddenly, hooves driving firmly into the hard earth like she'd been trained, while Eld threw the lance with their combined force through the air, buoyed by sulessence, faster than its weight would normally allow. There was not as much grim in a lance as a sniper's arrow, it could not carry as much memory. But neither was it as light or as likely to stray. And in her essence enhanced rage, Eld had given it perhaps thrice the power she'd been able to summon in regular exercise. Wondering eyes, both gold and burning Eurthani, watched the dart of metal sail through the air, its path strangely straight, skimming the heads of the Eurthan Host, missing the dome of a tent frame, to land in the back of a shelled woman, phenomenally piercing a weakness below her shoulder armor, breaking it and skewering her, and for good measure, dislodging her Bane weapon from its housing.

A roar of cheering went up from the Host. For a moment Eld was disoriented, her head swimming as her essence enhanced sight snapped back to normal. Blinking, she could barely see the woman or the wounded Eurthan, but she saw enough: whatever death wish the cavalier harbored had been abandoned. Perhaps seeing the Eurthan fall made her come to herself. In any case she had taken her opening, dodging around her attackers, and was running back to the lines. It would be a hard task, even as foot lances covered her with burst and feeding strike, blinding her Eurthan pursuers where they could. But Eld had a good feeling the woman would make it.

"Eld!" Tafli called a few feet away in the direction of the ridge.

Eld looked at the muster; they were readying another foray. But what could she could do without her lance? She sidled Fiorseth to the right, closer to Tafli.

"I need to join the muster!"

"After you are throwing away you lance?"

241

"There's probably another to be found."

It was likely true; a couple of their sisters had been wounded. Eld scanned the field for one laying on the ground but nothing was in sight.

"We are needing strong essence for the trees! And quickly! They are trying to use the Bane-monster again!"

Eld snapped her head up, wishing she could sight like she had moments ago. But she only saw the waving branches of dense firs behind the fluttering new leaves of the maples. Then she looked down at the gap, now filled with the foot host surging forward, the Eurthans falling back, perhaps too readily. Athmod's gaping craw, Tafli was right. And if the weapon struck again, with no sinks to bleed off its power, they'd be lucky not to lose several foot companies.

## Chapter 18

# The Green Strike Gambit

Eld drove Fiorseth at a gallop to join Tafli, passing him, then dismounting where the ground was soft and steep. Not only would it be impossible for Fiorseth to climb, but the trees above would be too dense for her to move effectively in her barding.

"Stay near and be wary, sister," Eld whispered to her, patting her neck. Fiorseth snorted, shook her head and moved a bit aways to seek cover as she was trained to do. Eld secured her sword on her baldric as Tafli caught up, trotting lightly on a thick narrow root that rose out of the ground a couple inches in front of him as he moved. Eld fell in behind him, and they both ran on it up the sandy embankment. The root thickened to widen at places, forming shallow steps for them to run up. Eld had never seen this much practical wood-essence in motion. She wondered if the root was a collection of plants Tafli had forced together, or an underground vine he'd pulled up. But when they reached the top of the embankment, she saw it was a middling sized root from a large maple near the edge at the top. As she watched the entire length sank back into the soil.

"I hide it so others may not use it," Tafli said. "I can be calling it again if we come back this way."

Eld considered herself an adept hunter, well skilled at woodcraft. But Tafli found her skill wanting, for he grabbed her arm and pulled her off a place she was about to step.

"Rocks there," he whispered as if the rocks would hear. "Eurthans trap Dwen on stone, so we are wary. Follow me exactly."

Eld didn't argue. They ran together almost silently, zigzagging through the ridge of beech, fir and maple, until they stopped near the top, hiding behind a cover of great ferns and thorn bushes. There was no birdsong but there were voices. Eld was embarrassed she didn't mark the other Dwen until she was almost stepping on them, the Oak Dwen woman, Yeladrin and the Ash Dwen man, Aredheli. Aredheli made a shallow "oh" of his mouth and blew silently. For a moment Eld though he was being strangely suggestive. Tafli breathed a whisper in Eld's ear:

"Quiet."

They crouched in the ferns, almost supine on the slope, listening for several moments. The voices became more distinct:

"Id iz nod bossible!" one woman said, reckless of being overheard.

"Zavages don't have znipers! Zhust feeble arrowz vrom wud bowz widh dwine vor zdring."

"Dell thad do Darnyn and zhee odher dwo in Demple. One had do be dragged back vrom dhe Odherzide. Zo, keep ur garapace on, und zat iz an order!"

"How am Ey going do zee?"

"Yew don't need do zee do zdrike widh a Meduza, boob. "

"Vine. Where'z dhe liewdenant?"

"Dhat green girl? Ha ztill walking up dhe var zide ..."

Eld could barely make out the dialect, being as the Eurthans were speaking amongst themselves. But she joined the Dwen in raising their heads to peek above the ferns. Belatedly Eld worried her flout would give them away, but the Eurthans were at least twenty yards distant and their vision significantly restricted by their helmets and visors. Still Eld tilted her chin up so her flout was lowered from view. She noticed the leaves of all the Dwen's yastols had laid flat like Little Acorn's.

The Eurthans were only a couple, but completely shelled as Eld expected from their conversation. They stood around the weapon, the 'Medusa'; Eld wondered if it implied the same thing in their dialect, an Athmod-like godling or demon from humyn mythology. The weapon itself was more baleful up close: unlike the Bane-weapons perched on the armor, its striking end wasn't triangular, but circular, with many rods of some metal or glass clustered together in its two-foot wide squat body. One end was capped and rounded like a strike cannon, but instead of a place to put a hand, it had two hefty handles on either side. The entire contraption sat on a thick tripod three or four feet high. They might say it needed no sight to aim, but its design argued it was more effective if a Bane-warrior had her target in sight.

At the moment though, they weren't sighting anything. One armored behemoth was clearing the area around the weapon, kicking twigs, branches and debris left by the previous soldiers out of the way, while the other was clearing their firing line above the embankment, almost directly above the gap the Host could be marching through. She did this roughly, ripping branches with her hands, cutting larger ones with her sword. Tafli seethed by Eld's side, breathing with a hiss, but waited for the moment.

~Soon friends,~ Aredheli said in their minds, avoiding even a hint of breath on the air.

Eld wondered if they needed to worry about being heard. Even with elfyn ears, the Eurthans probably couldn't hear them with helmets. But she also knew the risk was great and she trusted the Dwen had good reason to appear overcautious. Then Eld saw it, motion around the base of the weapon. Ivy was moving, but faster than ivy ever invaded any garden, whatever a gardener might claim.

Long vines had been creeping across the forest floor, unnoticed among the forest growth. Now four or five wrapped themselves around the legs of the tripod, accelerating their speed, the growth of weeks or months happening in seconds. A strangled cry from the Eurthan clearing the ground revealed she'd noticed. The words that followed, shouting in alarm, were too quick for Eld to make out, but probably a string of profanities and cursing.

The other Eurthan leaped forward to cut the vines, making a great racket of clangs and sparks as her sword struck the Medusa and the legs. But the vines only tightened, and growth cut, like the legendary Bane themselves, sprouted multiple replacement vines, until the entire machine was almost completely overgrown in seconds.

"Now, stand in the sunlight!" Tafli ordered, pushing Eld into a dappled open space by a young beech just leafing with white flowers. "We are needing your essence to help!"

"I don't have wood-essence!" Eld protested, pulling her sword, expecting the Eurthans to spot her and charge any moment.

"No silly, your sulessence. We will grow faster if we twine together." Tafli rolled his eyes at the guarded look on Eld face. "No, we will not be 'rooted', that you should be so blessed."

Without further ceremony the beech next to Eld wrapped a long sucker around her hips and middle, then over a shoulder on her solstone epaulets, like a strange living stole. Large leaves sprouted all along its length, unfolding broad and green, typical beech leaves but much wider, as if their intent was to soak up as much of the sun as possible. In the curling branchlet Eld felt the strength of the tree, the flow of sap echoing in her blood, the power of the absorbed sun like breathing vapor, bright, crisp and cool, flowing directly into her lungs. The air was almost as bright as when she had thrown the lance, but this brightness had a green cast, and it wasn't something she could control but something that flowed from her. Much like a tree, she was stationary while the Dwen controlled the effects. And while the sucker did have a serpentine sinuousness, its embrace was firm but moved enough to allow Eld to breathe. Eld felt no fear it would suddenly trap or strangle her. Why had Roel made such a fuss in the Rowan Oak? It was so calm and relaxing to be a tree ...

Meanwhile Tafli had run up and into the top of the tree, standing where the bole branched. Tafli's balance and ankle twinings kept him in place, while he held onto two bole forks in each hand, his wrist vinings attaching themselves for stability or more essence contact.

Then the whole tree moved.

It wasn't the only one. Aredheli was perched in a maple, and another maple revealed Dwen activity, but from Eld's vantage she couldn't tell if it was Yeladrin or Olyeth. But she could see a ranger standing next to it, much like herself, wrapped in the embrace of friendly suckers, with new overlarge essence grown leaves. Surely Dwen didn't need Sula for this operation; Eld had heard of treeriders. But she imagined it made things easier, being a conduit of concentrated sunlight. Eld wondered how this would be managed when the tree moved. But just as Tafli had extended a root for them to walk up, this was reversed, so the place the suckers grew was left behind and the tree moved, roots rippling underneath the soil like the coils of a deep sea creature, the centermost deepest roots acting like anchors for stability, only moving last. It wasn't a fast action, perhaps a foot a second, but when one considered trees usually didn't move at all...

Above the crowns rustled, birds hitherto lurking silently quickly taking flight. The small casualties of bushes and herbs crushed or uprooted couldn't be avoided. The Eurthani were in a panic, spinning around, horrified at the moving trees. Eld wondered how they knew that wasn't an ordinary occurrence in these strange lands, far from their home. Apparently, in spite of living in cities far underground, they were conversant with the regular flora in the same way Eld herself was conversant with many customs of humyn tribes she'd never visited.

One Eurthan tried to use the Medusa, but it was so choked with the quick growing ivy, now thickened to the size of tree branches, it no longer pivoted. Her sister rotated the demon on her shoulder and a thick fork of blue strike cut the air. But it split almost equally between the three moving trees, and though it struck them, something odd happened: just like on the field when the blue strike hit the bright nimbus, the place it hit turned green. Eld felt a surge of energy through her feet, as if coming from the deeps of Eurath herself. Entwined with the wood-essence and her active sulessence, she understood: the blue strike was a kind of earth-essence, echoing the patterns of elemental motes that exchanged energy during a storm. This was why it looked so much like lightning. But while it had been made to destroy, at its root it was neutral, like water that could quench thirst or drown. Meeting sulessence under certain conditions shifted the blue strike into an energizing force that gave more power to wood-essence. In short, the trees moved faster, the vines grew thicker with greater speed, and while the three treeriders – Eld could see Yeladrin now – appeared shocked or startled, they were not hurt. The two Eurthans fled as a third shelled figure appeared, seeming to shout at them, waving her sword in an authoritative fashion for all the good it did. Then she faced the looming trees and seemed to freeze, sword forgotten.

It was impossible to see this newcomer's face behind the frosted crystal or glass of her visor. But the next moment she leapt forward, attacking Tafli's tree with her sword. In the blink of an eye, a branch the width of an arm whipped down and threw the armored woman back with a blow to her chest. She fell several feet away on her back. The trees moved on.

The trees were converging on the Medusa, which was now hidden under a mound of thick ivy. But Eld imagined a determined soul could free it, with fire if nothing else. And so the Dwen moved the trees around it, and for good measure sprouted and wove the lower branches into a barrier so thick no soul could see, much less get through. It was in this way Eld knew six millennia ago the Forest had barred passage from what would be future Federation lands after The Outrage of the Forest, an offense against Dwenoshire so great that even today it was discussed in hushed voices. Worse than the Burning, the shame drove the monarchy of Sunqueens to abdicate.

It also forced Sula to discover woodcraft and develop industries to make things that for millennia they had depended on trade with the Dwen for. When the border was lifted a century later, both nations had changed forever. Eld had seen the trees that remained from the Great Barrier, mostly daughter trees, but a few were twisted, suckered and wind weathered partitions of the original wall, kept alive by the wood-essence of the locals. It was possible millennia from now this edifice might still stand, a wooden cocoon of an ancient fell weapon.

The trees stopped moving, branches swaying in a final dance of whispering rustles, and the Dwen climbed down. The sucker that embraced Eld unwound, straightened, then froze. It would grow like this into its own tree in time. Absently Eld realized she still held her sword. She gripped it harder, looking among the ferns for where the Eurthan had fallen. The Dwen were standing around the area she was last seen. Eld heard Tafli say: "And now you will feel the revenge of the forest!"

Eld rushed forward to see the warrior was almost covered with vines and tree roots, not just seeking to bind, but to crush. Aredheli and Yeladrin looked on grimly.

"No!" Eld shouted, grabbing Tafli and jerking him around. "Our orders are to drive them home!"

"Your orders." He pulled himself out of her grip. "We will take our vengeance for the boys stolen. Do not take liberties with you hands!"

"Look, I know about you and Alhern!"

"You know what?" Tafli demanded, green eyes flashing. "That I bring kin to help is all you know!"

"Fine! But the commander has made it clear we are to let them flee if we can!"

"They do not deserve mercy!"

"Not for mercy! But so we don't give them a reason to return!"

Yeladrin sighed and looked away. She knew.

"This is true," the ranger said. Eld was shocked to see it wasn't Captain Draeyn as she'd assumed but Orinac, the ranger Tafli evicted. "I am not the best soul when it comes to the matter of men – " Tafli snorted – " ...But by letting them flee they may stay away. And not come back for revenge."

"They never needed a reason to invade the forest before except for sport," Aredheli said. "They have seen the might of the trees and two witnesses escaped. Let this one feed the forest!"

Mothers forgot that men too could be murderous if their calls for justice had gone unrequited. A horrible screeching sound of thickening roots squeezing metal came from where the warrior lay. Then the ferns suddenly exploded and Eld ducked to avoid flying pieces of armor.

Blinking she saw the vines and branches waving in active wood-essence, holding pieces or partial pieces of black armor. Leaping to her feet was the warrior inside, now only in the padded, black skin suit, grabbing her sword from the remains of her baldric harness. Either the shell had released automatically or she'd seen it was the only way to avoid death. She was tall, slightly taller than Eld, but slimmer, her strength compact and wiry. Her skin was a pale silver gray, eyes bright blue and her white cropped hair looked like nothing so much as a bowl upended on her head, the line ending just above her ears; the hair close to her neck was shaved almost to stubble. She sprang away like a cat, evading the roots and vines that sought to trap her again.

Eld glanced at the ranger Orinac and they shared a look of understanding: they needed to bring the woman down or herd her away before the Dwen got their roots on her again. Eld hoped Tafli would forgive her.

The Dwen's feelings were understandable, but they did not see the greater picture: the Eurthans who had harried and harassed the borders of Ta Dwenoshire for so long were simple greedy and venal adventurers. Such women were understood to be acting on their own and responsible for their own fate. But this force had the blessing of the Eurthan's government of mothers, and they seemed, however misguidedly, to believe they were exercising their rights. If any mother's daughter died irretrievably, Eld was certain there would be consequences. In their own history, elfyn lost irretrievably to humyn in border patrols near Sharitan, even Thyn horses, were avenged. Attempts were made to find the individuals responsible, who were killed without ceremony. If they no longer lived, the property or legacy given to their descendants, be it house or tent, was destroyed. Technically the laws had never changed, though retributive actions had not been taken for several centuries. However one felt about these laws – and some believed their time was past – the Eurthans seemed to have a much harsher view of nations they considered "lesser". It took no imagination for Eld to see them returning with a vast conquering force in retribution. Their best course for the nation, indeed, both nations, was to give them no reason to consider it.

And so Eld's arm shivered as her sword met the Eurthan's black grim blade. Eld imagined her sword would shatter, but, for the moment, it held, showering sparks over the damp forest floor. Orinac engaged the Eurthan on her other side, where, irritatingly, the woman was holding a long dagger that might as well have been a sword. She was skilled, even for elfyn. She spun and danced, unlike Eld, free of even light armor, or the shadow cloak the Ranger favored. Soon Orinac shed it, trying to entangle and blind the Eurthan, but such tricks didn't slow the woman down. She even seemed to have a knack of where to step, never missing a firm place in the soft loam, always on a fallen log or the only large stone for yards around. If Eld wasn't mistaken, the woman was enjoying herself, as if she rarely was challenged in practice.

But worse, Eld and Orinac weren't able to drive her back. Perhaps she didn't understand the condition of the Medusa, but she seemed insistent on reaching it herself.

"Leave it!" Eld yelled. "Just go and take your Bane-force with you!"

Instead the elf ran at them, spun over their heads to land behind them, but that was a mistake. Two branches of the maple tree snatched her out of the air and bound her feet so she hung upside down.

Still she held on to her weapons, trying to cut at the branch, only to be jerked around until she stopped.

"Hornz up! Zat iz unzpording!" she objected.

"So is violating our men!" Yeladrin yelled.

"What?" the Eurthan said. Yeladrin tried to take her weapons, but the Eurthan swiped at her dangerously. "Vree me!" she demanded.

Suddenly she fell, twisting at the last moment to land on her feet. Then she stood in guard, ready to fight again.

"Let us escort her back to her Host," Eld suggested to Yeladrin, holding one hand up, hoping the Eurthan understood she was trying to let her go.

"What?" Aredheli said. "So she may ravish more men?"

The Eurthan understood this time. But she didn't smirk—her eyes widened, twin fiery blue pools of alarm.

"Zy never do dhis!" she exclaimed. "Do any man!"

Tafli snorted in disbelief, but Aredheli's face changed to curiosity.

"Then what do you say when your sisters brag about their deeds?" Aredheli asked.

"What deedz?"

"Rapine!" Tafli shouted.

"No one doz dhiz! Whe are biouz und honorable!"

The Dwen looked at each other. Eld wasn't expert in truth, but the woman's words did not feel false.

"You cannot be possibly not be knowing this!" Tafli yelled. "Dozens of boys taken every year!"

But the Eurthan shook her head, baffled before his righteous anger. Tafli looked to Yeladrin, rolling his eyes.

Yet Yeladrin shook her head, her expression as perplexed as the Ash Dwen. "Her words are true," she said.

"Remember her sisters who fled?" Eld put in. "If I understood, they called her callow and young. You're an officer, correct? A lieutenant?"

"Dhird Lewdenant Brig, yez." Brig still held her weapons out in guard.

"Does it matter?" Tafli said. "So she is young and green, and they have not taught her the joys of despoiling men. One day she will be doing the same--"

"Never!" Now Brig's guard had dropped, outrage getting the best of her. "Zy do nod ever dake men!Against dheir will!" The last was added almost as an after thought.

Eld smirked. "I think she's a virgin."

"Zat iz a lie," Brig said, pointing with her dagger for emphasis.

"Well, this is truth," Eld said taking a serious tone. "Our commander only wants your forces gone. We've been ordered to avoid killing if possible. We already know this is some misguided exercise. But these are Federation lands and the Forest Nation. Your invasion is making mothers and men fear for their safety. And according our Dwen allies your people have been abusing and kidnapping men for some time. It will only get worse the longer you stay. If we weren't here," Eld motioned to Orinac and herself, "You would already be dead."

"Who are you to determine if she is to go free?" Aredheli demanded. "You're not even an officer."

Eld could have slapped him. The Eurthan didn't know that, and now it was less likely she'd take Eld as an authority.

"No, I'm not an officer," Eld added forcefully, "I'm Lancer Elderyn Farthal and I am intimate with the commander's house." If there was ever a time to trade on her liaison with Seth, it was now. "And I have heard her say to drive you back to the Void – her words not mine. What would happen if we killed your lot?"

"We marg under Godz will. Godz will not be zwarted."

"So you would return."

"Yez."

"Perhaps in a century?"

Brig stared at her. Then she laughed. "Zat iz a djoke." Her mood sobered. "Zy am only a lewdenant. Zy do nod make dhese dezisionz. Dhis land is vronteir zavage land – "

"It's not the damn frontier if people live there!" Eld barked.

"And we are not being savages taking other mother's men!" Tafli added.

Brig looked uncertain. "Zy have orderz to dake the Meduza."

"It's gone," Eld said, waving at the three trees twined together for emphasis. "And so is your shell. You should run while you can. Whether you have raped men yourself or not, these Dwen still want to murder you."

"Execute," Tafli corrected.

Eld sighed. "You can't call it an execution without a trial."

"We will have a trial," Aredheli declared.

"We don't have time ..."

But Eld's protests were ignored. Orinac glanced at her in sympathy but shrugged. Neither was eager to interfere with the twinings, literally or figuratively, of angry Dwen. Aredheli stood in front of the Eurthan officer Brig while ivy slithered around the forest floor towards her at Aredheli's bidding. Brig's glowing blue eyes widened in sudden fear, then she exhaled with relief.

"It's just the same vines covering the Medusa," Eld said.

"Zey loog lige znakes."

"I'm not found of snakes myself," Eld said while she stifled a laugh. An officer from the Bane-like legions was possibly a virgin and afraid of snakes. No poet could have invented such a tale. The next moment the vines were whipping around Brig, binding her in a cocoon.

"Do not move if you want to live!" Aredheli ordered.

Brig had dropped her weapons and now only her face was visible. The vines thickened, then stopped.

"Nowadays we do things differently," Aredheli said. "But we are far away from Ash City and old ways are still used in the deep forest. This is the trial of Truth and Thorns." Aredheli paused, knowing the fear that lurked in the woman now. "I could crush you into nothing, send you screaming through the Door. Or rip each limb from your body in turn. Mothers have done as much for vengeance before. But the cavalier wants your soul to be judged fairly, though there was no fairness from your people in stealing so many men and boys. Still, you will have this gift since we agree to help the Sula by their ways. But remember, as she said, were it in our hands, you would already be dead."

Aredheli took a step back. Little Acorn and Olyeth had just stepped into the clearing.

"Half the Wall is down!" Olyeth declared. "Suddenly it was easy! The Eurthans are retreating but slowly ..." Sighting the tableau, she paused.

"What is this?" Little Acorn demanded, her massive form looming near the bound Eurthan.

"A trial," Aredheli said. He looked like a king from a rare land, his yastol crown-like and erect again, his fine tree silks drifting on the slight breeze. "If your answers reveal a true heart, we set you free. If they reveal malice, you die by thorn.

"What is your name, Eurthani?"

"Dhird Lewdeant Aleen Brig ov Our Avatar's Holy Legions!"

Orinac and Eld shook their heads.

"They don't half think highly of themselves, do they?" Orinac said.

"Danshor has more humility," Eld added.

"Hush you both! Listen!" Tafli hissed.

"Why have your people attacked our lands?" Aredheli asked, continuing his interrogation.

"Zy, Zy am told we are do defend zhe borders, dat threats do dhe vronteir must be removed."

Aredheli's green eyes narrowed. "Have you ever attacked or despoiled a man or boy from our lands?"

"Never!"

Aredheli stepped closer, asking the next question almost intimately: "Have you ever attacked or despoiled a man or boy, or found merriment when hearing someone has?"

Eld was certain this last question was Aredheli questing for an excuse to kill the Eurthan.

"Never!" the Eurthan answered.

252

"Have you ever desired to do so and only lacked the means or opportunity?"

"Tresses, man!" Eld blurted. "What mother hasn't had an errant thought or two in her youth?"

Aredheli didn't even look at Eld, but threw his hand back for her silence, greatly assisted by a glower from Little Acorn.

Brig stared directly into Aredheli's eyes, her blue ones meeting his green, two souls from two vastly different worlds, each seeking to find fault or falsehood. But they both failed.

"Never," Lieutenant Aleen Brig said, her voice full of the same certainly that as she had in the righteousness of her literalist nation.

Something passed between them, the Dwen and the Eurthan. For a second Brig's eyes glowed a deeper blue as if she was excited or aroused. Aredheli stepped back suddenly, then caught himself, standing tall and haughty once again. The front of the cocoon unwove, leaving the form of Brig's body as she stepped out from its embrace. Slowly she retrieved her weapons. Eld gripped her sword, but Brig simply held the sword, reversing her grip so it hung down. They were the same height, Aredheli and Brig, and now there was no mistake they looked at each other with a deeper interest. Little Acorn narrowed her eyes, not looking pleased.

Eld walked over to where the remains of the Brig's armor lay and fished out her baldric with a little help untwining vines from Olyeth. Eld handed it to Brig and they all stood in silence while she arranged her gear.

"Zy vill tell ov dhis miztake," Brig said. "Dhat dhese are not zavage landz but are defended. But Zy do not know what will happen dhen."

"Then tell them this too," Aredheli said, pointing at the empty cocoon. The next second thorns the size of daggers erupted filling the inside, half a foot long and so thick, had Brig still been inside, she would have instantly died.

"Look and remember; we could have killed you. We are not savages, unless we are treated like savages."

Brig turned to go, then paused.

"Vat iz your name?" she asked.

"Aredheli, son of the Tree Mother Margynweld, of Haldwynshor. Our Sula cousins call it, Ash City. It is in the center of Ta Dwenoshire, in the north. I gift you a welcome. Ask for me if you find yourself there."

"Id vaz my pleazhur do meet you, noble zir," Brig said.

"If you would dare to return." Little Acorn interjected, using her deep voice, and it was deeper than most souls. "You would be wise to forsake this tribal arrogance. Your people forget the truth: we Five are One, our fore-mothers were all daughters of Er."

Er, the greatest elfyn city there ever had been, lost in the Cataclysm, de-stroyed by the Dying Star that ruined the Orb for eons after. It had taken millennia to repair the damage and much had been lost forever. But elfyn memory was long and the dreams of Er remained. Out of the ground two suckers of beech sprouted, about three feet apart, growing and thickening in seconds to just above their heads. While they grew, they twisted as if cir-cling an invisible cylinder, making a living helix. Halfway up the total height a sprout emerged from each coil, perfectly parallel to the ground, meeting each other in the center. From that center a point of wood extended both above and below it, the form finished until it made a perfectly symmet-rical four pointed star that appeared to hover in the center of the helix. This device was known to all of Er's daughters, the Helix Star or Astalyn, the an-cient symbol of all the Elfyn people. It was a monument size image of the smaller curios sold to tourists by artisans in Falls Gate.

"Only Eurthans are breaking the Taboo: elfyn do not war against elfyn ," Little Acorn continued, passing judgment on the wanting. "If you dare to return remember that. Remember Er. One People, One Duty. Always, and Forever. Now begone!"

Brig nodded, bewildered more than afraid, but ran, as if knowing Felkeni held a door open for her not much longer. In moments she had disappeared down the hillside.

"Now, how did you decide to let her being free?" Little Acorn demanded. "Is she Shindi? They do not cut their hair so."

"No, but her soul is clean," Aredheli said. "Sacrificing an innocent to satisfy vengeance will only bring more vengeance."

"I can't argue with that," Eld said. She was worried about what she was missing below. Being with the Dwen made time flow differently. Eld didn't know if it was the proximity of their auras or her interaction with wood-essence. But the Federation army did not tolerate tardiness for any reason.

"What's happening below?" she demanded, striding towards where the Eurthans had been ripping the trees for a better line of sight. Now it would serve them; she'd have a clear vantage of the ravine. Distantly Eld heard the occasional shout and several whistles sounded, but too indistinct to know their message. Orinac fell in beside her while the Dwen trailed behind.

"You said the wall is down?" Eld asked the Dwen.

"Half the wall," corrected Olyeth. "Suddenly we had the essence force and leverage, and it yielded."

Eld was certain that was where the green strike hit the ground.

"So the Host is marching through?"

"Slowly," Little Acorn rumbled.

They broke through the thin flora near the edge, but not so near they were in danger of falling. Eld was certain she saw the tree she'd been thrown against slightly below them. To the right was the remains of a tree shattered by strike days ago, a long straight pine, its bole removed, only its jagged stump remaining. The view was both stunning and illuminating:

Finally Eld could see the scope of the Eurthan operations, their camp dwarfed by white ridges of the Altans in the distance. Behind the wall, the open ground was bare before the first tents, the domed silk covered constructs mostly bare metal rods now, burnt fabric fluttering listlessly. The tents were spaced alternating, like cells in a bee hive, most of a size four women might fit, but Eld wondered how that would reckon with their armor. Did the shells stand in one piece when not in use? Or were they stored more compactly?

Then the regular lay of tents was broken, alternating with tents about twice the size, Eld would guess officers and personal staff, or even supplies. After came the massive tent that could be seen from the ground, not just to house an important officer, but the entire field command. On the other side of this, to the far north and east, was a collection of works Eld didn't grasp at first; three shallow domed pavilions and what seemed to be round stepping stones and metal mesh, flat-topped pillars scattered around them. Then she saw the great pots, large enough a woman could bathe in. It was an outdoor mess. There was even a well. And possibly a hospital. A handful of unshelled Eurthans lingered, along with a couple of white robed figures. Did they too have men assisting healers?

Wisely this hospital activity was to the rear of their lines. Below, where they stood, Eld saw a scrum of the Host rushing over the fallen wall, that, sure enough, was now chunks of rubble, at least up to where the green-strike had manifested. The Host was spreading out, filling the gaps between the tents, slowing wisely to reform in case they were surprised by hidden archers. The cavalry company rode up and down by the wall, remaining on the Sula side, giving the foot host cover by bursts of strike. The magi finally felt bold enough to hover high in the air above the wall; a keen eye could see large rocks dropping from the wall as if by invisible teams of sappers. The magi seemed to be opening the way, now and then a rock sailed through the air, as if by a catapult, into the Eurthan ranks, where the women either let themselves be hit, their armor freezing protectively, or struck at the missile, which didn't seem to do much to destroy or deflect it. The Bane-weapons, deadly to the living, weren't optimized to destroy structures.

On the Eurthan side, to the north, their ranks massed together, looming hulks of black metal in the early afternoon sun, waiting for the Host to get close enough to strike. It bothered Eld they clearly had no intention of being routed. It seemed both forces were pausing, seeking the best way to make an advantage.

Nearer, right below them, a wide column of a foot company started marching through the gap in the wall, somehow knowing the bane-weapon had been disabled. Ahead of them the Eurthans stayed just out of easy strike range while also guarding any path to the command tent. If no side gave soon, they would be forced to fight at close quarters and Eld didn't like their chances if it came to that. Unless they used the Dwen like the Dwen had used her....

"Where's Captain Draeyn?" Eld asked out loud.

"Down the slopes with the rangers," Orinac said.

Eld shook her head, watching her fellow cavaliers riding to and fro, strike bursting from the lances every few moments. She was suddenly concerned for Fiorseth.

"I should be down there," Eld said. "Look, we can't depend on a message of good will from a green lieutenant to get them to go away. Both of us will lose souls if it gets more fraught."

"What can be done?" Yeladrin said. "The ground is dry and rocky, the water deep, and we have little leverage from here."

"When blue strike meets sunstrike—like there!" Eld cried, pointing to where a blue fork of light struck a firing lance and a green halo surrounded both parties. "It enhances wood-essence! Feel it! When Brig struck at the trees ..."

"Yes, I felt that!" Aredheli said. "It was like a healing draught from Eurath herself!"

"I wonder if hitting their blue strike will make the same effect?" Eld mused taking out her signal whistle. As a regular troop, not an officer, she was only permitted to use it during operations as an emergency measure. "With enough green strike do you think you can do something with the plants there?" Eld asked.

"There's nothing but grass and brambles," Orinac muttered, but the Dwen smiled.

"Brambles are the humble defender of the forest," Yeladrin said. "We've already laid a root network to take down the wall. We can do more than some one thing."

Eld blew the whistle, a series of notes:

1st: new tactic, with urgency.
2nd: direct spare strike to meet blue strike.
3rd last: yield to Dwen action; prepare to move asunder.
It was much quicker in code; Eld repeated it to be certain the message was sent. She held her breath. Three seconds later an acknowledgement sounded, with notation the signaler would report the irregular action to command.

"Field command knows," Eld said. "Be ready."

Eld left them, running through the ferns and dappled quiet forest to find her way back down. In some ways it was easier. While she didn't have the moving root stair Tafli had made, it wasn't far down, maybe a twenty foot drop at the lowest point, and Eld simply let herself drop, rolling a little before coming to her feet. It was free of Sula or Eurthans, though the hospital tent could be seen. She cast her mind around for Fiorseth, calling the horse's name out loud.

Eld heard no response. Looking around at the ground, Eld saw the path the mare had taken, away from the battle, they way they'd come. She tracked her for a few moments, then stopped as the sounds of the engagement rose. They were closer, but more seemed to be happening, the thunder and cracking of blue strike through the air, the rush of sunstrike creating flames, and what sounded like a stampeding clang of metal. Eld smiled, hoping the green strike gambit was working. Then there was the sound of galloping ahead and Fiorseth broke cover, emoting elation on seeing Eld. Another horse with unicorn barding was with her, a roan mare who followed Fiorseth as if she was her sister. With a sinking feeling Eld could guess who owned the other horse. Sure enough, the sounds of cursing came from the brush behind the horses.

"Athmod rotting pair of nags!" Roel's voice sounded.

Eld quickly mounted her mare before Roel came into view.

"There you are, Farthal! You'll pay for this!"

"For what, exactly?" Eld wanted to laugh but didn't dare. Had Roel been chasing after the horses all this time?

"Your blasted nag has been a wayward influence on my horse!" Roel exclaimed.

"Surely the control of your horse isn't my or my mount's responsibility," Eld said. She failed to stifle a snort.

"You think this is funny, Farthal?"

"With apologies, emha, I must join my company!" Eld said driving Fiorseth forward into a gallop, Roel's horse close behind them.

They left Roel far behind. If she hadn't been so busy berating Eld, she could have mounted her horse with plenty of time. Now Eld had two horses in her care and that would not do. She made a detour to the commander's mound slowing down to explain herself to an aide.

"I found Lieutenant Roel's mount, but the horse appears to prefer to follow me instead of Roel. Could you care for her?" Not only would it be further humiliation, but the truth of it would be marked, aborting any complaint about Eld stealing or waylaying the mare.

A woman grabbed the horn on the roan's saddle and patted her neck, saying soft words making the mare stop.

"My thanks!" Eld said. "Any one have a spare lance?"

"Hark!" a voice called from the healers tent. A soldier hefted it and threw it high above Eld. She turned and galloped back into the field, timing it so she caught the lance without stopping. Then she headed to rejoin the battle.

The engagement was unrecognizable. Almost the entire foot host was now behind the ruins of the wall and they were systematically moving in disciplined ranks, striking in bursts as the Eurthani fell back. The cavaliers were leaping the wall, now with plenty of room to maneuver behind it and galloping to harry and herd the Eurthans north, then east, back to where the door to their land lay. Still they didn't flee outright, but that was in part because many couldn't. Among the bright flashes of Bane-strike, many were now striking the lightning-like forks instead of the warriors themselves. It both bled much of the force of the blue strike, and the remaining magical power turned green as it hit the ground. Almost instantly long grasses appeared entangling Eurthans' feet wherever they could. While this was mostly a nuisance, for the grasses came up in clods easily, it distracted the Eurthans and kept them from staying in ranks for fear they might be twined and trapped by something more serious.

That fear was real, for where a dormant seed of bramble was in the aura of the green strike, it spouted alarmingly fast. Some tribes of bramble came from the harsh and rain barren hills of deepest Sharitan, and while they could bear a gift of the blackest sweet berries in late summer, they could also be a nuisance, so vigorous they were with their sharp, protective thorns. Under the combined forces of elemental elfyn magic they sprouted fast and deadly, wrapping ankles, seizing swords, and even pulled some shelled women to the ground so, like Brig, they had to escape their armor and run away, leaving all behind. Seeing this, many Eurthans turned and ran but

258

could go no further than their fellows and were forced to run around them for their manner of battle and gear did not make directly fleeing in armor viable.

In that fray, to Eld's delighted astonishment, she glimpsed Little Acorn striding into a flank of Eurthans while vines and brambles thick as saplings erupted around her passage, a testament of how much her essence vigor equaled her physical brawn. She touched no Eurthan except through root and vine, entangling and snatching the armored figures, tossing them aside like children's dolls. Bane-warriors who came too close found swords and Bane-weapons snatched from their hands to be wisely thrown far from their grasp. Eld worried Peyteor would be struck, her own vigor being her bane, but, though the Eurthans tried, blue forks of Bane-fire striking her aura, a group of foot soldiers worked with her, sending rapid bursts of sunstrike ahead of her, anticipating the murderous intent of the Eurthans to destroy this savage master of murderous green-strike. But it was to no avail. Vines twined into deadly roots, roots joined into woody snakes grasping like octopi, ripping more than one armored woman off her feet, forcing her to escape her armor. One did not move fast enough and had the further ignominy of being seized by the scruff in Peyteor's hand and tossed like a doll for a handful of yards. She scrambled to her feet and ran, fleeing with the rest, adding to the disorganized scrum.

Eld laughed, then directed Fiorseth forward; it was time to rejoin the battle. She galloped to and fro, helping her sister cavaliers harry the Eurthans either with strike to protect the advancing foot soldiers, or adding to the green strike whenever they could. Eld knew without a sink she had to move quicker than the rest. She watched with satisfaction as a particularly large armored woman was caught by the ankles. The woman foolishly aimed her weapon to the ground. Eld grinned and sent a burst of strike hitting at exactly the same instant.

The blue and gold changed to green and the nimbus hovered, deeper and stronger than Eld had ever seen. There was no bramble at the Eurthan's feet, but the grasses swelled to the size of small bamboo, and twined around her ankles so fast that even though she willed her armor to break apart so she could escape, one ankle remained trapped. She tried to grab her sword from the tangle of fallen baldric but got her hand trapped for her effort.

Then another figure leaped forward, unshelled yet bold, and with one sword cut the woman's hand free, only slightly cutting her suit. The newcomer drove down another sword, no, a very long dagger at the grass holding the ankle, but already it had thickened to a small tree.

"Yew vant uz gone? Help me vree dhe Madjor!" the woman said. Eld peered through the bright flashes to see Brig.

No sooner had Eld seen Brig than the agile Eurthan woman sprang to change her feet, keeping herself from being trapped. The trapped woman glared at up at Eld hatefully, red eyes burning in a black face. Eld noticed some insignia at her collar, something that looked like small twin dragons. Major? Damn, that was an officer of note. Perhaps being saved would impress her enough to listen to the junior Brig ...

"Squint or you'll be blind!" Eld shouted. Then she struck the ground, but not on the woman's foot, for there was a real danger she might burn it to ash. No, she struck near the foot, focusing on burning the grasses. The woman shouted and swore, her foot burned, but whole enough to limp on. When the light cleared the woman was standing, leaning on Brig, a charred part of the grass root still wrapped around her ankle.

Suddenly Danshor was at Eld's side, lowering her lance for a burst.

"Easy as cooking fish in a weir!" she crowed.

"No!" Eld shouted, knocking the lance aside. The burst hit an already burning tent, the flames brightening for a moment and curling with smoke.

"What are you doing?"

"I have the same question, Farthal!" Alhern demanded behind them.

Eld spun Fiorseth around. Alhern was actually ten yards behind them, with two of her staff and four magi, a couple hovering overhead. With them a donkey dragged something on a cart about the size of a large plow covered with a black tarp.

"Well?" barked Alhern.

"They're fleeing!" Eld shouted back, glancing at Brig and the wounded officer limping back with her. They were far enough away from the ground seething with plants that a guard of shelled women surrounded them, hiding them from view.

"Get back here!" Alhern ordered.

Eld had Fiorseth canter to join the Commander's entourage.

"You too, cavalier!" This was directed at Danshor, who dutifully followed. Once standing next to Alhern's horse, the commander blew a series of notes:

Ranks were to fall back in a wide arc around her position.

Instantly the foots melted from the front to either side, until no soul stood on the ground now covered with burnt and broken Eurthani tents and gear, and masses of quick grown grasses and brambles that consumed abandoned Eurthani armor and equipment, smothering all under a carpet of green leaves and thorny vines.    If the Dwen didn't stop, the brambles would be impassible to horses and women.  Perhaps that was a good thing.

All the while they watched the clearing of this verdant soulless land, Alhern was demanding an explanation from Eld.

"Not of the release of the Eurthans," Alhern clarified.  "Of course we want them to flee.  But the irregular orders you signaled."

"Oh.  I apologize for acting out of turn.  But ..."

"Don't," Alhern cut in.  "It was brilliantly effective.  I just want to know how you came by this ruse.  Briefly."

Eld gave her an account of the Dwen disabling the 'Medusa' on the ridge.

"Hmm," Alhern looked above to their right, musing.  "Well, you're not the only one with an active mind, Farthal.   You'll want to move several paces to the side, women.  Ta Narin, if you please."

Eld and Danshor shifted their mounts as bidden, as the magi Narin pulled off the tarp in one sweeping motion, revealing a portable field solstone cannon.

"We use it at the abbey for research," Narin said.  "As you can see it's only half the size of a military field cannon ..."

"Better little, than bereft," Alhern said.

All size was relative.  It certainly was much smaller than the cannons fixed on the garrison's walls. The tube of solstone was several inches wide and a yard long.   The cart it had been carried on was stabilized into a platform, giving it some height.  Then it was placed on a tripod and cranked even higher so it now sat eight feet or so above the ground, the tube parallel to the ground, one of the magi standing with it on the cart to aim and presumably strike.  It had been years since Eld was tasked in class to calculate the sulforce of stone by length and thickness.  Besides, a target never wondered or cared how its pain was calculated on paper.   The fact was, even the strike from this small cannon could kill an Eurthan in her armor, if not by breaching it, then by cooking her to the core, especially on such a bright day.

But the afternoon was wearing on, and the sky, while still clear, was clouded by the haze of smoke and strike they'd made.  Alhern was doubtless alert to this and moved her horse forward a bit from them, holding a field horn in her hand.  In proper wars, there would be a herald appointed for this task.  But Alhern waved away an aide volunteering for the task, impatient for it to be over.

First she blew the horn, a long note in a universal signal to hark and listen.  Eld was a bit impressed at the length of the tone.  All elfyn were musical to some degree, but deep, sonorous instruments were something of a specialty, usually the province of orchestras. The horn was a deep alto and echoed throughout the ravine, up and over the ridge and around them. Later it was known to be heard from Falls Gate to the Green Barnsted Canal Station almost ten miles to the south of them. When the last strains had just about faded, Alhern spoke, her voice enhanced to echo, not quite as far, but it was clearly heard in Gate Step and the Abbey:

"Greetings, Host of the Eurthantian Realm, understood to be a nation ruled by the Avatar who claims to speak for the Mother Gods. We do not dispute these claims at this time. But we do object to your unprovoked and unjust attack on Federation Lands. As Commander Major Selind Alhern of Falls Gate Keep it is my duty to defend these same lands. We do not have a quarrel with your people except for these actions, and do give our word, as mothers of honor, that if you withdraw now, you will be allowed to escape without pursuit.

If you do not withdraw, you shall be forced to do so to the best of our ability. We have seen your great strike, a Medusa it is called. If you do not instantly retreat, you will see ours.

To parley, respond in reply. Otherwise you have but to leave. Instantly."

## Chapter 19

# Out of the Earth

Alhern lowered the horn. "Instantly" in military terms was a bit less so in real time. Practically it started with a cessation of all aggressive actions. An observer could say that had happened. However the mass did not move backwards. In fact, it appeared to move forwards, though a bit to the north, as if angling somehow to retake that part of the wall, though for what purpose no soul could fathom.

"Magi?" Alhern growled, scanning the Eurthan troop movements for meaning.

"It's hard to say," Ta Narin replied. "They don't appear to be advancing, but neither are they fleeing."

"I can see that," Alhern said acerbically.

"They've moved command," a magi with a familiar voice reported from above them. It was Ta Murdan. Eld glanced up to see her looking out in the distance ahead, arms crossed, black robes rippling in the winds above them. "The dome is empty," she added. "Whatever remains they plan to abandon."

Eld had a thought. "Perhaps there's another tunnel they're trying to get to."

"I hope so," Alhern mused. "Nonetheless, perhaps this will motivate them. Ta Murdan! You said the command tent is clear?"

"Yes," Murdan confirmed.

"Ta Narin, strike it," Alhern ordered. "At your time."

Eld's heart raced with excitement. She'd seen strike in training, but to be present during an action would be part of history ...

Eld was so taken with the idea she blinked and almost missed it. For a fraction of a second the air around the cannon was bright, a halo surrounding the magi operating it. Then a silent flash exploded on the great dome tent and the cloth went up in flames. A hole several feet wide was scorched out; as Eld watched, supports separated and fell. She had no way of knowing if they were made of a lesser metal, or if the joints were weakened, or even if the strike had actually defeated the hard grim steel. Only that the top of the tent burned vigorously until it was engulfed.

Then, just as suddenly, the fire vanished. There were soldiers walking through the ruins, in black coats with white circles around their arms at the shoulder. They held long metal staffs with arcane patterns on them like the celestial designs on magi robes. Eld shivered; they looked like the apparition; neither in padded skin suits nor armor, but uniformed troops, in black and white, waving their staffs in some operation. Wherever they went the fires fell down, then flickered out. The other soldiers rushed in to gather and salvage as much gear they could. Thus they looked to be planning to leave.

"Those are magi," Ta Murdan said above them.

"But, they're leaving, right?" Eld said.

"They are smothering the fire," Murdan said. "We can't have that."

Then the air around them shifted and a screech of fast thoughts scraped past the edges of Eld's mind. More magi rose to join Ta Murdan in a line above them, like beaters hovering in the sky. Now the air vibrated so strongly it was a force against Eld's ears. Even the horses objected, dancing back and to the side, as if trying to evade it. Looking up, Eld saw Murdan was making the same motions with her hands as in the Garrison Hall, as if pulling on ropes holding strong sails in a storm. Suddenly Murdan opened her arms out and Eld could feel a column of air rippling from the magi in the direction of the Eurthan command dome. A couple of the Eurthani magi waved their staffs around, but to whatever purpose, it was not effective. A second later the frame of the dome exploded as if a large creature had broken its shell. Unarmored Eurthans dodged away from the debris as it fell with a great noise on helmets and other ruined tents.

"Give us another strike, if you please," Ta Murdan called, sounding almost casual.

Ta Narin glanced once at Alhern; she was the field commander. Alhern nodded and Ta Narin struck again. It hit the same place and Eld wondered why. Then she saw the strike, instead of flashing and dispersing, had been contained in a nimbus, the work of Ta Murdan. Eld was excited, expecting the nimbus to sink to the ground, adding to green strike. That, however, was not Murdan's intent. Instead she held the nimbus in the air, moving it in the center of the large dome's remains. The sun appeared to shine brighter, a sure sign sulessence was being directed nearby. A warm wind pulled at Eld's flouted hair and a chill went up her spine. She knew what was to come.

The savage mind did not comprehend storms and imagined fickle, vengeful gods, striking mortals who displeased them with lightening. But scholarship had known storms were birthed from striving winds, often, but not always, bearing the breath of rain. So strong were these forces, they seemed to be powers unto themselves, roving the surface of Eurath in vast whorls of chaos. In time this understanding was found to be incomplete: the great force that drove storms and all weather, was the even greater force of Mother Sul. Somehow the ancient pagans must have guessed or dreamed, for in myth the very first children of Sul were Bright Solshar and Quick Payeen, personifications of light and wind. When Sul heated Eurath, deadly driven winds could birth; Ta Murdan used this principle to heat the air with the nimbus and drive the resulting winds to create a cyclone.

The rest of the dome was ripped apart. As one the entire Eurthan Host seemed to crouch, as if worried they might be blown away. Unmoored debris flew as the wind screamed and it was hard to convince the horses not to bolt. Eld worried that they would be injured, but any debris that flew their way was knocked aside. It seemed that the magi were divided into tasks on this: Murdan directing the whirlwind; the others supporting her efforts and keeping any deadly missiles from hitting the host with an invisible barrier. The center of the cyclone grew brighter, the air grew hotter, and suddenly the cyclone was a tower of spinning flames that sought to draw anything not tacked down into it. The Sula host was far enough away from the gale force, but not the Eurthans. Those armored crouched and did not move, those without shells clung to their armored sisters. The heat was now equal to a hot day in late summer. It must be unbearable to the Eurthans. And still they didn't flee.

But Eld saw a flicker of blue strike among the crouching Bane host, with it a rumble of false thunder. It rippled suddenly, flickering back and forth between warriors while above them the conflagration raged. Just before it discharged Eld understood: the Eurthans were using a type of feeding strike, the final force making a bolt of blue strike as powerful as the lost Medusa to arc over their heads with a peal of deafening thunder and hit the center of the flaming tornado.

The spinning flames instantly turned bright green, then dispersed to grow into the largest nimbus of green strike seen yet, enough to fill the dome had it remained whole. A gust of wind ripped past as the heated air fled to the sky, the day suddenly cool in contrast. As the green light hovered, the Dwen took this gifted chance: the ground erupted not just with grasses and brambles, but trees. It was hard to tell of which types because their growth was essence forced into attacking vining branches, their wood shaped into whipping thorns. The existing tangle of magically grown brambles and grasses put out a further burst of growth, finally becoming an impassable thicket to fill the ground between. The Host cheered. Then a line of Eurthan magi stepped forward to meet the thicket.

Walking like beaters into the soulless land of greenery, though the green light had vanished, Eld thought it boldly unwise. Sure enough, vines and murderous woody hands of twisting trees sought to grasp them. But they were prepared. They swung their staffs down, as if blocking a low sweep in a battle dance, and frost instantly covered the plants touched. Vines froze, shining black with ice, grasses stiffening, the magic-forced trees breaking under the sudden weight their own frozen water then shattering from within. The frost rippled over the field, slaying the new plants growing with a sudden magical winter. This was "calling the cold", used by butlers and talented cooks to chill certain foods. Sula did this by an inversion of sulessence. But Eurthans had a different way, as if they were creating water crystals, making so many that the air was chilled.

"Murdan, what in Athmod's craw is happening out there?" Alhern demanded.

"With respect, my dear girl, I am concentrating," Ta Murdan said shortly.

Alhern glared up. Eld followed her eye to see Murdan reach out with her hands, fingers spread as wide as a harpsichord player navigating a tune with a wide range. One of Murdan's hands seized into a fist, then she pulled the fist to her and sharply down and Eld felt strings of deadly essence shiver through the air. A shout went up from a couple women and Eld looked to see two Eurthan magi had fallen, one clutching her chest, the other screaming as if suffering a great pain, greater than the hardest birth. Eld's skin crawled. The same forces magi exploited to fly, throw rubble and stone, to corral winds, could crush a heart. But from this distance it would take a soul of great power or age, with the keenest concentration....Eld abandoned her feelings of wonder. Ta Murdan was obviously such an essence- powerful soul.

Thus it was no shock the next wave of feeding blue strike from the Eurthans struck Ta Murdan like a tower rod drawing lightening in a storm. In the horror at seeing false winter destroy the Dwen's work, most eyes hadn't caught the new thread of feeding strike growing between the Bane-warriors. Many assumed the Sula magi were at a safe distance; Eld certainly did. Like the bolt that quieted the firestorm, it forked to land into the ice blasted plants. But this was no mistake. It had been called or directed to the magi under attack and then, like the trick of a match re-lighting a candle using its recent smoke as a wick, the feeding blue strike had followed Ta Murden's personal essence trail back to hit her in a shower of blue lightning.

The Host cried out, some women gasping as Ta Murdan fell. Eld was close enough to tell she hadn't hit the ground with full force; her wizard sisters broke her fall, though whether that would help her or not was impossible to tell. Any lesser elf would have been dead, but she only looked unconscious and there were no holes piercing her body.

Alhern bellowed, "Strike, for the love of Sul! Disperse those demon magi!"

Ta Narin, looking grim, was already at the task.

Dispersal was much like a warning shot: usually fired in front of a force to drive them away. But instead the nimbus blossomed behind the magi troops, perhaps to avoid killing any plants the Dwen might be able to use. Or perhaps to vindictively trap the Eurthan women. This time the effect was more gruesome. A woman went up like a torch, not hit herself, but her clothes had caught fire. Her fellows, crouching in alarm, were late to put it out, making her wounds more serious than they might have been. How they put it out baffled Eld. They seemed to be sucking the air from the fire. A couple others had minor burns. But the ground where the strike hit glowed for several seconds, then seethed as the dirt and clay turned into lava near the center. The glow faded quickly; it would be hard and glassy by evening.

Finally the magi soldiers ran. The rest of the Eurthans milled in earnest, shifting to make a defensive wall out of the perimeter, but still clustered in the north and east, away from the obvious escape route.

"Commander," Ta Narin said. "I'm told they are preparing a retreat."

"Then why are they still in my field?" Alhern demanded.

"They are waiting for transport."

"Are you certain? Our friend is barely warmed."

"I think we should exercise patience."

"Patience is for men waiting for a proposal. Tend to your wounded and we'll scout. You two." This was addressed to Eld and Danshor. "Patrol the wall up to that end." Alhern pointed to the far northwest. "I want to know if they are seeing something we can't over here."

Eld and Danshor took off at a gallop parallel to the remaining part of the wall, in the direction of the north end. Eld's enthusiasm for heroics was greatly quelled after seeing one of their most powerful magi struck out of the sky.

"Why did you stop my strike?" Danshor shouted.

"What are you talking about?"

"The two Eurthans!"

"You're still thinking on that? Didn't you hear the Commander? We want to drive them away, not kill them!"

"And her timidity killed a magi!"

"I don't think Ta Murdan is dead!"

"Well, they almost sent you through the Door!"

"Look, if we kill them and they can't be retrieved, they'll come back for vengeance!"

"They didn't seem to worried about that when they attacked you and the commander's brother!"

"Then they assumed we were savages who couldn't defend ourselves!"

Danshor didn't reply until they came to the north end of the wall.

It didn't end so much as the ground rose slightly to meet it. Beyond, the ground sloped up slightly, then dropped away into a vast meadow, gently rolling down away far below them. There was another tree line, more fir and maple, but from where they stood, nothing that appeared to be an Eurthan military asset.

"So it's true the Eurthans were attacking both of you," Danshor said.

"What?" Eld looked at her quizzically. "Of course they attacked both of us!"

There was another rumble of false thunder, but no peal. Perhaps the Eurthans were sending warning strike as well.

"But wasn't the tale we heard about how the commander's brother – who, by the by, is far beyond your station – was attacked and you just happened to be hunting, or out for a stroll or watching birds in the area, and rushed in to save him? If they attacked both of you, that would mean that you were together from the start. And I suppose it wasn't the first time you'd been together. In the forest. Gathering herbs or summat."

Danshor was staring into Eld's eyes, much as Aredheli had stared into Brig's. Eld's heart pounded, the Eurthans nearby forgotten.

"Why do you care?" Eld demanded.

"I don't," Danshor said.

Eld glared at her.

"I mean, I don't care who you're milking dry like a prized stud," Danshor said. "But you've never shut me out before."

"You are beyond belief!" Eld exploded. "You want to question the reputation of the commander's brother in the middle of a battle because you're jealous?"

"Is there anything to question?"

"Are you in your seventh decade?"

Danshor did not rise to the bait. Much more worryingly, she turned Tuiric away from the slopping meadow, looked deep into Eld's outraged eyes, and calmly said:

"That's what I thought."

Then Danshor rode away at a light canter.

Eld's head spun. What would Danshor say? Who would she say it to? Had Eld been over cautious not to confide in Danshor? Gods, what fool would confide in Danshor with their career at stake?

Then the ground shook, driving all these petty worries from Eld's mind.

It took all of Eld's riding skill and her years long link of trust to keep Fiorseth from bolting. Danshor's stallion panicked, prancing in circles, wanting to shoot off in any direction. Earthquakes were rare and usually presaged by the actions of birds and animals. That neither beast nor any bird had given warning suggested a non-earth sourced event.

"Somehow the Eurthans are behind this!" Eld shouted.

"Truly?" Danshor shouted sarcastically.

Eld looked around while the ground continued to shake. Fiorseth neighed her displeasure loudly. The Eurthans were surging toward the wall. Shocked, the ranks of the foot host broke, fleeing before the mob of behemoths in a rout. The athleticism of women leaping en masse on the wall was impressive. For a moment Eld thought they would halt and make a stand, striking from the slightly higher ground. But no, they continued over and the Eurthans, shields up, swords at the shoulder, lumbered forward pressing their advantage. So much for their imperfect truce to leave. Eld felt she been played for a fool as the Host ran away, the cavalry line guarding their retreat with bursts of strike.

The Eurthans had been observant: they struck en masse, blue forks of bane-fire hitting the strike instead of the woman striking. While having no Dwen as allies, though it did not produce any attacking or entangling greenery, it did diminish the power of the sunstrike; like the feeding strike had bled the firestorm, the sunstrike grounded it in forks of green light, making feeble grasses instantly taller and sprouting seeds long abandoned in the earth.

Then the Eurthans reached the wall and stopped.

But the ground continued shaking and Fiorseth was about to rebel against Eld's elfyn stubbornness and bolt. Oddly the cavaliers engaged fifty or so yards away with the Eurthans didn't seem to be having trouble with their horses. Eld saw the ground break. Danshor shouted in alarm. At the same time all four of them understand this wasn't a passing tremor, but they were standing on the epicenter of something erupting from below. They were of one will when the horses finally bolted.

There were times the wise rider let her horse take the lead, only using her bond to guide the animal. This was one of those times. As the ground broke below Fiorseth, her hooves chose the best path, and soon that path was on the top of the wall itself, for the ground was collapsing and erupting at the same time, dirt and soil falling to Mother-Gods knew where, while chucks of earth and stone were being pushed up. Only the wall, made solid by ineffable Eurthani craft, resisted this, though it too must at least break and fall before a force that could shatter the ground. As Fiorseth's shoes showered sparks, like the storm herds of Payeen sending lighting to the earth as they thundered across the sky, Eld drew her sword and switched hands with lance and sword in a tricky maneuver that required throwing the lance back in a spin and catching it the same moment she tossed the sword handle across her front. It was risky but necessary, because the Eurthans were clustered against the wall on her left, and she did not expect they'd let herself and Fiorseth pass without a challenge. She could strike with either hand, but the sword was only usable on that side. At the best of times this action was hard. Doing it riding a wildly galloping horse balancing on a crumbling wall as the ground broke and rose behind them, it would be a miracle.

And so Eld was elated the next moment when she felt both the sword and lance firmly in her grips. The lance had been reversed and needed to be spun to return its striking head forward, but any cavalier could do that in her sleep. As Fiorseth galloped on, her sure hooves carrying them along the wall, Eld sent a sustained strike into the line of visors on her left side. It didn't matter if blue strike met it or dispersed it. It was only to hold them at bay with blinding brightness, so Fiorseth could pass without injury. It was brilliant and sudden, shining like a ray directly from Sul herself and many of the shelled women fell back, not even bothering to strike. Fiorseth galloped on. In several seconds they would come to the place the Dwen had broken the wall into rubble and they'd be free.

But then the ground rose alarmingly behind Eld, tilting so she had to lean back in her saddle to remain seated, standing in her stirrups so the horse could move freely. Fiorseth's mind coursed with new fear, but Eld calmed her body, focused the mare's senses, gave her all the access to Eld's elfyn perceptions so that the mare could dance on the smallest firmness of stone she needed to continue safely. They could not afford to tumble or fall. A horse could break her neck as well as legs during extreme maneuvers. A flash of reflection and a dim clash of fallen metal told Eld Fiorseth had thrown a shoe and it had hit an Eurthan. Fortunately it was a rear shoe. They wouldn't be on the wall much longer in any case. The stones underneath started to break and crumble as the ground rose steeply as a mountain slope. But this was all part of elite cavalry training. Casual riders were astounded that a horse could run down a slope so close to vertical; it made one swoon just thinking about it. And it felt as if they were riding vertically, only the fact they weren't falling corrected this perception. Eld's vision was bisected by the horn on Fiorseth's barding; her head lowered, the sharp spiraling metal divided the clustered Eurthans on the left from the open field on the right, that was scattered with both foot and mounted companies who looked to be cheering. Eld could not spare them a moment of attention.

Then she spied danger at the edge of her left field of vision, an Eurthan, shelled and bold, ducking under Eld's strike line with a sword high. The woman pulled it back, across her front, preparing to swing it at Fiorseth's legs.

Eld eyes blazed with rage and cursed the woman, her foremothers and the demonic literalist Avatar who sent her. More practically, Eld swung her own sword down to met the dark Eurthan blade. With the force of a horse and a righteously inflamed cavalier, the Eurthan had no chance. Her blow was knocked away with such power she stumbled forward and lost her footing. But it came at a price. Eld's sword shattered in a sparkling cloud, showering the Eurthans with shards of solstone enameled steel, a sword the smiths of the Shard Hills had never imagined would meet a pure grim-steel blade.

Then, past the Eurthans, Fiorseth leaped off the broken end of the wall, over the rubble, and Eld released the last line of strike, feeling exhausted as the mare turned to carry them away to join the rest of the cavalry company.

For a moment Fiorseth was determined to gallop all the way back to the barracks. Eld needed to firmly take control again, sending feelings of promised rest and peace that would come soon. But when they turned around and saw what had come out of the earth, Eld quailed.

The eruption had created a small hill, not dissimilar in aspect to those fire mountains, Cauldrons of Eurath, that scholars called volcanoes. At least there were no rivers of lava pouring down its sides. Instead a large edifice crouched on the top, the size of the entire crèche complex, with the proportions of a shallow upturned washing pan. It was shiny and bright, glimmering in the sunlight, only slightly streaked with soil from its journey below. If it reminded Eld of anything it was a massive crab or spider, for there were what seemed to be legs radiating from around its edges, some bent as if ready to push it up further, the rest perhaps anchoring it in place. Eld's military instincts told her it was a fort or transport, maybe both. Whatever it was, the power it took to break through layers of stone and soil was something to respect.

Whistles screamed through the air: rout to safety. Giving the order to rout had to have been painful to the commander. At least a retreat could be explained strategically. A route meant a mother had admitted she was not able for the fight. But the Host was already moving, soldiers running behind the command line, cavaliers galloping after the soldier's retreat, ahead of them all the healers loading their wounded who couldn't move into wagons and abandoning the tents. The magi descended from the air, hovering only high enough to act as lookouts, drifting above the Host as it poured out, a small cluster of them carrying a still unconscious Ta Murdan like black robed messengers from the Court of Heaven. Eld was almost relieved they were fleeing, until she couldn't see Danshor in sight.

Eld broke from the company, scanning the way she'd come. Danshor couldn't have been too far behind. Had Tuiric stumbled and fallen? Perhaps she needed help. With great resistance from an angry Fiorseth, Eld turned her back to race up the slope of debris. The ground no longer shook. She only hoped there was good enough footing.

"Where are you going?" Patrycan shouted riding in the opposite direction with Torin and a couple others.

"To look for Danshor!"

"Danshor?" Torin echoed.

"She's missing!"

Eld was ready to turn around in an instant, hoping they contradicted her, but instead she found Pat and Torin riding at her side.

"We were on the spot where this thing erupted ..." Eld started to explain.

Then Patrycan yielded, and turned down the slope to their left.

"I feel Tuiric!" Pat called.

Most cavaliers didn't try to meet their fellows' horses mind to mind. It was considered forward and could distract a mount. Eld had met Tuiric's mind a couple of times. He was very friendly and welcoming, but was always eager to run for a race or seek out his favorite watering holes or treats. It was a constant barrage of want and id, like a sprite child badgering their minder for sweets. Eld found it exhausting and was pleased her children were past that age. How Danshor managed she didn't know, though it was possible the stallion only did this with new minds, wondering what he could get away with. Eld worried on this day his impulsive nature married with Danshor's own recklessness would land them both in trouble. As the three women's horses skittered down a slope of scree to where Danshor was, Eld saw that day had come at last.

But Eld exhaled with relief. Neither was greatly hurt, but they were trapped, Tuiric's hind legs buried, pinning him. Danshor had dismounted and was throwing rock and stone out as fast as she could. Eld and the rest dismounted and rushed to help her, Torin reaching her side first. The stallion gave a deafening neigh and somehow it lightened their spirits. Eld laughed while tossing a stone the size of a woman's head:

"He doesn't think much of your riding!"

"Damn dowager nag should talk," Danshor growled. "He was doing most of the 'riding'!" She and Torin hefted a slab of slate the size of a small table and tossed it in the direction of the meadow, while Patrycan was making short work of plucking and throwing the smaller rocks Eld worked on. Suddenly Pat said, "Stop!" In reply to their queries, she said, "If we move any more it'll collapse and fill again." They looked warily at the mix of dirt, rock and stone. Only the stallion's lower legs were covered now, but it was hard to know what was covering the last couple feet. "Is there any weight leaning on him from the side or above?" Pat asked Danshor.

"He's a horse, not an engineer! He doesn't understand!"

"Well, he needs to lunge forward if he can and keep going in case it all falls again."

Danshor was sweating. Eld knew exactly the concern she felt for the stallion. Eld let her mind meet theirs and what she understood worried her:

Tuiric was unsure. He didn't like to run hindered. And they were shadowed a little by the mound so buoying his spirits with sulessence would be hard. But as far as Eld could feel, he was not longer pinned, the remaining rock being small gravel. She made a choice and hoped the stallion would forgive her.

"Now!" she said to Danshor at the same time slapping the stallion's rump.

Danshor almost lost her footing when the stallion reared in outrage. That motion itself made the rest of the debris around his feet move. Unfortunately, Patrycan had been right about the instability and the entire slope started to slide and threatened to bury them all. Tuiric leaped forward immediately, eager to flee, and Danshor mounted him the next instant as he galloped down the slope. Torin and Patrycan agilely remounted and followed.

Eld was almost not as lucky. The hill shook again and Fiorseth, seeing the horses running away, did not wait. Eld had to spring away from the falling rock, jumping from stone to stone before leaping onto Fiorseth's back as she ran.

"Inconstant steed!" she shouted with annoyance.

Fiorseth whinnied loudly in rebuke: it was Eld's fault for taking them back into danger...

Once off the artificial hill, they all circled back to camp. Eld half expected the area to be empty. But the rout had stopped. The entire Host and the command were staring up at the top of the hill. The cavaliers, not feeling danger or seeing pursuit, slowed and turned around to see the top of the hill swarming with Eurthans. Whatever the contraption was, it had open doors now and Eurthans were streaming inside, unshelled women first, while the still armored ones guarded their passage behind a shield wall. No swords were visible, but the bane weapons on their shoulders lurked, ready to strike if threatened. The Eurthans from along the wall were gone, their destroyed encampment abandoned.

So they really were leaving. Eld spied a tall, blue-eyed woman looking back a moment, perhaps wistful at the memory of a Dwen man's deep, green eyes. Then she was gone. Soon they'd all be gone, sinking back to their subterranean country where they imagined they had dominion over all the Orb. Asserting that arrogant territorial claim had been more than they had bargained for, Eld thought with a smirk. So much for the Mother-God's chosen.

"We should fall back," Patrycan said. "They might appear to be leaving, but we don't know what magic that thing has."

"They're leaving," Eld said certainly, but she moved back a couple paces anyway. What if Patrycan was right, and the contraption was able to strike? Or worse, it was mobile and could scuttle around the land like a fell crab carrying Eurthan troops to whatever "frontier" they fancied in their colonialist dreams?

Eld tried to shake the thought. If they had magical, armored wagons that could do that, surely they would have used them from the start. The last of the armored figures disappeared inside and the doors, which had folded open to make ramps, rose to close. The Host watched anxiously.

"What do you think, Farthal?" Alhern said as if they had been part of a conversation.

Eld had been joined by the commander, a mounted Captain Draeyn and a mounted foot officer. But it wasn't Roel because her insignia was that of a major. Eld barely recognized Galledan, the Red Major, her russet locks hanging down her back from beneath her helmet.

"Me?" Eld said. Her fellows sat on their horses nearby, shaking their heads as if to say, "Well, she's not addressing us."

"The rangers report you spoke at length with one of the Eurthans, making a well argued case for their retreat," Alhern said.

"Yes, I did."

"Well? Do you think they will act honorably?"

Eld sighed. "The one I spoke with will, without a doubt. The rest of her people?" Eld looked at the behemoth that loomed over them. "They have a literalist belief in the righteousness of their cause. They claim they are defending their frontier."

A moment passed. Then the three officers exploded with barks of humorless laughter, the Red Major laughing the loudest.

"Sul's tresses, there's a great bunch of ignorant hoods!" Galledan crowed.

Alhern was the first to stop. "Magi!" she called, whistling in case her voice wasn't clear.

"Yes?" a distant but clear voice said. Many magi could project their voices without horns, something to do with giving energy to the air as Eld understood it. The magi were clustered around Ta Murdan who was awake and sitting up drinking something, probably a vivifying potion.

"If your Aeon has recovered from her nap, prepare the cannon!" Alhern called.

"But they're leaving!" Eld objected.

"And I'd like to drive that point home. Don't weep for them, Farthal. If that shell of the contraption is made of the same metal as their armor, it will be but a love tap. But one they will remember."

Eld cantered to where Danshor and the rest stood.

"I don't think it's a good idea to provoke them," Eld said, feeling agitated.

"I agree," Patrycan said. "But I want them to pay for the lost horse."

Eld looked in the field at the sad mound. The barding had been removed and a healer crouched by it, perhaps making certain of its lost fate.

"Did the cavalier make it back?"

"You mean the one you saved by skewering an Eurthan with a throw Amer herself couldn't make?" Danshor said gleefully.

Eld was buffeted by praise and adulation for a minute, Torin being given to reenact the struck Eurthan as much as she could still mounted, to the laughter of the rest. Either Torin was less annoying or she was growing on Eld. And Danshor rarely expressed pride in her war-sister publicly. Eld assumed she never minded, so was surprised she felt so warm hearing it. Not that she'd tell Danshor. No, they would clasp arms and wrists firmly, laughing off the intimacy of a war-sister lest some soul who didn't know them assumed a different intimacy.

"To answer your question," Patrycan said, "Trannecyn made it, but is in a bad way. Two strike wounds from the Bane, one in the back, the other a leg. She might not walk for weeks. And she also has cuts from fighting them, and burns from our strike covering her. Couldn't be helped. But she'll be whole one day."

"She'll never be whole without her horse," Danshor said with finality. "Lenia, my first horse, died when I was eighty two. I still feel her loss though she died in peace of old age. I can't fathom what losing a horse in battle could do to a woman."

Patrycan sighed in sympathy. "It will get better."

Meanwhile the cannon was ready to fire. Its tripod was directly on the ground, no need to be elevated to give it a clear shot. To Eld's eye Alhern looked overeager, a fighter who had taken a beating in the arena, landing so few blows she burned to hit her opponent well at least once. Leaving aside motherly pride, there was elfyn pride.

The duty to care and defend was taken seriously, even by slack souls like Danshor. The greatest expression of that care was the building of the legendary city of Er, where it was said they calmed the very winds and managed the lands so that no bird, beast or Thyn lacked. The greatest failure of duty was the destruction of Er by the Dying Star. However faultless the elfyn had been, it marked their collective soul, and any failure in duty since was felt as a reminder of this first catastrophic failure. It would be easy for a mother in Alhern's position to become consumed with thoughts of self reproach if she did not make some accounting to be proud of.

As Eld watched, Alhern raised the whistle to her mouth. Suddenly Eld shivered, feeling the danger of an imminent moment. She cried out "No!" just as the whistle blew. The next second a peal of thunder broke over them and a bolt of blue strike erupted from the top of the edifice, as wide as a woman's arm, jumping through the air in a second to strike the cannon. Solstone and metal exploded apart, and the magi was thrown off her feet, flying through the air to land several yards away. Alhern did no better, her horse rearing, making her tumble off, as did Galledan's mount. Only Draeyn kept her seat with the cavaliers, though their horses all danced madly. Fiorseth was now angrier than Eld had ever felt. She was promised it was over, but these damn elflings kept doing something to bring danger back.

As if to vindicate Fiorseth's feelings, the ground rumbled. In spite of their collective lingering worries of the Eurthan's intentions, the edifice seemed to lower, its top coming even with the hill, then disappearing. It took several moments but the rumbling stopped as well, though the sounds of the eldritch thing falling through the earth, like a dragon's claws scraping the side of a cliff, still could be heard for several minutes. It seemed Alhern wasn't the only soul to want to leave a message of remembrance.

Though Galledan had landed on her feet, the commander had not. Alhern refused assistance, preferring to swear a streak as she leapt to her feet, watching her and the Red Major's horses gallop wildly back to the lines. Eld looked over to where the ruins of the cannon lay. The magi, Ta Narin, was picking herself up, her robes smoking, but otherwise unhurt. Eld looked back up at the low hill, free of Eurthans or contraptions. She had to know.

Sliding off of Fiorseth, Eld said, "Go back to the lines," with a directing touch. "Drink some water. I'll meet you soon."

Fiorseth didn't need convincing. She dipped her head, horn waving dangerously, then turned and trotted away. Eld, using her lance like a staff, started to climb the slope of stone, rock, soil and scree. The amount of earth moved in moments was phenomenal. Then Eld remembered the tunnel under the commander's house. Still, the tunnel was a much smaller work. But that might mean it was made with similar quickness, both impressive and frightening. The Eurthans could return whenever they desired and how would anyone tasked with protecting the Federation know? Eld supposed they should feel lucky that they hadn't considered Sula men and boys a commodity to harvest.

Or had they? The tales of the dark visitors and dark lovers from the outer lots came to mind. Well, as long as they were truly lovers and not euphemisms for rapine predators. Eurthan individuals could be attracted to the exotic like any mother, Eld supposed. And there were tales of men and women disappearing, very much like the tales Gaels told of Sula and Dwen, of children taken to the Land of Youth, many never to return. But while it was in general a ridiculous fantasy that Sula would have any interest in stealing humyn children, Eurthans stealing Sula or Dwen children would make sense if there was trafficking in slavery. Suddenly Eld was so offended she wished the cannon had been able to strike. There was no formal taboo against slavery because any true soul knew it offended decency to presume to own the souls of mothers or their children. Only humyn could be so dense. What had happened to the Eurthans that they had strayed so far from elfyn ethics?

Eld finally stood at the top. As expected, she was at the edge of a circular gap in the earth, large enough to swallow most of Step village. It had a flattened and compressed three foot wide rim, and in four places those areas were further pressed down, probably by the door ramps. Carefully Eld looked over, the distant sound of the descending vehicle still echoing to the sky. It was too dark to see much except for the deep vertical grooves that ringed the shaft, as if a clockwork-like mechanism was involved. There was what might be the black top just disappearing out of view. For a moment Eld had a mad thought to jump down. She'd made a game as a youth jumping off cliffs into a nearby swimming hole. It was descending, so landing would be soft, though not as soft as water. But how would she return? It was too mad and reckless. Perhaps Danshor would be interested.

"So they're truly gone?" Alhern said, joining Eld by the edge.

"Truly, emha. Sorry about the cannon."

Alhern shrugged. "I should have realized we'd won. They gave out so much, and we almost lost souls. We almost lost a magi Aeon, for Sul's sake. In the moment it didn't feel like winning but like letting a child run away from mischief unpunished."

They looked around. It was a pleasant view, the late afternoon sun now putting the meadow beyond in shadow, Sul's light reddened slightly by the lowering angle and the haze of smoke that lingered. A flock of ravens flew over head, returning to the ridge, likely Thyn who knew the danger was gone.

The white peaks that hovered on the eastern horizon, lost in the hazy blue distance over green hills, sat as they always did, ignorant of the events that had transpired. Behind the women, and below the new hill, the Host organized the tasks of retrieving equipment and returning.

"We won certainly." Eld felt this as a truth. "This thing was called to rescue them. The remaining question is whether they will they be back."

"Gods, I hope not," Alhern said, striking the open air above the pit with a gesture of dismissal, not exactly crude, but definitely rude. Light flashed in the air where her fingers had flicked. "May they stay and rot in their Bane hell and never return. Now come back from the edge, Farthal. If you fall in I will never stop hearing about it until the day I walk through the Door."

## Chapter 20

# The Debriefing and Aftermath

It was late afternoon when the Eurthans fled. With the enemy gone, the Host was free to dispose of the area at leisure, for which the healers were grateful. They took their time with the wounded who could not walk; those that could insisted on walking back with their companies. The rest would wait for more wagons. Another horse had died, but he was retrieved, though sedated. Animals that were not Thyn were often frightened and disoriented after revival. The cavalier would stay with her mount until he was ready to leave. It's what Eld would have done.

But the horse that had died was a sad tale. A lucky bolt had sunk into its eye, in spite of the barding. The barding having been removed, soldiers gently loaded the corpse into a wagon with the help of a winch. Eld did think it odd the body had not stiffened, but it was not unheard of for a corpse to go into rigor late.

"But surely if rigor has not set in there is hope?" she asked the senior healer present.

"It was not safe to tend the animal where it fell and the wound goes into the brain. This late we risk bringing her back in the midst of rigor setting and that is a horrible thing." The woman had the matrician temperament that was not unkind, but did not linger on sentiment.

"But if ..." Eld started. But another healer, a younger woman, caught her eye. She shook her head. "I see," Eld amended. She waited for the senior healer to move on. "So ..." she queried the woman.

The healer's white robes were streaked with mud, grass stains and blood. Her round green cap, much like a magi's but with no solstone gems at the quarters, was the only part of her free from blemish. Even her blond locks were dirty; healers did not wear a veil like magi. The woman did not look at Eld directly, instead placing a hand on the horse's chest where it lay. For a second Eld thought she saw the body inhale.

"You appear to have an interest in the health of horses," the woman said, still not looking at Eld. This was almost certainly because she planned to bend the truth; in being artless about it, she was communicating it was a deliberate confidence. "His ways and passages are clear. For general information it is possible to delay rigor."

"Yes, I know."

"You have training?"

"Yes. The Waiting Serum is part of a tending kit if a soul is too far away from a temple."

"Precisely. It is always part of a war healer's kit."

"But it needs to be administered soon after death. And she said the horse wasn't tended."

"It was dangerous to tend her. I know. I did it."

"Why haven't you told her?"

"That is Temple Prefect Olthan. She is a firm and just master. But she does not believe waiting serum is safe for animals."

Eld was worried for the healer. Temple discipline was very similar to the military in some ways.

"Is it? Safe?"

The woman sighed. "No one is sure. But a chance is better than none at all, certainly? Especially for a horse that has fallen in service to an elfyn cause?" Those words bought Eld's loyalty and silence in all but a sworn court interrogation. The healer leaped up into the wagon and shouted, "Drive on!"

Eld rejoined her company, all who were having their horses checked for wounds. Like Eld, Fiorseth had nothing but light scratches, but Eld was told Fiorseth should be unshod and left free for a week. Danshor received similar advice for Tuiric, who definitely had strains and pulls in his hind legs; while not serious, they could become so without rest. In Eld's partially qualified opinion all the mounts deserved to wander at will in fallow fields without a care for at least a week and she was pleased the cavalry horses were definitely in for that fate. However the women of the host would not be that fortunate; until Command cleared the emergency, they were still in watchfulness.

Along their return to the garrison they were showered with cheers and not a few flowers from the villagers lining the streets as they walked by.

"It's just like in the tales," Torin said, behind Danshor.

"Except they forgot the red rose petals," Danshor said, waving to one of her many admirers.

"Yellow petals," Patrycan called. She was somewhere behind Eld. "Red for war; gold for victory."

"The point remains these are yellow daisies, not roses," Danshor said.

"Given the victory was questionable at best, we're lucky the men didn't just gather dandelions and be done with it," Eld said, reluctantly giving a very enthusiastic boy in a lavender shift a nod and a wave. She didn't want to encourage any man she wasn't interested in, and there was only one man who held her interest.

"The dandelion is a noble flower of great distinction," Torin quoted.

"In medicine," Patrycan said while Eld and Danshor laughed. "No wonder you're lacking in male company if you think the common dandelion is an acceptable offering flower!"

Once inside the garrison gates, activity did not cease. Soldiers released from duty for the day made directly for the Kettle, the baths or the Temple. The Rowan Oak was shuttered, an unknown occurrence during the day; Tafli was always hungry for queens. Eld supposed he was still with other Dwen doing whatever they were tasked with.

Captain Aynath relieved the company from duty and the women dismounted, yielding their horses to the grooms who would remove their barding, feed and water them, and do whatever else was needed or desired. Eld hugged Fiorseth's neck a moment, sharing a feeling of relief that, at last, they were both truly in a safe place. Then Eld let her be led away with the rest. Garrison pages took their lances to storage. Only then did Eld wonder what happened to the hilt of her shattered sword. It was probably still on the battlefield.

"Farthal!" Alcas said, plucking Eld's elbow. "The captain is calling for you."

What now? Eld thought uncharitably. As the afternoon sun was dimming she became more aware of her exhaustion. And she was now truly hungry enough to devour the entire larder of Myngar, the Mother-God of wealth and industry, though the poets reported Jaro herself had failed at that task:

"You might as well drink the ocean, Daughter of Sul!"

Ignoring the persistently urgent pangs in her stomach, Eld found the captain.

"You're to report to the commander's house instantly," she said. She'd turned away to another soul before Eld could ask why.

So Eld made her excuses to Danshor and their fellows, and started trudging up to the commander's house. The women on guard were grim, interrogating her as if she was challenging the gates of Amer's keep. There were even ravens fluttering about, making a nuisance of themselves, demanding news of the action.

~this one I spied with the leaf elflings,~ a raven sent, perched near the porch. ~she is as good as our people. her sister is a loud crow.~

"And if that's not a recommendation, what is?" Eld said, eliciting the laughter of those nearby including the guards. "And I thank you, emha or effa raven."

The raven dipped its beak, croaking with laughter. ~i have laid many clutches in my seven-toes-two-wings-years. sun elflings are funni. you make marking of mother and mate so important but cannot see a mother of other people.~

"Truly, we are idiots," Eld agreed affably to more laughter and went inside.

The rooms inside were a disgraceful sight, much worse than when Eld and Danshor had fought the Eurthan warrior. Shards of glass and porcelain covered the floor and many windows were in the process of being cleared for repair and boarded for the night. A magi shoved Eld to the side, directing her to avoid places they were taking essence signatures; this entailed other magi touching the ground or palms in the open air in active psychometry. The house staff was carrying out shattered and ruined furniture. Eld walked through the halls, splinters of white wood scattered about, noting the lack of bronze sculptures or even curtains in some rooms.

"They took them," Seth said.

He was standing in a doorway, disheveled, face scratched and smudged but still as beautiful as ever.

"The curtains?" Eld replied stupidly.

Seth laughed, then started weeping in spite of himself. Eld grasped him in an embrace and he clung to her like she was life itself.

"All the Corinath pieces," Seth said. Corinath was an Aeon master metal sculpture now in her sixth century and still productive. "And many of the ceramic whites, those not shattered. And yes, the curtains. They were here to loot. The only reason they didn't take the treasury or our jewelry is they didn't know where to look. But worst, they tried to take one of the knaves. It was horrible."

Seth choked back tears, but more escaped, Eld feeling them wet her cheek as she held him. Eld was glad she could hold him, relieved she had not jumped after adventure. What a foolish thought. She might have never seen him, her children, or her family again. "Is everyone in the house uninjured?"

"We're fine!" Alhern barked. She'd entered the room with a member of her staff. Eld leaped away, releasing Seth who wiped his eyes, glaring at his sister. "You are being over familiar with an ensign, Farthal."

"Yes, emha," Eld said formally. Seth was still wearing a uniform and sword. "Apologies, emha."

"Join us in conference. Now."

Alhern walked on. Eld knew she had to follow.

"We'll speak later," Seth murmured, taking the opportunity with his sister's back turned to peck Eld on the lips.

It was strange being back in the same room where Eld had given her account of the Eurthans, then wearing only her running kit. Though it was late afternoon it was bright, the solstone skylight bending the best of Sul's rays to extract their light, but little heat, producing a calm, soothing effect. The room was crowded, officers throwing themselves into any seats available, shedding helmets and gauntlets in a clatter on the table. In armored field gear, battered, scorched and bloodied by the events of the day, the officers looked nothing like Eld had seen before, genteel women in cleaned and starched uniforms. Now they looked like a throng of vandals fresh from a raid. Stools were brought in so that officers of the cavalry companies could sit at the table with their equals, though it was every woman for herself. Eld was not particularly pleased that Lieutenant Roel had somehow captured an arm chair and Eld's own captain was forced to perch next to Major Galledan on a stool. Captain Aynath yanked her armored flout off and set it next to the major's helmet. Then she pulled off the thong holding her hair in place, and, thus free, it cascaded around her shoulders in a slightly masculate way. Eld herself longed to remove her own flout, but she didn't want to give Roel reasons to mock her. There was only standing room for the rest, a mix of regular troops, civilian engineers, magi and healers. Eld moved herself to stand next to Captain Draeyn, intending to inquire after Scout Orinac. But before Eld could ask anything Alhern spoke.

"Refreshment will be here soon," the commander said from the head of the table.

"Sun-soaked water I hope," Galledan said.

"We will do what we can," Alhern replied.

"I could fancy White Brandy," Roel exclaimed. "If anything was mother's business it was this!"

There was a mild murmur of approval at this sentiment, mostly from supporters of Roel. But none of senior officers pressed this point.

"Alas, this is not a public house," Alhern said in a voice bereft of regret. "The Rowan Oak will be open for trade this evening for any mother welcome there."

A couple officers chuckled, and Roel's face flushed with embarrassment. Roel's disastrous encounter with Tafli was now common knowledge.

Then Alhern dived into business, demanding reports from the officers at the table, followed by the magi and engineers. As the women took turns with their reports, Sonamor and servers drifted in and out, first with chilled water, then plates of cheese and sliced, buttered bread. Whether the water was sun-soaked Eld didn't know; she didn't feel forward enough to take a cup. The cheese and bread was to take the edge off their appetite while they conferred with events fresh in their minds. Eld did cadge a slice of bread because her hunger was desperate. She ate it quickly and was still ravenous.

About a quarter of an hour into the proceedings Seth entered, still in his uniform, uncharacteristically uncertain where to go.

"Yes?" Alhern said, holding a hand up to pause Lieutenant's Arthen-weld's report of Company Ter.

"You wanted all officers present? Even civilian commissions?" Seth asked.

"That's the point of the commission," Alhern said tersely. She waved that Arthenweld should continue.

" ...When I heard the irregular orders, my first thought was to confirm from field command. It seemed to be a stretch the Dwen could accomplish this feat. But a ranger reassured us it was possible ..."

Eld watched Seth make his way to the table, then pause, uncertain of his place. Eld slid past a couple of field sergeants to where Roel sat dipping a slice of bread in a honey bowl. Eld gently kicked the leg of her chair. Roel looked up, glaring at Eld.

"The commander's brother needs a seat, emha," Eld said quietly. Eld tried to put all her contempt for Roel in that honorific courtesy.

Roel stared insolently. "What of it, cavalier? If he's going to work as a mother, he'd better be quick as a mother ..." Roel trailed off as the women around her become distracted and turned to mark their conversation.

Alhern looked furious. "Is there something so pressing that you need to interrupt, lieutenant?"

Roel opened her mouth to object but Eld spoke first.

"Apologies, Commander," she said. "But the ensign doesn't have a seat at the table and I suggested Roel could yield hers."

"He's an ensign!" Roel objected, "Not a noble Laird of the Lots from times past!"

Yet in spite of this fact, all the seated officers, and most of the ones on stools, immediately jumped to their feet to offer Seth their seat.

"A stool will be fine," Seth said. But before he could take it, Roel leaped up.

"My apologies!" Roel said defensively. "I was remiss. And I've rested enough already."

Roel forced herself to smile at Seth while he murmured a gracious thanks. Then Roel glared at Eld, standing uncomfortably close to her. Eld didn't fancy moving away least it looked cowardly.

Alhern sighed heavily and waved Arthenweld to resume.

"How do the leaves fall on your boy admirer these days?" Roel said in a voice barely a soft breath of air in Eld's ear. "How would he feel about trysting with me again, do you think?"

Eld's heart raced with anger but she wouldn't grant Roel any satisfaction.

"Are you going to whisper sweetness to me all afternoon?" Eld breathed back. "I don't tryst with sisters."

"Do you think Althas would be willing to yoke with another harlot if I paid him twice as much?"

Eld felt her aura consuming the light above, eager to transform it into fire. It took concentration to not fluorescence or simply deck Roel. Eld exhaled, then became aware she was being addressed.

"Emha?" Eld said. It was the ranger Captain Draeyn.

"Scout Orinac reports you had intimate conversation with an Eurthan."

"Well, it wasn't that intimate."

This elicited laughter.

Draeyn said, "Tell us about this woman."

Eld did her best to be both accurate and fair, and included the later encounter freeing the Eurthan major from the vines.

"What in the Orb did you bother doing that for?" Captain Hawthorn asked.

"With respect, emha, they could hardly flee with her foot entangled," Eld said

"You could have just cut it off. They wouldn't be returning soon after that!"

Horrified at the idea, Eld didn't reply.

Alhern spoke next.

"Farthal, you seem convinced this Brig was acting in good faith."

"I am, commander."

"Then she's the naive idiot her own troops think she is," Galledan said. "How is an unprovoked attack 'defending' their frontier? The presence of a garrison proves this is land managed and defended by mothers. Do they think savages make fortified military structures for idle diversion? "

There were many words from the women in agreement at this.

"A greater question might be why, even with the Eurthan's arrogant view of encountering a 'lesser' country, they made no overtures of diplomacy or trade?" This was asked by magi Ta Narin. While not as old or powerful as the Aeon Ta Murdan, Narin seemed to have an administration rank among the wizards. "In our own history we have extended national friendship to Tamask, then a city-state, now the capitol of Sharitan."

285

"And examine how that story ended," Galledan muttered. "We gave them engineering. Now they call us demons."

"Regardless, we saw value in nurturing a humyn community because if they can care for themselves and thrive in health, all the Orb is the better for it and our duty is made easier. Like the management of children, it is best to try praise with humyn first, not punishment."

"For a magi you don't seem very well read," Galledan said. "Remember the Battle of the Blue Fields? To this day the Sultan has delusional dreams of conquering Federation lands. A disease has taken hold of the souls in that humyn realm. They now feel entitled to take whatever they can."

"That seems to be the same case with the Eurthans," Alhern said. "This Lieutenant Brig not withstanding. There are always individuals with divergent opinions. It does not mean they have influence. A social club of 'footers' exists among the army." 'Footers' were a fringe subculture who advocated freeing the domestic horse. "But none of them has a chance of abolishing the Federation Cavalry Host. The Eurthans' actions as a group prove the Avatar also sees herself entitled to take what she can. But, unlike humyn, they have the essence force to make good on that threat.

"Still, that individuals like Brig exist is a sign diplomacy might be possible. There is clearly a vast gulf between how privileged Eurthans see themselves as virtuous defenders of their nation and their actual colonial aggression."

"With respect," Galledan said, "They have violated the Taboo and are insensible to our Duty to the Orb as elfyn. They needed a Tree to remind them. I'm not optimistic about diplomacy."

"Understood," Alhern said. "But that will be for Command and politicians to decide. Thank you, Lancer Farthal. While we can't say for certain your work with our Dwen allies made the Eurthans flee, it was obviously a factor. As was the tactic of exploiting their Blue Strike with Dwen essence. This was your idea?"

"Well, emha, it wasn't all me obviously," Eld stuttered, a bit disconcerted to find every eye in the room on her, though Seth looking up in admiration was pleasant. "Without the Dwen ..."

"The idea was yours, however," Alhern pressed. "We don't have time for false modesty, cavalier."

"Yes, emha, the idea was mine," Eld confirmed.

"Well done," Alhern said.

"Thank you, emha."

There as a low whistling of approval throughout the room. Eld didn't bother looking at Roel; of course there was only spite to be found in that soul. But Roel had stopped trying to bait her with whispers about using Althas.

The meeting wore on, and, while it was interesting, hunger returned to consume Eld. Finally she took the lead of a foot corporal bold enough to pour a cup of water and reached for another piece of bread. Seth briskly took the bread out of Eld's hands and buttered it, along with a couple others, to appear he wasn't favoring her.

The bread was the best, working wholemeal bread, full of caraway, fennel, anise and currants. It would sate her for a while. And the water was indeed sun-blessed, made available in gill sized tin cups; Eld was certain she could down a pitcher in one draught.

Finally matters turned to the defense of the garrison and the report was decidedly mixed: while none of the Eurthans from the battle reached the keep walls, a handful invaded through the tunnel.

"There was a sudden mist," Seth said. Captain Vergant had already given the general report concerning the grounds; the tale of the house was left to Seth. "At first we thought it was smoke and the house was on fire. But magi told us it was essence induced. It filled all the lower part of the house and a great part of the ground floor, and dimmed the light so we wondered if strike could be used at all. Several women fell to small darts, imbued with poison to send them to dreams. Thankfully, not death. And then the Eurthans came and ransacked the house. Swords were useless, lances didn't have enough light for strong bursts. But we didn't make it easy for them. The women used chains to good effect on a couple of the shelled women, enough that the rest seemed to worry if they'd be able to escape with their gains. Finally a breach in the outer wall was exploited using an array from the Temple and we drove them back into the tunnel with bursts of strike."

Seth paused, his eyes open and haunted, staring at a memory as if it was still happening.

"Then we heard the knave scream." Seth swallowed. "We hadn't marked his absence. There were only a couple who took the double wages to work in the kettle today. His screams came from the tunnel. They were dragging him away." Seth looked up. "Can I not turn this tale over to the sergeant guarding the house?"

Alhern eyed her brother curiously. "Are you able to make a complete and truthful account?"

"Yes. I just feel odd reporting my own deeds."

"Get used to it, ensign."

Seth inhaled and continued. "I called out to inform the women of the boy's need. Then I ran into the tunnel. The mist was still thick there and it was dark, so I had no idea how far I needed to go. Several moments later I ran into the back of an armored woman. Though I couldn't see much, I found the knave by his sounds of distress. The Eurthan had him on her shoulder. I tried to pull him off but she threw me into the wall of the tunnel with a blow from her arm."

Not a woman made a sound now. They all knew the force and power of an Eurthan in their eldritch armor. Seth had sounded fragile when Eld embrace him earlier. But now his voice was deep and steady, even toneless.

"I pulled my sword but was afraid to use it for fear of hurting the knave. Hitting at her legs I forced the Eurthan to mark me and loosen her grip. The knave was able to twist free. I saw him shadowed against the light as he tried to flee, and I intended to guard his retreat. But the Eurthan snatched him by the arm at the last moment. I rained blows upon her anywhere I could, hoping to shock her into letting him go. She was also carrying a heavy sack of valuables, so I hoped she would consider that reward enough. But she was insistent, dragging the knave back while he screamed. I grabbed his other arm, and continued to hit her the best I could, but I could feel him slipping from my grip ..."

Seth didn't sob at the memory, but he stopped talking for a moment so he wouldn't.

"Just when I felt I couldn't hold on any longer, the tunnel was filled with light. Suddenly the knave was free and I pulled him down to the ground so our soldiers could strike at full force without hindrance. When it was over, the Eurthans were gone."

"And the sack she carried?"

"Alas, commander, gone as well." Seth's voice returned to its normal tone.

Alhern sighed. "You saved our knave. Well done, ensign. Your brave actions saved him from a fate we can guess. How is he faring?"

"Deeply shaken of course. But he's suffered no permanent harm."

Alhern moved on to other reports, the sergeants who had managed certain actions, notable skirmishes. It would have been much more interesting if the phantom of hunger hadn't returned. Eld noticed the light seemed to dim and she wasn't the only one.

"Sul is retiring," Alhern said. There was a point the when the sun's rays were too low to be bent by solstone. The light shifted towards a reddish orange and lamps above glimmered as the impending darkness activated their crystals to discharge light. "We will adjourn until after dinner where I will hear the reports from the magi, healers and civilian engineers. Gentles."

Every soul fairly leaped out of their chairs or stools, making for the door with speed . For all the affection Eld had for Seth, she moved to join them. The Kettle would be open late of course; they would have been warned to save a healthy portion for those being debriefed. So Eld was more than annoyed when a house girl blocked her way and informed her she was to join the commander's table.

Sitting primly at an officer's table worried about which fork to pick up was not the meal Eld wanted at the moment. She wanted to gorge and not care who was watching, especially if Roel or her cronies were present. But to refuse was unthinkable.

Eld followed the woman to the servants' washing room to clean up. It didn't have a waterfall, but there were large tubs and basins, and ample taps. There was no time to submerge herself, so she settled for splashing her face and hands, wiping the dust and grime from her coat as much as she could. She stripped off her shirt to better soak her right sleeve and try to scrub out the blood; fortunately, the light from the window was bright enough that, with toweling, she could use sulessence to dry it to dampness. At last she removed her armored flout. One wall was covered with mirrored panels; Eld knew from her own estates it was thus often said there was no excuse for staff to not look presentable. She'd missed some grime on the bridge of her nose, so she washed her face again and tried to make her hair fall in a presentable way. She didn't attempt guardlocks; without a comb her efforts would look worse than just letting it hang. It would need to be washed properly later; she could see and feel the grit just beyond her hairline. She wished she had a thong to tie her hair back, but it would do. Eld carried the flout like a helmet in the proper marching protocol and for once wished she had her cape.

Leaving the washroom, the servant woman was waiting, with an air of impatience she tried to hide. But they were all tired and she failed badly. It occurred to Eld the servants might be late for their supper.

"Sorry if I was keeping you," she murmured.

The woman shook her head. "It is an awkward time for every soul."

Eld was led to a dinning room she suspected was not used for formal occasions. The room was square, the ceiling above vaulted in a decorative oval, with a skylight that was exactly above the placement of a modest table that could seat seven comfortably, more if a little crowded. The skylight emitted redly, but was overwhelmed by the four hanging lamps in the ceiling's corners. They were directional, meaning they were made so their light could be directed to shine brightly in a direction, or be diffused to give the impression that somehow daylight filled the room with little or no shadow. It was clear this room was regularly used for intimate breakfast dining: the east wall was covered with what appeared at first to be dark mirrors, but were actually tall windows, not unlike the windows along the south wall of the Rowan Oak common room. The table itself, it's length parallel with the windows, a rectangle of white holly-wood with corners rounded and ornamented with leafy scrolls, was laden with abundant but simple food. No aspics, stuffed roasts, or layered tea cakes to impress visitors. It was all basic mother's food and much of it:

A vast tureen of potage sat in the center, stewed to an indistinct beige green that suggested pulses, roots, kale and whatever vegetables were nearing the end of their use. It had a cast of yellow, as if turmeric had been added, but this was not a common custom in the north Crownland. Another platter was piled with fowls roasted in olive oil with a sauce of olives, grapes, rosemary and green herbs and salt; also too were several rounds of the same bread served in the Kettle. There was no salad, but various leaves from the garden, mostly lettuces and mustards, and bowls of sour cream sauce, seasoned with mustard and dill; lastly sat a round of cheese alone on a plate, it beeswax covering broken and torn where a large knife had cut it in two, one half being further cut into uneven and slightly broken slices. It was the kind of cheese that leaned on the dry side with a sharp flavor. There was also a bowl of radish sauce and other condiments common to a civilized table. As Eld watched, a large silver pitcher of water was being set down at one end to match one closer to the commander's seat at the head. The ware was like most things in the commander's house, of excellent quality but simple: translucent white porcelain plates with a dusting of gold on the rim, and helix handled silverware. Though there were two spoons, Eld was relieved there was only one fork, the basic supper trident.

"Given the state of the kitchen, we raided the Kettle," Seth explained from where he stood behind a seat opposite the commander, "I had the cook add some Gashoreen curry for a bit of flavor." Like the women, he still wore his uniform, minimally cleaned for the occasion.

"Hunger is the best sauce," quoted Captain Aynath who stood by Alhern's right. That was the Heir's place, or the most notable visiting mother. If Alhern had an older daughter, the visitor would go on her left. Eld wondered if that was where she would sit. But instead she was led to a seat next to the captain, exactly in the middle of the table side. To the right was an empty seat, on Seth's left. On Seth's right, no doubt to his irritation, was the nephew's keeper, Effa Tanmor, looking even more dour and joyless than when Eld had first spied him at the award ceremony. While Sil always dressed respectably, this man's robe was a smooth, cream white shift, free of any suggestion of ornamentation, unless one counted the weave in the cloth, that might be a basket pattern. His locks where bound tightly with ribbon so thin it looked like common white twine. Tonight he wore a shoulder cape, a snug fitted garment cut circular, made to hang just off the shoulders, buttoning in the front in a high collar. The keeper had occulted seams, so the buttons were not visible: oh what a tale they might share if they were not hidden!

The nephew, Solafi, was much as Eld had seen him before: full of spirits and also with the desire to be seen so sophisticated he had not a care. In other words, he was a typical adolescent. Solafi still looked like a daffodil, wearing a yellow robe covered with white birds woven in the fabric, while his kirtle-shirt was off-white, similar to what his keeper wore. Today his hair was in trilocks, the back half bound in a pony tail, all with gold ribbon. In fact his fondness for ribbons might scandalize the same women who obsessed about merry men painting their feet: several bands of wide white ribbons were wrapped around both arms just above the elbow, large bows secured at the back. There were thinner yellow ribbons around his wrists, but they were crisscrossed in a way that either took quite a bit of time or practice, or both. He wore no glimmer except for a faintest dusting of gold on his lips. Eld could only imagine what efforts the keeper had made to keep the nephew from applying the glimmer like gilding wax.

Solafi aimed for the seat next to Eld, but the keeper directed him firmly to the one next to himself, directly across from Eld. Solafi complied with a voiceless sigh, and an ever so slight roll of his eyes. As everyone took their places before seating, with the seat to the left of both Seth and his sister empty, Eld saw the table had been divided on the diagonal by sex. Somewhere within lurked a metaphor on the focus of contrasts in Sula society.

Once everyone was in place, the commander intoned, "In abundance is our gratitude."

"Always and forever," they murmured before sitting down.

It was common to wait until the mother of the table had taken the first bite before others did. Many men took this further, waiting for first the mother, then the man of the house before eating. This explained why Effa Tanmor firmly held the foot of the nephew's goblet when Solafi reached to fill it.

"Patience," the keeper intoned quietly.

Solafi sighed and looked at his aunt and uncle in turn.

Eld was quite in sympathy with the boy because, while it was custom to wait and eat, once gratitude had been given, serving was open at will. But this wasn't even to be allowed because, springing from the back of the room, two house girls, in dark green coats and trousers much like Sonamor, descended on the table to ladle potage into the large bowls and pour water into their crystal goblets. Idly Alhern picked up a mustard leaf, dipped it into sauce and took a bite. Eld saw her wink at her nephew, taking a sip of water for good measure.

The boy grinned and tucked in with gusto, as did the rest of them.

Eld had some idea she needed to watch the table to see what the custom of the household was. But, with the exception of the prim keeper valiantly acting as a model of masculine restraint, everyone ate with the abandon of the starved, first attacking the potage, their bowls refilled within minutes, and piling plates with bread, fowl and cheeses. It tasted better than any meal Eld had eaten in a while, and vanished even faster. Soon all the women and Seth were on their third portions, though Seth had slowed down. Eld wondered if it was because the keeper kept sending him sly critical looks, even though Seth kept his poise and manners like always.

Solafi thought this was all amusing.

"The women are going to devour everything!"

"It is natural for mothers to have great appetites," Effa Tanmor said, emphasizing the word "mother".

"As does anyone who works as a mother," Alhern said diplomatically.

Seth of course said nothing on the subject. Instead he reclaimed his role as conversational provocateur:

"Tell us, Captain Aynath, how are the women of cavalry host?"

"It is kind of you to ask, effa. Exhausted but in fine spirits, having done their duty and been victorious."

Alhern and the captain paused to toast each other in camaraderie.

"Victory in Duty!" they chorused.

Eld wasn't included so she just took another bite of bread and cheese.

"Of course the loss of a horse has saddened us," Aynath continued.

Alhern nodded soberly. "And we almost lost the rider as well. Tell us, Farthal, what makes cavaliers reckless fools?"

Eld swallowed quickly to answer, hoping her wits were with her:

"Boldness and bravery are expectations. Perhaps individuals take it to extreme."

Alhern smiled. "There's no 'perhaps' about it, Farthal! The extreme has become a standard with girls and their horses!"

292

"Don't let my sister fool you," Seth said. "She wouldn't have it any other way on the battlefield."

"Even on the field boldness should be calculated. Charging an army of Bane-warriors, on foot no less, is well outside the purview of cavalier 'boldness'."

"Surely allowances will be made for the shock of loss?" Aynath asked.

"Of course," Alhern agreed. "But it can't go unmarked. She ignored orders to return to the lines and almost got herself killed. That was a phenomenal throw, cavalier," Alhern added, looking at Eld with unabashed admiration.

Eld felt her cheeks flush. "Thank you, emha."

"No, thank you. You skewered that Bane-armor, saved a soul and now I'll get to yell at her. When the healers let me, of course. I'm thinking a permanent rebuke will be sufficient. And a short suspension of pay. No need to summon an entire court-martial. She clearly wasn't herself."

"I agree," Aynath said. "This offense usually entails labor duty ..."

Alhern waved a hand. "We can apply her time in Temple. Those wounds are punishment enough."

"Verily."

"Now this one," Alhern pointed to Eld with a fork, "Is greedy for medals."

Aynath and Seth laughed at this; Solafi giggled.

"I wouldn't say that," Eld ventured. Modesty might not be desired in a debriefing, but it was essential to prove humility while socializing.

"What would you say?" Alhern asked. What unnerved Eld more than the question was Alhern's smile. In fact Eld was sure she'd never seen Alhern smile so much in her entire time at Falls Gate Keep as during this meal.

"Be wary, cavalier," Seth said. "She's laying a trap."

"I would say I was doing my duty as much as any mother given the same opportunity." Eld was proud of herself. It was a true and humble statement, but not obsequious.

"Well said," said Aynath.

"Yet not completely true," Alhern added between bites of fowl. "It is not true any mother would have attempted diplomacy with one of the enemy Eurthans. I will leave it to Command on whether that should be rebuked, since you are neither an officer nor in a position empowered for diplomacy. But I will recommend the attempt should be commended, not punished."

Aside to Eld, Aynath said, "Practically that means you will probably not be punished and count yourself lucky."

Alhern smiled at this speculation but didn't contradict it. She continued: "The other action that would not occur to 'any mother' was whistling orders for the Green Strike Gambit. You find that amusing, Farthal?"

"No, emha. It's just I called it something like that in my mind."

"It's an apt name. The insight into the strike effects was worthy on its own. Doing so in the midst of a real action, is remarkable. But putting that insight into action, with the support and assistance of others not obligated to follow you, that is a mother greedy for medals."

"She commends your duty and your extraordinary action in the midst of danger," Seth said as if translating a foreign dignitary.

Aynath laughed and Solafi giggled again. He stopped upon seeing his keeper glower.

The boy cleared his throat and asked, "Will Uncle Seth be decorated for bravery? He saved the knave!"

"He assisted the soldiers," Effa Tanmor corrected. "I believe he needed saving himself."

"You will find it is few mothers who will claim success without any assistance on the field," Alhern said with an authoritative deepness. "That assistance does not take away from bold or brave actions. It supports them. We'd be in Athmod's own vise if all we had was a handful of bold champions acting on their own. Ensign Alhern's actions will be reported and I expect there will be recognition."

That was the end of that matter. Seth had stopped speaking, looking sightlessly into his half empty plate. Eld wondered why. Surely it couldn't be because of the keeper's dismissive words. Effa Tanmor was quiet now, as if punishing the company for not taking to heart his wisdom.

"Can I be a page?" Solafi asked.

A military page was a volunteer position. Originally for sending messages and looking after officers, pages were now used for general minor tasks not covered under any department. They were mostly girls, but there were boys depending on talent and interest.

This question stirred the keeper. Effa Tanmor said nothing to Solafi but turned a baleful eye on Alhern. Finally this was his purview. "Surely this would be unsuitable, emha. Solafi has trouble as it is remembering the limits of respectable leisure activities."

But Alhern was too savvy to walk onto this uneven ground. "I don't think my sister would approve," she said. "And it is true you have trouble listening to instruction from the men running the house, nephew dear. How can you convince me you will follow orders that cannot be tried with familial affection?"

"It would be different," Solafi said. "And I could wear a uniform!"

"Now that's a reason I believe. A new fashion to impress your friends. You'll have to abstain from a profusion of ribbons. If this isn't a passing fancy, and you can come up with a better explanation, write it down and I will ask your mother."

"Thank you, auntie," Solafi said, perhaps too smug that he'd thwarted his keeper. "I felt like such a lump hiding in the wardrobe! That's where we fled after the cellar was overrun."

A moment later the keeper asked, "Have you eaten your fill?"

"Yes, but can I take a quarter loaf with me?" This question was directed at Alhern.

"Of course not!" Effa Tanmor said. "You weren't birthed from a vagrant tinker!"

But the boy wasn't even marking him. He faced Alhern, keeping a pleasant smile on his face.

Alhern didn't look up from her plate. "Brother?"

"I'm sure a platter for snacking can be sent to your room."

"Thank you," Solafi said, not specifying whom. He was already becoming adept at household politics.

"Then we will retire," Effa Tanmor said, standing in one graceful motion. "And leave mother's business to mothers."

The nephew stood less quickly, clearly wishing to linger. They said their goodnights and left.

"I should go too," Seth said.

"You don't have to," Alhern said, echoing Eld's desire that he stay.

"The day has been long."

"And no doubt made longer by a man all but telling you you've forgotten your place and no matter what uniform you wear you will never be considered a mother's equal."

Seth didn't deny this. "That doesn't relieve the burden, true."

"You mark his words too much," Alhern said. "Give him his orders and don't dwell on it. That's why I put you in that uniform. During these times of watchfulness, he obeys. And so must you for that matter."

Seth's humor returned, smiling at his sister grimly. "Remember, sister, watchfulness will not be forever."

"Oh, I'm aware, I am well aware. You will have your revenge anon."

"And on that thought, weariness bids me retire. Sorry." Seth added this last seeing Eld's eyes pleading with him to stay.

"The truth is weariness is about to take us all," Alhern said. "We do have business that should be discussed. You are welcome, brother, but your presence isn't required. Go if you must."

"Then I bid you gentle worthies good night."

The women stood as a house-girl stepped forward to pull Seth's chair out for him to rise. Never had an ensign been treated so regally. Eld eyes lingered on Seth's retreating form until Alhern said, "Stop mooning, Farthal. I expect you will have a chance to see a beautiful man soon enough."

Eld coughed, saying, "Sorry, emhas," and sat back down.

"What's your preference, Farthal?" Alhern asked, as Aynath drained the last of her water.

Preferences in spirits were another political and wooing gauntlet. Ask for something too expensive and a mother might be judged presumptuous or greedy. Ask for something too humble, then judgment might lean to unsophisticated and callow. At least it wasn't a man of the house asking: like lot fortune tellers who had pressed Trump cards into an apocryphal oracle of ill repute, her answer would be picked apart for the meaning the men fancied. What Eld wanted most of all at the moment was barley-mead. But that would be too simple by far. So she fielded the safest answer:

"What the the woman of the house chooses will be good enough for me."

The captain and commander laughed.

"When you're a politician, remember we simple soldiers!" Aynath said.

"Send for the Ishca Ba," Alhern said. "Bog Mead," she said by explanation to Eld. "It's not actually a mead at all, though the brewery is in a bog. It's grain brandy, if you haven't had it."

"Tyreens and Gaels call it whiskey, correct?" Eld ventured.

Alhern nodded.

"I haven't had it often," Eld confessed.

In fact Eld didn't favor it at all, preferring proper brandy. But she was unlikely to be drinking much, unless Alhern had lured her there for very grim news. In moments the house-girl came back with a bottle, dark green and unadorned, stoppered with a sealed cork. The woman broke the seal and set the bottle down.

"You and the staff may retire for the rest of the eve," Alhern said.

"Thank you, emha," the woman said, bowing and retiring from the room.

"The poor magi and healers will want for refreshment," Aynath ventured.

"There will be plenty left on the board. I want to finish our business with my favorite cavalier."

Eld raised an eye brow at this. "Should I be worried, emha?"

296

"Caution would be wise," Alhern confirmed as she poured three crystal goblets with a couple finger fulls of pale amber liquid with a sharp peaty scent. "I call you my favorite cavalier because my brother favors you. And it would be awkward in the long term to disagree with him. Thus I'd prefer to not have any reason to."

Eld started to nod then stopped herself. The door was shut and she was certain she was alone with these two women, the captain of the cavalry host and the commander of the garrison. All that was missing was her company lieutenant and sergeant, but Sergeant Tarl had a trick of making herself unreachable to superiors when she preferred to be making merry. Eld wished she'd had that talent but she seemed to be drawn into the thick of events. Eld waited patently for Alhern to express her mind, or at least pass her a goblet.

Finally Alhern set a goblet in front of Eld. Aynath took one of the two remaining. But Alhern didn't touch hers so Eld didn't feel free to drink yet. Instead Eld sat back, exuding what she hoped was humble patience. A full minute passed before Alhern said:

"What did I tell you about Lieutenant Roel the last time we spoke on the subject of that soul?"

Eld's mind flew back. It wasn't that she'd ever forget, but she wanted to recall it correctly.

"You said I should not swagger or boast about Roel's humiliation. And to consider myself even."

"Why?"

"Because I baited her."

Alhern sipped her whiskey. "Tell us what Roel complained about this time, Aynath."

"The lieutenant claims Lancer Farthal had her thrown from her horse deliberately. Roel added that Farthal's horse was a – " here Aynath pulled a leaf of paper from her jacket, " – 'an unwholesome influence on her own horse, causing it to stray, ignoring her calls for at least a quarter of an hour'."

While it was clear both the captain and commander found this greatly amusing, Eld didn't dare laugh or smirk.

"That's rather good penship," Alhern muttered. "Considering it's in pencil. As neat as printing."

"I think she didn't want to miss one transgression," Aynath said. "She even left room for an unabbreviated signature."

Eld decided having a sip of whiskey was the best way to keep her composure.

"And she submitted this right after we returned to the garrison?" Alhern asked.

"No, just before we left the field."

"Well, Farthal, Roel seems quite motivated to report your, and your horse's, actions with alacrity," Alhern said.

"Yes," Eld said, her throat raw from whiskey.

"Not to fear, cavalier. I'm sure we can manage to save your horse from a court-martial."

"I would be truly grateful," Eld said, fully knowing this was a jest, though she kept her face neutral.

"Jesting aside, you cannot so easily avoid that fate," Alhern said solemnly.

The merry mood drained from the conversation.

Eld waited for Alhern to speak. There was no point in protesting her innocence.

"Did you throw Roel deliberately from your horse?"

"Yes."

"Why?"

"She boasted about using a man I was friendly with. No one you know," Eld added. She didn't want Alhern to worry over Seth's safety.

"Did she force herself on him?" Alhern asked.

"No. But —"

"Yes, Farthal, you will have to explain how jealousy over a man excuses abusing an officer's person and thwarting her duty in the middle of a battle."

"It wasn't jealousy!" Eld objected. "He told me himself! Roel sought him to take her vengeance out on him."

"But she didn't force herself on him," Aynath said.

"No, she paid him," Eld confirmed. "But she humiliated him, making him understand it was because of me ..."

Eld grabbed the goblet and downed the rest of the whiskey, wanting to obliterate the disgust she felt.

Alhern mused a moment. "Is your friend willing to report Roel actions? Even if it's not rape, it may fall under unworthy conduct of an officer."

"No. At least when I asked him. He was adamant he would talk to no woman about this."

"And while she rode with you, did Roel go into details?"

Eld didn't want to break Althas confidence. "They were things few men choose to do, but many harlots are paid for."

"That's baiting," Aynath said. "In the course of duty."

"That defense has merit, " Alhern said, "But, baiting or no, throwing an officer deliberately during battle is the greater offense against duty. It requires a court-martial unless Roel waves it for a rebuke.

Now Eld laughed humorlessly. "Roel would have me in a Dwen pit of spikes if she could just because her horse hates her."

"Yes," Alhern agreed, "It is unlikely Roel will consider she shares any responsibility. You're about to be the first soul in centuries both awarded for actions in battle and court-martialed for the same. But there are other options."

Captain Aynath spoke:

"It's been such a long time since these things have been needed. The laws are nearly obsolete but have never been stricken. Most think of duels as informal fights of private arrangement. But the military duel is still part of regulations. It can only be invoked in specific circumstances: the honor of the mother or her family or associates must be tangibly offended. And the offense must happen in such a way that it had threatened to prevent a soul from discharging her, or his, duty by disruption, distraction or obstruction."

"What you have described as I understand," Alhern said, "is being baited by Roel through the abuse of a man's honor. No," Alhern held a hand up to Eld's expected objection. "You do not have to confess the details. Nor does he need to be publicly named. But his name must be in documentation."

Eld inhaled and sighed. She wanted another portion of whiskey but Alhern hadn't offered one. "There are papers to sign I expect."

"Absolutely. A military duel is a contract. If Roel accepts."

"And if she refuses?"

"Because you requested the duel based on tangible offense and distraction from duty – both recognized legally – this puts Roel's complaint in a dithering light."

"Put simply, had she not gone out of her way to cause offense, it is unlikely you would have acted against duty," Aynath put in.

"That's part of why we must offer Roel the option to wave a court-martial and settle for a rebuke," Alhern said, "As much as we think she will refuse. If she was a wise soul, she would take this. A formal rebuke of the sort you earned is a permanent mark. But if you duel, win or lose, there will remain a doubt on record that Roel's complaint ever had justification. If she refuses, the doubt will be stronger."

"I see," Eld said. "But if I went to court ..."

"Farthal, you are as guilty as a spriteling caught in larder of sweets covered with honey," Aynath said impatiently. "The court might be sympathetic as to why you threw her, but there is no mitigation that would affect the legal outcome. At minimum you will be drudging and have your pay suspended for weeks."

"Three months, I'd guess," Alhern said, "We really would prefer the hero of the garrison not be humbled so. But it is your choice. Which will it be?"

Duels had their own risks. Outside of the power struggles between adolescents, Eld had never witnessed a proper duel. Not even the arena fights that Danshor liked to wager on. It wasn't a sport Eld found compelling. Risk included not just the chance of injury, but the weather was fickle, assuming they wouldn't be fighting inside. Eld didn't like the idea of a cold fight in a cellar arena, but at least they were fair in that neither party could access her sulessence.

But the certainty of suspension of pay decided her. Eld was already skint. And the truth was the idea of beating Roel and doing it legally, greatly appealed to her.

"Very well," Eld said. "A duel it is."

"I told you," Alhern said, holding a hand open towards the Aynath. "Five queens was it?"

Aynath laughed. "It's no queens at all, because I refused the bet!"

"Oh, that's right!" Alhern said. In a serious tone she added, "I think that will be all for now. Rest up, Farthal. We will settle the formalities tomorrow."

# PART II

# ꝒAꝛ ~ ꝶONOꝛ

## Chapter 21

# Settling the Wounded

Leaving the commander's house was only difficult due to the various obstructions and repair scaffolding, the maze-like feel having faded with familiarity. Outside, though there was still light in the sky, the sun had set leaving a red haze over the western horizon. The fresh night air was somewhat marred by the scent of burning, and in the hours after the battle a haze had settled over the valley. Much like after a wildfire, the lingering smoke was likely to cause mist or fog, especially as the night was still crisp and cool this time of year.

Yet none of this dampened the celebratory spirits of the souls in the garrison and the village. The lights from The Step, filtered through the new leaves of the hedgerow trees, could easily be seen, singing and music echoing in the distance. Nearby, as Alhern predicted, the Rowan Oak was active and glowed, the center of shouts and general sounds of revelry, flautists and drummers vying merrily with each other. Alhern would find no comfort in Tafli's bower tonight. The commander was not likely to sleep for a while in any case. Eld had never been certain where the conference room was from the outside of the house, but now she could see a faint glow emanating from the center of the roof, beyond her line of sight. Surely this was the light of lanterns falling up into the sky. Eld's thoughts turned to other rooms but she didn't dare seek them at the moment. It wasn't late enough, and she'd be marked by someone. She had not made arrangements with Seth, but wanted to call on him all the same. He had been brave in his report, but Eld suspected he still felt troubled.

Revelry didn't appeal to Eld so she instead made her way to the Temple. There were wounded sisters to visit as well as the cavalier who had almost thrown her life away.

The Temple was a misnomer for it was really a hospital. The name was traditionally applied to ancient places of worship and meditation dedicated to a Mother-God or Goddi; more specifically, to places for rest and healing, traditionally in houses of Lorthensul, Physician of the Gods, that fraught birth from Sul's tryst with Eurath's son Theedwen, Laird of the Forest. Lorthensul's symbol, a wand of foxglove or thorn twined with a helix of snakes, was much like the Astalyn. It was called a snake-branch or Tathum, and implied poison could be medicine, but only with the wisdom of a trained soul. Many were the folktales of both heroes and villains being assisted by snakes with their magic.

While the myth of Athmod had cast permanent suspicion on the serpent as a creature of questionable intentions, most depictions of Lorthensul, robed in the mantel of the ancients, still had a serpent twined like a pet around each arm. The garrison Temple was small, thus the statue of Lorthensul was equally modest, certainly not life sized. Yet it was a good work in white stone, one hand holding a cup, the other, a wand, but no twining snakes. Instead the figure wore a belt with an interwoven snake pattern, binding a long shift ancient women of respect wore. Her hair was bound in a single plait of four strands, one for each Airt, where the ancients believed healthy "airs" originated: Euphoria, Calm, Rapture and Melancholy. These were imagined as birds: the hummer, the heron, the hawk and owl, and thus they perched on and around Lorthensul, blessing her with the wisdom of the healing arts. Now it was known the source of health was a balance of the Motes of Life; like a good brew, a healthy body and soul encouraged vigor and discouraged the blossoming of motes of disease. And while, true, fresh air was desired, it did not carry anything special medicinally from direction or time of day. Still there were people who warned of placing dining rooms in the west lest excessive calm inhibit their digestion. Or made a point of bedrooms sitting in the east to rise with pleasant spirits. But it was all errant philosophy. One proof was that hospital temples put patients in rooms irrespective of the Airts and they all thrived equally.

Lorthensul's statue stood above a small pool near the Temple doors, two pillars flanking the way, the only design elements hearkening to the ancient past. In every other way the Temple was a modern practical building, windows and doors topped with plain, half-circle arches, all a single story on a wide but compact design, allowing for as many rooms to have arrays above the beds. Up to a quarter of the garrison population could be comfortably housed at a time, a situation that would be considered disastrous. It had never been this full from wounded or sick soldiers, though now and then it was given over as emergency shelter for women fighting wildfires or locals driven from their homes by storm or flood.

Now the Temple was near capacity, but at least every soul that needed an array had one. It was even more crowded because each woman had a steady stream of visitors. Eld seemed to remember that the Temple forbade bringing food. Healers wanted to know their charges were being fed properly for recovery. But so sudden was the influx of bodies, and so serious the wounds, the healers had given up on policing food. A healer pursed her lips in disapproval at a couple soldiers boldly bearing two full hampers of various rolls, meats and sweets, oblivious to her glaring eye. They were greeted by cheers and disappeared to where their wounded sisters lay. The healer sighed forcefully and strode on. The fact was the Temple kitchens couldn't keep up with the need at the moment.

Eld walked through the halls packed with women, greeting a soul here and there, now and then stopping to hear news. One soldier wanted to wander, gripping a blanket around her shoulders, wary of all the faces around her. Her hair was loose and she looked a touch mad. Her sisters kept guiding her back to her room and telling her to breathe. Women in passing touched her lightly on the arm or shoulder, and it seemed with every touch she was more settled. Eld rested a couple fingers on her shoulder as she walked passed and wishing her peace.

"Elam," said a women nearby. "She died and we almost lost her through the Door."

Eld nodded, having guessed that was so. Death was to be avoided, and this was why. The woman would recover, but the shock of passing and returning was not to be underestimated. Some women never completely recovered; if she couldn't settle to be fit for duty she wound be discharged with honors.

Eld wandered on, knowing who she sought and almost afraid of finding her. She did accept a sip of a goblet from Galdas, the soldier who had both wrists broken. She was in fine spirits, the bones of one wrist set enough she could use it if she was careful, the other still splinted, now wrapped with woody vines.

"That Ash Dwen man did it. It still hurts but it stays in place without bandages cutting off my blood. Why don't we have Dwen men in every Temple?"

"And they're not half nice to gaze on either!" another woman added to general laughter.

"Watch your words," Eld warned. "Keep your appreciation respectful or suffer the fate of…."

She stopped herself, knowing using this moment as an excuse to humiliate Roel was indulgent.

"Idiot officers who can't catch their horses?" one woman suggested.

Laughter buffeted Eld from every direction. "I didn't say it," she said, walking on.

Eld quickened her step. One soul launched into a retelling of the events of the Rowan Oak and Eld thought it wise her presence wasn't noted when they came to the most amusing bits.

Eld came to clearer, calmer halls, with visitors talking quietly or women in healing sleep. That was where she finally found the wounded cavalier, Trannecyn.

Trannecyn was from the 1st company so Eld didn't know her or her sisters, though one of the two women looked familiar. Probably a customer of Patrycan's. The women were speaking; Trannecyn herself was unconscious.

" ...and I sent her sister a letter by the canal station. Seemed safer than using post that goes through Falls Gate ...Hello?"

"Al met," Eld said, pausing at the door. When there was no objection she stepped in. The women's eyes widened in recognition.

"You saved her," the one who had been talking breathed.

"I guess I did," Eld said looking at the figure lying unconsciouses.

"Bless you, Gilded Hero!" the other cavalier said, clasping her wrist.

"Yes, of course," Eld said absently, wondering how much pain Trannecyn was in or if she had been given so much draught she was senseless. Woody vines wrapped a good third of her body, including an leg and an arm. Unlike most patients she'd been completely stripped of her clothes as well as armor to treat the burns down one side. Half of her hair had been scorched off. One leg was suspended in a sling by a twisted wood frame added to the supports of the bed. She was covered by a light sheet draped over a wicker-like collar so it did not touch her burns. Eld only half heard the continued expressions of thanks from Trannecyn's friends. Looking at her, Eld didn't feel she'd done a very good job of saving this woman.

"They say she could be healed in three months," one woman was saying.

"Good," Eld said absently.

"But it will be hard without Boad."

"Boad?"

"Her horse."

Boad. The image of a wagon with a white tarp swam into Eld's mind. She remembered her talk with the healer. Where was the body now? She wondered. Waiting serum only lasted for a couple hours. Eld shivered, feeling danger, a reverie without vision. Either the horse lived or it didn't. But if it did, how much more distressed would it be returning to life without it's rider? There would be only one touch that could calm it and she was lying here.

"Where did you last see Boad?" Eld blurted.

"Being taken away in the wagon," one of the women said.

So they didn't know.

Eld dashed out the door, through the halls and outside. Animal healers tended to their patients in barns or paddocks. There had been a couple of injured horses. But if Eld was trying to retrieve an animal that had become fraught, she wouldn't keep the animal near the rest if she could help it. But where?

Looking around there was a paddock. She saw shadowy equine figures. Eld trotted in that direction. First she'd check which horses they were. But she slowed to a stop, having extended her mind and finding that while yes, they were horses, neither was so distressed that it could have died recently. Maybe the healer had failed.

Eld changed direction towards a large stone building, if she could guess, the Temple supply house. She heard the sounds before she felt the mind: a low indistinct voice speaking calmly and a whinny that rose and fell with agitation. The door was unlocked. Eld walked in.

The interior was a wreck. Barrels had been kicked over, and a stack of grain had fallen, a couple bags ripped, spilling their contents across the slate stone floor. A whole shelf of goods in glass jars and clay pots had toppled over with predictable messy results. Only things in bottles were spared, though these too had been kicked by the beast, making footing dangerous. At the end of a rope lead the healer hung on close to tears:

"He won't settle!" she said. "What am I going to do?"

Eld looked at the horse. He seemed healthy on the outside, with the sole exception of the gaping wound where his eye had been.

"I can't even seal his head! He needed to wake or he'd be gone. It's not like with Thyn where you can explain and keep them near ..."

"Yes, I know."

"I have someone getting a calming drought. But it's anyone's guess if he'll drink it ..."

"I know who will calm him," Eld said. "Give me the lead."

"But they said she's deep in dreams...."

"I know. Maybe they can help each other." Eld took the rope and placed a hand on the stallion's neck. "We are going to her," she murmured, touching his mind.

It was roiling with fear, pain, loss, horror ...suddenly Eld understood.

"It's not just the death. He thinks she's gone. No, come with me. I will take you to her."

Almost instantly the horses thoughts calmed. There was still anxiety and pain, but now there was anticipation and hope. Boad yielded to Eld's guidance and walked out of the storage silo, the healer following relieved but worried.

"How are we going to get Trannecyn out? She's not supposed to be moved."

"We aren't. We're bringing Boad in."

"But beasts aren't allowed in the Temple..!"

"I think this time an exception will be made."

"You don't know Temple Prefect Olthan."

"Olthan? I think I met her after the battle." Eld shrugged. "Guess I'm fated to meet her again."

While Eld was far from adept at thought speech, the fearful anxious thoughts of the young healer were almost a palpable thing lurking in their wake, reminding them of the threat of challenge and discovery. But such times the only true danger was hesitation and timidity. As long as they kept to their course and acted boldly, they would be unchallenged, at least until they had reached their goal.

And so Eld guided Boad at a brisk walk, astonishing both visiting soldiers and patents with the presence of a horse entering the Temple halls, not the least being the cavaliers who had understood this particular horse had been lost irretrievably to death.

"That's Boad!"

"It's not possible. He laid too long in the field!"

"Ai, but I marked he wasn't stiff when he was covered and I wondered then ..."

"So it's possible?"

"Well, that's not a ghost horse walking, now is it?"

Eld ignored them all, particularly the astonished healers who were too shocked to object. Perhaps they guessed at her goal. She was grateful for the company of her healer ally, for Eld's mind was so occupied with calming and reassuring the stallion's mind, and keeping the worst of his pain at bay, she'd lost track of where exactly Trannecyn's room lay. The healer guided them into the familiar corridor. Hearing the sounds of a horse coming their way, both of Trannecyn's friends stepped out. Unlike their fellows they were utterly speechless.

"We think Trannecyn's touch will calm him," Eld said.

"He's having a hard time setting after retrieval," the healer explained. The woman glanced outside the hall then stepped into the room, moving quickly.

"There is not much time," she said, pulling the sheet down from Trannecyn's form to move her least injured and unbound arm out. "Bring him closer."

Eld guided the stallion until his head stood over Trannecyn's bed. Aware of the danger if, for whatever reason the stallion was upset or tried to bolt in a panic so close to his injured rider, Eld had taken to hugging the horse's neck so there was no chance their contact could be broken. She settled in thought, meeting his mind, waiting to guide it. Through Boad she felt the palm of Trannecyn's sleeping hand being placed against his nose. Boad jerked back, uncertain, still in shock, it was wrong, she wasn't there....

She sleeps, Eld corrected, keeping her thoughts positive, using her own essence to search for the presence of the sleeping woman's soul. This was something the healer would be more adept at so there was nothing to do but wait and reassure the horse. Eld tried to recall memories to help Boad, but it was hard. They were over-shadowed and pale against the vivid event of his recent death. But she found one: Boad stood by a stream, greedily drinking after a pleasant run across a meadow. It had been a lazy sunny day, and Trannecyn laughed beside him, splashing water over her face, then patting his neck and saying words of fellowship and praise –

And then Trannecyn was with them.

Eld had closed her eyes. For a second she saw Trannecyn's soul, a cavalier geared for battle, but surrounded by a blinding light. Boad shivered, making a sound that might have been a whimper. He neighed so loudly Eld was sure the entire garrison must hear it. Then he was silent and all the tension lingering inside him melted away, his soul, now secure it was safe to stay, finally settling into his mortal form. Eld could feel the healer's essence rushing in, taking the opportunity to seal Boad's wound, removing as much of the cause of pain as possible. The most pressing matter was his brain; enough had been repaired for life, but one half was doing the duty of two and the injured side would need to be restructured using the whole side as a map. Inevitably memories were lost from these injuries, though with Thyn most could be recovered from dreams. Eld pulled her own essence out as the healer sealed the remains of Boad's left eye lid, essential to reconstruct his eye, a work that would take months.

When Eld opened her eyes, she was pleasantly surprised to see Trannecyn had wakened, her gold eyes amber in the low light, tears streaming down the side of her face into her hairline.

"How is this possible?" she whispered hoarsely, her hand still on Boad's nose.

Eld's own throat caught with emotion. She intended to let the healer explain except, at that moment, the dreaded Prefect Olthan burst into the room.

"What in all of Athmod's unholy legions is going on here?" Olthan demanded using the deepest of her voices.

She was indeed the same matrician woman Eld remembered from after the battle, the kind who embodied institutional sternness and authority; it was hard to imagine her ever doting on children. When Eld was younger, much like the healer next to her, she had been intimidated by this sort. But now Eld understood it was a type of aspect such women wore. An unbalanced soul wore it as armor more than they needed, but underneath most was a mother like any other, who simply took their commitment to institutional duty seriously. With sudden insight, Eld saw it wasn't much different from Alhern's commanding aspect. That made facing the prefect easier.

"Well, as you can see, emha, we're reuniting a cavalier with her horse," Eld said, trying to keep her voice light but not flippant.

Olthan peered sharply at Boad. "That horse died!"

"And has been retrieved. He had trouble at first, but once reunited with his rider he settled right in."

Olthan looked at Trannecyn, Eld, Boad, and finally at the young healer. "You used the waiting serum."

"Yes," the healer said, her voice almost a whisper.

"Good thing too!" one of Trannecyn's friends exclaimed.

But Olthan ignored them as if they were furniture. "That was reckless and foolish. If its soul could not settle it could have run on a rampage. And if its body isn't tended ..."

"It could decay in situ," Eld said feeling bold enough to speak. "It is rare and so best dealt with by prevention."

"Cavalier, as much as I respect your many well discussed deeds, this is a Temple matter and I will thank you to hold your tongue."

"With respect, emha, I have training. I understand commitment to Temple custom ensures the habit of duty. But less time spent berating your healer and letting her tend to Boad's system will prevent the very thing you fear."

Eld almost quailed under the intense stare of Olthan's deep gold eyes. She was older than she looked in passing, not a couple centuries, but a vigorous three centuries, perhaps three and a half. The force of the decades pressed on Eld's aura. If an elf lived long enough, she acquired much of the force of a magi adept without having to train. And a healer was simply a type of magi.

But Eld had faced death, Eurthan Bane contraptions, and interrogation by the commander over her liaison with Seth. She could weather the storm of this worthy's disapproval. What could she do? Send her through the Door?

~If I was a murderous mother with no scruple, yes, I could,~ Olthan said in thought.

Startled to hear the thought, Eld's eyes widened, but she held Olthan's. They stayed locked while Olthan verbally said, "Healer Tarasik, take this beast to the paddock and tend it until dawn. I will send another to take over the task and it will be watched day and night for corruption."

"He's fine!" Trannecyn objected, though she barely had the strength to speak.

Olthan broke eye contact with Eld to stare at the wounded cavalier, and her tangle of Dwen bindings, bandages and burn salve. "You should be resting in dreams. Your healing will be faster that way. If you refuse to rest you will be given another draught."

Trannecyn was silent but glared at Olthan. But the senior healer had returned her attention to Eld.

"You, Lancer Farthal, have meddled enough. Since you are not injured, you are banished from my temple until such a time that you are."

"Emha," Eld said, nodding in an abbreviated salute, acknowledging Olthan's authority before walking quickly out. The women she passed peppered her with questions, begging her for the tale, but she didn't dare stay. Olthan was like her namesake, a dragon protecting her lair. She'd probably returned from the commander's meeting and wasn't expecting horses to be roaming the Temple corridors. What would Olthan do? Eld wasn't a healer under her authority, but Tarasik was. Like Eld, Tarasik would face discipline. Healers weren't court-martialed, but an inquiry was close. Eld would testify in Tarasik's favor if she could, but her fate was ultimately with the Temple Prefect's Council.

Outside the night air was crisp and refreshing, though it still carried the taste of burning. Eld looked up to see an odd star here and there, but haze and mist obscured most of the sky. Near the ground it diffused light so that all places still alight with activity, the Crèche, the Temple, the Rowan Oak, even the distant village, seemed to glow with a magical warm light. It might be three hours or less before midnight. Not as late as Eld might preferred, but perhaps, with so much activity, enough women were not marking the commander's house and it was safe to approach the back garden.

Eld walked down the path until she was as far from any light source as to be shadowed and unrecognizable even by friendly eyes. From there she watched the house and saw a cluster of magi leave, followed by a couple of women dressed in civilian garb. Eld let a minute pass. Seeing no other soul besides the guards pacing, Eld set off to the back of the house, tacking to the shadows much as she had the first time. It was even easier now; she knew after a handful of visits exactly which glass door to approach and every other window on the ground floor was dark. Had everyone abandoned the house to celebrate?

Still, Eld walked as quietly as she could. There were lights in the upper rooms and she suspected the commander slept there. Why she let Seth sleep on the bottom floor Eld wondered. Was it to allow him to leave discretely, for whatever reason?

Eld spied Seth's door and for a moment thought she saw a warm light. But it winked out. Carefully leaning into the glass, at first Eld saw nothing but a weak reflection of herself lit from the glow of distant lights. Then, as if slowly manifesting from the dream world, Seth appeared, his face replacing Eld's reflection as he leaned close. It was unreadable and emotionless. The door eased open the barest part of an inch. Then Seth vanished leaving Eld to open it and slip in, closing it behind her.

"Pull the curtain," Seth said in a subdued voice.

Once Eld did this, Seth opened the shutter of a table lamp. Amber glass filtered the solstone light so it was a deep, warm orange. The room was much as Eld remembered her last visit, but Seth was much changed from when she'd seen him earlier.

His hair was loose and he wore a tree silk dressing robe with a fabric scattered with small woven suns, their rays touching each other at quarter points. The color of the cloth was hard to tell but probably pale yellow or white, because in the light it took on the same orange cast as Seth's skin. He slowly sat on the bed, apparently insensible to Eld's presence, his eyes resting on the arm chair nearby where his military uniform was draped, as if the body it encased had vanished suddenly leaving it to fall on the chair's padding.

"I can't stop seeing it," Seth said, grabbing the bedding to either side of him in fists. "The boy. That thing trying to drag him away. I held on and could feel him slip from my grip no matter how hard I hit it. We were showered with so many sparks. I am surprised it didn't break."

Then Eld saw the sword on the floor, unsheathed, lying as if it had been dropped there. It's edge was chipped and scratched in a way swords from the Shard Hills never were. Eld remembered the sparkling shards lying in the battlefield, all that remained of her own sword. She would be issued a new one soon. It was lucky Seth's sword hadn't broken. But it was damaged beyond use.

"You'll need that replaced," Eld said.

"I never want to touch it again!" Seth shouted. "I can still hear him screaming! Our knave! Peleen! He's only eleven decades! I kept hitting it, but he was slipping away! If the women hadn't been able to strike, he would have been taken and ..."

"Seth, you need to stop ..."

"And it would have been my fault!" Seth shouted. Then he broke down and sobbed. "I never want to hold a sword again! I never want to see that thing again ..."

This time he didn't mean the Eurthan warrior but the uniform that lay empty of body and purpose, a cloth ghost that haunted Seth's mind.

Eld looked around and spied a mantle hanging on a hook. She threw it over the chair, covering the uniform. Seth blinked and looked up. The spell appeared to be broken. But Seth's eyes swam with tears.

"I can't stop seeing it," he said, his voice breaking from grief.

Eld knelt in front of him, as if proposing, taking his hands into hers.

"You saved him. No, listen: you saved him. Had you not held him for as long as you did, had you stopped fighting for a moment, he would have been lost. But you held on until help came. Sometimes that's all you can do. None of us are as brave as we'd like to be. And even when we are, none of us are as graceful and poised about it as we imagined. Remember the attack in the glade? I wished I could have danced as lightly as a sprite, evading that strike that almost killed me. You saved us there too: without that waxed paper we would have been done for."

"But that was nothing. Everyone knows waxed paper seals air."

"You improvised with something you knew. It was bold and brilliant, and allowed us to flee with our lives. Fighting is always messy business, even when life and duty aren't at stake. You need to forgive yourself for not being the perfect warrior. No woman is; why should a man expect to be?"

For a second Seth was his old self, staring at Eld with a hint of offense. "That's your argument? I should expect less of myself because I'm a man?"

"If it will bring you back from despair, I will weather whatever offense you send me, my noble laird."

Seth shook his head. "You are impossibly bold, cavalier."

"And you are truly expecting too much of yourself. No, not because you're a man," Eld said quickly to avoid argument. "Because you haven't been trained. Yes, you can use a sword. But it's not the same as drilling, as doing the acts of battle even in practice. It disciplines the body, mind and soul, even dreams. It becomes second nature, so even in the face of fear or the unexpected, a part of you is secure that you have the means to meet the foe. Without training your doubt is greater than your skill; it is that doubt that makes you rethink the event over and over. Your soul is trying to understand and see how it can learn to do better. But trauma is a terrible teacher. Repetition without wisdom will wear the spirit down to aught."

Seth sighed as if he'd held the breath of an entire week inside him. "Well, that is truth. I think I could sleep a month."

313

"It wouldn't hurt." Eld rose. "I'll leave you--"

"No!" Seth exclaimed, seizing Eld's arm. "I don't want to be alone. Just lie with me?"

Eld thought a moment. "I must leave very early."

"Why? I know you all are free of duty for at least a day."

"I have watch coming soon. But, more importantly, I need to be in the stables so your sister can summon me."

Seth's brow furrowed. "Why?"

"To face discipline for offending an officer. You'll learn about it soon enough. That's what we discussed after you left."

"I see." Seth's curiosity seemed spent. That itself was a sign he was mentally and emotionally exhausted.

"How is the knave?" Eld asked.

"Are you staying or not?"

To answer Eld started unbuttoning her coat. "I shall chastely sleep on the sheet covering you, effa."

Seth smiled slightly. "If you must. Peleen is well enough. He had a draught for shock. I suppose you'll suggest I have one as well."

"I suggest you speak to a healer. A settling would be better."

Settling was an essence operation by which a healer untangled traumatic memory, giving the patient a revealed understanding. A simple settling might be done for children after a serious accident, or for animals disturbed by thunderstorms. Most of the wounded would have been settled as part of their basic treatment.

Seth didn't reply, turning his attention to brushing his hair before weaving it loosely for the night. Eld took that time to remove her boots and untuck her shirt for comfort. She dumped her coat on top of the mantle that hid Seth's uniform.

"Did you ever get a settling after the attack?" she finally asked.

"No."

"Why?"

Seth paused a moment before replying.

"I didn't want a woman in my mind after being threatened with rape."

"There are male healers."

"Would you want anyone in your mind after that?"

"I ...wouldn't know."

"See, women don't understand the threat, do you? That you will be humbled forever as a slave to another's soul and never, never be considered worthy or effective because once a woman overpowered you for her pleasure. Never will you be allowed to recover your dignity. Unless you are that rare

314

man who can fight as a mother's equal. But they are never attacked so, are they?"

"There's truth there," Eld confessed. "Some women fantasize about dominating 'war-kings'. But they're much more afraid of the humiliation if they fail. So they mostly avoid them, apart from talking nastily behind their backs."

"Assuming they are brothers of passion."

"Yes."

"So, no, under the stormy weather of these expectations, I will not be opening my mind unless I absolutely must. We should thank all of Paradise, them being stray vandals, we were spared anything like a formal inquiry."

"I saw one," Eld blurted.

"What?"

"The first time we formally encountered the Eurthans. One of the attackers was in the ravine. In Bane-armor. She threw me into a tree."

"I hope she suffered for that."

"I don't know. I was knocked out. Danshor played with her a while." Eld sat on the other side of the bed, waiting for Seth to recline. "I understand. No, not the fate of man, but why you don't want to bare your thoughts to a strange woman. But saving the knave seems to have affected you more than the attack in the wilds. Consider it. Most of the women wounded have been settled. So it wouldn't be a slight on your sex."

"You should be a legal notary," Seth said, finally slipping under the sheets. "You argue your case well."

"Will the court consider it?" Eld asked. She laid beside Seth, pulling a light coverlet halfway up over them both, but not so far to hide their separation.

"Perhaps," Seth said shuttering the lamp. Then he lay with his back to Eld, pulled her arm around him, so they rested, folded together. "If you don't leave before dawn."

Eld nuzzled him, kissing his neck, falling into the warm scent of his skin. Then, in spite of the early hour, they both fell into dreamless sleep, exhaustion conquering whatever vague ideas Eld might have had to coit in dreams.

Dreams Eld had, but they were simple dreams of a sleeping mind making sense of events and emotion:

She was standing before a court of healers, the most stern and unforgiving prefects a soul ever imagined, Prefect Olthan acting as judge. The healer Tarasik was dressed as a legal notary, in shirt and vest, yet with her healer's cap. But she was too afraid of Olthan to say a word, so Eld was forced to speak in her own defense, pointing to all her medals to prove her deeds. Then Fiorseth took the stand and spoke verbally as if she was Aelgyn, and accused Eld of exposing her to danger. A parade of horses Eld had known accused her of using them carelessly. Even Hollar accused Eld of being slow and deficient in her healing. Only Tuiric and Boad spoke in her favor: Eld had given Tuiric carrots once, and that should be considered. And of course Boad was grateful to be returned to his rider, but this only underscored the issue of reckless elfyn danger so it didn't matter. Olthan pronounced her sentence: Eld was to be cast into the Void. Suddenly seized by two armored Eurthans, Eld was dragged to the door, that had turned into a portal leading to the black wastes between stars. Eld screamed for mercy while she heard Fiorseth say, "This is for your own good ..."

Eld opened her eyes, apparently waking, feeling her heart race. But something wasn't quite right, the quality of light was still of dreams. She was still hugging Seth from behind, facing the door. It had been cracked just an inch. A gold eye about the height of a woman peered in, the rest of her obscured. Eld blinked and raised her head.

Then she truly woke. The door was still shut and the light much darker, a cast of blue presaging the coming dawn. Very carefully Eld rolled off the other side of the bed, trying her best not to disturb Seth, still deep asleep. Eld first stepped to the door and put an ear to it. She heard no one, not even sounds of retreat. She felt sure the presence she'd seen was Alhern; was she watching them from dreams?

Eld pulled her boots on and retrieved her flout and coat, not bothering to put it on until she stepped through the door out to the garden. Yes, she felt certain it had been Alhern, as she buttoned her jacket, carrying her flout in hand. Whatever their arguments, Selind and Sethshorn were brother and sister, and they were as close as Traith and Shedann. Alhern would know Seth was distraught and she had come to check on him. Leaving now was for the best.

## Chapter 22

# The Challenge

The way to the stables was thick with mist, which struck Eld odd as the air wasn't that cold. It seemed to drift in waves from the village, as if one of the valleys had filled with vapor and was spilling over. But mist was a manifestation of cold, moist air. It did not "flood" like a river in Eld's experience. When she arrived at the stable, the guard challenging her was at least near her age.

"Strange morning, Ai?" she said.

"Ai," Eld agreed.

"You weren't the only one lodging elsewhere. Half the garrison is in The Wildling, I think."

Eld smiled at the exaggeration and entered the stable. There was much truth to it; a quarter of the cots were empty, including Danshor's. Eld was relieved. They seemed to have moved past their argument about men, but there was no reason to revisit it. Stripping her clothes off and settling to sleep properly, Eld didn't have much time to wonder whose company Danshor was enjoying before falling back into a much needed rest.

It seemed like the next moment Reon was tapping her bunk.

"I abhor disturbing any resting mother on a free day, but there's a summons from the commander's office."

Eld blearily took the folded, sealed paper Reon held over her face and sat up, her loose hair falling around her shoulders like a cape. It was well after dawn and bright.

"Who was he?" Torin called.

"No one you know," Eld muttered, breaking the wax seal in the shape of a flint-sun and reading the contents. It was as she expected, a formal summons to respond to a complaint. She was warned she could be court-martialed unless she made a challenge. A duel. She was to report dressed for duty at noon.

Eld rubbed her face, then set about gathering what she needed for the baths. She had to expect Roel to be present and would be damned if she looked like a vagrant or Wildling in that soul's presence.

"What's this?" Danshor asked, picking up the summons from where Eld dropped it on her cot. "A duel?"

The entire barrack fell silent.

"Ai," Eld confirmed absently. "An officer has made a complaint. It seems I can avoid complete disgrace if I fight her."

The silence bothered her. She'd gathered her bathing kit (sandals, towel, hand scrub and comb), and was dressed in her drudges: heavy, dun linen, loose trousers, much like those worn by townies, and a long vest of the same material with an abundance of pockets. It was the uniform women wore when doing work on duty, like cleaning the stables. It was also a practical stand-in for a morning robe. A couple others were prepared to jump in the baths much like Eld, but most of the company was dressed in various civilian garb: bracs or town pants, with shirts and vests. While all eager to be off to enjoy their free days, they lingered in collective uncertainty.

"What did I say?" Eld asked.

"You plan to duel?" Danshor asked, her voice with a hint of uncharacteristic worry .

"Your concern is touching," Eld said, annoyed at her tone. "I'd think you'd have a bit more faith in someone you keep teasing as a "Gilded Hero". It's not like I don't know how to fight."

"This is different," Danshor said, her voice more serious than Eld thought the matter warranted. "Roel is a minted officer."

"Minted, sponsored or spawned from the ranks, what difference will it make?"

"In a duel, everything," Patrycan said with authority. She spoke while she laid out various bits of wares on her cot and the one beside it, preparing to do a bit of trade. "An officer spawned from the ranks, well, she's like us. She fights well and fights to win. In any way. Sponsored officers usually come from old families and have a taste for the culture of politics. But she also likes the practical experience so spends a couple years living like us beyond the task weeks the academy requires. They learn soldiering by living it and leadership by example. The Red Major was sponsored. Most of the good officers were."

"The Commander?" Torin asked.

"Commander Major Alhern is a complex case," Pat said, relishing her audience, perhaps hoping they'd come back later to buy something. "The story is she wanted to enlist as a regular foot, but was pressured to go into the academy. The Alherns put a lot of stock in upholding tradition. If you look at the roots of their tree, at least a third of it has been in military service for millennia. The commander is one of those mad women who enjoys hardship as a hobby. She's climbed three notable Altan peaks, several Cambrian sea cliffs, sailed to and from Seahome in a tiny boat with a couple other mad adventure seekers, and has hiked across the Federation on foot at least ten times. Marching in full kit would be another holiday for her. But her grandam pressured her to be an officer, not a lowly foot. I say, pressured, but I think she was bribed..."

Eld wasn't completely comfortable with this conversation. "You gossip more than a lot helper," she said.

"Information is trade," Pat said unabashed. "Now minted officers, learn their officering – "

"Not an actual word," said Althone.

" – from the same sorts who run any school or college. Sure, history, geography, politics and maths, and the rest are taught. But when it comes to officering, it's combat. It's supposed to be tactics and strategy, but somehow all the minted hoods spend every free moment learning how to fight in every modern system and several obsolete ones. And because they're mostly from moneyed old estates, and every soul thinks she's the most precious child since the birth of Jaro of the Dawn, they constantly duel over the most ridiculous things. It's considered better than the alternatives and makes bullies scarce. Because a bully doesn't like to duel for the same reason you may not be as able as you think you are: the rules are sacrosanct and you must win within them, not like how we beat the Eurthans with any means at hand."

Pat paused, letting her words sink in.

"What she's saying, sister," Danshor said, "is you need to be trained up." Danshor picked up Eld's bathing kit and paused at the door. "What are you waiting on? We need to discuss strategy."

Eld argued with Danshor all the way to the baths.

"We dance all the time. I think I have some knowledge of martial arts," Eld opined.

"And what do we strike when we dance? The air ...not another mother evading us and trying to strike back."

"You of all people know how much we've been fighting ..."

"On horses," Danshor cut in. "With strike. You won't even be allowed a sword, you know. It's not like you're a lor's gallowglass from feudal times bringing a thrall to bear."

"Alas," Eld said grimly. She didn't have a romantic attachment to those fraught times. But if anyone deserved to feel the worst of them, it was Roel. "Look," she said as they entered the baths, "Roel might not even accept."

"She'll accept," Danshor said with certainty. "If she doesn't, it's as good as admitting you were justified flouting her. What did you do anyway?"

"Are you going to tell the company?"

"Probably. Be reasonable. We have a right to know; we'll all be betting on you."

"I shall be a source of revenue. I'm in bliss."

"Hold your sarcasm and consider the opportunity: you can bet on yourself."

"Is that allowed?"

"It's not like Pat or any other shifter here is working for the coliseum."

Eld had stripped and sank into the water, Danshor sitting cross-legged nearby, guarding her things. No prankster would get lucky this morning. Submerging herself once, then surfacing to sit on the underwater ledge, Eld said, "It's pointless anyway. I'm out of queens."

"Not if I loan you a stake. I take it out of your winnings."

Eld took the hand scrub, a small square of rough matted fiber and started scouring her skin all over. "You seem very confident of a win."

"Well, once we've seduced Fate by training you."

"You should think less of philandering with Goddi and more about who is betting against me. If they're going to bother."

"All us rich estate brats can't help gambling. It's in the blood."

"It's somewhere deeper and fuller than that," Eld snorted. "You all want Fate to approve your inherited gains by blessing you with more. It's like you're guilty of something."

"Nothing recent. Oh, we have watch tonight. Sergeant stopped by."

Eld made a sound of disgust. "And here we're supposed to rest after our labors."

"We're in watchfulness until command gives the order otherwise. I know who to go to for training."

"We're back to that again."

"I assume you want to win?"

"Let's wait until Roel agrees to duel first."

"We can go after watch. It's the first one of the night and we'll have about an hour before retiring to make the arrangements."

Eld gave up arguing. A focused and ambitious Danshor was not to be thwarted when she scented arena winnings. And the truth was, being skint, it would be nice to pay off her debt and not have to live like a stoic until the next quarter. Eld was only wary of the propriety; betting on a formal duel was seen by many as in bad taste.

When they returned to the stables, it was empty except for a couple of souls napping. Eld dressed with Danshor bizarrely acting like her valet. It was strange being the object of Danshor's attentions, but it was certainly a help when it came to threading her flout. Eld had gone back and forth over wearing a flout or guardlocks. Like all cavaliers she was proud of their style, but was sick of being compelled to wear it for the entire round of the day during this time of emergency. On the other hand, if Danshor was right, that the entire company and possibly the other mounted and foot companies, would support her if she dueled – and Danshor knew arena fights as well as she knew men – Eld felt an obligation to represent the cavalry company. And so she would wear the flout for the morning with her full uniform.

Eld was somewhat relieved that a cavalier's full uniform didn't require a sword or lance when on foot. Some women did strap their swords to their backs as a personal preference during actual battle, or carry them when unmounted on a baldric if they fancied, but the saddle scabbard was standard so it wasn't a uniform requirement. And, of course, it would be ridiculous for her to carry a lance just for show. That left Eld with her dagger in a sheath at her back, and an eating knife on her belt. It would look absurd to savage eyes that she would be challenging the Great Elfyn Warrior that Roel was sure to look if she was allowed, complete with helmet and ancient aspect.

"What are you snickering about?" Danshor asked as they walked to the commander's house.

"I'm wondering if Roel is going to kohl her eyes like a Sunqueen's champion."

Danshor boomed out a laugh loud enough to make people nearby turn their heads. "She'll come buffed and polished, but I doubt she'll go that far. That would maker her look like a sissy."

It always annoyed Eld when Danshor said things like this. "You understand many of those women you bet on as a hobby are 'sissies', right?"

Danshor shrugged. "Not that many."

"More than you want to know."

"It's doesn't matter as long as they win."

"And it might be wise to drop the habit of calling sisters 'sissies' when you're in the presence of officers who have just as many 'sissies' as arena champions."

"But they don't prance around about like Crandal and Fenath."

"They both come from theater families!"

"Keep telling yourself that tale."

"This was like that time with Lancer Carn from 1st Company. The sole reason you don't like her is she's just as bold as you but doesn't favor men."

"She's an arrogant hood."

It was Eld's turn to boom out a laugh. "*That* soul is an arrogant hood? Maybe you have more in common than anyone thinks. One might wonder why a bold mother like yourself even cares about what Carn does as a 'sister'."

Eld walked a couple of steps before realizing she was alone. Danshor had stopped and was glaring at her, the air around her almost crackling in the sun.

"Tresses, that offends you?" Eld asked.

"Jesting about mother's vigor is always dangerous," Danshor growled.

"Unless it's about me being prettier than you," Eld said. "Because that's not *your* mother's vigor, which is the only important one in the Orb."

Danshor still glared, but Eld didn't have time to nurse her ego. Eld walked on, thinking maybe she'd be free of Danshor the arena trainer at last.

But Felkeni wasn't so kind. In a couple moments Danshor was striding beside her again, speaking as if there had been no conflict, the only acknowledgment of Eld's point she should expect.

"So when you're done we should meet at the Rowan Oak. It will be time for lunch anyway."

"Yes, fine," Eld agreed. They'd come to the steps of the commander's house. Danshor's escort ended here; being a free day she was no more eager to wear their uniform than any other mother.

"Remember everything," Danshor said, jauntily saluting the guards before taking off at a run for the Rowan Oak.

"Everything?" Eld muttered, as she walked up the stairs. She expected she didn't need to be a trained legal clerk to accomplish that feat today. She was well warmed by the sun, and rested enough to feel the alert nervousness that exhaustion had numbed the day before.

A duel. The women were right; it wasn't going to be like roasting an Eurthan in Bane armor in the noon sun. Even if they were fighting in the sun, they were both Sula. Unless Roel had more essence training.

Eld stopped herself from praying to Gods she didn't believe in. It was considered the worst luck even by literalists to be inconsistent with one's devotions except to ask for heavenly favors, especially for mundane matters like a duel. As it was said, let the Gods defend Heaven and leave the rest to Mothers of the Orb.

This time Eld was confident of the way, but she was expected and so intercepted and escorted by the butler.

"We are seeing you quite frequently," Sonamor said.

Eld laughed nervously. "Soldiers say that's a bad sign."

"All signs come and go as the Heavens turn," Sonamor said.

Eld said nothing, thinking that safest. Soon they were at the open door of Alhern's office.

"The Lancer Farthal," Sonamor announced.

"Enter!" Alhern boomed.

Eld stepped into the room, saluted and stood waiting for instruction, noting in a second all present:

Alhern was, of course, sitting at her desk. Major Galledan sat in a chair, reclining but alert. Captain Aynath stood behind Alhern, like a ghost in a play hovering to inform the hero of the villain's deeds. A little behind the Red Major stood Roel, in a patch of sunlight. If Eld hadn't been at attention she'd have laughed.

Roel was in her dress uniform, something slightly suspicious to Eld's mind. Had Roel been warned a duel might be offered? They were only required to be dressed for duty, not a soirée for the Federation Field Marshal's wedding. Eld hadn't bothered with her cape. But Roel had bothered quite a bit, polishing all her brass so that it fairly twinkled. The Federation Army officer dress uniform was much like the regular field uniform with some differences:

The gold accented sage coat was a close woven fine linen and so had a shiner quality than the regular uniform coat with its heavier and more practical weight. The fawn facings were lighter and brighter, and not wool but linen velvet, only slightly less expensive than silk velvet of any kind. Thus the officers twinings were made more striking as it seemed they were golden helix paths in a field of the minutest ripened grain. The back, unseen for the moment, had a larger twining of gold, as if a helix was circling a woman's spine. As with all dress uniforms, the brass buttons were plated with real gold. Her breeches were bleached a brilliant white, her black boots so polished reflections from the furnishings could be seen. At her neck where the high collar discouraged bad posture, her lieutenant wings glimmered, accenting her helix guardlock clips, shimmering so they gave the impression of spinning. The top of her hair wasn't parted, but pulled straight back , bound behind the crown; of the two main styles accepted in the military, the peaked version was considered slightly more dignified than the parted version. Either could be worn with the back locks pulled into a tail, which is what Roel had done today. Where the sunlight struck Roel's hair there was ever so slightly a hint of glimmer. Nobility, politicians, and women attending special occasions, like a graduation commencement or a birthing, often lightly dusted their hair with glimmer dust. Nothing that could be seen casually, but would catch the light as if blessed by the Gods. Eld was sure some officers who attended her awards had touched their hair. But this wasn't even a formal event. So Roel must really feel she had to make an impression, feeding Eld's suspicion Roel had intelligence of what was to pass. Furthermore, Eld doubted Roel had done all this work herself. In her experience women as entitled as Roel had very little tolerance for domestic tasks, even those required of a soldier. And Roel had availed herself of the option of wearing a cape: white, lined with gold, the fabric on one side thrown back over her shoulder, presumably for style.

"As you see cavalier, Lieutenant Roel has gone to some effort to mark the time," Alhern said deadpan. Captain Aynath coughed, covering a laugh. "So we should get on with it," Alhern finished.

"If I may be permitted," Roel said with the air of a noble granting a boon, "Before this unpleasantness is doomed to go further, I am willing to accept an apology of sincerity. Were I to hear the truth of such words, I would willingly withdrawn any complaint as the understandable heat of the moment when all our fires were ascendant in our duty."

Eld watched Aynath's eyes wander during this small, florid speech, only discipline keeping the captain from rolling them.

Alhern gave Roel a long look. "I am pleased to hear you acknowledge that a woman inflamed in the course of duty might be given allowances, as well as the acknowledgment the time of battle should be the focus of such duty and nothing else. Lancer Farthal, do you think you can offer a truthful, sincere apology for your actions?"

Eld wanted to bark a laugh like Danshor. Roel had a full belly making such an offer. She'd been told and thought she'd cleverly twist out of the very net she'd woven; if the complaint was dropped, there would be no discipline or duel. They could go back to loathing each other from a distance. But what of Althas? Or in fact any man who found Eld's company? Was Eld to forever worry that Roel would prey on her lovers for sport? Althas might not want vengeance, but Eld did. She wasn't so full of herself to think her dignity had been as abused as Althas', but it offended her to her core that she was the cause of it.

"Farthal?" Alhern queried.

"No, emha, I cannot offer a truthful, sincere apology." Eld remembered the points they discussed the night before. "Lieutenant Roel offended my honor by gloating to me about using a man I am friendly with. Thus was I distracted from my duty where I otherwise would not be." Roel wasn't the only one who could speak floridly.

"Alas, cavalier," Alhern said, "that is not an excuse. In battle at all times discipline is the task master of duty and all other passions should yield to this. As it stands you face court-martial for abusing an officer and flouting her reasonable orders."

Roel couldn't help smirking at these words. But the smirk vanished as Alhern spoke on.

"However it is also true, as an officer is owed obedience, her duty compels her to not invent barriers or distractions to those she is demanding obedience from. Surely if you want a soldier or cavalier to obey, you neither do nor say anything to thwart that obedience? That was a question, Lieutenant."

Roel stood straighter if possible. "Yes, emha! Of course!"

"I am pleased that is understood. And that is why, even though Lancer Farthal can be court-martialed for a technically justified complaint, she may also testify she was provoked by offense to be distracted from her duty."

Alhern slid a leaf of paper to the opposite side of her desk closest to Eld, along with a stylus pen with ink.

"Write down what offended you, Farthal."

"Emha," Eld said once, snapping to attention. Then she bent down and wrote as briefly as possible before returning to attention.

Alhern picked up the paper, careful to wait a second for the gall ink to dry.

"Lieutenant R. boasted of paying for – a man's name – company and lascivious acts she did knowing the man found them unpleasant and that it would discomfit me to hear of them."

"I paid for that harlot!" Roel exploded.

"Careful, Lieutenant," Galledan's voice rumbled like distant thunder.

"I apologize," Roel breathed. "But I doubt I have to answer for offending the sentimental feelings of a delicate cavalier mooning because I gave her boy the good riding she couldn't."

"You have to answer for it if you used it to bait or goad Lancer Farthal deliberately," Alhern said. "Otherwise complaining about her insubordination makes for an incomplete tale."

"She's saying," Galledan explained, "Had you not goaded Farthal, she wouldn't have been insubordinate, dammit."

Roel's mouth twitched. "I offered to drop my complaint if she apologizes ..."

"I think we all know that's as like to happen as me sprouting dragon wings," Alhern said.

"Well, then court-martial the villain!"

"Are you dictating how I should run my command, Lieutenant?"

"No, emha, of course not ..."

"Good."

"Discipline must be maintained," Galledan said. "Either Farthal submits to a court-martial. Or Farthal objects she acted in justified outrage and requests the court of combat. Either can be done. One must be done."

Roel was sneering at Alhern's desk, where something landed with a gentle thud. The Gauntlet of Jaro, a stylized, armored glove, gilded in gold, and worked artistically with spirals in patterns evoking a bygone era filled with godly magic. It was a real gauntlet, but a ceremonial object, usually used in the blessing of new military buildings and breaking the ground for construction. But it was also the gauntlet thrown down to issue a challenge to duel.

"If a duel is your wish, Farthal, you may throw it at Roel's feet," Major Galledan said.

Eld picked up the gauntlet. The sun had shifted so the metal glove shimmered in the light and felt weightless in Eld's hand. She wasn't sure if this was because it was lifted by unconscious sulessence or it was only a light costume piece. Eld held it a moment then looked at Roel.

Roel was mulish, her sneer barely contained, her eyes flashing gold with warning. Eld could almost feel her thoughts. Then she heard clearly:

~You don't dare, common vagrant spawn. Take the damn apology and count yourself lucky. Your harlot was paid fairly.~

Eld didn't betray Roel was baiting her. The officers might even know, and wanted to see how it played out. Instead Eld quietly walked to stand an arm's length in front of Roel, holding the gauntlet, eyes lowered as if in thought.

She may throw it at Roel's feet. But that wasn't the only acceptable way to offer a challenge. Any gauntlet would do. For the rules said a hand or gauntlet was to be offered. It was only early modern custom that weighted it towards the gauntlet.

Eld grabbed the gauntlet with her left hand and with her right hand struck Roel across the face with a blow that echoed loudly in the office. Roel was so shocked she didn't even cry out, one hand holding the left side of her face, eyes and mouth wide in disbelief. Then Eld dropped the gauntlet at Roel's feet. The muffled thud was anticlimactic. Not a soul seemed to breathe. Eld stared into Roel's eyes, pushing her thoughts out as she rarely did:

~ You haven't paid enough,~ Eld thought.

A slight twitch in Roel's eyes told Eld she heard. Then Roel's face changed, her ugly sneer making it savage like an animal, and, in spite of the brightness, it was like a dark cloud shadowed her soul. Roel snatched up the gauntlet.

"I accept!" she spat, then slammed it into Eld's chest.

"I guess we should finish drawing up the details then," Aynath said lightly.

"Never a drab minute with our girls!" Galledan added.

"Indeed," Alhern intoned, her eyes pleading for a return to decorum.

Eld turned away from Roel and returned the gauntlet to Alhern's desk. It was an awkward wait while Alhern's clerk was called to draw up the rest of the documents. Eld would duel Roel, and, as the Mother-Gods of the ancient pagans blessed her foremothers, Eld intended to win.

## Chapter 23

## Visitors in the Fog

Danshor was laughing indecently at Eld's recount as they walked to the Rowan Oak.

"Could you try to restrain yourself?" Eld said. "Every soul is watching."

"That's your fault for making such an entertaining spectacle. You have any idea when the duel is?"

"The Red Major said we would both be notified. And until then – "

"You are to abstain from each other's company," Danshor said. "Coliseum rules. It's not fair to those who invest in the wager if one or the other is sabotaged. Roel'll probably work out an arrangement where she isn't even in the garrison until the fight."

"She can't," Eld said. "Watchfulness is still in effect."

Just then a rider sped through the gates on a white horse. White horses were reserved for messengers, both civilian and military. Many thought it was because a higher number of white foals were afflicted in the womb, requiring an essence surgeon's treatment to be birthed whole. And thus these animals served in some vague sense of gratitude. But, while the issue of diseased white foals was true, their use as messengers was more practical: white horses were the most visible, even at night. The horse's saddle and trimmings were white, gray and pale blue, the colors of a Federation messenger steed. The woman herself wore a blue sleeveless coat, much like a vest, with white facings. All of her hair was drawn back into one close braided tail at the nape of her neck, in an inverted weave that kept it close to the head and less likely to unravel. She also wore white breeches and dark boots, though not as hard heeled or stiff as cavalry boots. If she needed to, the messenger could run over terrain; though if she was on foot running duty she'd have running sandals and the tunic. Though women called out to her from all sides – messengers were badgered by soldiers more than men for attention – she ignored them, heading straight to the flag tower where the mustering bell was rung. The messenger didn't even dismount, riding around the base as she dropped a mail bag while a woman rushed forward to throw on the outgoing into her saddle bag. Then the messenger withdrew a sealed scroll and tossed it up to the other woman on duty who caught it eagerly and instantly unrolled it. But she did have a heart. As a sop to the mob eager for news, she blew notes on her signal whistle as she cantered back to the gate:

Falls Gate Command to Falls Keep:
Watchfulness lifted,
More to follow

"There," Danshor said with an air of smugness. "Roel will beg for a holiday away from the garrison and we'll train you up without prying eyes."

They continued to argue all the way to the Rowan Oak.

"You tell her, Noble Laird of the Wood," Danshor said to Tafli.

Tafli's brows arched high as he set a platter of nuts, cheese, cold meat and various fresh greens in the center of the table. They were sitting with Patrycan, Torin and Alcas, and the ranger, Orinac. Also with them were the Dwen, Yeladrin and Olyeth.

"What is this I am to be saying?" Tafli asked.

"That she needs to train for this fight," Patrycan put in. "And not count on her heroism."

"There, you say it. She has heard. I do not need to say it as well."

"But she's not listening!" Danshor said. "They won't tell us the exact time or place until it's three days upon us. It could be inside--"

"And then we'll be even," Eld said.

"Or at midnight--"

"Much the same--"

"It's a military duel," Patrycan put in. "They'll tell the time soon. And they're traditionally outside. No matter the weather. That's where Felkeni will have His amusement."

Eld had a flash of slipping around in muddy ground with Roel, barely able to stay on her feet. But it was just an anxious thought, not Reverie.

"I still don't understand," Yeladrin said.

"It is a Sula thing," Tafli said. "They are making everything more complicated because they are seeing everything in the light and dark."

"Excuse me, 'noble laird of the wood'," Eld said, taking a more sardonic tone than Danshor had. "We weren't the ones who insisted on stopping the battle for a formal trial and execution!"

"What?" Danshor said. "When did this happen?"

"When you were running around the Eurthan encampment setting things on fire."

"Well, that is bring different," Tafli said. "That was a matter of stolen boys."

"Which the Eurthan was innocent of."

"And because of the trial we are knowing that. Now, I cannot be standing here all day."

While Orinac explained to Danshor the details of the events on the ridge with Olyeth's input, Patrycan was trying to explain to Yeladrin military discipline.

"And so you see the only way to satisfy both honor and duty is a formal combat."

Yeladrin's yastol bobbed as she rocked her head side to side in a lateral nod, a common Dwen gesture.

"I understand trial by combat. What is baffling is how this insubordination seems more serious. Not for the offense which has harmed no one, but because a member of your officer class has been offended. Those who protect the Forest are not divided so in Dwenoshire. Ranks grow up from Green-root to Sky-crown, tree runners to border weavers, in one class of tree, the whole oak is our body of defense, and it is not ruled by mistletoes, or worse, ivy entangling the upper branches. This is a strange tree you have and if I was the crown of your command, I would prune it."

"In a manner of speaking we are," Danshor said. "Or rather she is," hugging Eld's shoulders as if she had been lost in the wilds for centuries.

"My anticipation knows no bounds," Eld said.

"It should," Pat said, standing up to pull a long vest over her shirt. It had many pockets and was just the thing if one was dealing in small wares, buttons and string. "You can pay your debt off with you winnings."

"Because otherwise she might have to report you being in arrears," Danshor added, glee in her eyes.

"You both know I don't make a habit of being in arrears. Danshor is just trying to pressure me to be her gladiator milk cow."

"Apples will fall whether you make cider or not," Pat said. "Opportunity and abundance is profit."

"And training is surety," Danshor said.

"I'm looking forward to watch tonight," Eld said. "It will be a welcome break from this chatter."

The cook was in her element today on the patio at the back of the Rowan Oak, a bare armed Sula woman from the village who rarely spoke to matrons. Today a couple hogs had been harvested and gifted by the lots to the garrison Kettle and the Rowan Oak. Eld had seen the cook once, hair bound on her head, wrapped in a white scarf, wearing aught but a leather apron and bracs while sun-frying meat on a grill surrounded by mirror flashing. Eld knew from experience it was enjoyable, hot work, but needed a careful touch to avoid charring the meat. It was of course something impossible for

Tafli to do. Tafli would only allow sun-frying or boiling outside in the summer, with the odd coal fire if absolutely needed, so all the cooking had to be done from the moment the sun hit the grill bricks in early morning to whenever Her rays could no longer be bent. During this flurry of activity, any thing to be warmed with ambient heat was set out on a tray. Because of these customs, rainy days were the worst for the Rowan Oak, for while Tafli was a remarkable dab with cold meats, particularly considering Dwen weren't exactly experts with meat generally, it was on a cold day the Sula mother craved heat the most, meaning, contrary to most military conventions, women clustered in the Kettle for the hot if tedious fare, only afterwards visiting the Rowan Oak for drink. But Tafli didn't care. He called it his rain holiday and the cook was paid the same so she had no complaint.

So there were slabs of fresh bacon matrons were left to thinly slice and pile on bread with sauces and trimmings and cheeses of their choice, along with thin acorn flour pancakes rolled around fruit, or as Torin tried, used instead of bread, much like the plate breads of Sharitan. Froths were offered; like the cakes, Eld suspected it was for the Dwen guests, for the original foods of the forest were nuts, eggs, honey and greens.

A froth was a common breakfast drink in Dwenoshire, and adopted many places where mothers took serious exercise. Froth was made by separating an egg, whipping the whites stiffly, and the yolk with tea, juice, ale or barley-mead. Herbs or spices might be added with the milk of nut or cow; children liked a touch of sugar. Then it was remixed creating a thick drink not unlike winter eggnog, but not as rich.

"These are not being for you," Tafli said to Torin as he set down a couple of froths in tall, bottle green, glass tumblers. The foam on the top was slightly yellow from the yolk and it smelled vaguely of carrots. "I am putting acorn milk in for my forest friends and it is too strong for a Sula tongue. I will be bringing some with other milk."

"Yelam," murmured the two Dwen women. Yeladrin sipped the drink, smiling with pleasure, the foam hovering on her lips for a moment. Torin pestered Olyeth for a taste. Olyeth downed hers in one draught, except for a small part at the bottom.

"I warn you, friend, it is a strong taste to those who do not have sap in their veins," Olyeth said.

"But the cakes are acorn and they're fine. Why wouldn't acorn milk be fine as well?" Torin asked.

"Because Tafli is serving Sula and gets the flour that is leached the finest. We leach a bit in the Forest but not so much because we can take the flavor."

"Then I can take it too!" Torin exclaimed, and downed the remains of the froth.

Once when Eld was a child, she had eaten a fresh acorn. The bitterness overwhelmed her mouth and dried it so she needed to drink almost of pail of water to be rid of the taste. So when she saw Torin's face change from expectancy to disgust she knew exactly how Torin felt. Everyone, Sula and Dwen, burst with laughter, while Torin gulped down water and grabbed the rest of Danshor's barley-mead to wash her mouth out.

They were still laughing when Tafli returned.

"So you did not listen I am hearing," Tafli said, setting down more froths, for all appearances identical. "Now you are knowing better. This are the milkings of hazel and will be better for Sula tastings." Tafli's yastol waved as he walked away, shaking his head.

"What do you want to bet he's pranking us?" Pat said.

"I have every faith in his good intentions," Orinac said, taking a glass.

"You of all people should be careful," Eld said.

"I know I was an inexcusable hood, but I don't expect revenge."

"You really don't understand men, do you?" Danshor said, snorting.

"Perhaps Sula men," Yeladrin said, taking a sip. "Dwen men don't hold a grudge after they've taken satisfaction. Orinac's help on the ridge would cancel her offense as they have agreed. It's spiced well with angelica and anise, but the base is insipid. Perfect for the Sula palate."

The "insipid" drink was medicinally sharp and spicy, but had no bitterness. Only after observing them all drink good portions was Torin assured it was safe for her. At which point she took to the froths so well, she had two more. The rest of them perhaps drank too much barley-mead (or whatever passed in the Rowan Oak for barley-mead), so found themselves happily without ambition, idling the rest of the day, walking or chatting for pleasure. Afternoon found them in the field south of the garrison wall, with Torin wearing Olyeth's yastol. She'd been standing for minutes trying to feel wood-essence while the rest of them lounged on the grass watching a distant laysaid game, the dominant form of football in the Federation.

"I can hear wind rushing," Torin said, slowly spinning as she was wont to.

"That's the air," Olyeth said. "It should rustle over your head, like wind in branches."

"No," Torin said, frowning. Her eyes were closed now. "It's like wind on a lake. Or going over a mountain. And it's so bright ...I feel I'm floating ..."

Torin opened her eyes and promptly unbalanced and fell over. They laughed while she tried to get up again, but Olyeth steadied Torin's arm and guided her to sit down, taking back her yastol.

"I think that's enough wood-essence for the day. Sula magi take years to learn to touch the wood. You won't be doing it in an afternoon."

"If at all," Alcas muttered.

Eld took out her signal whistle and started to play the tune to 'Tortin of the Boggy Glenn'. Torin's name was so similar, it sparked Eld's imagination. Alcas never found recalling the words to a tune hard, and she was just as adept at inventing new ones for japes. The character, "Tortin", was "a cad and a cheat", and the song was the tale of a dishonest vagrant worker who seduced sons and stole from the mothers who hired her. A light hearted, amusing song, it was perfect to be turned to the moment:

Alcas sang:

~

*She falls off her feet*
*when men come to meet;*
*Torin the clumsy Dwen!*
*She stepped on a bole*
 *and fell in a hole;*
*Torin the clumsy Dwen!*

~

*Torin the clumsy Dwen!*
*How will this story end!*
*She'll fall off a branch*
*in a bramble patch,*
*Torin the clumsy Dwen!*

~

Torin was affronted at first, often being the butt of company jests. But the Dwen leaped up and invited her to dance in a three way Dwen jig and reel. Torin's steps started unsure and indeed a bit clumsy. And there was the part where the Dwen linked arms and keep her feet from touching the ground, scissoring ridiculously. That made Danshor laugh. Yet, as Torin got into the spirit if it, the clumsiness vanished, until it was an ironic refutation of Alcas' new lyrics as Torin leaped and somersaulted almost in time with Yeladrin and Olyeth:

~

*Torin the Clumsy Dwen*
*how will this venture end!*

*It's quite neat*
*When she lands on her feet!*
*It might be belated*
*and that's how it's fated!*
*We'll see her again,*
*stuck in a bog or a fen*
*Torin the clumsy Dwen!*

~

They all whistled and clapped, the Dwen including Torin in a three way bow facing each other.

Suddenly a man's voice exclaimed, "That's was brave dancing, Bec!"

They all looked to see a young man smiling at Torin as brightly as his yellow kirtle-shirt. His windswept hair was ribboned with yellow as well, and something about how the fronts of his tunic hung made Eld think he wasn't wearing the more restricting undergarments many men did.

"Ai!" Torin said, both a greeting and surprise.

"You know this fine flower of the Lots?" Danshor asked sardonically.

"Who is 'Bec'?" Olyeth added.

"I'm told she's a clumsy Dwen," Alcas said. "Her mother, of the Torin estates, named her 'Beclyndwol'. We call her 'Beclyn' or 'Bec'. When we remember."

"Or Becee," Danshor said, grinning. "It's the reason she volunteered. In service we're all called by our estate names."

Torin ignored all of them, eyes only for the man. "It is a fine thing to see you, Adamys! How may I serve you?"

"One tryst and they're about to wed," Danshor muttered.

"I'm in a situation!" the man said urgently.

"Village shops out of ribbons?" Alcas asked deadpan, then exclaimed, "Ow!"

Torin had booted her.

"Say on," Torin added.

"I'm a century and five, and I do all the petty errands of the house, yet suddenly I'm not allowed to go to a day fete at Fern Lake on my own. But ama said if I found an escort she approves of, I could. That's just an excuse to push her favorite on me. I want to find my own soul!"

Torin stepped forward to link the man's arm like a chaperone. "I will be honored to be your hero!"

They walked off mutually pleased, while Alcas and Danshor sang:

~

*"Torin the clumsy Dwen*
*See how the story ends*
*on a man again,*
*in a bower or a glen*
*Torin the clumsy Dwen!"*

~

"Who was he?" Orinac asked.

"One of the men from my barracks revel, I think," Eld said.

"But men aren't allowed in the barracks," Orinac said.

Eld, Danshor and Patrycan burst into laughter.

"Is now the time to tell you those Hal Suldan's gifts of your youth didn't manifest by your spriteling virtue?" Danshor asked.

"Of course not," Orinac said seriously. "They are gifted by Winternight."

Eld was certain Orinac was being clever, but Danshor laughed. "You still believe in Winternight?"

"No, but I knew you'd assume so." Orinac looked smug.

"She is not being as naive as you think," Olyeth said.

Eld put her whistle back in a pocket and jumped to her feet. "I should get to the stables and nap before watch."

Danshor was lying back, arms behind her head, eyes closed enjoying the warmth of the sun.

"Good idea," she said without opening them. "Fighters need to get all the rest they can. And food. And abstain from men before they duel...."

Eld held up a finger for silence as she creped away.

"She's sneaking away isn't she?" Danshor said as Eld turned her back. "We'll discuss this further!" Danshor called.

Eld reported for watch alone, having prepared Fiorseth, dressed and armed herself, then rode to the report station, just a short distance outside the gate. Normally she'd be worried; Danshor was typically late, but Tuiric was standing there waiting. Looking around, Eld saw Danshor walking from the direction of town, a dim figure in the deepening night gloom.

"Where were you?"

"Making arrangements," Danshor said, mounting Tuiric. The stallion whinnied, dipping his head, eager for adventure. Fiorseth on the other hand was full of subdued and wary feelings. What foolishness were the elflings planning this time?

"It's just watch, girl," Eld said soothingly. "We'll patrol the outpost ..."

"Actually cavalier, you'll be joining the ravine patrol," the watch captain said. She strode out on foot from the small hut that looked like a kitsch version of a Wildling tent. It had no real walls, being little more than four posts and a roof, with some hooks for tackle and slate boards and chalk. "The place is already thick with mist. We suspect essence activity though none of the Eurthans have been sighted. So stay sharp and whistle if you see anything."

Eld did her best to keep her mind light as they trotted up the road then turned onto the way to the ravine. The passage of the Host left a wide path easy to follow even by starlight. Starlight however wasn't needed because, with the lifting of watchfulness, the lights from the town broke the darkness, glowing late into the night. High above the Abbey lights twinkled. Eld continued to think soothing thoughts as they entered the place where the healers tents had stood: yes, they were going back to the fraught place, Eld admitted to Fiorseth, but there were no dark warriors or Bane lightning …

"I'm glad Fiorseth can't speak Sulanilish," Eld said. "She'd be cursing us now."

"Tuiric doesn't mind, do you, boy?" Danshor said patting his neck. "We're much the same."

"A witless horse with a witless rider?"

Before Danshor could retort Sergeant Tarl rode up.

"Al met, girls! Looking bright?"

"Never brighter," they chorused dully.

"Though its a strange thing to say at night…." Eld put in.

"Grouse later, Farthal. We have a camp at the base of the Hole," –Tarl waved to a spot slightly west and north. "Not too close, but we should see if those Bane demons poke their heads up. You'll patrol the entire field just like in a regular patrol: one will walk the border, while the other walks the front, then switch on return. See anything, whistle. There should be no souls wandering at this time in these fields." Tarl saluted as she rode off.

"I bet they have a spread at the camp," Danshor said.

"Just remember to bring something back for me when you sneak off there."

"I am the soul of duty."

Eld turned Fiorseth into the darkness and urged her forward at a walk. Very reluctantly she obeyed.

"Don't you want to draw lots?" Danshor called.

"Why bother? We both know you want to loaf, pacing back and forth on the front. And I've saved you the effort of trying to cheat."

Danshor muttered something Eld didn't try to catch. Soon Eld was out of easy earshot. Eld wanted to be alone with her thoughts for a while, if one could count being mind linked to one's mount alone. Still Fiorseth was good company as they picked their way around the field, past the rubble of the broken wall, a place they had to take care. The greatest tangles of thorny bramble remained, presumably as a barrier. Eld worried that Fiorseth might step on something sharp, a shard of steel or broken armor. Without the sun, the mare didn't benefit as much from Eld's senses. At least she was unburdened by unicorn barding. Passing the ruined wall the gloom deepened, and Eld took to waving the butt of her lance into the darkest parts, slowing Fiorseth to stop with what seemed every second step. Eld decided to pause and let her eyes adjust further. There were few clouds so starlight was unhindered. It was abysmal if she needed try to read anything, but was better than nothing.

Now when they walked, Fiorseth almost entirely relied on Eld to guide her. Horses didn't make a habit of walking around at night for a reason, and Fiorseth was miffed that she had to. It would be so pleasant to stand in her stall, nibbling hay, sheltered from the wind...

Eld could almost scent the hay, so strong was the smell in Fiorseth's thoughts. They were now further along the ravine, circling the back of the ruined Eurthan tents, the frames of the broken domes making spidery shadows against the starry sky. There was an abundance of mist, hovering over the ground, obscuring it in the dark, though now and then an abandoned piece of armor or a ruined and bent lance would reveal itself, glimmering faintly in the starlight. Eld started, seeing what looked like a head rising out of the ground. But it was only a helmet, its visor frosted and obscured like a glass curio of the damned. The magical rime had long melted, leaving dead and frost blackened plants. Still, enough of the green-strike growth remained, particularly the bramble thorns. There was no point in patrolling the center of that area for it had become impassable to horse and woman. It was quiet, so quiet it made Eld wonder. The normal sounds of animals and birds rustling in the night were absent. Even before she saw the thick white embankment ahead, she suspected Eurthan activity.

The mist. It was cover for their activities, probably to reclaim any gear they found. And they weren't coming up through the Hole. They were coming through the mountain door where they first started their foray. If it was up to Eld she'd let them. Less reasons to harass Sula and Dwen lands. But those weren't her orders. Because she saw no one, she didn't whistle. That felt premature. But she turned Fiorseth around to ride back to the line where Danshor waited, assuming she was back from getting refreshment. Eld would gallop to the base and report once she informed Danshor of the activity.

Or that's what she intended. Suddenly the cool air felt more chill, and the fog bank Eld was certain was a hundred yards away surrounded her, its impenetrable thickness as high as Fiorseth's flanks, the rest hovering around them like cold steam.

Fiorseth shied, whinnying. Then she reared as a Bane warrior appeared out of the mist, looming over their side.

Eld didn't even try to strike. She shoved the lance between the neck and the Bane-weapon that had turned its sights on her, and drove Fiorseth around the warrior in tight fast circles. The weight of the horse forced the woman to spin on her feet the best she could until she toppled. With a snap and screech the weapon was freed from its moorings, and fell with a thump out of sight.

That was good enough for Eld. She dropped the lance and drew her sword while she blew her whistle. But it sounded feeble, as if the air had been stilled and refused to carry sound. Eld cursed. That was exactly what had happened. Meanwhile the Bane-warrior was rising. And so she leaped off Fiorseth and prepared to fight.

"Go back to the line! To Danshor! Tuiric!" Eld said.

Fiorseth cantered in a circle around her a moment, offering her a chance to remount.

"Go! Get help!"

Fiorseth galloped off as the Bane-warrior drew her black steel blade.

Eld didn't like the idea of fighting on the ground with this thing, but she liked less the idea of Fiorseth getting wounded or killed. And if the wait was too long, Eld knew the terrain; she could run if she had to.

Eld almost ran after the first time their swords met. The blow shook her entire body and she had no sulessence from the sun to mitigate it. The hardness and momentum of the Bane-armor was frightening in the dark. Eld wondered how long her new sword would last before bending or breaking before the grim-steel. If it was destroyed, or the Eurthan was able to retrieve her Bane-weapon, Eld would run and hope the Bane-warrior didn't follow.

The moments lengthened to minutes and it was clear Eld's sword wasn't going to last. It shivered and chipped after blocking a particularly savage blow, then spun from her hands. Eld slipped, falling to her chest on the ground as if she was preparing to do a press-up. And while she'd planned to spring to her feet and run, her hand landed on the handle of a sword. A cold sword of dark metal.

Eld stood, drawing the Eurthantian blade from the debris, feeling almost as bold as if she was standing in sunlight. She might not "have the essence", but it was a well made blade, much lighter than she expected from its crystalline dark aspect. It was perfectly balanced and the grim seemed to want to link to her soul and tell her things, of its long dark journey through the Void, for the main ingredient in grim-steel was meteoric iron. But it was passing through Airts to the earth or its exposure to the essence source of the Orb that made it grim. No one was sure which, for while the Dying Star that destroyed Er left grim deposits, it would not explain the sheer abundance of grim the Eurthans had access to. Did they make it?

The warrior seemed to pause uncertainly. Then the part of Eld that was a soldier needed to know: with this blade could she win?

The blades screamed as they met, showering a fountain of sparks over the two women, like a fireworks display at a waterside festival. The warrior was not significantly stronger than Eld, but she had the momentum of the armor; there was simply no getting around the fact, no matter how well Eld fought, the armor made the woman impervious to injury. Still Eld danced with the warrior, hoping to unbalance her, maybe find a hitherto unknown weakness in the shell-like hide, but there was nothing. Green eyes glowed behind the faceplate, excited or outraged, Eld couldn't tell. She knew she'd have to abandon this game, for it was indulgent. And it was possible she was being distracted.

Then more of the armored figures loomed out of the fog until Eld was surrounded. Still holding the sword she dived for her lance, prayed the charge it had would be good enough, and rolled back to her feet, spying the weakest point of the circle to run through. But as the lance glowed, a voice called out:

"Ztop! Ve are nod do engage!"

Eld panted, watching her opponent warily, but the woman had stopped.

"Driadz up!" a voice said. It appeared to be coming from the fore of the figures. The order, whatever it meant, resulted in all the Bane-weapons on their shoulders pointing straight to the sky. The figure stepped forward, her faceplate glimmering with a faint blue glow above the collar of her armor, each side flanked by a single bar of gold gilt metal. Eld remembered the same bars on the collar of this person's skin suit. It was rank. The faceplate rose to reveal the bright blue eyes of Third Lieutenant Brig. She loomed over Eld in armor.

Eld slacked her arm holding the lance. "You again."

"Zat is nod zo vreidly, Landzer Vardhal," Brig said, but she was smiling.

"What's not friendly is your villain attacking me!" Eld exclaimed.

"Zhee attacked me widh her equid!" the warrior objected, her own visor raising, green eyes blazing in a bronze-tan face. "Knocked me over, broke my driad!"

Brig looked perplexed between them.

"She spooked my horse sneaking up on us in the middle of a battlefield at night!" Eld exclaimed. "Pardon all of Paradise if I assumed I was being attacked!"

"Ey zee," Brig said. "Yew miz underztand."

"I misunderstand?" Eld said incredulously.

"Ve are nod here vor war. Ve gum do reglaim." Brig gave some more orders and the women drifted away in the mists to resume their tasks.

Eld sighed. Of course. Like the attackers in the glade that seemed like months ago, they had orders to leave nothing behind.

"If your command is thinking gathering every scrap of grim will keep the knowledge of your country a secret, it's too late."

"The land of Godz jozen cannod be hidden!" Eld rolled her eyes at these words. "No, ve must keep dhees out ov dhe handz ov zavage razes."

"Not attacking their countries will go a long way to accomplish that," Eld said acerbically.

"Ey am zorry. And Ey musd dake dhat." Brig gestured to the grim sword Eld was still holding.

Eld switched her grip to hold the blade reversed, under its hilts, but she didn't pass it over yet.

"Did you know about the looting?"

"Yez, we hav heard. Dhey are punished. Looding iz against regulazhuns."

"Do you know they tried to kidnap a boy?"

"No." Brig paused. "Iz he ogay?"

Eld felt Seth's rage. "They would have used him, you know. And maybe sold him. Is that against regulations?"

"Ey-- ey know yew vill nod believe it, but yez. Ve are to use brodhels or willing men. But zome do no listen. Even dhe rape of unbious men iz a grime."

It took Eld a moment to parse Brig's accent. "It's not as serious a crime with pious men?"

Brig lowered her eyes. "Id iz drue. But nod an excuse!"

"You are naive. What about slavery?"

"Slavery vaz abolished by Nalinard dhe Virst! All vay are vree!"

"Fay?"

"Dhose daken millennia ago vrom above. Dhere descendants sdill live among uz."

"And what of those taken more recently?"

"Dhad iz nod common. Only vor dhe rich ..."

"So it's still legal as long as it's just a few boys kept as pets."

"Ey don't know…."

Eld turned away, inhaling then exhaling, trying to control her outrage. It was a pointless conversation. One to be left to the diplomats. Brig was just a thread in her culture's rotted tapestry, and being angry with her would accomplish nothing.

"Gan Ey asg iv Aredheli iz zdill here?"

Eld looked askance at Brig in her black Bane-armor, looming in the mists on a field where her people had brought the threat of wreck and ruin … and she was sweet on an exotic Dwen man. Was that really where the path to peace lay?

"They left for Ash City. Look, you Eurthans have men right? You're not spawned like some tales say?"

Brig laughed. "Yez, ve hav men, but he iz zo beautivul, zo bold…"

"Listen, friend, the Gaels of Cambria have a phrase…"

"Ey do nod know dhese elvyn."

"They are humyn. Though they have more than their share of aelg—elf-born. Anyway, they have a phrase: "Is glas iad na cnoc ibhfad uainn". It means the green hills farther from us are greener. At least I think that's what it means. My Gael is unpracticed."

"Why are dhe hillz greener? Are dhey covered widh malaghite?"

Eld didn't understand for a few seconds. When she did she laughed.

"I suppose you have emeralds instead of grass!"

"Don't be zilly. Emerald growz in clusters or poolz, not lawn dew. Bud lawn dew iz more dhan green: zome iz white, brown, even blue."

"Very well. Perhaps the Dwen aphorism is better: the star you adore may long be gone."

Brig looked up. Belatedly Eld realized Eurthans might not understand stars. But Brig seemed to comprehend their existence. The Mother Bear hung above them. Amid the sight of the true stars the giant orb Mynge, named after the Mother-God of plenty Myngar, danced. Mynge had many moons, not just one, easily seen by elfyn eyes.

"Vhy wud a sdar Ey zee be gone?" Brig asked.

"True stars, cousins of Sul, may be so far from us in the vasty distances of the Void, we only see the ghosts of their light after death."

Brig scanned the sky. The clouds in the east glowed with the imminent moon rise.

"Zhat iz zad," Brig said. "Ey like sdarz. Our zities hav one skylight fixed above dhe blue dome in day. At night id iz alzo dark, bud the sdar iz nod tdhe zame. Jusr zhimmer in dhe dark. Ey lige dhez bedder."

342

"The point is, we always think we want what we don't have. Aredheli is beautiful, but I'd beware of Little Acorn."

"Dhe one who remindz me ov duty."

"Yes."

"Ey hav been reading. Id iz a pagan tale vrom dhe dimes of Gueens. Ey don't know. Iv we were one, we are not now. Bud duty, yez, iz vorever. Ey vill bray on thiz. God vill reveal dhe druth. Vee are almost done," Brig said. "Ve are leaving dhe scraps underneadh dhe plant dangle. Dey are doo small vor any uze." She held out her hand for the sword.

Eld passed it to her. "As far as it doesn't conflict with my duty, I wish you luck, Brig."

"Dhe zame do you, Vardhal."

They saluted each other, Eld's hand open to the sky, Brig with a fist on her chest plate, making a dull clang.

"God und Avatar," Brig added.

"And the Blessings of Sul's court," Eld said.

Brig turned and walked away, her armored hulking form soon swallowed by the mist.

As it thickened Eld grew calmer, part of her feeling the Eurthan's anxious minds retreating. Then imperceptibly the normal sounds of the night returned and the mist started to retreat.

A few minutes latter galloping hooves approached.

"Where are the Bane-spawn?" Sergeant Tarl demanded, trotting to a halt with Danshor and a couple other cavaliers, Fiorseth in their wake. Fiorseth circled so Eld could mount; she'd found her sword and lance while she waited.

"The Eurthans were back to collect what they could," Eld said. "Then they left."

"Didn't hear or see a damn thing," one woman said.

"They called up mist to hide themselves and quieted the air. But they really are leaving."

The sergeant wasn't satisfied until they swept the entire field, or at least the parts free of bramble thorns. They found nothing for two hours except footsteps from the Bane-armor, indeed walking away from the ravine. Eld and Danshor were released from watch as the Abbey bells rang the hour before midnight.

As they walked back to the garrison Eld was deep in thought. She'd fought the Bane-warrior but only survived by the intervention of Brig. It made her think on her other fights, her victories and defeats, of how most of them were not formal or were as a soldier, free to win by any means. The truth was, after so many wins, she wasn't taking the chance of a loss seriously. It wasn't just her ego or reputation at stake. It was also Althas, for if she lost, Roel would see that as a blessing from Heaven that Eld's offense meant nothing and Roel had done nothing wrong. Thinking previous victory meant the future was guaranteed was a dangerous state of mind for any mother to fall into.

After they reported at the gate and turned the horses over to the night grooms, Eld stopped Danshor at the door to their barracks.

"Fine. I'll do it."

"Do what?"

"Let you train me up."

"I knew you'd say that."

"What do you mean?"

"I Reveried while you were singing about 'Torin the Clumsy Dwen'."

"And you're telling me?"

"Only what has already happened. I didn't say you won."

"Well don't!"

"Relax. Let's go meet some friends before we retire. It won't be long."

## Chapter 24

# The Gladiator Shifter

With the lifting of watchfulness, the garrison yard was full of clusters of women around lamps or under the stars, chatting or singing about this or that. A game was often made of spying constellations and planets. Not every elf's sight was as keen, nor the woman as knowledgeable about what she saw. Usually around this time, there would be few women out free from duty. But so many had leave, it was like a holiday. The Rowan Oak's lights were still bright; Eld knew Tafli would stay open as long as trade was brisk. It was anyone's guess where any soul was at the moment and Danshor seemed particularly miffed when, after they had trudged all the way to the regular barracks in the northwest quarter, hardly anyone was there.

The general clusters of army barracks were in that area of the garrison: most for the infantry companies and one for the officers, all sitting in the west of the garrison, the officers' barrack slightly apart and center, closer to the Crèche. That was an older building, perhaps as old as the Crèche, three stories, with vaulted gate windows inset with a round pane at the top, so that the second story was blessed with regal round picture windows giving the residents a fine view. These apartments would be for the senior officers. The first floor would have graceful, well crafted, but more humble panes. But the ground floor was actually a mix of stables, kitchens and servants lodgings. The roof had a flat area placed amid the necessary peaked architecture for drainage. It was there officers held private fetes to the occasional nuisance of the nearby barracks.

Those barracks were their destination, several long, low buildings of the same simple, elegant but serviceable design as their own stables. The barracks were placed around one of the west field used to muster infantry for morning roll and general announcements. Where it did not hinder military function, raised gardening beds for herbs and fruit surrounded the buildings, mostly bare except for the first sprouts of nettle, angelica, lovage and other herbs. Angelica was a particular favorite of soldiers to chew; it was a reputed tonic from the days of Queens. It also explained the hint of carrot in the air. Outside the barrack doors lanterns hung, though a couple had a flaming torch or two for ambient light. Women sat outside on lawn stools, eating and drinking under the stars. Danshor led them to a hall, second from the edge of the field. They briefly made account of themselves to the soldier more or less on duty before entering. It was clear Danshor was a regular visitor.

But few souls were within the long, open building, that had more the air of a university dormitory than a barracks. Unlike cavalier barracks, the cots were slightly wider and had posts designed to allow them to be stacked in bunks. However, at present, they were not, making only a simple spread of forty cots, a score on each side of the hall. Space was available such that the trunk of every soldier was not under the cot as in their own stables, but against the wall beside it, each with a tall narrow window to herself, and a couple of wall hooks in addition to those on the cot posts. Some women had tables against the wall over their chest, with a folding stool and even small shelves. Most extravagant were the couple of souls who had tented their beds with netting for privacy, rigging extensions on the posts that Eld was sure had to be packed away during inspection. Similarly some found it expedient to rig light draping so that each area was divided as if walled, and so the impression of minute apartments was complete. There were hooks from the rafters above, but most of them were empty.

"They have so much space!" Eld breathed. "I feel like we're sleeping in our sister's pockets half the time."

"We have the horses," Danshor said. "If you add the stable space, it's about the same."

"But we're not sleeping in the stable space!"

"Aw, is our noble cavalier too delicate for the mother's life?" an amused voice called out, chorused by the laughter of women who had been drinking.

The barracks hall was invaded by about a dozen women, clearly all foots. Some wore bracs and shirts, others some form of their uniform unbuttoned and loosened post duty, all bonded in the life of sisters who marched together and found those who didn't wanting. Presently they took to their cells, either leaping to rest on beds or fishing out a bottle, book or stool, or returning to the one cell near the door, crowding around the cot or carpeted portion of floor to join the throng around a popular mother of the hall. This worthy pulled back her curtains, hooking them open and jumped up to sit against the headboard like an old lor holding court in a castle. She took a goblet someone had poured with amber wine and toasted Danshor though she didn't offer any.

"It's our flint hungry friend, Danshor," she said, taking a draught, then pulled her guardlock clips off. "That's better," she added shaking her loose hair. "You brought a friend."

"In their scholarly best," some soul jeered. Others took up variations on the jape:

"You going to a graduation?"

"You'll be a real magi now!"

"Very droll," Eld muttered. She knew it wouldn't last but the women had to have their fun. The masculate style of cavalry always invited ribbing from those souls who marched on Eurath's blessed face.

"I do say, my fine laird, that is a most sparking accessory this season!" one bold soul said, hands hovering over Eld's flout. "Where does one get these fashions?"

"Only on the brightest streets in the most fashionable quarter of Ta Mel!" another said in a ridiculously high voice mimicking a fastidious male. "But I'm far more interested in this fine foot wear! They would look so broll with my moon meet reeds. So slim would be my feet not a soul would sight them as I dance in the moonlight! Do you dance in the moonlight, my fine laird?"

"She's got to because as sure as Jaro's tits she's not marching in those!"

Buffeted by laughter Eld glanced at Danshor, who seemed to be sharing some private jest with the woman holding court, their eyes locked, both smirking at each other.

"You know," Danshor said in a moderately deep voice, "This is the Gilded Hero who saved the commander's brother."

This reminder brought many of the women out of their mocking merriment; they weren't exactly apologetic, but they started speaking like normal souls. Yet a couple others continued, though their tone was less mockery and more merriment, offering Eld a plate of fruit and cheese.

"As Jaro came to the mothers of the Bright Plains, so you grace us with your glory! Please, an offering from we, your humble servants!"

Eld took a small cluster of grapes. "Fine, Elam etc. Are you all entertained now?"

The "lor" waved her hand, a signal to stop the silliness. "It's not everyday two elite cavaliers visit us. And it's the butler's holiday."

This elicited more laughter while a couple stools were found for Eld and Danshor.

"This is Sergeant Ald Dolanmeer," Danshor said by introduction. "Patrycan shifts things. Dolanmeer shifts chance."

"On fights?" Eld asked.

Dolanmeer shrugged. "Fights are a common thing."

"Wagers," Eld said.

"What mothers decide to do with their queens is not the business of this soul," Dolanmeer said.

"We're here to discuss a coming wager," Danshor said.

"What coming wager?" Dolanmeer asked. "There's nothing until the next vagrant camp travels through."

"A duel," Danshor said. " You haven't heard?"

Eld was curious herself. If Dolanmeer didn't know, how was Roel getting her knowledge?

"I heard a rumor. But the source was a vain braggart so I didn't credit it. Not until I learn more."

"Well, here's the cause," Danshor said gesturing to Eld.

"Officer Roel and I duel," Eld said. "But I don't know when."

"But when we know, she needs training up," Danshor added,

Dolanmeer rose from her cot, looking at Eld intently. Dolanmeer herself was a well made woman, slightly taller that Eld, though not as built as Danshor.

"Lieutenant Roel challenged you to a duel?"

"No, she offered to drop her complaint if I apologized." Eld noticed the women were suddenly quiet.

"And you didn't?"

"Of course not."

"She slapped her," Danshor said with a grin.

It was a low noise at first, a collective gasp of disbelief, then a sudden explosion of laughter. Just as suddenly Eld found herself being hugged by Dolanmeer like a sister returned from death. Then the woman held her at arms length, looking her up and down while the women decided this was a cause for more celebration.

"You're solid. But you're used to dancing on a horse. You need to be trained up for the arena."

"I've been singing that chorus," Danshor said. "That's why we're here. Who's the best?"

"Sergeant Tershol. But she doesn't approve of fights."

"This is an official military duel," Eld said, having trouble making herself heard over the revelry.

"In that case, she should be a willing soul!"

"Lieutenant Roel is really disliked?"

In response Dolanmeer just laughed and poured them ample goblets of amber wine, the revelry of the barracks renewed for who knew how long.

The woman at watch poked her head in with a mix of annoyance and curiosity.

"You're all lucky most of us have leave. What in all the Mother-Gods of the Heavens is going on?"

One of the merriest teasers earlier shouted, "The Gilded Hero is going to thrash that hood Roel back to the shard pit she crawled out of!"

## Chapter 25

# Wagers

Finding Tershol was another task, but Dolanmeer agreed to hunt her down the next day. It was better this way, since Eld wouldn't be seen coming to the barracks. They all arranged to meet at the Kettle during breakfast. The only thing Eld objected to was rising early after a late night of drink.

"It should be your last revel until the fight," Danshor said.

"Yes, that would be wise." Eld was nearly finished with the trencher of porridge, sausage, scramble, pancakes and elderberry syrup. The Kettle had also made a brave effort at a froth, served in a tankard: whipped egg blended with cream, nutmeg and curry. But while it tasted well enough, it didn't have the body of Tafli's drinks. "I wonder if we'll be having forest travelers?" Eld ventured.

"Why bother? The Wildling serves a fine enough one."

"Both are frauds."

"The matrons don't care."

It was true. Eld's own children, adoring all things Dwen, ate more than their share of acorn stew, cakes and breads. The forest traveler Sula knew, unlike most traveler sandwiches, was a hot dish of sliced elk, venison or bacon layered on bread, with mushroom sauce poured on, often garnished with a sprig of horseradish. Actual travelers in Dwenoshire – for there was no such thing as a "forest traveler" among Dwen – used acorn pancakes in a soft bark shell, covered first with an herbed green mayonnaise, then layered with cold salted meat or fish, tart fruit jam of whatever locality, then was packed with mustard, radish, or kale leaves. It was a meal meant to be enjoyed after a hike or hard labor, not sitting at a table, and certainly not with a fork and knife.

"Looking bright?" Dolanmeer said, taking a seat across from them. She was in civilian garb; the uniform wasn't required in the Kettle unless duty was imminent. Eld and Danshor were also in shirts and bracs, but they would have to change for dinner because they were to patrol the field again.

"Never brighter," Eld said. "Who's this layabout?" she added.

Tershol was at Dolanmeer's side. They both sat down across the table with their trenchers.

"Careful, Farthal. You might get hammered as well as gilded," Tershol said.

Eld noticed a couple souls glance at Tershol, then look away.

"No, that's Master Sergeant Tershol, you nit!" some elf said.

Eld frowned.

"Oh, that's my hue going before me," Tershol said wryly. "Now that everyone has sighted our Dwen allies with tan or red-bronzed skin, some have taken it into their minds I am one."

"I think I'm having a reverie," Dolanmeer said, lowering her eyes theatrically. "I see us practicing ...with strike! Something no Dwen can do."

Tershol grinned. "She's like an oracle." Her grin vanished. "So what's this about you fighting, Farthal?"

"It's not a fight," Danshor said. "It's a formal duel."

Tershol started to demolish the food on her trencher, speaking between bites.

"So you're the one."

"You've heard?" Eld asked.

"The date's been set for a week from now."

"That's not very far," Eld said feeling like a hunted animal. "Danshor made so much of needing training. Should I even bother?"

"It's not the best, but yes," Tershol said. "There are many reasons: while you can't gain any new strength in that time, you can become more efficient with what you have. And your essence can be focused. But it will mostly be tuning what you already know and eliminating the worst of your weaknesses. Are you still on watch?"

"Yes. We patrol tonight, then have free time tomorrow-"

"As of now you have no free time," Tershol interrupted, then swallowed some froth. "Not for drink, revelry, or men. So if you have a boy, you better tell him. Take the time this afternoon to finish any small business so the next week isn't interrupted. After dinner, return to your barracks, do a basic essence form, then nap until watch. I'll meet you there after your patrol."

"How is this duel going?" Sergeant Tarl loomed over them from behind Eld and Danshor.

"Should be well, now she's my charge," Tershol said.

"Good. None of you worthy souls know anyone shifting contraband from the battle do you?"

"Contraband?" Eld asked.

"Profit is being made from the found Eurthan armor."

Danshor shrugged. "Didn't they loot the commander's house? Why shouldn't we trade in their Bane-gear?"

"Because, cavalier, Command has declared all abandoned Eurthan weapons and armor to be Federation property dedicated to formal scholarly examination. Any soul in possession of so much as a grim tooth pick will face discipline."

Eld's heart skipped a beat. She still had the crossbow bolt that almost killed Hollar. Eld didn't want to be glowered at about it, so she said nothing, but made a note to turn it over later.

"Some soul is selling Eurthan grim as curios," Tarl continued. "She needs to stop. You know aught of this?"

Adrenaline flowed up and down Eld's spine like ice. But it was a question she could truly answer: "No," she chorused with Danshor.

The sergeant paused, then appeared to be satisfied with what she heard.

"Good. You've got a week to win, Farthal. Be happy. In the olden days challenges were at noon and combat the same time the next day."

"I've done my part here," Dolanmeer said standing with her empty trencher. "Spread the word I'll be at the Rowan Oak," she added to Danshor. "The usual place."

Danshor nodded.

Tershol also rose. "Now don't go teasing Felkeni. That's one man who should forever and always be treated like a prince."

"Not a king?" Sergent Tarl ventured.

"There's only one Goddi who is King of the Heavens and I'm not foolish enough to spark a war between the Moon and Fate."

"In old tales Felkeni was an aspect of Lun," Eld offered. "That's why half his face is covered; he's the unsettled moon, half full, or half empty. Only later was he a separate person married to Myngar."

"That's our plan, see," Danshor said, "When she utters these poetic morsels of wisdom, Roel will fall into a stupor from boredom."

"I can't agree, cavalier," Tershol said thoughtfully. "The best warriors in history were poets. See you tonight, Farthal."

Dolanmeer and Tershol left.

"Remember, girls, we're cleaning the stables and barracks tomorrow," Sergeant Tarl said. "Danshor, you're with Alcas on soil duty. Don't worry, Farthal. While you're training you have leave to be free of drudging."

"But I'm supposed to be managing her," Danshor said.

"Managing your wagers on her, you mean. I thought I heard it was Tershol doing the actual training."

Danshor glowered at nothing.

"If you don't sulk, you'll find it easier to haunt the Rowan Oak plotting with souls wanting to invest queens. As for you, Farthal, your duty it clear: win, dammit."

Sergeant Tarl left.

Eld and Danshor rose to leave themselves and saw they were the center of curious looks from the women still eating, many lingering hoping to learn more.

"Is it true, Farthal?" the archer Camden said. She was wearing sage and green civilian hunting garb today.

"If you're asking about the duel, yes."

"That'll spark the stones!"

"And if you want to support our Gilded Hero, ask after us at the Rowan Oak," Danshor put in.

"Yes, of course!"

"So it's true?" another soul said.

"When?"

"They haven't announced the time yet," Eld said. "But expect to hear soon."

"And be ready with your queens." Danshor added in a louder voice, "Seek us at the Rowan Oak!"

"I think enough souls know and we should leave now," Eld said, walking briskly to the door.

Danshor joined her after confirming to more women wagers would be taken.

"You worry too much."

"You don't worry enough. Just because the duel is popular doesn't mean the regulations about wagers have been suspended."

Gambling wasn't exactly forbidden in the Federation military. But there still lingered a sacredness to practices once used as spiritual devotions, such that some souls felt it was tempting Felkeni's wrath. For the only one who never saw the dark side of His face was His wife Myngar. By seeking to profit by chance a soul was admitting they might not be basking in Myngar's favor and therefore was in the sights of Felkeni's dark face, making it unlikely that he'd be gracing the mother in question with winnings. Or worse, was trying to force or trick Felkeni into showing his bright face, thus perhaps robbing all mothers of their rightful plenty. Or so the argument was made by literalists.

A stoic mind saw the problem in logical terms: as all essence in Ta Pangeal and the Orb was contained, that is, once the final balance of the Source flow was made, there was no excess, so in the final balance of Chance, there were equal winnings and loses. Yet no mother knew what portion of that story she lived in. It was irrational, gross arrogance to presume one could harvest a segment of that time for profit.

But these arguments were more apt for the games of pure chance, like cards or dice. In the military these were considered slightly unwholesome distractions, and games played for profit were private and encouraged to be held outside the walls. And even in games for profit, there was a custom of paying Felkeni, if not in a donation to a temple or shrine, then the mother or keeper of the house.

Working chance was different from pure chance: that included all races, fights, sports and other wagered events where work, skill and talent were involved. This was the province of Myngar and She was neither as offended nor as fickle as Her consort. But She was more demanding. And much more vengeful against those who would cheat, though Her punishments were considered fair. So wagering on sport was less objectionable, but the exchange of money was still considered incompatible with military discipline by Command. Taking wagers was forbidden on garrison grounds. But the Rowan Oak was not technically ruled by the garrison.

Certainly regulations prevailed in the public spaces of the Rowan Oak. That was why the women were restrained in expressing their joy at Roel's humiliation in the commons. But Tafli rented rooms on occasion, or allowed them to be used with profit in mind. These were private, and his arrangements were with the souls as women, not soldiers. Thus they were free of regulations. All women had to do was speak of it in a way that did not encourage wagering. And in this case certainly no soul needed to be encouraged. Walking to the Rowan Oak, Eld noticed a vast crowd trailing them at a distance. This made Eld wonder.

"If all the foots and cavaliers are wagering on me, and all the officers on Roel, how can that balance out?"

"It doesn't," Danshor said. "That's something of the point: one side will win and be richer, and the other side will lose and be poorer."

"But there are fewer officers."

"But they have more money."

"But betting on who you want to win, isn't the same as them winning."

"Now you're getting epistemological. Yet you have a point. Maybe we should be a little less certain of you winning. Perhaps talk up Roel and work in your defense of a man's honor."

"You will not mention his name!"

"Very well! But we have to give the tricklers something to consider."

"No marching or riding mother is going to throw her queens away if I'm expected to lose."

"That's why we talk you up for the Host and train to win, and, at the same time, stage a conversation to be overheard by an officer about your weaknesses and how worried you are that Roel could win."

Eld stared at Danshor. "I didn't know you could be this devious."

"A hunter has to be. And wagers are hunts, make no mistake."

No sooner had they stepped inside the Rowan Oak, then Tafli said: "Upstairs, with a leaf on the door."

Tafli didn't look at them, shooing the new knave to gather cups because he'd paused to grin at Danshor.

"Isn't your son the same age?" Eld asked.

"Thanul is barely past ninety. That knave has to be a ripe century. There's no crime in looking."

"I hope his mother agrees."

Eld had never seen the second floor of the Rowan Oak. The stairs were something fantastically grown out of the building's structure, alive with grafted branches. They curved to the right, horizontal branchings from the left wall reaching out to a series of saplings embedded in the opposite curving wall to meet and twine together, making, more or less, even steps. The steps weren't particularly wide and they were rather steep, though to a people used to walking high on tree branches, Dwen like Tafli probably thought them excessively accommodating. The former stairs were long gone, removed when the dub was replaced with weavings. One certain clue was the broad maple leaves that sprouted from the wall around a tall, narrow window halfway up the staircase. There was also a skylight of simple glass over the upper landing. While Dwen used light gems and other artifacts of Sula magic, they preferred plain glass if solstone was not needed to extend daylight.

But what Dwen preferred best of all was open windows with no glass. This was apparent from the cool air circulating on the upper landing. The single hallway appeared to be a gallery of arching boughs. A window at the end of the hall faced them, bare of glass or screen, its shutters open to a glimpses of blue sky and the road to the village beyond. There were five doors in all: a large one in the center of the left wall, and, further down on the same side, a smaller one close to the window. From placement and probable size of the room, Eld would guess that was Tafli's private chamber, the other door perhaps a closet. The three doors on the right would be the rooms Tafli let. All of the doors were closed, but the middle one had the shape of an elm leaf impressed in the center. Danshor tapped once and Dolanmeer opened the door.

"There you are," Dolanmeer said.

They walked in and Dolanmeer shut the door firmly. The room was simple: there was a small bed to one side, shelves growing out of the wall on the other, with an abundance of hooks. A reasonably sized window of the same peaked gate-style faced the door, its shutters open, looking south over fields and rolling country of orchards and ranches. A few patches of grain, likely oats and barley, could be seen, still young, looking like tall green grass. They had over-wintered, being planted in the fall. But the ground was not the best for grain this close to the Altans. This was mainly a country of fruit trees, pulses and dairy stock.

The blossoms of various trees were already falling like pink and white snow, but some trees were still showy in their orchard rows. While the sun shined directly on this face of the building, the eaves were so deep it wouldn't touch the inside of the room for an hour.

"It's a fine view," Dolanmeer said. "But can we shut the window? We wouldn't want trade notes flying away."

"But you'll be skint for light," Eld said sympathetically, reaching to pull one shutter closed. It cut down some of the wind. "Unless you brought a lamp with you. Tafli doesn't allow burnings."

"That's why there's no hearth," Dolanmeer muttered. "No matter. We've had a good take so far and there's more on the way." She gestured to the bed where a pile of queens and and smaller coins clustered on the wool blanket.

Danshor was shifting a small table as far from the window as she could without blocking the door. There was a chair and a stool, and on the table was a soft ledger of the sort school children used for sketching. Dolanmeer sat on the chair and Danshor perched on the stool.

"I can lie on the bed," Eld offered.

Dolanmeer chuckled. "Your friend has suggested you should be pure and above reproach. I agree."

"Meaning?"

"You stand outside the door," Danshor said, opening the ledger and scanning it. "Let the mothers see what they're supporting."

Eld stalked out, stepping to the hall just as three women in uniform trotted up the steps.

"You have to be a spriteling not to trip on those!"

"You don't need to be a Tree to dance on a branch ..."

They stopped talking on sighting Eld.

"Al met, as we breath in the Orb, Farthal!" one said, clasping Eld's forearm. "Within?"

Eld nodded.

It was a more practiced form of "speak not and tell no lies". Every soul understood this was the place to make a wager on the duel. But while many did wish Eld luck, the words "wager", "money", "queens" or any reference to currency was not uttered. Eld could hear clearly enough, but no sense could have been made without context. Women walked in, mostly saying Farthal or "Gilded Hero", were told a series of numbers that could only be odds, and asked how much. This was apparently written down because Eld never heard it. The first bets for Roel came from a couple of officers who said nothing but stared at Eld as if she'd personally insulted their foremothers. What was Roel telling them? They must have paid with trade notes because Eld didn't hear the clink of coins. They left without another glance or word.

It was a tedious business. There was a lull for lunch where they took a break and ate shaved pork loin on a bed of greens with spicy aioli. Eld felt Tafli had been somewhat generous with the horseradish. As the afternoon wore on, Eld worried they might linger too long and not have time to prepare for watch and eat supper. At one point Tafli made a stool for her, a bundle of three sticks joined in the center, expanded and formed, with one end in a triangular seat of thick ridged mesh. This took less than a minute.

"Set it by that window when you are done," he said pointing at the end of the hall.

"Elam."

"I do many things for my favorite cavalier." He looked up at the vaulted roof. "I am thinking of opening the roof. Freeing gaps between branches to the sky."

Many questions filled Eld's head. "Won't that be brisk and breezy?" she asked.

"Yes, it would being lovely."

"And when it rains?"

"That is being the only problem," Tafli said, nodding seriously. "This house is not built with floor drainings like a proper loft. It might not be easy. Can I get you something?"

"A bun and barley-mead would be nice."

"For the Gilding Hero, anything. Provided you are winning."

"That is my intention."

"Good."

Tafli walked away briskly, his bangles jangling with every step.

When he returned a woman came with him. From the looks of her bright, clean, but worn linen shirt, heavy, dark brown bracs and knee-high field boots, she was a local farmer. Her hair was parted in locks, the rest hanging loose, but not mussed by labor or wind. That, and her vest, cut out of a green fabric woven with exotic arabesques, a fine piece tight around the muscular "V" of her torso, implied she'd made an effort to look trade worthy. As a stranger, to Eld's eye she was ageless. Usually such souls were somewhere between their second and fourth century.

Tafli gave Eld a plate with a couple of buns and a footed cup filled with mead.

"This woman is seeking you. And perhaps others who are wagering."

Tafli turned on heel and left as soon as he spoke, presumably to avoid being a witness.

Eld stood, putting the plate and cup on her stool.

"You are Lancer Elderyn Farthal?" the woman asked.

"I'm your elf. Um, I'm off duty, if you're wondering at my lack of cavalier aspect."

The woman looked Eld up and down. "I suppose you're as able as any mother."

"For?"

"To win." The woman's tone had been neutral, but now dipped an octave, her face heavy with repressed anger. She pulled out a letter with a broken seal, from the imprint and ink, it had been sent by military post. "Halda Oldenmor ga-Mores, in service," she added. Her name suggested she was birthed of a daughter stream of the Mores estate, famed for its amber wine. "And no, I don't have a bottle with me. Our concerns are cheese and cream. My other concern is my son. You know him as Althas."

Eld stood as straight as if she was at attention. "Yes, I know Althas."

Halda glanced at the letter. "I certainly hope so."

"We, uh, trysted once."

"So I gather."

"I'm fond of him, but he's like a brother now! I don't want you to misunderstand my intentions."

"It's Althas' understanding you should be concerned with."

"I am certain I have not misled him."

A moment passed, Halda gold eyes staring into Eld's.

"Very well," she said at last. "Then can you explain this?"

Halda handed Eld the letter. The contents were much as she expected: it was from the commander's office telling Emha Oldenmor her son was the cause of a duel; she was being informed as was her mother's right.

"What do you want to know?"

"Why."

"Has Althas said?"

"No. He refuses to discuss the details and tried to forbid me from 'causing a stir'."

"I'm under the same prohibition."

"But you know."

"Yes."

"I'm his mother. I have a right to know if my child has been hurt."

"Without betraying confidence, I can say Roel used him to get revenge on me."

"Did she force herself on him?" Halda rumbled dangerously. The light around them seemed to brighten. "If so I will burn her to ash before you have a chance to duel."

Eld shivered at the truth of her words. "No," Eld said, glad they were the truth. "But she ...no," Eld amended.

"But she did the closest she could and be safe in the truth and law."

"As I understand."

Halda nodded, taking the note back. "I don't blame you, Emha Farthal. Althas is hard working and dutiful, and deserves his leisure moments. But he has romantic ideas of what cavorting with soldiers entails. Those damn magazines don't help. Yet you are responsible – for teaching that hood a lesson. The wagers are within?" she added.

"Yes, emha," Eld said.

"I'm betting on you, cavalier. A wager of a hundred queens. I can spare it, but I would prefer to use the profit to send Althas away to learn healing properly as a trade. If you truly care for Althas like a brother, you will do your best to win."

"Yes, emha."

## Chapter 26

# The Abbey

The conversation with Althas' mother felt more dire than any glower from Commander Alhern. It was the difference in situation: Seth's prospects might suffer if he let himself be courted by a common soldier, but it would be his choice. What happened to Althas was forced on him. A mother's wrath was never to be tempted.

Suddenly Eld was more anxious about the outcome than she previously had been. How would she face Emha Oldenmor if she lost? Eld supposed she could gift Halda money for a school with a loan from her own estate...

These thoughts haunted her during patrol, even as they caught an elf scavenging the fields. Fiorseth loved this new game which did not involve dangerous leaping and rolling, or hurtful stings.

Eld realized she couldn't outflank the fleeing woman because any unburdened elf was faster and more agile than a light cavalry horse. So she threw her lance like a javelin into the ground in front of the woman, drove Fiorseth down one side with instructions to corral, anticipating the direction of the woman's dash to evade the horse, then launched herself from the saddle to tackle her. The elf still might have gotten away: unburdened with a riding coat and gear, the woman would have out paced Eld in the unfavorable terrain. But Eld had blown her whistle before and no magic silenced the air. The riders from the camp surrounded the woman moments after they rose to their feet and she was arrested formally. There was much implied pretense on her part that she was an innocent wanderer. She was actually a soldier from Company Ter.

Yet even through all the excitement, Eld was seeing the amber gold eyes of Althas' mother demanding a victory to avenge her son's dignity. Even the news of the closed shaft was barely a distraction: the Eurthans, perhaps the same night they retrieved their gear from the battlefield, had closed up the shaft, moving some of the earth and soil back, though Sul knew how. Much still remained mounded. But the shaft had been sealed at the level of the bedrock just below the local water table. It was still unknown how stable and safe it was so visitors were forbidden to walk on it. At least no soul would accidentally fall down to Athmod knew what fate.

So when they returned to the stables and Eld saw Sergeant Tershol waiting, she was eager to begin training in whatever way to ensure a victory.

"Get out of that and into loose shirt and bracs," Tershol said, herself in similar clothes with a dark mantle thrown around her shoulders. "No, not your running kit; you'll take time to get your blood up as it is."

As soon as Eld changed, they walked briskly away from the lighted areas.

"We want to avoid spying eyes," Tershol said. "It won't be possible to avoid them all, but we must make them work for their gains."

Once in the darkest shadows they made for the gate.

"Where are we going?" Eld asked as Tershol showed the women on duty a paper.

"To engage in research," she said.

"We're going to the Abbey?"

"Not today. Not until we find out if another party is using it."

"So you mean all spies except our own?"

From the sound of Tershol's voice she was smiling. "Cavalier, only in the minds of poets are heroes so noble and blessed to win without intelligence."

They were making for the south field just outside the garrison wall, the same used for laysaid and picnics. They had to be as far from the wall as possible to avoid the lights. Finally they could see the night sky where only wisps of clouds hovered in the high air. They paused under the starlight, to check that the field was empty before striding into the uncut herbs and grasses only now beginning to need shearing.

Tershol bid Eld to stand in the middle of a flat patch of grass.

"Move through the basic dance form, slowly."

Eld stepped, turned and spun, speeding up only if she needed to leap or flip. She was pleased her healing appeared to be complete; she could breath deeply and feel her ambient essence with the flow of her blood and breath. When she was done, her hands clapping soundlessly above her head; no fluorescence forthcoming, she lowered them to her sides.

"Good," Tershol said. "Now go faster and try to fluorescence."

"Fluorescence?" Eld asked incredulously. At night she didn't see how it was possible.

"It's not just a gesture of over-high spirits after the Dance. It shows your sulessence is flowing strongly and you need to be as strong as possible."

Eld wondered if this was a jest. "But Sul has long been asleep ..."

"And therefore you only have your sulessence from the day and none to draw on?"

"Well, yes."

"I thought you were smarter than Roel. You know she's training at high noon so she can practice frying you. It's not allowed, but she thinks she'll be forgiven if she flares a little from the excitement. But she's wrong."

"Oh, I don't doubt she wants to fry me. She's able."

"But she's wrong that training when Sul's the strongest will make her su-lessence stronger. You gain strength by increasing resistance and adapting. All Roel is doing is getting more practiced with the essence she already has. And we shall not correct her in this error. We shall do it correctly. You know the stars are Sul's distant cousins. Close your eyes and feel their essence."

Eld did as she was bidden. "I just feel a slight breeze," she said. "The air is cold."

"Open your eyes. Pick out a star, a bright one. Look at it like you sight through sunlight."

Eld's eyes landed on the Spindle Star, also know as the Guide Star, or simply the North Star. Though bright it wasn't the brightest, but with so many souls marking it for so many lifetimes, it might be easier. Seconds become minutes. Then something happened.

"It looks brighter," Eld said.

"Good! Your eyes are responding to the light. Close them and mark how you feel."

It was very slight, but it did feel as she was in very weak sunlight, perhaps filtered through a north facing cellar window. "Pull it into your aura. When you feel it over your whole skin – don't rush! --then, slowly, dance."

It took several minutes. And it wasn't helped by the fact, being night and standing still, Eld started to get chilled. She'd bring a mantel herself next time. When finally she felt the whisper of starry essence around her, she started dancing.

"Slowly, Farthal."

"I'm cold."

"Don't lose your touch. If you do, stop until you feel it again."

Eld slowed slightly, alarmed for a moment that the starry essence flickered away for a second. But it came back and stayed with her throughout the form. She still couldn't fluorescence.

"But I felt lighter!" Eld said excitedly.

"You have essence training, correct?"

"As a healer of animals."

"Your sensitivity is what we build on. Now again."

This time Eld was warmed enough to feel comfortable taking the time and feeling the light in her aura. Then she spun faster than she intended on a turn, the lightness exciting her, but she lost the feel and had to start all over.

Now she felt the distant starry essence as soon as she looked at the Spindle Star. She danced, slow and steady, making her moves controlled, coaching the starry essence to flow through her. While the air where her hands struck didn't fluorescence, she felt the discharge and was encouraged. When she clapped her hands over her head, she fluorescenced but so subtly she almost missed it. It was the faintest pale glimmering of her aura, like it had been touched for a moment by weak moonlight.

"Well done!" Tershol breathed. "Now we go together."

Tershol cast off her mantle and joined Eld, first facing each other, crossing their hands over their hearts, palms facing inward, as an acknowledgment of their opponent. Then they sharply pulled their arms apart so that the right hand struck with its heel the air farthest from the right hip, while the left did the same thing to the air farthest above the left shoulder and away from the head, while twisting left with a slight shift of their weight to the left knee, in a shallow lunge. This was the Whirling Salute, the start of all proper fights in the elfyn martial arts. In a fight the ruling mother or appointed referee gave the order to begin. At that point the women had the count of a minute to make a move. Most burst into action immediately, but those who knew they were evenly matched often waited, hoping to gain some small advantage by her opponent's first motions. Failure of either party to move meant a draw.

"Begin," Tershol said.

They didn't wait, but they moved slower than in a real fight: this wasn't to practice Eld's combat, but to keep the force of her essence flowing, even with such a weak assistance. Simply sparing at night was hard enough, and perhaps that was the point. Without the force of Sul in the offing, it would force her to avoid sloppy form and improve drawing on the distant su-lessence of the stars that did, however slightly, make sparring at night easier.

Eld was a good fighter and an excellent soldier. But there was a reason Tershol was a training master. She wasn't just fast; her blocks were solid, her blows unerring. Eld wasn't eager to fight her vigorously as she knew it was going to hurt. The lack of sunlight – even sunlight filtered through clouds was a tonic to Sula –did not seem to depress Tershol. When they finished, they parried with their right forearms in a mutual downward block. Where their arms met, the air flashed a ghostly white. Eld knew that Tershol was responsible for most of that discharge.

Then they stood facing again, arms crossed over their chests a moment before relaxing.

"Well done, Farthal. I have an idea where our time is best spent. That will be all for tonight. We shouldn't meet like we did again. You are still on free days?"

"We're drudging, but I've been excused to train."

"Then I'll send a page to fetch you after breakfast."

Tershol was true to her word. No sooner than Eld had cleaned her trencher than a fresh faced girl in a page uniform appeared at her table. This was a partied tunic vest of green and brown, with dun colored leggings and light leather shoes. Her hair was pulled back into a tail at her nape, held with a brass clasp. The girl looked to be in her early eighth decade, just before her body manifested true strength after her first shedding. She still had sprite quickness and the enthusiasm of youth. Saluting smartly she said, "Hail, Lancer Farthal! I am here for your summons!"

"What did you do now, Farthal?" some elf teased.

"She's clearly for the Temple," another said. "That must be why she's not in drudges."

Indeed, every other member of her company was in loose linen work clothes, with varying degrees of annoyance or resignation. Only Danshor understood the whole of the tale, but like Tershol and Dolanmeer, wasn't going to shout it to the Orb.

"You know Farthal's too delicate for real work," Danshor said. "All that poetry."

Danshor winked at Eld as she left with the page.

Eld was aware that, again, most eyes in the Kettle were on her as they walked out, but it didn't bother her much since she expected most to support her. But the pressure of expectation was growing and she knew she had to put it out of her mind to stay focused. The day was gray and overcast, something that would have made Eld unenthused before training with starlight. But filtered sunlight was stronger than even the reflected moon.

Meanwhile the little spark walked briskly, almost at a trot, taking a path from the Kettle, around the Crèche, and then to a foot path through a lavender thicket that lead to the Temple.

"Where are we going?" Eld asked.

"I've been ordered not to discuss anything with you, however small," the girl said.

"Oh."

363

Already the secrecy before a wagered fight was beginning. Finally, they entered the Temple through a side door into a small hall with a couple of benches.

"You are to wait here, Lancer," the girl said. She saluted smartly and left.

A few minutes passed. Eld had a sense she shouldn't call attention to herself. But a soldier in civilian garb lurking around the Temple was bound to spark curiosity. Today Eld wore her training vest under a loose shirt. She preferred to keep her paps as still as possible when there was spinning and tumbling in the offing. She'd bound her hair in one tail with a thong, much like the page, and wore sandals like the night before. Finally she heard a soul coming. A moment later a magi entered the hall.

In a blink the woman threw Eld a bundle of black clothes of slightly worn linen.

"Congratulations, Farthal," Tershol said. "You're an adept now."

Astonished Eld asked, "Is this allowed?"

"As long as we don't claim to be magi or take payment for essence work, there's no prohibition against actually wearing the robes."

"So if someone asks, we must reveal ourselves," Eld said pulling the long black shift over her head, followed by the full cut mantle.

"No, we must only reveal we are not qualified magi. Any elf who doesn't know us will assume we are students; that's why there is no tracery."

Sure enough the silvery designs were absent from the robes. Tershol helped Eld with the veil, that unintuitively hung under the back of the head and was clipped together on the crown, so the black fabric completely covered the bound hair. The round cap, with four solstone gems at the quarters, covered the rest, pinned securely in place. Eld shivered, feeling her aura aroused.

"That's the crown affecting you," Tershol said. "They are of the same high quality solstone on our epaulets. Sitting on your head they can be overwhelming to the untrained."

"Like a Sula wearing a Dwen yastol?"

"Yes. Try to breathe and focus while we walk outside. Even with cloud cover they can exhaust a soul."

"Where are we going?"

"To the Abbey, of course."

It was a good day for a walk in spite of the gray sky. The air was brisk but not cold. There were a couple of paths to the Abbey: one branched off the crossroad in the middle of town by the post, taking a winding road up the steep hillside. This was the way to the front doors and used to deliver supplies. But Tershol took them up another way, turning right and south as they left the gate, onto the Queen's road as it curved past Falls Gate Keep in the direction of the Green Barnsted Canal Station. A wagon park sat near this intersection, its stable yard placed conveniently for carriages to drop off travelers, many destined for The Wildling, a relatively short walk away. A little past the yard an unimproved path broke off from the road, winding into the scrub woods, then climbing up the the worn jagged hill of maple, herbs and young oak, young being no more than a century. The path was a mix of gravel laid earth, woven tree roots and rough cut stone steps, scraps from masonry building. As they rose higher, a lay of the land Eld didn't usually see opened around them:

The white walled garrison of Falls Gate Keep was as laid out like a map, easily copied by a keen eye and firm hand. Forest hugged its west side, the place where they met the Dwen on the border, where it opened to the south field. That field rolled away, changing into brush and bracken before the land came to the lots, more fields bordered by white stone fences, with sol-stone gravel scattered at the edges to burn out weeds. Houses, simple but elegant wood frames of ash-lime daub on stone or brick foundations, tended to cluster together where fields met, mothers and men building infrastructure for those tasks best done by community, like threshing, pressing, washing and baking. No linens were to be seen hanging. This would not be a good day to wash nor sunbake. Smoke rose from chimneys, the residents surrendering to using charcoal until Sul threw off Her drab raiment. Cows and sheep meandered in green fields, eagerly taking advantage of the new spring turf. The land rolled away, cut with patches of Greenway, that forest and wood set aside for Thyn beasts, usually elk and wolves, to pass through. Hunters could use the Greenway with care: no mother was allowed to use a bow until she was adept at distinguishing Thyn from their common cousins. A river could be seen wending between the lots and Greenways, cutting a path south and east. This would feed the canal, or turn into it. Eld hadn't examined a map properly. Unlike the usual view, the mountains were out of sight except for part of the range marching southeast, disappearing in a hazy of blue dimness. The south terrain disappeared into hills of solstone mines that came before the vast fields beyond that made up the cornucopia of the nation. It was a fine view, but one thing disturbed Eld.

"We came this way to avoid spies," she said, as they climbed a long stair. "But the trees still haven't leafed fully." Eld pointed to a maple in flower, its leaves dark clusters at the end of its branches like tightly closed fists.

"Which is why all they'll see are two magi."

Ahead, an actual magi appeared, trotting down the steps, black robes billowing.

Eld's heart skipped, but she just smiled absently as she passed on her way down the hill.

Finally, at the top of the steps, they'd reached the Abbey grounds.

A couple of thorn trees flanked the way, their trunks twisted slightly, as if made from clusters of scaly rope. Many thorns twisted, growing persistently in uneven soil, unfriendly winds and crowded by other trees. But these had not been so challenged and grew, if not straight, then robust and tall for their tribe, perhaps forty feet. These had leaves forming already, getting more sun earlier in the day, their branches scattered with spots of green. Soon they would expand, ready for their notable use as a heart tonic. A few weeks later, when most fruit blossoms were spent, they would burst with white flowers. But now the only accompaniment to their leaves were the thorns. These were mature trees and their thorns were as long as a small finger. They were used to thread hide and netting, or even as sewing tacks.

Beyond this living thorn gate was a sward of green grass, trimmed and tended with deliberateness, bordered by bushes and modest trees of birch and maple. The space was as large as a small parade field. Eld was surprised.

"I thought the Abbey was a cramped tower filled with stargazers," Eld said.

"Advanced students travel to study here or learn practical essence skills. And remember there is a school."

An old beech tree lurked to the left on the north side of the grass, branches lost in the midst of a green cloud of many budding leaves. Around it sat a circle of black robed students, palms up in the air as if they were juggling invisible balls between them. It wasn't a ball, but a stick, a small baton of the kind used for drums. It spun over their heads, passing to each soul in turn, never actually touching their hands in practice. Eld shivered, not with fear, but the echo of a memory. It was said, much like speaking mind to mind, at one time all elfyn could easily move essence the way magi did.

Then a soul fumbled and the baton fell. The magi laughed. It was tossed into the air and they resumed.

In the opposite part of the field, twenty or so souls danced in long, loose, dark pants that were cut as full as robes, with a white tunic shirt, some women opting for white training vests. The moves were much like the Dance the Host practiced, but with less striking motions and more fluid gestures, as if they where sifting the sands of the air for a rare shell or tide-washed treasure. Some scholars did describe the quality of essence as an ambient fluid; that never made sense to Eld until now. Then the dancers did a series of motions completely absent from the martial form Eld practiced:

They leaped and spun, then, on the toes of the supporting foot, they rose in the air, hovering for a second. Eld blinked, not certain of what she saw, but then they did it again, hovering longer, this time strafing and striking the air with visible strike before jumping off the 'step' in the air, cartwheeling into spinning forms.

"The strike is like from starlight ..." Eld muttered. "Except brighter."

"Filtered sunlight is a step away from strike at night," Tershol said. "You haven't said anything about the Triad."

Eld blinked, scanning the field for a stone circle, then felt foolish to have missed the raised circular garden in the center of the field. In fairness, from their perspective, one stone was obscured and their presence was less stark for the tall, yet-to-flower rhododendrons that had been planted in a circle around them. But once sighted they could not be forgotten. Though modest for menhirs, only twenty or so feet high, they had a presence. Yet they also seemed to want to slide away from the eye, the air around them rippling like heat waves.

"There's no room for a proper sadol," Tershol explained. "This Triad is linked to the sadol at the post office in Falls Gate." Sadols, circles of odd numbered great stones, were an established form of distant communication throughout the Federation. Every large post office had one; offices that didn't had dedicated messengers to take dictated missives to the nearest sadol. It was first thought by scholars the sadols in humyn countries were abandoned ancient elfyn works. But most of those stone circles were imitations used for places of worship, ignorant of the exact construction, materials and purpose. A Triad was the smallest workable sadol, but its range was much restricted.

"I didn't realize the Triad was open to any soul," Eld said, increasing her pace to reach the low, white wall that surround the elevated garden. Shallow steps of white ash-lime were placed at each quarter. Hugging the border were low bushes of lavender and mint just putting out new leaves. The place where the stones sat was paved with smaller bricks, placed to give the impression of rings around their base, as if they were sitting in water on a windy day. In the exact center was a round paver that glimmered even in the diffuse light, shot with mica or quartz or, like the loci sinks, with something more potent. Eld felt drawn to stand there, certain she could see the country if she only stood on the spot. But even with the elevated garden, the view was obscured by the trees and scrub except for the highest mountains

in the north and northeast. She was sure she could sight Ramoth's Ridge and the Passage Cataract. Then the air shimmered and she felt minds, seeking and aware. Suddenly the insides of the jagged stones were covered with spiraling symbols and letters. But they shifted as in a dream, images glimmering just under the surface of the rock like leaves sinking in a lake.
"There are words carved here," Eld said with wonder, an urge to understand compelling her to peer closely to catch them.

"No, there's not," a woman's voice said.

A magi had joined them, dressed as they were but with glimmerings in her robe.

"You are seeing with your soul ambient patterns of meaning that have been or will be sent," she explained.

"Or 'will be'?"

"None but the master wizards of Er know exactly how sendings work. There is a hypothesis that sendings work because the stones know what will be sent."

"That makes no sense."

"It makes as much sense as Reverie. How they know is the mystery. Now I must bid you to come out. It is linked with the post sadol and only those with duties should be standing near. And the children think we are being unfair."

Eld stepped out. Her awareness of the minds vanished and the surrounding lands seemed to diminish. Indeed there were a cluster of children looking very put out:

"Why does she get to stand in the Triad?" a girl said loudly.

"Magi have leave to use it in their duties," a man replied. He dressed much like Sil; Eld assumed he was a keeper of some sort.

"Say nothing to anyone except myself," the magi said, turning to lead them inside the abbey. "As children say … ~Speak not and tell no lies,~ she finished in thought. ~If you are asked to identify yourselves, say you are guests of the abbess.~

Rows of windows in serried levels overlooked the back gate to the grounds, tall and narrow in a gate-style, but newer than the Rowan Oak and built of ash-lime dressed stone. Deep eaves covered the length of the porch as they walked under and through double doors in the same peaked gate-style that stood open for the day. The air was laced with the scent of smoldering incense – cypress, fir, mastic and other resins – a mixture burned in temples since ancient times to evoke the memory of the Mother Tree. They passed visitors and townsfolk who came to the Abbey for the library, tutoring and scholarship. Soon Eld and Tershol found themselves in a covered, pillared corridor that ran to either side, doors at regular intervals suggesting rooms for institutional purposes; the halls turned out of sight, implying they followed the outer foundation of the Abbey. Another gateway opened ahead, revealing a large, paved, inner courtyard open to the sky. In the center was a strange building of ornamented arches and gables, with twisted, almost florid, designs of snakes, birds, trees and flowers around its many pillars. The building was made of stone, primitive yet well crafted, but not of elfyn design; it was the size of a modest house and covered with a dome, four turrets at each of the quarters. Eld only had a glance before they turned left.

"What is that?" Eld asked.

"The Temple," the Abbess said. "It was built by humyn who traveled from a land of lush forests in the far south and east. We think they were related to the Indus tribes; they share their art and a writing system. They built many monastic temple communities and schools throughout the southern Altans. These were used later to escape the wars of their rulers. Little is known of their life here. They were in decline when the lots expanded to this area. For millennia this was all overgrown. This Abbey is a only a couple thousand years old.

"I have made it clear you have arranged to use this north room." She opened a door into an ample room bare of furnishings, but filled with sunlight. "You may also use the grounds at your leisure after lights have been shuttered. But you take the risk of being observed if you do. Practice well, 'initiate'. Soldiers are not the only ones who wager."

The Abbess left and they slipped in quickly, closing the door and shedding their magi robes. There were no lamps as the roof was a solstone skylight dome. That was why the light was so bright: most solstone skylights were made to produce even light regardless of cloud cover. They were least active at night and at high noon on a clear day.

"What did she mean, 'initiate'?" Eld asked.

"A magi joke. This is student wizard dress."

Eld took off her shirt and sandals as well, and felt reasonably comfortable. She walked to the center of the room preparing to spar, but Tershol said, "No. First you drill."

Eld spent an hour practicing spinning, springing and falling, a good fall being one that was either transformed into an attack or at least brought one back to their feet. The tiled floor became a frequent sight as she fell forward many times, catching herself then pressing up forcefully enough to land in a guarded crouch. Then she tumbled sideways, first in cartwheels, then rolling on her shoulders, feeling like a ball. Then backwards, onto the high part of her back, immediately springing to her feet again; Tershol didn't let her stop until she returned to her feet fast enough to satisfy her.

"If you fall, your first task is to return to your feet!"

Then came the flip fall, not really a fall, but a backward spring turning the force of what would have been a fall into back flip. A skilled fighter could work in a kick to their opponent's face while evading. Perhaps the most enjoyable was spinning fast in lateral rolls across the floor, like an errant log of timber, again ending in the guarded crouch.

Then came all kinds of sweeps, Eld working so low that after half an hour her thighs started to burn.

"You feel it?"

"Yes!"

"Why?"

"What?"

"If there is anytime to exploit your sulessence it's now! Breath deep. Deeper. Keep breathing until the pain starts to ebb."

Tershol gave all these instructions while Eld was still in a long crouch, knee bent close to the floor in a deep side lunge, open palms up and guarded. She bit back the snarky things she wanted to say and tried to breathe. It was very hard in that position, but Eld knew it was going to be harder during the duel. It helped to exhale as much as possible. Her legs shook with effort. Then she inhaled and they stopped. She forced her breath out again and inhaled fast. Light filled her aura and the pain eased. Another couple of breaths and the pain, was just a slight soreness.

"Good," Tershol said. "Now do the sweeps keeping the essence flowing. Pull the light into your aura to quench the burning."

And so Eld did it all again, but it was easier this time, though she knew she was tiring. The sulessence made her feet lighter and when she was done the burning had vanished.

"Stop," Tershol said. Eld stood up, at ease.

The next moment there was a knock. Tershol opened the door. No one was there, but a platter with food and a tall jug and tin cups were sitting on the floor. Tershol brought them inside and they sat cross legged to have a snack with water.

"These gifts will arrive on the hour," Tershol said. "No, you go ahead," she added, taking only one of the fist sized cakes. "After you eat, we'll do some essence forms for rest."

The cakes were rich, made of ground barley and pulse flour, butter, eggs, cream and honey, leavened with soda. Sel's Small Cakes they were called, made energy dense especially for magi, though soldiers and athletes also ate them. They weren't exactly tasty like a sweet. But they were flavorful and satisfying. Eld could feel the core of her stomach eager to absorb this new energy. She was surprised she'd eaten three of them before she was sated.

Then they stretched a bit before standing in the center of the room facing each other to connect with the Source.

Source meditations were at the core of all elfyn magical practice, spirituality and mysticism. The Source, called by the mystics Affeegon or Avigon, was understood to be the life force of the Orb, deep inside Eurath, that all the living on Her depended. For while Sul gave the Sula power, Eurath gave all the peoples shelter and sustenance. Mystics saw the Source as the ever growing child of Eurath, she who would birth a new Sul if ever there came a day that Sul would die. For had Eurath not birthed Sul's most famous daughter Jaro at dawn? The Sun inside the Earth even had a nod from scholarship; the deep fires in Eurath were the source of volcanic activity. Religious poetry aside, the Source was the origin of magical power as experienced in the universe of existence or Ta Pangeal, the Net of Time. It appeared in dreams and visions at the center of the Orb Eurath, yet volcanoes, while revered by humyn as holy or damned places, were not any more essence rich than a cold peak of the Altans. Many details of how essence flowed from the Source remained obscure to scholarship. But it was a fact confirmed by True Dreams that meditating on the Source strengthened a soul's power and connection. Roel would probably sleep in meditation if she could.

They started eyes closed, standing relaxed and balanced, feet slightly apart, arms hanging loose. First Eld reached into her aura feeling where the light touched it. She inhaled and saw it brighten even through closed eyes. Eld shifted her focus to the part of her aura under her feet, seeking the light from the Source. She exhaled and almost instantly felt threads of essence rooting down, racing and branching through the dreamsoul of Eurath like roots of light until, the next second, they touched the Source. Eld perceived a vast nimbus of white-gold light rising as she inhaled, diminishing as it filtered through the many layers of Eurath's body, until it touched the floor beneath her feet.

Her aura shivered much as her legs holding the lunge, but there was no pain, only essence euphoria. Eld raised her arms, drawing the nimbus up through her feet, the seat of her womb, her heart, her throat and finally to a point above her head where her fingers tips met. She shivered like a tuning fork and felt as if she could float away.

"Open your eyes and control it," Tershol said.

Eld did as bidden but could see very little, the light around them having become so bright. Tershol mirrored her and the glowing nimbus above her must also mirror the singularity that hovered above Eld. She wasn't sure what she should do, but tried to breath like she did lunging and was pleased it worked. But she didn't know for how long.

"Let it settle and fill the nodes. You're a poet; you know all the old correspondences."

"But that's arbitrary literalist nonsense," Eld objected.

"Imagination is an essence tool. That 'nonsense' can be used as a tool. Talking about a lathe will not make a bowl, but using a lathe will."

The mystics put Sel above all. Next came the Dragon, the Voice of all Creation. Then Sul shining at the center of one's heart. Then Myngar or Maer, depending on the mystic: was the seat of the womb flowing? Or the growth of abundance? Or even Lun, who moved mothers to grow in the first place? For this, Eld preferred Myngar. Lowest, yet not low, was Eurath.

As they drew their nimbuses back down, the room dimmed. It was like a tide receding leaving the ground well watered, but not waterlogged as the essence singularities sank back into the earth and dispersed through the roots. Slowly all the light faded, returning brightness to normal, though it felt dimmer in contrast.

"Did you pull up your roots?" Tershol asked.

"Um, no."

"Sloppy. When you draw them back up, you leave an echo making it easier for you to put them down quickly. It's a magi trick."

"Did you train?"

"No. I have a sister at Trillium University in Ta Meloshok." Trillium was one of the smaller magi colleges. "We should practice those roots –"

A cheer from outside distracted them. Eld ignored it, returning to stand, closing her eyes and touching the light through her aura, preparing to repeat the form. But the cheer grew louder, and the voices more shrill, children's voices, always easy to pick out, almost singing for joy. One word was heard clearly: "Dragons!"

Eld's eye flew open. In a moment she was a sprite again, her eyes pleading with Tershol. "Master, a moment won't make a difference, will it?"

But Tershol wasn't hard to convince. Only the deadest mother's soul could not be moved by the sight of dragons.

"Come on," she growled. "Be quick!"

They raced out into the field, for no one knew how long the dragons would be visible. 'Hothyn' was the Sulanilish word for 'dragon', but dragons of the sky were called 'Thyngalu'. If they were lucky there might be a murmuration, a rare sight of Thyngalu wheeling high on the surface of the air just below the Void, like sparrows dancing in the dawn or dusk. But typically it was only one or two great souls flying high at the edge of sight, passing over without event. They'd run out of the eaves and stood near the Triad like many souls, Eld leaping up on the wall, though it was unnecessary for the dragons were almost directly above them, near the sky's zenith.

The clouds had cleared somewhat but still covered Sul. There were three great souls, their saurian outlines little more notable than skinny featherless geese, long necks stretched out before them, wings spread on either side, a snake like tail training behind. Oh, if there was just a ray of sun, Eld prayed. Then, as chance blessed the mothers of Eurath, there was. Not so great as to reach the ground, but a parting in the clouds above allowed a ray to glimmer across the dragons' paths and throw them into illumination.

A gasp went up. And with Sul's essence in the air, assisted from Eld's recently Source-charged state, the Thyngalu rushed into focus as if a telescope had been suddenly thrust before her eyes:

They were massive, so large it was hard to wrap one's mind around it. Were she to alight on the ground, the lead mother would stand easily as tall as the hill the Abbey sat on. Sapphire and gray scales glittered like glass in the sunlight, while the shadowed, light blue, under scales that rendered them nearly invisible in misty weather, shimmered underneath. Their saurian forms, taken when they manifested in the Orb during the Cataclysm so many eons ago, were frightening and predatory, yet soul piercingly beautiful, more so than a lion or an eagle. Their eyes had three irises or perhaps two with the whites: white, misty blue and violet; violet eyes were rare among elfyn and never found in humyn. The pupils were open now, not in slits or diamond stars as most painters gave them, but deep black pools that had seen stars birth and die. And so, like a shade of the visiting dead, their eyes were filled with stars.

~ELFLING~ a voice said in Eld's mind.

Eld gasped and felt dizzy. The mind that touched hers was so vast....

~BE WELL ON THIS DAY~.

And then it was gone.

Eld blinked and the next moment she was falling.

"Cavalier, I swear--" Tershol began.

Eld's training took over. It was too low to flip, but she spun herself sideways and landed as if she'd just finished a sweep.

"Good landing!" a magi nearby said.

"It had damn well better be," Tershol muttered.

Then a peal of thunder exploded over them.

The children squealed with delight, pointing up at the sky where dragon strike was splitting the air, in short, the Thyngalu exhaled lightening.

"Is that why the wind roars in their passing?" Eld asked.

"Yes," Tershol said, but the magi nearby said, "No" at the same time.

"It's an understandable mistake," the magi said as if launching into a lecture. "Dragon strike, like the Eurthan Blue-strike, does cut the air so fast it thunders. But we couldn't hear that so quickly from the ground. That is the speed of their passing. Only Payeen herself can go as fast and do so silently."

Then they heard the distant rumble the dragon strike birthed.

"Except in these times we worship knowledge and discovery, not romantic personified notions of the forces of the Orb," the Abbess added. "Let us not disturb our guests."

Eld followed Tershol briskly back to their room, where a platter of luncheon waited. They each had a bowl, pulled roast fowl on barley and steamed greens with another cake. Then Tershol told Eld to nap an hour. Tershol left on some errand, while Eld rolled her faux magi robes into a pillow and reclined under the skylight. In moments she was drifting into dreams.

Eld walked barefoot in the bright dreaming sunlight, still wearing the clothes she trained in. The air felt restful; she knew she would wake refreshed, ready to train. She wondered if in the short time she could visit Seth and what he would look like. An expert dreamer could communicate mind to mind with the waking. Eld wasn't expert, but perhaps she could leave an impression. She didn't expect to meet him before the duel.

And it was the stray thought of the duel, with all the force of her subconscious worries, that derailed any chance of her sighting Seth. Instead she found herself standing on the roof of a building where she could see most of the garrison grounds. The grounds were abandoned, empty except for a couple souls walking around near the Temple, along with a horse and a handful of hounds. These were the only dreamers active, everyone else being awake. Still Eld felt the force of a couple of presences near her and heard, as if from a distance, the Red Major say, "Ai, look up! There's a sight! Thyngalu above us!"

Eld looked and was so shocked she almost woke. Unlike what she saw waking outlined by the high light of the sun, massive forms circled the building no more than fifty feet above her head. Their minds were full of playful mischief, laughing in dreams as they made a whirlwind, and Eld felt herself rise up in the air as if plucked from the ground by a cyclone.

~YOU HAVE COME TO FLY WITH US LITTLE ELFLING?~

"I'm napping! How can you be dreaming if you're not asleep?"

~DREAMING IN SLEEP OR WAKING FLIGHT IS ALL THE SAME TO A DRAGON MIND~

"Oh!"

~ WE LEAVE YOU TO REST~

Suddenly the Thyngalu were gone, but Eld still hovered in the air. Then she knew where she was and the voices confirmed it:

"Well, that's a sight that brings luck!" Major Galledan exclaimed.

"Why?" Roel responded peevishly. "Are they going to devour that villainous cavalier for me?"

Eld wanted to laugh as she slowly sank down into darkness and felt her body wake. Tershol walked in the door as she opened her eyes.

"You've caught the time perfectly."

"Roel's training on the roof of the officer's garrison," Eld said.

"Are you spying?"

"Not on purpose."

"See that you don't. The rules are strict: no spies or sabotage."

"Which in practice means not to be caught spying."

"On your feet. Drills will drive these errant thoughts away."

## Chapter 27

# Inspection

And so they drilled the rest of the day, breaking again for dinner, this time at the garrison. Eld kept the magi clothes to use for the same ruse the next day. After supping, she napped again, rising to meet Tershol outside the gate an hour after dusk. They took the same path to the Abbey. This time they used the grounds furthest from the building, returning to practice essence resistance with starlight. Everything Eld had done earlier she repeated until she was exhausted from the effort of drawing on the stars. Tershol had a draught for her, an essence potion brewed by temple and magi shops, a general tonic crafted for essence users. She also had a small cake for Eld to eat on her way back.

"We'll meet again after breakfast like today."

Eld slept well that night, and the night after. This was their habit without fail for five days after which Eld felt she could almost dream and fight while she walked awake. She'd never felt so invigorated except for moments while studying healing and during the times up to birth.

Meanwhile those invested in the outcome, whether for the honor of their favorites or the money they wagered, had not been idle. Danshor, between drudging and helping Dolanmeer take wagers, had printed bills to announce the duel:

**OUR GILDED HERO**

**VS**

**A NOTABLE OFFICER**

No other words were needed. There were even images to represent them: a stock plate of Jaro holding a thick snake with spikes, The Spined Eel, above her head in a fist. Roel was shown by a stock cartoon of an officer, at attention, slightly exaggerated. But that was only the beginning.

No sooner than the ink had dried and the bills had been tacked in the usual places – around the Crèche, outside the barracks, the stables, the Rowan Oak – than partisans started to gradually deface them. Soon women were stopped and searched for pen and ink after new slurs materialized, usually overnight. Roel's image was defaced in the most common way, snakes had been added to her hair, implying she was as shifty as Athmod, the wayward daughter of Amer by Lun. Words were often added to the effect "it took a Hero to defeat a Bane Spawn". In literalist times it might be a slander, but now it was a schoolgirl insult and not serious enough for a report. There was a response to the effect, "It takes one Bane Spawn to Know another." That would be the limit of vengeance on that count.

Eld found the Jaro image on one bill altered to have thick rounded eyebrows, the ears cropped to suggest she was humyn. The words "she's brave but not very bright" were added. It made Eld laugh.

A couple days later, new bills were printed and posted, clearly from Roel's supporters who spared no expense. An intricate border of swords and stars ran along the top and bottom. A stock image of a general or marshal in profile represented Roel, while a thin spindly sketch of a rider on a horse was meant to be Eld.

## LIEUTENANT ROEL
## VS
## A COMMON CAVALIER

The words "DUTY" and "HONOR" ran in small print under the top border and above Roel's cartoon.

The women had even more fun with this one. While for the most part insults directed at Eld included witticisms like, "A pity she can't bring her horse" and "Surely a Wildling ruffian, not a cavalier", Roel's cartoon was graced with not only snakes in her hair, but the eyes had been outlined to suggest she wore kohl, with sparkles around her hair implying glimmer. One ambitious soul altered the rider so she too was holding a snake like in the first bill. This was altered further by Roel's supporters to be a vining tree with words suggesting Eld was at the root a tree with Forest sympathies. Since Dwenoshire and the Federation had not been at odds for at least two millennia, this was ridiculous. But the next alteration, appearing late on the fourth night, cause the greatest stir:

On the bills where the rider held a snake-cum-tree-branch, it had been extended up to end suggestively under the cartoon for Roel, with very large letters aslant asking:

### *"YET WHO IS IT WHO SEEKS DWEN HARLOTS TO BE ROOTED?"*

An hour before dawn on the fifth day, the entire garrison was roused. Lights glaring, the muster bell clanging, Sergeant Tarl was terse:

"Rise! Awake! Inspection on the field in a half an hour! In full uniform!"

379

Surprise inspections were usually close to quarterly exercises. No one knew why and any attempt to ask was met with remonstrations to "Hurry up!".

"Any cavalier not bright and shiny in full uniform at the appointed time will be doing presses. So anon and quickly!"

"Is it our dress uniform?" Torin asked unwisely while Eld was already stripped and grabbing a towel to run to the baths.

"Your dress uniform?" Sergeant Tarl shouted. "Are you going to the Sun-queen's court at this early hour and belated millennia?"

"No, sergeant...."

"Then obviously not! Now move faster unless you want to kiss our Mother Eurath!"

Eld couldn't hear them anymore. She joined the dash to the baths. They would be quick, jump in, wet their hair, jump out, dry themselves while they took turns combing each other's hair. Only when Danshor was dragging the comb over Eld scalp was there a fraction of time to speak.

"What do you think this is about?" Eld asked, just as Danshor finished, bound Eld's locks in a thong to be threaded into her flout later. They switched places.

"No idea," Danshor said, jiggling on her toes.

"Stay still!" Eld said. "It'll go faster!"

The next couple of seconds she was done. They grabbed their towels and ran back dashing around the entire scrum of arrivals.

"It's not just us but the entire garrison!" Eld exclaimed astonished.

"Well, I didn't do it, what ever it is!" Danshor said.

"How long do we have?" Eld asked, throwing her gear out of her trunk and dressing fast.

"Less than twelve minutes," Patrycan said, already pulling her coat on.

Shirt, breeches, belt, socks—Eld fell on her cot to pull her boots on, then yanked on her coat. Danshor tossed Eld her flout and she caught it, while Danshor wrapped Eld's tail of hair in a thin narrow scarf and spun it so tightly it felt like it would twist off. She grabbed Eld's flout and threaded it, Eld pulling the flout to sit down securely on her head. Then the scarf was yanked out. It took all of thirty seconds. They switched places and Danshor was flouted a half a minute later. Then they ran out to the field, buttoning their jackets as they went.

It was utter chaos. Every woman was doing her best to beat the time. Eld felt sorry for the foot companies whose barracks were farther away from the Crèche baths, yet over half of them stood in ranks, many buttoning their coats just like herself. The officer's barracks would have their own baths. Yet Eld saw only a couple of those blessed souls. Were they exempted?

They were all in the same places during the awards, but neither Seth nor the men were anywhere in sight. Alhern stood as straight as a monument, eyes flashing as dangerous as a dragon's. The Red Major joined her on the steps of the review platform saying something. Whatever it was Alhern barked a humorless laugh, and Major Galledan trotted off. At the last possible moment the officer's barracks disgorged the rest of its spawn, who rushed to take their places, some seeming uncertain where to go.

Then the time was out, the mustering bell clanged thrice.

"Stop!" Alhern bellowed with the assistance of her horn. "Any soul not in her place of duty report to Sergeant Tershol."

Eld's stomach sank. If Tershol was caught up dispensing discipline, her training would be disrupted.

There was a pause in the mysterious proceedings while an officer asked Alhern something.

"Yes, even if you're minted, dammit!" Alhern bellowed. "Be lucky you will simply stand and count out the presses!"

A handful of officers trotted over to join Tershol.

"Attention Host!" a master sergeant bellowed. "Prepare for inspection!"

They stood at attention as the sergeants carefully checked them over like the rest. They were none too pleased at losing sleep; that perhaps explained how they didn't seek every unpolished button. But some things could not be ignored.

"Lancer Torin, what's this?"

"What's what, Sergeant?" Torin asked anxiously.

Eld didn't dare look.

The next moment Torin exclaimed, "Ow!"

"Your grooming scarf was hanging out of your flout."

"Sorry, Sergeant!"

"So am I. Join the rest with Tershol."

"Yes, Sergeant!"

Torin dashed off to join those doing press-ups.

Then the most incongruous sound was heard, the meowing of a kitten.

It was somewhere across from Eld, in one of the foot companies.

Alhern brought her speaking horn up, but didn't bellow this time.

"What ridiculous soul has brought a kitten on the field?" she said.

A woman stepped forward, turning smartly and saluting, all with perfect precision, except for the small matter of holding a white kitten close to her chest in her left hand.

"Emha, Corporal Selden of Company Par, emha!"

"And you are carrying a kitten why, corporal? As you know, regulations only allow animals in military service to reside in barracks. "

"Emha, she was part of a litter suddenly orphaned. I had planned to send her to my estate as a pet for my nephew after breakfast this morning. But we were mustered and I couldn't leave her in the barracks unwatched. Emha."

The woman was far too savvy to blame the surprise inspection for the animal's discovery. The woman's sergeant faced her at close quarters, making her repeat herself to hear the truth. The sergeant turned back to Alhern and nodded.

Alhern announced, "Messenger Captain, confiscate that animal and send it to this soldier's estate with the appropriate care and instructions."

An officer saluted, strode over to the soldier and gently extracted the kitten, causing it to meow louder. She saluted again and then rushed off the field to execute the task. Animals were regularly delivered by canal boat. An infant animal like this would be sent with a page. Eld could only imagine how fierce the competition would be among the girls to get this task.

"Now that we are no longer operating a kennel for strays, you fine mothers of the nation are wondering why I have roused myself out of bed at such an early hour to stare at your plain faces. We will have to wait for those who were tardy to finish their five score press-ups before I explain. So be patient and think on your deeds."

It was silent on the garrison grounds except for the breathing of women finishing a hundred push-ups. The way these things went, if a soul could not continue for whatever reason, they were allowed to rest a minute, then continue on. Above them the sky turned from black to blue then gray and pink as the eastern clouds slowly revealed Sul's arrival. Those who finished with their discipline ran back to stand in their ranks. Torin sped past, her skin shiny with sweat. It must have been hard without even filtered sunlight. Finally only two women remained, the officers under discipline forced to stand at attention, while one counted.

"Eighty-nine, ninety, ninety-one ..."

At this point a woman paused, arms extended.

"Oh, for Sul's sake, how do we get these lumps in our Host?"

The voice wasn't Roel's but had the same tone of entitlement and arrogance. She might have no idea her voice carried, or was so used to making snarky asides it didn't occur to her what she said was undignified for her station.

383

"What did I hear, Master Sergent Tershol?" Alhern asked, returning to a boom through the horn.

"Emha, Lieutenant Golwind has asked how we get these lumps in our Host."

"Thank you, lieutenant, for calling the deficiencies of our serving mothers to our attention," Alhern boomed.

Eld shivered. She didn't think Alhern was offering thanks at all.

"Since you are clearly an expert in military standards of vigor," Alhern continued, "please show this woman by example how it is done."

Golwind looked around like a hunted animal. "Commander, you want me to do presses for discipline?"

"No, lieutenant, that would be below your station. I want you to demonstrate how to do the last, what is it, nine? Yes, nine presses with this soldier so she may learn from your example. One of your fellows can hold your coat and sword."

"Emha!" Golwind said.

Eld heard the anger and outrage in her voice. Officers did not do this kind of discipline in public. Alhern's description aside, every soul knew Golwind was being punished for her arrogant words. One officer took Golwind's baldric, the other her coat, and she set to kissing the earth with the soldier for a final count of nine.

"Don't forget to count, lieutenant," Alhern said. "You must set a fine example."

And so the final nine was somewhat easier for the soldier as Golwind counted first, did a press, and then waited for the other woman to do hers. When they were done, the soldier walked to her company, bound to be her own minor celebrity. Golwind replaced her coat and baldric, and with the other disciplined officers, marched back to their own spaces with all the pomp of escorting the ashes of a long dead ancestor being re-interred.

Alhern made them all wait a few minutes more. When she finally spoke the clouds had shifted from pink to orange then gold, and Sul's first rays warmed the commander's form. Alhern wore the command circlet, a feminine form of the hastol, a crown of enameled brass with four acute points, with solstone gems sitting on the points. Alhern was a handsome woman of course, well-formed and smart in her military dress, but on this morning her aura sparkled forbiddingly. Eld's sensitivity to essence moods had been heightened, and today this was not a woman she wanted to cross.

"I sometimes think our cavalry host is a group of unruly girls playing with horses," Alhern began.

There was chuckling from the younger officers. "Similarly, "Alhern continued, "young officers seem to think their duty is an unending schoolgirl holiday full of pranks and japes."

No one laughed now.

"As all of you know, because of these two dread forces in the Orb, there is a duel in two days. In anticipation, certain bills were printed, reasonable enough in announcement, though clearly partisan. This was not objectionable. But the defacement that followed is.

"I will remind every soul standing here, as a soldier serving in the Federation Forces, you have a duty to  represent our nation with dignity and grace. Part of that duty is that the dignity of motherhood is to be upheld at all times."

Alhern held up a bill. Eld couldn't see its details, but the formatting looked like the one printed by Roel's partisans.

"Suggesting either participant hires harlots for the purpose of receiving sodomy is a gross breach of the dignity of motherhood. Lieutenant Roel and Lancer Farthal, step forward and present yourselves!"

Eld moved with alacrity and Roel must have done the same, for they stopped at the steps below Alhern's glowering form at the same time.

"Lieutenant Roel, are you or your partisans, with your knowledge, responsible for this obscene defacement?" Here Alhern held the worst bill in question in front of Roel's face.

"Emha, with respect, why would I--"

"Answer the question!"

"No, emha!"

Alhern turned to Eld. She looked forward with perfect discipline.

"Lancer Farthal, are your or your partisans, with your knowledge, responsible for this obscene defacement?"

In truth this was the first time Eld had a chance to look closely at any bill, being as her life had been limited to training, eating and sleeping. It was obscene but  also funny: this one had altered the 'Roels' eyes so they appeared to be popping out of her head with surprise.

"No, emha!" Eld shouted, hoping amusement didn't obscure truth.

"In that case, you will both impress on your partisans this is not acceptable."

"Yes, emha!" they chorused together.

"And to answer your question, lieutenant, it is not unheard for those so lost in the spirit of competition to stage an attack on themselves so as to smear the character of their opponents. Do either of you know of such activities?"

"No, emha!" they chorused again.

"Good. Whatever the circumstance behind this coming duel, such customs remain because they bring the Host together and remind mothers of their collective duty in service. But since some souls have seen fit to drag a noble custom into the realms of a Wildling traveling circus, I am forced to remind the mothers serving here of their obligations. I never want to see or hear of this filth again!"

Alhern motioned to an aide who carried out a metal washing tub and set it at Alhern's feet. It was filled with bills of both print styles, collected from where they had been tacked. The majority of them had been graffitied in some fashion. Alhern raised the one she held to the dawn sunlight. She lit it easily and threw it into the tub. In a flash they burned quick and bright.

"There will be no more bills posted. At this point any soul who has an interest already knows of it. All free days are canceled until further notice. This is a drudge day for all souls except those on duty, and of course Roel and Farthal who will continue to train. At dawn tomorrow we will muster again with a full inspection. Yes, even our precious young officers. And Heavens help the mother who does not report with alacrity. Dismissed!"

They fell out, Eld exhaling as if she'd been on trial and gotten a reprieve.

"Can we go to the Kettle now?" she wondered out loud, joining the crowd heading in that direction.

"Most of us," Danshor said. "Alcas is being held back."

She wasn't the only one. Sergeant Tarl collared a couple more of their company, and Eld saw something similar happening throughout the grounds with other companies.

"They're marking those with gall stains on their hands," Patrycan whispered in Eld's ear. "The commander is taking some measured criticism for how she commanded the engagement with the Eurthans. That, and the earlier incident with her brother's attack, has led some souls to mutter about discipline."

"The duel hasn't helped," Eld suggested.

"No, not at all. That crack about a Wildling traveling circus has a source. It's not like this will change anything that's happened – "

"But it'll keep souls from straying in the future." Eld said, finishing the thought.

And so the garrison drudged while Eld returned to training. Sergeant Tershol wasn't away much. Besides, Eld knew by now how to best get her heat and essence moving with meditation and practice forms. Tershol was present to spar, and in the last couple of days that was the bulk of their work. Blocking drills, dodging drills; falling and recovery drills. And when

Tershol thought Eld was sound in them all, she had Eld repeat it under starlight.

Except the nights were becoming progressively cloudier, until on the sixth night there were no stars to be seen. This no longer bothered Eld. She had become used to dancing without the sun's rays, simply calling to mind the image of the guiding star was a comfort. So it was a shock to her, at the end of a form, her aura glimmered for a moment.

Tershol grinned at Eld's surprised face. "Well done, Farthal! I think you're ready."

There would be no more training that night or the next day. Tershol wanted Eld to rest, suggesting she take a walk. No riding, she cautioned. Horses or men. Eld was to avoid risk and not waste her energy.

"We should pause a moment to thank our host before we leave," Tershol said as they folded their magi garments.

"The Abbess?" Eld said.

"No. But she can explain it best."

They found the Abbess on the front steps, the first time Eld had been at the entrance. She'd always intended to visit the Abbey on a free day, but some distraction or another delayed her. It was too dark to see the lay of the land in any detail, but below, to their left, the lights of the village twinkled and distant revelers could be heard. The garrison was behind them and obscured by the hill and trees, as was the winding road that serviced the Abbey. The stoop of the actual entrance faced east, to the mountains, but they were dim, only the whiteness of their peaks visible like ghosts as they reflected the leavings of starlight.

The Abbess stood on the wide porch near an elevated statue of some importance: it was twice life size, with two figures standing back to back. The light from the gable lanterns glimmered on their surface; they were a dark metal with patina steaks, possibly bronze, standing on a high stone base.

"You have come to bid us farewell," the Abbess said gazing at the stars like so many before her. There were only a few thin clouds at the moment.

"And to give thanks," Tershol said. "Farthal is not familiar with our host."

The Abbess turned to face not them, but the figures. "Her name was Anda. Her remains were found in a funeral urn that rests in the base of this monument. It sat on a memory stone and that is where we get most of her story:

"These humyn, Anda's people, came from the east and south, from warmer lands, but with a desire to build places of learning and spend lives meditating on the mysteries of Ta Pangeal. What their order was or their exact beliefs are lost. But they too watched the stars and the marked the passing of death by burning. Quite civilized for humyn."

Eld remembered Dwen buried those who passed and wondered if this was part of Sula prejudice.

"They lived well here," the Abbess continued, "but they were in decline by the time these lots were established. Many returned to the mountains, others joined the Cambrian migrations. Until only an old humyn woman with a man was left. The man died in an accident, and the woman might have died too had her grieving not been heard in the dreams of a farmer. There was no village then and Falls Gate was little more that a post station for the garrison. This place was already much overgrown. The mothers below had no idea any but ravens lived here, and the community had been reclusive by nature. A friendship blossomed between the old Anda and the farmer, and soon Anda had regular visitors bringing her supplies. In turn she offered hospitality and entertained many with her stories. Anda lived another decade before being found dead in her rooms. She was burned on a pier here in the manner of her people, or as best we understood it. The alien temple within our courtyard is the only structure that remains of Anda's people. They say she had writings, but they have never been found. This is her image in life as it was known."

The Abbess pointed to the figure that faced west, where the road came. Eld stood closer, then pulled back in shock, the lined face of an old humyn somewhat alarming. It was an open, kind face that had smiled much. The eyes were intelligent and curious, her unaccented brow ridges in no way implying dullness. There were many wrinkles on her forehead and creasing her face, the mouth slightly flat, perhaps from tooth loss. A small dot sat in the center of her brow, a custom still practiced by modern Indus. From what Eld knew of humyn, she looked to be in her ninth decade. But she wasn't stooped, though she was depicted holding a staff for support.

"But that is not the form of her soul seen in dreams."

Eld was bidden to see the image facing east. Now she understood it was the same woman, but younger, slightly taller, with the full form of a dancer, her face rounded and slightly heart shaped. Her hair was thick, parts of it coiled in some custom, a fine veil hanging over the back. The clinging garments of layered mantels and scarves suggested the celebration of a full life of industry, building, learning and children. Then Eld felt a deep sadness: this Anda in her youth looked not so different from elfyn, yet humyn were doomed with the passage of time to lose sight of how their souls truly appeared separate from a body that withered after barely a century. That they could seize all the joy of life in this brief time was humbling. If Anda's people could thrive so, then Eld had no excuses to not do her best with the abundant talents she'd been gifted with. This underscored the reasons for their collective duty: elfyn did for the Orb because they could. And because they could, there was an obligation to do.

"Thank you for your hospitality," Eld murmured up at the lovely face forever gazing east to the lands of her ancestors.

## Chapter 28

# Duel

The day of the duel dawned gray and heavy. It was not exactly dark and there was no storm predicted. But after Sul rose, it was hard to tell where exactly She sat in the sky. Fortunately the military had relied on clocks for the last several thousand years.

Eld rose before the muster bell, did an essence meditation, then bathed. She was eating breakfast in the Kettle when the rest of the company arrived. No one wished her luck: on the day of an event begging Felkeni for his favors at the last minute was insulting Fate.

"Looking bright?" Patrycan said, perhaps being the tenth soul to greet Eld thusly that morning.

"Never brighter."

Eld did in fact feel good. She wasn't certain that she'd win, but neither was she fearful of losing. Her soul felt perfectly in balance with the Orb and Fate. What would happen would happen, she was just present to do her part. "Or at least never sounder," she added.

"Where are you going from here?" Danshor asked, ripping apart her bread.

"The duel is at noon. I think I should meditate and prepare myself."

"You sound like a newly married virgin."

Eld snorted. "I doubt any man old enough to marry is a virgin these decades."

"Coliseum gladiators meet with their partisans in the hours before. Dolanmeer and I think that we could get a bit more trade if you ..."

"I'm not a gladiator."

"In all but name. If you just ..."

"No, Danshor." Eld was firm. "I'm not a gladiator, this is a formal duel and I think we've tempted Fate, or at least the commander's temper, enough for one year. So I won't be glad handing partisans hoping for more wagers."

"Very well," Danshor said almost meekly.

"It's not about money."

"The stake I loaned you says otherwise."

"If it comes, it comes. There should be plenty as is, right?"

Danshor's head bobbed like a Dwen nod. "Probably. Yes, if the numbers are sound."

"Then that will be good enough."

Eld walked around the grounds, avoiding speaking to anyone. Women did whistle or cheer their encouragement; she waved or nodded, then walked on. Eld wasn't actually nervous, but the weight of what was to be done grew as the hour drew near. Tafli crossed her path at one point, saying nothing but offering her a large cup of water. It was dew or rain water(knowing Tafli, a mix), caught in the morning. It tasted sharp and brisk, like melted snow. Eld thanked him and walked on.

After briefly visiting Fiorseth, Eld lay in her cot and closed her eyes. In what seemed no time Danshor roused her, tapping the cot with her foot. Eld's eyes flew open. The light was still shadowless and flat. But Eld could feel the day had grown.

"It's time," Danshor said.

Eld rose and dressed, most of the women in the barracks trickling in to help or join the honor guard that would escort her. As such they wore their uniforms or some adjacent species of it. It was not an event that required women to be in uniform, nor was it explicitly forbidden to wear, say, the cavalry coat or flout with civilian clothes, provided a woman was both an actual cavalier and she was not on duty.

And so they marched together, their arrival greeted with deafening cheers, flouted to show their cavalry pride, the sole exception being Eld, whose hair was on the top of her head, the tail wound in the same grooming scarf used to flout, now instead tied down in coiled warrior knot. She wore her leather training vest and had chosen the flared dancing trousers used by the magi. On the walk she wore sandals, but neither participant would be allowed footwear during the fight. She had no ribbons or honor reeds. She thought them ridiculous and showy. So it didn't completely surprise her that was exactly what Roel was wearing.

Roel also marched between two lines of partisans, young officers who had chosen to wear their dress uniforms. Like Eld, Roel trailed the twin column as it passed though the crowded throng filling the parade field. And like Eld's partisans, when they stopped, they parted and faced each other to create a passage for their hero. There the similarities ended. The officers, mostly younger women, raised their swords over Roel's passage so she had a glittering roof of blades over her. Roel's hair was in trilocks, the back third coiled into a warrior knot. Wasn't she worried her guard locks would get in the way? Perhaps Roel hoped they would strike Eld by chance. She also wore her laced training vest but with white riding breeches. It wasn't a bad choice: unlike the magi dancing trousers they would not swish or move. Only Eld felt her essence flow better being less confined, especially after so many days of continuous practice. The dancing trousers were light and wouldn't hinder her, but watching Roel walk with such a confident spring in her step made Eld wonder if she'd made the right choice. However the reeds Roel wore were another matter.

Warrior reeds referred to many historical military or martial customs of decorative scarves or fabric. The gilding honors after a victory were one. Some wore the bands wrapped around the arm, wrists or hands, originally to support the joints, but becoming their own statement, advertising clans, families or estates, even schools of training. The most elaborate of these were long narrow bands of silk twined around the hand and wrist for support, then spiraling around the forearm to tie in a hitch knot behind the elbow, where the extra fabric would flow in streamers a couple feet long. This was what Roel was wearing, the silk bandages a pale yellow, a color too close to gilding for a humble soul. Most gladiators who wore reeds chose white or red.

And, much like Roel had in Alhern's office, she had the finest dusting of glimmer for all the good it would be on this gray day.

They faced each other at opposite edges of a fifty foot circle marked out at the center of the parade field in chalk. At the edge, halfway between the participants, a scaffold had been set up to offer an elevated view for the commander and other notable observers. Seth was there, but Eld kept him distant in her thoughts. They would be together soon enough. Alhern and her staff sat together at the very top. On the lower elevated step were more staff, along with a couple of civilians Eld didn't know. She knew a broadsheet agent was traveling from Falls Gate. She might be the woman in the purple vest holding a notebook. A man sat next to her, with much the air of a keeper of children but dressed far too brightly in sky blue robes with a yellow kirtle-shirt, cut for both masculine style and practical movement. At first Eld assumed he was a secretary, but instead of a notebook, he held a clip easel and a charcoal crayon. He was the broadsheet artist. In front of the scaffold, having brought their own chairs and stools, appeared to be all the men of the village, settled in as if they had come for an afternoon at the theater. To the side were tables with simple refreshment, fortified by a solemn Tafli serving civilian women who had also come to see the proceedings, or perhaps to escort the men. Eld was mildly surprised to see Althas. He sat near the center of the group, next to his much more merry friend; Althas looked as solemn as Tafli. He'd brought a bag of straw and was preparing to weave a straw braid of the sort used for making party hats as he watched. They both wanted satisfaction. Now was the time to gift it to them.

As Eld and Roel stood at the edges of circle and shed their sandals, the cheering died down to utter silence. Sergeant Tershol and Major Galledan stood by their respective charges. It was the first time their coaching had been publicly acknowledged. Eld felt irrationally resentful of the Red Major, as if she'd been betrayed. Eld had always liked her. Now Tershol and Galledan would act like referees. Nearby a handful of healers from the Temple had volunteered to serve if needed.

"Remember, there is is no forfeit at the start of a military duel," Tershol whispered in Eld's ear. "So if you plan to delay, be ready when the whistle sounds. You win when one of you does not rise, or one has pinned the other."

Eld nodded tersely, already pulling the sun's filtered light into her aura. It was so easy now, much easier than dancing in starlight. The air seemed to shimmer, full of energy.

Alhern didn't offer a speech nor bother with a speaking horn. Instead, using her deeper voice, she said, "Let's finish this foolishness."

There was a low chuckle that faded almost immediately.

"Approach and salute." Alhern intoned.

Eld walked forward, the stones feeling cool under her feet. Lines of white chalk had been drawn to show where they should stop. Facing each other, their eyes met, filled with dislike. But Eld surprised herself in that the feeling was distant and not overwhelming. Eld was here to win, not to punish Roel's tarnished soul. They crossed their hands over their hearts and waited for the word.

"Begin," Alhern rumbled.

They pulled their hands apart sharply, facing each other in the Whirling Salute.

Neither moved for almost a minute.

There was something to testing the impulsivity of one's opponent. Or her strength to hold the salute for a time. But neither of them wanted this moment to last too long. Once they started, speed, vigor and momentum would determine victory. And there was a danger of losing focus.

Eld breathed in essence every second she stood, opening her mind's focus, trusting the training of her body and soul to move correctly when the time came. Like a good game of chess, these first moves would mean nothing, they would be testing each other and, in the process abandoning tactics, while new ones manifested. It was foolish enough for a general to assume she could plot a battle from start to finish past the first engagement. Even more so for a single fight. The air brightened and for a moment Eld thought the clouds had cleared. But it was their auras. A murmur rippled around her, the sight being noted.

Then Roel exploded into motion.

A good minute was spent spinning around each other, evading blows from both hands and feet, exchanging parries, Roel's lip curled up revealing teeth bared in aggression. Eld didn't like it, but found herself pushed ever so slightly towards the edge of the circle. She waited until Roel's position changed to give Eld an opening to cartwheel past her and back towards the center of the circle, throwing a kick as she did.

But this was easily evaded by Roel, who blocked Eld's foot, trapping it a moment, forcing Eld to spin horizontally to free it. Then Roel had to let go or be unbalanced herself. Eld landed in a deep lunge, ready to leap up again, which was good because Roel was already rushing forward, then spinning, intending to kick Eld in either the face or the torso. Eld spun too, but stayed low, sweeping Roel's turning leg, forcing her to redirect her momentum into a backward flip. Roel landed on her feet, crouched with one hand on the ground to steady herself. But Eld was already rushing her, landing the first blow with a fist to Roel's face as she rose, followed by a knee to her center. It felt better than Eld expected just to be able to hit the hood; she tried to bring her elbow down to strike Roel's back, but Roel was already gone. Correctly seeing the threat of entanglement, she had dived under Eld's arms to roll behind her.

Eld spun not a moment too soon. Roel was already on her feet, flying back at Eld with a flurry of blows, yellow reeds flashing through the air. Somewhere in the parries there was a rip and the extra fabric floated to the ground, almost causing Eld to slip when she stepped on it. It was against the rules to seize hair or clothes, or use anything like a weapon. But Eld didn't put it past Roel to hope for a chanceful accident. So when Alhern bellowed "Stop!" it wasn't a surprise.

Eld and Roel separated, hovering at opposite sides of the circle, while Major Galledan rushed in and grabbed the ripped fabric off the ground. As soon as the major left the circle, Alhern shouted, "Begin!"

They didn't bother saluting, instead circling each other. Eld felt like an adolescent meeting a rival in a field. Circling could last as long as a Whirling Salute. But then Roel spun and Eld felt what was coming: this time Roel led with flying and wheeling kicks, but Eld blocked them easily, responding with her own, feeling so light on the air she attempted a spinning kick to be followed by another in quick succession, aiming to end with another punch. But after the first kick landed, Roel lunged with a fist, and though she missed her first target, Eld having shifted out of the way, Roel drove at her with the elbow of that same arm and hit Eld right under the rib cage. Again in danger of entanglement, this time it was Eld who sprang away in a back flip.

And so they continued to spar back and forth for nearly an hour.

There was no reprieve from the sky, the cloud cover persistent and unbroken, though a slight breeze came now and then, bringing a welcoming coolness to Eld's skin. Elfyn did sweat though it usually evaporated immediately, like the sublimation of ice or snow. But Eld and Roel had sparred for so long without the sun-heated air they now both glowed with perspiration, rivers of moisture starting to roll down Roel's neck. Eld expected she looked much the same.

What Eld had not expected was to feel invigorated, like a runner who had found her deeper wind after miles. She had an awareness she would tire and should therefore conserve her energy until she knew she could secure a win. And Eld found this easy now, almost restful as she spun, blocked and parried Roel's attacks.

And Roel's attacks were relentless. Unlike Eld, Roel had not reached that place of calm action nor found her deeper wind. She was driven by rage, fists flying in a flurry of pistons, hoping by sheer number Roel could unseat the equilibrium of Eld's defenses. And Roel had landed more strikes, as had Eld, but none of them were damaging or even winding. The women seemed to be evenly matched souls.

Then Roel leaped and flew at Eld, apparently intending to kick, but Eld saw the kick pulled back, followed by a another flurry of punches and then a spin for another kick, all midair-

But it was a Vision, a lesser cousin of Reverie, briefer, immediate and unlike Reverie, not a fixed future.

Roel was still flying at Eld but, seeing what was to come, she refuted every argument presented by Roel's attack. For a moment they were both in the same moment, so close no blow of any power was possible, though they both managed to land a couple of slaps and chopping strikes. And then Roel sneered and she seemed to slow.

In the battle there had been moments when the time shifted, but Eld had never experienced it in a one-to-one fight. She inhaled, keeping her focus centered, easily refuting Roel; Eld knew she shouldn't let herself be taken with elation for that was the one way the spell would break. This was Eld's chance, she could beat Roel with ease. Eld abandoned her desire to punch Roel in the nose or humiliate Roel in an obvious way. She would land a blow to Roel's center to wind her, another to keep her wind out, and then knock her down. And this calm plan worked at first: Roel gasped in shock as Eld's foot landed deep in her belly. Then with another spin she unbalanced Roel who, still gasping, stumbled. Finally Eld punched Roel on the side of the chin and Roel fell slowly backwards, her body giving no sign of twisting or springing into a recovery. Eld felt relief. It was going to be over.

And that's when Eld snapped out of the spell.

Roel did fall, flat on her back, only her tucked neck keeping her head from hitting the stone. She gasped, eyes wide and laid there for several seconds. The healers nodded to Alhern: Roel was not seriously injured. Major Galledan walked into the circle placing herself between Eld and Roel. But Eld was already backing away, keeping herself near the center. If Roel didn't rise, the duel would be over. She lay there a long time without moving. The day had brightened. It would be a great jest of Heaven if the clouds cleared after the duel was over.

Then, like a revenant, Roel moved. At first Eld thought she was sitting up slowly. But instead Roel rolled back, pulling her feet over her head, then arched her back and sprang to her feet, eyes blazing with fury, her guard lock clips hitting each other with a snap. A cheer went up from her partisans. No sooner had the major stepped out of the circle, than Roel rushed Eld, spinning with kicks and punches like a whirlwind.

Eld berated herself for her premature feelings of relief. The duel wasn't over, no fight was ever over, until it was finished. Eld blocked Roel effectively, but it felt like work again and Eld knew she needed to seek that center of calm. But that might be impossible now. They were both showing signs of fatigue. Eld seemed unable to land any strike now, and Roel was becoming crazed and reckless in her attacks, in her need to humble this upstart common cavalier. Roel's thoughts started to bleed through, Eld must have been taught magi tricks to have humbled her so, why didn't Eld just go down? She would make Eld kiss the earth! But none of it was useful, nor gave any insight into Roel's tactics or motions. These were simply the feelings of resentment and entitlement Eld already knew. They whirled around each other, striking, parrying and blocking, evading or leaping free of attempts to sweep each other to the ground, until the thing they both had avoided for over an hour happened: they were entwined, locked together in an attempt to overthrow each other by sheer force. Roel's hostile thoughts seeped into Eld's mind, and worse than that, Roel became aware of it.

Roel's lips curled at the edges, as if she'd found the key to unlock her victory and it filled her with dark joy.

Suddenly Eld's mind was flooded with images, memories of Roel's past:

Eld was Roel, lying on her side in an ample bed, the furnishings and lights informing Eld she was in a room at The Wildling. Eld expected to be around Althas, perhaps holding him down as Roel rode him, to be shown this as a way to gloat that Roel had taken Althas more deeply and completely, as if that mattered. But it was worse than that. Althas was bound with scarves, his feet together at the foot of the bed, his arms stretched above his head, anchored to a bed nob on the headboard, the length of his lithe, naked body stretched out. Roel was embracing him from behind, fondling him to keep him firm. Althas' face was blank, unreadable, as he endured and it was clear why: across the rumpled sheets and bedding lay gold coins, queens, perhaps ten in all, cast as if Roel was gambling on pieces of Althas' dignity. The coins were the only reason Althas did not demand to be released or scream for rescue. It was the earnings of a month for modest labor of either sex on a lot, and many children felt an extra pride if they could gift their mother's house with a portion of their earnings. Eld, as Roel, kissed his neck slowly, then reached for something that made Eld's soul shiver with revulsion: a dagger.

Not to cut or injure Althas. That would have already been discovered as a crime. There was a game some women liked to play, usually with harlots as most men refused. The handle of the dagger seemed to be made for such games, thick with a rounded end, all smooth to avoid serious injury. Roel held the dagger at the bottom of the blade where there was no sharpness. Then she shoved the length of the handle up inside Althas.

Althas shivered in revulsion and possibly pain, making no sound, while Roel, both then and now, smiled with satisfaction.

~Well fertilized by your harlot, my dagger was,~ Roel thought, her poetic phrasing the final insult.

The air was suddenly warm but all Eld saw was a red haze. Roel's smile vanished, perhaps seeing the furious fire she'd lit was much brighter and stronger than she expected.

Eld felt no tiredness now. Roel was forced to defend herself as it was now Eld whose fists came at Roel in a series of piston blows, like a spring flood driving the workings of a mill to beat cloth or metal into a new form. Several blows landed causing Roel to gasp. She rolled with them, tried to redirect Eld's attack, to steal the force of her river to drive her own mill. But Eld was relentless, as steady as the turning of the Orb, as unstoppable as a dragon in flight, dragons whose blessing Roel had dismissed as worthless if they would not do her bidding. Eld didn't even let herself think about the abuse of Althas, or her own feelings of disgust with Roel, instead letting pure force fill her aura, driving the essence as if she had the power of the Sul and the force of Heaven behind her.

Then with mild surprise Eld realized she did. The clouds had parted and the sun shined on them unhindered. That was the reason for the sudden brightness, not just Eld's inflamed passion.

Roel felt it too, and tried to call on streams of flames, the essence tracers that fluorescenced during the dance. But it was no match for the training Eld had done under the distant essence of the stars, now coming to fruition. For Eld now taking power from the full force of Sul was the simple work of a thought. Burning Roel alive would be so easy, but would be a crime as well as violating the terms of duel. Instead Eld drew the sun's power within her to drive her actions which were quick and brutal:

First she punched Roel on the chin, followed by an under cut kick. Roel would have fallen back, except for the next kick to her center, making Roel fold forward. Finally, Eld leaped up over her, and as Roel tried to press herself up from fall, Eld brought down the heel of her hand on the base of Roel's neck, slamming her into the stone. Eld heard a tooth crack.

Roel didn't move.

This time Eld kept her essence active and moving as she stepped back, the major again stepping between them. The crowd was cheering, Eld's partisans the loudest, but Eld knew it wasn't over.

Suddenly Roel sprang up and rushed forward, and Eld prepared to deflect any blow. But Roel simply tackled her around the waist and they fell together on the ground.

Roel in her fury became savage, clawing at Eld's face and eyes, trying to find purchase on her throat as they rolled around. She'd lost all discipline and focus but was still dangerous, using her raw strength at close quarters to try to tear Eld apart with her bare hands. But then Eld was straddling her, and landed a punch that cracked Roel's skull and took all the fight out of her body. She went limp.

But Roel's mind didn't.

Now Roel invaded Eld's mind, like she'd invaded Althas' body, and Eld was Roel again, riding Althas, still bound, dropping another coin on his chest while Roel smiled and took her pleasure being around him.

~He was firm, your harlot,~ Roel thought, her mind vigorous with spite though her body was exhausted.

Eld's aura exploded with sulessence. She punched Roel again and again, pressing a hand to Roel's chest so she couldn't evade, her nose streaming blood, the blood curdling from heat. There were shouts among the cheers, then Eld felt strong hands drag her off Roel and she smelled scorched hair....

Eld found herself kneeling alone, the light slowly dimming as her aura cooled. The sunlight was weak, but strong enough for Eld to draw it in to cool herself, for had she not drunk starlight? Moving sulessence to calm herself was nothing. The vile memories Roel forced on her faded along with the rage, until Eld finally felt she was completely herself again.

Blinking Eld turned her attention back to the circle where healers hovered around Roel, the stones scorched black in places. Eld couldn't see Roel at all.

Tershol stood over Eld. "What happened?" she demanded.

Eld was too tired for euphemisms. "She forced me to see memories of her sodomizing then coiting Althas," Eld said. "I could have burned her alive. I wanted to."

Eld wasn't proud of it, but neither was she ashamed. Tershol nodded once and walked over to Galledan. The Red Major looked furious, possibly because her coat was ruined, one sleeve scorched to the elbow. Whatever Tershol told the Major, did not improve her mood. They both approached Alhern while the buzz of the curious crowd increased in volume. The healers withdrew from Roel who sat drinking from a cup, either water or healing tonic.

Roel looked terrible. Her vest lacing was charred, leaving the garment half open, the remaining laces threatening to separate entirely. The lower half of her guard locks were ragged and scorched, the lock clips barely holding together what remained, and her face, chest and shoulders were covered with white salve to speed her healing. The sunlight would help; already the angry redness of the adjacent skin was receding. The reeds that had swathed her forearms were long gone, burnt to ash and lost to the air. Roel did not meet Eld's eyes. She had been defeated and there was nothing left than to see how their actions were judged.

"Get up," Alhern said. "Both of you."

Eld sprang to her feet, eliciting a cheer from her partisans. She didn't need to watched Roel clamber to her feet ungracefully in her condition. They both stood before Alhern, her gaze still stern and forbidding. There was a clattering as a couple of small, metallic things fell. Glancing to the ground, Eld saw Roel's lock clips had dropped from the seared remains of her hair.

"It seems Farthal was unclear that burning an opponent in a duel is not permitted. This is not an ancient wizard battle. But because it was fluorescence triggered by a mental provocation, also not permitted in duels, we have agreed these actions shall both be forgiven. Leaving the winner Lancer Farthal."

The cheers, whistles and shouts were like a dragon's roar, and nearly drowned out Alhern's final words:

"The rest of the day is a garrison free day until dusk, at which point, Sul and Heavens permitting, life shall return to normalcy. Dismissed!"

But the women only gave the commander's call for normalcy the briefest acknowledgement, their souls already on holiday with the joy of their now truly Gilded Hero's win: Tershol, assisted by Dolanmeer, Danshor and others expert in the custom, 'gilded' Eld, wrapping her torso crosswise with a long sash of gold silk: around the back of her neck, crossed over her heart, then crossed over the small of her back; then brought forward, wrapped around at the waist but not knotted, the ends hanging off the side of each hip. The extra lengths hung in tails to her knees.

"Kneel," Tershol said.

Eld knew this. It was an old custom, part of knighting champions in both the times of lors and queens. She faced south, sinking on her left knee, palms of both hands on her right knee, waiting for Sul's blessing. Eld rarely stared into the sun. While a Sula couldn't be blinded by looking at the sun, they could be made insensible and drunk. But a little drunkenness was acceptable now. Her face was bright, a disk hovering beyond the clouds, beyond the Orb they lived in, a distant world of flaming fields seen only in the dreams of magi. Perhaps one day Eld would visit that place.

Then Eld felt Tershol's thumb marking a cross on her brow with glimmer.

"Rise victorious, Gilded Hero!"

At last the name was free of mockery. Eld felt herself buffeted on all sides by cheers, women wanting to touch her, to share in the grace of the moment. Althas was there, offering a cup of water which Eld drained greedily. Then Althas kissed her, full on the lips but brief, a goodbye to their trysting tale. She hugged him, while Tafli also embraced her other side like another brother, and much was made of how many men Eld would have flooding her way. But the only man for her was Seth, lingering on the scaffold. Their eyes met. Seth smiled and winked. They would meet anon. This might be the brightest day of Eld's life and she looked forward to sharing it with him. Perhaps it was time to tell him of the reverie.

Eld looked for Roel, but she was gone. So was Alhern. There was no medal, no award, nothing except the gilding sash to commemorate her win and perhaps a ballad if a soul was moved. The reward for winning a duel was satisfaction and forsaking any further compensation.

Eld was borne away by her partisans for revelry at the Rowan Oak.

# PART III

# TER ~ OBLIGATION

$\phi\pm o\text{j}\phi o\text{q}$

## Chapter 29

# Drudging

The tale would travel far with or without the help of the broadsheet agent and her artist companion. But the broadsheet, Herald of the Dawn Country, would ensure the tale traveled around the Federation and Her territories. The other civilian was revealed to be a professional bard. This was not obvious because she'd dressed as conservatively as a legal scribe. At the Rowan Oak, where Eld was introduced personally to these worthies, the bard explained she didn't dress as she did for performance so as to blend with the moment. Eld was careful what she said, perhaps even more so than with the agent and artist; a good song could last longer than a nation and her people. Of course Eld spoke no untruth, something the agent would be trained to hear, but she felt she had to work to politely evade questions about saving Seth. Eld did feel proud of herself by adroitly directing the artist to talk to Sethshorn in person since they were both artists and would have much in common. This was well received, perhaps too well received. On reflection, given the habit of gossip among men, Eld had misgivings she'd been as clever as she thought.

Questions lingered about which souls exactly were responsible for the obscene bill defacement. Alhern was all but calling in the Hounds to find the culprits. A corporal had been detained who confessed to drawing the suggestive branch. But she truthfully denied scribing or painting any words. Some words had been in brush strokes, like the art, but most of the lettering was by quill. All this was concurrent with the investigation into Eurthan contraband. The woman Eld collared was just a scrounger for an itinerant dealer not under the authority of Command and apparently not yet found. If the dealer was wise, she'd left the area and any of her custom would be silent about it until the day they walked through the Door.

But it was hard to be too worried about mays or maynots of the future in the afterglow of victory and celebration. Women's spirits were high, barley-mead, true mead and ale flowed freely, and the cook had a task keeping up. Tafli was doing great trade, both he and his knave dancing on their feet but pleased with the queens that flowed from women's purses. And the village men had come, mingling with the women, free of fear or worry. Something had happened on the field that refuted the philosophy of the mother who believed she could exploit the dignity of men. Even Althas was there, eventually sitting on Patrycan's lap; they both seemed pleased with this arrangement, his spirits perhaps further buoyed by the full leather purse he held.

For it was the time for wagers to be paid. This was done in public, but with the briefest of exchanges: a woman, or her agent, gave her name to Dolanmeer and was given a purse. Only after she left the table Dolanmeer fortified did she talk excitedly about her winnings. Of course none of Roel's partisans were present. Some soul reported they were holding a wake for their loss in the officer's tower and Roel had dungeoned herself in her private rooms.

"Lieutenants have private rooms?" Torin asked, sipping a froth which she now preferred even to mead. "I thought they had to bunk in fours until they were at least captains."

"They're probably being respectful of her loss," Pat said to the laughter of the table.

"And what a loss it was," Althas added. "To our Gilded Hero!"

And so Eld was toasted for perhaps the twentieth time that afternoon.

Eld was grateful for the honors and equally pleased with her winnings. Less the stake of what she owed Danshor, she had such an abundance she was able to pay off her debt to Patrycan and the stable accounts and have plenty left over. She'd get the mites presents, and give an offering to the estate, and there would still be plenty for her to gamble, drink and harlot away if that had been her temperament. She could buy Seth something nice. In truth she had so much left she wondered how it could have manifested. She'd been kept ignorant of the odds given or how much Roel's partisans had thrown in to defend the dignity of their stations. Had they really thought Eld was a bumbling fool when she wasn't on a horse? Or had they thought Roel was that masterful?

"You shouldn't look too closely at a gift from Felkeni," Pat said. "But I can tell you Roel's partisans bragged to anyone in the village who would listen that Roel had been a white ribboned fighter in the academy and was an adept in the Dawn School. There's no reason to think they were lying."

Eld watched the table where Dolanmeer paid out wagers from a chest sitting on the floor. If the Eurthans wanted to loot, this would be a perfect time. Though they might be disappointed: modern queens were only plated with gold. The rest was a mix of silver, brass bank markers and trade notes.

"Whereas I was a bold but unknown cavalier," Eld said.

"I imagine they might have bet differently if they'd known you were training with magi under starlight," Pat said.

Eld stared sharply at Patrycan who was grinning.

"Really?" Althas said.

"Oh yes," Pat said. "They were quite impressed. Don't be unsettled, sister. Magi trade like any other mother."

At that moment a group of those same black swathed individuals entered the Rowan Oak. For a second the house quieted as if Sel herself had stepped from the stars among them. Magi did not usually drink at the Rowan Oak, preferring The Wildling closer to the Abbey. But when they immediately made for the table Dolanmeer sat, spirits lightened. Magi were normal mothers of the Orb after all, not dragons in elfyn form. They took their winnings and left; Tafli did not think much of this, but he couldn't complain as he had more than enough trade.

The rangers and Dwen also came, Captain Draeyn, Yeladrin and Olyeth collecting their winnings. But Scout Orinac came directly to their table to congratulate Eld.

"It was a fight worthy of the ancient duels!" she said.

"And your enjoyment has been rewarded!" Eld said.

But the ranger looked sheepish.

"No!" Alcas and the man with her said in astonishment.

Eld looked to all their faces, understanding settling on her. "You bet on Roel?" she asked Orinac in disbelief.

"She was a noted fighter at the Academy!" the ranger protested. "Her partisans spoke truth and said it was a certain thing!"

"There is no such creature," Patrycan said as the table exploded in laughter.

"Sit down, traitor," Eld said, laughing with the rest. "You've been punished enough. I suppose we have to buy your drinks as well?"

This was unfortunately true. The ranger was skint until her quarterly pay.

It was time for another round and Eld volunteered to get it, her rising causing another collective toast from the matrons in the house. She met Danshor at the bar while they waited for Tafli to return from serving food.

"I get a feeling they're cheering more for their full purses than my victory," Eld mused.

"They're one and the same, sister."

"So can I get rid of this gilding?" The gold satin still wound around Eld's form marking her from the most distant of eyes.

"No," Danshor said in a voice as firm as Tershol's. "You wouldn't glad hand them before, so they deserve to see their hero now."

"Very well," Eld sighed.

Tafli returned, took Danshor's coins and pulled a couple of cups of cider from the barrels. Tafli and Danshor were not exactly friendly but much more civil than before. After Danshor left, Tafli dropped the coins in a merchant's chest drawer just below the back of the bar. He briefly ran his finger tips across the gold and silver coins.

"I like my queens," he said lovingly.

"You are a rare man," Eld said, 'rare' in this instance being a polite word for strange.

"It is true," Tafli said, then suddenly shouted, "No burnings!"

A woman had struck a match for some reason, but blew it out instantly. She was being remonstrated by her sister on Tafli's ways.

Eld ordered more of the same for their table. As Tafli set each cup on a tray for her to carry, something about his hands caught Eld's eye.

"Your nails!" she exclaimed.

"What?"

"They're lacquered!" She had seen them shine with a dark green polish, revealing the color was a bottled essence, not a Dwen stain. It wasn't unknown for Dwen men to lacquer their nails, but Tafli didn't as a habit.

"Yes, I am a man," Tafli said with a smile. "This surprises you?"

Eld wanted to object, to point out he never did. Then, as Tafli set the last cup on the tray, she saw a darkness under his nails that could not be explained by lacquer or paint. Black gall ink was hard to wash out and Tafli wouldn't be practiced with a brush or quill as he preferred impressions in wood. Eld thought as a Dwen he should be able to remove it with wood-essence. But perhaps gall tannin was hard even for Dwen to clean.

Tafli saw Eld's eyes on his hand and snatched it away.

"Take your drinks, Gilded Hero," he said, green eyes intent. "As your wise Patrycan says, do not be looking at too closely the gifts of Felkeni lest they are vanishing into mist!"

Eld shivered and returned to their table.

Conversation had moved to the coming awards and a promise of the feast they'd been cheated out of after the first Eurthan attack. News came that the final report on Alhern's actions during the battle fell on the favorable side, any defects the understandable consequence of being surprised by a formidable opponent and sabotage that prevented reinforcements from arriving. Command declared it a win for the Federation, though that seemed to be stretching the tale; in Eld's mind it was a draw, both to luck and impromptu diplomacy over shared elfyn values. But that wasn't her concern. Let the Eurthans correct the record if they wanted to file a complaint.

If the women expected Alhern to give them more latitude because suspicion of her command was lifted, they were mistaken. There would be drudging the day before the awards, then muster and inspection, of the Host, the barracks, the stables and the kennels. Only after would the awards be given. Alhern seemed to want to drive home the lesson that the days of allowances were over. Awards would be presented at noon and, like before, the afternoon would be given to the many heroes mixing with villagers and staff, another opportunity for trade and festivities. A light meal would be offered in the Kettle before the feast, which was mandatory. They would wear their dress uniforms.

"But where is everyone going to eat?" Eld asked. "The commander's house is large, but not that large."

"The grounds," Danshor offered, finally finished dispensing the largess from the wagers. She was fingering a note which she folded and slid in a pocket. "Whoever isn't blessed to sit at the commander's table or in the house will eat in pavilions outside."

"Except for Roel who will eat in her rooms I expect!" Torin said.

There followed much laughter at Roel's expense as every soul wondered how long she could hide from the Host.

"She'll have to report for duty some time," Patrycan pointed out.

Eld pitied Roel just a small bit. But Roel only had herself to blame for abusing Althas. And a soul had to wonder how many men's dignity she'd been careless with over the years.

Late in the afternoon they left to prepare for dinner and finally Eld could shed her gilding sash, folding it and placing it carefully in her chest. She released her hair from the warrior knot and put it in loose trilocks, smirking a bit as she did, knowing it would be a while before Roel could wear trilocks as her burnt hair grew out. Eld exchanged her dueling garb for a casual shirt and bracs, though she decided to wear her boots. Her feet were slightly sore from dancing on stone.

Eld's arrival at the Kettle turned it into another public house. The cooks were generous, forcing Eld to be generous in turn: she didn't actually need to eat another whole round of bread or another half rabbit. Patrycan was happy to take them both.

"Althas and I thought we'd have a late picnic," she said, wrapping the rabbit and bread in a large napkin of waxed paper.

"Keep that close," Eld said. "I could save your life."

"The rabbit?"

"No, the waxed paper. I meant to ask, could you recommend a cache office? I seem to be awash in winnings and I think it's time I nurture funds separate from the estate."

"I've been telling sisters that for years! Its grand when you're young, but there comes a time you don't want the estate to know all your business. I'll write down some names tomorrow."

"Elam."

"Nabi Cuanaiya," Pat said, waving her hand.

Draining the last of her barley-water, Eld considered her next course. Seth wouldn't be available for hours, and Eld expected Danshor would insist on parading her to the other barracks. Considering these women had contributed to the wager, Eld wasn't inclined to object as long as she left early enough to meet Seth at their usual time.

"I'm for the baths," Eld said standing up. "I think I can still scent Roel's sweat on me."

Those within earshot recoiled with mock aversion.

"You'll be back later for some rounds?" Danshor said.

"Yes, yes, you can show me off like a prized mare," Eld said throwing her arms up in a gesture of surrender as she left. The Kettle burst into applause at her passing. Eld tried to project both thankfulness and humility, making a last salute before exiting. She was looking forward to the end of the days of being anyone's hero.

The baths were free of souls apart from the towel girls, and thus free of the threat of pranks. Afterwards she visited Fiorseth, then took a trip to the Temple to visit the souls still in residence, but the young healer, Tarasik, warned Eld, gilded or not, Olthan would not be welcoming. So instead Eld visited the paddock where Boad and his rider were; Trannecyn was feeding him carrots. Eld was surprised she could walk: one leg was still wrapped in a Dwen wood twined cast, as was her entire upper torso. But her burns were healed, her only complaint being, due to the nature of the casts, she could only wear a shapeless mantel when she went outside.

"I look like a damn ancient bard about to launch into the lay of the Cataclysm," she opined.

"I expect you felt like you'd been there in the flesh," Eld said.

"Been there and knocked out by a piece of the Dying Star. But it would have been worse without your lance skewing that spawn. They say I'm healing faster than they expected. That's down to him."

Eld looked at Boad who, apart from the sealed eyelid, seemed to have recovered from death quite well, now nibbling grass without a care.

"We're retiring when were healed," Trannecyn said. "Command isn't happy. The record says my wounds were a result of 'reckless action'. But our estate's legal notary was persistent. I get my discharge with honors, medals, but no monetary heroes award. Apart from Boad. But that's enough. And I'm a veteran at a hundred and fifty two! Not many souls could want more. Except maybe hair."

They laughed; Trannecyn's head was a patchwork of healed bald spots. Like most elfyn she refused to cut the remaining locks for evenness. Instead she planned to wear a magi veil in public until her hair had grown to her shoulders, then shear it evenly.

"I'm sorry I missed the duel."

"Some soul is bound to tell you about it over and over again. Just wait."

Dusk was falling and the healers were chivying patients back inside. Eld said her goodbyes and Healer Tarasik escorted her to the Temple bounds in case there were questions.

"You're still serving," Eld said. "I expected to be summoned if there was an inquiry."

"Fortunately, the Board of Prefects, while appalled I took the risk, were equally impressed Boad was brought back after so long. So I have been re-buked in the strongest terms. I also have an invitation to study at the Labrys Academy, the top school for essence surgery."

"Well done!"

"Yes, I am pleased. But I am careful to be humble about it. Good eve."

No sooner than Eld had come to the end of the Temple path, than Dan-shor waylaid her and their tour of the garrison began in earnest. It was good Eld hadn't had any strong drink after the duel because she felt obligated to accept a drink from every barracks she visited. The hospitality was over-whelming; Eld was offered the best seat or cot while they drank to her health and their new wealth. Defying math as Eld knew it, every elf seemed to feel she was gifted with a small fortune. But perhaps some of the younger mothers had never had any extra coin for themselves. Eld was mildly appalled their first cache was made gambling. She said nothing of course, as the visits fell into a pattern: first showers of greetings and praises, then asking how she felt about the match, immediately followed by souls flooding her with their feelings and which parts of the duel they liked best. These were covered in exhaustive detail, even acted out, presumably for those who had an obscured view. It was all Eld could do not to remind some mothers, yes, she'd been there. But she wasn't going to rob them of their excitement. As tiresome as it was for her to go over the event again and again, it did bring the women together. They all had wagered and won, and felt part of the glorious hero's tale, except for the few who bet on Roel. Eld found herself defending these souls, reminding the rest that Roel was a minted officer and an expert in many fighting forms from the academy.

"Not enough!" one wag shouted to laughter.

Finally, long after the sunset, they were finished. Eld heard the clock from the Abbey in the distance: an hour before midnight.

"I'm going for a walk," Eld said to Danshor.

"Are you going to keep this pretense that you and the commander's-"

"Stop!" Eld shouted. "You don't know what you're talking about!"

Danshor looked mulish, regarding Eld coolly. "You have been forbidden to discuss it. Why didn't you just say so?"

Eld stared at Danshor, mute with astonishment. Finally she said, "If – and this would be a great 'if' worthy of the ancient philosophers, – if I had been forbidden to discuss any topic, by that same token I would be forbidden to tell you about it!"

Eld stalked away towards the Rowan Oak. What she'd do when she got there she didn't know. She had an idea she'd ask Tafli to hide her in one of his spare rooms. But she looked back now and then, marking Danshor's path. Danshor disappeared between the two vast stables. Which didn't mean she wasn't watching.

So Eld tried a different tactic. She walked out the gate, and then around the perimeter of the garrison, a casual walk often taken by locals on a nice day.   In the time it took to navigate the outside of the wall, and a couple of breaks in the path due to drainage ditches, Danshor would have given up her spying. Hanmet Danshor was a determined soul in battle, betting and men, but easily bored. By the time Eld returned to the gate, she was confident enough to approach the back of the commander's house with a minimum of stealth.

Seth opened the door from the garden as soon as Eld arrived.

"I started to wonder if the village men had carried you off," he said. He was wearing a robe bound at the waist and nothing else. From the look of the vanity he'd been brushing his hair; it still hung loose.

"The village men have moved on to other mothers, my dear laird. After the battle, there are heroes for the dozen."

"But none that won a duel so brightly."

Seth kissed Eld full on the lips, and Eld slid her arms over the small of his back, pulling him to her.

"So why did it take you so long?" Seth asked, eyes glittering in the lamp-light.

"The men didn't carry me off. But the women were another matter. They all wanted to meet the source of their great fortune. Well, Danshor insisted."

"She's a baleful influence."

"She a good sister. Yes, she drives me mad, but she's the reason I'm not skint anymore."

"You bet on yourself?"

"Actually Danshor bet my debts on myself. "

"It was a good investment. Our kettle staff are happy."

412

"They're allowed to gamble?"

"Selind didn't like it, but I explained they were going to do it anyway. So we took their money in escrow, paying the wager ourselves. That would keep the young and enthusiastic from wagering more than they were able. They are happy to have a small winnings. Alas, except for our butler, Emha Sonamor. She bet on Roel."

Eld fell back on the bed laughing. "Someone must have told her Roel was a master of the Dawn School!"

Seth tumbled into her side, "And did you know she was white ribboned at the academy?"

"Then bet the entire mother's cache! We can't possibly lose!"

Eld kissed Seth as if celebrating their new wealth. Soon they were embracing in earnest and Eld pulled the sash holding Seth's robe together.

"Shall we have no poetry at all this night?" Seth asked.

Eld pulled him close. "The only poetry I need is a vision of your soul."

"Flattery will do, I suppose," Seth said.

They kissed again and spent a pleasant hour before falling into dreams.

They both woke in the early dawn, knowing they would in their separate ways have much to do. For today was drudging, and while the commander's house was not under military discipline, the cleaning would carry at all the seriousness of a battalion of uncles descending on an estate before Sol Suldan.

Seth lay on his back trying to muster the will to rise while Eld dressed.

"I tried to excuse Solafi and his keeper, but I wasn't able to find either of them yestereve," Seth said sleepily. "I would rather they spend the day away. Neither is of any help in their own unique ways."

Eld kissed Seth, then stood to leave. "I am informed you are a capable man of many talents," she said. "I am certain you will find a way to keep equanimity."

"Not without a dungeon and chains," Seth muttered, closing his eyes.

Eld slipped out, feeling the hour hunted her. It was later than she preferred, any trace of true darkness gone. Only the late rising souls reveling the night before kept the paths empty enough Eld was unmarked. Once she was away from the commander's house, she walked briskly, taking a path one might assume she'd come from the Crèche and an early bath. At the stables she was surprised to run into Danshor, fully dressed, apparently having spent the night away from the barracks as well.

"Al met," Eld said warily. She didn't want to row again, but neither did she want to discuss Seth, however indirectly. "Where were you?"

"What? Are you the only soul allowed to cavort overnight, away from our modest abode?"

"Are you drunk?" This thought genuinely worried Eld. It took quite a bit of the strongest distilled liquor to bring elfyn near a state of drunkenness.

"No, simply awash in the afterglow of many free men. I might not have slept much, if at all."

"Drink some of Tafli's sun soaked dew water," Eld suggested. "It refreshed me after the duel."

They stepped into their dim barracks, and Eld wasn't surprised to see it as much a mess as it had been after her first celebration throng. She helped herself to food still lurking on a table: a local cheese spiced with herbs, slices of a fig-filled sweet bread roll, and several salted crackers and walnuts. A few cots were empty, women out the last night or to the baths, but a couple seemed to be more full than they should be. Patrycan in particular had over her, instead of a blanket, a man, his long pale hair covering both their faces as their breath softly whistled. Danshor was pointing and grinning because the man's robe was up over his hip on one side, exposing a buttock. Danshor mimed swatting him, but was quelled by Eld's glare. Danshor grabbed a bunch of crackers instead. Patrycan was completely nude.

Eld leaned to a window, working to open it as quietly as possible. Men were usually evicted while the dark could hide their passing. They would be lucky to escape presses after drudging if they were caught.

"Wake Pat up!" Eld whispered. "Quietly."

"Hard to do without touching that fine laird covering her!" Danshor said in a normal tone of voice.

Eld looked furious.

"What? We're not going to be able to smuggle him out in a chest. Our fate is sealed ..."

"What fate?" Reon asked looking up. "I didn't hear the muster bell-- Athmod's Tits, do we still have men here?"

She was wide awake and a second later helping Eld with the window.

"I'm glad another soul understands the seriousness," Eld said. "Alhern is on the march. Never mind the ladder! They're fit and agile farm lads! They'll just have to jump."

By this time more women had wakened and were either helping or found it a good excuse to leave for the baths. Danshor sat stupidly on her cot, grinning.

"What's wrong with her?" Althone said irritated.

"A night of coiting, drinking and no sleep," Eld said. "She claims to not be drunk--"

"Cavaliers, sergeant approaching!" the watch outside announced.

Eld ran to Patrycan's cot where the lovers were at least sitting up, smiling at each other.

"I think everyone sees us," Althas said.

"Yes, and you have to leave," Eld said. "Now!"

Eld was happy Althas had recovered his passions after Roel's abuse, but wished he was moving faster. She seized Althas by the arm, firmly pulling him off Patrycan. Thankfully they weren't still joined in any way. "Straighten yourself up and get out the window!"

"Oh yes, I remember," Althas said. "There's a ladder--"

"No time!"

Now Pat was fully awake, herself, and comprehending, unlike Danshor who fell back on her cot and laughed at their efforts. Pat demanded a soul throw her a mantle. In a second she had it wrapped around her like an ancient poet, one end draped over an arm, her loose hair covering her shoulders and fronts as she strode out the door.

"Sergeant Tarl!" Pat said gregariously, "Morning and Al Met! The mustering bell hasn't even rung, what brings you so early ..."

Another man in green robes was already hopping up and adroitly slid out the window, landing like a cat. He blew a kiss before running off. Althas was still dithering over not having a ladder.

"Al met, yourself," Tarl said. "There's an Emha Oldenmor inquiring after her son, who she knows came to watch the duel. His name is Althas."

This acted on Althas like a tonic. Suddenly he was willing to chance jumping out without a ladder and accepted Eld's help. But just as he stepped onto the ledge he cried out, or would have if Eld hadn't put a hand over his mouth.

"My mother's winnings!" he whispered urgently.

Cursing, Eld leaped down and rummaged around Pat's cot, her rumpled bedding and discarded clothes. She found the leather purse and dashed back just as Althas was being lowered by Reon and Althone. Eld thrust the purse out to him. Althas snatched it.

"Run!" Eld hissed. Then they shut the window.

Meanwhile, Pat was saying, "Althas ..."

"Yes, cavalier, Althas. If you're dragging the time out--"

"Oh, I do know an Althas. We had several drunks together yesterday in the Rowan Oak--"

Eld rushed out before Pat bent the truth too far.

"What's this about Althas?"

Sergeant Tarl looked between them, too wise not to know when something was being occulted. She pushed past and inside the barracks.

"My, what an early rising, eager lot you are," Tarl said.

No one replied to this.

"I hope this means this will be the best drudging ever seen in these barracks."

The women murmured various forms of affirmations. Just then the mustering bell clanged.

"Outside in ten minutes, in drudges!"

"Yes, sergeant!" they all chorused.

They worked quickly after she left, but it was nothing like the surprise muster Alhern had called. The drudges and sandals were easy to throw on, and flouting was not required, most, like Eld, opting to pull all their hair back or on top of their heads with a thong. As Eld ran to the field she caught a sight of Althas out of the corner of her eye and a snatch of conversation:

" –And then it was hard to get back. Now I have retrieved my mother's winnings I really must return home..."

Standing at attention, they listened while Sergeant Tarl informed them of their life for the next couple days:

They would drudge all day cleaning their barracks, assisting with the stables, and, if they were finished, they would help any other barracks or garrison office that needed it. After dinner they would clean and tend their uniforms to present themselves as worthy mothers of the Federation. Exactly at dawn the next day would be a formal inspection of persons and barracks.

"We will be hosting Command including worthies from the Federation Field Marshal's staff. If any soul makes us look unworthy, woe be unto her and her fellows. And let woe fall particularly on those harboring forbidden guests. After inspection you will breakfast and have a couple hours of freedom before the awards. Then you will lunch at your pleasure and be free for another hour before the Hero's Feast and Gala. Attendance is mandatory. Heaven help the souls that brings dishonor upon the garrison in front of our hosts.

"Finally for those mothers who have recently acquired a small fortune, be aware that gifts from Felkeni were due in part to wayward encouragement, leading townsfolk to lose more than a reasonable amount in wagering. We strongly suggest each and every one of you give custom to the fair and the village Step after the awards and be generous with your queens. Dismissed!"

And so they drudged.

The bedding was stripped and sent to the laundry, but their blankets were hung outside to air. Their clothing was soaked, scrubbed and beaten on boards, or in that friend of helpers, the bucket agitator. The clothes needed to be cleaned first so they had time to hang and dry enough to be ironed and pressed, and ambient sunlight was best for that. While the clothes dried and their blankets aired, the barracks were cleaned top to bottom, swept, mopped and dusted, the brass polished, the wood shaved and oiled where needed. Women who were adept with the tools were tasked with examining the furniture to hammer, screw, tighten or otherwise repair. The windows too were a separate task: a cracked pane had been discovered and it needed to be replaced. If it couldn't be done before inspection, it would be marked as "work to do" and not count against them.

When they were done with their quarters, they moved to the stables. Most women had some experience on their estates with livestock, but a few came from cities or towns, and cleaning after horses was either a novelty or abhorrent, depending on the individual. So Eld felt a little guilty when, due to her talent to ease horses not her own, she was assigned to the group given the task of walking the horses while the stable was cleaned. Danshor was not pleased as she watched Tuiric led away.

There was a peculiar legend among humyn in the North, especially the Prithi, Tenes, and Nords, that elves were eager to labor the night for saucers of milk, or do such labors of magic like spinning grain into gold. What anyone would do with that amount of gold wire, Eld couldn't fathom. It was true elfyn were faster, stronger and more perceptive than humyn. It was equally true the labor the women did in a day would have taken humyn of the same number and skill several days, especially to the high quality expected in the Federation Army. But the fact remained it was work and it took time and energy. How these simple people found the idea elfyn would be gifting such labor, especially for the cheap price of milk, or worse the exchange of a humyn infant, was beyond the average mother's comprehension.

Those who studied savage folklore speculated these "gifts", "blessings" or even curses from "elves" or "fairies" were a muddled humyn understanding of the elfyn people's role in taking care of the Orb, the blessings for those who respected the ways of nature, the curses for those who flaunted them or tempted Fate with greed. It was simply beyond the humyn mind to comprehend how vast elfyn works were and how their people had been sheltered from the worst of the turns of Fate for aeons.

The women drudged not for trinkets from savages, but because it was part of the duty expected of a soldier. And, as some souls ruefully observed, they had no men to do it for them. It was another vast difference of military life: the army of uncles, keepers, knaves and other members of the male population of a household pressed into service were absent. The only exception was the officer's barracks, which was assigned servants from the academy students, managed by a civilian butler. Eld did not envy those girls with Roel in residence.

They walked the horses along the Old Farm Road and found themselves further away from the garrison than ideal when the time for lunch came. As chance would have it a Wildling camp had arrived nearby; they had heard of the coming fair the next day to mark the awards. The village was enjoying some celebrity being so close to the Bane Incident as the broadsheets were calling it, and felt proud to have supported the garrison and the action. This fair was shaping up to be a much larger event than the one after Eld's first awards. So every itinerant crafter, tinker, and merchant in the area was drawn, as well as farmers, foragers, brewers and smiths. Wildlings had all these women, and good food besides.

The women were well fed eating authentic Dwen traveler sandwiches, the thick pancake bread wrapped around many slices of boar ham, kale, green onion leaves, and green mayonnaise mixed with elderberry jam. It also had soft white cheese, as Wildlings, having more Sula streams among them, used milk derivatives not found in native Dwen cuisine. It was a perfect meal, quite satisfying even for those who objected to these not being "Forest Travelers" as served in inns.

"Sula have a wide imagination," one of the men said, smiling. His eyes were lined with black gall, like thick kohl, with a triangle of three dots tattooed on each cheek. Like Dwen, his eyes were green but his hair was bright gold and his yastol, like many Wildlings, had no leaves, little more than a crown of decorative branches, woven with moss and lichens.

"I have a Dwen friend," Eld said. "His yastol moves."

"Ah, he is feeling and flowing with the wood," the man said. "Alas, I feel it but cannot flow with it. I can spark however. If we need fire, no need for flint. My mother's mother twined with a Gold man. I am blaming him!"

They all laughed at this, and conversation birthed about who could do what and their family legends about why. It was still vigorous by the time the company women left, leading the horses back to the garrison.

The work on the stables was impressive. The wood shimmered with oil, and the dust and straw cluttering the corners of the inner courts until familiarity made them invisible truly had vanished, making the area feel twice as large. The horses didn't care one way or the other; in fact they slightly disapproved, the scents of the newly cleaned floor and tackle a shock to their senses. But they felt their elfyn sisters pleased and that put them at ease, especially when they were gifted a bag of unsold vegetables from a local grocer, still sound but slightly withered. The horses were watered and fed, then turned over to the grooms to brush. Eld wanted to brush Fiorseth herself but she had no time. Their clothes needed to be tended or they would dry stiff, then need twice the work to be made presentable.

It was a perfect day for ironing, the sun was unobscured but a light breeze kept heat from being excessive. They had wood planks covered with linen and irons, a typical domestic creature, with a smooth steel face. It could be placed on a stove or heated with charcoal. But the women just held them in the sunlight and treated them like lances.

"Don't strike your clothes, girls!" someone said.

"I don't think thats possible."

Then Torin actually tried to do it out of curiosity and she wasn't alone.

Eld sighed. "They don't have solstone enamel or grim," she said patently, as she ironed a sleeve of her coat. "All that will happen is ..."

Suddenly the air around Torin's iron flashed brightly, giving off heat as the wayward essence fluorescenced and dispersed.

" ...that." Eld finished.

Disappointed, they returned to ironing.

Eld was flattening one of the pockets of her coat that seemed to be twisted, then realized something was in it. A stone. As her hands fished it out, amazed it hadn't been lost in the water, she remember the felkinoc she had found weeks ago. Seeing the Astalyn in her palm made her shiver with excitement; it had been with her all this time, through the battle. Eld was not a literalist, but it was hard not to think Felkeni was turning his bright face to her. For had she not also won a great victory over a foe? But no. Eld rejected the idea she was beholden to the Goddi of Chance and Fate, no matter how alluring. She did value the stone, not because it held godly magic, but because it connected Eld to the foremothers who tended these lands and worked the lots in times past. Eld was grateful to be part of the magic of their legacy. Perhaps she would give the felkinoc to her mother or grandam when she visited the estate next.

"My shirt is still too wet," Torin said, irritated.

"You never mangle it thoroughly," Althone said shortly. She still didn't have patience for Torin.

"Maybe try a little sulessence," Eld suggested.

"What?" Althone said.

"I read if one is very careful, and lets the essence flow across the fabric, water can be released minutely without burning."

"You read too much," Althone said. "Training at the Abbey doesn't make you a magi."

"I didn't say it did. Only – what's Torin doing?" Eld wondered.

Torin was walking with one of her shirts to a place on the grass where she had plenty of room and sunlight.

"No, she's not going to actually try it ..." Eld said.

"Don't do it!" several woman called, with others telling Torin the opposite. Torin held the bleached white, linen shirt, tails and sleeves waving in the breeze, and her aura glowed as she pulled sulessence into it.

Eld almost ran to yank the garment out of Torin's hands, but she froze in fascination. What would happen? Torin could barely control her lance. She struck powerfully, but with no finesse.

The air grew brighter. With a sudden whoosh Torin's shirt went up in flames.

Eld held her head in her hands, while many souls laughed and Torin stamped on the shirt in a desperate attempt to save it. But it was lost, too scorched for even rags.

"Be of cheer," Danshor said between laughter, "At least you don't have to wash it again."

Torin was in a foul mood for the rest of the day, refusing to speak to either Eld or Danshor.

As the day wore on, and their tasks one by one were finished, Eld was looking forward to simply resting in the barracks, perhaps reading a book, or socializing with the company in a way she hadn't for a while. She was also behind on her letters home. It did not improve her humor when she was informed she and Danshor had patrol again that night.

"But we still have to finish our uniforms!" In truth all she had was buttons and boots to polish but she didn't like rushing them.

"Then do it fast," Sergeant Tarl said. "Or before sleep. Or get up before dawn. There are many choices in the Orb, cavalier."

Eld seethed. Danshor kept her objections to a stream of profane speculations about no one in particular and kicking the wall.

"Language," Crandall said.

Torin snickered quietly to herself. Eld and Danshor pretended not to hear.

The only good thing about the patrol was it was uneventful. Such that Eld was certain it was a waste of time, time better spent tending to her uniform and oiling her blades. When it was finally over, she found herself sitting on her cot by a lamp half shuttered still polishing her boots at midnight. She wasn't the only one. Finally, as the distant Abbey clock chimed the first hour after midnight, Eld could go to sleep.

On the morrow they dressed, closed their chests and secured them under the cots neatly before marching out to muster well before the bell was rung. The entire garrison seemed to be standing in the fields. Stragglers trotted to join their companies, running suddenly as the bell rang, standing in file when it's last peels stopped.

"Attend!" Sergeant Tarl and others shouted.

All the women snapped to, standing as straight as pillars. Thus began one of the longest hours of Eld's one hundred and thirty years.

## Chapter 30

# Awards

Sergeant Tarl had not been exaggerating about Command visiting. General Sallaryn of the North Crownland Battalion they expected, the crimson facings of her coat advertising her rank for those too far away to see the dragons above her twinings. Sallaryn's hair flowed, even floated, on the air, one of those souls who bound it as minimally as she could and still be within regulations. Seeing her aura glow, apparently without effort, Eld suspected why: General Sallaryn was either old, magi trained, or both, and such individuals preferred garb that did not hinder essence flow even more than the average elf. In addition to helix guardlock clips, one small clip bound the top of her locks at the back of her head where it flowed with the rest of her hair, hanging almost to her waist. Even Sallaryn's light steps suggested she could make the air her promenade and chose to walk on the stone paved ground as a courtesy. Alhern accompanied the general, talking easily together as they inspected the Host.

Ahead of these two and slightly apart was a woman of different character. She wore a black jacket, making the gold helix on her back stand out starkly for all to see. She also wore a flout, and, given her senior position with respect to both the commander and the general, that meant one thing: this was the Federation Army Marshal Egalsh Tantilaan, the woman at the apex of all Federation military offices. Even the Admiralty answered to her. It was known Tantilaan had spent most of her nearly seventy years in service as a cavalier; marshals had the option of wearing the flout if they had served as cavalry. How were they blessed with the presence of so notable a mother? She didn't glow like the general, but her posture and presentation implied her essence flowed tightly around a tall, rooted core, rising to the stars. Tantilaan was ambitious and, if not a politician, had learned their ways and was comfortable in that world. Eld was also surprised to feel an instant dislike on sighting the marshal. It was irrational: she couldn't possibly be as loathsome as officers like Roel or she'd never have risen so far. Eld put it out of her mind; there were many mothers in the Orb and they were not all destined to be sisters.

The hour dragged on, Alhern guiding her guests through the foot company ranks, leaving the cavalry for last. When finally the trio came near, Captain Aynath and Sergeant Tarl saluting at their approach, Sul had freed Herself of the low clouds of dawn and a brisk wind was blowing. A gust made every woman's tail of hair fly forward, falling in front or on top of their shoulders, ruining the disciplined effect they had worked so hard to achieve. But the Marshal laughed.

"The winds of Payeen play with us!" she boomed heartily. "Now these are the bold mothers I remember in the patrols of my past!" She was a mother's mother, Heaven's help them, all her polish and advancement aside. Eld deeply hoped the Marshal wouldn't be haunting them at the feast. Her eyes were bright and piercing, doing nothing to diminish Eld's first impression. "So who is the boldest one of these cavaliers? The one who first fought the Eurthan Bane, and later skewered one in a feat worthy of Jaro, and conceived the Green Strike Gambit? No, don't tell me." She held up a hand to stop her companions. "Let me hunt her out."

Now Eld felt loathing. She was hungry, tired from labor and lack of sleep, and bored from standing almost an hour doing aught, and the Federation Field Marshal wanted to play "Hunt the Vole".

"Not you," Tantilaan said to Lancer Carn, a noteworthy soul in the first company. Danshor had butted heads with her once and now they avoided each other. "No fool would challenge you. Heroism often has an element of deception," the Marshal continued. "The most notable ones are not marked until their deeds."

With that logic, the Marshal was going to mark Torin, Eld thought snarkily.

But when the Marshal started walking down the line of Eld's company she didn't mark Torin. Apparently Tantilaan was more discerning than a trite aphorism. She paused in front of Danshor.

"No. You look the part."

The Marshal walked past Eld, and, for a second, Eld was relieved and smug at the same time.

Then Tantilaan stopped and took a step back to stand in front of her.

They were about the same height, Eld and Tantilaan. And while the Marshal didn't glow, Eld could feel a very subtle pressure of a stronger aura touching hers. Eld did her best to look forward over the Tantilaan's shoulder and into the blue distant sky.

"I sense an essence rich, romantic soul. Were you born at dawn, cavalier?"

Ignoring the implied reference to the legend of Jaro, Eld answered formally, "No, emha. It was some unnotable time in the afternoon, emha."

"And humble as well. She probably me wants me to stop staring at her. All the ranks and most officers do once you become a Marshal."

The commander and general were the only ones who chuckled. Even Aynath only smiled briefly.

424

"Well done, cavalier!" Tantilaan added.

"Emha! Thank you, emha."

"General Sallaryn will have a word with you. With your commander's permission, of course."

"Of course," Alhern said.

Sallaryn approached Eld while Tantilaan continued to look over the cavalry host.

"Step out and join me, Lancer Farthal," Sallaryn said with a friendly but not too friendly smile. "We have much to discuss about the Eurthan Host."

Eld stepped out and fell in beside Sallaryn, dropping back half a pace as they walked. Being so close to the general felt calm. Eld liked Sallaryn.

"I am privileged," Eld said.

"Yes, but so am I," Sallaryn replied. "I'm not sure any trained officer, minted or otherwise, could have brought a diplomatic conclusion after so violent a beginning."

"With respect, if you are referring to the Eurthan officer Brig, the Dwen had a great hand in that."

"Yes, but they would have killed her without you being there, and we would be facing Sul knows what kind of war with an enemy we still know appallingly little about. Tell me everything about your encounters with the Eurthans, from the very first attack."

Eld spoke as openly as she felt she could without revealing anything unnecessary. Still Sallaryn's eyes twinkled when Eld mention Seth, however briefly, but the older woman didn't pursue the matter. When Eld was done, Sallaryn didn't say anything for a moment. They were standing near the Rowan Oak.

"This Brig might be the best point of diplomacy if we can get a message to these mothers in a way that convinces them we aren't 'savages'."

"Emha, there's the door."

"Yes, the Hidden Door. To our eye aught but a small room with smooth walls of stone. I don't like that they can just appear anytime they please. It's unsettling. Not to mention rude. Your commander is not forgiving the looting any decade soon. I should return you to your company. Thank you for your time, Lancer Farthal."

"Emha."

They started walking back.

"Another thing, cavalier. The soul you dueled with is a distant niece of mine. No, no, I'm not making excuses for her. Nor am I saying either of you should forgive and make a pointless show of dishonest reconciliation. That only plants seeds of resentment, equally as dangerous as unrelenting ri-

valry. But I will say the wise mother seeks a path that can lead to civil cooperation in the future, once all the passions of the moment and their causes
have receded. You will never be friends. But take it from a mother who has
lived over thirty decades and served in the army for fifteen of those: a soul
never knows when duty will bring them together in a joint cause."

"Emha," Eld said in acknowledgment.

"Be assured, I will speak to Lieutenant Roel privately. Now I return you
to your company."

Eld took her place while Tantilaan and Sallaryn rejoined the commander.

Just when they all thought it was over, the women set to tour the barracks.

Eld could feel the thoughts of the rest of the Host, a general upset and resentment, even a couple words seeping through to her mind, and none of
them polite. So they stood another half-hour while the officers toured the
stables, the stable barracks and the foot host and officer's barracks, until Eld
felt her stomach rebel with hunger. If the officers weren't wary, they would
trigger the first mutiny in millennia.

And then it was over, the entire Host having been found worthy. When
they were dismissed most of the cavalry women immediately strode to the
Rowan Oak, it being closer than the Kettle.

Tafli was well informed of their needs because he was prepared with a
welcoming board; it was not uncommon in inns to offer light refreshment
while matrons waited to be served. These light snacks were weighted to the
Dwen or Yino palette: various nuts, honey soaked pan bread, cakes baked
with dried fruit and filtered rainwater. Because they were among the first arrivals, they didn't wait long, yet Danshor had already grabbed some honey
bread and slathered it with strawberry mayonnaise while they hovered to
settle on a table. All Eld had time to do was grab a handful of nuts. She
popped a hazel in her mouth while they sat around a table suited for four but
a couple more drew up stools to avoid waiting. Reon and Algath joined
Danshor, Patrycan and Torin with Eld. They weren't long getting food or
drink: for drink most thought it wise to stick to water or weak barley-mead
(or whatever it was Tafli served) with the awards coming anon. Beef was
the order of the day, sun seared steaks cut into fine slices, layered over saffron barley, all drowned in wine and mushroom sauce. This was all placed
in a deep bowl-like platter of pressed wood leavings, tightly woven with
wood essence and water proofed. Tafli refused to be fussed with breaking
crockery, for the same reason he served most drinks in tin cups and goblets.
The edges of the platter were garnished with lightly steamed mustard and
kale. Their portions were abundant and, after their labors and long wait, the

women ate greedily. Eld was aware Tafli seemed to be running about on his own.

"Where's your knave?" Eld asked during a pause.

"He is not being able to come," Tafli said breathlessly. "It is a big day for his family and he is needing to be at home."

This wasn't surprising. This time the entire lot community, and village in particular, felt an ownership in the victory over the Eurthans. Every mother and man had done their part and now they would participate in the preparations and celebrations to the fullest. A good many would even be coming to the awards; civilian advisors would be honored as well as soldiers.

"It's going to be madness soon," Eld said suddenly.

"It isn't already?" Reon said.

"We're having a civilian invasion." Eld stood. "I'm going back to rest before the awards."

"She's going to work on her speech," Danshor said. "Just remember to thank those steady companions that stood beside you unwavering in battle."

Eld replied deadpan, "Never fear, Fiorseth and Tuiric will be noted."

Laughter echoed behind Eld as she left.

The horses were inside and resting. They had no idea their sanctuary would soon be swarming with visitors, for after the awards the garrison was to be opened to civilian guests until the evening feast. After stopping to check on Fiorseth, who was not at all bored with a lack of running around day and night under threat of danger, Eld withdrew to lie on her cot hoping to recapture a portion of the rest she'd lost polishing her boots the night before. It helped a sunbeam was shining, making the air both warm and refreshing. Several other souls lurked with similar plans, napping or reading while they waited to be showered with honors. The hour seemed to pass quickly, but Eld was more rested and glad she had time to make adjustments to her uniform.

Then it was time for them to muster again. The field was filled much as it was for Eld's first awards, but the platform was larger to accommodate the guests and their men. A place was made for civilian attendees, both from the village and soldiers' families who were able to come. None of Eld's estate was present. The unprecedented Eurthan threat had caught them in the middle of lambing and cheese production. After the beginning of spring, the men were taking over management of residences for the coming social season, driving the women to perhaps more hunting, fishing and other industry than they would as craft projects sprawled throughout the drawing rooms and would do so until the hawthorns flowered. Then it was said all preparations were best done until the Sul Suldan. Eld would have liked to see her own ama and dame, and of course Traith and Shedann. But she expected leave soon and, after the fright of her children being at the garrison during the first attack, she preferred to know they were safe.

Like before, they were called to attention and Alhern gave a speech touching on the expected themes of duty and bravery. Then she let Marshal Tantilaan step forward:

"Looking bright?" Tantilaan called out in a deep voice that carried far without a horn.

The Host replied as one body, their many voices rumbling like distant thunder after dragon-strike: "Never brighter, Marshal!"

Tantilaan grinned, somehow making her teeth visible as far as her voice was heard.

"That's the Host I remember! I served as cavalry for two decades… let's hear from our cavalry!"

Eld groaning inside. How long was she going to spend reminiscing and grandstanding?

But Eld saluted and called out "One duty!" with the rest.

"Nothing like running with the wind under a clear, blue sky, right sisters?"

"Yes, emha!"

"It's that spirit of duty that defends our nation, that nurtures watchfulness, and gave us victory over the Eurthan spawn…."

A hiss rose up, as if from a thousand snakes, as every mother and man listening expressed their feelings about the Eurthans. Then Tantilaan spoke on, sounding less like a mother introducing awards and more like she was standing for the honor of provincial governor. At least Tantilaan found time to praise the foot companies before yielding the stage back to Alhern. Eld suspected Alhern greatly abbreviated what she had been going to say in respect of the time.

Among the first to be honored was the Temple with their healers, "… Without whom some of us would not still live in the Orb," Alhern said by way of introduction.

Individual healers were named, those who served on the field, as well as those who put themselves at risk to tend the wounded. Tarasik was amongst them, earning whistles of applause from Eld and the rest of the cavaliers for retrieving Boad; she bowed, keeping her aspect humble. After the healers came various civilian consultants, engineers and workers. Then came the magi, neither military nor strictly civilian, as civilian implied no explicit duty to risk life. But the Order of Magi were duty bound to serve the nation according to their charter, which was almost twice as old as the Federation. Then came the first of the military awards, the pages, girls around the age of Seth's nephew who served under military discipline, but not strictly as enlisted mothers. Most had been stationed in the garrison or around the village, but two older ones had served during the battle, earning themselves a Battle Lion or "The Jaro". It would be the most common award given that day, the most unambitious or otherwise mediocre mother still honored for discharging her oath to defend her nation by risking death in battle.

And so women were called up to present themselves by company, the logistics of numbers precluding the individual attention Eld had been given before. Yet, being trained for efficiency, the process proceeded faster than a soul might expect. The Foot Host of five companies and their noncommissioned leaders were first, before all others, followed by the Cavalry Host of two companies; officers were awarded after their companies. Apart from Battle Lions, the most common award was the White Phoenix for great bravery or extraordinary deeds.

Awards in the modern Federation inherited the mystic themes of ancient philosophical magic: the Gold Sun or Dawn, the White Sun, the Red Sun and the Black Sun. Gold tended to signify rescue; White, bravery; Red, risk or injury, and Black, death. These were the hues or aspects of awards. The classes were Lions, Phoenixes, Unicorns, Rods and Stars. Lions were for civilian mothers, the sole exception being the Battle Lion or 'The Jaro', which was the oldest of them all. Phoenixes were for soldiers, who were expected to rise even from death to fulfill their duty. Unicorns were for deeds unique to cavaliers. Rods and Stars were given to healers and Magi respectively, but were limited in aspects. There were others who did not fit the pattern, like The Rose Shield Eld had been awarded. And there were the obsolete awards like Cups; given to Thyn who served in the ancient past. The Cups had been literally colored bowls the individual would drink from, then the bowl would be taken and placed in the hall of heroes, for what use did Thyn have to carry around medals? Eld supposed a raven might insist on something shiny.

Still ordinary animals could be awarded the Dawn Lion, also given to children, horses or hounds of any serving mother. But that would be for actions they had taken of their own initiative, like rescue or performing under extraordinary duress and not yielding to their instincts to flee. In Eld's opinion Fiorseth should be showered with such things, but cavaliers were biased. So Eld was mildly surprised when, among her many awards, Fiorseth had in fact been honored with a Dawn Lion. In addition to her Battle Lion, Eld also received the Dawn Rider, a Unicorn class award for daring, the White

Phoenix for bravery, and the Ruby Torch for sending help, Eld had to assume this was because of the events with the Dwen on the ridge.

"I told you she was greedy," Alhern said. "You'll need pins to keep those all in place." It helped the aspects were given different lengths of ribbon, so they would hang one below the other, the Gold the highest, the Black the lowest. But Alhern was right: the Dawn Lion and Dawn Rider would try to occult each other.

"She has as many as I do!" the Marshal said grinning.

It suddenly struck Eld as odd and somewhat frightening this was true. Even Sallaryn only had a handful of medals pinned to her left so the ribbons draped slightly. Alhern, as of yet, had none, though presumably she too would have a Battle Lion, perhaps issued from Command. What strange times they were in that a soldier or cavalier serving less than a decade had as many medals as an officer who had served more than half a century.

"But this is the best of them all," General Sallaryn said, giving Eld a small sealed roll of parchment. Not paper, for this was not a common offer. The seal was gold wax with not a flintsun, but a helix. Eld felt her heart skip a beat. "Your leadership was vital to our victory over the Eurthans," the general continued. "You are also of good character, courage and have the respect of your fellows. Such souls are worthy of sponsorship for a commission. If you choose it. Your commander will discuss the details at a later time."

Elds eyes flickered between them in astonishment. She was speechless. Then she saw Seth standing with the other men at the back, smiling. The possibilities unfolded. She could court Seth properly. Even marry one day...

"Farthal, you're crowding the stage," Alhern said.

Eld snapped to attention. "Emhas, I am honored."

"Indeed you are," the Marshal said with her terrible friendliness as they exchanged salutes and Eld stepped down to let Danshor approach.

The rest of the awards passed before Eld in a blur, her mind turning with this unexpected event. It was a small scroll, but precious; she slipped it into an inner pocket. Everything Alhern had said about Eld before had been true: Eld was not burning with ambitions to rise through the ranks and was perfectly content to serve her time, build a cache and find an industry to apply herself. She'd thought vaguely of either draying or training horses.

But the truth was this was a common path that almost always defaulted to working for one's mother's estate. It was secure, but if Eld was honest with herself, she would never be completely content if she settled into a life limiting her opportunities for travel or society for decades. Why serve as a soldier, when she could have just as easily worked and raised horses at home? Why Seth, when she could have any pretty boy happy to be taken by a uniform? They also loved poetry. But there was a satisfaction of knowing she was with a man who appreciated the works of the ancients as much as she did. Seth wasn't just a tryst of passion, he was a companion soul. Similarly Eld's service wasn't just an exchange of duty for queens. She felt called to see the Orb and challenge herself. For did a mother ever know her true self without being challenged, whether by drive, force or fate?

These thoughts weighed on her, not unpleasantly, but persistently, haunting her mind while exchanging congratulations in the barracks after they were dismissed from the field. Captain Aynath personally congratulated Eld on her sponsorship. Much was made in good humor about how she was too big for her boots and of course she was doomed to be an officer: she was, after all, a sensitive poetic soul. Danshor was oddly subdued:

"What's the matter?" Eld asked during a lull. They'd stripped off their jackets and capes to relax a bit before lunch. Hungry as they all were, the Kettle was going to be tardy because of the awards. "Not happy with your awards?"

"You still have more," Danshor said, but the joke felt forced. "I need to catch up. That's not likely now the Eurthans are gone."

"You never know. They might come back."

"But you're certain they won't."

Eld shrugged. "Probably not."

Danshor suddenly stood. "I need to post a letter to my son. See you anon."

"Anon," Eld said. There was something sad in the air as she watched Danshor leave, as if she had taken the first step away from Eld's fellowship. And Eld understood: Danshor, the self-involved hood with no regard or care for anyone but herself-- or so she preferred it to be known – was unsettled that Eld might leave her society. And Eld, seeing this truth, found herself unsettled too. Though the women joked, and were genuinely proud and happy one of theirs was advancing, they were already pushing Eld away, preparing for the day she would step away from them into another world. It would be a death of sorts, and if she returned to serve with them, it would not be as a war-sister, but just another helix to be saluted and obeyed. The sadness of it hit her.

Then Sergeant Tarl barked her name.

"Yes?"

"Farthal, you haven't been commissioned yet so don't get lost in dreams as Field Marshal ordering us about."

Eld forced herself to laugh with the women as she took a folded sealed paper. It was from the commander's office. She was to report for lunch. Eld pulled her coat back on.

"Where are you off to?" Torin asked. "The Kettle isn't open yet." Her Battle Lion and Gold Phoenix for helping free Tuiric had put her back on speaking terms with Eld and Danshor.

"The commander has summoned me," Eld said.

"She's realized her mistake!" Alcas said. "It was some other cavalier she meant to sponsor!"

Eld left her cape in the barracks while more jests were called after her.

"Don't worry, Farthal! We'll probably let you stay in the company!"

But each step towards the commander's house felt like a step away from the company, a family of sisters who were as important as any family by blood. The day seemed brighter than it should, the sunlight overwhelming, and Eld was relieved when she stepped inside to the relative dim coolness of the commander's house.

Yet cool though it was, patches of light shined brightly in the centers of many rooms, solstone skylights illuminating the center floors like shafts of sunlight piercing clouds. And the activity was far from restful, house-girls, knaves and grounds staff running to and fro with a variety of preparatory tasks under the direction of the butler or cook, the lor and laird of the domestic realm. There also seemed to be a roving argument from room to room, but just out of sight, between Solafi and his keeper:

"No, you may not leave to meet with your friends," the older man was saying. "You will remain for luncheon so you will be at the feast at the hour."

"But the feast is hours away!" Solafi objected. "I will return with plenty of time!"

"Yet, you did not last night."

"I apologized for that delay."

"Young effa, hours after dusk is more than a delay!"

"But I did apologize!"

"But it has not been explained."

"It is easy for a soul to get lost if they don't know the way!"

"That statement is general to the point of meaninglessness," Effa Tanmor said without amusement.

"I already said I was with friends."

"Obviously," Seth interjected.

Eld pulse raced at the sound of his voice.

"But as Worthy Tanmor has stated," Seth continued, "that is not an explanation. And it will need to be given."

"I am glad we are in agreement in this, Effa Alhern."

Eld was surprised the two men seemed to be in alignment at last.

"We are," Seth confirmed. "However, it is not an explanation that needs to be given at this moment. Cease this complaining, Solafi. Will not your friends be at the gala? There will be a spread available in the pavilions on the parade field. And I am certain the fair and carnival after will continue for as long as there are queens to be made. You will have ample time for society later. Now we have much to do."

"Ai and the Orb," Solafi muttered.

"What did you say, young effa?" Tanmor demanded.

"Yes, uncle," the boy added with a resigned sigh.

"Cavalier," Emha Sonamor said, manifesting so abruptly Eld jumped in surprise. "Apologies," Sonamor added. "If you follow me ..."

Eld knew the way now, but she wasn't being led to the dining room. Sonamor took her to Alhern's office. The commander wasn't at her desk, instead sitting at a small table nearby in a patch of sun. Two places were set, each with plates piled with trout and roast, saffron barley with raisins, asparagus and greens. On the table was also a bowl of oranges and a tray of small cakes. Alhern looked up as Eld entered and waved away her salute.

"At ease, Farthal," she said, then started to eat. "Hurry up, or the sun-blessed taste will fade."

Eld took her place and eagerly had a bite. She paused as the flavor hovered in her mouth, like the nose of a good wine, as if she could taste the sunlight where the trout had recently swam in life.

"Good, isn't it?" Alhern said, stabbing an asparagus stalk.

"Yes!" Eld affirmed. "We don't often have sunblessed cooking."

"The Roan Oak's cook grills everything outside in the sun, I thought. 'No burnings'."

Eld nodded, smiling. "Yes, our Tafli is strict on that count. But by the time the meat comes to us, it's been cooling."

Alhern made a noncommittal noise. They ate for a while with little talk. When their plates were almost empty, Alhern asked, "What do you think, Farthal?"

"About sponsorship, emha?"

"Yes, Farthal, sponsorship. You're not being invited to display your table manners, though they have been noted as above reproach. Men talk," Alhern added to Eld's questing look.

"Oh. Well, it is an honor of course," Eld said.

"Stop being a politician."

"Very well. It offers possibilities I hadn't seriously considered. I don't just mean courting your brother." Somehow saying it made Eld feel bolder. Meeting Alhern's eyes was not a hard thing anymore. "My family would be honored. My children might advance in ways unknown, though they are too young to know the path of their passions. And I feel the need to engage with the larger world more than I have. I suppose it wasn't a thing on my mind until I spoke with the Eurthan Brig."

"Traveling to other nations reveals perspectives previously unconsidered," Alhern said. "For good or ill. Our wisdom grows for it. It is one of the many reasons bigots are shortsighted idiots. By refusing to see others as they truly are, they rob themselves of insight into their own condition and are doubly blind for it. Elfyn may be one people with one duty, but we are also many tribes and there are many paths to fulfill that duty.

"If you were to take the path of sponsorship, you would finish out your quarterly service, then be sent to the academy for year to drill in customs peculiar to command, as well as the basics of leadership and military strategy. Don't worry, you'd be apart from cadet culture. You will study with the general body, but those sponsored from the ranks lodge in their own barracks. Instructors adore the sponsored barracks for their mature presence, free of weekly challenges to duel. Not that you would suffer on that account." Alhern's mouth twitched in a smile.

"Thank you, emha," Eld said.

"Incidentally, do you know who was vandalizing those bills?"

Eld's fork paused in the middle of cutting a piece of cake. "I thought it had been determined that soul was from one of the foot companies."

"Soldier's gossip. We think men are masters, but they are but naifs compared to idle women in a Host. Where did you hear this?"

"The Rowan Oak," Eld admitted feeling anxious. It was coming time Eld must evade or confess because the truth could not hide forever.

"Did you also hear that elf was was not found to be responsible for the most slanderous elements?"

"Yes, emha."

"Do you have any idea who was? A partisan sister of yours, perhaps?"

Eld looked up, eyes pleading. "I would rather not say."

"Are you complicit? I didn't want to say anything until after the wagers were settled. It will remain between us. But you must tell me."

Eld sighed. "Very well, emha. It was a partisan, but not a sister."

"A man?"

"I think it was Tafli."

For a second Alhern stared blankly. Then she burst out laughing in a way Eld had never seen before.

"And you were not complicit?"

"No," Eld said finally relaxing.

"Well. I suppose those leaves have blown away. Taffellyni is not under military discipline. But I should have a word with him nonetheless. Never fear, a friendly word."

Eld felt tension return. Under no circumstances did she wish to have a discussion about how friendly Alhern was with Tafli. She was certain they trysted, and she was equally certain this knowledge was unknown and Alhern wanted it that way. Eld did not wish to be caught out that she had that knowledge. "You were saying about the Academy, emha?"

"Yes. After a year, you'd come back as an cornet attached to an officer mentor for another year. Then you sit another exam, as well as the practical test of your understanding of tactics and strategy."

"The Game," Eld said. It was a legendary version of a child's story game, played in a permanent installment near the Crownland Academy grounds. Two opposing forces had to outwit each other in a strategic maze involving traps and various challenges. The details always changed, but it was well known that the point was not winning, but how one conducted themselves whether they won or lost. It was equally well known that the game was run so cunningly participants soon forgot this fact, their own drive to win fueling the pressure of the test. Quarterly exercises were lesser cousins of The Game but with none of the weight. No one failed as such during an exercise, though a commander might decide her women needed more discipline or practice. But a cadet or sponsor could fail the Game by temperament or behavior. No one knew what would happen until play began. And they said play began as soon as The Game was announced for the season.

"But that's a long way off," Alhern said. "Presuming you accept. What do you think?"

"I think it's a decision great enough, even if I was certain, I should take time for my soul to settle on it."

"A wise answer. You have a month. Meanwhile, do you know your chess?"

"Modestly," Eld said. She put aside memories of being thrashed by her cousins in youth.

"Let's play a game."

It was a compelled invitation or a friendly order, depending on one's view. Invitation to a game of chess was common in military or politics, giving an ambitious mother a chance to show her mettle, whether by skill or by losing with grace.

The board was wood, the thirty two pieces, half black, half white, finely carved marble. Eld was mildly surprised the board was set up so that she would play White.

"You have an objection, Farthal?"

"No, commander. Only shouldn't we draw lots for the colors?"

"That is the custom. But I have a curiosity. And, as you know, White has advantages, which I am yielding to you."

"Very well," Eld said. "Commander."

" 'Emha' will do while we play."

As White, Eld would make the first move. She hadn't played for weeks, months perhaps, and the practice of her youth being pitted against older cousins haunted her. They claimed to be teaching, but it was their excuse to show off. Eld knew she hadn't truly learned the game, but she'd been driven to play aggressively, though this did not reveal itself until after they both had made a move, an innocent foray that advanced each pawn in front of their Heirs until they sat face to face in the middle of the board.

Now the Heir, (or Cradle, or Child) was the most valued piece, sometime a carved figure in a Princar crown, but here in the old style of a cup on a pedestal with a ball in it, giving the impression of a goblet holding a pearl. The object was to capture the Heir while protecting one's own. The Heir might be the most valued, but it was a weak piece by move: it could only capture pieces right next to it. At its side, at the start of the game, was the most powerful piece, the Queen or Mother. She could move along any rank or file, and capture any piece provided she was unimpeded. She was so powerful players forgot she could be captured if used carelessly. Flanking the Queen and Heir were Advocates, modeled on the administration of ancient healer and magi schools. Their pointed caps gave the impression of helmets and they moved on diagonals. The Champion was the iconic chess piece, a unicorn head, and the Castle or Rook, could take several forms but Alhern's set had a tower with a dragon's head emerging from the top. The pieces were carved in more details than a typical set, so the pawns, usually blank-faced rounds topped with a smaller round, were foot solders from the feudal era of Lot Lors; from their hair spooled on their crowns and arms crossed over their hearts, they looked much as Eld and Roel had at the start of the duel. Romance of that era aside, these footwomen were often daughters of a mother's house pressed into service with threats of cruel punishments if they refused. The pawn was a memory of their use, valued for their sacrifice with little, if any, compensation to their families. Some over-intellectual souls had the conceit Chess was a metaphor for life. Eld certainly hoped this wasn't so. Chess was, at its best, a stimulating mental diversion that disciplined the mind in strategy and tactics using strict logic. But a soul needed more than brutal mathematics to find joy in life.

Eld felt the years fly back, Alhern taking the place of a smirking cousin sitting across from her, smug in her superior skill. Eld's mind knew Alhern had no such thoughts, but her emotions felt otherwise. And game of logic or no, a player's emotions colored their actions. Eld picked up her Queen and flew her right on a diagonal, to the far edge of the board. She immediately regretted this. It was a bold play but only caught the foolish, inexperienced or distracted unawares. Masters were wary of the Flying Queen and admonished students who dabbled in such tricks. It was also insulting to an experienced player, whom Alhern most certainly was. But Eld had made her move, and by the rules of the game she must abide by it.

There were a couple of firm refutations to the Flying Queen, some that played with expectation, others that stopped the gambit in its tracks. The worst refutation was to advance a pawn in an attempt to block Her with the threat of capture. What Alhern did wasn't that bad; she advanced the Champion's Horse, threatening a capture. But Eld took her Queen and made her fly left, capturing the first pawn Alhern had advanced and putting the black Heir in check. The old elation came back to Eld, the rush of the hunt, for when the Heir was in check, one's opponent must move the Heir to safety or block it from danger. Here most players blocked with the dark footed Advocate, for if one blocked with the Black Queen, a very confident player would simply take it, though it would cost them their White Queen. It was possible to play a vigorous game without any Queens on the board.

Eld moved her Queen two squares to the right, intending to take a black pawn and then, if Alhern was inattentive, the Rook. This was the glory of the Flying Queen: it was possible to wipe out half of an opponents valuable pieces and destroy their defense early in the game, even if it did not end in checkmate.

Alhern advanced the pawn at the edge of the board to threaten the Queen. Excited, Eld captured the black pawn. Her plan was working. Alhern moved her Advocate back to protect the Heir in anticipation of the Rook's capture, for that would put the heir back in Check. Eld greedily captured the Dragon headed tower wondering what Alhern could do next. Eld's queen was behind the Black lines and the Heir pinned!

Alhern simply advanced her other Champion. It was then Eld saw it was she who was pinned between the Advocate, Champion and a couple of well-seated pawns: her Queen could not move or escape without loss. Thus the adventure of the Flying Queen came to an end.

They said nothing as they played on. Alhern proceeded to trounce Eld. Eld had managed to rescue her Queen at a cost, but lost it soon after by inattention, along with one Rook, the other gamely defending the Heir to near the end, when it, too, was lost, leaving Eld with only the Heir and a white footed Advocate. Finally, with all her pieces gone except the Heir, she was forced to valiantly try to prevent Alhern's Queen from advancing a pawn, which she did, with a simultaneous checkmate.

Eld toppled the cradle of her Heir and sat back.

Alhern was already setting the pieces back, a slight smile playing on her lips.

"You gave me more trouble than I expected after that bold opening."

"I meant no disrespect, emha. A habit from youth."

"A bad habit."

"Yes, I know."

"But one that wasn't completely unprecedented."

Eld blinked. "You were toying with me."

"If you thought that was cruel, the Game is much crueler. You had only to resist the urge to charge boldly. No one compelled you to send your Queen Flying but yourself, cavalier. And you could have recovered, but you lost focus. Think on that. We will play again. But not now. I am time's slave."

They stood.

"Thank you for the game, Commander."

"Thank you, Farthal. Oh, one more thing: my brother and nephew need an escort to the gala. Seth has dropped many hints that this would be a good time for the public to see his favorite. I was thinking you could choose one of your sisters, though I'm dubious of the soul that would be your first choice."

"I love her like a sister, but I am the first to admit Danshor is a mother's mother."

"She's a venal braggart and a fraternizes overmuch with harlots," Alhern said bluntly.

"But she is good with children."

"Truly."

"Yes."

Alhern sighed. "Well, don't let my nephew hear he was described as a child. He's past his fire and thinks that makes him free of obligations. Oh, Solafi is a good boy. But I worry that he's surrounded by soldiers and not girls his own age. The end of virginity is inevitable. But it should happen with equal souls."

Eld saw the opportunity and took it. "If I may ask, how old is he? Your nephew."

One of Alhern's eyebrows arched. "Has someone expressed interest I should know of?"

"Not as such. Just women talking in the theoretical, 'should he be old enough', etcetera."

Alhern motioned that Eld should follow her out the door as they talked.

"I can imagine what 'etcetera' covers. Well, you can discreetly reveal to these lechers he is ninety-eight and therefore two years too young. You might also remind them he is some mother's son, as most of you are mothers. Understood?"

"Absolutely, commander."

"You and your war-sister will report here at sunset. The bells will be rung for the time, and we all shall proceed to the hall. It's shaping up to be the social event of the spring for the locals. The mayor of Gate Step is coming, if you can imagine."

Alhern said this sardonically, glaring at the baskets, vases and pots of flowers; others filled with ferns, branches and baubles being carried to and fro. Her house of elegant feminine décor of white, bronze and gold had been overwhelmed with masculine sky blue and lavender drapes and ribbons, all twined with strings of lights. Glass vases full of shimmer, larger versions of Shedann's wishing orb, seemed to loom on every available surface, the sparkle within in constant motion by some magical process.

"If the Eurthans return, I'd happily exchange this flotsam for the return of my Corinaths."

"Perhaps we could soirée them to death, emha," Eld suggested.

Alhern chuckled. "Thank you for that cheerful thought, cavalier. Anon," she added, walking away.

Dismissed and alone, Eld set off seeking Danshor to inform her of their gala duty. It was a long walk that was somewhat diverting. After checking the Rowan Oak, the Kettle and the stables, Eld was directed to the fair grounds, a place she planned to visit in any case. She wanted to get Seth something special, but not too forward. As chance would have it Eld had discovered one of Seth's fallen hairs on her coat. Elfyn hair shed much less frequently than humyn hair, perhaps a handful of strands a month. Daily brushing and combing caught most of them. That one had escaped to travel on her coat felt meaningful. After first holding it up to the sunlight to feel the echo of Seth's essence, confirming it wasn't one of her own, Eld carefully coiled it in a small circle, then folded it in a scrap of paper. She had an idea what to do with it.

So while Eld was looking for Danshor, she also took her time, enjoying the sights, the various tents with games that this time she abstained from, and performances by musicians, dancers and acrobats. The best of these was by Yeladrin and a Wildling girl as they demonstrated Dwen stick danc-ing and sparring with six foot long poles that could morph and twist around an opponent or her stick, as they leaped and vaulted around each other. The girl seemed to "flow with the wood" like any Dwen, bending her stick into a great horseshoe shape and trying to grasp Yeladrin's. Yeladrin yanked the girl off balance; she recovered, keeping a grip on Yeladrin's stick to spin around it, then release it, landing on her feet as her stick resumed its default straight form. They did this for gratuity, a Wildling young woman guarding a deep, narrow basket about waist high. Eld was generous with her gratuity, remembering the words of their sergeant.

Eld wandered the merchant tents after buying some Tartar Orbs, a large round of grilled, spiced, ground beef or mutton mixed with breadcrumbs, of-ten with an onion or olive at the center, and glazed with meat sauce. She needed something to feed her before the feast and she had no idea how long they'd be escorting before actually eating. Finally she spotted Danshor, predictably with a couple of men, using her talents to win anything she could to impress them. Eld sighed. She wasn't her sister's keeper. Let Sergeant Tarl berate her for her grifting ways. Eld would catch Danshor up when she was done.

Finally Eld found the tent she was looking for, a peaked frame of twisted wood making a shelter of four shallow gated arches, like a gazebo growing out of the cropped grass. The Wildling woman wore the same shimmering vest of gold fabric; she had just finished selling wishing orbs to a couple of girls. They leaped away, spinning their new baubles on their chains in the sun, gleeful at the swirling blue sparkles.

"Al met," Eld said.

"And to you, Gilded Hero. It has been an eventful and profitable time since we met."

"You placed a wager?"

"Not I, but a cousin. Who I had to convince strongly not to wager on your opponent."

Eld sighed. "The Master of the Dawn School."

"Precisely."

"What convinced her?"

"Reverie. I saw you over her, seemingly trying to burn her alive. It was possible that would result in a draw. But it certainly showed she wasn't a victor."

"You knew you would come to the duel?""

"After seeing that I did. How can I serve you?"

Eld pulled out the paper holding Seth's hair, then plucked out one of her own, wincing.

"Elfyn hair is deeply rooted," the woman said.

"From the feel, right into my elfyn skull," Eld muttered. Checking first the root was not bleeding, she handed it to the woman and explaining what she wanted.

"Woven or twined?"

"Twined I think."

"Not certain?"

"I'm sure of the man. Not of my prospects."

"So it could be a remembrance or promise. That should be simple enough. I assume you want it in gold?"

"And solglass."

"I will have to charge a whole queen for such a bauble."

"I have enough," Eld said. It was quite a reasonable price.

"No one is having enough to be taken!" Tafli said, manifesting from somewhere, a basket of goods on one arm.

Startled, Eld said, "Al met and what?"

"You are to being careful with Wildling merchants," Tafli said, looking suspiciously over the baubles and trinkets of glass, hammered copper and twisted wood. "They will sell orbs of rose-gold sparkle that is aught but mead and ground flint."

The merchant locked eyes with Tafli, the gall shadowing making her baleful mood look menacing.

"I assure you, cousin effa, my orbs are of the highest quality gold water, with essence of madder. Except for the blue, which instead contains indigo."

The truth of her words was like a hammer on the anvil of their ears. Tafli fell back under the force of it, blushing.

"Well, it is often the case," Tafli said defensively.

"But not now, not here."

"I never had a doubt," Eld said firmly, fishing a queen out before the woman became so offended she banished them. "When might it be ready?"

"Easily in an hour, emha."

"I will return then. Come on, Tafli," Eld added, firmly taking his arm, though she worried he might resist, or worse, twine her. But he did neither, and let himself be guided away.

"I'm astonished at you," Eld said. "I would think you of all our people would be sympathetic to the condition of Wildlings." She let Tafli's arm go after they were out of earshot of the merchant.

"It is hard yes, but they are always begging."

"Tafli, she's not begging! She's a jeweler selling her wares! And I'm certain she has wood-essence. I thought that made her Dwen regardless of ancestry?"

"By birth and stream maybe, but not tribe," Tafli sniffed. "It is hard enough Sula thinking Dwen are for cheap labor and all Dwen men harlot without a tribe of carnival barkers and horse traders lurking about."

"Tafli, I am very fond of you, but hearing this bigotry makes me wonder if you've spent too much time with Sula."

"Very well, then next time I will let you get gypped!"

Tafli strode off in high dudgeon, yastol erect, green eyes flashing. "What are you looking at?" he barked at a young woman marking his form, particularly his legs. Like always, they were covered with green leaf felt, but not obscured by a robe. "My legs? Perhaps you are a virgin who wonders what a man guards between them?"

The woman and her friends were both abashed and amused, barely containing laughter as they choked out half hearted apologies.

"Sorry, effa!"

"You are sorry for nothing except you are being caught and I say it boldly unlike Sula men who cower for fear of what other Sula men say! You are ridiculous girls not fitting to birth yet! Be standing there and think on it!"

And stand there they did, for the grass had suddenly grown around their feet.

But this was to them the life of a day and they hooted louder: "We are twined sisters! Come back King of the Wood! Let us buy you a goblet of something!"

But Tafli was a fast walker when angered and he was soon gone, as was the effect of his wood-essence. The grass stopped growing and while it didn't untwine, it was a simple matter of yanking their feet free, with some clods of turf. The women continued on, the more merry for their rebuke from a beautiful Dwen man.

"Look!" a bold voice shouted from the opposite direction. "The Gilded Hero graces us with her presence!"

It was Danshor, a laughing man on each arm. They had wrapped long ribbons around their necks, flowing like streamers of gold, blue and pink, bits of straw still clinging to them from being bound in prize bales. One held a small burlap bag of what must be sweets that they were all eating in turn.

Eld strode over, her sudden remembrance about their coming duty making her urgent.

"You were so bold!" one man said to her. "I was there! And Althas tells us ..."

"Truthful things, I'm sure," Eld cut in. "Look, we have duty this eve," she said, addressing Danshor.

"No, we don't. I checked and double checked the roster. I even spoke to the elf minding it. We are free to indulge in the company of beautiful men!"

For emphasis, Danshor pulled the two closer to her, eliciting vocative murmurs of delight.

"Well, you are right about that," Eld admitted. "But it won't be these men. Sorry, effas, we are doomed to escort men from the commander's house."

The men pouted. Danshor looked positively furious.

"For how long?"

"I don't know. The commander said for the gala, so I expect we might be with them at the feast after."

"The gala is going to be in the hall," one of the men offered.

"And on the grounds," the other said.

"But that's for the common soldier. The officers and heroes will be in the hall."

"Brother, they're all heroes now ..."

Eld and Danshor stepped a little away while the men argued amiably.

"Does this have anything to do with your sponsorship and the commander's brother?" Danshor asked.

"I think that's why Alhern suggested it."

"Could you leave me out of it? Some of us just want to enjoy the pleasures of the Orb."

"I said you were good with children."

"Children?"

"The nephew is the other male to be escorted."

Danshor looked to the Heavens for patience. "So while I could be around two fulsome men, in whichever order, instead, I'll be escorting a child."

"He's not that young. At ninety-eight ..."

"He's still too young to take unless we were betrothed somehow."

"I'm not saying you should marry him. Only that you'll be able to have some form of conversation. You're a hero and he'll ask questions. And since you love talking yourself up with the lads ..."

"Lads I can tryst with freely! I thought that was obvious! When are we doomed to meet?"

"At dusk."

"Then you'll excuse me if I try to get some adventure in while I can!"

Danshor stalked away, put on her charming face again with apologies, followed by suggestions the men found intriguing. They all walked off together, away from the fair, likely to find a free glade, wood, or even a barn, Eld thought snidely.

In a couple hours Eld had retrieved the orb, holding it up to Sul's afternoon light, pleased with what glimmered within. She put it carefully back into the small box she'd been given with it.

"It's perfect, emha."

"And this too." The woman handed Eld a small, square envelope. "The balance of the strands not used."

"Elam. And please excuse my friend earlier. He seems to think he's protecting me from a grand swindle."

The woman tilted her head side to side. "It is unfortunate some of our cousins will focus on our differences, not our common duty to the Forest. As if we do not have enough Golds seeking strife through division. No offense, emha."

"You speak more truth than you know. Good eve."

Eld first stopped in the barracks for her cape, and to check she was perfect for the night, polishing her boots and removing any stray grass or straw that might have followed her. She brushed her flouted tail and for a moment regretted not having glimmer dust, for that touch of magic in the right light. But she wasn't Roel and put it out of her mind, making haste to the commander's house. The most important preparation was that she should be on time. If only Danshor complied.

To her relief Danshor was already there, waiting by the steps just as the bell rung to mark dusk and Sul's retirement to bed. Above them, in the violet darkening sky, fireworks blossomed white and gold, upstaging the new twinkling stars. There were only a handful of pops, a flourish to call attention to the time; there was to be a grander show later.

"Come on!" Danshor called on the top step. Eld ran up as the garrison band started to play in earnest from the ramparts, making the whole of the keep a music chamber.

Alhern waited in the entrance with Marshal Tantilaan and General Sallaryn and their men. The general's married consort was as tall as herself, with intelligent eyes and a strong jaw that suggested resolve, stubbornness, or both. Unlike most formally dressed men, he did not wear a pillar gown, but instead a wide cut robe that hung from a line around his chest to flow around him much like magi's robes, if magi robes were bright, red satin. Wide reeds – scarf-like streamers on formal wear – of fine red silk hung from his shoulders, both at the back and in the front to either side of a square neckline. His hair was in the Meridian style, the bulk of the top locks woven down in a tail in the back, the locks to either side bound loosely in coils of gold wire. On his head was not a hastol, but a wreath of gold edged red leaves mimicking the laurels given as awards to ancient poets. His lips were brightly glimmered with red-gold; he had no other accent or jewelry. He smiled instantly at Eld, friendly without coyness or suggestion, for his arm was linked with Sallaryn's and it was clear they were equally entwined souls.

The man standing next to the marshal was surprisingly young. Not as young as Seth's nephew, but little older than Eld, which, considering the Marshal was near her twentieth decade, seemed divergent. He wore a short cape of mail over his white robe, but didn't wear it well, in that he was obviously uncomfortable in it, his shoulders shifting constantly. His gold eyes flickered, as if marking everything lest he be caught in error. His hair had a modest dusting of glimmer, as did his lips. In fact his entire ensemble could be described as deliberately modest. He was thin, almost too thin, and at least two inches shorter than Tantilaan who was clearly his wife, her hand under his elbow as if he was a bauble that might roll away. He wore simple trilocks with a hastol that was barely a circlet, with eight minute quarter points, though it did flicker with a glow when the light caught it just right. Both men had lacquered gold nails.

A short ways away stood the keeper Effa Tanmor with Solafi, the boy still looking much like a daffodil, though tonight a white and yellow daffodil: white wing reeds of silk streaming off the back of his shoulders, his hastol flickering with subtle rainbow hues. It was only now seeing Solafi standing in a group Eld appreciated he was almost adult height, his slack posture and errant attention usually obscuring this. His keeper, as always, looked dour, but perhaps a little less so. Eld imagined Tanmor might have the evening off if they were escorting the nephew instead.

"The bell has rung the start of evening," the Marshal said heartily, but her voice betrayed irritation.

"We should remember," Sallaryn's consort began, "The feast is not ruled by martial law. You should try to enjoy yourself, emha."

Sallaryn whispered something to her consort that did not carry except for the word "agreeable." His reply was wordless, hugging Sallaryn's arm more firmly and beaming as if he was filled with joy, while his eyes flashed rebelliously. Eld felt he did not like the marshal at all.

"I am only observing that our host's brother is a little late," Tantilaan said. "Given that he manages our worthy host's house, it is odd he has forgotten the time."

Now Alhern's eyes glowered balefully, a tight smile pasted on her face.

"Well, you know men," Sallaryn said, playing diplomat, and perhaps wishing to demonstrate the agreeableness she had encouraged. "When it comes to looking their best, there's never enough time."

"How right you are, darling," her consort agreed.

"I often feel this way!" Tantilaan's consort blurted, his voice high from nerves.

"And yet you have been disciplined to avoid such tardiness," Tantilaan added with a mix of pride and repressive firmness. They had all been smiling politely in various degrees. At this point Eld's smile vanished. But she didn't know she was glaring at the Marshal Tantilaan until Alhern addressed her.

"Farthal!" Alhern said, snapping Eld's attention back to the moment. "Had a pleasant afternoon?" Alhern's eyes seemed to say, "Go carefully."

"Yes, emha, quite. The awards were overwhelming. It was good to have time to reflect."

"Reflection is good for the soul," Alhern said. "Solafi, here is your escort," she added, gesturing to Danshor.

The boy beamed as if his day of birth had come early. "I'm to be escorted by a cavalier!" he effused.

"That's the nephew?" Danshor breathed at Eld side. Eld looked at her. She looked to be in shock.

"Yes. He was at the awards before, remember?"

"But I hadn't heard his voice," Danshor gasped. "I knew he looked familiar ..."

Eld was about to ask what Danshor meant. But then Seth stepped into the entrance and Eld only had eyes for him.

Seth wore his hastol, his blond white hair hanging free except for his guardlocks bound in gold ribbons. He wore a simple robe, a white shift cut to flow fully, but hugging his torso to the waist. No pillar gown for him this evening; he wished to dance. Seth wore no mail, only a decorative gold chain with crystal and aqua that was pinned to border the square neckline of his robe. Sky blue wing reeds flowed off his shoulders, and his wrists were bound in gold filigree bracers. As usual his glimmer was minimal and tasteful, and his nails weren't lacquered. The length of his robe was measured perfectly to not reveal his shoes, yet hovered just high enough not to drag on the floor.

"I understand I'm being escorted by a bold cavalier," Seth said looking about as if searching for this soul. "Who is this rare elf?"

Everyone found this amusing except for Marshal Tantilaan, who smiled tightly while the rest laughed.

"Effa," Eld said formally, stepping forward to offer her arm. This time she had remembered to throw her cape back rakishly in advance. "Perhaps you will find me suitable."

Seth looked into Eld's eyes, his own twin gold promises of a full night to come.

"I suppose you will do, cavalier."

## Chapter 31

# Gala

The nephew needn't have been concerned about missing the society of his village friends, for the path of their procession, lined with decorative pillar lamps for the occasion, was thronged with sight seers, and of the many excited boys dressed in their holiday best and ribbons, Solafi's friends were certainly among them. Doubtless they would contrive to meet later, for while the soirée was a formal event to honor the victory of the troops and notable worthies, both civilian and military, anyone was welcome, servant or soldier, provided they did not have duty and did not make a nuisance of themselves. There was a certain democracy to the event which would have had consequences for Seth had he been proud minded. Alhern, as the commander of the garrison, walked first with the man she chose to escort, in this case, to Eld's mild surprise, Effa Tanmor, the nephew's keeper. In normal times it would be Seth on her arm, in the place of the courted or married consort Alhern did not have. After Alhern, walked her most senior guest, the Marshal Tantilaan and her consort, Tinyan. Being a military event, order was determined by rank, not relation, so General Sallaryn and her consort Rathi came after, then Major Galledan and a series of officers from various departments. Once the last of the garrison command staff stepped out the door, Eld and Seth proceeded forward, followed by Danshor and Solafi.

The music echoed around them, its source now indistinct, for musicians played on the ramparts and on the fields, great tents full of lights covering the space where they had been inspected. The tents weren't completely necessary at the moment, but there was often a little rain after dark in the spring season, and so they were there as a precaution, their sides currently tied back to make glowing canopies in the coming night. Musicians would also be playing in each great canopy and Eld knew, like when a group of talented unknown souls met in an inn by chance, the smaller orchestras would play off each other, harmonizing the dominant mood, then, at other times, wandering where talent and whim took them. So as the commander's entourage promenaded along the lit path to the garrison hall, the music surrounding them took the tone of a brisk cheerful march. Eld would tell herself most times she was indifferent to these social events. But with Seth on her arm, and every eye looking on them, she found her opinion quite changed. Eld's heart grew three times larger, filled with affection for the moment, that she could walk with the man she was falling in love with, that thought itself avoided for so long. Of course she would accept sponsorship. Why had that ever been a doubt?  And Seth could finally have the satisfaction of being seen in society as more than an errant masculine soul who shared the fate of so many men who were not offered marriage: appreciated in their mother's house for their labors, but rarely with access to public life unless their talents  brought them note in the worlds of publishing and art.  Even those who chose a mother's life often found themselves limited to practicing their skills on the family estate, though there were exceptions.

One such expectation was the artist who accompanied the broadsheet agent.  They both returned for the gala in style, the artist in a dark red pillar robe, wound with reeds of gold satin so he resembled a helix, his hastol accented with red glass.  It was a bold color for a man, red being the color of angry or passionate mothers.  When an unmarried man wore red, their were implications of harlotry, in this case not alleviated by the lack of sleeves or shoulders, the garment being little more than a tube of cloth hanging on thin straps.  A transparent scarf of gold silk wrapped his shoulders, suggesting modesty as an afterthought, and he was wearing all the proper undergarments.  But the playful smile that never left his red gilded lips showed he knew the effect he had and enjoyed the thoughts, both the appreciative and scandalized, of what would happen should those straps fail.

The broadsheet agent surprised Eld with her dark blue coat.  In the military Eld was used to dress uniforms as women's formal attire and forgot civilian women could be as colorful as men.  The coat wasn't the great coat of industry, though that was what the mayor was wearing, its high, broad collar standing up stiffly to cradle the back of the neck.  The great coat, whatever the color, was always trimmed in silver or gold.  The coat the agent wore was much like Eld's own cavalry coat, the modern coat taking its cues from cavalry costume. It wasn't actually dark blue, but sapphire with black brocade, black silk reeds hanging from the back of its shoulders, marking it as a garment intended for formal dance. A silver waist coat lurked underneath, and below that a white silk shirt worn for these times. Her black trousers were long and snug, with blue town shoes on her feet, little more than sturdy slippers. Blond hair hung in simple trilocks, lightly glimmered for the occasion.  It was a typical feminine civilian ensemble, varying only in color and hue.

Though the agent and her artist came to the garrison hall together, they did not act like a couple, even for the purposes of escort.  From their behavior, while they were certainly enjoying the event, they were working as well, seeking acceptable gossip and tales for their shop.  They worked the crowd by gender, the woman charming the men, the man, charming the women.

450

"Be careful," Seth breathed in Eld's ear after finishing pleasantries with The Wildling's owner. "Law prevents them from acting with mercenary malice, but any true thing said in public is acceptable grist."

"I thought you'd find common cause with the man," Eld said. "You are both artists."

"I do like Effa Fathil Borin, or 'Fathi' as he insists. And I hope we will be friends. He'll be dining with us later. But his duty here is to his employer. Never forget that. They will harry the crowd like hounds, not with teeth and barks, but pleasantries and flattery. Say nothing true you do not want the Orb to know."

The transformed garrison hall was perfect for the purposes of these hunters of tales. The lights dazzled the eye and seemed to be in greater abundance than on the day of Eld's arrival. In addition to the usual lamps and strings of lights, ribboned globes of sparkling gold water hung from hooks in the ceiling, and generally it looked less like a garrison hall and more like a ballroom of an ancient estate, which was surely the intent. One large difference from Eld's welcoming gala was the lack of a vast spread. There would be the feast at the commander's house later and abundant food to be had in the pavilions outside. Thus the only refreshment was light sparkling wine, and chilled sunblessed water, with the sort of small cakes and simple snacks one might find in a parlor.

The bulk of the activity was dancing and as soon as the commander's retinue arrived this was engaged in earnest. The musicians on the stage played for the inner court, the music of the grounds muffled to obscurity. An astalyn had been painted on the floor in silver, white and blue, the star in the center marking the point all the courtly style dancing would revolve around. And so Eld danced with Seth for a long while, so lost in their spinning steps, passed now and then to others but always returning, insensible to their own smiles or the whispers about the cavalier with the commander's brother. Seth had no eyes for any woman but Eld, and no man had ever held all the parts of Eld's attention, body, mind and soul. She was the luckiest woman in the Orb and every eye knew this.

The current dance ended and Eld was shocked to see the clock marked that almost an hour passed. No wonder she felt parched.

"I'm thirsty," she said.

"Then you should get us something," Seth said.

"What, you're not coming?"

"I can't just spend the night sweeping the floor with my favorite cavalier," he said. "I'm also responsible for representing my sister's household.

Don't worry," Seth added, pecking her cheek. "I won't let anyone carry me off before you return."

Eld shivered at the touch of his lips. It wasn't the kiss, for they had shared much deeper and more intimate kisses. It was the fact he'd done it publicly. Now Eld heard the faint gasp from the most discreet of observers and, if she'd been inclined, she could have tuned her ears to what they said. But it was obvious from glittering eyes and knowing smiles they marked her as the one who must have prospects, for why else would the commander's brother be so bold? Oh, did you hear, she's been offered a sponsorship. Ah, then that was understandable. The rumors of her deeds must be true if she's fated to be an officer. And she won a duel against an officer, a master of the Dawn School no less…

Eld didn't hear all these details exactly, but the pieces she did hear were part of the expected tapestry of the tale.

Then the Dwen arrived.

Tafli was attractive in his exotic way, but Eld had never seen him like this, an elegant Laird of the Forest. Gone was his bark vest tunic and instead a corset of sorts wove and twined around his torso, flat strips of blond oak, curling in spirals and interweaving patterns, covering his torso like a breast plate of wooden filigree. Flowing from his hips and shoulders were reeds of white treesilk, floating with every step he took. Dark green velvet accented portions of the wood at his shoulders; then Eld realized it wasn't velvet at all, but living moss. Similarly what looked at first to be green lacy bracers covering his forearms were living fern leaves, wrapped tightly from wrist to elbow. The same sage green leaf-felt covered his legs like always, but his sandals, still twined at the ankle, now had a white flower blooming on the top of each foot. His yastol today was green, no shaped wood, but a band with rowan leaves growing out, though how this was done, Eld didn't know. Clusters of white flowers dangled from either side, stark against his red and brown hair, obscuring his ears. His eyes were outlined, not with his usual glimmer, but black gall, as were his lips. This must be Dwen in their formal aspect. Eld had never see Tafli without his glimmer or bangles.

His two companions, Yeladrin and Olyeth, were changed as well, though not as dramatically. They also had corsets of wood in spiral patterns, but reeds only flowed off the back of their shoulders. Their arms were bare except for wood bracers of the same style as their vesting, and living ivy vines that seemed rooted at their wrists, wrapping around their lean muscled arms ending in several erect leaves hovering above their shoulders. Their yastols were also alive: both women had oak leaves and clusters of faux acorns hanging by their ears. Their legs were covered with russet leaf-felt, and their eyes, exactly like Tafli's, were outlined in black gall, though their lips were not. The Dwen women looked both slightly masculate and more savage.

A hush fell on the crowd as the Dwen entered. The musicians faltered. In a clear voice used to berate souls for burnings, Tafli said:

"I understand there is to be dancing."

This elicited laughter and the musicians started to play, then stopped. Eld saw Alhern speaking with one. Then they started again, a flautist playing several long notes at haunting dirge speed, the beginning of a traditional Dwen air. The three Dwen took to the floor, equal distant to each other. Then rapid drumming began and the Dwen danced so fast it was hard for the eye to follow. They leaped and cavorted, spinning and twisting, tumbling between each other, somehow never letting their reeds tangle or otherwise missing a step. Then they would rest in an interlude, if rest one could call it, with quick hopping steps moving them between each other as they continued to spin and cavort, the sound of their wooden sandals snapping against the floor as quick as oil crackling with water in a hot skillet. Something of the traditional Dwen dance was observed and recorded in the jigs and hornpipes of the northern humyn Gaels, but without the leaps and tumbles that were beyond the skill of most humyn. And then the 'rest' was over and, after a couple more springs and leaping twirls, the three Dwen whirled around each other like a cyclone with three cores, ending on the final beat, each of them facing out in three equal directions, saluting the audience with both hands to applause.

"He's so bold," a familiar voice said next to Eld. It was the ranger Orinac. Her dress uniform also had a cape, but it was longer, hanging to the knees, black with green lining. They were both near the table with cups and drink.

"He has caught the eye of many," Eld said, observing women, both soldiers and civilians who had come alone, drifting towards Tafli to try their luck.

"He refused me," Orinac said.

"I thought you wanted to forget that."

"No, not then. I was a hood and I'm not proud of that. I asked to escort him. He was kind, but said he was already being escorted. Do Dwen usually share men like this?"

"I think Tafli just wanted to come with friends. I don't claim to know all their ways."

"He told some elf he was with a woman."

"Did he?" Eld said.

"And must a man always be with a woman?" a male voice queried.

It was the broadsheet artist, perched on a nearby tall stool, sipping from a glass goblet.

"I wouldn't say must, effa," Orinac began, perhaps a little too excited a man had engaged her.

Eld took the opportunity to seize two small cups of sparkling light mead and escape before the subject of whom Tafli might be with returned. Then she ran into Danshor who looked as pale as a ghost.

"What's wrong with you?" Eld asked.

"I need to talk to you. Now!"

"I can't! I have to return with drinks before the commander accuses me of ignoring Seth."

"Don't you mean Effa Alhern?"

"It seems the charade may be over soon."

"I'm so pleased for you."

"You don't sound pleased. And where is Solafi? You're supposed to be escorting him."

"Never fear, he's safely gorging on cakes and sparkle."

Eld looked over and sure enough the white daffodil was near the table, chatting animatedly with a couple boys his age.

"Alhern's coming," Danshor said, and then was gone.

"Not ignoring my brother after monopolizing him for an hour, are you, Farthal?"

"Not at all, emha. Just getting refreshment." Eld gestured to the cups she held.

"Hmm. What's wrong with Lancer Danshor?"

"I don't know. She looks a bit ill."

"Nerves likely. Some of the bravest women on the field quail before engaging in society. It is the realm of men. Well, don't let my brother die of thirst."

"Emha."

Returning to Seth, Eld found him talking to the village mayor and the broadsheet agent, with a couple of men listening, one being the mayor's son.

"Yes, she has been offered a commission, and here she is to tell you about it." Seth took one of the cups Eld was holding and beamed at her.

Eld did her best to speak both humbly and proudly about her deeds, and why she thought she'd been offered sponsorship. She tried to speak in vagaries, but when the agent started pressing Eld fell on that career soldier standby: obstruction by ignorance. She didn't know exactly why Alhern offered her for sponsorship. But her betters were more experienced and wiser, and she was sure they had good reasons. Seth saw her awkwardness and helped steer the conversation back to her brave deeds, at which point the listening men drove the talk so firmly into this track, the agent's attempts to ferret out any comments suggesting their trysting was driven into a ditch. The agent toasted Seth, her admission of defeat, before drifting on.

Eld was relieved. Then one of the men caught her eye. His face was narrow and he was on the thin side, but not fragile. He looked familiar but she couldn't place him.

"Excuse me, effa," Eld said. "Do I know you?"

The man laughed, not unpleasantly, but more like a mother might. He was not a coy creature.

"Yes, we are acquainted, Lancer Farthal. I have seen you in your most intimate moments: specifically near death."

Eld's alarm at this news, and the look Seth gave her was mollified by the knowledge he must work as a healer.

"She once said I should wear more glimmer if I didn't want to be mistaken for a girl," the man continued to much laughter at Eld's expense. "She's brave and able, but I wonder if we tended to her head as skillfully as we thought!"

Of course it seemed absurd looking at him now, with his pale yellow kirtle-shirt and green satin surcoat robe, much like a woman's great coat if it hung to the floor. His guardlocks were bound with green ribbons, and he had a simple gold or brass circlet on his head. And, now, his lips were glimmered. Thus society knew he was a man and Eld was a fool.

"My apologies for our previous misunderstandings," Eld said, letting the laughter roll over her. "I maintain you are a prickly and contrary man, but I also know your skill at healing is irreproachable."

"Well," the man considered. "That is all truth. We see what we expect to see. So I might forgive you. She's a healer herself. Of horses." He launched into the tale of saving Hollar's life on the battlefield.

"I'll get more drink," Eld breathed to Seth.

"I don't need another yet."

"I do," Eld said emphatically. She looked around, wanting to avoid the agent and her artist, who now seemed to find the ranger the most fascinating soul in the Orb. Trusting Orinac was unlikely to know anything scandalous, Eld gave them a wide berth, glad the man had found a different victim.

Then the lights dimmed and another dance began, a traditional courtly pace, the kind that friends and acquaintances could engage in without drawing eyes. Yet eyes were drawn, not to Seth, who was taking a turn with the mayor, but Alhern who was literally cavorting with Tafli.

The commander didn't know, Eld was sure, because Alhern never socialized with Tafli in public. But Tafli never stepped or swayed quite like he did when holding Alhern's hand, and when it was time to spin into a brief embrace, every sinew of his resisted the next moment that he must spin away. His twinings betrayed him, the fern leaves and flowers seeming to always reach back towards Alhern.   Alhern, for her part, was as she always was, ridgid and erect, military discipline in every bone, and honestly Tafli was her equal. It was only his twinings that gave him away, and perhaps the blazing stare they shared was too harsh for a causal acquaintance or friendly turn on the floor between sibling souls. If Alhern was lucky what was seen would be dismissed as the crush of a savage man who didn't know better. If she was seen as returning his attentions, of course it wouldn't affect her career.  But if she had some mad plan to actually marry a Dwen, the men of her estate might revolt.  The uncles of any estate were fierce if their domain was threated.  And many Sula men found the idea of sharing a household with a 'savage' an affront.

It wasn't just Sula men insecure in their position.  Eld caught a glimpse of the Marshal, who had been dancing with her consort, then maneuvered them both to the edge of the floor and broke off, to Tinyan's disappointment.  It was not in good form, and would have been considered rude in a soirée presided over by the lairds of a governor's palace.  But who was going to rebuke the Federation  Marshal at a military gala? At the end of the dance,  Alhern bowed to Tafli and they parted as if they barely knew each other, but Tafli's vinings said otherwise.

Then Yeladrin approached the commander's entourage. She bowed and offered to take Tinyan's hand for the next dance.  Before Tantilaan could sputter out a word, Tinyan agreed, all but leaping back onto the dance floor.  Tantilaan looked furious while Alhern, Sallaryn, Rathi and Seth converged and made small conversation.  Eld caught something about relaxing, to which the Marshal glared repressively.  So they all turned back to conversing amiably, ignoring Tantilaan as if she was a small, pouting child.  Eld thought it wise to stay away, at least until Tinyan was no longer in the 'savage' hands of a Dwen.

The light was still dim when Eld came to refill her drink, but hushed voices made her cautious.  She certainly didn't want to be burdened with others' secrets.  But, even talking in hushed tones, the boy's voice carried:

"Well, everyone is bound to make mistakes in the Orb," Solafi said. "It's learning from them that matters, is it not?"

"You are so wise for your age," a woman's voice said.  It was a voice Eld loathed and now hated: Lieutenant Roel. But surely the nephew was safe from Roel's predations. And how was Roel even present? Eld tried to look at her surreptitiously. Roel was in her dress uniform, of course, and her hair seemed magically recovered. But no, it was a clever barber's trick: false locks gummed to accent her hair like actors or vain men used. Whatever the case, at least at a distance, Roel appeared to have full guardlocks. Eld moved closer, feeling she should be certain of the nephew's safety before moving on.

As chance would have it a scaffold remained standing against a wall from the preparations, fabric draped decoratively over its front to hide its purpose. Presently a couple clambered down from where they'd been watching the floor below, perhaps exchanging surreptitious kisses. Eld stepped quickly, masking her climb with the sound of their giggling egress. Not only did Eld have a view of the floor, where the Marshal's young consort Tinyan continued to be swept around by Yeladrin to his glee, but Eld had a good view of the refreshments and was able to hear better.

Roel stood close to the nephew but did not touch him, not even a chaste hand on the arm or shoulder. Because Roel was seducing him by talk, and for her to be blameless in her entitled mind, she must let the nephew come to her. Eld seethed as she listened. At least Eld would be in a good position to shout out an alarm.

"My great aunt said much the same thing to me earlier," Roel said, dolefully. "Wise words. But certainly a charming young man like yourself is not alone?"

"Oh no! I'm being escorted by one of the hero cavaliers!"

"Indeed."

"No, not that one. Never fear, I won't reveal you to her."

"You are kind."

"But it is her war-sister."

"Oh?"

"And can I confess something?"

"Only if you want."

"She sounds like someone I met a couple nights ago."

"Does she?"

"If you must know, I too have made a mistake. I think. I went to a Garden of Lun."

"Truly?"

Eld's breath caught. Perhaps she misunderstood and it was a typical moon meet with a romantic local name.

"I didn't know there was one in a community so small," Roel said.

"It's run privately, never in the same place. News spreads by word of mouth. Or dreams. And I can dream quite well."

Gardens of Lun were usually found in large towns and cities, in a semi permanent installment near the local Temple of Lun. They were indeed gardens, night gardens with high walls, open to women and men who were read truthfully as being of age and free of obligation. Most wore masks or other means to obscure their identity because the Gardens of Lun were basically places to tryst or orgy, depending on one's desire. Eld had visited one long ago with friends while studying healing, but she'd been too shy to partake even though she was masked. For some women it was a welcome taste of excitement now and then, like eating spiced curry. And for men, especially young men who were of age, it was often the best place to let themselves be taken for the first time without worry of complications or social censure. For privacy was sacrosanct in a Garden: mothers and men were forbidden to use their real names, even if they came with fellows, frequent guests using pseudonyms from myth and legend. But for the institution to function as it should – a place where mothers and men might tryst and indulge erotic curiosity without judgment – the population must be large enough to support anonymity. And the management, usually a man attached to the Temple, had to be regulated by the city.

This local garden seemed to be a reckless venture with questionable management. And dangerous for men. A proper garden was the safest place a man might seek an unknown woman to tryst with him. Some back-lot, barngarden was the perfect place for a man to find himself seduced by pressure to do things he wouldn't otherwise.

"A friend of yours attended?" Roel asked cleverly, damn her. She knew what the boy would say, and was making it easier.

"No, I went. But it's not what you think!"

"What do you mean?"

"I didn't let anyone, you know, take me. Not fully."

Eld didn't know why she felt relieved. Perhaps because there would be no chance of complications from a stream. Women who had been cleared of rapine, yet still determined to have taken advantage of men and profited by pregnancy, had to pay the price, literally a dowry to the man's mother. While this wouldn't hurt the nephew, the legal discovery would be mortifying.

"Surely you left after your curiosity was sated," Roel said.

"No. I wish I had though."

"What's the worst that happened?"

"I kissed many women. I mean kissed them, deeply. And I am certain one was the cavalier escorting me."

"You are simply overwrought with guilt," Roel said soothingly. "She would know who you are and not touch you –"

"But she wouldn't! I had henna in my hair and glimmer in a way I am never allowed at home. It has worked for so long. And women only see what they want to."

"Whatever has happened it surely will not affect your prospects. Like you said, everyone is bound to make mistakes in the Orb. You should avoid suspicion by staying close to your escort. She doesn't know, does she?"

"No, I don't think so."

"Then she doesn't need to."

"Oh, thank you!"

The nephew trotted away, Roel watching him go. Then, to Eld's horror, Roel looked up straight into her eyes, smiling maliciously.

~ Just imagine the scandal,~ Roel thought. ~ A heroic cavalier being kissed in the nethers by Alhern's sweet, virginal nephew. I wonder how that will sit with riding the commander's brother. You've obviously been doing that for a while. No wonder she favors you. But for how long? ~

Then Roel walked off.

Eld almost leaped from the scaffold in rage. She took a breath and forced herself to step down and not cause a scene. It was just a kiss. Didn't the nephew say he hadn't been coited? It was stupid sure, kissing or coiting anonymous men in an unregulated Garden, but if that's the worst Danshor had done, maybe it wasn't so bad. As for Roel's thoughts on Seth....Well, let her say them aloud. They could duel again and Eld could scorch off the rest of Roel's hair.

Stepping back on the floor in time for the music to stop, Eld was shocked at another confrontation. The Marshal was looming between her consort and Yeladrin, standing threateningly close. Tantilaan was taller than the Dwen but seemed insensible to the danger she was in; both Yeladrin's wood and ivy twinings had partly unwound to hover horizontally at her side, and her yastol had flattened. Having seen Dwen in the field under threat, Eld knew that Yeladrin had been startled and was ready to fight. Thankfully the floor was inlaid stone or a small forest might have sprouted.

Nonetheless, Eld strode over but was beaten by Alhern.

"It was but a dance, Marshal Tantilaan," Alhern said soothingly. "I'm sure our Dwen ally had no plan to abscond with your consort."

"Yes, of course," Tantilaan said, valiantly hiding the force of her dislike. "It's only Tinyan looks overexcited and should rest."

"Overexcited" was one turn of phrase. Aroused would be a better one. Whether Tinyan was so overwhelmed or artless, and likely he was both, the young man was flushed and smiling. "It was quite a dance!" he said.

Very, very slowly Yeladrin's twinings withdrew and her Yastol raised. But though her voice was civil it was warningly deep, almost a baritone and her eyes remained hard. "And I was pleased to step with you, effa. It is a mother with weak roots who is so threatened by a Dwen touching a man like any mother here."

"I said nothing about your race or nation, emha," Tantilaan said with bluster. "I am simply ..."

"Lying to yourself, emha," Yeladrin said, her voice deeper if possible. The entire hall was silent and the music had stopped. "You have been staring at us with thoughts of reproach since we stepped into the hall, thoughts sending strongly of lies that we hunger after twining your Gold men with force. Why should we do this ridiculous and offensive thing, hunger after Gold men? Our men are both beautiful and bold, and we prefer their boldness to fragile compliant flowers. Bright mothers like you slander us with these tales to hide your own guilt over your inner darkness, the Athmod inside you deny. It was not the Forest who committed The Burning, betraying your fostered Sharitani refugees by setting their boats on fire while they fled the plague in Gashora. It was not us who drove Dwen from burnt forest land after the God Storm, whose descendants now wander homeless as The Bereft, A'Yinomehey, 'those who have lost all'. You persist in calling them "wildlings". They call themselves 'Yino'. Who is it who is 'wild' in this tale? It was not our Queen's debased sister who took her sadistic band of followers to slaughter a Dwen village, saving a handful of boys for rapine.

"Yes, Sula worthies, that is the reason Her Humble Majesty's ancestor abdicated in shame: the Sunqueens, for all their grand and lofty vision, they failed to teach those with the greatest power to submit to duty. Instead they embraced pride and entitlement. It was for this Outrage of the Forest, not some minor tiff of trade, that we barred Sula from us from us the first time. And yet we come when duty calls. And still you insult us like this, with suspicions of your own guilt. It was Sula who raped Dwen boys millennia ago and yet we do not look on every Sula woman as a threat. Perhaps we should.

"Do not worry, Marshal of the Bright Plains. We will not trouble you further with our unwanted savage presence."

Truth vibrated like a tuning fork in the air, the throng was silent, the music inside dead. It was only then in the silence another argument was heard, though it faded as attention eager for any distraction turned to it: Tafli was remonstrating with Solafi, his voice low and furious.

The nephew. Eld felt stupid. "We see what we expect," the male healer had said. And Solafi had said, "Women only see what they want to." Of course Solafi was familiar: he worked, over-glimmered in henna red hair as "Farni", Tafli's knave. And now he was being berated for the deception and dismissed from service. Whatever was being said, as soon as he realized they had the attention of the entire hall, Tafli broke off and strode over to join his countrywomen. As one they bowed in three directions, then left the hall proudly, looking at no one, yastols erect, heads high.

The next several moments of silence were painful. Eld could only imagine what the broadsheet agents would make of it.

And then Seth stepped forward, his smile restrained and sad.

"We are bidden to apologize to those we have offended, past and present. It is clear there is much we can reflect on in our private moments of conscience, for none of us is blameless in life. However, the feast awaits and we are obligated to honor those who have labored so hard in our kitchens by not keeping them waiting longer."

Seth then strode to Eld, holding his arm out in a clear demand that she take it, and pulled them forward in defiance of their proper order of promenade. Eld resumed the lead, off footed slightly when Seth paused abruptly before Marshal Tantilaan, his gold eyes flashing up at her in fury. Seth's tone, however, stayed conversational though hushed:

"For a woman adept at navigating the sea of politics, I cannot imagine a greater blunder if a fool was left to the task. Try to remember, your status aside, Marshal Tantilaan, you remain our guest and guests do not make difficulties for their hosts by insulting friends and allies."

This time Eld was ready when Seth stepped forward, invigorated by his boldness, and yet terrified by what he'd just done. Eld was more happy to match his quick pace, to flee the hall and a vengeful marshal who might be now regretting signing off on her sponsorship.

## Chapter 32

# The Heroes' Feast

Their promenade back to the commander's house felt like a forced march at double speed. At least the mood lightened once they left the hall, the majority of eyes ignorant yet of what had transpired with the Dwen. It it would be widely known in the coming days, one of the many tales printed by Herald of the Dawn Country. Alas, it would not be the most scandalous one.

Already the tale was seeping into the gathering consciousness before they had taken their seats in a much grander dining hall than Eld had yet seen. The extraordinary labors with the décor – strung lights, shimmer globes, gold and white satin ribbons, red and gold tulips exploding from vases on pedestals in the corners of the room – surrounded a long table where a carved ice dragon stood tall over the spread of goose, lamb, roasts with forcemeat, whipped and creamed potatoes, carrots and parsnips and sundry grilled vegetables and sauces. All this grandeur threatened to be flooded by a somber mood more suited for a funeral.

Yet Seth stepped into this room, his field of battle, making for his seat opposite the head of the table. Eld was tardy in taking the place reserved next to him for his escort, but the butler, Sonamor, with several house-girls were there to remind her, as well as guide others who did not know their place with soft words: "Your seat, emha," or "Your seat, effa." It was a large table, oval at the ends, giving more space for intimates or favorites of either party. Effa Tanmor was to sit on Seth's other side, next to him, So-lafi, and then Danshor who did not look much better, her eyes hollow and haunted. At Alhern's end of the table, Tantilaan would sit next to her, then her consort, Tinyan, then General Sallaryn and her consort, Rathi. On Alh-ern's other side was the Red Major with a man she was escorting and more staff officers of the garrison and so forth. Thus they stood waiting.

After Sonamor made a motion for musicians lurking near the tulips to play, Alhern said some brief words about how hungry they must be, an ex-cuse to take their seats immediately and start eating, hoping to evade thoughts eager to be expressed. For the issue of the Outrage of the Forest was one that unfortunately drew out apologists of the nation, whether be-cause it had happened six millennia ago, or because it happened under a dif-ferent government, implying a government of mothers would never have al-lowed such a thing to happen. Yet it was under the government of mothers, through the Federation Council and the parliamentary Voice of Mothers, that the Burning did happen, as well as the Eviction of the Forest in the

Ethynsul. Neither the Council nor the Voice stopped the land seizure of what was now the New Forest. While many resisted drifting into these fraught conversational waters, some souls couldn't help themselves.

"It was of course a horrible event. But it was in a different time ..."

"Are you suggesting that the quality of Sula character six millennia ago is in essence different from what it is now?"

"I meant it was under a different government, one that had its flaws."

"As do we."

"But the government of mothers is the heir of that government."

"And does one forever blame an Heir for the actions of her Dame?"

"An apology of some sincerity beyond a concern for lack of trade might make a difference."

"We apologized millennia ago!"

"It sounded hollow in the aftermath of the Burning."

"I hear the lives lost in the Burning were greatly exaggerated."

"If humyn life is truly a loss."

"Worthy Mayor," Alhern boomed in her deepest voice, stopping all conversation. "I must ask you to remember humility in our collective duty. We are not above other Thyn in the Orb except in ability. And ability does not guarantee moral character."

"I apologize, commander," the mayor said, the truth of her words shivering slightly. She was certainly apologetic for saying them. "I forgot myself. My concerns drifted to the Plague which we must remember was endemic along the shores of the continent."

"But elfyn are immune to plague," one soul said.

"Not actually immune," woman near Eld said. "Our essence vigor destroys it before it progresses to disease. While this battle rages unseen, we can carry it."

The table was suddenly silent. Eld had never known this. Was it true?

"That's absurd," Major Galledan said.

"I assure you, being as the Temple is my lair, I know my business," the woman said.

"But elfyn are immune to disease," the man with Galledan said. "We're above humyn noxious airs."

"The only thing above elfyn, literally and in essence, are dragonkind," the healer said. "We might be immune to the effects of humyn disease, but we have our own 'noxious airs', like 'dread fever'. And the lurking Ghosts in the Bones it can summon."

Eld shivered. Dread Fever was a disease of essence, sapping strength and bringing on deep depression. If not treated, half of souls afflicted would walk through the Door in a dream fugue. Worse, it could trigger latent "ghosts in the bones", memories of ancestral diseases that would waken to horrific effect: blood could become unbalanced, bones brittle, even strange lesions appearing. Most didn't know they had these ghosts; it took an essence surgeon to find then. Fortunately, once dread fever cleared and essence vigor returned, the ghosts and any symptoms vanished. Eld had a deep fear of dread fever as a child.

"The point being, we cannot get sick, much less die from, plague," another woman was saying.

"But livestock can and livestock are valuable."

"And the fostered humyn were not?"

"I didn't say that ..."

"Surely after fostering these foundlings it's long past time they learn to manage themselves," Marshal Tantilaan said.

"Careful worthy. We might find ourselves with more maintenance costs. Between the Cambrian Protectorate, the Skerries and that bacchanal known as Tyrum ..."

"Tyrum more than earns its keep," Alhern interjected. "I might remind the worthy mothers present that the while the Sunqueen's fleets explored much of the Orb, it wasn't circumnavigated before the aqua driven city-ship the Black Ramothyn."

"One wonders if they would have had as much success had she been christened 'The Cabbage Moth'," Rathi said, eliciting the first true laughter at the table. "But your point is sound, commander," he added. "The talents of that aelg city are well fostered by Her Humble Majesty."

"I suppose it's a hobby of sorts, if one is stuck on a rock with savages," Tantilaan muttered.

Alhern sat back staring at the Marshal balefully as her superior cut into a thick portion of beef as if uncertain it was dead. Then Alhern's eyes flitted to Seth, who shook his head ever so slightly. They would not engage and hope the conversation moved on.

"We must remember the limits of our ability," Major Galledan put in. "And when one risks failing in duty because of these limits, one must avail oneself of willing talent."

"I certainly agree," Fathi said. "Grandam has finally decided we are to hire a Dwen to manage the garden. We're just not as able. But she wants us to seek a Wildling –"

"I think we're supposed to say 'Yino' now," some soul interjected.

Fathi sighed impatiently and continued: " – Because they don't charge as much."

Seth leaned towards Eld, breathing a whisper, "It was probably fortunate the Dwen excused themselves from the feast."

"That's very mercenary of your estate," someone was saying.

"Isn't thrift the virtue of a well managed house? I seem to remember many uncles boring me with that aphorism…."

"I was referring to the defense of our western Ethynsul shores, effa," the Red Major said. "Not hiring of gardeners. Before the Sunqueens, the only ships were merchant ships of the Lors, who were little more than pirates, happy to exploit a rival house's vessels. Our fishing boats always had defensive lances to protect women working on the water from humyn piracy or the aforementioned rival vessels. But they didn't patrol with regularity. So our shores were always vulnerable until the first watchtowers were built by the Sunqueens …"

It would have been an interesting lesson in history, but it wasn't a lecture hall, and even the scholarly minded were distracted by the good food, the late hour and the music, so Galledan was forced to work to get to any point. Meanwhile the woman next to Eld, who from her aura must be an older soul, kept trying to engage in small talk, but Eld felt ever so slightly intimidated, though she didn't know why.

"You don't recognize me, do you, cavalier," the woman said.

Eld looked at her. She wore a white vest with yellow scroll brocade, an emerald green coat, with black reeds floating from the shoulders over the back of the chair. Her guardlocks were bound in simple steel clips and she had no spec of glimmer on her hair. Her amber eyes were deep, her hair, dark blond. She did sound familiar.

"Apologies, but no, I can't place you," Eld said. "But I'm certain I will feel like a fool once once you inform me of our acquaintance."

The woman smiled widely. "You probably have never seen me smile. Before or after your healing, and certainly not while invading the wards lecturing me about my business." She laughed at Eld's look of shock.

"Temple Prefect Olthan," Eld said.

"They breath that like as if they're worried it's an invocation. I know you think me an unfeeling old dragon, like my namesake."

"No! I mean, well, perhaps a little. I understand you have your duties."

"Yes, I do. You know the tale of the Dragon who cast our foremothers from the Mother Tree?"

"It's apocryphal. And not supported by historical fact or dreams."

"Yes, much like all those tales of Mother-Gods and heroes our ancestors wove, it didn't strictly happen. But that doesn't mean it doesn't have truth for the soul:

"One day, the tribe of Sunseekers climbed to the highest tree, much taller than the tallest trees today, and saw the ice that had covered the Orb after the Cataclysm was gone and the snow was melting. And, more joyful to the Sunseekers, they found they could light a cone on fire and bring it down to the rest of the people. For the first time since perhaps Er – no one knows how long exactly though we accept it was at least a couple of millennia – there was light and fire and true warmth.

"Yet, though no tree was damaged, to bring fire from the sky into the wood was a Great Taboo. The guardian of the forest came, a great dragon of the wood, with antler shaped horns, each the size of a great oak, herself covered with moss green scales and as large as a mountain hill."

"So, the size of a typical dragon then," Eld said.

"True," Olthan said smiling. "It was her regret that she must revoke the tenancy of the Mother Tree and evict the three tribes. For the Sunseekers would never  feel at ease until they they found a place to  make their fires, the Stoneshapers would never be at rest until they ..."

" ... Found their calling as colonialist, slave trafficking, literalists?"

Several souls listening laughed, including Seth.

"You're as bad as my great-grandchildren. Stop interrupting."

"Apologies."

"The Stoneshapers would never rest until they found the gate to Eurath and the secrets of Avigon. Even the Treerunners had outgrown their home, for the world was changing and the forests would expand and they would be needed to tend them."

"And?"

"And so they left."

"Because a dragon told them to?" Eld said. "I'm not arguing. I've read 'On the Step of the Sky'. I'd also do what a dragon told me to."

Olthan smiled, taking a sip of her elderberry wine.

"The author exaggerates her experiences with the Thyngalu in places. For instance, I'm not certain any elf can safely be snatched from an avalanche in a dragon's claws without injury. No, she can't be lying. The publisher would know. I just wonder, in that exotic place, high in the air, whether she confused a dream for waking truth. At that altitude the air is thin in a way that affects the mind. Only Luserani are completely immune to these effects.

"Anyway, the Dragon in the tale did not tell the three tribes to leave out of malice or inhospitality. But because it was her duty. And it was their time to go."

Eld nodded, not sure she understood the meaning she was meant to take, but was glad the Temple advocate seemed to be genial.

"I hear Boad is well," Eld said.

"The horse is a horse. There is no corruption and that is pleasing. But it could have gone elsewise. That is why discipline in practices exist."

As the main meal was consumed, the conversation turned to poetry and sundry local gossip. One of many differences between a military and an estate gala was, during the feast, the estate had each dish trotted out to fanfare. Whereas a military gala was institutional by arrangement; much like tutor halls, universities, hospitals and temples, food was placed out at once so women might eat what they wished quickly if time was short. Sometimes the after sweets were announced, but here they sat on the table on pedestals and shelved trays, untouched until such a time that the man of the house announced them. Seth rang a small bell, then Solafi and many others took their desired cakes, tarts or cremes. Eld didn't much have a sweet tooth, preferring a thick shortbread baked with lemon custard on the top. A magi sitting near the middle shamelessly seized a whole quarter of a red velvet cake, layered with jam and cream. She was wearing a magi helm, striking a romantic figure from ancient times.

Magi helms were typical of wizards in ancient times. The solstone cabochons surrounding the hat were instead mounted in a crown. But now helms were considered flamboyant. The woman's hair was pulled back in a tail like most of the magi who weren't completely veiled. This wasn't just an aesthetic. In moving essence magi often generated gusts around their person and long elfyn hair was a hassle in contrary wind. A peculiarity of the magi institution meant that all adept magi were awarded the honorific "Ta" to be used with their birth name, something they shared with queens, heroes and dragons. Though outdated for work, magi helms seemed to be wizard formal wear. Instead of robes she wore a silver vest over a black shirt, with a black coat much like her work robes. Eld recognized the woman as Ta Narin.

Fathi, never shy to make a statement, said to Narin, "That's quite a meal! And after you desecrated that quarter goose!"

"Could we avoid such colorful descriptions, please?" Effa Tanmor opined, but he was largely ignored.

Ta Narin didn't even glance up as she attacked the cake with a fork.

"What do you think fuels essence, man? Dew and moonbeams? If I'm to advise the carnival magicians tonight, I'll need more sustenance."

"Be careful, effa," another woman said. "Those who mock magi rarely mock anything after!"

"I am awash in terror!" Fathi said dramatically.

"Oh, I want to see the carnival at midnight!" Solafi said.

"Yes, that would be fun!" Tinyan said.

"I would think such common entertainment would be something you've grown out of," Tantilaan said.

"I also think it would be fun!" Rathi declared boldly, daring the marshal to comment. "Did you arrange this too, dear?" he asked Seth.

"Alas, I cannot take credit for the carnival. Those arrangements were made with the worthies of Gate Step. The carnival is owned by a Yino clan, but I can assure you they were interrogated as thoroughly as any other venture allowed to conduct trade near the grounds."

"I can vouch for their tribe!" the mayor said, to Eld's mild surprise. Souls who thought little of humyn lives often consider the Yino travelers as bad. "They come every year at Sol Suldan, just after the Quickening. And, provided the snow hasn't kept them away, again, around Hal Suldan."

"Well, that seems alright then!" Tinyan said optimistically.

The Marshal did not looked pleased.

As they discussed what they hoped to see at the carnival, Effa Tanmor said to Seth in a low tone, "Not to dampen the festive mood, but I'm not certain it is wise for Solafi to go."

"No!" the boy objected with all the passion of youth. "It's only here for one night! And I'll be escorted surely!"

Here he glanced at Danshor who smiled tightly, a smile that vanished as soon as attention shifted from her. She seemed to be avoiding wine and mead, drinking only water, which Eld thought wise. Eld was more worried Danshor didn't have an appetite, something unprecedented. She had taken no after sweets; her plate still had remains from her first serving uneaten.

"Your time last eve remains unaccounted for," Seth said to his nephew in a soft but stern voice.

The boy looked upset, and his eyes flew to his aunt who, far at the other end of the table. Alhern could not possibly catch the details or context. But a subtle threat emanated from the lad's intense gold eyes; he could ask his aunt publicly, knowing neither male would want to openly explain the details of why they would prefer he stay inside. Eld felt Seth stiffen next to her. He was furious, knowing he was being played like an instrument. But there was nothing for it.

"Very well!" Seth hissed. "You may go. But you will be in the company of your escort at all times." These words made Danshor's eyes widen with horror. "And," Seth added, "First thing on the morrow, after breaking fast, you will disclose all that happened the night before."

"But my music tutor will ..."

" ...Will be told a family matter has come up and you will not have lessons tomorrow. Nor will you be receiving guests until we are satisfied," Seth said firmly.

"Yes, uncle."

The keeper wasn't happy, but nodded curtly in agreement.

"If you wish, you may have the rest of the evening free, Effa Tanmor," Seth said.

"You are very kind. I will accept. The last couple of days have been wearing."

And then another bell rang and the feast was over. Everyone stood, house-girls pulling the heavy chairs back for men to easily rise. Eld was intrigued to see when Ta Narin stood her vest wasn't over a black shirt but a long black tunic that fell to her feet. In truth she looked much like a feudal lor of the old lots would, except they favored dressing in jewel encrusted gold garments.

"Yes, I look as if I'm about to ensorcell a prince and perhaps charm a few stars out of the sky."

She was immediately joined by two other women whose auras vibrated together. They both wore civilian formal attire though all in black, with silver vests. Neither woman had a hat or helm, but they were obviously magi.

"I was explaining our formal wear. She probably thought I was just old-fashioned. Ta Fletharyn and Ta Hondal. "

"She stepped through the misty Triad as the first star appeared," Ta Fletharyn said like a bard beginning a tale.

"The range of that Triad is so mean," Ta Hondal said flatly. "It flickers out if either Sul's or Eurath's auras become excitable. If we could use it as a portal, for all that effort, we might as well have walked."

"It's about five miles in waking, three times that in dreams," Ta Narin said. "Calculations from the ancients suggest you are correct, Hondal: one would need a Triad about a mile and a half away to step through."

"Is that possible?" Eld asked. "We don't have portal doors only because they are calibrated for waking thoughts and dreams?"

"She's been listening to novice debates!" Ta Fletharyn said, laughing. "Briefly, to satisfy this curious whim all intellectual souls fall prey to:

"Calculations for the use of great stones, particularly portals, gates and circles, survive. Some think portals were for passing, gates, for viewing and circles for communing. Others maintain they could all be tuned to these purposes. There is an optimal mathematical distance for these purposes and it's understood in Er there were so many great stones of the same types and sizes attuned to each other, one could chose any structure for any purpose. So, say, our Triad, used to send message post to a Sadol station five miles away, could also be tuned to a station fifteen miles away for dream messages, or, in theory, and this is only theory, a Triad or gate structure, just over a mile and a half away to walk through.

"But remember, there is no credible evidence in records or dreams of a soul in life stepping through from one place to a distant place since before the time of Queens. If it was ever possible, that was long ago and we have lost the means. You party beckons for the carnival, Gilded Hero."

## Chapter 33

# Carnival

The carnival was held in a wicker-like dome in the same south field where
Eld had first sparred with Tershol, the only place large enough to accommodate it and not disrupt roads or traffic.  The wood weave was a larger version of the Yino tent, a cluster of poles bound at one end, set to stand in a
cone on the ground, then bent by wood essence to make a peaked dome.  In
this case it was a vast frame of twisted wood, large enough to hold most of
The Wildling Inn on its  circular floor. Five tiers of benches rose in concentric circles, also woven of wood.  This type of carnival tent was a re-pur-
posed Yino gathering hollow.  The main supports were eight to twelve foot
lengths of pole, from the thickness of two hands to the width of a dowel.
When not in use, they were stacked in special wagons, covered with oil
cloth and stored in wagon parks that served itinerant mothers. The women in
the traveling troupe, with strong bodies and equally strong wood-essence,
would have laid the poles out  earlier in the day, fusing them end to end, to
first make a "spider", which was the size of a Yino hut, but would actually
be the top of the carnival pavilion.  Then they carefully added and fused
poles to the bottom, at the same time propping the entire edifice up with
stray and scrap wood in a scaffold, as they went.  Once it was at its full size,
the poles would be adjusted in whatever way desired, then workers would
weave and attach the cross supports.  The end result looked much like a circle of bare trees that had been bent and flattened against an invisible bell,
their branches weaving and twining together at the sides.  At this point the
entire edifice was given any stability or rooting it required, after which agile
older children clambered among the supports adding more wood for decoration until it was all a dense filigree.  Strictly speaking it wasn't a tent so
much as a grange, for there was no canvas over it except in the worst rain.
But carnival troupes tried to schedule at times rains were infrequent, in the
heat of summer and the dry mid-winter, both  for their convenience and that
of their matrons.  Sula queens would not be easy to catch during a rainstorm.

Now it was evening and the whole of the tent was obscured.  Illumination
from lamps and flickering torches glimmered along the limbs of magically
twisted wood looming over the arrivals, promising mystery and excitement
yet to come.  A thick mist surrounded the walls, glowing with the  light from
within the dome, first amber, then yellow and green. The mist was  likely
magi made because the night wasn't chill enough, though the cold touch of
fine water droplets was real.  A vast, gate-style arch woven together with

sturdy poles marked the entrance, a baroque maw wide enough to straddle a road, swallowing the crowds of the curious gathering in the belly within. A light was mounted at the top of the arch, a warm, white globe making the way clear. Tall torches, real torches with flickering flames, surrounded the outside of the pavilion, adding to the savage mystery. Faint music drifted on the air, a haunting flute stringing together notes that could have been made by the wind through mountain trees on a stormy night. But, apart from the magi-induced mist, the coming night looked to be clear and full of stars.

Their party entered together, but soon Solafi darted ahead, excited to capture seats with the best view, Rathi striding after him. Danshor belatedly quickened her pace to keep up as a chaperon. Eld had tried to discretely engage her on their walk down, but Rathi was annoyingly friendly and gregarious, wanting them all "To be the best of friends tonight, now that ogre of a woman isn't here to confound the mood. Apologies, dear," he added to Tinyan. "I know she's your wife and she must be dear to you."

"Indeed, and I must protest you have not seen her at her best," Tinyan said dutifully. "I do apologize for her wayward words. Especially to you, Effa Alhern."

"It is she who should apologize, effa," Seth said. "But don't let it trouble you. I'm only sad my sister isn't here. She always loved the carnival as a child."

"I'm afraid that's my doing," Rathi said. "I knew this one wanted to go, and why shouldn't he? I can't imagine there's much chance for frivolity entertaining 'command' mothers."

"It is a duty that requires care and attention," Tinyan said carefully.

"Exactly. A recipe for unrelenting boredom. So, I suggested that I could go with, giving this outing the air of respectability the Marshal craves, and my darling Harneth could keep her company in the commander's lounge doing whatever important women do when men aren't around. Reading dispatch reports, news from the Voice, and...what else?" This was directed at Eld to her alarm. "Come, you're a hero of mothers; what do you think they'll be doing?"

"I wouldn't presume to include myself in the description of 'important women'," Eld said. "But I know the commander likes Cambrian Whiskey and chess."

"Exactly, chess," Rathi said. "They'll be staring at dull figures on squares of wood imagining they're reliving past glories of our nation, all the while drinking like barbarians. If we're lucky they'll have forgotten all about us after midnight. That's when they trade stories about whose daughter or niece they're proudest of. So fret not on the idea that you are too old for frivolity. I am twenty-seven decades and am certainly the senior among us. It's impossible for any of you to be too old if I am not!"

With these words, Rathi linked his arm with Tinyan like fast friends, which the younger man seemed happy with. They hurried to catch up with Solafi who was waving excitedly as he stood on the top of a seat in the midst of the thick throng. Seth slid his arm tighter around Eld's and gently guided her in a different direction. Perhaps it was his age for just as Seth did this, Rathi snapped his head around to look at them, red leaves like the crest of a jaybird. For a second he looked surprised. Then his red-gold lips curled in a knowing smile. Seth winked and continued on, dragging Eld in his wake, taking a path up the steps to where, Eld didn't quite know. With the light and fog it was disorienting, and stepping to avoid others also seeking a preferred location only made the exercise more precarious. They were at the top tier of the benches now, where it came close to touching the frame of the dome above them, sturdy branches one could carefully climb if one fancied. Eld spied musicians lurking ten feet or so above the highest tier, in curved seats of wood made for that purpose, their clothes as black as magi and their heads veiled to obscure them. Even their faces were painted or glamored in shades of black and gray, making them all but invisible except to a close observer. At this level Eld could see the entire inside of the tent:

It was arranged much like a typical coliseum, except instead of stone and brick, everything was made of wood twisted to be quickly assembled and disassembled, the tiers of seats looking like an ambitious and confused attempt to weave a basket of concentric circles, narrow planks of wood placed on the tops of the rings for seating. In the exact center of the space was a raised circular platform about as tall as a woman, twenty or so feet in diameter. Eld imagined this was where the Master of Ceremonies, or, as the Marshal said, "carnival barker", would stand. But she'd be pressed to stand anywhere except at the edge, for a pillar of smoke and mist billowed up from the middle of the platform in a thick column fifty feet high, obscuring whatever was at the center, though now and then what looked like thin branches appeared, as if rising out of the earth, the same place most of the light appeared to come from. Whatever was hidden in the mist and light could not be a tree for there was not enough space. A couple ravens fluttered overhead, black wings illuminated warmly, landing briefly on a tier or bench, then launching again. Eld wondered at their presence until one settled on a plank nearby.

~lost elflings?~ it thought.

"No more than any other soul," Eld said out loud.

~you have separated from your flock,~ the raven said.

"How considerate of you, Worthy Raven," Seth said. "Is your flock here as well?"

~ some of them. we fly to trade meat.~

"How do you plan to do that?" Eld asked, imagining a mass of ravens flying with dead rodents and other carrion in their beaks to the fair.

~silly elfling, we help youse coming under the great basket to sit with your flock or find fledglings.~

"Ah," Eld said understanding. "And then you will be given meat after."

~hark! you can count wings and toes!~

"Thank you, Worthy," Seth said. "But we separated from our companions purposefully. We are making for that space if we can." Seth pointed to the top tier opposite the entrance and above a dark doorway where presumably the performers would emerge.

The raven hopped higher and cocked its head.

~the way is clear. i will sit there and wait.~

It flew off to perch in a spot, doing as good a job as an usher or servant keeping spaces for them until they arrived. Once they sat, it flew off, presumably to help others.

"I'm not certain about the stability," Seth said as they sat down. The length of planking was warped, making the seat angle and curve oddly. Being tacked to the greater frame with wood-essence bound strips was the only reason it didn't wobble. "And it's rough."

Eld felt the surface. There was certainly a chance of splinters. She took off her cape. "Stand up and I'll put this down for you."

"My cavalier is so gallant," Seth said, cleaving himself to Eld's side when he was seated again. "What are you smiling at?"

"Being here. With you. Not hiding. I didn't realize how much I was hated hiding. And not just worrying your sister is going to banish me to the southern borders."

"She likes you, you know."

"No, I don't know. I wouldn't presumes to know!"

"Well, she does. And I should know... Ooh! It's starting!"

As custom, country shows of this kind waited until the last light of the sunset faded before starting. The lights dimmed, the yellow-green glow changing to green, then to a blue barely visible, like the color of a dying candle flame. The flutes were replaced by drums, beating first softly, then increasing in tempo, echoing and driving the beat of their collective hearts in anticipation. The blue mist thickened and billowed until the ground surrounding the platform was completely obscured. Then the fog cleared above them and the crowd gasped, because they could see the night sky as if there was no frame. This was a Vision.

Visions were popular in carnival shows but this was one of the best Eld had seen. There was no outline or shadow of the tent frame hovering transparently. Either this company had some of the best wizards, or the magi from the Abbey were assisting. The Vision was simple, the sky at night, not significantly different than any night sky. Then a magically amplified voice echoed around them, narrating what they saw.

"Welcome Mothers and Men of the Orb, and we bid you watch events that happened so long ago. What comes after you might see with new eyes and wonder, for it was a peaceful night all those eons ago when the Dying Star came and unseated the peaceful rule of Er!"

A sudden brightness appeared in a far corner of the sky, as if Athmod had lit a match deep in the Void. The brightness grew and the crowd gasped as a flaming ball of light flew overhead, growing larger and larger, and then, to all of their alarm they saw it was not going to pass harmlessly back into the Void but was doomed to strike the earth they stood on. In the Vision the mass of fire, white hot above them with a halo of red, slowed and a chorus of voices cried out operatically, falling and rising in despair and woe, drowning out many actual voices crying out from children and the excitable. Eld didn't blame them. It looked so real every nerve bid her to duck and find shelter. Instead her hand seized Seth's tighter, and he responded with short gasps as if they were really present in that distant past.

"So great was our doom, so absolute was death upon the Orb, all that remained was for the Worthies of the Great City to cry out to the Void, to the Heavens, to the Mother-Gods of Paradise, that if they ever cared for the Mothers of Eurath, to send salvation and send it quick! And they did!"

Suddenly the perspective of the scene shifted and they were seeing the Dying Star rushing over cloud covered blue oceans. But in the center the air seemed to bend, as if heat waves had made an invisible cyclone. For a second it shivered and bent, deforming the light around it. Then there was a flash and a flock of dragons erupted from it as if from a tear between the world known and the world of the Gods. The dragons tore through the air, faster than the eye could follow, silver and blue saurian bodies heading straight for the Dying Star. A great roar of thunder echoed making every soul jump as lightning erupted from the jaws of the dragons, breaking the threat apart. They flew faster, chasing the fragments of the Dying Star, some of the dragons flying so close in the Vision Eld reflexively pulled them both back as a body with glittering scales barely missed them. For these were the same tribe of dragons, the Thyngalu, Eld had spoken with in thought at the

Abbey. Had the one who spoke to her been there, so many millennia ago? Dragons lived much longer than elfyn, but how long?

"And so the Dragons came and we were saved. But not without a cost. For the Dying Star was so great, even the Thyngalu could not catch all the fragments before they abused Eurath's face."

Lesser meteors, but still greater than cities, struck the sea, turning water to steam instantly, while the land and sky burned. Around them smoke billowed.

"And if that was not enough, once the fires faded, a pall covered Eurath, threatening to hide Her face forever from her sister Sul. Having fled the ruins of Er and saved much of the peoples and beasts of the Orb, now we bade them find shelter, for the Long Winter was coming and we could only shelter until better days came. Even the dragons slept, in high mountain caves of ice and snow, resting after their noble labors. And we? We sought the shelter of the Mother Tree."

The smoke was gone. The snow fell so thickly and seemed so real, only the lack of cold broke the illusion. Everything was obscured, silhouettes of dragons on mountain slopes slowly disappeared, crouching under folded wings, heads tucked, first under snow, then ice, then more snowfall. Deep sonorous calls sounded, the noble race saying goodnight to each other before the Long Winter.

Then the light dimmed to darkness and the Vision vanished. New lights sprang forth, amber and red, growing back to yellow and green, and the mists around the center platform were gone. Revealed was indeed something like a tree, had the branches been somehow folded together in a bundle like a badly made broom. It towered over them, the full length of the column of mist, and now, very slowly, started to separate and expand, like a strange flower made of branches instead of petals. It was making a treelike form, but one constructed for dancers and acrobats, it's farthest branches touching, then twining, with the edges of the dome for greater support.

"And for many generations, three tribes of mothers and men lived in peace under the Mother Tree: the Sunchasers, the Treerunners and the Stoneshapers!"

The dancers appeared as named, rising from between the roots of the false tree. They were women and men in leggings and decorative vests made to illustrate their roles. The Sunchasers had gilded themselves with glimmer much the way Tafli did everyday. The Treerunners resembled Dwen, light green costumes twined with vines and leafy costume yastols. The Stoneshapers made Eld bark with laughter: they all wore caps that were a mix of shaped wood and paper paste to give the impression of crystal

crowns of sapphire, emeralds and rubies. Their costumes were black or dark
brown, with clusters of costume gems, probably glass, around their ankles
and wrists.

Seth laughed soundlessly at Eld's side. "Liberties have been taken with
the truth!" he breathed in a whisper.

"While the Orb sleeps through the Long Winter," the narrator continued,
"The tribes danced under the Mother Tree!"

The dancers started to tumble, spinning and somersaulting out from the
roots, then they danced acrobatically around the bole to the drums, now
joined by flutes and fiddles in a lively, spirited tune evoking adventure and
joy. They leaped up the tree and spun off branches into higher branches,
the disciplines of trapeze work and dancing melding seamlessly together. At
first the dancing tribes mingled together, around the base, then up through
the branches, until the tree was full of cavorting and spinning figures. The
light was first green, then yellow, then green again, as if filtered from far
away through leaves, though Eld seemed to remember the trees in that time
being only cedars and other conifers. Then some dancers, prancing and balancing on branches, dropped in a way they caught themselves and flipped to
tumble to a lower branch, or clasp the hands of another and spun themselves
to switch levels, until the distribution of the dancers changed: the Stoneshapers on the lower branches, the Treerunners in the middle area, pirouetting around the trunk, and the Sunchasers at the top, now gathering together
near the apex of the tree frame underneath a great yellow ball of light slowly
appearing above them. It took on the size and brilliance of the sun, and the
music slowed as if drifting from the center of a fast river into calm shallows,
the operatic chorus heralding the return of Sul's warmth and radiance. From
the base of the tree long batons were thrown up to the Stoneshapers, who
juggled them to the Treerunners, and then to the Sunchasers, who, once having caught them, all stood as high as the "tree" would let them and pointed
the batons to the bright Orb meant to be Sul, at which point the ends of all
the batons burst into flames.

The crowd gasped in delight, surprised they were real flames. The Sunchasers danced in the highest branches, joyful at calling fire down from the
heavens. Then, still holding the torches, they cavorted down the tree, spiraling around the trunk as if it was a circular staircase. They came to the very
base of the tree, to stand on the platform, and then leaped to the ground, one
after another, running in a wide ring between the base of the platform and
the lowest tier of seats. The flutes faded, leaving only drumbeats, while the
orb dimmed, no longer bright yellow, but a pale whitish blue, implying night
had fallen, the sun now becoming the moon. The Treerunners and Stone-

shapers sat or perched among the lower branches while the Sunchasers started to juggle the burning torches while still dancing and cavorting. The skill of the performers was appreciated by the Sula audience all the more because they knew most of the dancers were Yino with strong Dwen streams. Few, if any, would have the inherent ability to quiet errant flames like Sula did. If one of them stumbled and caught fire, they would need to roll ignominiously on the ground or to be smothered with the help of water soaked blankets nearby. But there was no such accident tonight. They danced and caught their torches flawlessly, ending with a final flourish of tossing, catching and spinning their torches to face outward, saluting the audience.

Whistles and claps of applause echoed around the tent for a minute. Then the "moon" dimmed and disappeared.

"Thus did the Sunchasers bring Fire back to the Earth! But this came at a price. The Forest has placed a bounty on those who call down Fire to threaten the wood!"

The light dimmed further. Then came the sound of a vast drum: BOOM.

The drum was either inside the platform or amplified in some way because it shook their very seats. It was struck again: BOOM. And again. And with every deep beat, the "tree" shook, and those dancers still perched in the branches fell as if shaken free, until the Treerunners and Stoneshapers tumbled off the platform to join the Sunchasers who now gripped their low burning torches, crouching in fear. Mist returned, billowing from the roots of the tree, and a new green light appeared, brightening as a form took shape. The tree changed and twisted, folding back together briefly, then parting in the center to make a lens shape, a gate around the brightening green light. Two sharp jets of air shot out of the center of the gate, as if a great beast had exhaled. Eld shivered.

"WHO DARES BRING FIRE TO THE SANCTUARY OF THE FOREST?" a voice bellowed in a very believable attempt at a dragon's ire.

The torches winked out, and the three tribes huddled together as a dragon appeared. It was partly a Vision, Eld knew, but she still felt fear for the dancers as if the gargantuan, green scaled head was truly present. Dragons of the forest, the Thyndwendesh, were much smaller than Thyngalu. But, being dragons, this was relative. The head of a flying dragon was the size of a large house, whereas the head of a forest dragon was only the size of a very large room. Their entire bodies being about two hundred feet long from snout to tail, they were the smallest dragons in the Orb. Found deep in arboreal forests across Eurath, forest dragons had back scales of variegated green that matched the places they lived, and under scales that were brown or earth toned. They had four legs and no wings, but instead a series of antler-like plates that seemed to grow from just behind their shoulders, like the bones of wings that had never come to fruition. On their heads were four elk-like antlers, which on older individuals were often covered with moss and hanging lichens. Their bodies were narrow and sinuous, the better to move between trees as they sought their main food, the fungi-rich decayed hulks of fallen or rotted ancient trees. And when their waste passed, it was called Forest Gold, for a mere handful scattered over a barren field would, once watered, return it to fruitfulness overnight. But it was rare to find fresh dragon spore. Most caches were left for years, even decades, well-aged, and found because of excessive lushness in one area. Thyndwendesh did not mind seekers of Forest Gold, and were reputed to enjoy the company. Still an elf had to be careful: a friendly dragon was still a dragon, and might hurt lesser beings simply by accident.

The dragon in the tale was not friendly, its duty to protect the forest precluding casual society. Her head rose from the green lit mists, exhaling steam from her nostrils, long rows of serrated teeth and fangs bared in a warning grimace. The mouth didn't move, implying thought speech like most Thyn. Only Aelgyn, that is, the class of Singers including elfyn, humyn, orukyn and aelg, were known to have vocal language. No Thyn quadruped could speak like an elf because they did not have elfyn vocal cords. Thus neither did dragons. The dragon's massive head was life size, hovering over the platform from between the lens shaped gate, eyes glowing yellow-green with the pure power of the forest. Dwen weren't the only souls with wood-essence. In fact the very pavilion they were under was inspired by remains of Thyndwendesh lairs.

The dancers bowed, undulating before the beast, humbling themselves in regret and apology. Then they leaped in a series of cavorting moves, gathered the dark torches and piled them before the Mother of the Forest, as she was sometimes called, their offering of sacrifice, before bowing and retreating in obeisance.

"I ACCEPT YOUR OFFERINGS OF APOLOGY AND PEACE. BUT THE LONG WINTER IS OVER AND IT IS TIME TO LEAVE THE MOTHER TREE. GO FORTH MY CHILDREN AND REMEMBER ALWAYS, HOWEVER FAR YOU WANDER FROM EACH OTHER, YOU ARE ONE PEOPLE WITH ONE DUTY: TO KEEP THE ORB WHOLE. FAREWELL!"

And the dragon exhaled steam one last time, slowly disappearing from view while flutes struck a sad, haunting tune of loss and longing, after which came hope and new beginnings. Spinning and pirouetting together once more around the platform, the tribes, one by one took their leave, first the

Sunchasers, breaking from the group to run around the platform before disappearing into the dark doorway beneath where Eld and Seth sat. They were followed by the Stoneshapers, then the Treerunners, until all that was left was the lens gate which now closed completely and twisted slightly in on itself. The mist and green light faded while, at the same time, a solar orb reappeared above the tree, bright as daylight, and it was something of a relief to see properly again.

But this was not the end of the show but a transition: the music of flutes, viols and drums thrilled energetically, like a triumphal parade. The crowd gasped and muttered, children in particular pointing to the light. A figure hovered, slowly descending as if she was an Eirok , that is, a Luserani elfyn, who could hover on the air without training in a Magi school. It was impossible to tell if this was truly the case or if she was being lowered mechanically.

"And so a new dawn came to the Orb!" the figure boomed, arms spread wide. "And the mothers worked, and the beasts thrived, and you will see them all, strange and rare wonders from the far corners of Eurath!"

"Orbs don't have corners," an extremely literal child said out loud.

"Hush!" a man's voice said.

The woman was clearly visible now, a typical Master of the Carnival, wearing a bright yellow formal coat that shimmered with many small gems of cut glass over its lapels. Long reeds of white tree-silk drifted from the back of her shoulders, and a vest coat of pale green velvet was covered with dark wood twining designs. It might even have been wood twinings, like the Dwen women at the gala. She wore white breeches and tall, dark boots with wood soles and twinings that sprouted up to wrap decoratively around her ankles. Her red hair was long and loose, brushed back from her forehead, floating on the air under a Yino yastol. She was a darker hued soul, such that with her green eyes flashing in the light, she reminded Eld strongly of the last Eurthan she'd fought. The woman was yards from the top of the platform, where she would land facing the the door, and therefore obscured from Eld's seat by the pillar of twinings that had been the dancing tree. One foot was extended, the other behind a knee, ready to gracefully step out of the air. Then she disappeared from view, but not for long. As she spoke, she walked around the platform edge, so all could see her clearly.

"As the lives of mothers and men are constrained by time, place, and duty, we bring to you sights and Visions impossible to find without making a life's work of sailing the many seas. Behold, the noble peacocks of the savage jungle realms!"

And out from the gate beneath them strutted a flock of blue birds, with long, thick tails of iridescent feathers. Like most, Eld had seen pictures and paintings of peacocks, and their feathers were easily found in shops. But she'd never seen one in life, only their cousins, the blue fowl bred from them for domestic meat on the western coast. Those birds had the same shape but were slightly larger, with no bold colored feathers. These birds were almost dainty in comparison as they strutted around the outer edges, a couple of wranglers dressed in blue and gold, walking with them. Once the birds had made a ring, they turned to face the audience and spread their feathers in great rainbow-hued fans to the sighing appreciation from the crowd.

"I read these are all males," Eld said. "The mothers are dull colored."

"Of course!" Seth replied. "We like to make a spectacle of ourselves!"

The birds turned around on the spot, as if hoping to catch the eye of a female of their tribe. As they did, another Vision filled the minds of those watching, of lush trees and large bright flowers, of bright sun and the call of other creatures the peafowl lived with. It reminded Eld of the style decorating Anda's memorial. Her people were certainly familiar with this jewel colored bird.

The Vision faded and the peacocks were marched out, most of their feathers folded. A couple individuals broke from the group to trot closer to the stands, fanning out their feathers hopefully to laughter. Eld realized they were begging, beadily eying Tartar Orbs and bread, before being shooed back to the door, a couple screeching horribly in protest.

"Yes, very beautiful," the narrator said. "But not much talent at singing, alas. Feast your eyes now on the Dragon of the Isle Forthos!"

The crowd gasped in alarm, for while this wasn't an actual dragon, it was a very large lizard-like creature that walked on two legs with a tail almost as long as its body. But it walked oddly, body not upright but forward, and when it opened it's mouth and called, it sounded like a roaring caw of the largest crow Eld had ever heard. It had scales, but, looking keenly, they were neither like dragon scales, nor lizard scales, nor even fish scales. Something about them suggested compacted hair or fibrous horn. It had a couple of arm-like forelimbs with claws suggesting hands. All its claws were easily as long as a finger, and its mouth was full of knife-like teeth. It looked at the stands with curiosity and Eld could feel its hunger barely sated. But she also felt a link; that was the only thing that made her relax. There was a soul she was linked to, imprinted from hatching, a woman who lurked under the seating, hiding to give the audience a thrill of danger.

"This creature's tribe was found and saved from loss long ago by elfyn caretakers, perhaps from Er of old. They are few and this one has been gifted to tour the Federation for but a while, before returning home. Only Forthos is as hot and humid as the place of their ancestors, with enough prey to fill them. But behold a most curious Vision! They share the soul of bird-kind!"

And they saw the island of Forthos, an even hotter place than the land of the Indus tribes. Giant ferns grew among palm trees and herbaceous plants that weren't truly trees, but grew so large as to make the difference academic. There were other types of this lesser dragon, strange creatures with horns and plates, that Eld was certain had souls closer to crocodiles. When the vision faded, the dragon was still standing before them, but had been joined by one of the ravens. They strutted around each other, the raven fluttering back if the dragon got too close. Perhaps it could not believe this beast was somehow related to it.

The raven's thought, ~uncanny~ echoed to nervous laughter of the onlookers.

Eld had never been certain of the assertion that birds held the echo of the Age of Petty Dragons, most of whom were long dead before the Cataclysm, their bones turned to stone, the only evidence they had lived in the Orb. But it was clear from watching the "dragon" and raven: their legs moved exactly the same way, with the same balance. And seeing this, the scales made sense: they were dense fused feathers, or rather, what came before feathers. Then the dragon called in excitement, so terrifying and loud, the raven took flight immediately.

"You are wise, Worthy Raven" the barker said as the wrangler ran out to seize the dragon's collar and drag it out of the ring like an errant hound. "Sometimes meeting our kin is not the pleasant event we'd like it to be, as we often learn around Hal Suldan."

The laughter was partly the woman's wit, but more relief that the dangerous beast, however interesting, had been safely withdrawn.

"I'm concerned about their wranglers," Eld murmured. "They don't seem to be completely in control of their charges."

"Are you always the master of Fiorseth?"

"If Fiorseth runs wild, the worst she will do is find a field with sweet apples to devour, not try to consume an elfyn child."

"Oh, surely the beast is only interested in sheep and goats," Seth said.

"Seth, I met its mind. If not for its link, it would attempt to eat anything it could catch. It might be a cousin of bird kind, but it sees us as ravens see carrion. I'm surprised they're allowed on the continent."

"Like I said before, their papers and warrants are all in order. Now stop fretting."

The menagerie march continued, striped wolf-cats from a distant, hot, dry land; a giant python entwined around a man wearing only a stick yastol and leaf felt, his eyes and lips outlined in black gall; he was introduced as Athmod's brother as he danced glamorously with his alarming charge, coming close to the audience, snake held high as it twined around his arms for support. Eld was relieved their seat was as far up as possible. The last of the menagerie was a mastodon, ridden by a man in a turban and red silks, a very romantic and wildly inaccurate portrayal of both Indus and Shari tribes. The Indus used elephants, certainly, but did not wear turbans, at least not jeweled fantasy things like the man did. As for the Shari, they rode camels and their rulers had degenerated into a cult of patriarchy, obsessed with the slaving of mothers, the ironic result being their men did not look at all masculine to the elfyn eye. This ingénue perched on the pachyderm with glimmer and gilded lips only vaguely looked like a savage humyn man, the lack of facial hair destroying any attempt at realism.

But there were two humyn warriors, Gaels from Cambria, necks circled with thick gold torcs, hair stiffened like horses' manes, wearing plaids of green, red, blue and white. They fought with round shields and bronze leaf blades, beautifully crafted for humyn, but far inferior to modern elfyn steel. They wore thick leather slippers and put on quite a show; one was a woman and the other a man, perhaps sister and brother, both elfyn tall but thicker in the body than elfyn with the same muscularity. And they had many tattoos of dots and complex intertwining knots. Yet they were partly a fraud, for Eld spied, hidden under the wild hair, they both had normal ears, and Eld was certain, like Roel's locks, their rounded brows and the man's beard was hair attached by gum. It was not as thick as a humyn beard, but their complexion, pale and ruddy, seemed real. Eld guessed they were Cambari, aelg or elfborn, fed by a father of the Cambrian tribes. The "savage" striped bracs, bound with thongs at the ankles, were bracs sold in any shop, dyed to expectations, the thongs hiding their mundane source. But the fight was entertaining, played broadly for spectacle, in the end both 'dying' tragically in a mutual embrace. Moments later they leapt up to applause, shaking their swords and shields defiantly.

"And now our time together draws to a close," the Master of the Carnival intoned. The light dimmed and the flutes blew sighing tones of wistful regret. "After the March of the Orb comes the night! Hark! And listen as the moths gather in the moonlight. For behold! Lun, the Laird of the Night himself, has come to sing!"

485

The orb dimmed again, and also shrunk, so a man could stand under it visible but not overwhelmed. He perched at the very tips of the pillar of branches, wound in flowing, white, silk reeds and vestments, a silver girdle twined helix-like around his body in a way many believed was worn in Er and, as poets imagined, all Mother-Gods and Goddi. The man wore a hastol of glittering silver and glass, his glimmer silver as well, making a more accurate Vision of Lun than Seth ever had. The song, "Ramparts of the Moon", was well known, as was the theme, a shepherd woman taken with Lun in the night:

*Long after the day*
*In the cool of the eve,*
*Looking up high*
*In the deeps of the sky,*
*I fell into sleep*
*Then woke in a dream;*
*Behold! and be there*
*Was Lun standing fair!*
*Crowned with his beauty*
 *And his white starry band,*
*With the breath of a kiss*
 *He took my hand ...*

~

*Far and away!*
 *We flew like birds ...*
*Far and away!*
 *beyond all worlds ...*
*Far and away!*
 *On the ramparts of the Moon!*
*Far and away ...*

~

*In the land of the Moon*
*Fall the leaves of the Sun,*
*Every house a silver palace*
*Of white moonglass spun*
*With starry magic*
*For the Fete of the Full,*
*When stars came to dance*
 *'Neath the White Laird's Rule.*
*In that bright domain*
*The Lors of the Stars*

*Hungered for his hand*
*But it was I whom he chose*
*Common shepherd of the land*
*Thus took he my hand ...*

~

*Far and away!*
 *We flew like birds ...*
*Far and away!*
 *beyond all worlds ...*
*Far and away!*
 *On the ramparts of the Moon!*
*Far and away ...*

~

*All night in his bower*
*Bedecked with moon flower,*
*We danced and we twined*
*Until heady with drink*
*From the cup of Lun*
*In which every mother sinks.*
*Then a horn sounded*
*The return of Sul!*
*Jealous her wrath,*
*Awful her rule!*
*And the Vision faded*
*In the mists of the dawn*
*Thus I woke cold*
*On the dew of the lawn*
*The touch of Lun's memory not long gone*
*When I in his land*
*Where he took my hand ...*

~

*Far and away!*
 *We flew like birds ...*
*Far and away!*
 *beyond all lands ...*
*Far and away!*
 *On the ramparts of the Moon ...*
*Far and away!*

~

The man sang in soprano and alto at the same time, a controlled voice that had a future in an opera house. No elfyn was unable to sing at all, but most souls could only master either their high or low voice. Professional singers could do both. Rare talents, like this man, could do both simultaneously. There was no Vision; he was no bard able to project the image of the story into the minds of listeners. But hearing a good voice was its own pleasure.

Yet there was more to the performance. The moths were not just a metaphor. As "Lun" sang, shadowy figures clustered against the underside of the tent frame and Eld saw they were small dancers, adolescents and children, dressed as moths. There were two kinds, white and tan, their caps with large leather costume antennae, their bodies covered in long vests of fur. Credible wings draped off their backs, some light framing with silk or paper. The "moths" did nothing until an instrumental break in the song, whereupon they "flew" in acrobatic trapezes to the music, using the tent frame to launch and land from. While admiring the skill, Eld could not fathom allowing either of her children to engage in such a performance, no matter how close the Temple was. This seemed much more dangerous than the tree dance; if one missed catching an undercut of the dome frame, there was no alternative except to fall to the ground. Their lighter weight made it a little safer, but not safe enough for the mother in Eld. But no dancer missed her or his landing. The dance slowed as Lun sang his last verse, and the moths landed around him as his arms raised. They covered him, his last echoing cords fading, all perched at the top of the bound branch tips, before the moths suddenly tumbled away revealing Lun had disappeared as he did in many tales. It was a fine effect and Eld whistled loudly with the crowd.

The drums started again, accented with a viol and flute for effect, while the Master of the Carnival started to rise into the air. Eld again tried to see what mechanics were behind this, but failed in the dim light.

"We thank you, Mothers and Men, and other Worthies of the Orb, for coming to our humble show. Lastly we leave you with this vision ..."

And once again the center of the tent disappeared as completely as if it had been wiped from reality and replaced, this time with a Vision of the Void. Black and full of stars, yet one star drew closer, bright and blue, with a smaller white companion. They flew past the companion Orb, only briefly glimpsing it's gray pocked surface, until the blue Orb filled their sights, vast oceans and lands made pastel with distance, covered with feathered white spirals of clouds. Here and there, in the part of the air that touched the Void, were tracers of flashing lights with hints of rainbow colors.

"You see the flocks of Thyngalu flying high on the old paths of Er, keeping the memory of all that was lost alive! Yet the Orb lives and so does our task, no matter how far we find ourselves from each other, know that we are One People, with One duty!"

It was a painfully beautiful sight, the Orb of Eurath, swathed in the blue oceans of Her sister Maer. Eld had tried to see it in dreams, but when her soul came close to the Void, she would always panic and wake in a sweat. Seeing it in a Vision was better than the best paintings. The magi must be assisting for this Vision needed the memory of someone who had Seen for the view to smote a soul to the core. The reminder of their connection as a race to their ancient duty was the closest in the modern nation to a shared religion. Unbidden every mother and man murmured, "Always and forever."

The Vision slowly faded and the amber light rose, glowing out of the platform, the mists long gone. The show was over.

Subdued music suitable for theatrical interludes played as the crowds started to make their way out, many girls making a game of leaping down the seats once they were cleared. Eld stood, looking for Danshor and the rest, but Seth held her arm, pulling her back to let others go out before them.

"Shouldn't we join them?" Eld asked.

"I'm sure Rathi with be able to manage without us," Seth said with mischief in his eyes.

They stood on the back of the seats as those around them filed out.

"I know your sister is taking to me," Eld said, "But I'm not sure I should test her."

"Well, in truth, my duty to her house is long done for the day. And since you're nearly respectable and Rathi is a discreet sweet thing, I'm certain he will only tell my sister that I'm out late with a bold cavalier. And," Seth added to forestall Eld's objection, "I know soon the lights will vanish."

As if on cue the lights did exactly that, plunging them into darkness.

"Because now there is to be the fireworks show," Seth continued. "Just at midnight. If we get to the top of the pavilion, we'll have the best view of any soul!"

Eld looked up in alarm, but before she could say anything, Seth was climbing adroitly onto the back of the highest bench where it came within stepping distance of the frame. The darkness didn't seem to hinder him, nor the concern of the twenty foot fall off behind the seats.

"This is too dangerous!" Eld objected.

"Don't be silly! I did this all the time as a child. Selind and I would sneak out when the carnival was in town ..."

"You were younger and lighter ..."

"And now I'm ancient and heavy with years ..."

"That's not what I meant! And you're not dressed for it...."

"Oh, stop being a grumpy Aeon! If a horse can carry you, so can this frame, and it can certainly hold me."

Then, maddeningly, he was gone.

Trying not to think how much Alhern would roast her if the commander ever found out, Eld shed her cape and clambered after Seth. In some ways his soft shoes made it easier, but his robe was another matter. Billowing in the light wind, his reeds fluttering like sails; they could easily be stepped on by accident. Seth was correct about the sturdiness of the frame. Many of the wood slats were even flattened or squared for ease of climbing. But Eld's cavalry boots were not the ideal footwear. Had she not been elfyn it would have been a deadly thing to attempt. As it was, it simply required more of her attention than she'd like, and made her desire to harangue Seth out of this adventure impossible. It didn't take long to reach the top, but the wind was stronger than Eld would have wished and the air was chill. She was surprised and pleased to find the apex of the pavilion was almost a crows-nest; where all the top poles met, it was reinforced with a platform, the extra length of the poles circling it about three feet high. The space was only a couple feet wide, but ample enough for lovers.

"See? I told you it was safe and stable," Seth said, his face glimmering in the starlight.

"Stable, I'll grant you," Eld said, bracing herself against the sturdiest poles and pulling Seth close, less for intimacy than to ensure he didn't fall.

Still, it was an excuse as good as any for Seth to kiss her.

"Now, isn't this romantic?"

The view without a doubt would be notable by daylight. But now the only sights visible shined with their own light: The Wildling and village street lamps, the watch towers on the garrison walls, and the field pavilions still aglow with activity. Scattered in the distance were glowing windows from farm houses. Above the night was deep and stars twinkled brightly as if to echo Seth's fancies.

"Yes, though it would be more romantic if I didn't worry about us falling."

Seth twined his arms around Eld's neck. "My poor cavalier. What's this?"

Pressed against her, he'd felt the lump in her inner coat pocket.

"Well, if you must know, it's a present ..."

Seth's teeth reflected brightly. "Should I seek it out?" he asked, hands on her coat.

"I'd rather you wait until we were firmly afoot."

"Were you planning to give it to me tonight?"

"Well, yes."

"My cavalier!" And without waiting he'd adroitly fished out the small box, Eld feeling powerless to stop him, their safety being more important than the trinket. She could replace it if she must. Eld wondered if he was giddy from exhaustion or excitement like Danshor had been earlier.

"It's such a small box," Seth said, frowning in mock disappointment.

"Rings come in small boxes." Two could play coy.

"But it couldn't possibly be a proposal. You're not allowed yet. And I'm not interested in eloping when we both know we can get what we want honestly. So ...perhaps a ringling?"

A ringling was Dwen inspired style of ring, given as favors to lovers. They were twined out of wood or twigs by Dwen as tokens of affection. The Sula version, made of gold or silver, was considered a step to betrothal.

Eld was beaten. The quicker he opened it, the quicker he'd be to get a firmer grip, on both his mood and position. "I suppose. Your only option is to open it."

"I suppose," Seth echoed, smiling.

When he opened the box his smile changed to look of astonishment.

Eld was surprised too. The orb, an inch in diameter, glowed even though the night was dark. It could have been residual, but it didn't fade. In fact it drew brighter, but not as warm as it might be in sunlight. It was the starlight, for it was within Eld's aura and now channeling starlight was almost as easy as the sun. Eld tightened her grip on Seth's waist as he drew the orb out and wrapped the fine gold chain around his fingers. Inside was rose-gold water and gold sparkle, not simple mica. But instead of a helix of hammered brass or gold, two strands of hair were wrapped tightly like a tiny rope and then further twisted with skill into a spiraling "8" shaped loop so that it fit the inside as perfectly as a glittering metal coil. And they did glitter in their own way, one strand blond white, the other, Eld's, golden honey colored, the memory of living essence trapped in the strands like an insect in amber, shimmering where the light caught it. And around the outside, extending from the hanging loop, a thin tapering thread of hammered gold was coiled like a vine.

"That's us twined together," Seth said. "You stole my hair."

"It traveled on my coat actually."

"Well then, that's Fate," Seth said. "It's… it's glorious."

"Thank you. Now put it on before it falls and I have to get a new one made."

"You truly know the romantic poetry of the ancients," Seth said as he clasped it around his neck. With that brief motion the shimmer inside started to dance and the glass glowed brighter. In spite of herself Eld was moved. It was a beautiful work and it warmed her deeply Seth adored it. And he was right, this was romantic. What did it matter the they were perched over thirty yards in the cold windy air. The Temple was indeed nearby.

Still holding his waist firmly, Eld kissed Seth deeply and he responded enthusiastically as fireworks erupted in the sky over them.

## Chapter 34

# Euphoria

"Are you both utterly mad?" the wizard shouted at them, her magi helm glowing in the starlight. "If we hadn't been up in those rafters working nearby-"

"Please, emha, if you do transform us into anything, be assured we are the same creature," Seth said clutching Eld's arm.

Eld felt pleasantly happy about this. "We could be birds," she said. "Falcons on the air!"

"Oh yes," Seth agreed. "And we would fly under the wings of dragons!"

They were near the pavilion, the fireworks long over, but people were still about, and while they lingered, the food mongers and performers also lingered. Carnivals were an opportunity for the casually talented to try themselves in the public for gratuity. Thus tall baskets stood in places next to women, and some men, juggling knives, eating fire or even sword dancing, a Picti or Gael custom, Eld couldn't remember which. There were also sorcerers creating Visions with torch or starlight, or "wizard juggling", which was just another way to describe making small objects float around a soul with essence. Many of these would be magi students working for pocket money. Eld had forgotten how magical a carnival could be and was filled with a feeling of deep equanimity and happiness, especially when she remembered kissing Seth at the top of the pavilion.

However, this was a minority opinion. Ta Narin's aura and eyes glowed as brightly as if they were under the day sky at noon.

"I'm shocked at you, Effa Alhern!" Narin said. "I know you to be a sensible man and can only assume you are not yourself, or I'd wonder what kind of idiots would perch on the top of the grange just to share a kiss!"

"That, noble wizard, would be the romantic kind." Seth said this with a smile of deep satisfaction. It sounded like a perfectly reasonable explanation to Eld, so she was perplexed why Ta Narin continued to look affronted. Her mood was not improved when Seth added, "And if it bothered you to see us kissing, you had only you look elsewhere."

"How could we miss you?" Ta Narin said, eyes still blazing. "You glowed so brightly a soul could see you for miles!"

"Really?" Eld said, finding she was smiling. "Even from Falls Gate?"

"That's a very nice thought, isn't it?" Seth added.

Narin's face became blank and unreadable, but at least her eyes stopped blazing a little. "I see," she said, as if pronouncing a judgment.

Then they were joined by Rathi, the torch light shimmering blood red where it hit the satin of his robe. Danshor and the rest of their party were right behind him.

"Thank you for seeking me, Ta Narin! I hear you've had an adventure, darling," Rathi added to Seth.

"Oh yes!" Seth said. "I'm giddy with delight!"

"You certainly are giddy," Rathi said briskly, peering at him.

"I suppose we are," Eld added, smiling wider. She didn't usually smile this much if there wasn't a reason to laugh. Then Seth did laugh, and Eld laughed with him, and they spontaneously took each other's hands and turned in a couple of dance steps. Danshor didn't seem to like this because she started glaring just like Ta Narin. Eld wondered if she'd ever seen Danshor so dour. Something troubled her, but Eld couldn't remember exactly what. That must be the reason.

Rathi stepped close to Narin to whisper, "Were they found ... twined?" he asked.

"They're not Dwen," Narin said crossly.

"I mean, were they found coiting? I'm attempting discretion."

Solafi giggled uncontrollably.

"Oh. No, I don't think so. They were completely clothed during their reckless adventure."

"Well, at least there's that." Rathi sighed, peering at Seth and Eld in turn. "Try to stand still, darling. And you, try to remember you are on duty as a chaperon."

This reminder did seem to bring Eld out of her buoyant mood enough to stop dancing. "He's right, Seth. I should be escorting you, properly." She secured Seth's arm in her own and Seth sighed, leaning into her side.

"This is the second infatuation," Rathi said like a healer issuing a diagnosis. "When auras become suddenly entwined it induces intoxication. My wife and I went through this a couple of times. It fades when equilibrium returns."

"Equilibrium?" Solafi asked, still giggling.

"There are a couple of means, but the only one we need to discuss in public is food and sleep."

"I don't recall this happening with Egalsh, before or after marriage," Tinyan said.

"The Orb doesn't wonder, dear," Rathi said. "Well, can you remember your duty to escort Effa Alhern, cavalier?"

This was addressed to Eld.

"Yes, my duty!" Eld replied. "Always and forever!"

Seth sighed. "My Gilded Hero."

"Sel preserve us, I suppose that will do. Come, my gallowglass." This last Rathi said to Danshor, implying she was his personal mercenary, like the Gael warrior of the same name. "I swear you to secrecy."

"Effa, I'm not sure ..." Danshor began.

"Not literally. But there no reason anyone needs to know if they don't ask."

"Us as well?" Tinyan asked seriously. "The marshal is my wife ..."

"Oh, child, if you don't learn how to have your own life in marriage, you will go mad before your second century. This wasn't a military maneuver, and no one, thank Sel's Starry Orb, was hurt. Let's get some food in them-selves before we return. Look, there's a sausage monger."

Rathi strode forward, a firm grip on Seth's other arm, to an open charcoal grill near a table lit with torches. The coals were orange-red, spent and dy-ing, a dozen or so cooked links skewered for convenience, resting on the grill for warmth. They were the last of the day. These were not the fancy novelty kind, long narrow links, twisted and twined to cook in interesting shapes, but thick and simple, a reasonable light meal.

Rathi gave some flint coins to Danshor to pay for the food, thanking the Yino cook, then passed out four skewers; Danshor had waved away the offer of one. The men brought out rough muslin napkins, carried in their robe pockets for such purposes. Officers also had napkins as part of their uni-form, but they weren't required of the regular host. Eld only remembered to bring them when her children were around, so she borrowed one of Seth's. The meat was delicious, spiced with peppers, cumin, clove, onions, dried apple and sage. What meat was often a subject of debate.

The sausage was a barbarian food. There were elfyn foodstuffs with the same concept: scrap meat ground and mixed with spices. But these were boiled in muslin, or baked inside fish or fowls, or breads, or even grilled like pancakes. The idea of putting such a mixture into the cleaned intestines or stomachs of beasts was, to put it politely, odd to the elfyn mind. Gut and of-fal was useful for so many other practical things and not seen as suitable for food stuffs, no matter how clean. Such food had been considered beneath cultured society for millennia. Several Sunqueens, or their scribes, wrote in sympathetic distaste of the ".... Wretched barbarian of such low means she is forced to feed her weanlings such poor and desperate fair!"

But with the Diaspora of Yino, who often camped, lived and twined with both humyn and Dwen, the practicality of sausages for a nomadic people was invaluable. First exposed to elfyn through traveling carnivals, children in particular took to them, as well as Tartar balls, fried cremes (deep fried, raised bread, filled with fruit, spiced nuts or custard) and tonic sodas. Several centuries later many households served sausages with breakfast or luncheon, but they were still considered unsuitable for the dinner table. And some souls considered them an offense against modesty.

"But sausages are indecent!" Tinyan exclaimed, both thrilled and appalled, holding the skewered meat uncertainly in his napkin.

"Oh, for the love of our ancestors," Rathi said. He took a large bite, his teeth snapping impatiently. "Eating food that vaguely –and if you've been marking yourself bathing it is quite vague, dear boy! – vaguely resembles our nethers is not going to turn you into a harlot! Or shift your passions to brothers. One wonders how the Marshal ever got those two sprites out of you ..."

The nephew had a hard time eating because he couldn't stop laughing, then got a bad case of hiccups. The cure for that was a sweet tonic of lemon water, and there was such an abundance at the end of the day they were encouraged to drink as many cups as they wanted. Then they were briefly waylaid by a gold faced, black garbed tumbler and contortionist, a very thin woman who mimed first shock and surprise at seeing them, then appeared to be dragged by an invisible beast or foe, unseen by anyone as it grabbed her feet to throw her several feet to one side, than the other, holding her upside down, then pushing her away, though she struggled against it. This was all expert miming, but the sounds were quite convincing. Solafi and Tinyan were fascinated, but Rathi was short of patience for this sort of performance.

"For Sul's sake woman, get eaten and be done with it!"

Eld pulled Seth close. "Where's the beast?"

"You're still witless, are you?" Rathi asked. "There is no beast!"

"But we can hear it." Seth said.

"That, dear metee, is because, in addition to being a mime, she is a ventriloquist."

"No, she's not," a voice said that appeared to come from behind them. "A beast stalks us! A fell ogre–"

"Not as fell as my temper!" Rathi said throwing a couple coins down. "Good night and begone!"

After one more brief struggle with the invisible ogre, the woman tumbled to snatch up the coins before cavorting out of sight.

It was well after midnight and the grounds were clearing as the carnival crews prepared to retire. Eld saw the 'dragon' being led away in a halter and chain. Unlike in the show, she wore a sturdy muzzle but was otherwise placid. Eld felt none of the worry or alarm she had before. Obviously the wranglers knew their business. Unseen, several harsh calls of a bird rang

496

out, somewhere between a the loudest owl and a rooster. It could only be the peacocks: Eld had read, like parrots, their rich plumage was at odds with an unlovely voice. They were all in good spirits as they walked back to the garrison gates, with the sole exception of Danshor who continued to glower and speak in monosyllables. When they passed within, Eld and Seth made for the commander's house, but Rathi stopped them.

"Hold there, Jaro and Lun!" Rathi said. "I think you've been escorted quite sufficiently for the night, Effa Alhern."

Eld had the idea the consort said this as a reminder. Yes, looking around, they should be discreet. She would just kiss Seth on the cheek. But when she tried, Danshor of all people yanked her back by the arm.

"Thank you, cavalier," Rathi said to Danshor, having taken a firm hold of Seth. But that was well, Eld thought. They stood smiling at each other while Rathi spoke. "Once they're rested, I'm sure they'll return to themselves. The women will be waiting, my poor wife bored to despair, so we should go. Farewell and good eve."

"Effa," Danshor said, bowing low, Eld belatedly imitating her.

When Eld stood she felt dizzy. Seth was walking away, looking back. Why did he have to walk away?

"Come on," Danshor growled. "The sooner I put you in bed, the sooner I can get a drink."

"Why are you so unsettled?" Eld asked as they walked to the stables. "The carnival was a spectacle to fill the soul!"

"Maybe the infatuated soul," Danshor muttered.

Eld didn't know what to say to this. Happy as she was, she was tired and the prospect of sleep and dreams was welcoming so she didn't inquire further. Once in her cot she fell almost instantly into sleep, feeling herself fall in a way that preceded the soul waking in true dreams.

Eld woke and stood on a pathway in the air, high above the clouds and sea below, a dizzying sight. Yet Eld was invigorated by the sight and not troubled, certainly less troubled than she had been at the top of the pavilion. Perhaps this was because she knew in dreams she could fly, and injury from death or fall was impossible. The pathway was a thin ribbon of opal-blue light, shifting as the winds shifted but constant all the same, and it twisted away meeting other paths of light, weaving together, going everywhere and nowhere. The old philosopher's question rose: what was the name of the road whose destination was yet to be determined? The naming of a road began with the first step and until the final step anything else was a suggestion. And there were many suggestions, many possible paths. As Eld watched, the paths seemed to spiral down and away into the starry darkness below the

Orb of Eurath that she hung over. Flickering in and out of her sight were figures, elfyn figures, robed in mantles that floated on the lightest breeze like the man who sang as Lun at the carnival. And like him, they wore girdles that wound helix-like around their bodies, tight at the waist, then ending in open points above their heads and below their feet where they hovered. But it was no silvery costume metal or cloth, but something different, a translucent metal that twisted like wood and flowed like water, yet kept its form. Even after changing briefly into mist, it would return to the form that mind essence bid it.

It was what Eld imagined etheric metal to be like, the mythical substance used in Er to manifest all the wonders attributed to the ancient world, especially the control of weather. Like the Master of the Carnival said, dragon flocks followed the memory of these old paths. And here they existed, but only in dreams.

"Eesh no hea, athlee maan oo," an echoing voice said. Eld was surprise she didn't understand because dream speech, like thought speech, was usually mutually intelligible.

~That is because you are in a place of both Dreaming and Wakefullness,~ a man said. ~ Our languages have drifted much over time.~

He was the most beautiful man Eld had ever seen. Layers of opal white, lavender and blue reeds hovered around him, making the robe of the same shifting colors hard to discern. He hovered several feet away from her, in a helix of starry metal and mist wrapped around him that seemed to twist and twine in places this individual preferred. On his head was a crown-like headdress of spiraling tendrils of the same etheric substance, suggesting both horn and a yastol, if a yastol grew and never stopped. Parts of it would vanish, and then reappear. His skin was white, not pale or ruddy, or even milky, but it glowed from a light within, as if it was transparent and his body was filled with starlight. His hair was striking in that it was so long it fell to his feet, or would have if it wasn't constantly hovering. It was also the palest silvery blue, something never seen naturally. He had no shoes, though some of the silvery, glassy metal twined around his ankle and instep. She half expected his eyes to be black and filled with stars like the dead. It wouldn't have surprised her if he was a shade or ghost of Er. Instead his eyes shined white, with stark black pupils floating, twin imperfect eclipses of the sun. And those eyes could see everything.

Eld felt her heart race, though she shouldn't. Her body felt real, so real she looked down to see herself naked, exactly as she slept.

"Where are we?"

~You are at one of the Edges.~

"Edges of what?"

~The Twilight.~

"The Twilight? The lost Guardians of Er?"

The man smiled. ~We are not lost. We know exactly where we are. You, however, have strayed from you regular paths. The casual dreamer usually only comes to us through Euphoria.~

"Euphoria?"

~Your passions were excited in some way far beyond your usual harmonic.~ he said, his thoughts echoing with interest and excitement. He was somehow very close, yet very far away, as if Eld was aware of both her body's place in her bed and her soul's presence in the dreaming land. If she had been a literal soul with no education, she'd been certain he was a Goddi, perhaps even Lun himself.

~No, I am not a godling, but I am here. And you are an attractive soul, full of adventure, bravery and passion. We may twine if you wish.~

It was not often a mother met, much less was invited to the bed of, a man who looked like a goddi, whatever he said. He hovered closer and Eld felt inflamed. He was so beautiful, so painfully beautiful, like a vision of an aria in the flesh. Eld pulled away, shaking her head.

"You are too beautiful," she said.

~An odd complaint.~

"I think it means that even if I felt free to coit you, I know there is another better suited for me."

And in that instant Seth appeared beside her and she knew it was truly Seth, not a Thought.

"Where am I?" he asked, astonished at the view. "And who is he?" he added, wonder mixed with suspicion.

~The one who has lost the contest for this mother's attention,~ the Twilight man said, but his eyes smiled with amusement and acceptance. ~You are easily the victor. Now I will do you both the service of moving you away from the Edge.~

The path twisted, spinning Eld and Seth, the scene shifting, and for a second dark patches of void rent the mantles of the twilight man, revealing windows onto distant stars and nebula. Then they were no longer hovering in the air above Eurath, but instead standing on the top of the pavilion where they had kissed. But sky above was twice as full of stars as in waking, and the platform was much larger, surrounded by small trees that grew out of the top pavilion branches. They stood in a grassy glade complete with white flowers, improbably lofted into the air.

"What a vision!" Seth said.

"Yes, but I prefer the one I'm seeing presently," Eld said drawing Seth close.

"Knowing I was chosen over a goddi is an inflaming thought."

"How inflaming?"

"Let me show you."

They kissed for a while, enjoying the feeling of kisses in dreams that were as electrifying as deep kisses exchanged instead of joining. Then when they did join, their souls shivered together, and they fell up into the sky, drifting for all the night in the pleasure of that starry sea.

## Chapter 35

# Scandal

The night was long and restful. At some point it rained, leaving the air cool, lingering with the scent of water. Eld felt so refreshed that rising was easy. But she also recalled the events of the night more clearly and was somewhat mortified. She felt deeply thankful for the presence of Effa Rathi Sallaryn, clearly a man of experience without whom she and Seth would have made even greater fools of themselves. Even Danshor impressed her, but then she remembered what weighed on her war-sister and Eld gently pushed aside her pleasant memories of dreaming with Seth. It was only a little before dawn, but Danshor was already awake and dressed in training vest and shorts. It was to be an ordinary day: they would dance, run, break for lunch, then return to practice riding maneuvers.

"Al met and good morn," Eld said to Danshor, trying to sound casual.

"Lover girl is awake," Danshor said, but not loudly. It was a pale effort of her usually robust self.

Eld rose, changed and made her cot while they spoke.

"I owe you thanks for escorting all of us," Eld said. "I was distracted greatly."

Danshor laughed. "That's one way to tell the tale."

"Speaking of tales, about the Garden of Lun –"

"Not here," Danshor said shortly.

The more alert Eld became, the more she remembered of the evening, and the more urgent she realized the situation might be. She motioned for Danshor to step outside the door. Danshor frowned, her worry pregnant as Eld leaned close. "Roel knows something."

Hard gold eyes shimmered in the subdued light of the overcast morning. "How?" Danshor breathed.

"She was friendly with the nephew at the gala dance ..."

"That little harlot ..."

"Is the commander's nephew!" Eld said in a quelling tone.

"Fine! That wanton slet! Is that better?"

"Not really."

"And what's your Wood King doing hiring the commander's nephew, anyway?"

"Tafli didn't know. I saw them arguing before the Dwen stormed out. It's possible no one will know ..."

"Except Roel knows I was at the Garden."

"Yes, and ..."

The mustering bell interrupted them and they were bidden to run to the field.

The tents remained from the night before and would likely stay up until the air cleared enough to dry them by sulessence. Everything else was packed away. But in the case of the cavalry host their regular exercise field was clear.

And so they danced, then ran, this time Eld being fit and whole, pleased to keep up and pleased at the path her life was turning to. No sightings of distant Eurthans troubled them, nor any other cause for worry, though on their return many were sad to see the fair tents being struck and the Yino pavilion of twisted poles being slowly dismantled. Eld wondered if some food mongers might linger long enough to have a breakfast of Yino fare. But this was not meant to be, for no sooner had they returned, than they were informed their company was volunteered to assist the Hound's Master in rounding up livestock spooked by thunder in the night. They ate quickly in the Kettle and were on the road fifteen minutes later, armed not with lances, but lassos, seeking out water soaked sheep and cows.

In the best of times Danshor was simply adequate at this task. Under the pall of her worried thoughts, she was terrible, inadvertently spooking the animals with her aggressive emotions. She was finally told to stay back and hold the horses when they were forced to dismount and wade through a stream at the bottom of a steep, grassy slope. They were muddy and soaked when they were done, eager to visit the baths before lunch.

After lunch they would ride again, practicing lance maneuvers. No one was enthused about this as the light was watery and weak. But that was exactly why they were doing it, Sergeant Tarl explained. A preliminary report from Command advised more strike training on overcast days, which Eld agreed was a sound idea. But the women weren't used to it and grumbled, pointing out they defeated the Eurthans without resisted lance training. They weren't magi, for Sel's sake.

They had a little time before muster and spent it cleaning whatever mud was still stuck to boots or coats, and drying anything that was still damp with care.

"Remember, girls: just heat the hovering air," Althone said. "Not some magi trick of releasing motes of vapor any normal soul would need an adept degree to master."

"How many shirts do you have left, Torin?" Reon asked to laughter.

"After my winnings, many and fine!" Torin replied, buttoning up a new, bright, white linen garment.

"But I will be happy to assist any soul drying ..." she offered, knowing they would refuse with mock horror at their garments going up in flames. Patrycan was already dressed, trunk open doing trade: a buckle, a man's flower broach and small funnel exchanged hands. Eld looked at the funnel enquiringly.

"Brew shed," the woman explained. Fizzy tonics were popular; soon hawthorn, linden, rowan,yarrow and elderflower would be in bloom, and brewing fresh seasonal cordials would be a common after duty hobby.

Just then Eld remembered she needed another charcoal pencil. She also intended to ask after the cache offices. As Eld stepped towards Patrycan's cot, Sergeant Tarl bellowed outside in her deepest voice: "Surprise Inspection!"

Eld shivered. Something bad was coming. This wasn't a disciplinary inspection. This was an inspection to find someone or something. Ridiculously Eld whipped her head around to check for men, but of course there were none. Most women rushed to throw things in their chests, shut them and stand at attention. Though she did it fast, Patrycan had the most to do. Items for sale were stripped off the top of her blanket, thrown in, the chest slammed shut, then kicked under her cot.

Then next second, Sergeant Tarl and Captain Aynath stepped in.

"Stand and attend!" Tarl shouted, unnecessarily in Eld's view as they were all easily within earshot. Then a black robed magi drifted in, aura strong and seeking.

It was Ta Narin, returned to her modern work habit. She gave no indication of their acquaintance. Whatever they sought, she would show no favor. And after last night, Narin was probably quite annoyed with Eld. While they stood at the end of their cots, Narin walked slowly up and down the room like a hound scenting something. Meanwhile Captain Aynath spoke:

"Good morn, my worthy cavaliers," she said.

"Good morn, Captain!" they chorused.

"However it may not be as good for one soul. Some elf has strayed from her duty. We will find that soul, never fear."

Eld's heart hammered, afraid not for herself, but Danshor. The wagers must have had irregularities, or funds were taken fraudulently. Violations of command code over debts and gambling could be expensive. At least Danshor had a rich estate to catch her if she fell.

So it was a shock when Eld's chest was singled out for opening.

"Just do it, Farthal!" Tarl barked. "That goes for the rest of you 'boys'. Save your theatrical sighs and looks of askance for the theater!"

503

Four of them, including Eld and Patrycan, were bidden to drag their chests out, open them and empty the contents. Eld swore if Danshor had put something in her chest "just for the moment", Danshor wouldn't need to be concerned about any scandal with the Garden of Lun. Eld emptied shirts, training clothes, underpants, her civilian bracs, sandals, mother's diapers (a type of underpant used once every thirteen months during shedding), sundry paper leaves and cleaning tools, the case with her stylus, metal quill and ink. And then she saw it, and her heart hammered in her throat: the Eurthan crossbow bolt she'd taken out of Hollar.

Eld stood up instantly. "It's not contraband!" she objected, quailing under Tarl's blazing eyes.

"Its certainly looks like contraband, Farthal!"

"It's the bolt that almost killed Hollar! I took it out after we healed her!"

"And kept it as a memento?"

"No, sergeant! I was going to turn it in! I just forgot!"

"She speaks truth," Ta Narin said. "But there is more." The magi swooped down on the envelope containing the unused parts of Seth and Eld's hair. Eld had taken them out of her jacket pocket in the morning before chasing sheep. Eld felt affronted and made to snatch it back. But Sergent Tarl shouted:

"Stay that hand, cavalier!"

"It's not military or magi business!" Eld objected.

"True again," Ta Narin said simply. "But its essence signature is very strong. Apologies." Narin gave back the envelope and moved on to Patrycan's chest.

Tarl snatched the bolt up. "Mind you don't forget again, Farthal!"

It took a long while for Ta Narin to go over Patrycan's stock. It wasn't illegal, what Pat did, selling trinkets and bits, provided what she sold was itself acquired honestly. Eld would be shocked if among the wine corks, cuff links, flasks, thongs, laces and buttons there could be one stolen object. Narin seemed perplexed too.

"It's here," Narin said waving at the whole of Patrycan's area. "But none of these things are it."

Pat's face was blank when Sergeant Tarl stepped forward nose to nose: "Where is it, cavalier?"

"What, sergeant?" Pat said.

"The contraband!"

"Contraband?" Pat repeated. Repeating wasn't a lie.

"Are we in a cave, cavalier?"

"No, sergeant!"

"Then why do I hear an echo?"

"It was a question."

"Then here is your answer: someone has been selling Eurthan grim artifacts from the battle."

Pat said nothing.

Eld felt her stomach sink. She sneaked a look at Patrycan and saw a face as still as marble, a rabbit in an open field, knowing it's been sighted by a hawk. Doomed, it still freezes, hoping it will be spared...

"Ah," Ta Narin said. She knelt down and reached into the chest, adroitly removing a false bottom. Then she withdrew the vest Pat often wore when trading outside the barracks, for it had an abundance of pockets. Narin dropped it on Pat's cot and reached inside a pocket to withdraw inky shards of sparkling, bluish-green, black metal.

Sergeant Tarl and Captain Aynath stared at the grim in Narin's hand, then Pat.

"Out in the stable court, cavalier," Captain Aynath said coolly.

Pat walked out. At least the first company was less likely to hear. Ta Narin fished out the rest of the grim shards, putting them in a small bag while the captain followed Pat. It felt like they were watching their sister go to execution.

"At ease," Sergeant Tarl growled. "But stay inside. Exercises will be delayed."

Then she went outside as well.

It was quiet for several moments, only the sounds of Narin gathering the metal were heard as they rattled and clinked together. The light brightened, Sul again making a brave attempt to gift them with light, but the cloud cover was insistent. In the distance thunder rumbled. Then the inner yard exploded with Sergeant Tarl shouting, Pat answering with as little emotion as possible.

"How did you come by this contraband, cavalier?"

"I didn't know it was contraband," Pat said, the truth bending in their ears. It wasn't a lie but that wouldn't help her.

"You did not know of the order for all Eurthan artifacts to be turned over to command?"

"Sergeant, with respect, they aren't artifacts but shards of artifacts."

"Shards of artifacts?" Sergeant Tarl bellowed. "Well, aren't you a legal scholar! Look, we have our own legal scribe! Whether they are whole armored shells, swords, shards or sand as fine as fay dust, all Eurthan grim has been commandeered for study so we can know more about this Bane-spawn if they strike again! I take it you have some interest in defending this nation, your family and your hide, correct, cavalier?"

"Yes, sergeant!"

"I'm glad to hear that! Because what it looks like is a mercenary mother looking for profit to spite the spirit of regulations! Are you that mother, cavalier?"

"I confess to trading for a reasonable profit. I have never cheated a soul ..."

"How did you come by this contraband?"

"I didn't gather it."

"We know that, idiot! That's why we patrol the fields! So how did you come by it?"

"I bought out the stock of a woman selling. She hired field scroungers ..."

"The same scroungers your war-sisters caught?"

"Possibly."

"And it didn't occur to you to report this?"

"The edict explicitly says artifacts are to be turned over. These are useless scraps."

"Why does any mother want them if they're so useless?"

"Souvenirs, mostly."

"Souvenirs?" Tarl bellowed. "You violated your oath of duty to sell souvenirs?"

"It may not be a violation of her oath," Captain Aynath said in a quieter but still angry voice. "But you knew it might be seen that way, Lancer Patrycan. That's why you hid your trade. Dungeon her for the day, sergeant. I'll let you know what the commander's office recommends."

"What are you waiting for?" Tarl bellowed. "Get back in there and pray Athmod swallows you up because I'll be back for whatever is left!"

In moments Patrycan walked in, not meeting anyone's eyes. She quietly busied herself replacing the contents of the chest. Narin walked out and Tarl stepped in just long enough to say:

"Company, get mounted and ready to practice!"

Eld tried to meet Pat's eyes, communicate some sympathy, but Pat remained focused on her tasks. Eld supposed if it was herself, she wouldn't want to talk to anyone either. Patrycan was well respected, so it felt like a coming funeral thinking she would be separated from them.

The exercises in the field were lackluster. Eld was the best, but she had no heart for it and Sergeant Tarl's praises at the power of her strike in spite of the weather felt hollow. Her thoughts were on poor Pat. It wasn't as if she'd kept something dangerous. But Command was in its rights; all the

Eurthan grim held clues and a soul never knew what would be important or not. It was, in short, not a choice Pat had a right to make.

They returned to the stables in subdued spirits, Danshor doubly so with her own burdens. And Eld saw the ramifications of those burdens could affect her in ways that Roel –damn Roel! –certainly understood in an instant: this could cost Eld her sponsorship. Were it not for Danshor's humbled mood Eld would be furious. She fought her urge to corner Danshor and yell at her, instead trying to focus on what they could do. First Eld had to learn exactly what happened, assuming Danshor could remember.

They were dismissed from duty for the day. No sooner than Danshor had dismounted Tuiric and turned him over to a groom, than she ran out of the horse stable. Eld patted Fiorseth and followed Danshor, finding her in a dim corner of the inner yard, bent over, hands on her knees, heaving. Nothing came out, presumably because Danshor hadn't been eating.

"Maybe we should go to the Temple," Eld suggested.

The tail of hair hanging from Danshor's flout shivered as she shook her head. "There's nothing the Temple can do." She straightened up, gasping, eyes flickering to the side. The company was curious, but more interested in the Kettle and food.

Suddenly Danshor laughed humorlessly, leaning back against the wall. "That night was a smear of lights, drink and blurred faces. But as soon as I heard that boy's voice, I can't stop seeing him. He was part of a gang of wantons, their faces all gilded as if their skin was metal, wearing cheap costume yastols, thin robes and nothing else, bidding us to touch them. And now I see his gilded face unbidden down ..." She glanced down to her own nethers, then shivered as if trying to shake the memories free. "I fondled many," she added, "but I swear, I rode none."

"Why not? I'm glad you didn't, but that seems strange for you."

"I never ride men in the Gardens. It's the best place to get a free kiss, but I'm not having some slet's estate stalk me for money claiming my birthed were fed by him. That happened to a previous sister of mine. Too much trouble."

Danshor shivered again as if fevered, saying through gritted teeth, "He's the same age as my son."

"Your son is ninety-two right? Solafi is actually ninety-eight."

"Thank you, scholar, that's a much improved situation."

"It might be, truly. That close to being of age, and clearly obscuring the fact they weren't, you might only suffer a fine."

Danshor looked up into the high rafters, considering. "It'll be the mother's choice. If she's anything like the commander, I'm doomed."

"Farthal?" a voice called.

Eld looked around to see Captain Aynath.

"You've been invited to dine at the commander's house. Don't dawdle."

Eld looked herself over. She was adequately presentable though she wanted to wash her face.

"Go on," Danshor said.

Eld wanted to tell her to be quiet, not to do or say anything until they knew more. There was even a chance she was wrong. But the nephew did seem to recognize her. And if Eld said anything, it could be interpreted as helping Danshor evade responsibility. That word and others weighed on her as she walked to the commander's house:

Responsibility. Obligation. Duty.

Was Eld duty bound to say anything? Danshor did not seek out the boys, so she wasn't a danger to mother's unripe sons. But Danshor had been reckless. An unlicensed or wild Garden of Lun was tempting this kind of trouble. At the commander's house, Eld was immediately taken to Alhern's office.

"Farthal," Alhern said. Her face was blank, but tense. "Dinner is tardy. Let's play a game."

The chess board was set up and waiting, the white pieces again sitting in front of Eld. They sat and Alhern waited.

"I have white again?" Eld asked.

"You have white again."

Eld opened with the same piece, moving the pawn two spaces forward, in front of the Cradle.

Alhern met it with her own pawn like before.

Here Eld could have tried the Flying Queen again. There were ways to change Her path before it became futile, to avoid getting Her trapped. But the truth was, against a greater skilled opponent, such tricks were a waste of effort. So, instead of moving her queen, Eld moved the pawn in front of her queen two paces forward to stand next to the other pawn. They would go into battle together as war-sisters, doomed to fall before the end of the game.

And so they played. The commander won again but it took time, and Eld felt proud that she had lasted as long as she did before toppling her Cradle.

"That was a much better effort, Farthal," Alhern said.

"Thank you, emha."

"You are slow to sacrifice, but once you start, you become impatient."

"I like to get the worst over once it's inevitable, emha."

"I see." Alhern motioned that they should rise. "The summons should be soon. We may as well get on our way. While we walk, consider: who would you sacrifice first if there was dire need: Lancer Patrycan or Lancer Danshor?"

Eld froze in shock. "Why do you ask, emha?"

"Does it matter?"

They resumed walking and Eld was haunted by a thought: this was a test.

"I understand your reluctance," Alhern said. "On one hand is a respected fellow, on and off the field, resourceful and reliable. On the other, your close bond with a war-sister who is loyal but also an embarrassing, obnoxious braggart. You must sacrifice one. Perhaps it is easier if I say you must save one."

It was a horrible thought. Eld knew the answer and loathed why.

"You know," Alhern said, as if feeling Eld's thoughts. "Don't tell me. Just know and understand why."

"Danshor isn't just a hood," Eld blurted.

"I didn't say she was."

"I'm not proud to admit I was not my best yestereve."

"I have heard a summary," Alhern said, a slight smirk on her lips.

"Danshor kept us from being more of an embarrassment than we might have."

"Are you gilding Danshor's virtues to explain why you'd save her and let a cavalier of better character die, or because there is something more serious you want to mitigate for your war-sister?"

They stopped outside the dining area used the night before. The door was open and they could hear the voices within. It was bright, but Alhern kept Eld outside, in the shadows of the hall.

"These theoreticals are small things to what will come," Alhern said. "When I gave the order to send your company to charge with the goal of breeching or taking the Eurthan wall, as you know we had no idea there were crossbow archers hidden. Had I known, it wouldn't have mattered. We needed to neutralize its tactical use, either by destruction or advancement. Harrying the Eurthan camp was to support that goal; in disarray we'd planned to move the foot companies in. I was ready to sacrifice a quarter of the cavalry company for that goal. Don't be shocked; had it been taken sprightly, the fallen could have quickly been tended, though some horses might have been irretrievably lost. Then the Eurthan archers destroyed our momentum. Without the Green Strike Gambit, it is unlikely we would have won without more losses. Your sponsorship comes with this future burden: it is easier to be a hero and sacrifice yourself, than rule the field and sacrifice others. But, like in chess, it must be done when necessary."

"I hear your sister," Rathi's voice echoed from within. "What's she doing lurking in the hall?"

"That's our signal, Farthal."

It was the same grand table, but with a much smaller group. Seth and Effa Tanmor were at one end of the table; at the other end the Marshal and Major Galledan sat to either side of Alhern's chair. The place where Eld sat before was open, but it was so close to Seth she felt it exposed them in this more intimate group. It didn't help that this time Marshal Tantilaan was on the same side of the table, her seating next to Alhern meaning her consort Tinyan would be on Eld's right side. Tinyan glanced at her, flashing a quick, shy smile. On the opposite side of the table General Sallaryn and Rathi sat almost dead center and very close to each other.

"There she is, giddy no more, I see," Rathi said smiling. "Your war-sister not with you? Like I said, commander, she served us quite well."

"So I hear. Sit down, Farthal, so the rest of us can eat."

Seth smiled as Eld took her seat next to him.

"I must apologize," Seth said. "For both of us. Yestereve was overwhelming and it took quite a while to return to myself."

"The carnival seems to have been a greater success than the gala," Sallaryn said. "If only I had seen it."

"It'll be a while before she forgives me, my metee," Rathi added.

"I thought we had a grand eve," Alhern said. "You seemed to enjoy yourself abundantly, beating us all at chess, then Brandubh and Gains."

Brandubh was a barbarian game of strategy, played on a board like chess, but a different creature all together. Gains was the popular card game played with picture trumps as well as the regular deck of five suits: darts, lunats, rubies, clovers and orbs.

"Those Gains wins would have been forfeit any other time," Tantilaan said peevishly. "Unless you were playing with Magi or Aeons."

"There is an alternate interpretation," Rathi began. "It could be you simply aren't as good – "

" – Good at finding agreeable fellows of the right challenge," Sallaryn said, talking over her consort.

They didn't pull apart, but Rathi was cool with his wife for a while.

"The carnival was quite invigorating," Tinyan said. "Thank you so much, effas, for welcoming me with you. It'll be a while before the sprites are old enough to really enjoy it ..."

"And then they will be exposed to entertainment worthy of their foremothers," Tantilaan said over him.

There was no playful tone of affection as had been the case with Sallaryn, who the keen soul could hear was herding Rathi away from argument. Eld was appreciative of the Marshal's support of her sponsorship, but nothing the woman did since alleviated Eld's first impressions: Eld did not like the Marshal, and in particular she did not like how she spoke down to and over her consort. It wouldn't have been so awful if Tinyan was a feisty and spirited man. But the consort was more like a foster child to be tutored than a partner of the soul. Worse, the Marshal gave every indication she was pleased with this arrangement, though Tinyan was obviously exhausting himself trying to uphold impossible standards.

"Farthal," Alhern said, calling her attention, a note of warning in her voice.

Eld realized once again she was staring at the Marshal with naked contempt. "Yes, commander?"

"Something appears to be on your mind."

Eld looked around, trying to appear casual, then noticed a perfect rejoinder. "I don't see your nephew, emha. Will he be joining us?"

"Alas, no, the lad is feeling out of sorts," Alhern said.

"I did caution yourselves," Tanmor said. "All that excitement after an already long day. Staying out far past midnight. And that foreign food couldn't have been at all good for a delicate young man. Tartar balls and root-beer! It's a recipe for stomach upset!"

"Not to mention the sausages," Rathi said, smiling toothily.

Eld laughed with Seth and Tinyan, though Tinyan quickly stopped when the Marshal looked up without amusement.

"I hope my consort's appetite for frivolity has been sated for the while," Tantilaan said. "As if these demon spawned Eurthans weren't trouble enough, we've had a dispatch about movements near the Bay of Gashora. The Sultan of Sharitan is organizing his forces."

"Foot or cavalry?" Major Galledan asked.

"Neither. Though there is a small army mustering along the southern border. But it's the sea his eye is on. We've watched him build new ships of war for the last half decade. Command was certain he was planning another raid on pitiful islanders in the South Straits near Nomclar, more conquests to steal resources or expand his pathetic 'empire'. But our dreamers can find no intentions in that direction. We will know more anon."

"That's why we must abandon you this eve, sweetest," Rathi said to Seth. "The women want to be at the Falls Gate sadol to speak through the stones in person. You never know what gets lost between scribe and messenger in missives."

"And then we continue on to the Crownland command office," Sallaryn added. "By wind, road or water, we'll know more then."

"But you must come to the estate for Sol Suldan," the Rathi effused. "And you as well," he added to Tinyan.

"That's very kind of you," the young man said.

"Haven't you been away from the estate long enough?" Tantilaan said. Her voice was light, but her meaning obvious.

"It's true," Tinyan agreed. "I miss the sprites. And they miss us terribly."

"Then the solution is obvious!" Rathi exclaimed. "Bring them along!" Effa Sallaryn beamed, his eyes blazing in aggressive friendliness, challenging Tantilaan to disagree.

"You will be more than welcome," General Sallaryn added with a more credible show of fellowship. "We must allow men a break from our incessant talk of politics, regulations and horses."

"I will consider it." Tantilaan said politely.

"It will of course depend on what tasks we have," Seth said. "But I will--"

"Go." Alhern said. "If you want. If we are not compelled to need your presence. But I don't see why, not at this time. The house will manage. Not as graciously, but it will manage."

"Thank you sister, that is good to know. I might however request to pick my escort on the road."

Seth winked at Eld and smiled.

The rest of the dinner was unnotable, though the intermittent awkwardness remained throughout, unrelenting until the general and marshal, with their men, took their leave. They had packed earlier in the day and only needed to walk down the drive where the coach waited. As the men waved to each other, a messenger on foot ran up the steps directly to Alhern. Major Galledan took Eld aside. She had a cavalier's cape over her arm.

"I believe this is yours, Farthal," she said placing it in Eld's astonished hands.

Eld's mind flew back to the previous evening, her memory obscured by the giddiness of euphoria and dreams. Hadn't she retrieved it? But no, they had climbed down a different way ...

"Thank you, emha," Eld said. Yet even in her gratitude she felt a shadow of resentment.

"Something troubles you, cavalier?" Galledan asked.

"No," Eld said, not wanting to sound petty. "Nothing of note. I realize it was foolish. It felt odd seeing you with Roel. At the duel."

Galledan smiled. "You thought me a partisan to her cause? Ah, but don't you see? In a formal duel, she deserved as much support as yourself. If there's not an advocate to show someone at their best, how can we judge them fairly when they stray? And your victory over an unsupported, untrained and friendless foe would have been worthless."

"I see your point. I just don't like to see it with Roel."

"Well, that's all over, thank Paradise. I'll be off, Alhern. Finally we have a free moment. You want to join us at The Wildling?"

"Unfortunately, a family matter has arisen," Alhern said holding a missive she'd unfolded, the light card tacked together with a drop of wax. "Tomorrow and anon."

"Anon."

When the Major left, Alhern reread the card.

It was a scribed missive sent through a sadol activated by magi, with readers and speakers at all involved stations sending messages on a schedule that was published for the publics' convenience. This was cheapest way to use the stones. Less frequent and more expensive was speaking directly, as the senior command officers planned to do later in the eve. But that was a privilege of those who had public duties. No ordinary mother could access the stones to chat about, say, the weather at a whim. Speaking through was scheduled; only in the most urgent circumstances was the circle held open to wait for a soul at the other end to arrive. Some of the oldest estates had sadols, or more likely triads, deep in their cellars. But most of these were no longer active, nor linked to the wider net of circles. The first circles were set up by magi and other schools in the Queen's realm to share knowledge. Now linked sadols were accessible to all but the remotest hamlets, allowing news to travel much faster than it ever had in the early days of the Federation. It was said had the sadols been as robust in the 10th century, the God Storm would not have been as devastating, for the south Alansatal and Myngarth could have warned the west Ethynsul and Cambrian Territories, who suffered the worst. By the 20th century sadols were instrumental in warnings of coastal piracy and coordinating the fleet patrol. Now it was common for every city or village office to know the current and expected weather throughout the nation, another duty magi were tasked with. With the ease and habit came expectation of access, until the sadol office was managing more missives, private or trade, than ever in elfyn history.

For all that, Eld preferred regular post. The stones were quick, but there was no expectation of privacy during the transfer of missives. Thus private news sent through the stones tended to be terse and formal. Yet sometimes terse and formal was exactly what the occasion demanded.

"I suppose I should be leaving as well," Eld said. "Thank you--"

"This is a reply to a missive I sent at noon, Farthal," Alhern interrupted. "My office. Now."

The tension Eld had perceived in Alhern's voice was no longer hidden. Eld was caught by surprise and had to trot to keep up. At her office, Alhern held the door open in perfunctory politeness. Eld caught a glimpse of Seth, who had followed them curiously. Their eyes met. But Eld only had time to shrug before Alhern shut the door.

The office was a different place after dark. The long curtains were closed and lamps gave the space a warm glow, casting the ceiling into shadow. The hearth glowed with red embers, a charcoal fire started at dusk to remove the chill, but allowed to die this time of year unless it was wanted for ambiance.

"Sit," Alhern said taking a larger, comfortable chair near the hearth. She gestured to the same sturdy seat Eld had used during all of her visits. Once Eld sat, Alhern handed her the missive. "Read this."

Nervously Eld looked the paper over. It didn't seem too noteworthy:

To My Loving Sister, etc;
Have Solafi packed for travel. I see myself there in 3 days. I look forward to questions being answered.
Yours,
A.T. Alhern & Estate

The room seemed to spin. Eld felt dizzy. Her soul knew the shape of the matter, even if she herself didn't know the details.

"You feel the seriousness?" Alhern asked.

"Yes," Eld said.

"My nephew has found himself in an embarrassing situation," Alhern said. "A situation that involves your war-sister Danshor. Do you know about this?"

Eld swallowed. "I was recently made aware they had an unfortunate encounter."

"You really will be a politician one day!" Alhern said. "'Unfortunate' is quite the understatement. My nephew and his bold friends gilded themselves to deliberately obscure their youth, then finagled their way into a Garden of Lun. Not a proper one, of course. They would have never passed a notarized gatekeeper at a city temple. No, this was a slipshod affair catering to the local Moon Meet and adjacent voyeurs, and those seeking cover for their clandestine adventures. Regulations don't forbid soldiers from attending such places, but they do warn of the risks. Trysting with those below age is one. The Hound's Master has been informed."

"I have to interject, emha," Eld said. "I understand Danshor didn't actually join with anyone."

"Nor did my nephew. He reports being fondled and kissed quite a bit, as well as kissing many women deeply in the nethers. Yes, you might blush to hear this. It certainly wasn't pleasant for me to interrogate my nephew about these activities. But his mother is coming and I must know the worst. For me, that was watching him weep in shame. No, not because he went. But because he was found out. And, as my brother never tires of reminding me, society is much less forgiving of a boy's intimate adventures. I will not allow Solafi to be publicly humiliated if I can help it."

Eld's head snapped up. "Roel did this."

Alhern frowned. "How did you guess?"

"I ... She was charming it out of Solafi at the gala, then boasted about it in thought."

Alhern glowered, even the dim light brightening around her. "Roel was too clever to come to me herself. She found your cloak, used its return as an opening to speak to Major Galledan. Leave Roel to me," Alhern growled. "Just leave it, Farthal! It seems using men as tools for revenge is a habit with the lieutenant. But as self serving and vindictive as it is, where Danshor is concerned, it doesn't matter. Adult mothers accessed my sister's son while I fostered him. She has a right to know and I have to consider what I will do with Danshor.

"I like you Farthal. And I like to see my brother happy. Which is why you are going to tell me everything you know."

Eld didn't hesitate.

When Eld was done, Alhern said, "I won't lie: my sister is a blunt, unforgiving ogre the best of times. She's not the artist my brother is, nor the traveler I am. Arumil is focused on what is right before her and is impatient with fay ideas and frivolities. So far only Danshor has been identified. But if Danshor helps the Hound's Master get the organizers, I may be able to save her from court-martial or worse. If not, you will need to think on the question of sacrifice.

"You would save Danshor over Patrycan, though by any objective eye Patrycan is the more worthy sister. Yes, Farthal, it's obvious. Danshor's habits and actions might madden you, but you are loyal to her because you see her as a puppet of fate to be excused, because she harbored no ill intent. Well, remember the Dying Star that destroyed Er had no intent one way or the other, yet our world was shattered all the same. Choices were made then. Animals and humyn were abandoned to their fate. If elfyn mothers did not save themselves, the Orb would have been utterly doomed and neither race nor beasts would have survived.

"Sacrifice and survival go hand in hand. Young Jaro who loved all beasts had to kill the first Ram to eat. The Thyngalu are said to have abandoned their home in another realm to save us. There is no great deed without sacrifice. Your sacrifice will be much less costly: you might be forced to chose Danshor ..."

"Or Patrycan?"

Alhern laughed humorlessly. "Patrycan is battling her fate quite adroitly. She's hired a reasonably skilled legal advocate and plans to defend herself on the finest particulars. You might be pleased to learn, considering her otherwise pristine service, she will probably emerge with her honor intact, though she will have to forfeit the dragon's share of profits she made. By which we mean all of her profit. No, the choice you might be forced to make is between your war-sister and sponsorship."

## Chapter 36

# A Bright Walk in The Step

Patrycan no longer lived in the stable barracks with them. Her gear was gone when Eld returned from the commander's house, the chest under her cot empty. A folded letter lay at the head of Eld's cot, not sealed or tacked, but with Eld's initials, a private message for her alone. It was a list of three investment houses, signed with Patrycan's initials. Eld smiled to herself sadly, thinking, "Elam, sister."

Danshor was reclining on her cot, back against the wall, holding a small book.

"So you've come to that stage where you leave endearing notes to each other in secret places?" Danshor said.

"No. How would we? Any stray note is sure to be discovered by his cleaning staff."

"You could leave some here," Danshor said, turning a page.

"You'd adore that. What are you doing anyway?"

"Reading."

"I thought that was for scholars and lost souls with cold beds."

"It's the Falls Gate Sadol timetable. I want to speak with ama and dame before news gets to them."

Eld pulled off her flout and undressed, getting ready for sleep. "You haven't been told anything else?"

"No. I expected to be dungeoned like Pat. They're taking her to Falls Gate to be interrogated by Command. Anyone in possession of Eurthan grim is questioned. Something about its effects on auras. She's been carrying it around and sleeping with it under her bed. So ..." Danshor shrugged. "But me, I'm just waiting before they come to throw me off a cliff."

Defenestration from "a peak of Eurath" was an ancient method of execution.

Eld let her voice fall to a volume below the background mutter of other conversations. "I had to tell 'A' everything I knew," Eld said.

"A? Who is A?"

"Danshor, even the savage Nords, with a rude literacy of simple runes, understand the significance of the first letter of a written name."

"Oh, 'A'. Ai! The sister of 'S'."

"Yes, full marks. 'A' knows everything, from myself and Roel. You'll be summoned for your account. I don't know what the terms will be. But try to remember who managed or hosted the wild Garden and any other soul you can identify. You have three days until the mother arrives."

While Danshor wasn't dungeoned to quarters, she was forbidden from leaving the garrison except during exercise and maneuvers. At times she was escorted away and back by a watch patrol. Danshor said she was questioned about the garden and those she could recognize. Eld suspected Alhern wanted to keep the matter from becoming a topic of discussion and that would be difficult if the entire company was asking her why Danshor couldn't leave the stables. But it also meant Danshor couldn't send to her estate like she planned. Falls Gate was at least a couple hours away on horse; even if she was allowed to leave, Danshor would need a free day to return before the gates closed.

"It's been a while since I've heard her swear like that," Eld said to Seth as they walked down the village street. Eld was escorting him for the day while he did small errands. "She was shouting into the rafters of the inner courtyard for a while."

Seth hugged Eld's arm closer, his eye wandering to a window across the street. "I'm sure I could sympathize more if I was told of this grand scandal."

"I'm not trying to keep anything from you--"

"Are you certain?"

"I don't think it's my place to say more than whatever your sister has told you."

"Well, my sister hasn't said much beyond telling me Solafi and his friends slithered into a wild Garden, gilded for sale, and that your war-sister had seen them. It does explain him being out of sorts. Nothing distresses an adolescent more than being caught out in public. Let's go there."

Seth gestured across the street to a shop with windows full of glass bottles. Like most displays it was lit with a directed skylight or mirrors, full of dramatic specimens to catch the eye: tall vases with narrow necks spun out of sapphire glass that glittered, round bowls with layers of yellow and opalescent white, and the center piece, a massive two handled rose-gold goblet as large as a helmet, cast or carved so the outside was a filigree lattice, itself shimmering with a glow of gold over-glaze. Whenever Eld walked through the village it caught her eye: it would be the perfect Aeon gift when her grandmother ascended. She'd considered it beyond her means, even to save for. But if she was an officer, that would enlarge her finances considerably. For now it would remain where it was.

Eld stepped forward to open the door for Seth. While she held it, she became aware of a cluster of boys on the opposite side of the street, full of spirits and enjoying the bright day, their mix of blue, violet, yellow and white robes decorated in an abundance of contrasting ribbons around the arms and wrists. A young man in white with red ribbons jumped and waved to get her attention, his long hair bouncing and glimmering in the sun. Eld gave him a parade smile, friendly but sisterly, and a short salute. Civilians always welcomed a salute. And this did please the lads, who all saluted back with enthusiasm and laughter, but none of the proper technique. Eld smiled and followed Seth within.

Inside was a typical shop, the rectangular floor surrounded by tables and cases, behind them all glass cabinets and shelves rising above their heads. A long, narrow skylight followed the outlines of the center floor, illuminating the interior and the many shimmering glass pieces. There were few bottles, bowls or vases like those in the window, and the pieces that were similar were much smaller, placed in areas of prominence among the displays. By far the most common objects were bottles and jars of various sizes, in clear, amber, blue or green glass. One large case seemed to duplicate the selections around the store. Eld wondered why; the glass was clear and unnotable like the rest, except that the case itself seemed to be better lit. Then Eld realized the glass bottles themselves glowed, as if weak sunlight was leaking out of them. These bottles and jars were all made with solstone glass. Opposite the entrance, behind a table, was a door. No shopkeeper was in sight. Seth walked among the tables and cases, quick but careful.

"I need to replace some of my jars destroyed by those Eurthan marauders," Seth said. "Basic things."

"We should send them a bill," Eld suggested.

"If only. My sister still grumbles about the Corinaths. Especially the horse. I helped ama chose that horse when Selind was commissioned. I hope it curses whichever Eurthan soul has it now."

"Should we look for help?"

"Not yet."

While Seth continued browsing, Eld took a closer look at the case of solstone glass. It was the same type used in the wishing orb Seth was wearing now, but much less magical in both their mundane shapes and their abundance. Still, they were nice to look at. Eld knew some men used them for evening and night cooking. They were more expensive than regular glass, but most households had at least one bottle of flavor – rose, lavender or vanilla – stored in a solglass bottle. It was a common personal gift for a newly married man.

No bell on the door had sounded to announce their arrival. Either a woman was within earshot or they were being watched. Many large shops had a narrow mezzanine around the top where a "shop eye" could watch the floor. Eld had worked a season as a shop eye for an aunt who dealt in porcelain ware in Ta Meloshok. The store was a much larger affair, with many rooms, and Eld was only one of a dozen shop eyes employed. If a matron seemed to want assistance, there was a bell the eye rang where the women lurked in the accounts room. If there was trouble, usually children testing their watchfulness pretending to steal, the eye was to call out. A great bell was rung for actual thieves, echoing throughout the building. Eld had never had the chance to do that, probably because she'd only worked the floor with the large platters and vases. Older girls or apprentices worked as eyes for the floors with smaller, finer, or sol-enameled jewelry and trinkets. Here Eld expected a younger relative to be the eye, or perhaps a village girl.

Finally Seth was ready and walked to stand in the center of the floor. Eld joined him, stealing a kiss on his ear.

"Stop it. They'll see." Seth said, but he leaned closer to her.

"I've been that bored child," Eld said. "She's forbidden to speak of tiny embarrassments like ear and nose pickings, and ..."

"Trysting on the floor?"

"Not something I ever saw. But it was a shop full of porcelain ware ... "

The door opened and they instantly pulled apart.

"How may I serve you?" a woman in a dark blue vest asked. She was ageless, implying a soul who was much older but keeping in good health and vigor. Certainly she was physically vigorous, her wiry muscled arms and shoulders looking as if they were chiseled; she wore no shirt with the vest. Her physicality and a faint glow around her slightly disheveled guard-locks told Eld she must have come from a workshop beyond.

Seth briskly showed her what was needed, and bottles and jars were plucked from shelves accordingly, wrapped in brown paper and placed snuggly into Seth's basket. It was already full of muslin scraps from the draper and fine brushes from a scribe's store almost as large as one in a city. Eld supposed trade from the Abbey made them more prosperous than they would have been in a small village. After paying the woman and taking their leave, they stepped out the door to be mobbed by the young men who had saluted Eld.

"How do the leaves fall, my fine cavalier?" one boy said, flashing a winsome smile.

They were older than they had appeared, about Solafi's age and eager to practice their charms on any available mother.

"They fall brightly, young effa," Eld said. "Thank you for asking. Alas, I am on duty, so I may not linger. Good day."

"Farewell," the boy sighed as if all his hopes were vanishing into mist.

Seth stifled a laugh as they walked away. But the disappointed boys muttered among themselves and none too softly.

"Whatever is he wearing? No glimmer and dull brown, not a ribbon in sight!"

"I suppose he does need an escort. Some artist might mistake him for a rough canvas and take a brush to him!"

They all thought this was the wittiest thing of the day and burst into peals of laughter.

Eld considered going back with some motherly words, but Seth held her arm tightly, pulling her on. To Eld's surprise Seth was laughing softly.

"Those same vain creatures were certainly singing my praises at the gala," Seth said. "That is, before our resident 'King of the Wood' upstaged me."

It was true Seth was in a less glamorous aspect today, with no glimmer, his hair in basic trilocks. He'd chosen the workaday kirtle-shirt and a light mantle because of the morning chill. Now Eld was carrying the mantle draped on her other arm.

"Truly, you do not have to defend me from those young drakes. They'll learn soon enough how much work keeping up a glamorous aspect is all day."

Eld frowned. "I still don't like it. If they are so free throwing snide words at an escorted man, they must be brutal little bullies with their peers, and should learn better."

"Never fear," Seth said. "I know a couple of them lurk in the circle of the mayor's son. I will have a quiet word with the mayor's consort. Don't look, but they are preening, hoping you will look back. At which point they will pretend to not notice."

"Why do men do that?" Eld asked expressing an old bewilderment.

"What?"

"Play a perpetual game of keep away."

Seth laughed. "Having captured your attention with our bright feathers, we seek to increase our value by making ourselves scarce. A mother is less likely to consider a man a valued addition to the estate house if he is overly free. Which some see as a sign of excess and lack of thrift."

"The worst transgression of a mother's house keeper," Eld muttered.

Seth smiled, eyes twinkling in the sunlight.

"And what of you and your secret wanton ways?" Eld asked.

"I am aware how fortunate I am serving in the house of an understanding sister. I am not idle. I manage her house and fine society. In exchange, I have lodgings, freedom to indulge my hobbies, and I make a modest profit from selling my paintings. I indulged myself with whom I like because I am discreet. For Selind's part, she is not troubled by vetting a keeper, nor the domestic quarrels that breed around them as we have observed. Selind has no interest in marriage, though I have warned her I will not keep small children. It is an amicable arrangement that suits us both. I am quite aware of the freedom and security I enjoy compared to many of my fellow men.

"Not to sound unappreciative of your availability..."

"I see your mind," Seth said, guessing what Eld would say next.

"But wouldn't it be better for men to be direct about what and who they wanted?"

"And be seen as 'an overly forward harlot'?"

"I know of no woman who calls a man such a thing just for speaking plainly."

"Are you sure? Even if he plainly rejects the advances of, say, a soldier like your sister Danshor?"

Eld thought a moment. "Danshor, Heavens bless her, is a hood."

"And you think she is as rare as grimsteel?"

"Well, no, but she's not every woman."

"I will suggest her kind of woman is more common than you think. Remember Roel?"

"I'll never forget," Eld growled.

"Exactly. They do not always reveal themselves outside of the private torments they direct at men. But it isn't just women who discourage forwardness; other men do so even more cruelly. Like our little friends back there."

Eld sighed. "Yes, I've seen that before, the biting gossip and intrigue. What a senseless waste of time."

"I agree it's a waste, but it isn't entirely senseless."

"Of course it is! While two peacocks snipe at each other over who has the brightest feathers, the woman whose attention they were vying for is long gone, either off to her business or with a third, moderate tempered man. Like lioni battling each other...."

"But darling, the point of lioni fighting isn't to win the affection of mother lions. It's to make certain his rival loses. If that means a third goes first, so be it."

Eld shook her head. "Men are irrational."

"We prefer to remain a mystery."

They'd come to a small grassy round near the center of the village. There, a moderate country sized lane intersected the Queen's road that made the village main street, making a crossroad: the south lane zigzagged up the hilly ridge to the Abbey; the north, through a cluster of houses and small lots, eventually fading to the country track near the ravine where the battle had been. Most of the more frequented shops were west of the crossroad, along with the town hall, its doors facing the hill. The grassy round was just before the entrance, a drive circling it. There were a couple mature cherry trees, thick with aging pink blooms. Tafli was there, in his usual garb, hand on the trunk of one tree, as if listening while it whispered its secrets. A couple baskets sat on the grass nearby.

"Effa Reffayn!" Seth called. "Bright day, is it not?"

Eld wondered who Effa Reffayn was, the answer obvious when Tafli replied.

"Bright and brisk," Tafli said. "How do the leaves fall?"

"Well, you'd certainly know better than I!"

Tafli smiled, looking rueful, then saw Eld and his green eyes seemed to cloud.

"I am seeing this cavalier often in my house," Tafli said, his old friendliness returning. "She is very brave and bold. But is burning too many trees."

Eld said nothing to this, smiling tightly. It was a judgment she must accept. Then she saw a wishing orb around his neck, sparkling flecks swimming among blue liquid.

"Yes," Tafli said, seeing where Eld was looking. "I get this from a Yino cousin after my friend reminds me I should not assume all of the traveling Bereft are cheats."

"You chose blue," Eld said.

"Of course. Blue water is of the sky reflected in lakes and rivers, feeding the wood. Red water is wrong and only Sula are thinking this attractive."

"Regardless of our differences in taste, our kitchens appreciated your vegetables," Seth said. "I'm only sorry about the gala ..."

Tafli waved a hand. "We do not speak of this now. I will bring good greens anon. And maybe your sister, she is yelling less?"

Tafli snatched his baskets up and strode into the sun, taking a path directly down the center of the white paved main street.

"Luckily for him there's little wagon traffic," Eld said.

"I don't think Dwen really understand how Queen's roads work," Seth said. "I do wonder what Selind and Tafli were arguing about yesterday. In the middle of the day!"

"There was a row?"

"Yes, a very loud one. The staff was talking. I feel everyone is keeping things from me."

"This one I think I can tell you," Eld said. "But I'd rather –"

"Yes, you're terrified of my sister."

"She is my commanding officer!" Eld protested.

"Just tell me something!"

"Your nephew was working at the Rowan Oak as a tavern knave."

Seth said nothing for a moment. "That's it?"

"You're not upset?"

"At my idle adolescent nephew showing industry? Why would I be?"

"If you saw him, your opinion would be changed. In addition to his efforts to disguise himself as 'Farni', covering his face with glimmer and making his hair red, he imitated Tafli's style. I think he liked the attention of women more than the money."

"Oh." Seth exhaled.

"Tafli found out who he really was at the gala. I assume that's what he was arguing with your sister about."

"You know my sister and Tafli –"

"There is nothing I want to know about your sister and Tafli," Eld said firmly.

"I see." Seth sat on one of the stone benches and Eld settled beside him. "Very well. Let's rest and discuss something else. Your two sprites."

"The joys of my life."

"May I ask after the sire?"

It was a conversation they had yet to have. Only in serious wooing did the questions of the history of children arise. Novels written for men suggested old paramours might lurk disguised as the new knave, waiting to poison the new consort, or even children, in a jealous rage. More common in life was simple awkwardness, a betrothal that was abandoned, or never offered though expected, yet those families would be linked forever through the children. This was how the society of motherhood made and kept links, no matter the embarrassment or disappointments of the parties. And it was reasonable for a man looking to marry into a family to ask of those who went before him.

"I don't think about him much, truly," Eld said. "His estate sends the children trinkets on their birthing day. It was a young romance, just after our first fires. We planned to travel the country, visit all the memory stones and menhirs. Then he decided his interest in poetry and history was a passing fancy, and the offer from the blacksmith's daughter suited him better. I was growing with Shedann when we broke."

"He never visits?"

"I don't mind and they barely know him except as a name. I only ..." It was hard to say. Eld hadn't thought of it for decades. "I only wish I hadn't found out about his changing affection by seeing him and the baby smith's auras entwined in dreams."

Seth squeezed Eld's arm in sympathy. But Eld felt lighter than she had before. She breathed deeply, the air feeling light and clear.

"I hadn't realized it weighed on me still."

"Well, I assure you I think your sprites are adorable"

"Even though you refuse to keep small children?"

"I just tell Selind that so she doesn't take my labor for granted. Anyway, I've seen the fate of men who cast all affection aside to marry for ambition."

"Like the Marshal's consort?"

"Oh, that poor thing! I think he didn't understood who he was marrying. He's a caged bird."

"There are women who prefer men who don't challenge them."

"But that wasn't always true of the Marshal." Seth looked at Eld slyly. "Have you ever heard of Tergani?"

"That name echoes with familiarity. But I can't place it."

"He was the boy victor of the Quickening in his youth and danced for the nation. He's also the most accomplished man to hold a magi degree in the last thousand years."

"So he should be Ti Tergani."

"All magi work as mothers, regardless of sex, remember?"

"Then Ta Tergani?"

Seth shook his head. "Tergani doesn't work as a magi. He's married to an admiral of the Tyreen fleet and lives in Tyrum."

"The Island of Wild Elfborn."

"And the seat of Her Humble Majesty in Exile. He's friendly, even an intimate, of Her Humble Majesty. But the relevant fact is, at one time he was to marry Tantilaan. They seemed perfectly suited for each other, two great and powerful souls destined to inspire the nation. Then, to the shock of all, one day they broke apart. No one knows why, but they never speak of each other. I can assure you Tergani is a man able to challenge any mother as an equal. And, not that it should matter, he is a beauty."

Eld looked at Seth slyly. "Is he?"

"Too late, cavalier; I've already ensorcelled you."

"I only meant if a man as fine looking as yourself is saying he's a beauty, then ...."

"I know what you meant. Be wary, emha, I will keep an account of every test and tease. Then one day have my revenge."

"I look forward to it."

Seth became serious again.

"They say Tergani's essence is like the perfect marriage of sun and moon. It was a minor scandal when he not only broke with Tantilaan, but married an naval officer."

"And what was Tantilaan at the time?"

"A major. Cavalry host, of course. But she was already being groomed for her current prospects."

"Yet Ta Tergani married an aelg."

"It is a mystery. Another thing about Tantilaan that might explain her consort's reluctance to leave: she has the Touch of Lun."

The "Touch of Lun" described a woman who could inflame any soul with complementary amphermones. If a man's, or woman's if that was her way, aura met hers, they would be aroused so strongly as to want to tryst instantly. Any man a woman with the Touch wanted almost always yielded to her. But it would not make a man fall in love, or create affection that did not exist. It was solely physical arousal. While it did not compel a man to give himself, it was very hard to resist, especially if that man was young or inexperienced. It was perfectly possible the Marshal's consort Tinyan had mistaken this feeling for love. Whether deliberate or unknowing, such a woman never had a cold bed. For a while Eld though Danshor might have the "Touch". But Danshor was just a mother with rough charm, adept at common seduction. The "Touch" was always used to describe a mother. Some men certainly had it, but it would be impossible to mark casually since all men seemed to be capturing some women's eye, and most women readily admitted being attracted to their beauty.

"So Tergani's marriage must be a soul match," Seth said. "The Tyreen Admiral being aelg... Well, you know. To some people that's as bad as joining with a humyn."

"But aelg who are born in the Federation and territories are citizens and subjects. Unlike humyn, who can only be guests."

"They can also be citizens or subjects. If they perform a great deed for the nation. Remember the Gael-Prithi bard Tomas? He was a powerful dreamer and warned the Ethynsul coast of a raider's alliance to attack the seaboard."

"Yes," Eld said, remembering her school lessons of the 30th century. "Wasn't his own tribe part of the alliance?"

"And for that he was banished. They would have killed him, but magi with the fleet patrol saved him. He was taken to Tyrum and lived in the Exile's Palace for seven years as a condition of proving his character before being granted citizenship for life. A humyn may also seek a boon from the Queen to be a subject and then request citizenship from Parliament. The Voice of the Mother's Council has never denied Her Humble Majesty in this. But you know there is a tribe of mothers in politics who would deny the Queen if they could. Her time is done, they say. We are a nation of rational mothers, who should not allow gifts of chance from Heaven to reign over our fate. Yet that is why they would deny a humyn with an elfyn soul society: because fate caused them to be born without active essence."

"You really believe some humyn have elfyn souls?"

"How else do you explain it? All their sorcerers, poets, druids, bards, shamyn ...those who truly see in dreams even if they cannot use essence?"

"All Thyn dream truly. Some are better at it than others. Their best is something we think them incapable of. So we find it notable."

"Perhaps. Very well, let me tell you an amusing bit of gossip at the Marshal's expense, since we adore that soul so."

"I must only listen," Eld said.

"She sings like a messenger of Paradise. She's a natural soprano and they say she could have gone into opera. But you know our Marshal. She only speaks in her low voice and will not permit any soul to hear her sing a note. Not her, the mother of mothers to be heard chirping like a son of Sul!"

Eld, in spite of her stated resolve found herself smirking. "She could just sing with her low voice."

"Apparently her low voice is out of key and terrible."

"So she doesn't sing at all?"

Seth laughed. "You said you were only going to listen!"

They ate at The Wildling before returning to the garrison. Eld had yet to get used to being both stared at and spoken to with respectful formality. Seth reminded her as an officer she'd have to expect it. They parted at the Rowan Oak, making plans for a ride the next day. Alhern finally declared the battlefield safe and Seth wanted to see it; Alhern agreed provided he was escorted. With these pleasant thoughts Eld walked inside and into a large spray of ferns.

A pot filled with living ferns was sitting on a table near the door. Eld had been so surprised she knocked it over, but caught it before it fell to the floor.

"Fine catch, sister," some elf said.

"What are you doing?" Tafli said alarmed, darting from behind the bar. "Has any frond broken?"

"No." Eld gently returning the ferns to the table. "That is quite a cluster. Perhaps they shouldn't sit so close to the door."

Tafli sighed. "You are maybe right. You are second drunken bear today. Put it by the hearth," Tafli added pointing, his wrist bangles jingling for emphasis.

Eld sighed and picked it up. "Don't you have a new knave by now?"

"I am thinking of only hiring knaves through the mother's house. Many Sula do this and I now am seeing why."

Eld was too savvy to ask for the details, and the abundance of ferns, long, lush and accented with snowdrops was making it hard to see her way. "This is heavy," she added. The pot was a woven burlap mesh lined with moss and, from the feel, contained enough moisture to fill a bucket.

"Yes, it is the way to keep it alive as it should be," Tafli said, unconcerned for Eld's efforts. "Yes, there, on that seat nearby. No one is using that."

"I use that!"

"When you have a poet's mood and no beautiful man to be escorting, yes. So I am thinking you will not be using that seat for a while."

Eld put the ferns on the seat and stood back with Tafli. The afternoon sun warmed the green frilly fronds, the snowdrops nodding their white heads with approval.

"I am liking ferns," Tafli sighed, beaming. "She knows and gives this for apology. Not clusters of cut dead flowers like most Sula."

Eld did not ask who, or why, and wished Tafli would stop speaking about his paramour. Eld knew he didn't do this on purpose, but it felt like she was being tested when he did. So she firmly drove the conversation back to what she wanted to drink. Then, because there was no one she knew inside, she sat on a bench next to the potted spray of ferns.

"We make a fine pair," Eld muttered to it, sipping her cup. She touched a nodding snowdrop, a small white flower with four petals that seemed to look over the moss covered edge. Eld felt a sudden rush of affection, regret and longing. She pulled her hand back lest she felt anything else. Eld wasn't an expert with the practice of seeking moods or impressions from touch. But if she could put a face to the woman with such feelings it was definitely Alhern. She was beginning to resent keeping this secret and had to force her mind to recall that Alhern was her ally, though she might be Danshor's doom. Then she saw a captain making her way through the growing afternoon crowd. It was Captain Aynath.

"There you are, Farthal. You have a fine companion."

"We met at a farmer's sale. He's very pretty, but I don't think we have much in common."

Aynath smiled at the joke, then gave Eld a folded card. It wasn't a missive, just a message. Eld popped it open anxiously.

"As you see, you and Danshor will report to the commander's house tomorrow after breaking fast."

"The commander's sister is arriving."

"That's my understanding. Look, Farthal, everyone knows you're a loyal and sound war-sister. But there comes a time you have to protect your own path. Cleave to companions who make the journey easier, and forsake those who create obstructions."

So the captain was another soul who would vote to abandon Danshor to her fate.

Eld said nothing out loud. Aynath was offering her support and she should feel grateful. But as she watched Aynath greet other women and laugh, a mix of officers from various companies, another resentment grew adjacent to the one keeping the commander's secret. If Eld allowed it, soon there would be a forest of resentments: the nephew for being an adolescent harlot, the women who allowed the boys into the secret garden, Roel for making it a matter of importance, women concerned with the fate of their sons, and men for making it a life and death issue in society. There was even a perverse part of her who wanted to blame Seth for becoming so important to her, that dismissing the offer of sponsorship was out of the question. How else would she be able to court him with the goal of marriage, an idea she'd never imagined considering before coming to Falls Gate? Maybe the ancient poets were ultimately to blame, for without Seth's challenge at the fete so long ago Eld wouldn't have dared to say a word to him.

But that wasn't right either. It was Danshor who spoke first, Danshor who annoyed Eld with her flawed verse, that bated Eld into joining the contest.

It was Danshor. And it was ultimately Danshor who was at fault for visiting a wild Garden and whatever else had transpired. Danshor had been Eld's war-sister for the last five years. They had gambled, harloted, laughed, pranked, rode and fought together. Eld couldn't imagine life in the company without Danshor. But now she had to. For Eld might not be in the company at all even if Danshor was saved from ruin. Thus returned the question of sacrifice.

Eld would never sacrifice Danshor to advance herself. That would make her a hollow simulacrum of herself, a creature of ambition like the Marshal, respected publicly, despised by the private discerning eye and, likely, hollow inside, a shell of ego around nothingness. Eld pitied the Marshal's children – how could they know peace and security with such a mother? No, she would not abandon Traith and Shedann in spirit by becoming such a thing.

The fading sun cast a warm glow over the table, the cup and Eld's silent leafy companion as her final  thoughts came to the dusk of the issue. She would sacrifice not Danshor, but her society. She would accept the sponsorship and leave the company. But first she had to save Danshor. Or what kind of war-sister would she be?

With that thought, Eld drained her cup and left the Rowan Oak.

## Chapter 37

# Secrets of a Wild Garden

Though the commander's house was bright as always, without red or black drapes for mourning or wake, it still felt like Eld had interrupted a funeral. The festive décor of the gala had long been cleared away, and the servants and staff were hardly visible, heard only speaking in hushed whispers. There was no sound of Solafi arguing with his keeper. In fact, there was no sight or sound of Effa Tanmor at all. He was probably packing with the boy.

Eld waited outside the closed conference room with Seth and Alhern, Seth on a small settee, Alhern pacing; Eld herself was seated on yet another armless, well-made, but hard chair that did not encourage comfort. Within legal notaries both civilian and military wrangled. Danshor was finally allowed to send a missive through the Falls Gate sadol and her family had spared no expense hiring the services of the best legal advocate available in Falls Gate. This would have been a blow if Alhern was vengeful and wanted Danshor utterly destroyed. Soldiers had a right to representation by a military advocate, but they also had a right to choose a qualified civilian one. Now their barracks was fielding messengers with leaves of paper, on the hour, until late in the night. Eld knew that the advocate had traveled to Gate Step, and was staying at The Wildling. But when Eld left for the commander's, Danshor didn't come with her, though she assured Eld she would be along.

"And you are certain you told Danshor she was to come?" Alhern asked Eld.

"Yes, commander," Eld replied. She felt odd sitting while Alhern stood, but Alhern simply had abandoned her own chair, preferring to pace.

"And what did she say?"

"That she'd be coming as she was advised."

"Did she now." Alhern resumed her pacing. "As advised. A law trick. Very well. I suppose we wait."

For a moment voices raised within, then lowered before Eld could discern meaning. Finally Alhern, a woman used to knowing exactly what was transpiring, couldn't help herself and yanked the door open and stepped inside, shutting it sharply behind her.

The small settee was opposite the door; Eld was on one of two chairs flanking the door.

"I assume you know now," Eld said quietly.

Seth glowered. "That your war-sister is involved in this wild Garden affair? Yes, sadly! Why were you so secretive?"

"It wasn't my place."

"Solafi is my nephew!"

"I assumed Alhern would say something if ..."

Eld trailed off at the sound of boots walking briskly towards them. Expecting Danshor, she was surprised to hear a strange woman's deep voice, "No worries, I know the way!"

She sounded like another woman used to giving orders, so Eld was further surprised when this new worthy appeared. She was not an officer or even a soldier. A cloak was draped over one arm, steaming slightly with damp. Neither as muscular as Alhern nor as beautiful as Seth, she seemed to be ever so slightly, perhaps an inch, taller than both. It was only something about the shape of her face that betrayed her as a sibling of Seth and Selind. Her hair, in wind-blown trilocks, was darker, her eyes harder and glossy, with no warmth. She wore a black trimmed emerald drayer's coat and one could believe she'd driven the horses of the carriage herself all the way from the Alhern estate. With the whip at her belt, it was unlikely she was a friendly soul at the best of times. Not that any animal should fear. Whips were used only to drive by sound or scare away wild beasts. A soul so different made Eld certain she was begat from a different father than Seth and Selind.

"There you are, brother," the woman said, as if she was speaking to the head knave of a house. "Al met, etc."

Seth stood. "It would be better met if you weren't tracking mud inside."

"That's what you have servants for. Where's your sister?"

At that moment Alhern reemerged, closing the door again.

"Here I am," Alhern said. "I thought I heard you stomping through my halls."

Eld had never seen Alhern so wary and alert in her own house. That look only haunted her face during dire times on the battlefield. Now another battle had come to the commander's house.

Her sister didn't seem bothered at all, a woman who dealt with her rages and fears by giving them no thought except to hunt down the causes and kill them. Eld couldn't keep her eyes from falling on the coiled whip while the woman spoke.

"I have just spoken with my son. What he tells me is distinctly unpleasant. Now explain to me, sister, how, after giving my child into care so he can learn discipline and be educated about our nation's military customs, instead I have received a stream of letters from Effa Tanmor, the latest informing the estate that, between loafing with his friends, and working as a common bar knave, he somehow found himself in a wild Garden of Lun?"

As a soldier, Eld was used to long winded sarcastic rhetoricals. But Alhern certainly hadn't been spoken to like this since she was a cadet. She opened her mouth to reply, but her sister continued her harangue.

"Apparently these events escaped the keen eye of my artistic brother and my sister, who they tell me is a commander of Falls Gate Keep. Effa Tanmor has been quite unimpressed with the suitability of these accommodations. With this latest news, I can't blame him. So oblivious was my sister, she sent me this –" Here the woman pulled out a letter that had been opened, holding it in a shaft of light angling in from a skylight in an adjacent room. " – Explaining how, after feeling the excitement of the battle, my son desires to make a further spectacle of himself by becoming a military page."

Eld started in surprise as the letter burst into flames.

"That is not an event that will come to pass," the woman finished as the remains of the paper fell to the floor in hot ashes.

"Have a care, will you?" Seth exclaimed.

Eld started again when Seth's sister stamped on the remains of the ash, grinding one heel down on the edge of a carpet. "Stop whining, brother. If you used your servants instead of befriending them –"

"Don't speak to our brother in that tone!" Alhern growled. "He manages the house admirably."

"Is that what you call it? Well, I'm rescuing my son from this 'admirable management'. He will be returning to the estate."

"He might be needed for testimony," Alhern said.

"He will be returning as adroitly as duty permits, is my meaning, as you well know." The woman's voice had raised as if correcting drivers in some laxity.

"We can hear you perfectly!" Alhern said.

"I have often wondered…"

Eld rose slowly, not wanting to call attention to herself. She'd felt like a child in the middle of a row among adults. Seth had stood and was now close enough she could chance a whisper.

"This is your sister?" Eld breathed.

But the woman's ears were excellent.

"Yes, I am," she said, staring at Eld as if she was a wolf harrying her livestock. "I'm Arumil Trythe Alhern and these are my sibling spritelings who still seem to need my watching."

"She's a decade older than us," Seth muttered.

"And still a century wiser! Where is the seducer, sister? I have a length of hide that needs warming."

"You can't flog her, " Alhern said sighing.

"Oh, yes, I can." Arumil advanced a step. Alhern didn't back up, so they were nose to nose. "I have had plenty of time on three carriages and one boat to review the law. Sentimental mothers in Parliament aside, the flogging of seducers is still accepted for settlement. Even in the case of a willing youth in the throws of wild passions."

"After a civil trial," Alhern said. "The woman in question is a cavalier. If it comes to that, first she has to be court-martialed."

Arumil made a savage noise in her throat.

"Is this the one?" she demanded, staring at Eld.

Eld was so shocked to be under Arumil's baleful glare, she was speechless a moment.

"No," Alhern said.

"You sure? She feels guilty of something."

Alhern sighed. "This is the woman's war-sister."

"Is she, now? So you were part of this Garden adventure, sampling the unripe fruits of youth?"

"No!" Eld protested. "I didn't know anything about it!"

"For a soul who has such a feeble opinion of poetry, that was quite a florid description, sister," Seth put in.

Arumil ignored her brother, her murderous eye fixed on Eld, fingering the coiled whip.

"As if we don't know soldier-talk about the boys they have," Arumil said, looking into each of Eld's eyes, seeking a lie.

"I was elsewhere that night," Eld said, wondering why she was defending herself as if her career depended on it and not Danshor's. "You have to understand it's easy to lose track of Danshor's men because there are so many."

It was nerves speaking, but from the looks on Seth and Alhern's faces, they did not think much of this defense. Eld resolved to say as little as possible.

"I'm almost certain you have no children," Arumil said.

"My children aren't relevant!" Eld shot back in temper, forgetting any thought of restraint. "I have two sprites actually. And Danshor has a son –"

"And she probably lets him harlot himself," Arumil said evenly.

It was rare Eld felt the desire to punch a civilian. Feeling her hand seize in a fist, she held it, instead raising her own voice as it deepened:

"Danshor is many things and I should know. I've ridden with her for half a decade. But her son is dear to her as any mother's child. He is not responsible for your wrath nor does he deserve slanderous speculations of him being a harlot!"

The hall was quiet. Seth stepped to stand next to Eld, slipping an arm around hers, giving her the grace of his presence, making public the link they shared that one day might mean he would leave his mother's estate and join Eld's. The wise mother avoided making alliances harder than they must.

Arumil's eyes flickered down, noting the gesture, then back to Eld's eyes. But this time Eld didn't care. If anyone had suggested something of the like about Shedann...

"Now that was truth," Arumil said.

"Another truth is you are menacing my cavalier. Cease and step back, " Alhern said in her familiar commanding voice.

Arumil looked between them and stepped back. "I expect this is the one our brother is mooning over. I forgot myself. My apologies. I should confine my outrage to true events and those guilty of them. Is that her?"

Eld snapped her head around and saw Danshor had arrived, like Eld, in full uniform, standing stiffly near Alhern waiting for acknowledgement.

"Lancer Hanmet Danshor," Alhern began, "this is Emha Arumil Alhern, my worthy elder sister, and the mother of my nephew. Arumil, this is the cavalier who had an unfortunate encounter with your son and ..."

"And who I am going to flog like a flint serf if I have my satisfaction," Arumil finished. She advanced on Danshor, but Danshor stood at attention, not moving. Only some one who knew her saw Danshor was alarmed, not only with the woman's ire, but her whip was not to be ignored. Arumil was as tall as Danshor and had she wanted, had the frame to be her equal in size. But Arumil found her vigor in righteousness, holding the coiled whip under Danshor's nose.

"You have nothing to say for yourself?" Arumil breathed.

"Again, sister, I must ask you...."

"Let her speak!"

"I have been advised to not speak until my advocate is present," Danshor said in a shaky voice.

"Have you?"

It was fortunate at that moment the doors opened.

A younger officer from Alhern's office held the door like a butler.

"They are ready commander," she said.

Before Alhern could say anything, Arumil, still gripping her whip, abandoned Danshor and pushed past into the conference room. The rest of them followed.

It was much like it'd been after the battle, but there were no goblets, bottles or refreshments. Instead missives and leaves of papers with scrolling, professional calligraphy covered the table. Three women were at the far end; two women, including the one standing, were military advocates, officers with gold sashes crossing their fronts. The other seated woman was plain faced and ageless. She wore a dark maroon waistcoat with no decoration and a white shirt with a gold neck scarf. Over this she also wore the mother coat of industry and trade, something professional mothers felt the need to don when meeting among themselves, but most discarded as soon as they come inside a house. But this was her armor for this legal battle, the high stiff collar and broad shoulders looming behind her neck, oversized and conspicuous. As they entered, she waved a lazy hand to the chair beside her.

"Lancer Danshor should sit here," she said, while still scribing a paper with a metal quill pen.

Danshor moved with the same speed she did to obey any order.

"Harthyn Bellarn," the woman said, by introduction. "And I am pleased to report, Emha Alhern, your estate will be happy this unfortunate event is about to be put to rest."

"Is that so?" Arumil demanded. She sat down next to the military advocate, and glared belligerently across the table at Harthyn, slamming her whip on the table top for emphasis.

"Yes, it is," Harthyn said evenly ignoring the threat. "After a few more clarifications are made. I'll allow the senior military advocate to explain."

Arumil glared at the officer, a little older than Arumil herself, shifting through documents before meeting her eyes.

"Apologies, Emha Alhern, for this unpleasantness. Having three grown children and many grandchildren I do understand your outrage. However, as the facts stand, no crime of seduction or rape has been committed. Which is not to say no wrongdoing has transpired. Recklessness and indiscretion have certainly been afoot.

"First, we have a group of boys, solidly past their first fire, aged from ninety-five to a hundred and three, dressing in a deliberate attempt to deceive women into believing they were all old enough to be taken. Of the three women they accused, those identified as accompanying Danshor to the Garden, none suspected the boys to be below age. This has been read as truthful.

536

"Second, is the matter of soldiers and cavaliers visiting the Garden in the first place. The women were reckless in the legal sense. They knew, as a wild Garden, it would not be managed with legal care. None of them knew underage boys would be offering themselves, but it is the real consequence of shoddy practices. We have identified the operator and that information has been turned over to the Hounds Master's office.

"That is not to say there will be no discipline. But this falls into the category of a reckless accident, not a felony. None of the boys have been hurt. A Garden with no oversight attracts seducers. Command has been reluctant to forbid mothers from Gardens. But commanders of garrisons can rule their own Hosts in these matters as needed. Given the local situation we recommend forbidding soldiers from local wild Gardens and the serving women involved to be disciplined with a suspension of regular pay and drudging. Because this cavalier in particular was identified, and this was a cause of upset and embarrassment to the Alhern estate, the offer of a written, formal apology has been made, as well as a verbal obeisance from Hanmet Danshor herself. I understand your feelings, Emha Alhern. But nothing was taken from your son. He simply kissed women. But if getting a deep kiss was all it took to birth, I'd have birthed five children before my first century."

No one laughed at the joke, but it lightened the mood ever so slightly. Adolescents were discouraged from fulling trysting, and the truth was most were too shy and uncertain to try until they were near adulthood. The intimate kisses of nethers was their domain.

Eld settled into the chair next to Danshor; Seth sat near her but with his chair a little distant. Commander Alhern stood at the head of the table, looking over the shoulders of the military barristers.

"Do we need more testimony and readings?" she asked.

"That depends if Emha Alhern will be satisfied. If she truly believes her child has been injured by this, it is reasonable for her to pursue it."

"Might I offer some insight?" Harthyn said.

Arumil glowered at her but didn't object. Harthyn continued:

"I'm not a native of this area. My mother's estate is on the edge of the New Forest and I worked in the offices in Ta Meloshok for two decades. I took the case of settling a fraught legacy after the passing of Aeon Corlyn, better known as Corlyn Bezhrad, of the Bezhrad public house in Falls Gate. I traveled here to work and never left. I think unknown to my soul I hungered to see mountains. There are subtleties of the culture and customs those not familiar with the life of the outer lots might miss. There are few temples and the usual infrastructure we take for granted is absent. Thus Moon Meets are free romps in the woods involving most of the adult male population, not in established glades reserved by private clusters of men. And women, while not permitted in the main rituals, neither are discouraged from discreet observation. There is a game where "hunters" seek "prey", that is, male attendees who wander from the circle wanting to be taken anonymously allow themselves to be found, much like in a Garden of Lun. But there are codes they exchange to confirm this, or at least release each other from blame. And the size of communities means true anonymity is impossible. Participants pretend to be unknown to each other, and the chance of any mother joining with some unripe boy is unlikely without a disguise produced by magi quality illusionary skill. A local boy would simply not attempt to do this in such a situation. The boys here certainly were taking advantage of the fact soldiers were unlikely to be as discerning and, forgive me, your son's naiveté. So were this to become a public case, you would not find as much local sympathy as you might expect. And if the local boys involved became known, they could well make it impossible for your son to ever visit again in comfortable society.

"As it stands, the only parties aware of the situation regarding your son are the four soldiers and everyone in this room. Not even the Garden host has been informed who exactly has complained; only that it was one of the boys' families. And had it not been for the vindictive manipulation of your son by an officer with a vendetta against Danshor's war-sister, you would not have known, and no one would be harmed more for it."

"So you are saying the real crime is that I know about it?" Arumil said.

"No, only the shame wouldn't have been this great without someone determined to exploit it for revenge. Which brings us to my last point. If protecting your son is your goal, I would advise a joint effort with the estate I represent to censure this Lieutenant Roel."

"Tell us more," Commander Alhern said before her sister could speak.

"It would have to be through military law," Harthyn said.

The seated army advocate was nodding. "We'd need a request with justification, but there's ample here. We could expedite it in a couple hours."

Alhern looked at her sister as if willing her to see reason.

"This is the best satisfaction you are likely to get. I know you're longing to flog a woman, but he wasn't raped."

Arumil sat back, arms crossed, still clutching her whip.

"I don't like letting mothers dance away without payment."

"Cavalier Danshor is facing a cut in pay and extra duties," Alhern said, sounding impatient. "Without free days during that time. That is hardly dancing away freely."

"I want compensation," Arumil said insistence. "It's the principle."

Seth sighed forcefully but said nothing.

Harthyn looked over the papers in front of her and shrugged. "I can ask the estate. But unless you can show your son was damaged –"

"He feels humiliated and hurt. He was put at risk."

"And you should definitely pursue a complaint against the Garden host. But you'll want to go carefully for the reasons I explained. These small lot communities have few secrets."

Arumil looked mulish.

"The family needs to discuss this," Alhern said. "My brother will ..."

"Your brother will sit right here," Seth said. "I'm no longer your ensign. There is refreshment in the main sitting room. Or ask the staff for whatever you wish."

Eld stood up with Danshor and the advocates.

"She should stay," Seth said, indicating Eld.

"You're confused, brother," Arumil said. "It is her house you'd be joining with if you marry, not the other way around. There's no reason your future maybe wife should be present in our intimate affairs. However, I'd like that one to stay and account for herself."

Arumil pointed to Danshor.

"I don't advise this," Harthyn said.

"Then I must decline, emha," Danshor said formally.

Eld looked at Alhern. She nodded towards the door, and Eld understood she was yielding to her sister's wishes.

"We will call you both back when we are finished," Alhern said.

And so they left, and waited to be summoned.

Eld found herself useful to their group. Neither officer had visited the garrison before, and neither Sonamor nor staff appeared as Eld would have expected. She suspected they were being discreet to avoid embarrassment or learning something they did not want to be burdened with. So Eld was their guide, the only one who knew the wild paths of the house, and they arrived at the sitting room without incident, a spread of light refreshment and barley-mead awaiting as promised.

They sat and the officers talked readily with Eld, taking especial interest in the recent duel. Slightly apart from them Danshor spoke quietly with Harthyn. The officers treated Danshor like furniture that needed to be aired and generally ignored her. While Danshor was determined not to have committed a felony, mothers were wary of laxness with women who had became intimate with an underage adolescent, however deceptive the circumstances. Danshor would have to weather this, a penance of suspicion, until she regained trust.

Eld understood because she had a son; Danshor surly understood for the same reasons. What would Eld have done if it was Shedann? If she knew that he had deceived the women as throughly as the nephew had? Eld would want to beat the mothers involved senseless. But she also knew she'd be demanding of Shedann what he thought he was doing. She hoped he would have learned long ago to not take such ridiculous risks. But how? Did boys even listen to their mothers when it comes to these things? The men of the house should guide them. But if the men of the house were judgmental and reproving of every expression of spirit, a boy may well ignore them too. Perhaps sons were doomed to be at risk of seducers.

After about an hour, Alhern appeared. She looked grim.

"We're ready."

They returned to the conference room, seated as they were before, but Alhern didn't rejoin them yet. They sat in awkward silence until she arrived a couple of minutes later.

"Sorry to keep you worthies. I had to summon Lieutenant Roel."

Eld and Danshor exchanged a look. Eld could hear Danshor's heart racing like her own. Why bring Roel?

"There are questions she should answer, notarized with witnesses," Alhern explained. "And it is necessary to compel her cooperation. I know some parties feel very strongly about Roel. I am going to ask you conduct yourselves with restraint." Alhern reached up high on the wall. Well made solstone skylights had a place that could be touched to diminish their force during the day. Alhern did this and the air felt less energized, less easy to, say, set someone's guardlocks aflame.

While they waited, Arumil tersely communicated what was acceptable so far: the formal apologies, written and verbal, and the suggested discipline. But Arumil considered this a place to start, not a conclusion. She still felt this was too lenient and had more questions about Danshor and her character. And so Eld found herself giving testimony.

"You understand you are compelled to speak truly from the soul, with no intent to deceive directly or by omission, on pain of oath breaking?" the senior advocate asked.

"Aiyn," Eld said, the ancient submission to the Mother Gods, chanted in the temples of the Sunqueens in hopes of reaching Sul's ears, reduced to the common acknowledgment of "Ai" in these lesser times.

"And in speaking truth, you open your mind to all reasonable paths that it may be confirmed, withholding only that which is truly outside a court's right?"

"Aiyn," Eld repeated.

Every soul had an anxiety that they'd either be censored for telling the truth imperfectly or else revealing some unrelated embarrassment in thought. While this wasn't a court, Eld was being read to a court standard, not just the general sound of truth in her words, but the thoughts behind them. Well trained, powerful or old minds could block a court reader, but that would be contempt. Rare talented souls could not only block their thoughts, but replace them with false memories to support a false tale. But to succeed, one had to somehow also give an aura of belief. This was so rare to be unheard of, if for no other reason than no matter how much one might have glamored her own thoughts, she hardly had the ability to do so with every possible witness. In short, reading of truth was considered as reliable a test as it was in the ancient days of the Mother Tree.

Eld couldn't imagine the process was any more pleasant for the souls of her foremothers. The head advocate was a patient, calm soul. Often magi were employed for this task, and they were preferred by some. Magi were expert at reading and speaking in thoughts, and the touch of their mind was like a calm trickle of a quiet country stream. Magi were also seen as neutral outsiders. Women like the head advocate made a soul wary they would be judged before their time. Eld was relieved the woman's mind on touching hers felt like a light breeze, insistent, present, but not unpleasant. It could have been much worse. Eld also felt a visceral awkwardness, as if she was two souls in one body. It was going to be a deep reading; her body's responses watched as well as her thoughts. She shivered briefly, then was able to bear the discomfort. While the head advocate read her, the other one asked questions.

Eld was asked how long she'd known Danshor and gave an honest and unflattering account of her first impressions, which seemed to cheer Danshor up.

"You find this funny, cavalier?" Arumil demanded.

"Pardon, emha. But she's always so sensitive."

Eld glared at Danshor, forgetting for a moment she was being read. "I could walk out and leave you to your fate, if you'd prefer," Eld said with feeling.

"I'm only telling the truth," Danshor said with an air of innocence. "It's not my fault which lots you chose ..."

"She cheats at lots," Eld said bluntly. "And dice. And Gains when she can manage it. No, not with essence. She just bends her own and leaves false impressions."

"Those who go looking for impressions instead of playing properly..."

"And droning on about her conquests to distract other players ..."

"I thought you were a sheltered poet with a cold bed. You might have learned something –"

"Would you stop saying I have a cold bed?"

"You're still mad about losing that tree flask."

Eld crossed her arms and sat back, shocked the anger still burned after five years. "It was a present chosen by my sprites."

"Truly?"

"Yes!"

Danshor looked at the advocate. That worthy was not amused to have her services bent to such a mundane matter, but she nodded once. "I thought you just said that to get it back. You shouldn't wager your birthed gifts in a dice game."

Eld seethed because she agreed. "I usually don't. But I was tired of you gloating over your wins all night, and hoped Felkeni had had enough."

"Felkeni likes me," Danshor said, still lost in her wonder about Eld's flask.

"The Goddi of luck and fortune likes you, you say?" Eld said. "Is that why I'm sitting here trying to help you and being needled for it?"

"I had an adjacent thought," Alhern said.

"I apologize," Danshor said with a sigh. "That was ill said."

"I think we are wandering into rare fields with few shards," Harthyn interjected. "Are there more relevant questions?"

"I have one," Arumil barked. She still held her coiled whip, hoping to use it. "Have you ever seen your war-sister lust after boys?"

"Allow me to interject here," Alhern said, " the common soldier often refers to young men who are of age as 'boys'. It's not uncommon in civilian life either, if we're being honest."

"If we're being honest, it's clear my question is about lusting after boys below their majority," Arumil said acidly.

"With respect, I have never lusted after children," Danshor said between gritted teeth.

"I'm asking your war-sister, Cavalier."

"Never," Eld said.

"Not even in the, what's that wildling public shack called? The Ash Oak?"

"The Rowan Oak," Alhern corrected. "And it is a contracted public house."

"A sign might clear the confusion," Arumil said. "My son recognizes Danshor's voice because he spent some time sitting on her lap making merry. Did you ever observe this?"

Eld thought, breaking into a sweat searching her memory.

"I don't recall that," Eld said.

Arumil glanced at the advocate reading then back at Eld.

"What do you recall of her words or actions with my son?"

Eld swallowed. "She made the same comments other women did the first day he worked as a knave. He was using the name "Farni" and the same deception of identity and age. He was enthusiastic and caught many women's eye. Danshor said something about not being partial to younger or older men. But she was discussing men, not children."

"And you had no idea he was not of age?" Arumil directed this at Danshor. "Even when you saw him as a bar knave?"

"No," Danshor said shortly.

"Is he typical for your type?"

"If we're going to discuss all the men I've been with we'll be here all day."

"Cavalier," Alhern warned.

"She has a point," Harthyn interjected. "It is no crime to tryst with half the available men on the continent, though surely it would be exhausting."

"I'm just trying to fathom how a mother, with a son near the age of my own, could be so insensible to the fact Solafi was barely past his fire, no matter how much glimmer and glamors he was wearing."

Eld prayed again to Gods she did not believe in she would not be interrogated on that count and be forced to reveal that's exactly what she and Patrycan said when Torin and Danshor ogled the nephew.

"As the testimony from the other soldiers and your own son show, he was very convincing to many souls. And in a night lit garden ..."

"So tell us of the oldest man you've wooed," Arumil demanded.

"It's not as if I request details from their estates!" Danshor snapped.

"Maybe you should!" Arumil shot back. "Because the more I hear, the more I am convinced the only reason you haven't taken a boy in your reckless adventures is bold, brazen luck!"

"Very well," Danshor said through gritted teeth. "There were two brothers I won many ribbons for at the fair. They're old enough to be married off and were trying to get some adventure in before that joyous time. One of them might have been older than me. A worthy mother doesn't badger a man about his age. And a couple weeks earlier I was graced with the company of a beautiful, bored and neglected keeper of children. Does that please you all? Should I write down methods of seduction for those wanting?"

"You forget I have a child," Arumil said. "Your prattling is meaningless."

"One child proves you'd trysted exactly once and were lucky to share vigor," Danshor said. "Almost a century ago. How warm is your bed now?"

"Cavalier!" Alhern bellowed. "You will master yourself!"

"Commander, apologies, emha. I do not seek to seduce boys below age. Read that!"

"But you are reckless," Arumil said. "It's in your character and had you or my wayward child been more persistent – "

To Eld's relief someone knocked. Seth stood up to open the door while the advocate reading Eld and presumably Danshor said, "I'll release your mind for the moment. Be ready in case more questions come."

Eld nodded, exhaling softly. She could still hear and feel a mind touching hers, but it had withdrawn from her body. The next moment she leaped to her feet in alarm because Roel stepped in.

Eld understood why Alhern had dampened the power of the solglass above. Eld hated the sight of Roel, hated the ingratiating smile Roel gave Seth, how her eyes for the finest part of a second lingered down the front of his robe. What she might imagine doing to him if she thought she could get away with it. Eld would relish catching Roel in the attempt. Relish burning her alive...

Roel in contrast was ignoring Eld admirably, saluting Alhern and acting such that no one would know they were enemies. "At ease and sit down," Alhern said. "There are questions about your involvement in a matter that need to be answered."

Roel to Eld's chagrin took the seat at the opposite end of the table, close to Seth. Seth sat back down, closer to Danshor, deciding being nearer to the accused was preferable to whatever Roel was.

The barber's trick of gum and false locks was less obvious. Or perhaps Roel's hair was growing faster. She leaned back, certainly not relaxed, eyes neutral but calculating. Was she pleased at the chaos she'd midwifed? Concerned she would be censured? Did she have a pat story that danced between motes of unpleasant truths? Whatever the case she looked unreadable.

The head advocate said the same thing to Roel:

"You understand you are compelled to speak truly from the soul, with no intent to deceive directly or by omission, and pain of oath breaking?"

After all of Roel's 'aiyns' , to everyone's surprise it was Alhern who started interrogating Roel.

"Why were you speaking with my nephew at the gala?"

"Commander, we fell to talking after I overheard a concerning conversation."

"Conversation between whom?"

"The boys from the village and your nephew."

"And you just happened to overhear their conversation?"

"They were clustered around the refreshment and artless as boys who are not yet men are. Their voices carried with enthusiasm."

"And what were you doing yourself? You did not dance."

"But so many did and so well. At a point I sought refreshment."

"You sought refreshment? You did not seek to hear the boys better?"

"I walked over to pour myself refreshment," Roel said.

"Did you seek to overhear the boy's conversation?"

"I had heard something concerning about the Gilded Hero's war-sister. I thought it would be helpful to understand that tale."

"Helpful to whom, lieutenant?"

"Helpful that we know if mothers are taking advantage of young boys."

"Fine. Now answer directly: did you seek to hear the boys' conversation."

"Yes."

"Before or after you heard them speak of Lancer Farthal's war-sister?"

Roel's lips pursed. Oath breaking could result in an automatic court-martial. "Before," Roel finally said. "I had a feeling."

"What? A reverie?"

"No."

"A hope?"

Roel said nothing.

"So when you did speak with my nephew, were you aware he was, in fact, my nephew?"

"Of course, commander."

"You pretended to be his friend, correct?"

"I respectfully dispute that characterization."

"Well, please explain to us how an adult mother would be discussing the intimate activities of a young man, a man below his majority, without some pretense of friendship. Because a true friend would not betray his activities to feed a personal vendetta."

Alhern didn't raise her voice, yet the effect was much as if she had yelled. Roel looked humbled but only for a moment.

"With respect commander, had I said nothing the boy might still be throwing himself unwisely at mothers. Now he may be guided by the wise council of his house."

"So you came to Major Galledan with a concern that Danshor had seduced my nephew because you were concerned for his welfare?"

"And the honor of the Host!" Roel added.

Even in Eld's untrained ear the sound of truth snapped and shattered. And it calmed her. She could see now all she had to do was sit and Roel would scorch herself.

"The honor of the Host, indeed," Alhern said. "You have broken the oath and perjured yourself, Lieutenant. Let me tell you what I think: you did this for revenge. You've known the knave 'Farni' was my nephew for some time, correct?"

"I didn't think it was my place to say--"

"Were you hoping to revenge yourself on the proprietor with embarrassment? Perhaps getting his contract voided?"

Roel said nothing, her face like marble.

"And you knew about the wild Garden because you were invited. Yes, after asking around it wasn't just cavalier and foot companies who attended, but a handful of your officer friends. In your one act of wisdom you declined to go. Why?"

"It is, as you say, not wise to be found in such a place."

"But your friends report you being quite encouraging, that they should spread the word any mother who seeks adventure will find village boys aplenty. By which we mean young men. But you claimed to be overtired from the duel. It was a gambit with only a prayer, but you hoped to bait a trap knowing that cavaliers are known to take risks. It wasn't Danshor you wanted at all, was it? It was Farthal."

"What?" Eld blurted, utterly surprised by this turn.

Roel's eyes became hard. "With respect, commander, I did not force those boys to attend the garden."

"But you made certain they were invited by your proxy, Lieutenant Searin. You didn't particularly target my nephew, true. But you knew he had a throng of friends full of their fire and looking for daring."

Roel said nothing.

"What is wrong with you, Lieutenant?" Alhern demanded. "Your compulsion for revenge is unnaturally persistent."

"Revenge is as natural as birthing, emha," Roel growled.

"But abusing the honor of a boy who has done you no harm is not!" Alhern bellowed. "You deliberately befriended him to exploit his trust!"

The room was silent a moment.

"I looked into your past, Roel," Alhern continued. "Your family was compelled by law to send you to Temple for an adjustment when you were sixty-three. Do you remember why?"

"Not really," Roel said, voice echoing with resentment. "It's true." She waved at the advocate,who nodded. "I only remember being angry."

"Since you've been so free with my nephew's secrets, I will share this relevant one of yours, though on the condition it does not leave this room." After everyone nodded, Alhern continued. "When Roel was in school she tried to strangle a friend to death. Why, you ask. Because the girl received a pony as a gift, the same pony Roel had an eye on. Only the intervention of the other girls saved her friend. Now Roel finds reasons to take her errant passions out on men. I have already requested information from your previous posts, lieutenant. By the by, your request for a transfer has been denied. We don't honor irregular transfers for mothers embarrassed by losing duels. And I have no intention of being responsible for any more victims of your rage. It ends here, in the Temple with an adjustment, under discipline, or in court-martial and banished from our service. An officer is to always behave herself as a worthy gentle. The entire point of being a Federation Army officer is to protect the lives of mothers and men, not act like an aristocratic thug!

"Now you will apologize to my nephew's mother and feel very lucky she is not allowed to use that whip."

Arumil grasped the coiled leather harder as Roel stood at attention, faced Arumil and intoned, "I apologize for the offense to your nephew and family. My actions were ill considered and I regret them."

The words were rote and not required to be truthful. This was fortunate, because, from the sound, Roel did not regret her actions, though she agreed they were ill considered.

"Get out!" Arumil shouted.

"In a moment, sister," Alhern said. "Lieutenant, you are confined to the garrison until further notice. Now you are dismissed."

Roel saluted and left sprightly.

"I told you an investigation, not floggings, would get to the source, " Alhern murmured. "This entire situation was artificial. However, that does not mean there is not blame to be assigned. We still must dispose of the rest of the matter with Lancer Danshor."

They argued over particulars until noon, at which point Danshor was given leave to dine and return in the company of her advocate. Regretfully, the advocate insisted that Eld not accompany them to The Wildling; it was clear Eld was entangled with the Alhern family and this was against Danshor's interest. Eld would have been free to accept Seth's invitation, but Arumil insisted on a family luncheon and Alhern indulged her sister for the peace. So Eld found herself eating at the Rowan Oak alone. She thought it safer that the Kettle. Eld felt the first true loneliness while serving as a soldier. At least her seat by the ferns was available and they were as good companions as any.

When they resumed conference a couple hours later, the finalities were made. Unfortunately, while other women were involved and they would be rebuked formally and their families notified, Danshor was the only one the nephew himself could name and identify as having intimate contact. Arumil intended to make her an example by insisting on her mother's satisfaction: in addition to the formal written apology, and Danshor's verbal apology in person, she wanted a settlement of a thousand queens.

"It will not be said I let my son be used and there was no consequence."

Eld thought that demanding money because her son might be thought a harlot was not the way to disabuse that idea, but said nothing. Harthyn did not argue, simply agreeing to pass it along to the estate. Arumil also objected to Danshor remaining stationed at Falls Gate: her son should not have to see the cause of his shame if he visited. It had to be explained to her, since there was no felony and she was waiving civil satisfaction – the whip was never far from the conversation –the military could not punish Danshor for anything more than "acting with reckless disregard". The estate agreement of apology and possible restitution was more than fair. But Arumil didn't seem to see that. Eld had a flash of insight: Alhern had this exact mood when she ordered the magi to fire on the Eurthan transport as it prepared to leave. The sisters had that in common, being unable to feel a victory while hungry for vengeance. The same fire that drove them to success made it hard for them to stop when they had achieved their goals.

As if reading Eld's thought, Alhern said to her sister, "You have won. No matter how long we sit here arguing, there is no path that will allow you the satisfaction of a flogging."

"Do not dictate to me what suffices satisfaction, worthy sister."

After another hour, even the military advocates' patience was wearing thin. Unlike Harthyn they were not being paid a retainer beyond their salary. Unless there was a crime, they would be finished with the matter.

At which point Arumil declared she would hire her own advocate gallowglass from estate funds.

"I thought you wanted to spare your son embarrassment!" Alhern exclaimed, also out of patience. "Why do you think I offered military advocates? If you request estate funds, grandam will demand to know every detail! Is that what you want? If we can resolve this here, it is over, for the estate and your son!"

Eld was pleased to finally see the commander that she knew. Alhern might terrify her now and then, but she was firm, reliable and fair.

Arumil slammed the whip down on the table and crossed her arms rebelliously.

In the pause Seth said, "Has anyone considered what Solafi wants?"

"Mothers don't leave these matters to the sentimental minds of boys," Arumil said.

"He just wants it over," Seth said. "He doesn't feel abused or taken advantage of. But he does feel oppressed and embarrassed so much is being made of it. Sister, he just wants it over. Please."

There was a long silence. The light dimmed subtly as the afternoon grew old. The advocates silently shifted their papers. Eld even heard a distant whisper in her mind that might indicate they were speaking in thought.

"Very well," Arumil said, her mother's concern for her child winning over unending vengeance. "I don't like it. And I will be pursuing the party responsible for the Garden. So, let this be done."

Thus papers were signed and Danshor apologized, and never sincerer words had she uttered in Eld's presence. Danshor's pay was suspended a month and she was to have no free days, but report for patrol or drudging after duty during this time. There was a relief in the barracks, for it couldn't be too bad, whatever had happened, if Danshor was still with them. With the loss of Patrycan it was hard for the company as it was. Althone was managing the cache now and she was far less lenient about arrears.

Arumil Alhern left after dinner that same evening with her son and his keeper, Eld imagining the prim Effa Tanmor smug in his righteous alliance with the mother. Eld dined in the Kettle with Torin and Reon; Danshor was again at The Wildling with her advocate, finalizing the last of the settlements. It was strange to not have her eating with them. Oddly, Torin dominated the conversation.

"Felkeni knows what went wrong there," Torin said. "Danshor and I went with a couple sisters from Company Par. A group of officers were loudly endorsing the place, but I don't know what happened."

Eld broke into a sweat. Torin was at the Garden of Lun?

"What happened is some idiot let burning boys in," Reon said. "They got ridden dry, yapped about it and a mother complained."

"Where did you hear that?" Torin asked.

"I didn't," Reon said. "It's what always happens at these wild Gardens. You have to be wiser than that, Torin. Or you'll find yourself disgraced or flogged."

"It's good I left early," Torin said, eagerly devouring a leg of roast fowl. "Those boys were energetic, but something was wrong with them. They had no idea what they were doing. So I met up with Adamys, apologized and, well, you know. "

"What?" Eld said in shock. "How did I miss you courting Adamys, much less having a tiff?"

"The Orb doesn't turn on your or Danshor's fortunes, you know. Maybe if you weren't arguing over your tedious secrets, you'd know what other sisters were doing."

Eld sat stunned while Reon laughed, slapping Eld on the back. "She's speaks truth you know."

"Ai, now and then, she does," Eld admitted.

Some soul slapped a leaf of dull rag paper down on the table, the kind used for quick missives and dispatches. It was printed with dense tiny capitals with no care for punctuation or format except what was needed to keep the message clear.

"Have you elves seen this dispatch?" a foot soldier in archer's garb exclaimed. Eld recognized Camden from Company Par. "The sand druids are actually going to do it!"

Eld ignored the mild slur for the moment. She'd spied words in the hard to read text that chilled her soul.

"They really intend to attack the Federation," Eld said hollowly. "They plan to sack Gashora? Do they understand Gashora dwarfs their greatest city, Tamask? It will be the Battle of the Blue Fields all over. They won't last a quarter hour."

"Except it will be at sea," Reon put in, reading over Eld's shoulder.

"Ha! Our patrols will scorch them on the water and they'll have to paddle home!" Torin said a little too gleefully for Eld's taste.

"Humyn have souls," Eld said. "And every soul counts."

"If they care about their souls so much, they should keep their bodies in Sharitan," Camden said.

"Doesn't Gashora have the largest solstone cannons defending the bay?" Eld asked. "Not counting the Federation Patrol fleet ..."

"It won't been the Patrol Fleet," Reon said. "That's letting them get too close. Admiralty will be requesting use of the Tyreen aqua driven fleet to meet them on the open sea."

"Then they won't have a prayer," Eld said. "Has anyone tried diplomacy?"

"Magi dreamers are seeking open souls all the time," Camden said. "But the Sultan's circle has convinced his people we are demons and any dreams we send should be ignored. The few who do listen either have to flee and seek asylum or are executed horribly as traitors. We've done our duty. They will not listen."

"The tale of humyn since the Beginning," Reon said. "My grandam says the country should be razed."

"What?" Eld said in shock.

"At least the corrupt rulers. They're all mad. Sharitan is a country were men rule like mothers and mothers are slaves."

"How would that work?" Eld said trying to imagine and failing. "Who would build everything?"

"Men apparently."

"Humyn men? That's even less believable."

"Well, they are primitive works. Including their laughable war fleet."

"So they will die," Eld said.

"And the sharks will sing. Keep it bright, sisters!" Camden said. She left to share the dispatch with others.

"I wonder what the wagers will be?" Torin asked.

Eld stared at her, remembering the Eurthans betting on their fate around the Medusa during the battle. They were not so different, Sula and Eurthani …

"Well, it won't make a difference to their fate," Torin said. "What's the harm in wagering?"

"The thought is tasteless and disrespectful of the life in the Orb we're supposed to protect?" Eld said.

"It's also pointless," Reon said. "They'll be quickly routed. No one would bet on a race between a horse in her prime and a crippled nag."

Eld sighed. "At least the war will be quick. And will not be between elfyn."

*Chapter 38*

# Parley and Restitution

Hoping to meet Seth, Eld dreamed that night. They planned to ride to Fern Lake in the afternoon the next day, spending time exploring its many pools and mossy banks, thick with ferns and wildflowers. They would go after viewing the field of battle, but Eld had no idea if they'd have the opportunity to tryst. Now she was allowed to escort Seth in public, the worry was they'd be so scrutinized, Eld's visits through the garden would be noted. So they hadn't trysted outside of dreams since the gala.

But Eld had trouble waking to true dreams. She floated in the darkness between waking and sleep, seeing many images: her children playing, with Sil watching; the filigree chalice from the shop display; sitting in the Rowan Oak cramped by a spray of potted ferns; sparing with Sergeant Tershol under a starry sky. Then the images all faded and were replaced with a pale, silver-gray Eurthan face with glowing blue eyes. Eld was so shocked she woke.

She lay in her cot, listening to the soft breathing of the company around her. It was frustrating. Once the process of settling to dream and travel was interrupted, it was hard to resume. The distant Abbey bell chimed the second hour of the night. Eld curled on her side under her blanket and accepted she might only dream simply for the night. Thinking of good trysting places they might ride to, she fell back into sleep.

Eld stood on a white paved Queen's road, the sun bright but the air hazy. The scene was indistinct, perhaps a meadow or farmland. It was hard to tell with the haze and mist, but the road was very clear. It ran forward a bit, then parted into two paths in a way Queen's roads rarely did, a perfect fork with Eld walking the length of the divining rod it made. As she looked at the roads, one led to the sea, and though the sky was clear and the wind calm, the waves rolled and crashed as if there was a great storm in progress. The other led to a concert hall where a gala was in progress, the event seen as if a wall had been removed. Every officer and worthy Eld knew was dancing with every man Eld fondly remembered. Right in the place the road forked stood a massive chess piece, the Cradle, so large it could serve as a washing basin. A curiosity to know what was inside seized Eld and she ran forward. But instead of a round ball symbolizing a babe, an actual babe lay there, small and thin as elfyn newborns were, with fine hair and blunted, curled ears. It was a girl; at intervals she was awake, then asleep; one moment smiling with bright, gold eyes, then sleeping, mouth moving as if trying to unravel the mystery of speech in dreams. A man's hand appeared on the edge of the Cradle.

"Which will you choose?" Seth said.

Suddenly the cradle was full of flames, the babe gone, in her place a crystal globe that reflected all the stars in the night sky and the possibilities therein. Eld felt the deepest part of her gut quiver. Looking down the globe was inside her, smaller, glowing softly. Was she …?

"Excuse me, I don't mean to interrupt, but I believe someone is trying to reach you," a woman said.

Eld suddenly was awake in the dream and was facing a magi in black robes; she recognized her as Ta Murdan from the battle. Now she had no veil, her pale hair streaming in the breeze. They stood on a road, white stones flickering with symbols. Eld couldn't read them, as she often couldn't in dreams. There was music in the distance, the most beautiful music in the Orb. But it was familiar because she had heard it before.

Eld looked sharply in the direction of the music and saw the Door. But this time seeing it didn't make the wind stronger because she wasn't mortally wounded. Eld grabbed the hands of the magi, looking for something to brace herself. How could she keep a soul from the Door and get help from the Temple?

"My dear girl, that is very thoughtful of you, but not necessary," Ta Murdan said, gently pulling her hands out of Eld's. "I've said my goodbyes and am ready for what is beyond. I was seven hundred and eighty-three, for Sul's sake."

"Was?" Eld looked in her eyes and was shocked. They were completely black, without iris or pupil, but like windows into the night sky, full of stars.

"You'll know if you live long enough. Once all those who were close to you are gone and you've seen all the sights the Orb has to offer, satisfied every passion, well, it's really time to go on, isn't it? I will say I'm glad I was here long enough for the battle! Being struck from the sky with Bane lightning! How invigorating!"

"I thought they might have killed you," Eld said slightly appalled at Murdan's casual attitude towards death.

"No, not me! Perhaps a less vigorous soul. No, it is simply I've become bored. What strange souls, these Eurthans. But my curiosity about our foes was not enough to keep me. You, however, have one of them trying to speak through dreams. She says she comes as an agent of truce and parley. It sounded important anyway, and she does speak truthfully. I had just stepped out and I saw her flickering in the stones. We had words; I thought I'd go look for the woman she sought before moving on."

"Lieutenant Brig?" Eld asked.

"The very soul."

Just then the wind increased. Eld gasped because the Door had jumped closer.

"You are in danger, girl," Ta Murdan said. "Step there."

She pointed down. The path was split, as if a great ax had sundered the road down the center making two smaller ways. The side the magi stood on the stones now all said "farewell". Then it started to fade away behind her. On the side Eld stood it became more solid, white and blank, but ended suddenly in the direction of the Door.

"Stay on that side and you'll find the way back soon enough. Your Eurthan friend seems to have a problem projecting herself. Sadols are made to shorten distances. Tell Ta Narin I've given you permission to use the Abbey's. Good luck, Gilded Hero."

She smiled and winked, then walked to the Door.

Eld no longer felt the wind. She watched as the path behind Murdan disappeared behind every step until the magi was at the threshold. Curiosity kept Eld watching. Would she see an Amerling? They were visions reported before the dead passed the Door, tall, pale women, with scythe-like curved swords, robed in the black rags of night. Some legends said they divided the worthy dead from the unworthy, to keep the Afterworld free of evil. Unworthy women and men had their heads severed and thrown into the Void to join Athmod and the Ghosts of the Bane.

No such apparition came. The light from the Door brightened as Murdan stepped on the threshold, the singing piercing Eld's soul. She could see where, had she been in despair or had nothing to live for, her soul could willingly step through and her body would never wake again.

But Eld harbored no such despair, and so watched as Murdan stepped through, the light obscuring her for a moment. Then the Door, the light and the music vanished, leaving Eld on the familiar path of waking, a path of white stones disappearing in the distance in either direction.

What had Ta Murdan said? An Eurthan was trying to parley a truce? Brig!

Eld woke instantly, sitting up in her cot.

It was still dark. Eld dressed quickly, in boots, bracs and shirt, and ran out of the stables ignoring the greetings of the guards. Should she rouse Sergeant Tarl? The captain? The commander? But what would she tell them? A dead wizard told her to speak to an Eurthan through the stones? They'd tell her to go back to sleep. She knew it wasn't just a dream, but it sounded like one. She had to prove it and speak to Brig first. Through the stones. A sadol. "Use the Abbey's," Ta Murdan had said. The Triad.

Luckily watchfulness was over. Eld ran through the gates not sparing a word, an act that could result in discipline. She would beg for forgiveness afterwards: at best it could advance her career, at worst she lost some sleep chasing ghosts. Eld knew well how precarious a dream or thought link could be. She had no idea what problem Brig was having, or her essence skill, or how long she would keep trying. Eld took the path up the hill she'd gone with Tershol, a mix of dirt track, gravel and stone. Elfyn night vision was excellent even with no moon, but thanks to her training under starlight, Eld's sight was so clear she was able to run up as fast as she could in daylight. She sprinted up the paths and stairs in a handful of minutes, pausing only to get her bearing before running over the night-gray grass, past the swaying beech, flowers spent and now full of leaves. Then Eld leaped on the white wall around the raised ground where the Triad stood to stand before the three fingers of stone.

Two made a gate before her, the third a distance away equal to the width of the gateway. Eld felt the air shiver, saw a ripple in the starlight between the stones, but nothing else. She wasn't sure what to do so she stepped forward and backward by partial paces, trying to calibrate a connection. A loud buzz shivered through the air as if a giant bumblebee had zoomed through. A pale image of a woman flickered in the center for the briefest moment.

"Brig?" Eld called. The air shivered with a loud buzz again. Clearly there was a link, but Eld didn't know how to make it work.

"Step in the center!" a voice called.

Eld looked around. The shadow of a woman near the back doors, presumably a magi in residence who knew sadol use. So Eld stepped forward.

There was a buzz again, then a hum vibrated through her body and soul as if she had been struck by a small fork of lightning. It was uncomfortable and Eld wondered if this was always the case. Then she saw she wasn't standing exactly in the center on the small embedded metal marker. As soon as she did, the discomfort vanished, though there was still a slight hum. At the same time a woman manifested in front of her.

It was Brig but dressed in a uniform much like the first Eurthans who had attacked Eld and Seth weeks ago. The coat was red, but longer, more like a cavalry coat and trimmed in gold. Instead of yellow circles at the shoulders around her arms, a thick gold braid looped around, attached to either side of a short rigid collar, a style not common in Sula fashion. A gold bar at an angle was pinned on either side where the collar met under her chin, clearly her rank; they were the same bars on her black skin suit and armor. Her breeches or trousers were tucked into high, black, cavalry style boots which aways birthed questions about Eurthan cavalry in Eld's mind.

"Horns up and Al Met!" Brig said, blues eyes alight with excitement. At her core Brig was a friendly soul. "I was despairing of reaching you or any soul!"

These words surprised Eld. "How is your Sulanilish perfect?"

Brig grinned. "And I would say your Druzan is fluent. I think it has something do with the Skein transferring our thoughts. Like true dreaming, where even Shindi from the most remote ice caves have no accent. Otherwise, Saints know what they're chattering about."

"Uh huh," Eld said. "Sorry, I don't understand any of that. But we have a ranger who mentioned meeting 'Shindi', was it?"

"Not completely surprised. Don't mistake me, Shindi are our best rangers and trackers, especially in the Athlantal. But Avatar help the woman who insults their 'honor'. Those reaping swords aren't for roasting game!"

"Look, sister, I'd love to have a long chat about our countries and customs, but you had an urgent message? Only I'm not sure how long we have."

"Right you are! There is a hope of truce. I still don't know what the War Office is thinking. But I managed to convince the Major if we returned what was stolen it would prove our good faith."

"The Corinaths?" Eld's heart skipped a beat. Seth would be delirious with joy.

"I don't know who or what that is."

"The bronze sculptures. Especially the horse."

"Oh yes! They say it's some of the finest primitive work."

"Corinath is a celebrated master sculptor of our people!" Eld exclaimed, surprised she was offended.

"I believe you. But it is still a work without earth-essence. It's simply impossible to get perfect detail with primitive melting and casting techniques. Still, excellent effort!"

"Why thank you." Eld's voice dripped with sarcasm. She felt like a sprite being praised on her first watercolor painting.

But Brig didn't mark it. "I've managed to get all the items reclaimed to be deposited by Door NW24."

"Door Northwest twenty-four? Where is that?"

"The door we first came through."

"The Hidden Door?"

"I suppose it would be on your side. Only we don't want to just dump it there for brigands and adventurers to find. I wanted to tell someone. But we don't have an easy way to do that."

"Yet," Eld said. "It needs to be said and said again: no souls were lost irretrievably, so there is no need for our nations to war."

"Agreed," Brig said.

It was an effort not to berate Brig for the transgressions of her people, or point out it was entirely their fault they were in this tricky situation. However Eld felt, she was wise enough to see the results of their parley could be momentous. If trust could be built here, it could lead to truce and the elimination of the Eurthans as a threat to the Federation. The Forest would benefit, for the Dwen would have a means to bring their complaints to the attention of the Eurthantian government. And with the aggressive actions from the Sultan of Sharitan, the Federation would benefit from not having another hostile front.

Instead of sniping over the actions of the Eurthan army, Eld said, "While I am not an officer, I have been offered sponsorship for a commission."

"Well done!"

"Thank you. There is a command office in Falls Gate. That is the town to the north, right next to the great cataract."

"Yes! We have all the major water ways in Eurthantal and Athlantal mapped."

"Then you should find it easily. Send civilian diplomats like normal souls, in good faith, then you should be received well. I can organize a party to retrieve the items looted from the commander's house if you can have a guard there until we arrive."

"How long? It's late in the day and the troops are off duty in a couple hours. And I can't be there; they're still debriefing me about the battle."

The air shivered as Eld thought quickly. If she took the road from the Abbey and commandeered a horse from The Wildling stables.... "I'll ride there myself. Within the hour." She hoped.

"I'll send a guard instantly."

"Thank you. And if we ever meet again ..."

"We'll have drinkies," Brig said grinning. "Your treat!"

"My treat? My people didn't invade your lands ..."

But a harsh buzz shivered in the air, shaking Eld's body and soul, and the vision of Brig vanished. Eld was suddenly cold in the night air. She'd never used a sadol or triad like this. Part of her was elated. It had been like a wizard in ancient times....

"Don't you have something to do?" Ta Narin said.

She was standing below near a bench, where another magi sat. Eld hopped down and trotted over.

"That was you!"

"You would have been there all night without our help," Narin said.

"Thank you! And you," Eld added to her companion, but the woman didn't move.

Eld took a step back, her throat thick. It was Ta Murdan. Her face was peaceful, only beginning to shows lines of age. She still smiled gazing up at the stars. Spontaneous tears steamed down Eld's face. The passage of death was a sacred thing and no elfyn soul was unmoved by the moment.

"Yes, it is sad and I will miss her," Narin said. "But it was expected. The first Sunqueen stepped into the stars like this when she was weary of her labor after twelve centuries. Few of us have the desire to haunt the Orb that long these days. We should lay her to wake soon, before she stiffens. Now, cavalier, you will need to run if you're to get to the Hidden Door in under an hour."

Urgency returned to Eld's mind. "Yes," she said wiping the tears away. "I need a message sent to the garrison."

"A cart and escort, yes. I'll arrange it. Go!"

Eld ran through the doors of the Abbey, held open by other magi who, speaking in thought, understood what had passed. Across the shadowed inner court, through the front doors, past the ever watching image of Anda, Eld tore down the road, turning sharply to her left when she came to the crossroad at the bottom of the hill. Had it not been night she would have run straight on by foot, but at the speed she needed, a horse was better on uneven ground in bad light. Between the steed's instincts and Eld's elfyn senses, they could both move at speed with surety. It would have been much better with Fiorseth or another mind-link trained horse, but any horse would do. The street was dark, the lamps shuttered at midnight, and to Eld's wonder a pale horse was walking in the middle of the white paved street, followed by a woman clutching for the reins.

To Eld's further astonishment it was Fiorseth.

The mare reared and whinnied as Eld ran up.

"She was making a racket," Torin said. "Stirred out of dreams and wanting you. Handel is like this sometimes. Danshor wanted to look for you when we saw you were gone. But she's not allowed so I came. I caught up and secured her at The Wildling porch, but she somehow slipped out …"

Eld embraced Torin like a long lost sister and kissed her full on the mouth.

"I could marry you!"

"Ugh!" Torin said pushing Eld away.

But Eld was already leaping on Fiorseth to sit bareback and hoped she didn't need cavalry maneuvers dependent on stirrups.

"The garrison will get a message soon from the Abbey for a cart and escort," Eld said. "Tell the commander the Eurthans are returning the loot!"

~ Forward!~ she added to Fiorseth and they flew through the night air like the wind.

Fiorseth's strong body carried them up the north lane to where it met the Old Farm Road, then across dim fallow fields and soundly through the scrub and battle scarred ravine without incident. No brigand, elf or otherwise, was about when Eld came to the place. For a moment she saw the shadow of a woman in Bane-armor and Eld's heart raced. Eld had no weapon, not even a knife. She'd be reduced to using rocks and sticks like the painted Waudans of Azhinazu. Eld had no confidence her use of starry-essence was strong enough to defend herself and Fiorseth against an armed foe.

The armored figure raised one hand, then ducked away, melding into the darkness of the rock wall. Eld had Fiorseth slow to a walk, ready to dart, dive, fight, even flee if they had to. But the closer they came, Eld could see no one was there. Instead a pile of crates sat, made of what looked like heavy paper board reinforced with metal. Eld felt the essence of the air the best she could, looked into the chamber were the door was supposed to be. Like before, it was a blank room with smooth, stone walls, no door to be seen. But now there were signs of passage, scrapes and steps in the dust, great steps of the armor, and stray gravel on the floor. The Eurthans had come and gone, and the night was still.

A few minutes later Eld saw the lights of a wagon approaching with an escort. The rest of the early morning was spent loading the crates and transporting them back to the garrison. A little before dawn they were parked outside the commander's house, lights blazing from all windows, the astonished staff unloading the wagon driven by a Yino youth hired from a camp along the Old Farm Road.

"My best pot!" a man who might be the cook or head knave exclaimed. He held up a great copper cauldron of the kind used to simmer soup in sunlight. "Oh, but those demons dented it horribly!"

Eld shivered a bit, the chill before dawn keen, the eastern horizon thick with haze. There would be more red dawn's until the memory of the battle faded from the air. Eld wanted nothing more than a hot breakfast and to return to sleep. But it was a duty day so she resolved to spend her lunch napping. She felt she should stay to manage the activity, at least until a more authoritative soul arrived. Sonamor was directing the house in a dressing robe, no aspect or uniform, as house-girls trotted up an down the steps carrying boxes. Finally Alhern appeared, fully dressed, Seth by her side, having thrown on his work kirtle-shirt.

"What is Sul's blazing tresses is this, Farthal?" Alhern said. "It's not even dawn. I'm being told the Eurthans have returned our property?"

"Personal delivery of your Corinaths, as desired, emha," Eld said saluting.

Seth rushed to open the clasps and lids of the boxes. They were cunning and secure, requiring agile hands to twist and release, but Seth was a clever dab with such things. Soon the lids were opened and removed, while Alhern tried to reign in her brother's mania.

"Yes, there's the eagle," Seth murmured. "And the lion pair, and the tree with the hidden owl. Oh! One of the branches has broken! But where ..."

"We can take a complete inventory inside, brother."

Seth ignored Alhern, rushed down the steps past Fiorseth and descended on the last box being unloaded. The woman carrying it set it down for fear of dropping it as Seth attacked the thing. It was more securely latched, bound in straps of tin. It was obvious after a moment there was no cunning involved. They needed to be cut. Once a house-girl did this, Seth ripped off the lid. Then he stood back, hands over his mouth, overcome with joy and relief.

"The horse!" he exclaimed, tears in his eyes. "Your horse has come home, sister."

It seemed the most natural thing for Eld to slip off of Fiorseth and embrace Seth.

He clung to Eld. "Thank you so much for this."

"It wasn't all me. The Eurthans wanted to return their loot."

"Well, they should, considering they stole it in the first place!"

"I take it a certain Eurthan was involved?" Alhern asked. "A young officer Brig?" Her eyes were on the open box as it was carried into the house, a look on her face Eld hadn't observed before, like a mother seeing her child had been safely found.

"Yes," Eld said. "We spoke through the Abbey Triad."

"Ta Narin has informed us. Come inside, Farthal. We'll have a moment of celebration before the day starts."

Eld's arm remained around Seth's waist as they walked up the stairs. Then Seth excused himself to finish dressing. Eld followed Alhern to the now familiar study just as the rearing horse was being restored to its place of honor. Suddenly a hand gripped Eld's shoulder with alarming strength. Alhern was even dangerous when she was grateful.

"Well done, Farthal. Well done." Alhern released Eld and set about preparing three goblets. "Whiskey?"

"If you insist, commander."

Alhern smiled. "You don't like it."

"I prefer a good mead."

"A good mead it is."

Bottles clinked as the commander retrieved the liquor from a cabinet.

"That was the sort of initiative and organization we need in Command, Farthal."

"Thank you. But I was thinking it would be the best path to diplomacy."

"And vision," Alhern added, handing Eld a goblet of deep amber mead. "It's no use, Farthal. You can't deny you have grown a temperament for command. The only question is when will you accept sponsorship?"

Eld inhaled, uncertain why the issue was so intimidating. Her life would change forever. Perhaps that was the reason. A great change, even desired, was intimidating. "I'll do it," she said. "It feels right." then she gulped down half her mead.

"About time!" Seth exclaimed as he entered. He'd thrown on a green robe with vining flower patterns over his kirtle-shirt and divided his hair in trilocks, but wasn't wearing glimmer. "I've been wanting to write about you to friends for weeks, but some soul has been urging restraint until you decide the obvious."

"Good woman," Alhern said smiling with approval. "I'll recommend you as a diplomatic attache if we ever get that far with the Eurthans. It's a perfect position for a cadet, whatever their path to commission. Sit down for Sul's sake."

"Not there," Seth said, pulling Eld away from the armless chair she usually sat in. "Unless you want to feel like a school girl perched to recite your Amenrah. We'll sit in comfort by the hearth. When they come to light the chill fire, I'll send for breakfast to served here."

"Of course," Alhern said. "Though I'm not so sure I want to be too welcoming to the woman who plans to steal my brother."

"Not even after she's paid for me with your bronze horse?" Seth's eyes glittered mischievously.

"That trap is so brazen not even the dullest humyn would fall into it, brother. You are warned Farthal, he'll bait you into bottomless debates about his value. When he's bored."

"I'll endeavor to avoid boredom, then," Eld said.

"Good luck to you, cavalier. It's an effort I have failed at."

"With respect, having sprites keeps one far from boredom," Eld added.

"True. And how does my brother who refused to keep small children think of this?"

"I think her sprites are adorable," Seth said, sipping his goblet. Then he made a face.

"Whiskey? Truly?"

"You like whiskey."

"Not this early in the day! My head will be fluttery! Barley-mead with blackcurrant please."

Alhern sighed, and made her brother the drink he desired in a new goblet. "More whiskey for me," she muttered.

Breakfast came just as the mustering bell rang: scrambled eggs, ham, with bread and cheese and they ate well. Alhern told a page to inform Eld's company she had a free morning just as a missive was delivered by messenger. Eld and Seth were organizing the itinerary for their ride in the afternoon when Alhern stood up and shut the door.

"And I'll show you where I get the best lilacs," Seth was saying. "They will bloom soon and are among my favorite flowers. That's a hint for you." Seth winked. Then he noticed Alhern looked somber. "What is it, sister?"

It was past dawn, the morning bright, but no direct light entered the office yet. The chill fire, a shovel full of charcoal burnt to warm the room after the night, was already dying, the coals falling to white ash.

"Our sister," Alhern said. "Damn her!"

Eld sat up. The news must be dire and it would be about Danshor.

"What?" Seth breathed.

"She's taken it on herself to hire an advocate privately with her personal funds. That advocate has contacted Command and demanded the transfer of Lancer Danshor. Command has strongly suggested that I comply to put the issue to rest quickly."

"She did this when we were children," Seth said. "Agreed to something only to lobby ama or grandam to change the agreement to her further advantage. Always with a cunning excuse, of course. No wonder her trade thrives at the expense of other drayers."

"She wasn't able to get the settlement monies," Alhern explained. "This is her revenge. She wants them humbled, as if they weren't already. There is more. Command wants all of Danshor's associates interrogated to 'ensure their character meets the standards of their duty.' What complete pixie waffle! I will never foster one of her brats again!"

"We adore our nephew," Seth said wearily.

"Thank you for that reminder, brother. Now what?"

Sonamor stood, now in livery, with letter on a tray. "Another missive from Command, emha."

Alhern snatched it up and snapped it open. She seemed frozen; only her eyes moved as she read it. Then she pulled a bell. An instant later a junior officer leaped in the door.

"Commander, emha!"

"Circulate this to the captains. We'll need volunteers ready by morning."

"Emha!" The officer disappeared.

"Sister?" Seth said.

But Alhern didn't answer. She walked to the window with her goblet, staring out a long time. Finally she said, "I need to talk to Farthal alone, brother."

Seth paused, looked at Eld, gold eyes shimmering with worry.

"Now." Alhern didn't raise her voice, but it was understood as an order.

Seth stood and left the room, shutting the door behind him.

Alhern turned around, backlit from the window. The indirect light made her eyes glow yellow, almost like an Eurthan.

"The Tyreen fleet of aqua city-ships is being deployed in a blockade to meet the 'fleet' of that insensible humyn ruler, the Sultan of Sharitan. He thinks he is going to sack Gashora and steal children for his harem. What will actually happen is his fleet will be scorched out of the water and, unlike the victims of The Burning, no one will weep for them. Not even Her Humble Majesty who has a soft heart for humyn. Still, to manage our national defense with certainty, the Federation Marshal will be traveling to Tyrum to coordinate with the Admiralty while the fleet is away. There is a concern that, with most of Tyreen fleet in action, the shore defenses will be weaker. I don't recall if the Tyreens have quay cannons. Command wants a guard at Landsbridge near Lethglean. It's the shipyards, you see; they will be vulnerable to sabotage. Thus the Marshal is gracing them with her assistance. Her coach will be traveling fast, with messenger foots and cavalry. With the recent Eurthan menace, the command office isn't willing to spare their women at the Falls Gate office. But they believe I have plenty, so there is a request for volunteers. I am going to rid myself of two headaches and put Danshor on that list; this is the sort of thing that can clear her offense. Or at least minimize it. She will leave at dawn."

Eld stood with her mouth open. It was so sudden. Danshor would be gone from her life and there was no time for proper good byes.

"What will you do Farthal?" Alhern demanded.

Eld blinked. What could she do? "I've already accepted sponsorship," she said, thinking out loud.

"That is an intelligent choice. You don't regret it do you?"

"No, but – "

"But what, Farthal? Your paths were already diverging."

"Yes, but – "

"But?"

"But I didn't think it would be sudden like this."

"What's wrong with you? Do you want to court my brother or not? If you feel compelled to follow your war-sister like a hound, I'm not certain you should have a commission."

"It's not blind loyalty, emha. What am I worth if I abandon my war-sister? She was there for me, when I was shattered after Fiorseth broke her leg."

Alhern's brow furrowed slightly in sympathy. "That must have been a terrible time."

"I was utterly useless," Eld said. "I wasn't even able to think clearly enough to find help and get a healer and wagon. Danshor did that. Fiorseth could have died. We were ever after war-sisters."

"You can't let her hold that over you."

"She never has!" Eld protested. "She's never mentioned it. Not once. She's a bold, brash soul, but not conniving. And if she leaves like this, the company will wonder again about her character. But if I go with her ..."

"They'll think it's the chance to distinguish herself in the Marshal's company because with the Braggart goes the Poet. And the Poet is going to be an officer who has her eye on the commander's brother. So they will of course be back. Am I correct?"

"I hadn't thought that far about it." A bold thought occurred to Eld. "If Danshor must leave, is there anything preventing her return?"

Alhern laughed. "That's not a gambit to be tried until I know my sister is sated and has let the matter rest. Still, there remains no reason why you must join Danshor in this exile, however brief."

That was true. Eld sat down thinking. Suddenly she stood, resenting the comfort of the chair as if it was trying to seduce her.

"To advance you need to prune your associations so your future grows in the shape you desire," Alhern said. "It's simple Farthal –"

"Yes, emha, it is simple," Eld interrupted. "But it's hard on the soul. I don't want to become like..." Eld stopped herself from saying 'the Marshal'. "Separated and unfeeling. Or what's the point? I feel like I'm being asked to divide myself in two."

"I see. Well, Farthal, I can give you until dawn tomorrow to decide. You have the rest of the day free to think on it."

## Chapter 39

# The Offer

Eld was starving for sleep and yet found it impossible to seek the slightest rest with her thoughts in turmoil over the future. The company was out on riding maneuvers when she returned to the stable. But there was one surprise: on her pillow was a flask, the front cast with Dwen-stylized tree of woven roots and branches. Eld found herself smiling as she picked it up, remembering when Traith and Shedann had presented it to her so proudly. Danshor was a deeper soul than even Eld credited. She swallowed, glad no one was there to witness her emotion. The moment was made more bittersweet by the new décor:

Over their barracks' doorway a long length of dull, orange-red cloth was draped, linen dyed with hot madder. This was the color of remembrance of the dead and start of mourning. The garrison office had been told of Ta Murdan's passing. The news of an Aeon's passing would overshadow recent events around the wild Garden, even the duel. It would be the last gift of Ta Murdan's passing. They would observe her death like any other hero of the nation. It wasn't strictly necessary since she hadn't died in the battle, but she had fought in it and was an Aeon. Anyone who lived to be an Aeon was accorded a respect for the their service in the Orb by the simple presence of their living essence. Alhern's office had discretion here and so hot madder would be hung from the gates and the entrance to her house. The other observations of mourning weren't required: the wearing of red at dusk, walking the round, waking the soul throughout the night in black, then singing her memory off in white garb as the sun rose, often during cremation. But an invitation was expected from the Abbey, and Alhern, or at least Seth, was certain to attend. Eld knew they would not be riding together today in any sense.

Instead Eld went to the Temple. There were still sisters not recovered from their injuries and she felt speaking with those who had survived the battle with less fortune might give her some perspective. She was welcomed on sight, still their Gilded Hero, but Eld didn't find it was overwhelming, perhaps because their powers were dampened, diverted from outer auras to heal their wounds. There weren't as many now: the worst broken bones were knitted solidly so the women could move, though they were forbidden to leave the Temple lest they exert themselves before healing completed. Only Boad's rider, Trannecyn, remained in splints, but they were reduced enough she could finally wear loose clothes and walk without a staff. She wore a black veil to cover her patchy hair.

"They're astounded at how fast I'm coming along," Trannecyn said. "But they won't let me ride yet."

"In fairness, Boad still has only one eye," Eld said.

"Ai, but we're linked and I have two. They just don't want us to enjoy ourselves!"

This was the general opinion of the remaining women, who had reached that point of healing when they felt they were fit and able, and wished to return to their activities. But any activity that might hinder healing was forbidden. A particular sore point was the lack of men.

"They have a couple here, but they'll freeze you to death with a look if you suggest paying for a kiss. Except for Dilarnis. She has the Touch so they always find a reason to 'bring her a cup of something' late at night."

"Well, she's still blind," another woman said. "I'll give her allowances until she can see again."

"She can still dream!"

"And so can the rest of you," a familiar voice said.

Prefect Olthan arrived and the conversation abruptly changed to bragging about who had the most medals. Healing temples had rules and from the sounds of it the women were bending them.

"Cavalier, I did not expect to see you here," Olthan said as if they had never conversed at the heroes' gala. "Are you injured?"

"I sense I might be if I linger," Eld said.

"Our amicable conversation at Alhern's table does not clear your previous offense," Olthan said. "I have discipline to maintain. As a soldier you should appreciate that."

"Yes, of course." Eld turned to leave, then stopped. A memory of her dreams flashed in her mind. The split path, the Cradle, the child. "I'm not injured. But I think I might be growing."

"I see. Come with me."

If Eld was growing it would make some decisions easier. She could take mother's leave. She could delay sponsorship and entering the Academy until the babe was weaned. It could make everything easier with Danshor. There would be no bad feeling between them. And, best of all, she could spend overdue time at the estate with her children and the family would be cheered at another addition to their line. But she'd also need to sort her heroes' award or she could lose Fiorseth. A cavalier had a right to her horse only while she was actively serving; in that sense the horses did serve the Federation like the Thyn herds had served the monarchy as individual souls. If not, the horse was given to another soul and there was no guarantee the cavalier would get the mount back.

Eld should have felt privileged she had the head healer's attention, but she suspected Olthan wanted to be sure Eld didn't continue to haunt her temple. They went to Olthan's office, a white room with tall windows and an array in the high ceiling above. Olthan set a stool down underneath it.

"Sit as straight as you can. Standing is better, but few souls can be as still standing."

As soon as Eld sat, she felt the filtered sunlight directed down into her aura like a cool stream of water running through the center of her being. Olthan's aura glowed as well, and the healer's hands made motions as if first feeling the outside of Eld's aura, then around the area over her stomach and loins. Watching the motions it occurred to Eld healers were just a type of wizard, magi directing essence within instead of without. It was an obvious thought, but obscured by custom and expectation. There were no great tales of master healers. Lorthensul was an important but lesser Mother-God, whereas Selis of the Fold defined elfyn identity through essence mastery.

"No, you are not growing," Olthan finally said. "But your womb is pensive; it harbors a seed. It's quite stable and protected. The best kind, really. It won't cause problems until it grows. Do you want it to grow?"

"I think so."

"I could force it to sprout. Or I could empty you--"

"No!"

"Ah, you are certain. But the time or circumstance doesn't suit. Correct? Well, you have anywhere from several months or more, depending what induced it. Local men's gossip suggest you are engaged in a High Romance. It's more than my prospects are worth to speculate on those details. But given the health of the seed, it looks like the cause was coiting in dreams or during Euphoria. In which case it might linger as long as a decade."

"And then?"

"Its aura will dissolve into yours and it will be absorbed by your body. Until either that, or it grows, you will neither shed nor birth."

"I see.

"You are a poet. Remember how Lun cursed Jaro with barrenness for upsetting the Game of Lun? It's an old story from before the time the pensive womb was understood. How this curse was resolved gives us clues:

'And the Barrenness of Jaro was lifted
for thirteen months later she would birth
The First of Jaro's House,

Ellushia the Starry Blessed
And all the Court of Heaven heralded her
as the Daughter of a New Age of mothers
Of explorers and great queens.
But one of the court would never see that day,
for as soon as Lun lifted the curse
Jaro felt her womb quicken
The full power of the mother returned to her.
Taking Amer's scythe
Jaro leaped to the Ramparts of the Moon,
Where Athmod had made her brood nest.
And after battling together a night and a day,
Jaro finally had the best of her aunt.
She seized Athmod by her hair
Of many hissing, and spitting and biting snakes.
But Jaro was unharmed for on Lun's ramparts
Jaro was close to her mother Sul
And Her power would not allow injury to her daughter.' ''

Eld could see the great battle in her mind as she imagined it as a youth, the beautiful, white, moon palace desecrated and in ruin. Eld took up the rest of the poem:

" 'Athmod first pleaded
Then begged,
Then opened Her mouth to utter the Final Curse
The curse of a God that could destroy the heavens and the earth,
And all that ever was or could be.
But before a sound could escape Her vile lips
Jaro severed Athmod's head and flung it far into the Void.'''

" 'And there it lives still,'" Othyn recited. " 'Now and then seen in dreams, screaming silently forevermore.'

"The Ancients had quite an imagination. You see 'her womb quickened' when the time was right."

"Because a beautiful man wanted something?"

"You say that as if things have changed greatly since."

"There's a problem with that interpretation," Eld said. "It would mean Jaro joined with Lun before. But they only became lovers after the defeat of Athmod and the restoration of Lun's palace."

"Doesn't it make much better sense that Ellushia the Starry Blessed, the founder of the great Renaissance of mother culture, was conceived by Jaro's first passion at seeing Lun?"

"That would mean they trysted after the Game of Lun."

"After a godling or hero chooses the man in Lun's palace who shares her passion, joining is expected. That Jaro chose Lun does not change that."

"I never thought of that."

"Or this could be an occulted tale by simple mothers from an early time who assumed a delayed birth was the result of a vindictive man's magic. The greater lesson is not to take myth and legend literally. If that is all, Lancer Farthal ..."

"Yes. Thank you, Prefect Olthan."

Eld understood she was dismissed and left the Temple grounds.

Having a pensive womb didn't give Eld the advantages she hoped for. She sought the garrison messenger's office for more answers. They didn't have a law clerk or advocate, but Eld was directed to a library in the Crèche. It was a small room to the side, the lower shelves given to children's books, the upper ones to mothers'. A handful of women were browsing; from the titles they held, brewing seemed to be on their minds. There was only one child, a girl of school age sitting at a table by her mother, a foot-soldier still in uniform.

"I'm going to make a bow!" the girl said loudly.

"That's ambitious of you," her mother said absently, scanning a page detailing types of gruit with large drawings of plants."

"It says here yew and elm are best," the girl added with authority. "We can hunt rabbits!"

"Little yew around here," another woman offered. "All our bows are elm or elm and horn."

"It doesn't matter if it's pine," the mother said. "It's her first bow. I'll keep an eye for elm if we pass it. Come on, metee," she added rising. "Leave the book. We're going to gather yarrow and vervain in the field."

"But first I have to make a bow!"

"We'll hunt rabbits with my bow and you can make yours later ..."

They left and the women chuckled softly.

"That child will scare all the rabbits away with her stray shots," a woman by the stacks said. Eld was shocked to recognize her voice.

"Patrycan?"

"I'm not a ghost," she said. She was in uniform but without a flout. "You look like you're on a free day."

"If you call it that. I have your letter, thank you."

"It was promised," Patrycan said shrugging.

"How are you?"

"As well as can be after being interrogated for what seems like a day and night. Don't worry, I'm not possessed by Eurthan magic."

"I heard you hired a legal advocate."

"Yes. I won't brag, but the order forbidding the possession of Eurthan artifacts and their sale was obeyed. Like I said before, all I had were broken, unusable scraps. I'm not blameless, but because I harbored no intentions to undermine our Great Federation, Command was forced to cede I had not violated my oath of duty. Lost all of my stock though. And I'm forbidden from managing barracks accounts or even trading until told otherwise. Hardest, I forfeit my heroes' pay. But I get to return with no loss of rank or wages. I have plenty cached. It could be worse."

"I'm glad to hear it," Eld said. "We've missed you."

"Don't go sentimental. What about you? Leaving for the academy soon?"

"Maybe. I have some questions about my next course. You're adept with military law. Can I have your ear?"

"If I can't help, I'll send you my advocate. What troubles you?"

Eld explained the tangle of Danshor, accepting sponsorship, her pensive condition and the Marshal's call for escorts.

"You don't want a simple weave to your life, do you Farthal?" Pat said.

"And you're the soul to speak of simplicity?"

Pat pointed to some books, narrow but dense, boring lists of protocol and procedures for soldiers in service. "This one is probably best. It covers mother's leave and adjacent situations. I know you're not growing, but a pensive womb could shift to growing at any time. Once our captain knows, it could be out of your hands and you might find yourself on light duty, being watched by the Temple."

"Olthan didn't seem concerned."

"The Temple only thinks of a woman's health. The military thinks of a woman's readiness. If at a second's notice you could be unready, well, they'll put you some place it won't matter. But that might be further from the path you want. Here's my advice:

"Request a Grace from the Temple declaring, in spite of being pensive, you are fit for duty. Accept sponsorship, but use the Grace to delay your admission to the Academy until after the action with Sharitan is over."

"So, one week?"

"At most. And that's counting the time between messengers and sadols. You might have to force growing if you don't start once you're rested. You keep Falls Gate Keep as your garrison of residence. Once you start growing, you go on mother's leave. Command's happy, Danshor is still friendly, you advance and marry the beautiful boy." Patrycan winked. "But tell him nothing of your plan. Nor Danshor either. One thing I have learned in the past few days is Command hates to feel played for the fool, even by heroes of the nation."

Eld had much to think on. Her first urge was to speak to Seth. But that wasn't possible for he had indeed gone to the Abbey to join the wake. And Patrycan was right: taking him into her confidence wasn't wise, if only because he might use what he knew to pressure his sister to his will.

So Eld returned to the stables. She saddled Fiorseth and prepared to ride to clear her thoughts, only to be waylaid by an angry Danshor returned from maneuvers.

"Did you know this?" she demanded. "About me being volunteered?"

Eld didn't want to speak of it now. "Yes."

"I should have kept that damn … Never mind! Did you make it happen? So you could have your bauble without the stain of my association?"

"No!" Eld shouted. "It was the commander's decision."

"So you were there. It must be cozy to be close to that fire ..."

"Stop making it harder, will you? Let a soul breathe…"

"And you'll stay here. I should have known. You criticizing me for all my trysting, but when the man of your dreams manifests, it's different –"

"I haven't decided if you must know! Hear the truth, war-sister, I haven't decided!" Eld was suddenly aware it was quiet, women looking at them warily then hurrying out of sight. In a calmer voice she said, "If you were thinking clearly, you'd welcome joining the escort. Alhern – the commander – says it will clear your stain. At least obscure it to an acceptable indiscretion. You can only benefit from it."

"Then why don't you join me, 'war-sister'?"

Eld stared back at Danshor, so full of defensive anger, expecting Eld to abandon her and so she quickened the path to avoid the pain of it. The wisdom smote Eld to the core. Her own anger vanished, but she was no closer to certainty about her course.

"I might," Eld said. "Like I said, I haven't decided."

Eld mounted Fiorseth and rode out of the stable, through the garrison gates and onto the unpaved north road. They rode far and fast, for no one was around except a Yino camp. Children ran and waved as Eld passed them. Then they were into the far fields, near where she'd sighted the Eurthans during the run. She paused Fiorseth on that spot.

It took a moment to sight where she'd seen the Eurthans in their distant black armor. It was only then Eld saw she'd been mistaken about the door. She'd assumed they'd disappeared from sight at the Hidden Door in the ravine. But that wasn't possible from the lay of the land. This entrance would be too far north of the ravine. The Altan peaks in the distance, still brilliant white, harbored far more doors to Eurthantal than the Federation knew. Eld appreciated General Sallaryn's worries for the first time. How many doors did the Eurthani have on their "frontier"? The Sulani Federation Army couldn't find them all, much less guard them, no matter how long they examined Eurthan armor and weapons. Diplomacy was the surest way to the security of the realm.

Eld dismounted and let Fiorseth wander after first being certain no plants harmful to horses lurked nearby. Eld unbuckled her baldric and hung it on a branch. She didn't have her lance, but she did have both her sword and dagger; while she was certain the Eurthans were gone as a menace, the memory of being completely helpless to defend Seth lingered.

In the sun Eld moved through essence forms, trying to find that peace and calm, if just for a moment. Then she sought reverie. It was an advanced magi discipline, fallen out of practice since the abdication of the monarchy, when Sunqueens felt duty bound to know the future to prepare for it. Seeking Reverie it had its dangers, recorded in tales of women seeking to know the future only to create that very future in the process. So Eld didn't push, but let her essence flow passively, open to any Vision that might come. But Felkeni was busy, perhaps laughing in amusement as Shari men begged him, as fate, luck, chance, the will of their Gods, in all His many names, to grace their venal cause. It wouldn't help many that humyn cultures imagined Fate as a woman. Little did they know the Goddi of Fate had graced them plenty in the past, when the Zoroaster culture that founded Tamask had a great friendship with the Sula elfyn, who encouraged humyn development of engineering and mathematics, without which the Sharitani civilization would not have birthed. But these gifts, like a bauble a child tires of, grew stale and instead of growing to maturity, the Shari chose to remain small children, putting their trust in the vain and power hungry, who forever demanded what was not theirs. So Fate was done with them and Felkeni's peals of laughter at their expense would reach even Athmod's ears and She might smile for the first time in Eons.

That was the only vision that came, of Mother-Gods that were not real, but comforting stories made to weave sense of life in the Orb. Eld had no reverie or true vision, only a persistent impression her time with Danshor was not meant to be over yet. But ultimately it fell to her to decide. She agreed with the shape of the matter as Patrycan had laid out. Looking in the book Pat recommended gave Eld further ideas. Being rehabilitated by joining the escort could apply to more than one soul. And Eld would not always

be a young mother, happy to dance on any crest or wave of an uncertain social sea. Her children were growing and she wanted to bring stability to the
estate. Thus her gratitude should manifest in keeping awkward, lingering
questions from haunting the quietude of the house. There was already a
seed of instability: Eld had figured out the identity of the bored keeper Danshor trysted with and credited Silalin with godlike discretion. When Eld
heard them at The Wildling she never suspected it was Danshor taking Sil.

For that matter Danshor's discretion was to be lauded. Even in her
anger, Danshor didn't use these things against Eld. There was a distant possibility Danshor could grow. Eld knew Danshor's first birth had been hard,
the result of deliberate rashness after her first fire, before Danshor had a
strong mother's body. While able now, the memory lingered strongly
enough that Danshor had her womb emptied as a matter of course every six
months to be certain. But, once growing enough to feel the coming birth,
many women changed their minds on the matter. Eld wouldn't make it a
harder choice because of awkwardness between their houses. Danshor joining the escort would cleanse any stain lingering on her honor, and with Eld
beside her, their sisterhood would be cleansed as well.

When Eld explained her choices to Alhern that evening, the commander
looked at Eld as if she was slightly mad.

"Farthal, I can't help but observe an excess of convolution in your
plans."

"Emha, I have a Grace from the Temple, as you see." Prefect Olthan had
seemed gleeful to sign it an hour earlier, if only to be rid of this cavalier who
kept troubling her temple. "I am pensive, and while not qualified for
mother's leave, I can request the sponsorship I've accepted ..."

"Be delayed, yes," Alhern finished, fingering the small leaf of paper from
the Temple. "You have been busy, Farthal. These are very adroit maneuvers to avoid choosing between your war-sister and my brother. I suspect
you had help from another cunning, adroit soul who has managed to save
her own honor. But why the delay at all, Farthal?"

Eld steeled herself. "Because I'm volunteering myself for the Marshal's
escort. Provided I can keep Falls Gate as my garrison of residence."

Alhern looked at Eld a long time. Eld had stopped after the Temple to
put on her coat, feeling a formal aspect was required. However she hadn't
bothered with her flout.

"My brother will not be pleased," Alhern finally said. "You won't be
able to see him before you go. The Marshal's coach rides past at dawn and
will not stop as the escort joins it."

"Oh." Eld felt moor-less a moment. "I didn't realize it would be that quick."

"They want to get to Tyrum in three days and have three provinces and two rivers to cross. Frankly the best time I see is five days, with river boats and rest. The horses simply can't go faster and I'm not sure there are enough fresh ones at messenger posts to trade a whole team. As we know, cavaliers cannot be parted from their horses." Alhern pushed a different leaf of paper across the desk to Eld. "You're certain about this boon?"

Eld took the offered quill and signed the boon without hesitation. "Yes. Waiving half my heroes award to claim Fiorseth after her retirement is more than worth it."

"And you are certain going to Tyrum is what you want?"

"It's what I should do at this time. Give this to Seth."

Eld was glad she had written and sealed a letter now she wouldn't be able to see Seth again for Sel knew how long. Alhern held it, perhaps feeling Eld's intentions.

"Very well, Farthal. Get your gear ready to ride in the morning. I'll tell your captain. Just remember, pensive or not, sponsorship won't keep forever."

"I know."

"Stay in touch. It was an honor to serve with you, cavalier," Alhern said.

"The honor was mine as well, emha."

"Damn right it was." Alhern saluted and Eld returned it. For one terrifying moment Eld thought Alhern might weep.

"Well, get out of here, Farthal. Don't you dare be late to join the dawn escort."

Danshor was shocked to hear Eld was going to Tyrum with her.

"But I thought you would stay and ascend to the Golden Helix."

"I plan to. Just not now. And, um, thank you."

"For what?"

"The flask."

Danshor waved the matter away. "I don't want your flask with a pretty tree. I was only borrowing it."

"For almost five years?"

"I can get my own. Something in my style… "

"I can imagine." Danshor wasn't fooling Eld. She'd coveted the flask for weeks before winning it. But Eld left the matter lie, saying, "So we ride again, for a while anyway."

"Well, good. I mean, who knows what souls will be going. Most are from the 1st Company. I wonder if that sissy Carn is coming?"

"I hope so," Eld said. "The real reason you grouse about her is she's as vigorous as you and we need all the vigorous souls we can get."

Patrycan was moving back in, bringing her own mixed news; though happy to have her back many women in the company were disappointed she wouldn't return to managing the stable accounts.

"Althone won't let one flint on credit," Reon complained. "It's not as if she doesn't know where she can find us!"

"If you have the queens, you should pay the queens," Althone said from her cot, not looking up from the book she was reading.

"It's not queens, it's flints!" Reon protested.

"Queens or flints, if you owe them and have them, you pay them." Althone turned a page.

"Sorry, sister," Pat said. "The cache is hers now."

"Hey, how about a final game of Gains?" Torin said, holding a deck of cards.

"Sure," Danshor said. "Let's draw lots to see who shuffles."

"Ai," Torin agreed, offering a cluster of straws in her fist.

"Oh, very well," Danshor said.

Danshor was disappointed because she liked to be the one offering lots. She had a talent at winning. But she would look churlish and so she drew with the rest, seizing a straw with certainty. Eld was shocked to see it was a very short one. But not as shocked as Danshor when it was revealed to be the shortest.

The women laughed at Danshor's look of astonishment. She almost always managed to win at lots, and had never lost to Torin of all souls. Torin was dancing with glee.

"It was bound to happen sometime," Patrycan said, as the cards flew to them while Torin was dealing. "Come now, sister, are you going to be a grumpy ogre in your final hours with us?"

"Fine," Danshor said. "I'll just beat you all and spend my winnings on all those fine, free men in Tyrum."

"Careful," one elf said. "Tyrum is full of aelg harlots with painted feet."

"Heavens, I hope so," Danshor replied, gathering her cards with an eye for profit. She sounded more cheerful than she had for days.

This cheer was quickly whittled down during play as Danshor seemed to have the worst luck Eld had ever seen: Blue Lunats led the first trick round, of which Danshor had none, forcing her to play the 10 of Orbs, wasting a moderately valuable card early in the game. Danshor also had the Queen of Orbs, but when she played it, Torin crowed "Gains", winning the round with the trump "Lun", his sly smile taunting those who had lost. They shared disappointment in a round led by rubies: Eld was sure she would win with the King of Rubies, knowing the queen had been played. Danshor crowed "Gains" right after her, throwing down the highest trump, The Orb, as in the world, not the gold colored suit. But then Patrycan, with a knowing smile, calmly laid down the card to trump them all, The Dragon.

There were two standard wild cards in elfyn decks: The Dragon and Athmod. Some chose to play without one or either. But many thought that practice rude to Felkeni. For if mothers of the Orb would profit by playing His games, certainly they should allow Him his fun. And so throughout the games played in the Federation, the most skilled calculator of chance must accept her hand might be cursed by Athmod, which always meant a loss of some sort, either a hand, or a portion of winnings. But so too could she be blessed with The Dragon, a card that trumped all trumps, and made the holder the winner of any hand, no matter how mean her other cards were. There was a certain poetry to Patrycan's wins and Danshor's losses, as if Fate himself was making commentary on recent events.

Eld stopped playing early on, wanting to have her gear ready before bed. And when she was done, knowing she needed to be fresh for the road, she laid down on her cot, looking up at the rafters, lulled to sleep by the chatter of women playing, now and then a voice whooping "Gains!" at her wins. She would miss them all when she left. Eld knew, even if she came back to Falls Gate Keep, it would never be the same. When she fell asleep, she neither traveled nor dreamed of anything of note, seeking only the rest of calm visions. It was early dawn when Danshor shook her cot.

"We should rise."

"Elam."

Danshor was half dressed. Eld didn't take long. They helped flout each other's hair, then made sure the grooms had readied the horses. The night before they had emptied their chests, small, unneeded or unwanted trinkets left on the common table, anything of value taken to the garrison offices to be sent to their estates by post. They stripped their cots of bedding; as they dumped their sheets at the laundry, the broad shouldered Carn was spotted doing the same.

"Sul preserve us, she is coming!" Danshor breathed.

"Shut up and let's breakfast," Eld said.

The Kettle was barely open and only had bread and cheese available, so they took double portions and some for travel; they had no idea how long they'd be riding at a stretch. Checking again, the coach was reported to have left, but might not arrive until after dawn. The volunteers hovered just outside the stables, not yet mounted. It was a common tale for those who served, the speed of waiting.

"Looking bright, Gilded Hero?" an elf said to Eld. It was Carn, pacing impatiently like many of the volunteer group.

"Never brighter," Eld said, trying to sound hearty as they clasped wrists.

"I heard that was quite a throw, Farthal," Carn added with open admiration. "Wish I'd been there to see it!"

"Ai, but I heard your tale! You commandeered a healing array to defend the tunnel under the commander's house!" Eld said. "I was told it was a mirror at first."

"There's mirrors involved," Carn said. "But you don't need to aim as precisely with a Temple array."

"What did Prefect Olthan say?"

Carn laughed. "She wasn't happy, that was certain! So many deeds that day. At least no soul was lost. When are we going to mount up?"

"As if sissies mount anything," Danshor muttered.

Eld rounded on her, too full of fraught feelings to have patience for Danshor's bigoted sniping. But Carn was already standing chest to chest with Danshor, angry but calm, almost bored. Danshor was mildly surprised, but had no intention of backing down. Eld was angry herself; Danshor was fortunate Alhern was giving her a chance to redeem herself and this is how she repaid it. Eld noted Carn's shoulders were ever so slightly wider than Danshor's. Getting between them was the last desire on Eld's mind. But keeping Danshor from making a mess of this opportunity required it.

"You know how many times I hear 'sissy' whispered by idiots who think I have humyn ears?" Carn asked. "What do you think I'm going to do? Sit on the ground and weep into my cups? I just note these souls whisper … like cowards."

Danshor looked mulish. "Very well," she said in a bold, loud voice. "Do siss –"

Eld seized Danshor's arm and yanked her back. "You have no doubt noted my war-sister has the sense of a gnat," Eld said. "I offer my apologies."

Carn's eyes narrowed in the dimness, still staring at Danshor.

"Is there trouble here, boys?" Sergeant Tarl asked.

"No!" Eld said.

Carn and Danshor parted and they all returned to waiting in the quiet predawn twilight. Eld was suddenly sick of it all, and Danshor's antics made her wonder if she was making the right choice. But she had made it and there was nothing to do at the moment except follow the road she'd chosen.

As the light grew they became aware of singing, distant as if from the heavens. From the Abbey above the wake was ending as the Magi sang their sister's soul off with the coming dawn. Eld heard there would be a reception to honor Ta Murdan at the commander's house, and gatherings at The Wildling and the town hall. The Passing of an Aeon did not happen every day. Seth would be busy. Eld hoped he forgave her.

Finally Sergeant Tarl informed the volunteers the time was near enough they should be mounted and ready. No sooner had they settled on their horses, than Seth, wrapped in white robes over a dun white kirtle, ran into the barracks, past the flustered guard as the volunteers cantered out to the gate.

"You know who I am!" he shouted at the poor woman. "Do not try me!"

"I'll see you at the road, sister," Danshor said, easing Tuiric past Seth and the guard. "I'd give them a wide berth and privacy," Danshor added to the guard.

The guard had taken Danshor's advice and disappeared from Eld's awareness. All she saw was Seth, slippers dusty and hair in disarray from a mad run to meet her before she left. Seeing him made Eld swoon. Part of her questioned her resolve and all her careful plans. It hurt her to see him distressed.

"You were going to leave without telling me?" Seth shouted, his voice deepening.

Eld slid off Fiorseth to talk face to face.

"I left a letter--"

"And I've refused to read it when I can speak to you as you stand in life before me! Oh, I have read enough novels to know of the letters left by noble cowards! Are you abandoning me?"

"No! Never! I'm helping my war-sister. It will be the best for all of us, in the long tale."

"Are you mad? My sister gave you a way out! You are not bound to that hooligan!"

"I know it's hard to understand, but I am bound by fate to Danshor. For a while. This service will clear Danshor of any suspicion. I can't leave her with that burden alone. I can't enjoy happiness and ambition knowing I abandoned her."

"Why not?"

"I'm her war-sister. I have a duty to her just like I have a duty to the Federation. Just like our duty to the Orb."

The more they spoke the more certain Eld was this was the right path. They would return with success, heroes beyond reproach, and there would be no obstacle to anything, not even Seth …

"And what will I do?" Seth demanded, voice breaking. "Visit you in dreams?"

Eld wanted to tell him her plans, but Patrycan was right. It would risk everything.

"I had a reverie," Eld said. Of the confessions, this was the least risky. "You were with Traith in my estate. She was older."

"Why didn't you say?"

"You know why. Felkeni is fickle and cruel and a jinx. I saw you and Traith. I did not see myself. But I believe I will see you again."

"Not if the Shari kill you! Women playing soldier have dispatches. But men are listening to souls who Reverie dire things! They say souls will be lost! Lost irretrievably at sea!"

"Well, I'll be with the Marshal's attachment on land –"

"Don't you dare be clever with me! You yourself aren't certain your Reverie means you live! Neither is standing on land a surety! But you know what is? Not going at all!"

Seth was weeping hot tears of rage now.

Eld clasped his hands between hers, pulling him close. Then she felt it, the stone in her pocket, a prayer to Felkeni from a long forgotten farmer, a gift of hope to the finder. Eld took the felkinoc out of her pocket. Seth gasped in wonder at it, the perfect helix star carved in ancient clay.

"I found it soon after I was healed from the attack in the glade. I'm not going to say it protected me in the battle. But I do feel it carries the hopes of our mothers before. Maybe it carries a protection to their children who live now."

Eld gave it to Seth.

"But then you should keep it!" Seth objected.

"And lose it on the way? Let it feed your hopes, not my fears. Do what is best for your future, Seth. I am either in it or I am not. I won't ask you to dwell or wait on the fading vision of an absent cavalier."

"How poetic! Is that you speaking or my sister?"

"It's a reminder I will not blame you if your feelings change."

"Have yours?"

"No, you are part of my soul now."

"Then don't leave me! Don't go!"

Eld had no reply to the anguish in Seth's voice except to kiss him, long, gentle and slowly, trying to share as much of her feeling and everything he meant to her, in the past, presently and the future she hoped for in that last embrace. Seth clung to her, his grip adamant in his despair at being parted, at the chance, however fine, Eld could irretrievably die.

Then Eld heard it at last, far away but coming fast; the trumpet of the coach's arrival. She forced herself out of Seth's grip and leaped on Fiorseth. She looked at Seth once more, still beautiful, eyes red with tears, gasping in disbelief that she would leave. Eld tried to speak, give him a final word of comfort or hope. But he had the Felkinoc; it would have to serve. She knew there was nothing she could say without her own voice breaking. The letter would be her coda. Seth would read it in time.

~Forward~ Eld thought, and Fiorseth shot through the stable door.

And so they joined Danshor and the departing escort, merging in the wake of the Marshal's coach, speeding away from Falls Gate, away from the Altans and mysterious Eurthan doors, and away from a distraught Seth holding the hopes of Eld's future. If Eld was blessed, one day she would return to Falls Gate and reclaim him.

# Coda

*Letter*

*Effa Sethshorn Alhern,*

*When you read this I may already be far away. After much thought, I have decided my duty lies with serving in the Host with my war-sister. I feel we will not have much time together, and it will cost nothing to keep society a little while so we may part amicably.*

*My sponsorship has been deferred. The details aren't important, but as soon as this threat from the sea is over, I plan to enter the academy.*

*When I came to Falls Gate Keep, I did not dream or expect to find such a bold and beautiful man, the sight of whom makes my heart leap even now. Your sister has said our auras are entwined and this must be true because knowing I'm leaving you I feel my soul is being parted. If I dared pray to Fate it would be to return without incident, and continue our courtship if that is also your will. There is so much I want to say but time is short. I'm about to tell your sister of my plans and expect she will try to change my mind. But I truly think the way I am taking away from you now is the one that will lead back to you.*

*When the children were visiting I had a Reverie. You were in the children's room, reading a story to Traith before sleep at my family's estate. Traith was much older. I can only hope it means what I want, and is not a bitter sweet vision to comfort me before a tragedy unforeseen.*

*But if that is so, then I know my children survive and you will be their friend, and that is a comfort now. I hope it brings some comfort to you as well.*

*Though Duty takes me away from you for a time, I will aways remember you with affection. Whatever may pass, I will find you in dreams.*

*Yours in duty and affection,*

*Elderyn Farthal*

# Glossary

## Military Ranks

### *Regular Army*

Gen-General
Maj-Major
Capt-Captain
Lt-Lieutenant
En-Ensign

Msgt-Master Sergeant
Sgt-Sergeant
Cpl-Corporal
Ft-Footer

### *Cavalry*

Chr-Charger
Capt-Captain
Lt-Lieutenant
Ct-Cornet

Sgt-Sergeant
L-Lancer

## List of Characters, Places & Terms

**A'Yinomehey**: The Bereft of the Forest. See: Yino.
**Abbey, The**: magi school built near the remains of an Indus humyn temple.
**Adamys**: a man from the local lots.
**Aelg**: Elf-born. Anyone with both elfyn and humyn ancestry.

**Aelgyn**: category in scholarship describing hominid races with vocal language in the Orb: Elfyn, Humyn, Orukyn. Aelg are sometimes included, but are more accurately a cultural group.

**Aeon**: an old, essence powerful elfyn individual, usually 500 years or older.

**Afleen**: a river that feeds into the Ath.

**Age of Light, AL**: reckoning from the first Sunqueen to the abdication of HSM Daris.

**Ai**: common expression of acknowledgment and agreement. Used informally for "yes".

**Airt**: discredited theory that attributed disease to an imbalance of winds from various directions. Also, a poetic description of the air or atmosphere.

**Aiyn**: formal, ritual or legal form of affirmation.

**Alansatal**: the south east province of the Sulani Federation.

**Algath**: A cavalier in 2<sup>nd</sup> Company.

**Alhern, Arumil Trythe**: The Commander's older sister.

**Alhern, Selind "Seli"**(Maj): Commander of Falls Gate Keep.

**Alhern, Sethshorn "Seth"**: brother of the commander.

**Alhern, Solafi**: son of Arumil Alhern and nephew of the Commander.

**Altans**: mountain range in the center of the Mother Continent.

**Althlyn**: a cavalier in 2<sup>nd</sup> Company.

**Althone**: a cavalier in 2<sup>nd</sup> Company.

**Ama**: Informal word for mother. Used like "mum" or "mom".

**Amenrah**: name of the alphabet in Sulanilish and Hiltekash. Taken from the first letters.

**Amer**: planetary Orb of Mars.

**Ameram**: also, Amer, Mother-God of War in elfyn mythology.

**Amerdwol**: Mountain in the Altan range.

**Amerlings**: "Reapers of Souls", legendary figures who stand at the threshold of the Door after death to divide the worthy souls from the unworthy.

**Amiantal, Ta**: (The Mother Land): name of the Mother Continent.

**Amphermones**: elfyn pheromones that advertise sex and sexual compatibility. Could explain why there is negligible sexual dimorphism, at least with the terrestrial tribes.

**Amynvar**: a mayor, usually head of a city or town council.

**An**: elfyn word for "one".

**Anda**: humyn woman, Indus tribe, last survivor of a monastic community that died out around 4000YL.

**Aredheli**: Dwen man, Ash tribe.

**Arthenweld**(Lt.): an officer.

**Ash-lime**: cement

**Aspect**: ritual makeup used by the ancient monarchy to show their mood to the public. Retained in theater and domestic service.

**Astalyn**: Helix Star. Ancient symbol of the Er and regarded as the symbol of the collective Elfyn tribes.

**Ath**: (snake) one of the two major rivers in the Sulani Federation.

**Atham, Athum**: the planetary Orb, Uranus. Named after Athmod.

**Athlantal**: The lands on the surface of the Orb.

**Athmod**: Disgraced Mother-God of shape-shifting and chaos. In early myths she is a trickster deity, Athmod the Dancer. Only later does she becomes venal and malicious. Beheaded by Jaro for her crimes. Athmod's head was then cast into the Void.

**Avatar, Our Holy**: ruler of the Eurthantian Empire.

**Avigon**(Afeegon): Mythical city in the center of Eurath.

**Aynath**(Cpt): cavalry officer.

**Azhin**: resident, usually humyn, of Azhinazu. Humyn Azhins are related to Waudans. Ancient Azhins of the Pharon culture were the first rulers of Tamask.

**Azhinazu**: land in the south of the Mother Continent, covered with jungle.

**Bedu**: indigenous tribes living in the deserts and wilds of Sharitan. Often exploited by the Sultan. Similar to Bedouin.

**Bane**: myth: demonic host threating the Orb in the early Days of Life. Metaphors for Evil. Also, a slur against Eurthani invaders.

**Baneweapon**: the Eurthan triad, a magical weapon powered with earth-essence.

**Barkcloth**: a Dwen fabric.

**Barley-mead**: the most popular beverage in the Sula Federation, barley-mead dates from the first settlements on the Bright Plains. It is brewed like mead, from a 50/50 mix of honey and barley malt sugar. Ale-mead is a cheap substitute of ale mixed with mead; it is illegal to sell ale-mead as barley-mead.

**Bellarn, Harthyn**: Legal Advocate and Notary of Law.

**Bereft, The**: one of many names for the Yino or Wildlings, descendants of those displaced from their ancestral forest lands after the God Storm of 999 YL.

**Bezhrad, Corlyn**: late Aeon dame of the Bezhrad public house in Falls Gate.

**Black Ramothyn, The:** Tyreen city-ship that circumnavigated the Orb in 2590YL.

**Bluestrike**: lightning-like discharge from Eurthan weapons.

**Boad** : cavalry horse assigned to L. Trannecyn.

**Borin, Fathil "Fathi"**: man working as an artist for the print shop, Herald of the Dawn Country.

**Bracs**: trousers of heavy linen or hemp cloth worn for heavy work and recreation. Based on a Cambrian garment bracci. Usually brown or black in the Federation, stripped or plaid in Cambria.

**Brandubh**: chess-like Cambrian board game of skill.

**Brig, Aleen**(3rd Lt): officer in the Eurthantian forces.

**Bright Band**: a reactionary political group.

**Bright Plains, The**: lands settled by the Sulani after migrating from the forest.

**Brother**: euphemism for a homosexual male. Often a target of fetish obsessed women, but not considered a threat to society.

**Cambari**: Aelg of Cambrian humyn ancestry, usually weak in active essence.

**Cambria**: territory in the north west of the Mother Continent occupied by humyn tribes.

**Camden**(Ft): infantry, archer.

**Carapace**: technical tern for Eurthan military magical armor. Once activated, it's joints seal to make the wearer virtually impervious to injury.

**Carn**(L): a cavalier from 1st Company.

**Cataclysm, The**: extinction level event about 25,000 years ago caused by the Dying Star.

**Coal**: always means charcoal

**Coit**: technical word for sexual intercourse in elfyn languages. Not offensive.

**Coiting**: to coit

**Command**: government body that manages all the Federation Armed Forces

**Consort**: a married man.

**Corinath**: contemporary master bronze sculptor, Aeon.

**Crèche**: a place in an estate house or town block where children below school age are managed while mothers work.

**Crèche, The**: complex in an institution that includes a crèche and other amenities, especially in a military base.

**Crandal:** a cavalier.

**Crownland:** Startolthia

**Dame**: ruling matriarch of an estate, usually the grandmother or great grandmother of the present generation. But she may abdicate and retire, either appointing a daughter or sister. If not, management of the estate might fall to a vote among eligible mothers.

**Danshor, Hanmet**(L): cavalier, 2<sup>nd</sup> Company.

**Danshor, Thanul**: son of Hanmet Danshor.

**Dawn Country, The**: old name for the wild, explored lands in the northeast, near the Altan range.

**Day Sea, The**: also The East West Day Sea; largest ocean of Eurath. Because of the placement of land masses, the Day-Sea, at it's widest, is almost 2/3 the circumference of the Orb.

**Dethglan**: garrison and township.

**Dilarnis**: a soldier with the Touch of Lun.

**Dolanmeer, Ald**(Sgt) : soldier

**Door NW24**: Eurthan designation for the Hidden Door.

**Door, The**: the place in dreaming through where a soul's consciousness passes after death.

**Draeyn**(Cpt): officer, ranger.

**Druai**: Druzan word for Eurthani.

**Drake**: an alluring, attractive man.

**Drayer**, draying: one engaged in the business of transporting goods.

**Drinkies**: Eurthan, upper-class slang for a round of drinks

**Druzan** : Dialect of Elfyn spoken by modern Eurthani. Based on ancient Eurthanilish.

**Dwen**: Dwenifee .

**Dwenhilish**: dialect of elfyn used by Dwen.

**Dwenifee**: Elfyn with active wood-essence. There are three main tribes: Oak, Ash and Red. Oak Dwen tend to be "tannin complected", with light tan to dark skin and variegated blond, red, brown or black hair, an effect called "roan". Ash Dwen have pale silver gray to gray skin, and long fine ash to black hair. Red Dwen have a red-tan hue and thick black hair. All Dwen have green eyes.

**Dwenoshire, Ta**: the forest nation to the north of the Sulani Federation.

**Dying Star, The**: meteor or small asteroid that caused the Cataclysm .

**Effa**: term of respect for a man in Sulanilish .

**Eirok**: Luserani

**Elam**: Sulanilish and Hiltekash word for "thank you".

**Elf**: informal word for an individual, usually female, though plural can be for mixed company. Used like "guy" in Modern English.

**Elfborn**: aelg

**Elfling**: common way non-Aelgyn Thyn address elfyn.

589

**Elfyn**: dominant Aelgyn race in the Orb. Elfyn are physically distinguished by accented ears and eyebrows, greater strength and speed, and average 6 ft/2m. tall. They are androgynous to humyn eyes; elfyn rely more on amphermones than dress and customs to seek mates; individual elfyn identity is primarily based on essence not gender or skin hue; these are considered "roles for a life". Elfyn essence vigor makes them immune to most disease resulting in slow aging and long life. Elfyn are genetically telepathic but only a small segment of the population develops this skill for practical use. It is difficult for an elfyn to pass off a lie even with each other, and nearly impossible for elfyn to be deceived by humyn. Elfyn also can travel in dreams as if in waking. This might be a side effect of native telepathy, but some humyn are known to dreamwalk so scholarship is uncertain.

**Ellushia The Starry Blessed**: myth; Daughter of Jaro of the Dawn by Lun. Credited with building the first civilization of mothers on the Bright Plains.

**Emha**: term of respect for a woman in Sulanilish.

**Er**: history/myth: ancient elfyn city destroyed by the Cataclysm.

**Erhilish**: oldest known language of the elfyn people. Few samples survive.

**Essence**: technical word for magic, magical force.

**Estate**: the buildings, properties and concerns run by an family, descended from, and inherited through, the female line. A basic institution of Sula culture, estates are the largest contributers to the economy.

**Etheric Metal:** legend? Essence concentrated metallic liquid or vapor used in Er to create planetary magical works. It's making is lost to scholarship and some dispute it's existence outside of legend.

**Ethynsul:** West Province of the Sulani Federation.

**Eurath**: myth; Mother-God of the planetary Orb all life depends on. Also elfyn word for the planetary Orb.

**Eurthan**: Eurthani

**Eurthani**: Elfyn who can manipulate stone and metal. In appearance they have skin tones in all the colors of the earth, from alabaster white to onyx black. North Shindi tend to be darker than Deep Druai. Hair varies as wildly as skin hue, black, gray, brassy and white, and tends to have a metallic shimmer compared to other elfyn. Eyes are red, yellow, amber, green or blue and always glow from active earth-essence.

**Eurthanilish**: indigenous Eurthani language. Has been replace by Druzan, an argot based on Eurthanilish.

**Eurthantal**: the subterranean lands of the Orb.

**Eurthantian**: of Eurthantal.

**Eurthantian Empire, The**: Eurthan theocratic expansionist state ruled by Our Holy Avatar.

**Falls Gate**: township on the border of the Sulani Federation and Dwensohire.

**Falls Gate Keep**: the garrison near Falls Gate.

**Farni**: serving knave in the Rowan Oak.

**Farsnah**: Garrison and township.

**Farthal, Eroli**: married consort of Tolen Farthal.

**Farthal, Reonalt**: Eldshorn's sister, Eld's aunt.

**Farthal, Salthyn**: Eldshorn's sister; Eld's aunt.

**Farthal, Shedann**: son of Elderyn Farthal.

**Farthal, Tiyed**: married consort of Salthyn Farthal, legally an uncle of the estate .

**Farthal, Tolen**: daughter of Salthyn Farthal, Eld's cousin.

**Farthal, Traith**: daughter of Elderyn Farthal.

**Farthal, Elderyn(Eld)(L)**: cavalier in the Federation Host, Lancer.

**Farthal, Eldshorn**: mother of Elderyn Farthal.

**Fati**: informal word children address their mother's married consort involved in their upbringing.  May or may be their sire.

**Fay**: marginalized cultural group who live in Eurthantal.  Descendants of Athlantian elfyn pressed into slavery millennia ago, mostly of Dwen ancestry. Most fay have pale white skin very similar to a human from northern Cambria and blue or green eyes.  Eurthani ancestry gives many of them white hair; those with more recent Eurthan blood have eyes that glow with active earth-essence.

**Feilithon Keep**: garrison where Elderyn Farthal and Hanmet Danshor met.

**Felkan**: the planetary Orb Saturn.  Named after Felkeni.

**Felkeni**:  Goddi of fate, fortune and luck consorted with the Mother-God Myngar.

**Felkinoc**: luck stone; charms made by early settlers of the Bright Plains

**Fenath**: a cavalier

**Fiorseth**: dappled white and gray cavalry horse assigned to Elderyn Farthal.

**Firelance**: farm and crafting tool using sulessence, similar to an army lance, but not as powerful.

**Firewind**: myth: Soltarlu

**First Fire**: elfyn puberty, around the 8th decade.

**Fletharyn, Ta**: a magi

**Flintsun**: stylized sun, symbol of the Sulani Federation.

**Flout**: metal or leather cone holding a rider's ponytail on the top of her head, perched like an erect horse's tail. A distinctive cavalry military fashion. Vaguely resembles an inverted funnel.

**Fluorescence**: sulessence discharge in a Sula aura.

**Footwomen**: infantry

**Forthos**: tropical island wild preserve of surviving petty dragons.

**Gaels, Gael**: humyn tribe in Cambria similar to the ancient Irish . Also, language of the same, represented by modern Irish (Gaeilge).

**Gains**: popular trick taking card game played with a deck of 98 cards: 5 suits of 14 cards, plus 28 trump cards. The suits are darts, orbs, lunats, rubies and clovers. The trump picture cards are sometimes used by superstitious men in fortunetelling.

**Galdas**(Ft): a soldier.

**Galeenwol**: estate, source of the Gallens stream.

**Galledan**, (The Red Major)(Maj): officer, infantry.

**Gallens-Farthal**: Full name and title of the Farthal estate but not used in modern times.

**Gallens**: Ancestral stream of Gallens- Farthal.

**Gallowglass**: Gael mercenary.

**Garden of Lun**, **Garden**: night parties run by Temples of Lun for people to meet and tryst anonymously.

**Gashora**: large cosmopolitan city on the south coast of the Federation.

**Gashoreen**: of Gashora, also a resident.

**Gate Step**: village near Falls Gate Keep.

**Glimmer**: a cosmetic made of finely ground solstone and pigment.

**God Storm, The** : hurricane event in 999 YL that devastated the west coast of the Sulani nation.

**Goddi**: myth; a male deity, usually consorted with a Mother-God.

**Golwind**(Lt): a young infantry officer.

**Greenway**: forested land set aside for Thyn beasts.

**Grimsteel**(Grim): a crystalline black metal with green and blue inclusions composed primarily of meteoric iron exposed to an essence source in the distant past. In the Athlantal found scatted on high mountains and plains. Also found in the deep ocean near the Cambrian Basin and the probable impact zone of the Dying Star. In Eurthantal it is much more abundant.

**Gruit**: herbs used to flavor ale.

**Guardlock**(s): bound hair to either side of the face in Sula fashion, particularly in the trilock style.

**Haflad**: Sulani name for Yafladan.

**Hak**: elfyn word for nonsense, crap, or excrement. Mildly offensive.

**Hal Suldan**: Sula winter solstice festival. Second biggest Federation holiday.

**Haldwynshor**: a Dwen city.

**Halva**: mountain river that feeds the Passage Cataract.

**Hastol**: decorative crown-like headdress worn by Sula men based on the Dwen yastol.

**Helper**: informal, from: house helper. Consort of the house, usually married.

**Hawthorn**(Cpt): infantry officer.

**Helix**: military slang for an officer.

**Helsyn, Ta**: myth. The Janus Scythe: also, the Labrys Inverted. Weapon made by Soltarlu Firewind for Amer to defeat the Bane. Later used by Jaro to defeat Athmod. Ta Helsyn has two concave cutting faces instead of the convex edges of a Labrys axe.

**Herald of the Dawn Country**: news publication serving Falls Gate and the surrounding area.

**Hethlyn**: a river in the Federation.

**Hidden Door, The**: informal name for Eurthan door(s) observed in the Falls Gate area.

**Hiltekash**: trade language based on Sulanilish, with elements of Dwenhilish, Aelgyn dialects, and Gael and Shari loanwords.

**Hollar**: a cavalry horse .

**Hondal, Ta**: a magi.

**Hood**: slang for a self-centered, obnoxious woman.

**Host, The** :  the assembled forces of an army.

**Hothyn**: Sulanilish for "dragon".

**Hound**: deputy of the Hound's Master.

**Hound's Master**: equivalent to a sheriff in rural lots.

**House-girl**: female servant working under a butler. Duties include serving at meals, and tending to the needs of the mothers of a house, residence or estate.

**Humyn**: Aelgyn closely related to Elfyn but less strong physically and mentally, and with low essence vigor. While humyn have no active essence, individuals have been known to develop passive essence becoming shamyn, druids and holy women/men among their peoples. Such individuals often can dreamwalk. But having a lifespan of barely a century, few humyn master these skills in time to accomplish much with them. Due to low essence vigor humyn are susceptible to a variety of disease.  Care should be taken with livestock around unknown humyn tribes.

**Indus**: humyn tribes or nations east of Sharitan, near the south of the Altan range. Physically and culturally resemble Indians from the Vedic Period.

**Janus Scythe, The**: myth: Ta Helsyn.

**Jaro of the Dawn**:   Hero of the Elfyn people.  In Sula myth she is the semi divine daughter of Sul, born at dawn to live among the mothers of the Orb to guide and inspire them. Also, the constellation Ophiuchus.

**Jendalis**: historic master painter .

**Keeper**: informal name for a married man of a woman's house.  Also can be a man hired to run domestic staff or manage child of the house. In an estate, a keeper is also a younger, lower ranking consort.

**Kettle, The**: kitchen in an institution, especially an army mess.

**Kettle**: a kitchen.

**Kirtle-shirt, kirtle**: men's shift, usually ankle length and warn under a robe of contrasting colors.

**Knave**: male servant.

**Kohl**: black cosmetic pigment around the eyes.

**Labrys Inverted, The** : (from Labrys=double-bladed ceremonial axe)  Ta Helsyn.

**Laird**: son or consort of a feudal lor. Also, a title among Gael-Picti tribes.

**Lakeson, The**: myth: goddi, son of a water deity tasked to ferry travelers for a price.

**Landsbridge**: unincorporated suburb of the coastal island city Tyrum.

**Laysaid**: dominant form of football in the Sulani Federation.

**Leaf-felt**: a Dwen fabric, flexible if the wearer has wood-essence.

**Ledowyn**: a politician.

**Lenia**: deceased horse of Hanmet Danshor.

**Lethglean**:  city on the south coast of the Federation.

**Light Impressions**: a type of photography.

**Lioni**: a male lion.

**Literalist**: a person who holds theist views and beliefs, that the Mother-Gods of the Court of Heaven are real persons.  Also may still hold on to discredited ideas and superstitions.

**Loci sink**: research tool made of ash-lime impregnated with grimsteel. Used to pick up essence signatures, dreams and impressions.

**Long Winter, The**: ice age triggered by  the Cataclysm.

**Lor**:  honorific of the matriarch of feudal ruling estates.

**Lorthensul**: myth:  physician of the Court of Heaven.

**Lot**: an area of land set aside for productive use and development, particularly agriculture. Can refer to the territory of a feudal lor. Also, a vote or the act of casting a vote.

**Lot War**: an emergency vote where qualified mothers and men are volunteered by being alloted by the majority, whether they want to serve in government or not.

**Lun**: a beautiful but aloof, high maintenance man.

**Lun**: myth: Goddi of the Moon, passion, dreams and magic.

**Lunat**: crescent moon symbol. Also a suit in a deck of playing cards.

**Luserani**: Elfyn who use wind-essence and kites to fly. Also called Eirok. Not frequently seen away from the mountains, but known to be thin and tall, with feather-like hair and hawk-yellow eyes.

**Maer**: Mother-God of the Sea and Oceans. Matron deity of the Meerfee.

**Maer**: the planetary Orb, Neptune. Seen by the elfyn naked eye, only formally recognized as an orb in the last couple thousand years.

**Magi**: order of wizards founded by Sunqueen Selastimor the Great to speak to the Court of Heaven. In the modern nation they are an empirical institution of magical research, teaching and discovery.

**Masculate**: describing a mother dressing or acting in a way considered more appropriate for a male, especially if seen as frivolous or weak.

**Matrician**: describing a woman with a serious, authoritative aspect.

**Meerfee, Meer**: elfyn with water-essence. Known to have dolphin gray skin and webbed hands and feet. All have blue eyes without tear ducts. They are excellent singers and use echolocation. Like cetaceans, they can hold their breath for long periods. Most live in or near the ocean.

**Meloshok, Ta**: city near the mountain of the same name. Capitol of the Sulani Federation.

**Meloshok**: mountain in the center of the Sulani federation rich in solstone deposits.

**Meltok**: garrison town.

**Metee**: elfyn for small child. Also, term of affection.

**Mite**: slang for small child, usually affectionate.

**Moon Meet**: a social and ritual gathering of men around the full moon.

**Mores**: estate known for producing amber wine, fermented from a golden raspberry and white grapes.

**Mother Culture**: matrilineal and matrifocal cultures of the elfyn peoples and their nations founded by mothers and managed to prioritize mother's needs and the welfare of their children. Men, while sometimes marginalized in the public sphere, are not second-class citizens as all men are some mother's son. The exception is the Eurthantian Empire, a true matriarchy where a man has no rights separate from his mother or wife.

**Mother Host:** an organized block of the Federation Army Host.

**Mother Tree, The**: history/legend; the legendary cedar that elfyn races sheltered in to survive the Long Winter. Historically, a forest of great cedars, probably on the north and west slopes of the Altan range.

**Murdan, Ta**: a magi, Aeon.

**Myngar**: myth: Mother-God of abundance, prosperity and industry.

**Myngarth**: south and central province in the Federation where most grain is grown. Named after Myngar.

**Mynge**: the planetary orb Jupiter. Named after Myngar.

**Nabi Cuanaiya**, also, Nabi Cwanaiya. Sulanilish: no worries, no problem.

**Nalinard I**(Holy): Incarnation of Our Avatar credited with freeing the slaves in Eurthantal.

**Narin, Ta**: a magi.

**Neh**: informal. Used like "nah".

**Nethers**: privates, genitals.

**Nit**: slang for a foolish, annoying person.

**Nomclar**: land in the South Straits.

**Nord/Nords**: humyn in the territory to the far north and west of the Federation. Resemble ancient Norse.

**Oldenmor (ga-Mores), Halda**: moderately prosperous lot farmer.

**Oldenmor, Althas**: Halda Oldenmor's son.

**Ollyn**(Ft): a soldier.

**Olthan, Prefect**: senior healer of the Falls Gate Keep Temple.

**Olyeth**: Dwen woman, Oak tribe.

**Orb, The**: the planet Eurath.

**Orb**: a planet. Also, a suit in playing cards.

**Orb and Rays**: script developed by poets during the Age of Light.

**Orinac**: a young Ranger, Scout.

**Orukyn**: Neanderthal humyn.

**Otherside**: The Afterlife, what is beyond the Door. Can also refer to the land of true dreams.

**Othyn**: dragonkind, word for dragon in the older elfyn languages. Dragons are the the most powerful essence users living in the Orb. They are also the largest beings of any kind in the Orb: forest dragons average 200 feet from nose to tail; flying dragons, if standing perched on the ground, would stand at least a 100 feet high. The origin of dragons is unclear though it is known a flock of Thyngalu (flying dragons) manifested during the Cataclysm.

Thyndwendesh (forest dragons) may predate the Cataclysm. There are also ocean and lava dwelling dragons. Black dragons that breath fire like Ramoth only exist in legend or dreams.

**Othynde**: "Dragon Seat". Peak in the Altan range.

**Our Avatar**: also Our Holy Avatar: ruler of the Eurthantian Empire. See Avatar.

**Pangeal, Ta**: "The Net of Time". Usually refers to all known reality. Also used to describe the known world of Eurath.

**Passage Cataract, The**: 1,000 ft waterfall at Ramoth's Ridge.

**Par**: elfyn word for "two".

**Patrycan, Heled**(L): a cavalier.

**Payeen**: myth: Sul's second child, Mother-God of wind, speed and messengers. Also called, "Quick". Matron deity of the Luserani. Also, elfyn name for the planetary orb Mercury.

**Pelan, Remlan**: master smith, head of the Falls Gate smith guild.

**Peleen**: knave who works in the commander's house.

**Petty dragons**: dinosaurs.

**Peyteor**: Dwen woman, Cedar Tribe, aka "Little Acorn"

**Picti**: a humyn tribe in Cambria similar to the Picts.

**Princar**: title of daughter of a Queen or ruler of an ancient city-state

**Prithi**: a humyn tribe in Cambria, similar to the ancient Britons.

**Queen**: a gold plated coin, basic denomination of currency in the Sulani Federation.

**Queen's Capitol**: most common script and print font in the modern Federation.

**Queen's roads**: network of major roadways throughout the Federation, paved with white stone or ash-lime pavers. Date from the time of the Sun-queens.

**Raffins:** rambunctious near-do-wells, often adolescent girls.

**Ramlachi**: "Eclipse". Myth male hero and War-king. Consorted with Amer.

**Ramoth**: myth: legendary Black Dragon in many myths, usually with a relationship with Selis of the Fold. Also, the constellation Draco.

**Ramoth's Ridge**: thousand foot high cliff overlooking Federation land near the wilds, and the falling point of the Passage Cataract.

**Rays of the Field**: Also, Rays. A type of cuneiform, Rays were an early script of the Bright Plains used where pottery culture developed.

**Red Major, The**: Galledan .

**Reffayn, Taffellyni (Tafli)**: Dwen man, Oak tribe, current lease holder of the garrison public house, the Rowan Oak.

**Regular host**: enlisted soldiers.

**Reon**(L): a cavalier.

**Reverie**: unique to Elfyn, the ability to have visions of the future. Always true, but rarely complete, or even relevant, and dangerous to try to control.

**Ringling**: ring formed of wood or vine given by a Dwen woman to a man she favors causally. A Sula imitation in gold, silver or glass used like an engagement ring.

**River Script**: First widely adopted written script used in the Bright Plains.

**Roel**(Lt.): young officer.

**Roan**: In Dwen, describes the variated shading of Oak Dwen hair. Typical colors, from crown to ends, are: red-brown, brown-black, blond-brown. The crown color is always lighter than the ends.

**Rowan Oak, The** : public house on Falls Gate Keep grounds.

**Ruger**: a type of rugby.

**Rut**: an unreliable, shiftless, or promiscuous man held in low esteem. Offensive; can be mildly obscene in context.

**Sadol**: circle of odd numbered menhirs used for long distance dream and audio communication. This elfyn technology has been imitated by humyn cultures without, of course, any functionality.

**Sallaryn, Harneth** (Gen): officer working in Command.

**Sallaryn, Rathi**: General Sallaryn's consort.

**Seahome**: collection of large islands in the southern seas Meerfee use as a base.

**Searin**(Lt): officer, Associate of Roel.

**Sel:myth**: Selis of the Fold.

**Selastimor the Great, Queen**: Sunqueen who lived about 12,000 years ago at the height of the monarchy. Larger than life figure credited with building the Queen's road, founding the postal system, and defensive works. Founder of the Order of Magi.

**Selden**(Cpl): soldier, infantry.

**Selis of the Fold**, Also Sel: myth/history In myth Selis is the foster-mother of young Jaro. She can shape shift into a dragon or is a dragon who shape shifts into a wizard. Selis is known to be based on a historic person but anything beyond dream impressions have been lost to history as she lived long before the Cataclysm or the founding of Er. Understood to be the greatest wizard that ever lived. *The Seat of Sel* = the constellation Cassiopeia.

**Shamyn**: humyns with passive essence who can travel in true dreams.

**Sharitan**: arid humyn country to the south of the Federation border.

**Sharitani**: inhabitants of Sharitan, including surrounding tribes subjugated by the Sultan. Resemble ancient Persians.

**Shindi**: marginalized Eurthani cultural group who live in the Athlantal, high in the Altan range. Trade and interact frequently with Dwen.

**Sídh**: Cambrian Gael word for fairies in their native myths. Also used for Elfyn.

**Silalin (Sil)**: keeper employed by the Farthal-Gallens estate.

**Sire**: biological father.

**Sister**: a close female friend, buddy, chum. Can be short for War-sister. Also an euphemism for homosexual women, especially when plural.

**Sissy**: a disparaging term for a homosexual woman. Mildly offensive.

**Skerries, The**: Cambrian islands managed as Sulani territories to keep the peace at sea.

**Skein, The**: Eurthantian essence communications network apparently similar to sadols.

**Skyrie**: Peak in the Altans.

**Slet**: a slovenly man of questionable morals. Rude, but not obscene.

**Sol Suldan**: Sula summer solstice festival. The biggest holiday celebration in the Federation.

**Solcannon**: a tube of solstone mounted to strike enemy forces with sunstrike.

**Solglass**: glass mixed or embedded with solstone powder. Commonly used for windows and skylights to extend daylight.

**Solshar**: elfyn name for the planetary orb Venus.

**Solshari**: "Bright": myth: the first child of Sul. Originally a girl, "Solshar", Solshar become masculinized to "Solshari" as the culture changed. Solshar was the Mother-God of light, hope and joy. Her role in myth was replaced by the hero, Jaro of the Dawn. Solshari is a Son of Sul, and the avatar of all masculine virtues in Sula society: beauty, modesty, grace and hospitality.

**Solstone**: a type of essence imbued sunstone, solstone is a pale gold, usually translucent, feldspar. Found in many places the largest deposits are around and near the mountain Meloshok and the Shard Hills. Ancient Sula settlers discovered they could use solstone to extend their natural sulessence. The basis of modern Sula magical technology.

**Soltarlu**: "Firewind": Mother-God, Smith of the Court of Heaven.

**Sonamor:** civilian butler employed to manage the Falls Gate Keep commander's house.

**South Straits**: tropical sea lanes to the south of Azhinazu and north of Nomclar.

**Sparkwit**: used like "nitwit".

**Spined Eel**: myth: massive demonic, snake-like creature with poisonous spikes that threatened to devour the Orb. Killed by Jaro.

**Sprite**: elfyn child between the age of 3 and 30.

**Spritehood**: a developmental age after toddler-hood unique to elfyn, starting around 4 years. Elfyn acquire motor skills about the same time as humyn children, but continue to improve and take longer to develop higher mental functions and essence control unique to the race. Sprites are full of energy and may know many words but don't have a mastery of language until about 30. Most use a types of sign language; mothers rely on dreams and mind links to communicate with their children during this time.

**Spriteling** = sprite

**Startolthia** (Star-tolthia = Crownland): North and central province in the Federation. Ancient seat of the Sunqueen.

**Staties**: (STAT-eez) upper-class, schoolgirl slang for relatives of an estate

**Stoneshapers**: Eurthani as portrayed in the legend of the Mother Tree.

**Sul**: the Mother-God of the Sun, matron deity of the Sulani nation.

**Sulani/Sula**: Elfyn with sulessence, the dominant ethnic group in the Sulani Federation. A typical Sula has warm, pale skin of a hue similar to a human from the north and east of the Asian continent, but with actual yellow overtones. This hue is called "Gold". Individuals can range from yellow tan to bronze, but people of strong Sula ancestry never tan; sunlight is a tonic to Sula and they are not harmed by it. They can't even be blinded, though looking too long at the sun will overwhelm a Sula's essence and produce temporary blindness. Sula eyes are shade of yellow, amber or gold, and their hair varies from white blond to dark, brassy gold.

**Sulanilish**: elfyn dialect of the Sulani.

**Sulessence**: technical word for the magical manipulation of heat and light, particularly from the sun.

**Sulforce**: measure of sulessence in artifacts.

**Sunbake**: baking using sunlight.

**Sunblessed**: food freshly cooking in sunlight. Also, water set out in sunlight.

**Sunchasers**: Sulani as portrayed in the legend of the Mother Tree.

**Sunqueen(s)**: Ancient Sulani Monarchy. Founded the Commonwealth of Mothers after the fall of the feudal lors. They ruled for about 10,000 years until abdicating 6,000 years ago. Descendants, stylized as Her Humble Majesty(HHM), are still the head of state in the modern Federation.

**Sunseekers**: Sunchasers

**Sunstrike**: discharge from military fire lances channeling concentration heat and light from the sun.

**T'hen 'Ok**: a Thyn Raven.

**Ta**: definite article of most elfyn dialects.  Also used to designate noteworthy persons combined with their birth name.  In the past the monarch was always addressed as Ta (Her name); likely the origin of custom with magi. Sulanilish has a masculine form, "Ti", but it is not used as an honorific in the modern nation.  Male magi are called "Ta".

**Tad**: Traith Farthal's pet cat.

**Tagathtal, Ta**: The Federation:  informal name for the Sulani nations.  Full name: Erdro Sulani Tagathtal -Western Sulani Federation

**Tamask**: capitol of Sharitan.

**Tanamin**: a cavalier.

**Tank, Eruption**: Eurthan military transport that travels through vertical shafts in the earth's crust.  Some tanks have tunneling capability.

**Tanmor, Melgan**: keeper employed by Alhern estate.

**Tantilaan, Egalsh**(Gen): Field Marshal of the Federation Army.

**Tantilaan,Tinyan**: consort of the Field Marshal.

**Tarasik**: a healer.

**Tarl**(Sgt): cavalier, 2nd Company.

**Tathum**: ceremonial rod of foxglove twined in a helix of two serpents, the wand of Lorthensul. Also a symbol of the Temple.

**Temple, the**:  institution of healers in the modern Federation.  Also, a hospital run by the same.

**Tenes-Cambri**: Subcultural group, usually Tenes who have allied with other tribes, but can also refer to elfborn.

**Tenes**: a humyn tribe living on the borders of Cambria and Dwenoshire. Similar to the ancient La Téne Culture.

**Ter**: elfyn word for "three".

**Tergani** (Ta):  former betrothed of Egalsh Tantilaan. The most essence powerful man to graduate from the magi universities in centuries, but does not work as a wizard.  Married a Tyreen naval officer and lives in Tyrum.

**Tershol**(MSgt): weapons master and trainer.

**Theedween**: myth: son of Eurath, Goddi of the Forest, patron deity of the Dwenifee.

**Thrund**: myth, Goddi of caves, vaults and passages. Called the Drummer in early myths. Consorted with Eurath. Also, tentative name for a planetary orb speculated by magi to have a path beyond Maer.

**Thyn**: scholarship: category of living beings with intelligence and language. Includes Aelgyn, Othyn(dragonkind), and animal counterparts with elfyn intelligence. Not all animals have Thyn; the most common are: ravens, wolves, elk, otters and whales.

**Thyndwendesh**: Dragons of the Forest.

**Thyngalu**: Dragons of the Air. Can "breathe" lightening.

**Tochrohan**: a painting master in history.

**Toleth Keep**: previous garrison Eld was stationed.

**Tolith**: garrison town.

**Torc**: thick neck ring of twisted wire worn by Cambrian tribes.

**Torin, Beclyndwol "Bec"**(L): cavalier, 2nd Company.

**Tortin**: roguish character in a Sula folksong.

**Touch of Lun**: a woman with amphermones so strong she can physically arouse compatible souls. Can be mistaken for love with the young or inexperienced. Can not compel someone to coit, but is very hard to resist in the woman's presence.

**Tracan**(Ft): a soldier.

**Trannecyn**(L): cavalier, 1st Company.

**Traveler**: a type of sandwich on a long roll of cut bread, usually making a good sized meal. Can also refer to Yino.

**Treeriders**: Dwen who use a tree for locomotion.

**Treerunner**: a Dwen messenger or scout.

**Treesilk**: fabric manufactured in Dwenoshire made from wood waste. Similar to rayon.

**Triad**: the smallest usable sadol of three stones. Also, an Eurthan weapon.

**Tricklers**: informal; taking an interest in gambling and wagers.

**Trilocks**: common Sula hair style of dividing the hair into three parts: sides and back. The back may hang loose while the guardlocks are bound in thong, ribbons or clips. Worn by women and men.

**Tuiric**: dark roan calvary horse assigned to Hanmet Danshor.

**Twining**: Dwen tool and ornamentation of twisted wood around their ankles and legs that assist with walking through trees. Can be used for protection.

**Twilight, The**: legend?: descendants of the survivors of Er who live in dreams. From dream observations, their skin shines white, like starlight(not like northern humyn), and their hair and eyes can be any color of the rainbow. It is uncertain if they have physical forms or are essence powerful spirits lingering after the Cataclysm.

**Tyreen**: of Tyrum, also a resident.

**Tyrum**: coastal island city in the south Ethynsul.

**Uncle, dowager**: older adult unmarried son of a woman in an estate. Has rank over Uncles married into the house.

**Uncle, estate**: a man with authority of the domestic estate matters due to marrying into an estate.

**Vergant** (Cpt): an officer.

**Vineflower**: name of Shedann Farthal's favorite toy, a Dwen tree doll.

**Vinings**: Dwen decorative accent of living vines, worn on the arms like bracelets. Can be used defensively.

**Vision**: a brief premonition of danger. Unlike Reverie, is not fixed or in-evitable. A Vision may also be an illusion for entertainment.

**Voice**: political representatives in Parliament .

**Voice, The**: the speaker for Parliament.

**War-king:** a man skilled in fighting and martial arts.

**Wasps**: Federation elite cavalry.

**Waudans**: tribal humyns who inhabit the Azhinazu jungle.

**Wildling, The**: Inn located in Gate Step famous for kitsch Dwen inspired décor.

**Wildling(s)**: common word for Yino, not exactly offensive, but many con-sider disrespectful.

**Winternight**: legend: figure who finds and protects lost children in the for-est. Supposedly leaves present for needy children around Hal Suldan. The custom has extended to all children, regardless of class or station.

**Yafelram Astersh**: "Long Night of the Stars" Dwen festival at the Winter Solstice.

**Yafladan**: Dwen village or township.

**Yastol:** traditional Dwen crown of leaves headdress used to regulate wood-essence.

**Yeladrin**: Dwen woman, Oak tribe, works with Federation rangers.

**Yino**: the least offensive name for the traveller culture known as "Wildlings". From, A'Yinomehey = The Bereft of the Forest. Displaced from their land after the God Storm.

**YL**: Year of Lots. Beginning of the modern Sulani calender. "Lots" refer to the first government of mothers alloted by vote after the abdication of the Sunqueen.

Illustrations

## Select images from the story and world

# Living Astalyn

JDC©2022

# Ta helsyn

# The Janus Scythe

JMC©2022

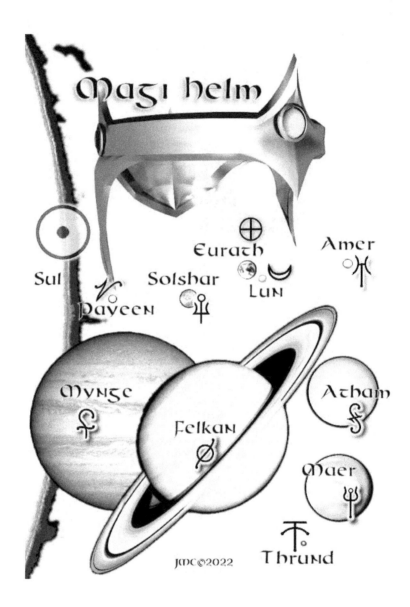

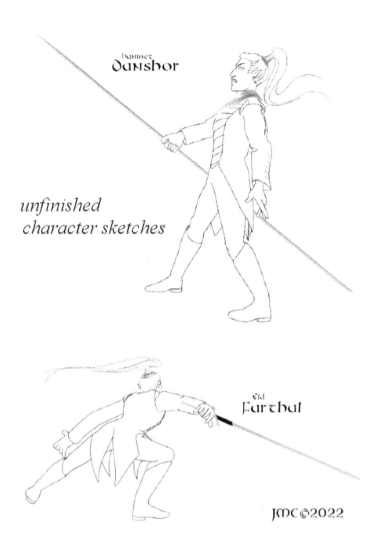

hammet
**Ðanshor**

*unfinished
character sketches*

Eld
**Farthal**

JMC©2022

Tafli

JMC ©2022

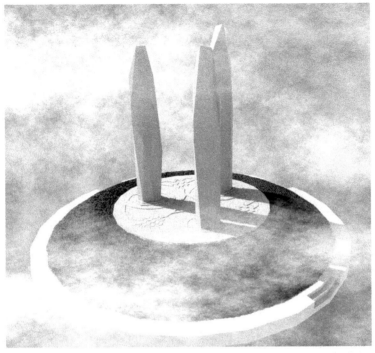

JMC©2022

# Triad Sadol

The smallest workable sadol, the
triad is three equidistant stones
calibrated for distance

communication.

Yino
Carnival Pavilion

JMC©2022

Mystic Astalyn

JMC©2022

# A Select Time-line of Historical Events

BL: Before the War of Lots. Historical reckoning before the founding of the Sulani Federation.
YL: Year of Lots. Historical reckoning after the War of Lots.
AL: Age of Light. Reckoning from the beginning of the first Sunqueen's rule to the abdication of Her Shining Majesty Daris Orvanae Halgyn.

| | | |
|---|---|---|
| 20,000 BL~ | | The Cataclysm: large meteor strikes the Orb about 24,000-26,000 years ago. An ice age follows. |
| 15,000 BL~ | | Ice age ends. Migration from the shelter of the Mother Tree. |
| 14,500 BL~ | | Bright Plains settled, agriculture developed and discovery of solstone deposits in the Ta Meloshok mountain hills.<br>Pottery and glass culture flourish with the use of solstone. |
| 14,000 BL | | Metalwork and smelting begin. The Elfyn Bronze Age. |
| 11,500 BL | | Rise of feudal lors and struggles to control solstone mines and placers. |
| 11,300 BL | | Iron replaces bronze as feudal lors seek military dominance. |
| 10,050 BL | | The first steel made by resistance sympathetic wizard smiths in Ta Wenthia(Meridian); the secret of manufacture is kept for decades. |
| 9800 BL~ | Year 1 of the Age of Light | Final rebellion and overthrow of the Lot Lors; the mothers of the nation are united under Elushian Trynador Halgyn who becomes the first Sunqueen. Solstone is declared a resource owned collectively by mothers and men of the Sula nation. |
| 9791 BL | 9 AL | Land allotment reforms. Mills, looms and various shop industries bring security and prosperity to the nation for the first time in hundreds of years. |
| 6000 BL~ | | Humyn in the Sharmain Valley develop primitive agri- |

| | | |
|---|---|---|
| | | culture about 10,000 years ago. |
| 5,120 BL – 4,730 BL | 4680 AL – 5510 AL | Rule of Sunqueen Selastimor the Great. Age of exploration and public works; Queen's roads built and national postal system founded. Order of the Magi founded. Grimsteel first used to strengthen steel edges. |
| 4000 BL – 3000 BL | | Migration of humyn from high Altan pastoral steppes, through the Sulani Realm and Ta Dwenoshire. Those peaceful are allowed to pass unhindered; those who act maliciously are culled. These tribes eventually settle in the far west and north of the continent in Cambria and include the modern tribes of Gaels, Prithi, Tenes and Nords. The history of the journey through elfyn lands are the basis of humyn folklore about elves and fairies.<br><br>South and east of the Sulani Realm, in the Sharitan flats, the agricultural settlements grow that will be the future city of Tamask. |
| 224BL | 10000 AL | HSM Daris Orvanae Halgyn is forced to banish her twin after an attempted coup. Her sister's followers pillage several Dwen settlements as they travel, leading to the Outrage of the Forest. First Barrier to the Forest raised. |
| 200-? BL | | In Eurthantal: Fall of the High Queen of Avigon. |
| 103 BL | | In Eurthantal: The Epiphany of the Empire of Eurthantal and rise of Our Avatar Emporator who founds a religious matriarchal state under the claim she is the incarnation of the One True Mother God. |
| 5 BL | 10219 AL<br>The last year of the Age of Light | Unable to find her sister's band to bring to justice, Daris abdicates and goes into self imposed exile, her house eventually settling on the island Tyrumaeve. Descendants of the Sunqueen's dynasty remain head of state but the honorific is changed from Her Shining Majesty (HSM) to Her Humble Majesty(HHM). |
| 0 | | The War of Lots. With the fall of monarchy rule, an emergency vote or allotment is instituted: mothers and men of the commons are bidden to volunteer those souls they consider to be worthy to guide the nation through the unstable times and build a new government of mothers. Being alloted to government office in an emergency is considered a duty not to be shirked; many |

| | | |
|---|---|---|
| | | "winners" of the vote are resentful and one woman is jailed for attempting to flee. |
| 19 YL | | The Midwife Government of six mothers and one man lay down the foundations of the Federation of Mothers. |
| 192 YL | | Pharon, ruler of the North Azhins, consolidates Tamask into a city state, the Tahmery. A lush culture of building and gardens flourishes until wars with competing humyn territories start desertification of the region. |
| 999 YL | | The God Storm: Lightning sparked forest fires decimate the Ethynsul hills driving the Dwen population out. Opportunistic Sula landowners expand their properties under the pretext that, without trees, the territory is no longer part of Ta Dwenoshire. The Voice and Parliament suggest mediation to both parties but don't intervene while the Dwen are evicted. Some travel north to Dwenoshire, but most try to regrow and squat only to be driven out and forced into a nomadic traveller lifestyle. They become the Yino, commonly called Wildlings. |
| 1000 YL | | First Sultan conquers Tamask, then unifies the lands Lin and Alon into the humyn nation Sharitan. Many Shari flee north to Federation lands. |
| 1201 YL | | The Burning: Plague strikes the western continent sea board. In Gashora, Shari humyn are scapegoated and flee, many killed as their boats are burned by hateful Sula in the Federation Patrol. Survivors reach Tyrumaeve, now called Tyrum, and are given sanctuary by Her Humble Majesty. |
| 1201-1295 YL | | The second Barrier to the Forest is made by the Dwen nation in response to The Burning. 1251 diplomacy reestablished but the Forest remains closed. |
| 1203 YL | | Battle of the Blue Fields: Last alliance between elfyn and Thyn horses against the Sultan of Sharitan's invasion. Solstone cannons scorch a quarter of the humyn army in the first minute of engagement. Soon the humyn are routed and driven out or killed. No ruler of Sharitan has attempted a land invasion of the Federation since. |
| 1257 YL | | Sultan's dynasty falls. Rise of Zorastar class that revere elfyn wisdom. 300 years of peace in the region |

| | | |
|---|---|---|
| | | follows. |
| 1542 YL | | Rise of second Sultan dynasty in Sharitan. |
| 2153 YL | | After expanding Sharitan territories, a mix of disaster, war and famine lead to the fall of the second Sultan's dynasty and the loss of the nation. The region is unstable for hundreds of years after. |
| 2201 YL | | Grim edged steel perfected in the Shard Hills, adding strength to the carbon wave process. |
| 2510 YL | | Piracy in NW Cambria becomes an unacceptable nuisance, causing Parliament to create laws declaring the sea lanes a Federation protectorate. Territories and humyn tribes affected are to be governed and midwifed to civilized standards. First roads in Cambria built. |
| 2531 YL | | Recognition of Tyrum as a Federation city, with maintenance to build aqua driven ships under the command of the Admiralty. |
| 2590 YL | | The Black Ramothyn circumnavigates the Orb. |
| 4680 YL | | A new Sultan rises in Sharitan, reuniting the nation under a religious patriarchal cult of the Eversky. The Sharitan Empire grows steadily for the next few centuries, mostly east and south. |
| 4922 YL | | First Light Impression images developed. |
| 5000 YL | | Invention and spread of the modern printing press. |
| 6016 YL Early Spring | | Eurthantal: Our Avatar's government must quell dissidents. Part of that plan is to expand the frontier, a popular distraction for the pious. Outpost reports opportunities for cargo, labor and profit near Door NW 24. But there is an organized heathen force nearby of unknown strength. Major Remil Velans proposes a testing exercise. A fortnight later her action is approved. |
| 6016 YL Merdow 2nd | | Soon after the spring equinox Lancer Elderyn Farthal's company arrives at Falls Gate Keep. |

# Ta Shum

## About Author

The author began writing fantasy fiction in the 1990's, mostly stories based in a world she created for her D&D campaign. Her first published story, "Hunt for the Queen's Beast", was in MZB's "Sword and Sorceress X". Since then J.M.Cressy has continued world building and writing while working as an artist.

After serving in the military, J.M. was trained in the tech industry. Interests include martial arts, the Society for Creative Anachronism, power-lifting, brewing, gardening, history, chess and the Irish language.

She lives in the Pacific Northwest.

CPSIA information can be obtained
at www.ICGtesting.com
Printed in the USA
LVHW020907220123
737664LV00001B/1